SHAUN HUTSON OMNIBUS

Heathen
Nemesis

Also by Shaun Hutson

ASSASSIN
BREEDING GROUND
CAPTIVES
COMPULSION
DEADHEAD
DEATH DAY
EREBUS
EXIT WOUNDS
HELL TO PAY
HYBRID
KNIFE EDGE
LUCY'S CHILD
NECESSARY EVIL
PURITY
RELICS
RENEGADES
SHADOWS
SLUGS
SPAWN
STOLEN ANGELS
VICTIMS
WARHOL'S PROPHECY
WHITE GHOST
TWISTED SOULS

SHAUN HUTSON OMNIBUS

Heathen
Nemesis

SHAUN HUTSON

A *Time Warner* Paperback

This omnibus edition first published in Great Britain by
Time Warner Paperbacks in 2006

Previously published separately:
Heathen first published in Great Britain by Little, Brown and
Company in 1992
Published by Warner Books in 1993
Reprinted 1994, 1995, 1997, 1998, 1999
Reprinted by Time Warner Paperbacks in 2002
Reprinted 2004

Nemesis first published in Great Britain by W H Allen & Co plc, 1989
Published by Sphere Books Ltd, 1991
Reprinted by Warner Books 1993
Reprinted 1996, 1998, 1999, 2001
Reprinted by Time Warner Paperbacks in 2002
Reprinted 2004

A CIP catalogue record for this book
is available from the British Library.

ISBN-13: 978-0-7515-3780-2
ISBN-10: 0-7515-3780-2

Printed and bound in Great Britain by
Clays Ltd, St Ives plc

Time Warner Paperbacks
An imprint of
Time Warner Book Group UK
Brettenham House
Lancaster Place
London WC2E 7EN

www.twbg.co.uk

Heathen

This book is dedicated to my wife,
Belinda, without whom there would be nothing.

‘Truth is rarely pure, and never simple’

– Oscar Wilde

Acknowledgements

The following is a list of people who, in some way, shape or form, helped with the book you are about to read. I am indebted to them all and, those whose names are listed should know why.

Many thanks to Gary Farrow, Damian Pulle (and Christina) and Chris. If a Pit Bull could walk it'd be called Gary. Thanks, mate.

To everyone at Little, Brown/Warner especially my ever-ready, ever-battling Sales Team. There are none to match them.

To Mr James Hale whose advice and expertise was, as ever, invaluable.

And, to the following who, as I said before, should know why they are listed here: Brian Pithers, Malcolm Dome, Jerry Ewing, Phil Alexander, Jo Bolsom, Gareth James, John Martin, Chas Balun, John Gullidge, Nick Cairns, Bert and Anita, Maurice, Trevor (and anyone else at Broomhills pistol club I've left out), Krusher, Steve, Bruce, Dave, Nicko and Janick. Rod Smallwood and everyone at Sanctuary Music. Merck Mercuriadis, Howard Johnson. Gordon Hopps, James Whale, Jonathan Ross, everyone at The Holiday Inn, Mayfair and the

Adelphi, Liverpool. Ian Austin, Zena, Julie and Colin (for keeping us fit). The quite marvellous Margaret Daly. Mr Jack Taylor, Mr Stuart Winton, Mr Amin Saleh, Mr Lewis Bloch and Mr Brian Howard. Indirectly I thank Metallica, Queensryche, Judas Priest, Sam Peckinpah, Martin Scorsese and Oliver Stone. As ever, I thank Liverpool F.C.

Special thanks to Mr Wally Grove, valued friend and pursuer of etiquette . . .

Love and thanks to my Mum and Dad for so many things I can't list them.

And to you, my readers, as ever, without whom everything would be a little bit pointless.

Let's go.

Shaun Hutson

One

The handkerchief was covered in blood.

PC John Stigwood cradled it in the palm of his hand and gazed at it through the plastic bag in which it was encased.

As daylight fled from the sky and night began to encroach, the sun was sliding towards the horizon. It left a crimson tint to the heavens. A little like the colour of the blood on the handkerchief, Stigwood thought.

He sighed wearily and glanced at his companion.

PC Andrew Cobb was older by two years. Older. *More experienced?*

'You do it,' Stigwood said, handing the bloodied parcel to his colleague.

'Does it matter which one of us does it?' Cobb said, a hint of irritation in his voice. 'Someone's got to tell her.'

Stigwood shook his head.

'I can't,' he said quietly.

'We don't even know if it's *him*,' snapped Cobb.

He glared at Stigwood then swung himself out of the car, slamming the door hard. He swallowed hard and began the short walk up the path which led to the front door. Jesus, he didn't want to do this. He pushed the handkerchief into the pocket of his tunic and rubbed his hands together as he approached the door. Dark wood. Elegant. Like the rest of the house. Large without being ostentatious, and secluded without being isolated. It was an imposing building, its dark stonework covered with clinging ivy. A moth fluttered around a lamp that was activated by a sensor, Cobb noticed as he reached the doorstep. He heard its wings pattering against the glass.

He had no speech rehearsed, no words ready on his tongue. All he had was the dreadful apprehension he knew his companion shared.

Across the street were lights in windows. He thought he saw shadows, figures moving behind closed net curtains, gazing out, wondering why a police car should be parked in the driveway of the large house.

There were no lights on in this house. Perhaps no one was home. Cobb told himself it would be better that way. He would ring the bell but there would be no answer. End of story. But he also knew that once the information was radioed back to base he and Stigwood would be told to wait until the occupant returned.

He glanced back; Stigwood was watching him impassively. The two policemen locked stares for a moment, then the younger of the two concentrated on the Escort's steering wheel.

Cobb slipped one hand into his tunic pocket

and felt his fingertips brush against the plastic bag that held the handkerchief. He closed his eyes briefly, sucked in a deep breath and held it for a second.

Come on, do your job.

He exhaled, opening his eyes in the process, one index finger aimed at the doorbell.

He noticed that his hand was shaking.

Two

Donna Ward thought she heard the two-tone chime of the doorbell and cocked an ear in the direction of the front door. The music continued to flow from the ghetto-blaster propped on the kitchen unit beside her. Donna wondered for a moment if she'd imagined it. She eased the volume down slightly, then continued with her task. She stepped back from the picture, trying to see if it was straight or not. She smiled to herself. Chris wouldn't even notice when he came in. She'd hung three small pictures in the kitchen, military prints of men in uniform. She'd found them in a box under the stairs a day or two ago. Chris had owned them for years, as long as she could remember. He'd once had a passion for military history. Years ago.

This time, when the ringing of the doorbell came, she *did* hear it. She jabbed the 'off' button and silence dropped like a blanket over the house as she walked across the hall towards the front door.

Donna didn't bother to check the spy-hole but she always left the chain in position and now, as she eased the door open, she only pulled it as far as the restraints of the metal would allow.

Through the gap between door and jamb she saw PC Cobb.

He nodded his head with such exaggeration it looked almost like a bow.

Donna felt a sudden, unexpected coldness run through her, as if someone had suddenly injected her with iced water. She didn't know why; perhaps it was just the sight of the uniform. She'd seen policemen often enough when her father had been alive. They'd arrive at her parents house to tell her mother that the drunken wreck she'd married was either too pissed to get home and was sleeping it off in the cells, or that they had him in the car outside.

But that, as the saying went, had been then. This was now.

What was a policeman doing ringing her door-bell at seven in the evening?

She brushed a hair from her face and looked at him impassively.

'Mrs Ward?' he asked, his tone subdued.

She swallowed hard.

'Mrs Donna Ward?'

'Yes. What is it?'

'Can I come in, please?' Cobb asked, running a

swiftly appraising glance over the young woman. Blonde, pretty. Slim. Late twenties, he guessed. She was dressed casually in jeans, sweatshirt and trainers. She had grey eyes, eyes which flickered back and forth, regarding him now with a combination of bewilderment and concern. He wondered for a moment if she was going to let him in but she pushed the door to and he heard the chain being slipped. The door opened to allow him entry, then was closed behind him.

'I'm sorry,' she said quickly. 'I was going to ask you in.' There was a pleasant smile on her face, but it never touched her eyes.

Do your job.

Cobb stood rigidly in the hallway.

'Mrs Ward,' he began. *Go on, you can do it.* 'I'm afraid to tell you there's been an accident. It's . . .'

She cut him short.

'Chris,' she murmured, her eyes riveted to the uniformed man.

'Your husband has been involved in a car crash. At least, we think it's your husband . . .'

She closed her eyes tightly for a second.

'Is he hurt?' she demanded, her voice cracking.

'We need you to identify him,' Cobb said.

There were tears forming in her eyes.

'How do you know it's him?' she said frantically.

'We're not sure; that's why we need you to come with us and look at him. We have this.' He reached into his pocket and pulled out the small, plastic-wrapped package. With a trembling hand he held it out towards Donna, who snatched it from him.

'Those are your husband's initials, aren't they?' Cobb said, indicating the CW on one corner of the bloodied handkerchief.

'Oh God,' Donna said, her eyes brimming with tears. She put one hand to her mouth. 'Is he dead?'

Cobb had been expecting the question but he still didn't know how to deal with it. No amount of training could prepare you.

'If you come with me, there's a car outside,' he said, trying to sound efficiently detached. 'We'll take you to . . .'

'Is he dead?' she snarled through clenched teeth.

'Yes.'

'Oh God, no, please.' She tried to swallow but couldn't. The tears began to flow.

Cobb felt helpless. So fucking, pathetically, screamingly helpless. Jesus Christ, he wanted to help this woman, but what did he do? What *could* he do, except drive her to the hospital to inspect the body of the man they were convinced was her husband?

There was a coat stand close by. Donna reached for a leather jacket and pulled it on, pushing past Cobb and out of the front door towards the waiting police car. He slammed the front door behind her and followed her to the car, helping her into the back, scurrying around the other side and strapping himself in.

Donna wiped tears from her face.

'We don't know for sure that it *is* your husband, Mrs Ward,' he said, as if that were some kind of comfort.

'Just take me to him, please,' she said.

The car sped away.

The sun slipped away, leaving the last of its colour to fade from the sky. Night closed in.

Now there was only darkness.

Three

She might as well have been blindfolded for the journey. Donna saw little or nothing of the houses and countryside that flashed by. Stigwood guided the police car along the streets with sometimes bewildering speed. She could see her own face reflected in the glass of the windows when other vehicles passed: her eyes looked blank. There was no expression behind them other than that of fearful expectation. Or desperate hope.

They'd said they weren't sure if it was her husband or not.

You're holding his handkerchief, for Christ's sake. Look at it.

It could be someone else.

Someone who looked like him?

It was possible.

Someone who had the same initials?

Please God let them be wrong.

There was so much blood on the handkerchief she could have wrung it out. As she sat in the back of the car she ran her fingers over the plastic. Occasionally she would clasp her hands together.

The silence inside the car was as uncomfortable as it was impenetrable, but what were the uniformed men supposed to say? Stigwood was too busy concentrating on the road to strike up a conversation and Cobb couldn't even bring himself to look round at the distraught woman. The only indication of her presence was the occasional sniffle.

If it wasn't Chris, then how did they know where to find her? From his driver's licence? She gripped the handkerchief more tightly, one part of her mind filled with the unshakeable conviction that the man she was being taken to identify was indeed her husband. The other part of her being fought to believe, prayed that there had been some terrible mistake. She tried to make herself think that there *could* be another Christopher Ward.

The police car slowed down as it approached a set of traffic lights, the glowing red in the gloom. The single scarlet circlet was like an unblinking eye. As red as the blood on the handkerchief.

Donna shifted position, pulling her jacket more tightly around herself, aware of the same bone-numbing chill that had enveloped her from the time Cobb had stepped into her house. But now that chill was deepening, freezing her blood, turning her bones to glacial props encased by bloodless skin. She had never felt cold like it.

Was death as cold as this?

Did Chris already know?

She closed her eyes for a moment but images of him appeared there, images she wanted to see but also ones she feared she might never see again. Images which would become only memories. Never again to be witnessed. She was to be left with nothing *but* memories, now.

In the night air the sound of sirens echoed stridently and amidst a blurr of flashing blue lights an ambulance hurtled from the main gates of the hospital.

Stigwood watched it go, checked that the way in was clear, then guided the car through the main gates.

As the car came to a halt and Cobb opened the door for her, Donna felt as if the very life were being sucked from her.

She brushed a tear from her cheek and followed Cobb inside the hospital.

Four

There were three of them waiting.

Donna had been guided through the labyrinthine corridors of the hospital by Cobb, hardly aware that her feet were touching the ground, seeing the activity around her but not registering it.

The nurse hurrying to casualty with packets of blood for a transfusion.

Two interns running along with a gurney.

Somewhere close she heard crying; always, there was that smell, simultaneously reassuring and nauseating. The disinfectant smell. It mingled with the stench of excrement as a nurse hurried to empty a bed-pan, walking past Donna without even glancing at her. Everything was happening in slow motion; the journey through the hospital took an eternity.

Until they reached the morgue.

That was where the trio waited to greet her, two men – one in a suit – and a WPC who smiled efficiently and took a step towards her, eyeing the bloodstained handkerchief that Donna still clutched.

The man in the suit also stepped forward, introducing himself as Detective Constable Mackenzie. Donna looked at him blankly and followed him through into the morgue.

Please God, don't let it be him.

The WPC took her arm as she moved into the small room beyond. It was grey and white, bare except for a single slab in the centre of the room. On that slab lay a shapeless form covered by a green plastic sheet. The room was barely twelve feet square, but it might as well have been the size of a football pitch. The slab seemed to grow in Donna's mind until it was the only thing she could see. The antiseptic smell was even stronger now.

She felt sick. Felt faint.

Please God.

The other man, dressed in a sweatshirt and trousers, said that he was the coroner, his name was Daniel Jordan. Something like that.

Donna felt a sudden feeling of light-headedness, thought she was going to faint. The WPC shot out an arm to steady her, sliding another arm around her waist, but Donna shrugged it off, pushing the offered support away from her with her cold hands.

Look at him.

No, don't look. Turn and run.

A tear forced its way from her eye and trickled slowly down her cheek.

'It won't take a second, Mrs Ward,' said Jordan, holding out a hand to beckon her closer.

And now every part of her mind centred on that shape in front of her. Moving like an automaton she stood beside Jordan, looking down at the sheet.

She clutched the handkerchief more tightly.

'All right,' she whispered.

He pulled back the sheet.

'Oh, no,' she gasped. 'No.'

Jordan looked at her, then at Mackenzie, who merely shook his head slightly.

'Chris,' murmured Donna, her eyes transfixed on the face of the corpse.

The corpse of her husband.

'No,' she said again, tears pouring down her cheeks. She studied his features, the awful gashes in his forehead and cheeks. She saw how the blood had soaked his jacket and shirt.

So much blood.

'Is it your husband, Mrs Ward?' Mackenzie asked.

Donna nodded and reached for her husband, touching one of his lacerated cheeks.

Jesus, he was so cold.

His skin was white, those areas that weren't discoloured by bruises or hideous cuts, as if all the blood had been drained from him. She smoothed one of his eyebrows, then touched his lips with her index finger.

So cold.

She touched her fingertips to her own lips and kissed them, then pressed those fingers to his cold lips once more.

She shook her head again, allowing herself to be eased back by the WPC, allowing herself to be guided towards the door.

She saw Jordan replace the sheet.

It was then that she collapsed.

Five

How many tears could the human eye produce?

As Donna sat sobbing she wondered.

How much pain was it possible to feel at the death of a man you loved? Could pain be measured, calibrated and categorised like anything else?

Chris would have known.

She felt a hand clasp hers; it seemed to exude strength and feeling.

The nurse who sat beside her was in her mid-thirties

(*maybe a year or two older than Chris*)

and she had the most piercing blue eyes Donna had ever seen. But in those eyes there was only concern now. The small room had yellow walls, two or three threadbare chairs and posters which bore slogans like

SAVE THE NHS

OVERWORKED DOCTORS ARE A DANGER TO EVERYONE: CUT HOURS

On the small table beside her there were tea cups; one was still steaming.

'Drink it,' said the nurse, holding the cup towards Donna, gripping her other hand firmly.

Donna looked at her, then at the WPC who sat opposite. She took the cup and sipped the tea.

‘Good girl,’ said the nurse, still holding her hand.

Donna swallowed a couple of mouthfuls then put the cup down. She sucked in a deep breath, as if to replace air that had been knocked from her, then sank back in the chair, one hand over her face, her eyes closed. Her sobs subsided into a series of quivering inhalations and exhalations. She could feel how wet her own cheeks were.

‘Oh God,’ she whispered, swallowing hard, aware for the first time of the heavy silence in the room and of the ticking of a clock above her.

11.06 p.m.

‘What happened?’ she asked, looking at the nurse and the WPC in turn.

‘You fainted and we brought you in here,’ the policewoman told her quietly.

‘Oh God,’ Donna murmured again. The words were like a litany.

The room was lit by a sixty-watt bulb that cast thick black shadows. Outside, beyond the closed curtains, she could hear the wind. The hospital seemed very quiet. Donna sat for interminable minutes just staring ahead, wondering why her mind was so blank. It was like a blackboard wiped clean of chalk, all feelings wiped away. She just felt a terrible emptiness, so intense it was almost physical, as if a hole had been gouged in her soul. Could so much emotion be expended that a person was left without feeling? When Donna looked down at her own body she saw only a shell, with nothing left inside. Just a husk, devoid and emptied of feeling.

She put down the teacup, touched the nurse gently on the back of the hand and released her grip, resting both arms on the worn arms of the chair. Tilting her head back she closed her eyes and took another deep, racking breath.

'How did it happen?' she asked finally, her voice low.

The policewoman looked at her and then at the nurse, as if for permission to speak.

'How was Chris killed?' Donna had no recollection of Cobb telling her about the accident.

'A car crash,' the WPC said quietly.

'When did it happen?'

'I'm not really sure, Mrs Ward,' the policewoman told her apologetically. 'I wasn't on duty when it happened.'

'Is there anyone here who could tell me?' Donna asked, smiling thinly. 'Please.'

The policewoman got to her feet, excused herself and slipped out of the door, closing it behind her.

The clock continued to tick loudly above Donna's head.

'You must have done this so many times,' she said to the nurse, 'comforted the grieving relatives.' Her voice cracked and a tear rolled down her cheek. She wiped it away hurriedly. 'I'm sorry.'

'Don't be,' the nurse told her, clutching her arm warmly. 'Don't apologise for the way you feel. I was the same when my father died; I was saying sorry to everyone. Sorry for being a nuisance, sorry for crying all the time. Then I realized that it didn't matter. You have a right to your grief. Don't be ashamed of it.'

Donna smiled, despite her tears. She touched the nurse's hand.

'Thank you,' she whispered.

The door of the room opened and the WPC re-entered. Mackenzie was with her. He nodded awkwardly to Donna before sitting down opposite her.

'You wanted some information about your husband's death, Mrs Ward?' he said.

She nodded.

'The crash happened some time this afternoon,' the DC said. 'We think at about four o'clock. His body was brought here for identification. It was easier to reach *you*.'

'*How* did it happen?'

'His brakes failed, as far as we can tell. He hit a wall.'

Donna felt that feeling of despair rising once more like an unstoppable tide.

'Was anyone else hurt in the crash?' she wanted to know.

Mackenzie hesitated, licking his lips self-consciously.

'I'm afraid there was another death. We . . . er . . . we found another body in the car with your husband. A young woman. Her name was Suzanne Regan.'

Donna sat forward in her chair, a frown creasing her brow.

'Oh my God,' she murmured. 'And she was killed, too?'

'Unfortunately, yes. Did you know her?'

'She worked for my husband's publishers. I don't know why she would have been with him, though.'

'She obviously knew your husband quite well?'

'They worked together,' Donna said, her confusion growing. 'Well, not really worked together. Like I said, she worked for his publishers. She was only a secretary, as far as I know. What makes you think she knew him?'

'Well, she *was* in the car with him, for one thing, Mrs Ward. I suppose he could have been giving her a lift home, something like that.'

'What are you trying to say?' Donna snapped, sucking in a deep breath.

Mackenzie clasped his hands together and looked evenly at the distraught woman.

'One of the reasons we couldn't identify your husband after the crash was because he had no ID on his person. No driver's licence, no credit cards, no cheque book. Nothing.'

'He always got *me* to carry his credit cards for him,' she protested.

'That's what I'm trying to tell you, Mrs Ward. He *did* have credit cards *and* his cheque book but *he* wasn't carrying them. After we'd taken the bodies from the wreckage we found your husband's cheque book *and* credit cards in Suzanne Regan's handbag.'

Six

'What are you trying to say?' Donna demanded angrily.

'I'm not trying to *say* anything, Mrs Ward. You merely asked me for some information and I gave it to you,' Mackenzie told her.

'I want to see her,' Donna said flatly.

'That's impossible, Mrs Ward.'

'You could be wrong about her. It might not *be* Suzanne Regan. I've seen her; I could identify her.'

'That's already been done. Her brother confirmed it earlier.'

There was an awkward silence, which was finally broken by Donna.

'Why was she carrying his credit cards?'

'We don't know that, Mrs Ward,' Mackenzie said, almost apologetically.

'What else did you find in her bag? Anything that belonged to my husband?' There was a trace of anger in her voice now.

'I can't disclose information like that, Mrs Ward.'

'Was there anything else?'

'There was a photo of your husband in Miss Regan's purse, and we found two letters from your husband to Miss Regan in her bag as well.'

'Where are they?' Donna demanded.

'Her brother took them. He took all her belongings with him.'

'And my husband? Did he have anything of *hers*?'

'Not as far as we can tell. There was a card – it looks like a business card – in his wallet, but it was blank apart from a phone number and the initial S written on it.'

'Suzanne,' she hissed, her jaws clenched.

The silence descended again and Donna sat back in the chair. Her mind was spinning. First dread, then shock, now confusion. What was next? What other revelations were to be revealed to her?

Why had Suzanne Regan been in the car with him?

Why had she had his photo in her bag? Why was she carrying his credit cards?

Why?

Letters. From Ward to *her*.

She raised a hand to her face once more, covering her eyes.

'I *will* need to speak to you again, Mrs Ward,' Mackenzie said. 'Once everything has been taken care of.'

'You mean after the funeral,' she said, quietly.

'I'll be in touch.' He moved towards the door,

pausing before he left. 'I'm very sorry.' And he was gone.

'I want to go home,' Donna said, her voice quivering. She sounded like a child, a lost child. And lost she most certainly was. She felt more alone than she could ever remember.

Seven

She'd been alone in the house often, but until now Donna had never felt truly lonely.

The silence and the desolation crowded in on her almost palpably. The clock on the wall opposite showed 1.32 a.m. She cradled the mug of tea in her hands and sat at the breakfast bar, head lowered. The central heating was turned up to full and Donna was seated close to a radiator, but she still felt that ever-present chill. She wondered if it would ever leave her.

The policewoman had offered to stay with her for the night, to call a relative. A doctor at the hospital had recommended sleeping pills. She had declined all the offers, accepting only the one to drive her home around midnight.

Home.

Even the word had an empty ring. How could it be home without Chris there? She sniffed back a tear then thought about what the nurse had said: '*You have a right to your grief*'. It was one of the few things from that interminable evening she *did* remember.

That, and Mackenzie's revelations that her husband had been in the car with another woman when he'd been killed.

Donna thought how her mind was trying to dismiss this particular piece of knowledge now in the same way as she had tried to shut herself off from the possibility that her husband was dead.

Another woman?

There was an answer, there had to be. There had to be a reason why Suzanne Regan had been in the car with her husband when he died. Had to be a reason why she was carrying his credit cards and cheque book in her handbag. Had to be a reason why she had two letters from him, and a photo.

There had to be a reason other than the most obvious one, that they were involved somehow.

Involved.

What a pleasing euphemism. It sounded so much more civilized to say that Christopher Ward, her dead husband, had been *involved* with another woman. So much more civilized than saying he was having an affair.

Was that what she was trying to deny now?

First his death, now his infidelity.

For now she had only nagging doubts, doubts which became more tangible the more she considered the matter. She got to her feet and wandered out of the kitchen, holding her mug of tea, snapping off the lights as she went. She walked into the hall, her footfalls soft on the carpet as she headed for the sitting room. She pushed open the door, flicked on the lights and the room was illuminated.

It seemed no more hospitable than the kitchen had done.

Over the fireplace hung the framed covers of three of Ward's books.

He'd written fifteen novels in the last twelve years, each one a massive bestseller. Two had been turned into badly-made and unsuccessful films, but he'd been well paid for the rights; Ward had washed his hands of the adaptations and continued writing.

How long ago had he met Suzanne Regan?

Donna sat in the chair where he always used to sit and where he would never sit again.

Never.

She gazed across the room at the television and saw herself reflected in the blank screen. There were videos beneath the set, her husband's chief form of relaxation.

When he was alive.

Donna felt a tear roll down her cheek.

Had he described the house to Suzanne Regan?

Donna got to her feet and walked out of the sitting-room, leaving it in darkness. Back across the hall she walked, to the dining-room with its large dark wood table and its bookcases where Ward's own books were displayed. She took one from a shelf and turned it over, studying the photo on the back, running one index finger over it. He had been an attractive man. It was hard to believe that this was the same man whose face she had seen earlier, gashed and bloodied by the crash. She studied his features carefully, the steely blue eyes, the shoulder-length brown hair.

Was that what had attracted Suzanne Regan?

Donna replaced the book, still crying softly, aware that she would never see that face again in life, never feel the touch of his hands. The unbearable chill seemed to close tightly round her, like a freezing glove.

It followed her into every room.

In the bathroom she touched his razor and ran her thumb across the blade, scarcely aware that she cut the pad. She watched blood well up from the small gash, forming a globule before running down past the first knuckle.

Every room she walked into and looked around, she picked out the objects which were Ward's, objects which made her think of him even more strongly. And the more she thought about him, the stronger the pain became. The chasm in her soul expanded with every recollection.

She paused at the door to his office.

Her hand quivered over the door handle.

She couldn't enter it.

The memories were piled high in there, as high as the copies of his manuscripts. As high as the filing trays, filled with their letters and notepads.

She closed her eyes and pushed the door open.

In the dull light from the desk lamp she gazed around. One half of the room was occupied by two huge bookcases, the other by his desk. On part of the desk sat a typewriter, an old portable manual model. Ward had never invested in a WP; he'd never found the need to fill his room with technological gadgetry. He wrote long-hand, then typed. It was as simple as that.

Beside the typewriter were loose sheets of notepaper with hastily scribbled notes. She saw a dictionary, a thesaurus, the pocket tape-recorder she had bought for him one Christmas. The filing cabinets and drawers remained shut, their secrets hidden from her.

Donna noticed that the small clock on the desk had stopped, its hands frozen and still.

Like Chris.

She flicked off the light and closed the door behind her, walking into their bedroom. The effort of getting undressed seemed too great; she sat down on the edge of the bed, her head bowed as if under some enormous weight. Tears were rolling down her cheeks, her quiet sobs loud in the stillness of the bedroom. Grief she thought she had expended at the hospital now seemed to crowd in on her. She fell back on the bed, her legs drawn up to her chest, and lay in that foetal position, her body quivering as she cried.

The darkness outside was impenetrable but it was radiant compared to the gloom in her soul.

And she knew this was only the beginning.

Eight

A dream.

It had to be a dream.

She heard the sound but thought it was part of her subconscious. The persistent two-tone bell.

She sat up quickly, her eyes wide and staring, red-rimmed. It was no dream. Daylight poured in through the open curtains of the bedroom. The ringing of the doorbell was virtually unabated now, occasionally interspersed with the banging of the brass knocker.

Donna put both hands to her face and felt the stiffness in her neck and shoulders, the beginning of a headache.

The ringing continued. And the banging.

Donna finally swung herself off the bed and moved mechanically across the landing and down the stairs. She paused beside the front door, she put one eye to the spy-hole and recognised the figure outside. She pulled open the door.

'I thought there was something wrong . . .' Jackie Quinn began. Then, as she looked at Donna, she realized that there was. Something terribly wrong.

Donna stepped away from the door, allowing Jackie into the hallway.

'Donna, what's wrong? What is it? You look

terrible,' Jackie said quickly, shocked by her friend's appearance.

'What time is it?' Donna mumbled quietly.

'Sod the time,' Jackie rasped. 'What's happened?'

'It's Chris,' Donna said, tears already forming in her eyes. 'Jackie, he's dead.'

The two women embraced, Donna clasping her friend to her with a strength born of desperation. Jackie could feel tears soaking into the shoulder of her blouse, could feel Donna trembling helplessly in her grasp. And she too felt that awful sense that someone had punched her in the stomach, knocked the wind from her. Shock struck like a clenched fist.

Jackie guided her weeping friend towards the kitchen and sat her down, keeping her hands on Donna's shoulders, stroking her hair repeatedly. She found herself looking into eyes that bulged in the sockets, eyes criss-crossed by veins.

Eyes without any semblance of hope.

At twenty-eight Donna was a year older than Jackie, but her face might have belonged to a person of forty. Beneath her puffy eyes the skin looked bruised, the lids themselves swollen. Her nose was red, her cheeks untouched by make-up. Her hair was unkempt, tangled like intertwined lizard-tails. Two nails were broken on her right hand and another chewed down as far as the tip of the finger. Her face was tear-stained and Jackie could see patches on Donna's sweatshirt and jeans. She thought the dark stain on her thigh was blood.

Jackie found tears coursing down her own cheeks, so touched was she by the plight of her friend.

Gradually Donna stopped sobbing. Jackie held her close again, rocking her as she would rock a child. She kissed the top of Donna's head, pressing her face against the other woman's hair. Donna pulled back slightly and looked at her.

'It happened yesterday,' she said quietly. 'A car crash. I had to identify his body.'

'Donna, I'm so sorry,' Jackie murmured, wiping tears from her own face before pulling a tissue from her handbag and wiping Donna's face. The older woman sat still and allowed her friend to minister to her.

'Have you been here on your own all night?' she asked.

Donna nodded.

'Why the hell didn't you call me? You need someone with you.'

'I need Chris.'

Jackie nodded slowly and swallowed.

'Have you slept?' she wanted to know.

'A few hours. I must have dropped off on the bed last night. You woke me up, ringing the doorbell.' She smiled thinly.

'Come on,' Jackie said, holding out a hand and beckoning her. 'You're going back to bed.'

'I can't sleep. I couldn't sleep. Not now.'

'You're out on your feet. If I hadn't woken you up you'd still be asleep now. Come on.'

'I'll never be able to sleep, Jackie.'

'I've got some sleeping pills in my handbag; you can take those if you have to. Please, Donna. You need some sleep now.'

Donna got to her feet and allowed herself to be led upstairs to the bedroom. There, Jackie drew the curtains and turned down the bed while Donna slipped off her clothes and threw them to the floor. Naked, she slipped between the sheets. Jackie sat on the edge of the bed stroking her hair until she saw her friend's eyes begin to close. It took a matter of minutes before she was asleep. Jackie took one more look at her then hurried downstairs.

In her sleep Donna rolled over, her lips parted slightly, her breathing even.

One hand slid across the bed to rest where her husband would normally have slept.

Nine

She awoke with a start for the second time that day, sitting bolt upright, her head spinning.

Donna looked round to see Jackie standing by her bedside, a tray in her hand. On the tray was a bowl of soup, some bread and two mugs of tea. Donna smiled thinly and sank back onto her pillows, pulling the sheet round her breasts. She glanced across at the clock on the bedside table and saw that it was almost two-thirty. A watery afternoon sun was trying to fight its way out from behind a bank of thin, high cloud.

'You should have woken me earlier,' she said, rubbing her eyes.

'You needed the sleep,' Jackie told her, setting the tray down on the bed. 'You need food, too.'

'Jackie, I can't,' Donna murmured wearily.

'I don't care whether you can or can't, you *need* to eat. Take it.' She pushed the tray towards her friend and perched on the edge of the bed. Donna looked so tired, so drained. Normally, the two women were not dissimilar in appearance. Both were blonde and about the same height, Jackie perhaps a little bigger around the hips and bust, but they shared the same well-defined features; on more than one occasion they had been mistaken for sisters. At the moment, Jackie thought, Donna could have passed for her mother.

Reluctantly Donna reached for the soup and began sipping it.

'The doctor will be here at about four,' Jackie announced, raising a hand to silence the protest she saw forming on Donna's lips. 'I don't care how much you complain, it's better he looks at you. He might give you some tranquillisers or something.'

'I don't need bloody tranquillisers,' Donna said irritably.

'You need something to help you through this,

Donna. They'll do you good. Our doctor prescribed them for my mum when my dad died.'

'What are you trying to do, turn me into a junkie?'

'He'll probably give you valium, not cocaine.'

Donna managed a smile. She reached out and squeezed Jackie's hand.

'Thanks for what you've done, Jackie. I appreciate it. I'm sorry if I've put you to any trouble . . .'

'Don't be so stupid. What was I supposed to do this morning, just turn around and walk away? What would you have done if you'd found me the same way?'

'Exactly what you've done. But I'm still grateful.'

She sipped more of the soup, then some of her tea.

'Do you want to talk about it?' Jackie asked quietly.

'No, not really, but I suppose I'm going to have to eventually. People will have to be told.' She sighed and rubbed a hand across her face.

'Chris didn't have any family, did he?'

Donna shook her head.

'Neither of us did, but there's my sister. I'll have to let Julie know.'

'It's all taken care of. I phoned her before I phoned the doctor. She said she'll be here tomorrow morning. She's taking time off work.'

Donna looked blankly at Jackie.

'She's your sister, Donna; she *should* be with you. You shouldn't be alone. Not now.'

'Thank you,' Donna said softly.

'So, do you want to talk?'

Donna nodded.

'It was a car crash, somewhere in Central London as far as I know. He was working there for a couple of days, researching a new book. He'd been using the British Museum Library a lot. So he said.' She repeated the sequence of events which led up to the identification of her husband's body the previous night.

'It must have been terrible for you. I'm sorry, Donna.'

'Jackie . . .'

I think he was having an affair.

The words were there but Donna could not bring herself to say them.

'What?' Jackie wanted to know.

Donna shook her head.

'It's all right,' she lied. Then, trying to change the subject: 'Did anyone ring while I was asleep?'

'Two or three people rang. They wanted to speak to Chris. I just told them he wasn't available.' Jackie shrugged. 'I didn't think it was my place to tell them the truth. You're not mad, are you? I suppose if I had done it would have saved you the trouble. Perhaps I should . . .'

'You were right,' Donna said. 'As usual.'

It was Jackie's turn to smile.

'The police rang,' she said after a moment or two, the smile fading. 'They said that you could pick up Chris's belongings whenever you wanted to. Some bloke called Mackenzie. He said he wanted to speak to you when you felt better.'

'He was there last night,' Donna said. Then she frowned. 'I wonder why they need to speak to me again? I identified Chris.' She swallowed hard. 'What more could they want to know?'

Some details about Suzanne Regan, perhaps?

Could you tell us how long your husband had been having an affair, Mrs Ward?

She wiped a tear from her eye and sniffed, pushing the tray away.

'I can't eat any more,' she announced apologetically.

'There's some stuff in your fridge, I checked. I'll warm it up for you later. Chops, that kind of thing.'

'I can't eat anything, Jackie, I told you. Anyway, you can't stay here all the time. Dave gets home at about six, doesn't he?'

'Dave is on a training course for a couple of nights in Southampton. I've got nothing to rush back for, anyway.'

Are you sure that's where he is, Jackie? Are you certain he's not driving around with another woman? Positive he isn't involved?

That word again.

'If you want me to stay the night with you I will,' Jackie said.

'I appreciate it, really, but I've got to face things sooner or later.'

'It's only the day after, Donna; be fair to yourself. Don't try to be *too* strong.'

'I'll be okay.'

'I'll stay until the doctor's been, how's that?'

Donna smiled and nodded, watching Jackie pick up the tray and head for the door. She heard her footfalls on the stairs and lay down, eyes closed for long moments.

A car crash in Central London. He was working there.

Was he? Was he really working?

On a book or on Suzanne Regan?

Donna opened her eyes, felt the moisture there.

Had it been an affair?

Somehow she had to find out.

Ten

It was about seven-thirty when Jackie finally left. She had tried to encourage Donna to eat something, using a combination of threats and cajolements. The two women had ended up smiling at each other across the kitchen table. Both of them knew that there was no relief in that smile, however; no hint of a respite from the suffering Donna felt.

The doctor had prescribed a mild dosage of Valium, just 2mg, the minimum dose, but Donna was wary of the drug and said she'd only take it if she found she had no option.

Alone in the house now, seated at the kitchen table dressed in tracksuit bottoms and a T-shirt several sizes too big, she stared at the bottle reproachfully and ran a hand through her hair. She had showered and washed her hair after Jackie had left, standing beneath the spray for more than twenty minutes, as if the powerful jets of water could wash away some of her grief.

She'd sat in the sitting-room and tried to watch television but the images on the screen did not register in her mind. She had flicked aimlessly from channel to channel before switching the set off and turning on the stereo instead. It didn't seem to matter what she did as long as she didn't have to put up with the silence. In the kitchen she had switched on the ghetto-blaster, but every tape she selected seemed to bring different memories. If she played one of Chris's tapes it made her think of him. If she played one of her own then the words she normally sang along to quite happily had added poignancy. He always used to joke with her about her choice of music, telling her the sad love songs she was so fond of would make her depressed. They never had. Until now.

She sat alone and silent in the kitchen, tapping the lid of the valium bottle, wondering if she should take just one.

It *might* help.

She shook her head. Tranquillizers helped to

alleviate symptoms of stress and suffering; they didn't remove the cause.

She got to her feet and padded barefoot from the kitchen back towards the stairs, climbing them slowly.

The phone rang again but she ignored it, allowing the message to be taken by the answering machine. The green light was already flashing three times but Donna had no inclination to learn the identity of the callers just yet. As she reached the top of the stairs she heard the click as the machine recorded the latest call and stored it.

The house was silent again as she wandered down the corridor that led off the landing to her husband's office.

It was cold inside there, colder than the rest of the house, she thought, but realized that this was merely fanciful supposition. She touched the radiator and found it was hot. She switched on the desk lamp and sat down behind the typewriter, running her fingers over the black keys as if it were a musical instrument.

There was a framed picture of her husband on the wall to the left of the desk, from a photo shoot he'd done in Madame Tussaud's Chamber of Horrors for the launch of his last book. It showed him standing beside the guillotine, pointing up at the blade and smiling.

Donna stared at the photo, her eyes filling with tears. She fought them back and glanced around at the other things on his desk. It was organised chaos. File trays were marked with white sticky labels, each one supposedly home, according to the legend on the sticker, to various documents.

CONTRACTS

RESEARCH AND NOTES

FAN MAIL

She picked a letter from the top of the tray and glanced at it. It was the usual thing. '*I enjoyed your books very much. I look forward to the next one. Please can I have a signed photo etc. etc.*'

Ward received a lot of fan mail and was always grateful for it. The readers, he used to tell her, paid their mortgage.

Did they pay for his mistress, too?

Donna slid open one of the drawers and peered in. More notepads, more envelopes. Elastic bands, paper clips, Tipp-Ex.

A letter.

She pulled it out and spread it out on the desk, scanning it through tired eyes.

Dear Suzanne.

Donna stiffened, sucked in a shallow breath.

Suzanne.

One part of her wanted to read the letter; the other part told her not to continue.

'Dear Suzanne,' she read aloud. 'Just a quick note to tell you that everything is taken care of.' She swallowed hard. 'I hope you are well and I will see you next Thursday. Love, Chris.'

Love.

Donna closed her eyes for a moment, her body shaking. Then she looked at the letter again. There was no date on it.

See you next Thursday.

She snatched at the letter and balled it up, crushing it between her hands, finally hurling it across the room with a despairing grunt. Tears were coursing down her cheeks. She glared across at the photo of her husband on the wall.

He smiled back at her.

'You fucking bastard,' she roared at the photo.

She didn't know whether her tears were of pain or anger.

And it didn't really seem to matter any more.

Eleven

Donna hadn't expected so much coverage in the papers.

She'd thought there would be a mention of her husband's death in the trade magazines, and perhaps a line or two in one of the nationals, but she was unprepared for what actually appeared.

Three of the tabloids ran two-column stories (one with a photograph) while even *The Times* mentioned Chris's death. A little ironic, Donna thought, considering how they had lambasted his books when he'd been alive. The coverage provoked a flood of phone calls to the house.

She moved around irritably, not picking up the phone, leaving the answering machine to cope with the deluge. Occasionally she would stand beside the machine and listen to see who was on the other end of the line, but by the afternoon she had unplugged all the phones except the one connected to the answerphone in an effort to get some peace.

She hadn't slept much the previous night and what rest she'd managed had been fitful. She'd woken twice from a nightmare but had been unable to remember the images that had shocked her into consciousness.

Car crashes, perhaps?

Funerals?

Mistresses?

She didn't go near Ward's office that day; she feared what she might find in there. The letter she had discovered had only reinforced her conviction that her husband had been having an affair with Suzanne Regan. What Donna *was* aware of was how little she had cried since finding the letter. More and more of the emotion she felt was tinged with anger now.

She ate a bowl of soup and some bread at about two o'clock and sat staring at the Valium bottle. She thought about taking one of the tablets but decided against it.

The phone was silent now. As she dropped her bowl into the sink, Donna decided to check the messages before a new batch came in.

The house seemed very quiet as she walked

through the hallway and flicked the switch marked 'Incoming Message'. She heard a high-pitched squeal, a cacophony of indecipherable noise as the tape rewound quickly then began with its catalogue of calls.

A reporter from the local paper.

Diana Wellsby, Ward's editor, offering her condolences.

Nick Crosby, Managing Director of his publishers, also offering his sympathies.

No message.

Chris's accountant; could he ring him? (Obviously not everyone read the papers, Donna thought.)

Her mother, who said she refused to speak to a machine but would ring back.

Donna smiled thinly when she heard her mother's voice.

Jackie. Ring her, just to let her know how things were going.

'Mrs Ward, this is Detective Constable Mackenzie. I'd appreciate it if you could call me as soon as possible. Thank you.'

Donna chewed her bottom lip thoughtfully. The policeman had called yesterday, too. What was so important? She reached for the pad and pen beside the phone, rewound the tape and took down the number he'd left.

'Donna, it's Martin Connelly,' the next voice announced. She smiled at the warmth in the tone. It was Chris's agent. 'I realize what you must be feeling and I'm very sorry about what's happened. I'll call you back later. Take care, gorgeous.'

One more call.

She waited for a voice but there wasn't one.

A wrong number, perhaps?

She could hear breathing on the tape, slow, rhythmic breathing. No background noise. Nothing but breathing.

Then the message was brought to an abrupt end as the phone was put down.

Donna flicked her hair from her face and was about to walk away from the phone when it rang again.

Her hand hovered over the receiver. She thought about picking it up but finally allowed the machine to click on.

Breathing.

The same breathing as on the message she'd just listened to.

Pick it up.

Donna stared at the phone, listening to the breathing. Then finally she heard, 'Shit.' The phone was put down, *slammed down* hard at the other end.

Donna backed away from the machine as if it were some kind of venomous serpent. If it was a crank call, it was either bad timing or a particularly sick bastard getting his rocks off at the other end of the line. She suddenly felt very lonely and vulnerable.

It was then that the doorbell rang.

Twelve

For long moments she hesitated, standing rigid in the hallway.

The chain was off.

Donna swallowed hard and took a step towards the door as the two-tone chime sounded again. She gently eased the chain into position and finally peered through the spy-hole.

She saw her younger sister immediately.

Donna hurried to open the door, throwing it wide and holding out her arms.

When Julie Craig embraced her the two women clutched each other tightly, unwilling to be parted. Finally Donna pulled back slightly, with tears in her eyes.

'Thanks for coming,' she whispered.

'Nothing would have stopped me,' Julie told her. They embraced again. 'Donna, I'm so sorry.'

Both of them were crying now, weeping softly against each other's shoulders. At last Donna guided her sister inside the house and pushed the front door closed.

'I'll get my stuff out of the car in a minute,' Julie told her, wiping a tear away. She touched her cheek and shook her head gently. 'You look *so* tired.'

'I haven't been sleeping too well,' Donna said, smiling humourlessly. 'You can guess why.' She wiped her eyes. 'I'm glad you're here, Julie.'

When she'd finished telling her story Donna didn't even raise her head. She merely shifted slightly in her seat, running the tip of her index finger around the rim of her teacup.

Julie watched her sister seated at the other end of the sofa, legs drawn up beneath her. She reached out a hand and touched Donna's arm, gripping it.

'Why didn't you call me as soon as it happened?' she wanted to know.

'There was no point. Besides, I could hardly remember my own name, let alone call anyone,' Donna explained, running a hand through her blonde hair. She looked at Julie and smiled. 'Little sister helping *big* sister out this time.'

'You've helped me enough times in the past,' Julie said.

There was only two years' age difference between the women. Julie, at twenty-six, was also a little taller, her hair darker, chestnut brown compared to her sister's lighter, natural colour. They were dressed similarly too, both in black leggings and baggy tops, Julie wearing white socks, Donna barefoot. They had always dressed similarly. They had similar views on life, men and the world in general, too. Best friends as well as sisters, they had shared a closeness throughout their lives most siblings only discover with advancing years. There had been no teenage rivalry between them, only a bond of love that had grown deeper as they'd developed. It had intensified when Julie left home first to attend photographic college and Donna had moved into her own flat after securing a job with a record company. The very fact that the women saw less of each other made their closeness more palpable when they met.

Julie had married when she was twenty-two. It was a doomed relationship with a man ten years older, whose affections seemed divided between her and the contents of whisky bottles. Their short marriage had ended acrimoniously less than a year after they'd promised each other, 'Til Death us do Part'. Alcohol, it seemed, was as effective a destroyer of marriages as death.

Julie had set up her own photographic business with her share of the settlement money, a business she now owned and operated with the aid of a partner, employing three people. It was thriving.

Donna had married two years later. Both had known love; both had known grief. The latter tended to predominate where men were concerned.

'How far have you got with the arrangements?' Julie asked. 'Sorting out the undertaker, things like that?'

'I haven't even picked up Chris's things from the hospital yet,' Donna said guiltily. She looked at her sister, opened her mouth to say something, then paused a moment longer before finally breaking the silence.

'Julie, I think Chris was having an affair.'

Julie shot her an anxious glance.

'What makes you think that?' she demanded.

'There was another woman in the car with him when he died,' Donna began, then went on to explain what had come to light.

'She could have been a friend,' Julie offered.

Donna raised an eyebrow quizzically.

'A friend? Yes, I suppose she could have been.' She shook her head.

'I'm not saying you're wrong, I'm just saying you've got more important things to think about right now.'

'More important things?' Donna snapped. 'My husband was having an affair, Julie. He died with the woman he was fucking behind my back. I think *that's* important.'

'You loved him, didn't you?'

'Of course I loved him. I loved him more than I thought it was possible to love anyone. That's why it hurts so much.' Tears were beginning to form in her eyes. 'I miss him so much but I'll never know the truth.' The tears were flowing freely now. 'And I have to know.' Julie embraced her, stroking her hair. 'I *have* to know.'

Thirteen

Donna was crossing the hall when she heard the car pull up outside.

She paused as she heard the car door shut and footsteps approach. She moved towards the front door, peering through the spy-hole. She smiled as she recognised her visitor and opened the door before he could ring the bell.

Martin Connelly looked surprised to find himself gazing into her face.

'I heard your car,' she said, beckoning him inside.

Connelly accepted the invitation and stepped in, turning to hug Donna briefly.

'When you didn't call me back I thought I'd come round and see how you were. I hope you don't mind,' he said.

'It's very thoughtful of you,' she told him as they walked into the sitting-room.

Julie was glancing at a magazine when Connelly entered. She looked up and saw him, smiled tightly and nodded a greeting.

'Martin, this is my sister Julie,' Donna announced. 'Martin Connelly. He was Chris's agent.' The two of them shook hands a little stiffly and Connelly looked at Donna.

'If I'm interrupting,' he apologised. 'I just

wanted to see if you were okay. I won't stay.' He smiled at Julie again.

'Stay and have a drink.'

'If I do it had better be coffee. I'm driving,' Connelly explained.

'I'll make it,' said Julie. 'You two talk.' And she was gone, closing the sitting-room door behind her, leaving them alone.

Connelly wandered over to the fireplace and glanced at the framed book covers that hung there. Donna studied him.

He was in his mid-thirties, smartly dressed (he was always smartly dressed, she remembered), his light brown hair impeccably groomed. He had been Ward's agent for the last five years. The relationship between them had never been business-orientated, though; it was something stronger than that. Although it was not powerful enough to be true friendship, there was nevertheless a mutual respect of each other's abilities coupled by a ruthless streak they also both possessed. It had been a formidable combination.

'You're okay for money, aren't you?' Connelly asked her.

'I won't starve, Martin.'

'I always made sure Chris had enough insurance policies and stuff like that.' He turned and looked at her. 'But if you need anything, anything at all, you call me. Right?'

She smiled.

'I mean it, Donna,' he insisted. 'Promise me you will.'

'I promise.'

He reached into the pocket of his jacket and took out a packet of cigarettes, lighting one with his silver lighter. He regarded her coolly through the haze of bluish smoke. Despite the dark rings beneath her eyes and the fact that her hair needed brushing she still looked extremely attractive. Prior to Ward's death he'd seen her dressed up, her make-up done to perfection. On some of those occasions the only word he could find to describe her was breathtaking. Now he ran appraising eyes slowly over her, a little embarrassed when she looked up and caught him in the middle of his furtive inspection.

'How long's your sister here for?' he asked, feeling the need to break the silence.

'For as long as she wants to be. Certainly until after the funeral.'

'Do you know when it is yet?'

She shook her head.

'I've got to sort all that out tomorrow,' Donna told him.

'Do you need any help?'

'I'll be all right. Thanks, anyway. It's probably better in some ways. The more I've got to do, the less time I've got to sit around and think about what's happened.'

'I know what you mean. No good brooding about it, is it?' He realized the clumsiness of his statement and apologised.

'It's okay, Martin. Say what you think. People can't tip-toe around the subject for the rest of their lives. Chris is dead, and there's nothing I can do about that. Ignoring it isn't going to make it any more bearable.'

'You know that he had it written into all his contracts that, if anything happened to him, you were to become beneficiary of all his money from royalties and advances?' Connelly said.

She nodded.

'I remember when we first met, before Chris was earning decent money from his books. People used to tell me I was crazy to stay with him, that he'd never earn a good living. Then, when he *did* start earning good money, those same people told me that was the only reason I'd stayed with him.' She shook her head.

'Jealousy. You'll always get it. The wives of successful men always get that thrown at them, that they're only with the bloke because of his money. It happens the other way round, too. Behind every successful woman is a spongeing bastard; behind every successful man is a gold-digger.' He smiled and took another drag on his cigarette. 'Of course sometimes it's true.'

Now it was Donna's turn to smile. The atmosphere seemed to lighten a little.

Connelly moved away from the fireplace and sat down opposite her, chancing another swift glance at her as she ran a hand over her face.

'How much did you know about Chris?' she asked.

Connelly frowned.

'What do you mean?' the agent asked, looking a little puzzled.

'I mean about his work, his character. What he did in his spare time. How much did you know about what he thought?'

Connelly looked bemused.

'Would you say you *knew* him, Martin? Knew him as a person, not just as a client?'

'That's a strange question, Donna. I don't see what you're driving at.'

Their conversation was momentarily interrupted as Julie arrived with a tray of coffee cups, milk and sugar. She set it down and poured cups for Donna and Connelly, saying she had some things to unpack. 'I'll leave you to talk.' She smiled at Connelly. 'It was good to meet you.' Again she disappeared and Donna heard her footsteps on the stairs.

Connelly dropped sugar cubes into his cup and stirred gently.

'What do you mean, did I *know* Chris?' he asked.

'You were pretty close, weren't you? I mean, he must have told you things. About himself, about his work, about me.'

'Donna, I was his agent, not his bloody confessor. If my clients want to tell me their problems, that's up to them. I care about them, and I like to think it's not just on a professional level.'

'Did Chris tell you his problems?'

'What kind of problems?' Connelly said, taken aback by her questions. 'What made you think he had any? If he had, you'd know more about them than me. You *were* his wife.'

'I hadn't forgotten, Martin,' she said acidly. 'But there might have been things he told you that he *couldn't* tell me.'

Connelly shook his head.

'Did he tell you he was having an affair?' she demanded.

The agent looked at her evenly.

'What makes you think he was?' he wanted to know. 'And even if he *was*, which I doubt, what makes you so sure he'd tell *me*?'

'You said you were close to your clients. He couldn't very well tell me, could he?'

'What gives you the idea he was having an affair, for Christ's sake? He loved you. Why would he want to screw around with other women?'

'Does your professionalism run to protecting him when he's dead, Martin?'

'Donna, I know you're going through a bad time, I understand that. But this is shit.' There was a hint of anger in Connelly's voice. 'Chris wasn't having an affair and if he was, he didn't say anything to me about it. You're on about that crap in the paper about him being found in the car with a woman, aren't you?'

'He *was* found in the car with a woman.'

'That doesn't mean she was his mistress. Jesus Christ, Donna. Think about it logically.'

'I don't know what to think any more, Martin,' she hissed. 'But I'll tell you this, if you're keeping quiet just because you think it's saving me hurt then you may as well tell me what you know. I couldn't suffer any more than I'm suffering now.'

'Just listen to what you're saying, Donna,' Connelly told her, trying to keep his voice even. 'Your husband is dead and all you can think about is whether or not he was having a fucking affair.'

An uneasy silence descended.

Donna rested her head on her hand, her eyes averted. Connelly kept his gaze on her. When he sipped at his coffee again it was cold. He put the cup back on the tray and got to his feet, taking a step towards her.

'He never said anything to me, Donna, believe me. I know as much as you.' He wanted to reach out and touch her shoulder but resisted the temptation. 'If I knew anything I'd tell you.'

'Would you, Martin?' she said, eyeing him challengingly.

'I'd better go,' he said quietly. 'I'll let you get on.'

She got to her feet and they walked to the front door where she paused on the step and pecked him on the cheek.

'Don't forget,' he said. 'If you need *anything*, just let me know.'

She nodded and watched as he walked to the waiting Porsche and slid behind the steering wheel. He started the engine and waved, watching her disappear back inside the house. Connelly pulled away, the house falling away behind him.

On the landing, hidden by the curtains, Julie Craig also watched the agent leave.

Fourteen

They had done all they could that day. The two women had risen early and begun the tasks which needed completion. Now, as night began to creep across the sky, they sat in the dining-room eating, occasionally glancing at each other and smiling.

Donna, wearing make-up for the first time in two days, looked pale and tired still but she also looked a little stronger.

There had been tears when they'd called at the hospital that morning to pick up Chris's belongings but Julie had expected that.

His clothes were now upstairs in one of the spare bedrooms, the blood-spattered garments laid out on one of the beds until they could be washed. It was as if Donna needed to keep looking at them; despite Julie's entreaties, she had returned regularly to the room that day to view the torn clothing.

Next to his clothes lay his wallet and his cheque book, similarly splashed with blood.

After the hospital they had travelled to the undertaker. He'd been helpful and sympathetic in his practised way, a fat, middle-aged man with too much hair that looked as if it had been dropped onto his head from a great height. He asked the relevant questions:

'Open coffin?'

'Cremation or burial?'

'How much did she want to spend?'

The enquiries had begun to blur into one another; Donna had left feeling that she was no longer in control of events. The undertaker would arrange everything, he assured her. She need have no worries. As she and Julie had left another group of people had entered, doubtless to be asked the same questions. Death had become like a conveyor belt, it seemed.

From the undertaker's they travelled to a florist's and ordered the flowers.

There were catalogues full of suitable wreaths and arrangements. Wreaths for all occasions. Donna noticed, with acute poignancy, that one page was devoted to 'The Death of a Child'. How terrible, she thought, for parents to be confronted by that particular ordeal.

Everything appeared ready now; there was just the funeral to come. The time Donna dreaded most. The awful finality of it all. At the moment, she knew the body of her dead husband lay in the Chapel of Rest. Once it was laid in the earth then it was as if he was to be wiped from her consciousness, not just her mind. All she had to look forward to now were memories.

Memories and pain.

And anger.

Donna pushed her plate away from her and sat back in her chair, exhaling deeply.

'You okay?' Julie asked.

'I feel so tired,' Donna told her. She smiled wanly at her sister. 'I'm sorry, Julie.'

'Go and have a nap, I'll take care of this,' Julie said, waving a hand over the dirty plates and glasses. 'Go on. I'll bring you a cup of tea up in a while.'

Donna thanked her and walked away from the table, touching Julie's shoulder as she went.

The younger woman smiled and kept on smiling as she heard her sister's footfalls on the stairs. The steps groaned protestingly as she made her way to the bedroom. Julie continued eating, looking first at her watch then at her plate. Eventually she, too, pushed it away, got to her feet and began gathering the utensils, ready to take them through to the kitchen.

As she reached the dining-room door she glanced across at a darkwood cabinet inside the room. There were a number of photos on it, each of them in a silver frame.

Photos of Donna and Ward together.

Julie stood close to them, gazing at the pictures for long moments. Then she reached out one slender finger and gently drew it around the outline of Ward's face, a slight smile creasing her lips.

Then she did the same around the image of Donna's face.

By then, though, the smile had faded.

Fifteen

He used to call it The Cell.

The room where he imprisoned himself for six hours a day, five days a week. The room where Christopher Ward sat, with only his thoughts for company, pounding away at a typewriter until a new book was completed.

The silence in the room was something Donna had always found unsettling. Only the sound of the water in the radiators broke the oppressive stillness. One day, jokingly, she had said to him that he had an easy job, just sitting behind a desk alone all day. He had locked Donna in there behind the typewriter. After just ten minutes she had called to him to let her out. Laughing, he had agreed.

Laughing.

She had almost forgotten what the sound was like. At times she wondered if she would ever hear such joyous noise again. Certainly not now, seated in The Cell, peering round her at the notes scattered over the desk, at the books and the files.

He had always kept his work private. What went on inside his head was his concern, he'd once told her. And what went on inside his office was his concern, too. He hadn't excluded her through any act of antagonism; he preferred to keep his work and his life with her separate. She had asked him about his methods of working, about how each of his books was progressing; she'd even been allowed to read portions of them before they were published. But as a rule Ward kept his work to himself. What little else she discovered was by reading interviews with him in newspapers or by hearing him on radio, watching him on television.

And now, as she sat amongst the remnants of his work, she felt a heavy sadness at this exclusion. Now it was too late for him to tell her, she felt she wanted to know every single stage of the processes involved in turning an idea into a finished book. But she knew it could never be.

She began by searching his attaché case, going through the papers. She needed the insurance policies, for instance.

She wondered why she felt as if she were intruding in the small room. It was as if she had no right to be in here, with the night closed tightly around the house like a tenebrous glove. Only the dull glow from the desk light illuminated the blackness.

Donna felt that chill she had come to know only too well over the last few days.

She found what she sought and pulled it clear of the case.

The photos came loose with it.

They fluttered into the air and then fell to the floor. Half a dozen of them.

Donna picked them up.

There was a publicity shot of Chris, unsmiling. His sinister face, he called it. She smiled thinly as she gathered the other photos, turning the next one over.

Chris again.

With other men.

She searched their faces but didn't recognise any of them. They were sitting at a large table, two younger men, no older than Chris, then her husband, then an older man. Very much older. She squinted at the picture but could not make out his features. It was as if that particular part of the photo were blurred.

It was the same with the next man.

Very old again and, once more, the image was blurred.

Not so with the last of the group, a young man in his early thirties, handsome but with cruel eyes and short dark hair. She could feel those eyes boring into her as she studied the picture.

The next one was the same, except that Chris was in the centre this time.

And again she saw those two blurred images. As she looked from one to the other she realized that it was just the faces that were blurred; the rest of the image was as sharp as a knife.

No one in the photo was smiling. Chris and the other five looked impassively into the camera. She assumed that was what the two older men were doing, too, just looking at the camera. She knew they were old from the wrinkles on their hands;

there were deep folds of skin around the knuckles and the base of the thumb. Their clothes looked old, too. Almost archaic, in fact.

What did stand out with sharp clarity was something on their hands.

Both the blurred figures wore rings on their left index fingers, large heavy gold signet rings.

She peered closer at them, aware that there was a symbol of some kind at their centre, but no matter how closely she looked she could not make it out.

Donna sat back on her haunches, breathing heavily.

Then she picked up his diary, flicking through it.

JANUARY 11th: Phone Martin.

JANUARY 15th: Confirm interview for next week.

JANUARY 17th: Shooting – 7.00–9.00.

The entries were mostly uninspiring, some scribbled in pencil, others in pen.

FEBRUARY 5th: Check train times.

She read on.

FEBRUARY 9th: Ring S.

Donna gritted her teeth and flicked back and forth through the diary. There were numerous entries of a similar nature. Sometimes just the initial. Others just bore the initial D.

Well, it didn't refer to Donna, that's for sure.

Another mistress?

Donna flicked to the back of the diary, to the addresses, and ran her index finger down the list.

Through the hotels and restaurants, the business addresses, the private addresses, the . . .

SUZANNE REGAN.

Donna read the address, then reached for a pen and scribbled it down on a piece of paper.

SUZANNE REGAN,
23 LOCKWOOD DRIVE,
NOTTING HILL GATE,
LONDON W2

She got to her feet, the piece of paper gripped in her fist.

Sixteen

'Where the hell are you going?'

Julie looked up in surprise as her sister entered the sitting-room, her long leather coat flying open as she headed across the room.

'Out,' snapped Donna, brandishing the piece of paper.

Julie got to her feet. She noticed that Donna had pulled on a pair of suede boots and tucked her jeans into the top of them.

'You were tired; you were going to have a nap. Donna, tell me what's happening.' She could see the tearstains on the older woman's face.

'I know where she lives,' Donna said angrily. 'I found her address in his diary. I know where she lives.'

'*Lived*,' Julie reminded her. 'And so what if you do?'

'I want to see where she lived.'

'Donna, this is crazy. She's dead. It's over. *She's* dead. Chris is dead. That's all there is to it. Stop this now, before it drives you mad. You're becoming obsessive about it.'

'And wouldn't you?' Donna rasped. 'You lost *your* husband to the bottle, but it didn't matter to you. I *care*.'

Julie took a step back, her face losing its colour.

'I wish I could argue with you,' she said resignedly. 'Yes, I did lose my husband to the bottle, not another woman. But the difference between us is I didn't blame myself for his drinking. It's as if you're blaming yourself for what Chris did before he was killed. It isn't your fault, Donna.'

'Then why did he need to have an affair?' she rasped. 'What the fuck was so special about this bloody Suzanne Regan? I want to know what she had that I don't. I want to know what she wore, what she smelled like. I want to know what kind of music she listened to. I even want to know what she bloody well ate.' There was a vehemence in Donna's words Julie had never seen before, a hatred that burned as brightly as a beacon. It danced in her eyes like fire.

'It's becoming an obsession with you,' Julie continued. 'I'm beginning to wonder which has upset you the most, the fact that Chris is dead or that he was unfaithful.'

'Well, perhaps even *I* don't know any more,' Donna told her. 'He's not here for me to ask, is he? I can't find out from him why he wanted her. So I have to find out myself. It might just keep me sane.'

'Why do you have to know?' Julie asked imploringly. 'Why do you have to torture yourself?'

'I told you, I need to know whether she was better than me.' There were tears forming in Donna's eyes now. 'I lost my husband, Julie, that's the worse thing I could ever have imagined. I don't want to lose my self-respect, too.'

For long seconds the two women stood staring at each other, neither speaking. Then Julie took a step forward.

'What are you going to do?' she asked quietly.

'Go to her house.'

'And do what?'

'Look around, see what I can find.'

'You're just going to break in? As easy as that?'

'I don't know what I'm going to do. All I know is, I have to see where she lived.' She handed the piece of paper with the address on to Julie. 'You're my sister and I love you. If you love *me*, then help me.'

'Help you do what? Go crazy? Because that's what you're doing. Please think about this, Donna. Think about what you're doing to yourself. Isn't Chris's death enough to cope with?'

Donna's stare was unflinching.

'Are you going to help me?' she asked, holding out her hand for the piece of paper.

Julie exhaled deeply and wearily.

'Yes, I'll help you,' she said finally.

'I want to go there now.'

Julie knew that it was futile to argue. She nodded.

'Let me get my coat,' she said. 'I'll drive.'

Seventeen

Number Twenty-Three Lockwood Drive was a converted house off Moscow Road, part of the maze of Notting Hill.

It was white, or had been at one time. Now the painted brickwork was grey with the accumulated grime of the years. Even the flowers in the window box on the ground floor looked as though they'd been sprayed with dust. It was difficult to tell which were alive and which weren't. A row of iron railings, rusted in places, protected the front of the house and a gate with one hinge missing guarded the short path to the front door. The neighbouring houses were in a similar state; many had FOR SALE signs displayed.

Lights burned in windows and shadowy figures could be seen moving behind curtains. There were few people on the streets and those that were hardly glanced at the two women sitting in the Fiesta parked opposite Number Twenty-Three.

Donna Ward gazed at the house, studying every

aspect of it: the colour of the front door, the curtains that hung at the windows. She saw a dark stain at the meeting of the roof and front wall and realized that water had obviously been dripping from a hole in the guttering. Somewhere close by she heard a dog bark.

Street lamps burned with a dull yellow light, casting deep shadows. Inside the car it was silent.

The drive into the heart of London had taken less than an hour. Traffic had been unexpectedly light and Julie had guided them skilfully to their destination. Now she sat in the driver's seat, one hand pressed to her forehead, her impatience growing.

'How long are we going to sit here?' she wanted to know.

Donna ignored the question, her eyes still fixed on the dirty white house across the road.

'It's expensive around here,' she said. 'A bit grand for a secretary's wages. Perhaps he was paying her rent, too.'

'Let's go. You've seen the place, that's what you wanted.'

Donna reached for the door-handle and pushed it open.

'What are you doing?' Julie asked, bewildered.

'Wait for me,' Donna instructed her, swinging herself out of the car. She walked briskly across the street and headed for the house, lifting the gate on its hinge as she made her way up the short path and four steps.

Julie, watching from the car, shook her head.

Donna studied the panel beside the front door and saw a number of names attached to the intercom buttons. She ran her index finger down the list:

Weston.

Lawrence.

Regan.

She gritted her teeth when she saw the name, then pressed the main door buzzer and waited.

She heard movement behind the door. A moment later, it was opened and she found herself looking into the face of a man in his sixties, short, balding and with tufts of white hair sprouting from each nostril. It looked as if two snow-white caterpillars were trying to escape from his nose. He was wearing impeccably-pressed trousers, a blue shirt that looked freshly ironed and a spotted bow-tie. On his feet he wore scuffed carpet slippers.

He smiled warmly when he saw Donna.

'Can I help you?' he asked.

'It's about my sister,' she lied, her tone sombre. 'Suzanne Regan.'

The old man nodded, his smile fading.

'I was very sorry to hear what happened. She was a lovely girl,' he offered. 'There's a family resemblance.'

Donna controlled herself with difficulty.

'My brother said he was going to call round for some of her things,' she said, sounding remarkably convincing. 'But I thought I'd better check whether he had or not.'

'No one's been round, Miss Regan,' he said, glancing down at her left hand, catching sight of the wedding ring. 'Or is it *Mrs*?' He smiled again.

She shook her head.

'My name is

(*careful now*)

Blake. Catherine Blake.'

'Mercuriadis,' he announced, holding out a hand. She shook it lightly; his hand felt soft and warm. 'I know it's a bit of a mouthful. Would you like to come in?'

Bingo.

Donna accepted the invitation and closed the door behind her, looking briefly around the hall. There was a small antique chest to her left with flowers propped in a vase on its scratched top. A pay-phone on the wall. To the right was the half-open door to the landlord's own flat, presumably. At least she assumed he was the landlord. Ahead of her was a flight of stairs.

'I'd just like to check my sister's flat if that's all right?' Donna said, trying to hold the old man's gaze.

'I'll get the key,' he said, and disappeared into the room on the right. Donna could hear the sound of television coming from inside.

Jesus, this was too easy.

See how easy it is to lie.

He returned a moment later clutching the key and ushered her towards the stairs.

'Did you see much of my sister?' she wanted to

know as they climbed the stairs slowly, the old man wheezing every few steps.

'No, she kept herself to herself. Very quiet. A lovely girl.'

'Did she have many visitors? I was always joking with her about getting a boyfriend.' Donna laughed as convincingly as she could.

'There was a young man,' Mercuriadis said. 'I saw him with her two or three times.' He lowered his voice into a conspiratorial whisper. 'I think he spent the night more than once.' He smiled.

Donna tried to smile but it came out as a grimace.

'What did he look like?' she asked.

'I can't really remember. Age plays tricks with memory, you know. My wife always used to say that, God rest her soul.'

Had Chris been here? Had he slept here with her?

They reached the first landing and Donna hesitated.

'It's up another flight, I'm afraid,' he told her. 'It's a good job my tenants are younger than I am. It never used to bother me, all this climbing. My wife and I bought this house forty years ago. After she died I decided to let the rooms. I don't like being in a house this size on my own. There aren't so many tenants now, though. I've had to put the rents up and some moved out. The recession, you know.' He nodded as if to reinforce his statement.

'Look, I can check out the room myself,' Donna

told him. 'There's no need for you to struggle up the stairs. I'll return the key to you on my way out.'

'All right, then. That's very thoughtful of you,' he said, looking at her.

Was it her imagination or did she see a look of suspicion in his eyes?

Come on, don't get paranoid.

'I'm surprised I don't remember seeing you before,' he said, still holding onto the key. 'I don't usually forget a pretty face.'

Donna smiled with impressive sincerity.

'Thank you. I live on the South Coast. I didn't get to see Suzanne as often as I'd like.'

Lying was easier than she'd thought.

He nodded again and handed her the key.

'I'll leave you to it, then,' he said. 'But I would just like to offer my condolences once again. I know what you must be going through.'

Do you? Do you really?

She smiled thinly, took the key from him and set off up the second flight of stairs, emerging on the next landing. She looked down to see the landlord making his way back down the stairs. She waited until she heard the door to his room close before turning around.

Only then, faced by four locked doors and with the key in her hand, did she realize that she hadn't got a clue which of the doors would lead her into Suzanne Regan's flat.

Eighteen

What the hell was she going to do?

Donna looked at the key, then at each of the doors in turn. They all looked the same.

Only one way to find out.

She crossed to the first door and edged the key into the lock, listening for any sounds from the other side. She didn't relish the prospect of having to explain herself to both an irate tenant *and* Mr Mercuriadis. She heard nothing and pushed the key as far as it would go into the Yale lock, turning it as gently as possible.

It wouldn't turn.

She withdrew it with equal care, looking behind her at the other doors just in case someone emerged and caught her at her furtive business.

She moved to the next door and pressed her ear close to the white-painted wood.

From inside she heard classical music. Someone was obviously in there.

Donna turned and moved towards the third of the four doors. Once more she pushed the key slowly into the lock and tried to turn it.

Again it wouldn't move.

She allowed herself a thin smile as she realized, by process of elimination, that the door she wanted was the last one. Donna pulled the key.

It wouldn't budge; remained stuck fast in the lock.

She swallowed hard and gripped it more firmly but still the recalcitrant object stayed where it was, held by the grooves and threads of the lock.

She had to free it.

There was movement on the other side of the door.

Oh Jesus, what if the tenant was coming out?

Donna pulled at the key again frantically but still it remained firmly wedged.

The movement behind the door ceased and she stood still for a moment, listening.

Across the landing she could still hear the classical music.

She waited a second longer then tried again, working the key back and forth this time, feeling it give a little.

And a little more.

She pulled hard and the key came free with a metallic rasping sound.

Immediately she heard footsteps coming towards the door from the other side.

She had to get inside Suzanne Regan's flat as quickly as possible. Donna took the three paces across to the other door, slid the key in and turned it.

The door of the flat next to her was beginning to open.

Hurry.

She pushed the door open, slipped inside and closed it. She leaned her back against it, trying to control her breathing as she heard footsteps on the landing. In the darkness of the flat she listened to them move towards the top of the stairs, the top step creaking protestingly.

For interminable seconds she stood in the blackness, awaiting the knock and the confrontation. Her mind was racing, her thoughts tumbling in different directions. She closed her fists tightly.

Closed one around the key.

The key.

As she stood in the darkness she realized that it was still stuck in the door, protruding from the lock.

Nineteen

On the landing the footsteps thudded back and forth, were still for a second then receded.

Donna listened to the silence. Like a spring uncoiling she slowly turned the handle, shot her hand out and plucked the key from the lock, pushing the door shut again.

She let out a breath explosively in relief.

She stood there in the gloom, waiting until she had stopped shaking. Then she slipped the key into the pocket of her coat, ran a hand through her hair and turned, feeling for the light switch. Her hand brushed against it and she flicked it on.

A sixty watt bulb flickered into life, illuminating the flat.

She was standing in the entry-way. Coat hooks had been attached to the wall to her right. Two short jackets and a longer wool coat hung there. There was a phone on a table close by.

Donna moved into the sitting-room proper and noticed how small it was. There was a sofa and one easy chair, a table and four chairs in one corner. These stood on a beige coloured carpet. On the other side of the room was an oven and hob and several fitted cupboards. A small fridge stood alongside.

There was a stereo, a small TV set, dozens of records, tapes and compact discs on a DIY unit with one screw missing at the top. A video recorder, surrounded by a number of tapes, lay at the bottom of the unit. The automatic clock on the machine was flashing constantly. Four green zeros flickering in the dull light.

The cooker was clean. There were no dirty dishes in the sink, no pots and pans on the hob. Everything seemed to be in its place.

A framed picture of a muscular man dressed only in a baseball cap and a thong stared down at her from one wall. Donna glanced at it for a moment, then wandered back towards the main door. There had been two others.

She opened the first and found herself in a tiny bathroom. Pulling the cord, she looked around at the contents. A bath which seemed to fill most of the room, a toilet and a sink. There was a cabinet on the wall and for a second Donna caught her own reflection in the mirrored doors. Clean washing was piled up at one end of the bath: blouses, T-shirts, skirts. A predominance of blues, she noted.

Donna opened the cabinet and peered at the contents. Some anti-perspirant, a Mudd Mask Facial Cleanser, nail varnish remover, some Lil-lets and two packets of contraceptive pills.

She moved to the next door and opened it, stepping into the bedroom.

This, too, was small; there was barely room to manoeuvre around the bed. Wardrobes and bookshelves covered three walls. On one of the bookshelves there was also make-up, perfume. Donna sniffed it, inspecting the bottle. It was Calvin Klein. Good perfume, expensive.

Had he bought it for her?

She opened the wardrobe closest to her and regarded the hanging clothes in there impassively. There was a lot of silk and suede.

How much of that had Chris paid for?

Shoes, boots, trainers.

She pulled open drawers and found underwear, more blouses.

The envelope was in the bottom drawer.

A brown manilla A4 envelope.

Donna sat on the edge of the bed and upended it, the contents spilling out onto the duvet. She rummaged through the pieces of paper, inspecting each one. There was a motley assortment. Bills, some paid, some unpaid. Bank statements, business cards, a couple of old birthday cards. She opened them to check the sender's name. Neither had been sent by her dead husband. A party invitation, a free pass to a London nightclub.

She found the first of the photos sandwiched between a Medical card and a bank statement.

It showed Chris and Suzanne together.

Pale. Unsmiling.

Donna swallowed hard and looked at another.

It was of Chris dressed in a leather jacket and jeans. He was smiling, leaning against a tree. The land behind him looked barren: only fields and hills.

Where the hell was that?

There was another of Chris, alone again, hands tucked in the pockets of his jacket.

Donna felt that all too familiar feeling building inside her, that combination of rage and sadness.

Then she found the last two pictures.

'Jesus,' she murmured, her breathing deepening as she studied them. For long moments she sat looking at the pictures then, as quickly as she could, she gathered the spilled contents of the envelope together and replaced them, shoving the manilla container itself back into the drawer.

The photos she tucked into her jacket.

She moved quickly through the flat, switching off lights as she went, heading for the main door, concerned to make sure she had left everything as she'd found it.

She paused at the door, listening for any sounds of activity from the landing or other rooms. Hearing none, she slipped out and closed the door behind her. She scuttled downstairs, the photos still tucked in her coat, returned the key to Mercuriadis, thanked him for his help and hurried from the house, resisting the temptation to run back to the waiting Fiesta.

As Julie saw her approaching she leant across and unlocked the passenger side door, watching as her sister slid in and buckled up.

'Did you find what you were looking for?' she asked, starting the engine.

Donna was staring straight ahead, but even in the dull glow of the streetlamps Julie could see how pale her sister was.

'Are you all right?' she asked.

Donna continued staring out of the windscreen.

'Get us home,' she said quietly, 'as quick as you can.'

Twenty

Julie was the first to see the police car, parked close to the front door of the house. Even in the darkness she could make out two figures inside.

As the headlights of the Fiesta illuminated the short driveway the car was picked out and held in the beams as if by some magnetic force.

'Donna . . .' Julie began but she was cut short.

'I can see them,' her sister said curtly. She gripped the photos inside her coat, tucking them into the waistband of her jeans.

One of the figures inside the car clambered out and watched as the Fiesta parked. Donna could not make out his features in the gloom.

Had someone reported her?

What were the police doing here at this time? She glanced at the Fiesta's dashboard clock and saw that the time was 11.23 p.m.

Had the occupant of the flat next to Suzanne Regan's reported mysterious movements in the dead girl's place?

How would they know to look for *her?*

Had Mercuriadis become suspicious?

Why should he?

Donna knew that the police could not possibly be at her house in connection with the visit to Suzanne Regan's, yet she felt uneasy, the way teenagers feel who have stolen penny chews from a sweetshop.

She swung herself out of the car and walked across to the police car and its occupants.

The plain-clothes man approached her, clearing his throat.

Donna Ward, you are under arrest.

'Mrs Ward, I'm very sorry to trouble you this late,' he said apologetically. 'My name is Mackenzie. I was at the hospital the other night.'

Donna felt a sudden, joyous feeling of relief sweep over her.

I realize this is a difficult time for you,' Mackenzie went on, 'but I would like to talk to you if I may.'

'Come in,' Donna said and the policeman followed her. When Julie entered she introduced them briefly. Then, as Julie went through into the kitchen to make tea, Donna ushered Mackenzie into the sitting-room.

'I hope you're feeling better,' the policeman said, standing self-consciously in the centre of the sitting-room.

'Sit down, please,' Donna said, slipping a hand inside her coat with her back to him, dropping the photos onto a coffee table. She pushed the newspaper over them, then turned back to face him and pulled off her coat.

Mackenzie perched on the edge of one chair, his hands clasped together as if he were cold.

'The other night, when you arrived at the hospital, I know you probably weren't thinking straight. It probably didn't occur to you it was unusual that a plain-clothes man should be present at an identification. I didn't think it was a good time to explain.'

'Explain what?' Donna asked.

'There were questions I needed to ask you about your husband; only trivial things. Well, trivial to you, probably.' He attempted a comforting smile but failed miserably. 'I need to know how often he had his car serviced.'

Donna looked puzzled, then she too smiled thinly.

'I know it sounds like a stupid question but it is important, believe me,' Mackenzie told her.

'He had it serviced once a year,' she said.

'And he never complained about it? About things going wrong with it?'

'Like what? Everyone complains about their cars, don't they?'

'Did he ever complain about the brakes?'

Donna met the policeman's gaze and held it, the colour draining from her face.

'It's a routine question, Mrs Ward,' the DS said quietly. 'When your husband's car was examined following the crash, his brakes were faulty. It could have been that which caused him to crash.'

'Are you saying the brakes were tampered with?' Donna said, her voice low.

'No, definitely not,' the policeman qualified. 'We have no proof that anyone interfered with the brakes on your husband's car. I'm sure it was an unfortunate accident and nothing more.' He shuffled his fingers together like fleshy playing cards, then looked at her again. 'And your husband was hardly the kind of man to make enemies, was he?' Donna shook her head.

'No, Chris didn't have any enemies,' she said quietly.

'None.'

'Well then, that's it. It was the brakes, I'm afraid.'

Julie arrived with the tea but Mackenzie declined and insisted he must go. It was the younger of the two women who saw him out.

Donna sat alone in the sitting-room, listening to the police car pull away. She moved the paper from on top of the photos, her mind spinning.

Enemies.

She looked at the photos lying on the table.

Enemies?

Twenty-One

'Why would anyone want to murder Chris?'

Donna looked at her sister in bewilderment.

'You said they were convinced that he *wasn't* murdered, that it was a mechanical fault with the car,' Julie insisted. 'It's just routine, Donna. They have to be sure of everything.'

The older woman nodded slowly and shifted her position slightly in the seat, looking down at the photos.

In particular of Chris and the five men.

One pile were those she'd taken from his office; the others those she'd taken from Suzanne's flat that very evening.

Identical.

The same young faces, the same blurred images of two of the figures.

Those same gold rings on the left index fingers.

Who the hell were these people?

'How could that happen?' Donna said, prodding the photos of the group, outlining the fuzzed shapes of the older men's faces.

'A fault in the emulsion,' Julie told her, inspecting the photos. 'But it's unusual. The negative could have been tampered with. The point is, why? Obviously, whoever these two men are, they didn't want to be recognised.'

'Then why have their photos taken in the first place?' Donna asked challengingly.

'Do you recognise the other three, the younger ones?'

Donna shook her head.

There were so many questions. She sifted through the pictures again, checking through both sets, looking for even the minutest difference, but there was none. The shots of Ward and the five men were identical in every way.

'Perhaps they were the ones that killed him,' Donna said finally.

Julie shook her head.

'For Christ's sake, Donna,' she snapped. 'The police said it *wasn't* murder.'

'I know what they said,' she responded angrily.

Julie studied her sister's features for long moments then broke the silence again.

'*Did* he have any enemies that you knew of?'

'He'd been threatened before while he was working on other books. Not threatened with murder but, well, warned off, I suppose you could say.' She glanced down at the pictures. 'He wrote a novel to do with loan sharks a couple of years ago, how some of the big Security Companies were in business with them. The security men would act as strong-arm men for the loan sharks. Chris was told he'd be beaten up if he published the book.' She smiled thinly. 'Nothing ever came of it, thank God.' Donna swallowed hard. 'When he wrote about the porn industry he lived in digs in Soho for a week; he worked in a peep show to get information. He used a false name, of course. When the owner of the club found out he was getting information, he thought he was an undercover policeman. Chris said they wrecked his room one day while he was out. They left a dead dog in the bed with a note stuck to it saying he'd be next.'

'There must be easier ways of earning a living,' Julie said.

'He used to call it the Method school of writing,' Donna said, smiling at the recollection. 'You know how actors like Robert De Niro research their parts, live them? Chris was the same with the characters he wrote about. He never knew when to stop pushing.' She looked at the photos again. 'Perhaps this time he pushed the wrong people.'

'If you think there could have been a link between Chris's death and the men in these photos, you should tell the police,' Julie urged.

Donna shook her head.

'What difference would it make? They've already decided it wasn't murder.'

'And what if they're wrong?'

'You're the one who keeps telling me they're sure.'

'That was until I found out about Chris's research,' Julie said. 'These pictures could be evidence, Donna.'

'No. The police said the crash was an accident. They have no reason to think otherwise, Mackenzie told me that.'

'And what do *you* think?'

'I don't know *what* to think. I just want to know who these men are and why Chris and *she* had photos of them.'

'Then tell the police, let *them* find out.'

'What am I going to tell them, Julie? "My husband and his mistress had identical pictures of five unidentified men. Could you track them down for me, please?" Somcthing like that?'

'So what's the answer? How do you find out who they are?'

'I have to find out what he was working on. Find out if these five men,' she tapped the picture, 'were anything to do with his new book. I have to find out who they were, but I'm going to need some help.'

'You know I'll help you,' Julie said.

Donna smiled.

'I know. But there's someone I have to speak to first.'

Twenty-Two

The banging on the door woke him up.

At first he thought he was dreaming, next that the racket was coming from the television, but then Mercuriadis realized that the incessant thumping was on his own door.

As he hauled himself to his feet he glanced across at the clock on top of the TV set and groaned when he saw it was well past two in the morning. He had, he reasoned, fallen asleep in front of the screen – something he'd been doing quite regularly lately. It irritated him, and when he got to bed he always had trouble sleeping properly. Better to doze in the chair, he told himself.

When his wife had been alive she had always woken him if he'd dropped off. Woken him with a cup of warm milk and reminded him that it was time for bed. He thought fondly of her as he moved towards the door. The loud banging continued. It seemed like only yesterday that she'd shared his life and he sometimes found it difficult to accept she'd been dead nearly twelve years.

'All right, all right,' he called as he approached the door, anxious to stop the pounding. He slipped the chain and pulled the door open.

'What the fuck is going on?' snapped the tall, dark-haired man who confronted him.

Mercuriadis eyed the man inquisitively, irritated by his abrasiveness. It was too early in the morning for profanity, the older man thought, although he was only too aware of this particular tenant's penchant for it.

Brian Monroe stood before him in just a pair of jeans, fists clenched and jammed against his hips.

'I'm trying to fucking sleep and someone's creating merry hell in the room next door. In number six,' Monroe persisted angrily, rubbing his eyes. He looked as tired as his landlord.

'What's going on, Mr Monroe?' asked Mercuriadis.

'That's what *I'd* like to know,' the younger man told him, running a hand through his short hair. 'I'm trying to sleep and there's banging and crashing coming from the room next to me. I've got to be up early in the morning; I can do without this shit.'

'Noise coming from number six?' Mercuriadis said, his brow furrowing. 'But that's, that *was* Miss Regan's room. It's empty.'

'Well, there's some fucking noisy mice in there then, that's all I've got to say. Are you going to check it out?'

'I'll get the key,' the landlord said, taking a bunch from a drawer in the bureau behind him. 'Is the noise still going on?'

'It finished about five minutes ago,' Monroe

told him. 'I've been banging on *your* door for two minutes at least.'

Mercuriadis selected a key from the ring and followed his irate tenant along the hall towards the stairs to the first floor landing.

'Perhaps one of her bloody relatives had a spare key,' Monroe said, stalking up the stairs two at a time.

'Keep your voice down, please, Mr Monroe,' the landlord asked, climbing the steps after him. 'Think of the other tenants.'

'Fuck the other tenants. I should think they're all awake by now, anyway, if they heard that bloody banging,' Monroe snapped, reaching the first landing.

Mercuriadis shook his head reproachfully and glanced at Monroe's broad back. Such profanity. It was difficult to believe the man was an employee of one of the City's top accountants. The landlord wondered if he spoke to his clients in the same way.

They began ascending the second flight of steps, the older man wheezing slightly as he struggled to keep up.

As they drew closer to the top of the stairs the landlord cocked an ear for any sound but he heard nothing.

Monroe was standing outside the door of number six.

'I'm going back to bed,' he snapped. 'I might get four hours' sleep if I'm lucky.' The door to number five slammed shut behind him and Mercuriadis found himself alone on the landing, the key to number six in his fingers. He inserted it gently into the lock, alert for any sounds or movement beyond.

Banging and crashing, Monroe had said. Could it be burglars? He paused, wondering if it wouldn't be easier just to go back downstairs and call the police. His heart was already pounding from the climb but it seemed to speed up as he thought of the possibility of a break-in. If the noises had stopped five minutes ago, it should be safe to investigate. He pushed the door a fraction, still listening.

The silence was total.

All he could hear was his own breathing and the sound of the blood rushing in his ears.

He pushed the door open, reaching for the light switch.

'Oh my God,' he murmured.

The room had been ransacked.

Everything it was possible to smash had been smashed. Damage of some description, it seemed, had been done to every single object in sight. The sofa was torn apart, the stuffing spilling from it like entrails from an eviscerated corpse. Chairs had been overturned. The television lay in the centre of the room, its screen shattered and holed, as if a heavy object had been thrust into it. Cupboard doors had been torn off their hinges, their contents scattered across the floor. Shattered. Destroyed.

Records had been pulled from their sleeves,

the black vinyl broken and scattered amongst the other debris. The video lay ruined against the opposite wall, as if thrown there with great force. The plug it had been attached to was still in the socket. The stereo too had been smashed, the turntable itself prized out and hurled to one side. CD cases, tape cases, videos and even books had been torn open. Mercuriadis could scarcely move without treading on some broken object.

His heart pounded harder, his head spun. As he looked around it became obvious that nothing had been taken.

The object had been destruction pure and simple, not robbery.

He felt a cold breeze against his hot cheek and realized that the bedroom door was open a fraction.

With infinite slowness he moved towards it, prodding it open slightly, just enough for him to slip inside. He fumbled for the light switch but when he flicked it nothing happened. Looking up, he saw that even the iightbulb had been smashed.

The duvet had been ripped to shreds; the pillows, too. Wardrobe doors, those that hadn't been simply torn from their hinges, hung open revealing the devastation inside: clothes torn and ripped, pulled from their hangers and tossed into the centre of the bed. A framed photo of Mel Gibson had been pulled from the wall and smashed, the picture snatched out, the frame smashed. Drawers had been upended, their contents dumped on the floor.

Mercuriadis felt a growing tightness in his chest, a sickly clamminess closing around him. He tried to control his breathing, aware of a growing pain around his sternum.

Sucking in deep breaths, he realized where the cold breeze was coming from.

The room's single sash window had been prized open, paint scratched and gouged from the frame where entry had been forced.

He swayed slightly and moved towards the window, wincing as the pain in his chest became more acute.

The bedroom door swung gently shut behind him, the sound causing him to turn quickly.

The figure loomed out of the darkness at him, stepping so close until Mercuriadis could feel the intruder's breath on his cheek.

His eyes bulged madly in their sockets as he stared at the intruder.

A heart already strained swelled and burst; the shock was too great, too intolerable.

His vision was clouded red as several blood vessels in his eyes simply erupted.

As he fell backwards onto the bed the intruder stood over him for a second, looking down. In his final minutes of consciousness Mercuriadis was conscious of its presence, and what he had seen – a sight he could not have imagined in even the most depraved nightmare. A sight which questioned his sanity as surely as it took his life.

The figure headed towards the window and

clambered over the sill, disappearing into the welcoming darkness.

Mercuriadis felt one massive surge of pain envelope him, spreading with staggering rapidity from his chest, along his left arm and up into his neck and jaw.

He felt the darkness descending upon him and he feared it but, after what he'd seen, the oblivion which awaited him was to be welcomed.

The flat was silent once more.

Twenty-Three

Martin Connelly sipped at the glass of white wine and peered out of the window of Silk's restaurant. He was seated at his usual table, to the right of the main door. The menu lay close by his elbow and a waiter came over to ask if he was ready to order. Connelly said he was waiting for a guest. The waiter nodded and passed on to another table.

Connelly glanced at his watch; it was almost 1.15 p.m. He wondered where his guest was.

The phone call had been completely unexpected. He'd arrived at his office in Kensington at around ten that morning, the drive in from Beckenham having taken him a little longer than usual. After listening to the messages on the answerphone, he'd returned those calls he thought important and decided that those not so important could call him back. Then he'd settled down to read an unsolicited manuscript he'd begun the day before. Unlike most unpublished material, it showed promise; Connelly was already beginning to wonder whether to invite the author into the office for a chat.

The phone call from Donna Ward had come about 10.30.

Could she meet him for lunch that day?

Connelly had agreed immediately, and told her he'd book the table at Silk's for one. He'd spent the rest of the morning wondering what she could want; she'd mentioned nothing over the phone. The fact that it was to be over lunch pleased the agent. It was less formal than her coming into his office. He smiled to himself, taking another sip of his wine.

He saw the taxi pull up outside and watched her clamber out. As she paid the driver, he took in as much detail as possible of her appearance.

She was wearing a black silk jacket over a white blouse. A short black skirt and black suede high heels showed off her shapely legs. The wind ruffled her blonde hair as she walked and Connelly felt his heart beating faster when she entered the restaurant. She was met by a waiter and then noticed the agent sitting close by. She smiled and joined him, kissing him on the cheek before she sat down.

'I'm sorry I'm late,' she said, running a hand through her hair and dropping her handbag beside her. 'The traffic was terrible. I had to leave the car parked in Golden Square and get a cab.'

Connelly waved away the apology. Unlike the previous day when he'd seen her, she looked tired but she was made up and her clothes were immaculate. She looked wonderful, considering the circumstances.

He told her so.

'Thanks,' she said. She smiled briefly at him and ordered a mineral water from the hovering waiter.

'I hope you like it here,' he said.

Donna glanced around the restaurant. The walls were covered in jockey's silks, riding caps, whips and pictures of racehorses. Paintings or photographs of famous jockeys vied for space on the walls. Rotary fans turned slowly like the blades of a helicopter.

'I usually bring clients here,' he said. 'This isn't business, is it, Donna?'

She raised her eyebrows.

'Sort of.'

'And I thought you just wanted the pleasure of my company.' He smiled and studied her across the table, gazing into her eyes a little too intently.

'How are you managing?' he wanted to know.

'Everything's organised, thanks to Julie. I don't know what I'd have done without her.' She sighed. 'I'm terrified, Martin. I'm dreading the funeral. Part of me wants it over; the other part hopes tomorrow never comes.'

'I understand that. Like I told you before, if there's anything I can do, call me.'

'That's one of the reasons I'm here now,' she told him.

The waiter returned and they ordered. Donna shifted position in her seat and looked at Connelly.

'How much did Chris tell you about the books he was working on, Martin? How much did you know about them?'

'Very little, until I saw the finished manuscript. You know how Chris liked to work, keeping everything to himself until the book was finished. Even *after* the book was finished it was sometimes a job to get him to talk about it. The publishers always wanted him to do promotional tours, interviews and that sort of stuff, but you know, he wouldn't do that for two of the books.'

'So he never talked to you about his projects?' she said. 'You never even had a *clue* what he was writing about, or what he planned to write about next?'

'He mentioned things here and there, rarely anything specific, though. Just plot outlines, ideas sometimes. That was it.'

'And his research? How much did you know about that?'

'Only what he told me.'

Donna shook her head gently.

'You were his agent, Martin, and you're trying to tell me you never knew what he was writing about, what research he did? Nothing?' She looked at him challengingly.

'Only what he *told* me,' Connelly insisted. 'It seems we've had this conversation before, Donna. I can't tell you anything different.'

The starters arrived. Donna prodded her avocado with the fork.

'What did he tell you about this new book?' she wanted to know.

'For Christ's sake,' Connelly said irritably, 'he didn't tell me anything. How many more times?'

'You arranged some of the interviews he did, didn't you? Or can't you remember that either, Martin?' she said cryptically.

'What is your problem, Donna?' he hissed, keeping his voice under control but not his anger. 'What do you want me to tell you?'

'The truth.'

'I don't know the truth. You asked me what Chris was working on. I don't know, but that's not good enough for you. Why did you mention his interviews?' he asked.

Donna reached down beside her and fumbled in her handbag. She produced Ward's diary and flicked it open, turning it around on the table so that Connelly could see it.

'October 25th,' she read aloud. 'Interview in Oxford.' She turned a few more pages. 'November 16th. Interview in Edinburgh.' She looked at Connelly. 'He was gone three days that time. And here, London, December 2nd. He was gone two days then.' She turned more pages. 'January 6th. Dublin.'

Connelly shook his head.

'Did you arrange those interviews, Martin?' she wanted to know. 'Or weren't they interviews? Was he with *her*, then? Did you know about it? Who usually went with him on promotional trips? Someone from the publishers, wasn't it? Someone from the publicity department? Or was it *her*?'

'Donna, I don't know what you're talking about,' Connelly said wearily. '*What* you're talking about or *who* you're talking about.'

'I'm talking about Suzanne Regan. My husband's mistress. Did she go with him on any of these trips?'

'I don't know. Really. Trust me.'

'What about these?' she said, pointing at other entries in the diary. Beside every single interview in London, Oxford, Dublin or Edinburgh was the initial D.

'Who was "D"?' she asked. 'Was that his pet name for her?'

Connelly could only shake his head.

'I really don't know what any of it means,' he said. 'I didn't arrange those interviews, if that's what they were.'

'Did you know he was going to be in those places?' she persisted. 'I thought you and Chris usually let each other know if you were going away, in case one had to contact the other urgently.'

'Donna, I wish I could help you. I can't

remember if Chris mentioned those trips or not.'

Donna reached into her handbag again, this time pulling out the photos she'd found of Ward and the five other men.

'Who are they, Martin?' she asked.

Connelly didn't speak.

'Recognise any of them?' she persisted.

He ran his eyes over the pictures.

'Where did you get them?' he asked finally.

'I found them in Chris's office,' she said, realizing it prudent not to mention she'd found identical ones in Suzanne Regan's flat. 'I want to know who they are and I'm going to find out.'

'How?' he enquired.

She flipped through the diary to another entry.

DUBLIN NATIONAL GALLERY

and beneath that

JAMES WORSDALE

The date was about a week later.

'I'm going to Dublin,' she announced defiantly.

'What the hell for?'

'To find out exactly what Chris was working on. To find out who these men were.' She tapped the photo. 'I think they're linked in some way. And I think they're linked to his death. I want to know how and I'm going to find out, no matter what I have to do.'

The rest of the meal was eaten in virtual silence and Donna finally left without having a coffee, having carefully gathered up the photos and the diary. She said goodbye to the agent and hurried out, flagging down a cab that was dropping off nearby.

Connelly paid the bill quickly and ran out after her, calling to her across the street.

Donna hesitated as he approached.

'When are you leaving for Dublin?' he asked.

'In five days,' she told him. 'Why?'

Connelly shrugged and smiled awkwardly.

'I thought you might like some company,' he said. 'I've been there a few times. Perhaps I could help you.'

Donna eyed him with something close to contempt.

'I'll manage,' she said and climbed into the cab. Connelly watched as it pulled away.

Twenty-Four

Julie Craig received the news of Donna's intended trip to Dublin with not so much surprise as weary resignation.

The two women were lying in bed, with only the ticking of the bedside clock an accompaniment to their subdued conversation. Julie lay on her back gazing up at the ceiling, listening to Donna recount her meeting with Connelly that afternoon. It was all she could do to stop herself telling Donna she was sick of hearing about the whole subject. Still she seemed obsessed with Suzanne Regan.

'Do you think it's a good idea you going so soon after the funeral?' she asked.

'The quicker I get this business sorted out the better,' Donna told her.

'And what if you don't get it sorted out? What if you don't find the answers you want?'

Donna had no answer.

'Are you going to let it haunt you for the rest of your life? Are you going to think about it for the rest of your life?'

'It's easy for you to dismiss it, Julie,' Donna said, irritably.

'I'm not dismissing it,' the younger woman said. 'But this has become an obsession with you.'

'Maybe it has. I'll just have to learn to live with it. The same way I've got to learn to live *without* Chris.' She wiped a tear from her eye. 'I have to do things my way, Julie. It's my way of coming to terms with it.'

They lay there in silence for what seemed like an eternity, then Julie broke the stillness.

'If you need me to help you, to come with you to Ireland, or anywhere else, you know I will,' she said softly.

Donna nodded in the darkness.

The light filtering through the window illuminated her face and Julie could see the tears glistening in the dull light. She reached across and wiped them from her sister's cheek, stroking her face.

Donna held her hand and kissed it.

Julie began stroking her sister's hair, smoothing the soft blonde tresses back.

'Everything's arranged for tomorrow,' she said quietly. 'The cars, the flowers, everything.' She continued stroking. 'The caterers will be here before we leave; they'll have the food ready when the service is over. I told them nothing too elaborate.'

'Sausages on sticks?' Donna murmured, managing a thin smile.

Julie smiled too, her initial annoyance giving way to a feeling of helplessness. She could see the suffering in her sister's eyes, feel it in her words, but knew she could do nothing to ease it. All she could do was stand by helplessly and watch. She carried on stroking, seeing Donna's eyes closing.

'Go to sleep,' she whispered. 'You need to rest.'

'Remember when you used to do this when we were kids?' Donna murmured, her voice low, her words delivered slowly. 'It always used to make me drop off then.'

'I remember,' Julie told her. 'You did it for me, too.'

'Little sister looking after big sister,' Donna said, her eyes closed.

She said one more thing before sleep finally overcame her, words spoken so softly Julie barely heard them.

'I miss him, Julie,' she said.

Then all she heard was her sister's low breathing.

She slept.

Julie stopped stroking her hair and rolled over onto her back again, glancing across at the photo on the bedside table of Chris and Donna, peering at it through the gloom.

It was a long time before she fell asleep.

Twenty-Five

Martin Connelly took the suit from the wardrobe and hung it on one of the handles.

He brushed fluff from a sleeve and inspected the garment carefully. He hadn't worn it for over two years, not since the last funeral. The agent noticed a couple of creases in one arm of the jacket and wished now that he'd left it out for his housekeeper to press. He shook his head. The creases would drop out once he had it on. What the hell. He selected a white shirt and then rummaged through his wardrobe for his black tie, hanging it neatly over the shoulder of the jacket. Satisfied that everything was ready for the following day, he wandered back into the sitting-room of the flat and poured himself a drink.

He sat down in front of the television and

reached for the remote control, flicking through channels, unable to find anything suitable. He wondered about watching a video but decided against it.

There were cassette cases underneath the television, both tapes leant to him by Christopher Ward. He made a note to return them. It would give him an excuse to return to the house.

He wouldn't phone first, he'd just turn up, surprise Donna one day. He doubted whether she'd be too happy to see him after their lunch that day. He regretted his suggestion to travel with her to Dublin.

You should have waited.

And yet what better time to speak to her than now? She was emotionally vulnerable, looking for kindness, wanting to be needed. As time went on and her emotional strength returned, his task would be more difficult.

Connelly finished his drink and poured himself another, rolling the glass between his palms.

It was one of a set Kathy had bought.

The thought of her brought the memories flooding back into his mind.

They had lived together for ten months and, whilst it had scarcely been idyllic, both had been happy. She was beginning to make a go of her career in modelling; she'd been signed up by an agency and the work had begun to flood in. At first he'd been overjoyed, proud of her and more than a little smug to think that his girlfriend was a fashion model.

When the nude work started to take over he began to change his mind. Kathy had never been ashamed of her body and when she was approached by a top men's magazine to do a spread she jumped at the chance. The pay was good and it opened up even more opportunities. Modelling assignments took her abroad. It got to the stage where they hardly saw each other and, all the time, Connelly was plagued by doubts. By thoughts of his girlfriend and a photographer he'd never met cavorting about on some sun-kissed beach in the Caribbean. He'd challenged her several times about it. Had she ever slept with a photographer while she was away? The usual thing. Blind to the fact that the only thing that interested her was furthering her career, Connelly had finally made life unbearable for both of them with his jealousy. As she reminded him, during rows over her assignments, he was always having lunch or dinner with female clients, editors or journalists. Connelly insisted it was different. Besides, the women *he* dealt with didn't sit in restaurants naked.

It took less than a year before she left him. He simply returned home one night to find that she was gone, all her clothes and belongings gone with her.

That had been almost two years ago. He hadn't heard from her since. He'd seen photos of her in some of the tabloids, looking decorative on the arms of rock stars or others of that ilk. Apart from that, he hadn't seen her or heard from her since the split. He'd lived alone ever since.

A housekeeper came in twice a week to clean the place and do his laundry, but apart from that he lived a more or less solitary existence outside working hours.

Connelly finished his drink, set the glass down and headed for the bedroom, glancing at the black suit hanging on the wardrobe door.

He wondered what Donna was doing now.

It was 12.36 a.m. She was probably in bed.

Bed.

Connelly tried to picture her lying between the sheets. It was a pleasing image.

He smiled crookedly.

He had failed that lunchtime, a trifle impetuous perhaps.

There would be other opportunities.

He had time.

Twenty-Six

There was a bird singing in the tree close to the grave. It chirped happily throughout the service, bouncing from branch to branch, rejoicing in the blue skies and the warmth of the day.

Donna heard its shrill song but the priest's words were lost to her. The words of the service were meaningless; it was as if he'd been speaking a foreign language. All she was aware of was that solitary bird in the tree. And the sound of a woman crying.

The crying woman was her.

Supported by Julie, she stood at the graveside surrounded by crowds of other mourners. Dressed in black, those paying their final respects to Christopher Ward looked like a menacing horde against the green of the cemetery grass. Splashes of brilliant colour afforded by the flowers at the graveside made the dark mass of mourners look incongruous in the peaceful setting.

A light breeze stirred the cellophane wrappers on some of the flowers, causing them to rattle.

Donna, looking down into the grave and seeing the coffin, was aware even more now of the appalling finality of the occasion. When they shovelled six feet of earth on top of that casket her husband would be well and truly gone. Nothing remaining except a marble marker which bore his name and an inscription:

CHRISTOPHER WARD, BELOVED
HUSBAND
SLEEP UNTIL WE ARE TOGETHER
ONCE MORE

Not much to signify the sum total of thirty-five years, Donna thought.

All around the grave others were standing in orderly lines, some with heads bowed, others gazing around as the priest spoke.

Beyond them stood the line of cars that had ferried the mourners from the church.

Again, Donna found it difficult to remember what had happened in the church or, indeed, since she had got up that morning. She had seemed to be moving like an automaton, not really aware of anything she did or said, or of anything which was said to her.

Julie had tried her best to coax her along but she too had found the solemnity of the occasion sometimes too much to bear. As she stood beside Donna now there were tears rolling down her cheeks. Inside the church she had stared at the coffin, raised up on a plinth and surrounded by flowers, her own mind struggling with the thought that inside that box lay her brother-in-law.

She had ridden in the leading car with Donna, neither of them speaking as the driver guided the vehicle towards the cemetery, never more than a few yards behind the hearse.

And then to the grave itself, yawning open to swallow the box that contained Christopher Ward.

Connelly had acted as one of the pall-bearers. He now stood on the other side of the grave, his hands clasped across his groin, his head bowed. Beside him were people from Chris's publishers, friends and relatives. There were even some fans there, readers of his books who had come to pay their last respects.

More than once Donna felt her legs weaken; she was sure she was going to fall.

Fall into the grave, perhaps?

But she held onto what little strength she had left and felt Julie's arm around her waist, supporting her but also needing that closeness herself. And Donna had felt this terrible feeling before, the night they had first told her that her husband had been involved in a crash. As she looked down into the grave she felt the same crushing desolation she'd felt as the coroner had pulled back that green sheet in the hospital morgue. How long ago was it now? Four days? More? Time seemed to have lost its meaning since his death. She wondered if *life* would lose its meaning, too.

As the priest came to the end of his service he stepped back a pace, beckoning Donna towards the graveside.

It was a monumental effort for her to walk those few steps; again she felt as if her knees were going to give way. Sobbing gently she made that short journey, Julie close by her. They both looked into the grave then Donna stepped back, her head lowered.

The breeze brought the smell of flowers to her, an aroma so strong, so thickly scented she felt sick. The cellophane rattled again and a petal from a red rose came free and fluttered across the grass towards the graveside, where it was blown in, floating gently downwards until it settled on the coffin lid.

Julie, trying to control her own emotion, led Donna away. The other mourners filed past.

From the tree close by the bird took flight, soaring high into the blue sky.

Like a soul en route to heaven.

Twenty-Seven

Donna stood by the car, a handkerchief clutched in her hand. The priest spoke softly to her but she heard little of what he said. She smiled every now and then, grateful for his concern but anxious only to be away from this place.

Julie stood beside her, reaching over once to pull a blonde hair from her sister's jacket. She lovingly touched the back of her hair as she did so.

The priest finished what he had to say and retreated, to be replaced by various mourners. Words of condolence were offered. Donna was confronted by a parade of people, many of whom she found it difficult to place. What she felt now was more akin to shock than grief; it was as if she was numb. Every part of her body and her soul, burned out. She looked at people with blank eyes, red-rimmed and glazed; she might have been on drugs.

Cars were beginning to leave the cemetery, mourners driving away back towards her house for the wake. Donna was suddenly aware how archaic the word sounded. Wake. The thought of having her house filled with people seemed abhorrent. She wanted to tell each and every one of them to leave her alone with her grief and her pain. Let her enjoy it unhindered. Their presence would only seek to prevent her complete immersion in despair.

Friends and relatives spoke words of comfort to her before climbing into their cars. She nodded gratefully at each word, unable and unwilling to answer.

Julie finally urged her to get into the car, wiping tears from her own eyes as she pulled gently at Donna's arm.

Martin Connelly walked over, arms outstretched, and Donna found herself embracing him. Embracing him and holding him tightly. His touch was reassuring and he allowed her to bury her head in his chest as he held her.

Only Julie saw the slight flicker of a smile on his lips as he spoke to her softly.

'It'll be okay,' he said. 'Just let it out.'

She sobbed uncontrollably in his arms.

Aware of Julie's probing gaze Connelly looked at the younger woman, their eyes meeting for uncomfortable seconds before he finally stroked Donna's cheek with one hand and she stepped away from him slightly.

'I'll see you back at the house,' he said and walked off to find his car.

Julie watched him go, then held out her hand for Donna to join her in the car.

'Come on, Donna,' she said gently, but then

noticed that her sister was gazing in the direction of the grave. Julie followed her gaze.

'I don't know who they are,' Donna said quietly, wiping her nose with her handkerchief.

There were three men standing by the graveside, the one in the centre tall and powerfully built. All three of them wore dark suits.

At such a distance Donna couldn't make out their features.

'Friends of Chris's, I suppose,' Julie said. 'You didn't know *all* his friends, did you?'

'Most of them,' Donna told her, eyes still fixed on the trio of mourners.

She noticed one of them kneel beside the grave, squatting down on his haunches and leaning over the edge, as if he were looking for something in the deep hole.

'Who are they?' Donna murmured, finally allowing herself to be coaxed into the car by Julie.

The driver asked them if they were ready, then pulled slowly away.

Donna turned in her seat and looked out of the back window.

The three men were still beside the grave, all of them standing again now, still looking down intently at the coffin.

The car rounded a corner and they were lost from sight.

Donna sank back in her seat, her eyes closed, the vision of the three men fading from her mind.

Had she been able to, she would have seen the tallest of the three kick a clod of earth into the hole.

It landed with a thud on the coffin lid.

Twenty-Eight

She didn't count the cars parked outside the house but there seemed to be at least a dozen, parked on the driveway and in the road.

As Donna moved through the sitting-room she glanced out of the window at the horde of vehicles. Inside, a low babble of chatter rose from the mourners who had returned to the house.

The caterers Julie had hired to provide food and drinks had set up a large table in the sitting-room, where they served guests with sandwiches and other snacks. In the kitchen they were using a tea urn and countless coffee pots to keep thirsts quenched.

The talk was subdued but interrupted by the odd laugh here and there. Laughs of relief, perhaps, now that the worst of the solemnity was over. A number of the men present loosened their ties.

Donna sat down by the window with a cup of tea in her hand, her eyes sore from crying, her head aching. She received the kind words and the advice with humility, concealing her desire that they should all simply leave her house as quickly as possible. They had paid their respects; now they had no reason to remain. But she pushed that thought to one side, grateful also for the concern.

Jackie Quinn glided across to her, kissed her on the cheek and squeezed her hand tightly, perching on the arm of the chair.

'Today seems to be lasting forever,' Donna said, smiling wanly. She squeezed Jackie's hand more tightly. 'Thanks for coming, Jackie.'

'I wish there was more I could have done to help,' she said, 'but your caterers seem to be coping.' She smiled.

'Where's Dave?' Donna asked.

'Getting himself a drink. I told him to get *you* one, too.'

'Jackie, I couldn't drink. Not now,' Donna protested.

'Yes, you can,' Jackie said quietly. 'A brandy will help you relax.' She turned and saw Dave Turner entering the room, a glass in each hand. He smiled at Donna and made his way past a group of guests standing by the door talking.

As he stepped clear of them another man almost walked into him.

Donna frowned as she saw him.

It was one of the men who had been standing at Chris's grave when the car had brought her away, she was sure of it.

The man apologized to Dave and made his way out of the room, followed by a companion.

Another of the trio of mourners she'd seen as she'd left the cemetery. Donna was certain of it. She still didn't recognize them.

Turner handed her the brandy and watched as she sipped, wincing as it burned its way down to her stomach.

'Thanks, Dave,' she said. He smiled down at her. 'That guy you just bumped into. Did you recognize him?'

'Should I?' Turner wanted to know.

'I can't place him. I saw him at the cemetery, him and two other men. I knew all of Chris's friends, or so I thought, but I can't seem to put a name to those three.'

'I wouldn't worry about it,' Jackie told her, squeezing her hand again. 'Drink your brandy.' She smiled.

Donna took another sip, wincing again, then she got to her feet, looking around the room.

From one corner, hidden from her view, Martin Connelly watched intently.

'Have you seen Julie anywhere?' Donna wanted to know.

Jackie shook her head.

'I'll be back in a while,' Donna said, excusing herself.

She made her way across the room, pausing to speak to Chris's publisher, then to a couple of magazine editors he'd been friendly with. More condolences were offered.

How many different ways were there to say, 'I'm sorry?'

She found more people in the hallway. They smiled politely at her as she passed, making her way upstairs, anxious to be away from everyone, wondering how long it would be before the guests started to leave. She paused on the landing for a moment and exhaled deeply. The top storey of the house seemed quieter, the atmosphere heavier. Donna crossed to her bedroom and entered.

Julie looked up in surprise as her sister entered.

Tears had stained her cheeks and her mascara had run, causing ugly black marks around her eyes. She wiped self-consciously at them as Donna entered, a worried expression on her face.

'I'm sorry, Donna,' Julie said, wiping her face. 'I didn't want this to happen. I didn't want you to see me like this.'

Donna crossed to her and the two women embraced.

'I wanted to be strong for *you*, to *help* you,' Julie said, angry with herself. 'That's why I came up here.' She sniffed and smiled. 'I'm okay.'

'Stay here for a while if you want to,' Donna said.

'It's me who should be saying that to you,' Julie told her, waving away the suggestion. 'I told you, I'm okay now.'

'You don't have to feel sorry for missing him, too, Julie. A lot of people will,' Donna told her.

The younger woman nodded slowly and stood up. She glanced at her reflection in the mirror and shrugged.

'Perhaps I'd better just touch up the worst bits first,' she said, smiling thinly.

Donna smiled too and walked out of the room.

She stepped back in only seconds later.

'Julie,' she said, her voice low, her expression troubled, 'did anyone else come up here with you? Follow you up here?'

'Like who?' Julie wanted to know.

'You haven't heard anyone come up here since *you* did?' Donna persisted.

'No,' Julie replied, looking puzzled. 'Why do you ask?'

Donna stepped back onto the landing, followed by her sister. The older woman was looking down the short corridor towards the door which was normally kept shut.

'I think there's someone in Chris's office.'

Twenty-Nine

As the two women approached the door, Donna noticed it was indeed ajar. From inside there was very little sound; just the soft rustling of paper on paper. Occasionally there came the furtive squeaking of a drawer or filing cabinet. Then there was silence.

Donna pushed the door open and stepped inside.

The man turned slowly and looked directly at her.

He was tall, his hair short and dark, cropped close at the nape of his neck. He had a thin face which rested on a very thick neck. Instead of looking surprised by the discovery, he met Donna's gaze with one of such intensity as to make *her* appear the intruder.

'What the hell are you doing in here?' she snapped, looking first at the man and then at the office.

He still had a piece of paper in his hand, taken from one of the open drawers in Chris's desk.

'Who gave you permission to break in here?' Donna hissed angrily.

The man smiled.

'I'd scarcely call it breaking in, Mrs Ward,' he said, his lip curling contemptuously. 'I realize that perhaps I should have asked your permission first, but you seemed otherwise engaged.' He made a theatrical show of dropping the piece of paper back onto the desk.

'Get out of here now,' she said, her angry stare never leaving the man.

'If you'd just let me explain,' he began.

'There's nothing *to* explain,' she told him. 'Now get out of here before I call the police. How *dare* you do this?'

The man looked at Julie, then back at Donna.

'I was looking for something which belonged to me,' he said evenly. 'Your husband and I had been working together. He'd borrowed some reference books from me.'

'Working together?' Donna said incredulously. 'Chris always worked alone. He never mentioned you or anyone else that he was working with. What's your name?'

'Peter Farrell. Your husband must have mentioned me at some time,' the man said, smoothing his short hair down with a large hand.

Donna shook her head.

'Why were you going through his papers?' she demanded.

'I told you,' Farrell insisted. 'I was looking for the books I lent him. I didn't want to trouble you. You seem to have enough to worry about.'

'Thanks for the concern,' Donna said, sarcastically. 'So, instead of worrying me you thought you'd just come up here and break into my husband's office?'

Farrell laughed and shook his head.

'Don't laugh at me, you bastard,' Donna snapped. 'If you're not out of this room, if you're not out of this *house* in one minute, I'm calling the police.'

Farrell shrugged and immediately headed for the door, holding Donna in that steely gaze for a second before passing by.

'I'd like the books back, Mrs Ward,' he said. 'I'll leave you my phone number. If you find them, I'd appreciate a call.' He reached into the inside pocket of his jacket and took out what looked like a business card. On the back he wrote a number and his name and then passed it to Donna.

'What are the books called?' she wanted to know.

'They're books about paintings. Catalogues. As I said, if you find them I'd appreciate a call.' He walked briskly towards the staircase and descended. Donna watched him from the landing.

'Do you know him?' Julie asked.

Donna shook her head. She glanced down at the name and number written on the card.

PETER FARRELL

Books about paintings?

'Jesus Christ,' Donna murmured.

'What is it?' Julie asked, looking concerned.

Books about paintings.

What was the entry in Ward's diary? JAMES WORSDALE: DUBLIN NATIONAL GALLERY.

Coincidence?

She looked over the bannister again and saw Farrell leaving, followed by two other men. The ones that had been at the funeral.

Donna walked across to the window on the landing and peered out, watching the three men as they clambered into a blue Sierra. Farrell sat in the passenger seat, glancing round once as the car pulled away.

A look of realization crossed Donna's face and she spun round, hurrying to the bedroom where she pulled open the bedside cabinet.

The photos she'd taken from Chris's office and Suzanne Regan's flat were there; she spread them out on the bed.

'I knew it,' Donna said softly, her voice barely audible.

'Look.'

She pointed to the photos of Chris and the five other men.

'I *knew* it,' she said again, more forcefully this time.

She recognised the dark cropped hair, the thin face and bull neck.

The image of Peter Farrell glared back at her from the photos.

Thirty

The last of the mourners left at just after six that evening and it was with something akin to relief that Donna graciously accepted the last words of comfort and bade the final farewells of the day. Those who had been friends of her husband told her to keep in touch, that they would ring her. The usual things people feel they have to say to widows. She wondered how many of them would keep their promises.

Martin Connelly was sitting in the kitchen when Donna walked in. He stopped chewing on a sandwich and smiled at her. She returned the gesture, wondering why the agent was still there.

Julie was pushing plates into the dishwasher.

Donna wondered briefly whether or not she should mention the incident with Farrell, then decided against it.

'He had a lot of friends, Donna,' said Connelly.

'Did he, Martin?' she said wearily.

Connelly looked puzzled.

'There were lots of people at the funeral, but I'm not sure how many of them Chris would have counted as friends.' She sighed. 'He was popular but I don't think he had any *real* friends. He couldn't give a fuck about anyone.'

'Come on, Donna,' Connelly began.

'I'm not being nasty,' she explained. 'I'm just telling you. People liked Chris but *he* rarely let anyone get close to *him*. People would ring him, write to him, but he hardly ever rang them back. You and a couple of others, that was it. He used to say, "If people want me bad enough *they'll* call *me*".' She smiled at the recollection. 'He was a solitary man. He liked his own company.'

And the company of Suzanne Regan.

'I think that's why a lot of women found him attractive,' she continued rather sadly. 'He genuinely *didn't* give a shit.'

Connelly dropped the remains of his sandwich onto the plate, wiped crumbs from his mouth and got to his feet.

'I think you're being too hard on him, Donna,' he said.

She smiled.

'That was one of the things *I* loved about him,' she said.

Connelly kissed her gently on both cheeks.

'I'd better go, unless there's anything I can do.'

'We'll be fine now, Martin. Thanks, anyway.'

He headed for the door.

'See you, Julie,' he said, looking at the younger woman.

She didn't turn to face him.

'See you,' she said and continued loading the dishwasher.

Donna walked with Connelly out to his waiting Porsche, watching as he fumbled in his jacket pocket for the keys.

'You're determined to go on this trip to Dublin still?' he asked.

She nodded.

Should she mention Farrell?

'Humour me, Martin,' she said as he slid behind the wheel and placed the key in the ignition.

'Is Julie going with you?'

'She's going to stay and look after the house.'

Connelly tapped the wheel gently and looked up at Donna.

'If you want company . . .'

He allowed the sentence to trail off.

'I'll speak to you when I get back, Martin,' she said sharply.

The agent nodded, started the engine and pressed down hard on the accelerator. The back wheels spun noisily for a second before the car pulled away.

Donna stood in the driveway, watching as the tail lights disappeared around the corner.

As she headed back to the house a cool breeze ruffled her hair and she shivered.

That involuntary movement might have been more extreme had she realized she was being watched.

It took the two women less than thirty minutes to check through the books in Chris's office.

There were atlases, dictionaries and at least a dozen books on weapons but not one about paintings.

'Paintings,' muttered Donna irritably.

'Donna, try his number,' Julie suddenly said.

The older of the two women hurried back into the bedroom for the card the tall man had given her, then picked up the phone and jabbed out the digits. Julie wandered into the room, watching intently.

Donna heard the hiss and buzz as the number was connected, then all she heard was the single unbroken tone of a dead line.

'Nothing,' she said. 'We should have known.' She tried once more, got the same monotonous sound and dropped the receiver back onto the cradle.

'His name's probably fake, too,' Julie offered.

'Maybe, but *he's* real enough and whoever he is he wanted *something* in Chris's room.' She looked at Julie, her brow furrowed. 'But what was it?'

Thirty-One

The roar of the Porsche's engine filled the garage as Martin Connelly left his foot on the accelerator a second before easing off. Through the open window he could smell the acrid stench of carbon monoxide fumes. He took his foot off the pedal and sat back, switching off the engine. It gradually died away.

Connelly rubbed both hands over his face and sighed wearily.

'I'll call you when I get back,' he said, raising the pitch of his voice slightly, imitating Donna's words. He swung himself out of the car and slammed the door hard.

Connelly walked to the garage door and pulled it down behind him, locking it from the inside. There was a connecting door through to his house; he didn't switch on the fluorescents inside the garage as he locked up. The only light coming into the garage was from a tiny skylight window above him. Glancing up, he saw that night was now in command of the sky. The blackness outside was almost as total as that surrounding him in the garage.

He could smell the drink on his breath. He'd

stopped off at a pub on the way home for a couple of vodkas. Neat. No fucking about. He promised himself a couple more when he got in. The agent selected a key on the bunch in his hand and slipped it into the lock of the door which joined the house and the garage. He stepped through into the hall.

The arm which snaked round his throat took him by surprise, both by its speed and its strength.

Connelly was practically lifted off his feet by his assailant.

He tried to cry out but a powerful forearm was wedged hard across his windpipe.

The tip of a knife was pressed against his neck just below his left earlobe.

The touch of it made him squirm; he felt his bowels loosen slightly.

'Keep still,' the voice behind him rasped.

In front, the shadows in the hallway seemed to be moving independently, dark shapes detaching themselves from the umbra and gliding towards him.

Two more figures stood close to him; because of the darkness he couldn't see their faces. They stood like sadistic spectators at some violent exhibition.

'Where's the book?' said one of them.

'What book?' Connelly managed to rasp as the arm loosed its grip slightly.

The respite was only temporary, however. The grip was re-applied with even greater ferocity.

The leading figure stepped forward a pace and drove a fist into Connelly's stomach with incredible force. The blow tore the wind from him and left him wheezing, wanting to drop to his knees but still supported by that choking grip.

The knife was pressed slightly harder into the soft flesh beneath his ear.

'You stupid bastard,' said the first man contemptuously. He leaned forward so that his face was only inches from Connelly's. The weak light coming through the hall window illuminated parts of the visages, but otherwise Peter Farrell remained bathed in shadow. 'Do you want to play games?' He snapped his fingers and the knife was handed to him.

He pressed the point to the tip of Connelly's nose and pressed gently, hard enough to make an indentation but not with sufficient force to draw blood.

'I don't know where the book is, I swear to Christ,' Connelly gasped, still held by that vice-like grip.

'Liar,' said Farrell. He began tracing the tip of the blade around the agent's cheek, pausing at the corner of his eye. 'I could have your eye out with one turn of this knife. You know that?'

'I don't know where the fucking book is, I swear to you,' Connelly gasped, his eyes bulging madly in their sockets.

'You were his agent. You knew what he was working on.'

Farrell trickled the knife point down to Connelly's bottom lip and pressed. Gently at first.

'No,' Connelly said, fearing that to move his mouth would cause the blade to cut it.

Farrell withdrew it slightly.

'Did he tell you what he was working on?'

'Some of it. He was very secretive about his work.'

'And you never asked?'

Farrell pressed the point against the underside of the agent's chin.

'Tell me what you *did* know,' the big man demanded. 'Tell me what you knew about the book.'

'I told you, he never spoke about what he was writing.'

Connelly's words were interrupted as Farrell pushed the blade up harder beneath his chin, hard enough to break the skin. Blood welled up from the puncture and ran down Connelly's throat, staining his shirt collar.

'Find the book,' Farrell said quietly, drawing the blade across the agent's cheek, stroking his earlobe gently with it. 'Find it. Someone will be watching you, not all the time, but you'll never know when. If you go to the police I'll personally come back here and cut your fucking head off. Understand?'

Connelly closed his eyes, aware that blood was still running from the cut beneath his chin.

'Understand?' snapped Farrell angrily.

'Yes,' Connelly croaked.

Farrell whipped the blade to the right swiftly and powerfully. The cut sliced open the lobe of Connelly's left ear. The fleshy bud seemed to burst, blood spurting from the gash. As the pressure on his neck was eased the agent fell forward, one hand clutching at the bleeding lobe. Crimson liquid streamed through his fingers.

Farrell looked down at the injured man as he opened the door, allowing his companions out first. He saw the blood puddling on the hall carpet as Connelly tried to staunch the flow.

'We'll be in touch,' Farrell said.

Then he was gone.

Thirty-Two

At first she thought she was dreaming, that the sound was the residue of a sleep-induced image. But as Julie sat up she realized that it wasn't.

She listened intently for a moment, the silence of the house closing in around her, then she heard it again.

Below her.

Movement.

Soft and furtive, but nevertheless movement.

She shot out a hand and pushed Donna hard, shaking her when she got no response. The other woman rolled over slowly and looked up, her eyes heavy with sleep.

'What's wrong?' she murmured, rubbing her face lazily with one hand.

'I heard something,' Julie told her, keeping her voice low. 'I think there's someone in the house.'

Donna blinked hard, her head suddenly clearing. She swung herself onto the side of the bed and sat there, her feet just touching the carpet, ears alert for the slightest disturbance.

'There,' said Julie as she heard another sound beneath them.

Donna nodded and got to her feet, moving swiftly and quietly across the room towards one of the wardrobes.

'Call the police,' she whispered to Julie, who needed no prompting and had already reached for the phone beside the bed. She frowned and flicked at the cradle. The line was dead.

'Nothing,' she said, a note of panic in her voice. 'They must have cut the lines.' She replaced the useless receiver, her attention now divided equally between listening to the sounds from below and watching her sister.

Donna slid the wardrobe door open, pulling the light cord inside. In the dull glow she was hunkered over what looked like a safe, a metal cabinet encased in oak. She took a key from the top of the cabinet and inserted it into the small lock, pulling the door open.

'My God,' Julie murmured as she stared at the contents.

There were four pistols inside the gun cabinet. The light reflected dully off their metal lines.

A .38 Smith and Wesson. A 9mm Beretta 92S Automatic. A chrome-plated .357 Magnum and a Charter Arms .22 Pathfinder revolver. Stacked at the bottom of the cabinet were boxes of ammunition.

Donna took the .38, pushed open a box of shells and flipped out the cylinder, thumbing the high-velocity ammunition into the chambers.

Julie looked on in disbelief, jumping involuntarily as Donna snapped the cylinder into position. She got to her feet and Julie found the image before her disorientating: her older sister, hair still ruffled, dressed only in a thin, short nightdress, gripping a gleaming revolver in her hand. It would have seemed absurd but for the seriousness of the situation.

'What are you going to do?' Julie asked, moving across the room, pulling her dressing gown on, glancing warily at the pistol Donna gripped expertly in both hands. 'You can't shoot whoever it is, Donna. This isn't a film, for Christ's sake.'

'I know. And whoever is down there isn't going to back off when someone shouts cut, are they?'

The two women locked stares, Julie blenching as she saw the determination in her sister's eyes.

'Come on,' said Donna, moving slowly towards the bedroom door.

Julie hesitated a moment.

'Do you want to wait until they're up *here*?' Donna asked challengingly.

Julie shook her head. Both of them paused by the door, listening.

The sounds were still coming from downstairs.

Donna heard a creak, a sound she recognized well.

One of the hinges on the sitting-room door squeaked.

The intruder was moving into the hall.

It wouldn't be long before he madc his way up the stairs.

Thirty-Three

'Open it,' Donna said, nodding towards the handlc of thc bedroom door.

Julie reached for it, hesitated, then closed her shaking hand around the cold brass. The chill seemed to fill her entire body. Goose pimples rose on the flesh of her forearms. She wondered if she would find the strength to force the door open.

What lay beyond in the gloom?

'Let me out first,' whispered Donna. 'When I tell you, put all the lights on.'

Julie nodded, remembering that there was a panel of four switches close to the door which controlled the lights on the landing, the stairway and the hall.

Donna gripped the gun more tightly, her own

body quivering slightly in anticipation as much as fear.

What if the *intruder* was armed?

What if she *had* to fire?

She remembered the hours she and Chris had spent standing on a firing range, the shooting designed as a hobby to begin with. As they'd attended more regularly they'd become proficient shots, then accomplished marksmen. When firing at a target, anyway, Donna thought.

Targets didn't shoot back.

Was he still in the hallway?

If so, what would be her best strategy?

Confront him? Hold him in the sights of the .38 until the police arrived? And how were they to arrive when the lines had been cut?

Thoughts tumbled through her mind madly.

What if he was already outside the door, waiting for her to emerge?

She closed her eyes momentarily, trying to push the thoughts aside, trying to clear her mind.

Come on, come on.

She could feel her heart thudding hard against her ribs, the blood rushing in her ears.

You can't wait all night.

Donna held the gun out in front of her.

Do it.

'Now,' she said, and Julie pushed the door open, allowing Donna to slip out onto the landing.

She scrambled across the carpet, the gun held

out moving awkwardly as she attempted to keep the .38 raised.

It was pitch black on the landing; the only light came from a small window about half-way up the stairs.

In the light from that window Donna saw a figure.

The figure was moving up the stairs.

'The lights,' she shouted frantically and Julie joined her on the landing, slapping at the switches.

The landing, the stairs and the hall were all bathed in light. In the explosion of radiance the intruder could be seen clearly.

Julie screamed.

The sound echoed off the walls and drummed in Donna's ears as she too recoiled from the figure's features.

She could scarcely find the strength to stand up as she saw him freeze, startled by the sudden appearance of the two women and, she thought, even more so by the sight of the gun.

Julie put a hand to her mouth to stifle another yell of terror as she looked at the man's face.

It was pale, almost yellow, the eyes only sunken pits. There didn't seem to be any whites. The flesh itself was rutted with a dozen or more deep gashes, some of which looked as though they'd partially healed only for the scabs to picked away again, revealing purple welts beneath. On the forehead and cheeks were large protuberances, nubs of flesh that looked like boils on the verge of bursting, brimming with corpulent pus. The man's head was covered by fine white hair that swirled around his ravaged face as he moved. The mouth was nothing more than a gash between the chin and nose filled with moulding teeth.

Julie took a step back, her eyes riveted to the horrendous sight.

Donna dragged herself upright, the gun still pointing at the hideous intruder.

As he began to move towards her she realized that the repellent features were not those of a man at all.

The intruder was wearing a mask.

The sudden realization fortified her and she took a step towards *him*.

'Stand still,' she shouted.

The venom in her command seemed to take the man by surprise. He looked at her, then down into the hall at something she couldn't see.

Donna heard the sound of the front door bolts being drawn, the chain being pulled free.

The figure on the stairs turned to run.

'I'll shoot,' Donna bellowed.

As she ran towards him the figure vaulted the bannister.

He either misjudged his jump or failed to calculate the distance from the landing to the hall.

From fifteen feet he crashed to the hard floor, landing with sickening force on his left foot.

The snap of breaking bone was devastatingly loud inside the house.

The man screamed in agony as he felt uncontrollable pain shoot up his left leg.

The cuboid and navicular bones in his foot had simply disintegrated under the impact and, so huge was the force with which he fell, the left fibula had snapped, part of it impacting into the talus at the top of the foot, the other part tearing through both the flesh of his shin and also the material of his trousers. A jagged point of bone projected from the leg like an accusing finger. The man screamed again as he toppled to one side.

And now, from over the banister, Donna saw that there were two intruders, one urging the injured one to follow him out of the front door.

Donna swung the pistol round and drew a bead on the injured man who was being lifted by his companion.

Kill the fucker.

The second man looked up and saw the wild-haired woman with the gun.

He too wore a mask.

Kill them both.

He hooked one arm around the waist of his crippled companion and the two of them hurried through the front door.

Oblivious to any danger she might be in Donna raced down the stairs after them, stumbling at the bottom.

'Stop,' she roared, her breath coming in gasps. But she could already hear a powerful motor start up. As she reached the front door she saw a car hurtling away from the house, its tail-lights disappearing into the night.

Donna banged the floor with her free hand and crouched by the door, the cold breeze rushing past her. She sucked in a deep breath and hauled herself upright. As she turned she noticed blood on the hall floor.

Julie descended the stairs slowly, using the banister to support herself.

'We'd better get the police,' said Donna. 'I'll go over to Jackie's and call them. One of them was hurt badly.' She smiled thinly as she said it. She tried to slow her breathing but it was an effort.

The blood on the floor glistened beneath the bright lights.

Thirty-Four

'It doesn't make sense,' said Detective Constable David Mackenzie. 'They disable the alarm, use a glass-cutter to get in, don't leave any prints behind and wear masks in case they're spotted. They cover every eventuality but they don't take anything.' He shook his head.

Standing in the sitting-room he looked around in bewilderment.

'Nothing's even been *broken*, let alone taken. Burglars usually ransack the place. These two look as if they were being careful not to disturb things too much. As if they didn't even want anyone to know they'd been inside.' Again he shook his head. 'I've never seen anything like it before.' He looked at Donna, who was sitting on the edge of the sofa stroking her neck slowly. 'You're sure nothing was taken, Mrs Ward? I know you say you've checked . . .'

'Nothing was taken,' she interrupted him.

The clock on the mantlepiece said 2.36 a.m. The police had arrived more than thirty minutes ago. Already they'd dusted for fingerprints but found none that shouldn't have been there. Donna had called them from Jackie Quinn's house, telling Jackie there was nothing to worry about.

Did she really believe that herself?

She'd told Mackenzie that one of the men had been injured, badly, as far as she could tell. Word had been put out to surrounding hospitals that all casualty admittances with leg injuries were to be reported.

The two women had not been able to help much by way of descriptions apart from recounting details of the horrific masks the burglars wore and that one appeared to be rather thin (the one with the broken leg).

Mackenzine had no doubt that the masks and the clothes they wore would have been discarded by now.

'You say no shots were fired by you *or* the burglars, Mrs Ward?' the policeman enquired again, checking his notepad.

'No. You only have to check the gun for that,' Donna said wearily.

'And you can verify that the guns are licenced?'

'My husband and I both held Firearms Certificates. We were members of a gun club; we shot there regularly. I'll give you the number if you want to check it out.'

'Just routine,' he said, smiling. 'Why did you have guns in the house, Mrs Ward?'

'My husband was away from home a fair bit. He said I should have more adequate protection than a burglar alarm. It was my husband who insisted I learn to shoot.'

Mackenzie nodded.

'Am I the one on trial, Detective Constable?' she said irritably.

'I have to ask these questions, Mrs Ward,' he said apologetically. 'I mean, this isn't New York. It's not every day a young woman pulls a gun on a burglar. This is new to me.'

'I didn't pull a gun on him,' Donna corrected. 'I was protecting myself and my sister. God knows what would have happened if he'd got upstairs.'

'Would you have shot him?' Mackenzie asked flatly.

'My house has been broken into, my sister and I could have been in danger and all you're concerned about is whether or not I would have shot the bastard who did it.' She glared at him for a moment. 'To tell you the truth, I don't know, but I'd like to think that I could have pulled the trigger if I'd had to. But if I had, it'd be me you'd be arresting, wouldn't it? To hell with saving my own life and my own property.' She ran a hand through her hair.

Mackenzie lowered his gaze a moment, his voice softening.

'Mrs Ward, do you think this break-in could have anything to do with your husband's death?' he asked.

'You're the policeman; you tell *me*.'

Mackenzie could only shrug.

'It was just a thought,' he added belatedly.

Donna was already certain there *was* a link.

Mackenzie looked around him. 'I don't think there's anything more we can do here now. We'll leave you in peace.'

Donna got to her feet, ready to show him out, but the DC motioned her to remain seated.

'There is one thing, Mrs Ward. The fact that they broke in but didn't *take* anything, and also that they were obviously professionals, makes me think they were looking for something specific. Something particularly valuable, perhaps. Can you think what it might be?'

Donna shook her head gently.

'Do you think they'll come back?' Julie wanted to know.

'Normally I'd say no, especially after having had a gun pointed at them. But if they *were* looking for something, and it's *that* important to them, then it's possible.' He looked at both women. 'Be careful.'

Thirty-Five

The pain was excruciating.

Howard James had felt pain before, but nothing to compare to the agony he felt from his shattered leg.

'Get me to a fucking hospital,' he said, frantically shaking the arm of the man who sat next to him.

Robert Crossley looked down at his companion huddled in the passenger seat of the Orion, his broken leg stretched out before him. The splintered bone was clearly visible poking through the rent in his trousers. Blood had congealed thickly on the end of the smashed fibula. There was dark matter oozing slowly from the centre of the bone which, Crossley concluded with revulsion, was marrow. The stench inside the car was almost overpowering.

'How much longer do we have to sit here, waiting? I need help,' wailed James, his cheeks tear-stained, his skin milk-white.

Crossley wiped perspiration from his face and looked at his watch.

3.27 a.m.

It was almost thirty minutes since he'd made the phone call, stopping off quickly at a pay-phone before swinging the car off the main road and into Paddington Recreation Ground. The vehicle and its two occupants now stood silently in a children's playground. The wind, blowing across the open ground, turned the roundabout and Crossley looked up nervously every time he heard it creak. Swings also moved gently back and forth in the breeze, as if rocked by some unseen hand. Beside him, James continued to moan loudly as the pain seemed to intensify.

'I can't take this much longer,' he hissed through gritted teeth. 'Please.'

Crossley nodded and looked round again, as if seeking inspiration from the children's slides and climbing-frames.

He heard the soft purring of a car engine and saw the Montego rolling slowly towards them, its driver flashing his lights once as he approached.

'Who is it?' gasped James.

Crossley didn't answer. He pushed open the driver's side door and clambered out, unsure whether to approach the Montego or wait. He decided to wait, watching as the driver switched off the engine and slid from behind the wheel. He walked with brisk steps.

A strong breeze ruffled Crossley's hair and made him shiver. Inside the car James was huddled in the seat like a whimpering child.

'What went wrong?' Peter Farrell snapped, looking at Crossley then down at the injured James.

'She had a fucking gun,' Crossley told him. 'I wasn't going to argue with a gun.'

'So you found nothing?' Farrell persisted.

Crossley shook his head.

'Did you check his office. Upstairs?'

'We didn't get that far,' Crossley said. Then, turning towards his injured companion, 'We've got to get him to a hospital, he's hurt bad.'

'The police will have put out checks on every hospital for miles. How bad is it?' Farrell demanded.

'Look for yourself,' Crossley told him and pulled open the passenger door.

Farrell saw the smashed bone sticking through skin and material.

'You were careless,' he said irritably.

'We were unlucky,' Crossley protested.

'Same thing.'

'And what the fuck would you have done if she'd pulled a gun on *you*?'

'Pulled one on *her*,' Farrell rasped, taking a step closer so that his face was inches from Crossley's. 'You could have jeopardized everything. We won't be able to get near the house for a while; they'll be expecting it. You fucking idiots.' He turned his back on them for a moment, hands planted on his hips.

'So what do we do about James?' Crossley asked. 'He needs help, for Christ's sake.'

Farrell turned slowly. His hand went to the inside of his jacket.

Crossley's mouth dropped open as he saw the taller man pull a gun into view.

The silencer jammed into the muzzle of the .45 made the weapon look enormous.

Farrell fired two shots into James's head.

The first hit him on the bridge of the nose, almost severing the appendage and taking out an eye as it exited. The second blasted away most of the back of his head, spraying it across the driver's seat and the side windows.

The body toppled sideways, the eyes still staring wide in shocked surprise, the mouth still open.

'Get rid of the body *and* the car,' Farrell said flatly. 'Call me when you've done it.' He turned and headed back to the Montego, pausing as he opened the door. 'Crossley, you fuck up this time and I'll kill you, too.' He climbed into the car, started the engine and drove off, his lights still out, disappearing into the darkness.

Crossley looked down at the corpse, the breeze bringing the stench of blood and excrement to his nostrils. He shivered and he knew it wasn't just the wind.

The roundabout creaked again. The swings moved gently back and forth.

Thirty-Six

The porter accepted his tip gratefully, nodded and glanced at Donna as he left, smiling approvingly when her back was turned.

She waited until the door was closed and then crossed to the window of her suite, pulling the curtains aside. The Shelbourne Hotel in Dublin overlooked St Stephen's Green and Donna gazed out onto the park for a moment, glad to be safely at the hotel. 'The most distinguished address in Ireland,' boasted the legend on the desk notepad. Donna stood at the window a moment longer, gazing out at the people in the street below. Finally she lifted her small suitcase onto the bed, flipped it open and began taking clothes out, sliding them into drawers.

The flight had been smooth but Donna didn't enjoy flying. It didn't frighten her; she merely disliked the physical act of getting on a plane and sitting there for the duration of the journey. Fortunately the Aer Lingus 737 had delivered her from Heathrow in less than an hour, so she'd barely had time to become bored.

She'd promised to phone Julie that night to let her know she'd arrived safely and to check on her sister. The break-in of the previous night had shaken them both, but Julie more so.

Donna finished unpacking and crossed to the desk where her handbag was. She sat down, reached inside and took out an envelope, removing the contents.

There were a dozen American Express receipts inside, each bearing the name of a hotel. One of them bore the name of The Shelbourne.

She flipped open Chris's diary and ran her finger down the entries.

She checked the date on the Amex slip against the entry for Dublin in the diary.

It matched.

So did the one for Dromoland Castle, County Clare.

And The Holiday Inn, Edinburgh.

The Mayfair, London.

Every entry in the diary was matched to a receipt. Only some of them had the initial D beside them; it was these which Donna was interested in.

It had been simple to find out which hotels Chris had stayed in. He always paid by credit card and he always kept the receipts for his accountant. She had merely unearthed them from his office.

How many of these places had he stayed with Suzanne Regan?

Donna swivelled in her seat and looked across towards the bed.

Had he stayed here?

She tried to drive the thought from her mind, feeling an all-too familiar surge of anger and sorrow. If only she'd been able to ask him why, perhaps it would have been more bearable. For a moment, Donna felt tears welling up in her eyes but she fought back the pain, forced the thoughts away. There would be plenty of time for them in years to come, she thought wearily. For now she replaced the receipts in the envelope and pushed it into a drawer beneath some clothes.

She put the photo of Chris and the five men in there too.

The diary she dropped back into her handbag.

Donna got to her feet and padded across to the bathroom where she showered quickly, rinsing away the dirt of the journey. Travelling always made her feel grubby, no matter how luxurious it was. She pulled on one of the towelling robes and wandered back into the bedroom, selecting clean clothes. A white blouse, jeans and some flat suede boots. She dried herself, dressed, brushed her hair and re-applied her make-up, then inspected her reflection in the mirror.

Satisfied, she slipped on her jacket and picked up her handbag, pausing to look at the diary once more and its mysterious entry:

JAMES WORSDALE: DUBLIN NATIONAL GALLERY.

As she made her way to the lift and jabbed the button marked 'G' she found her heart thumping a little faster than normal.

Outside the hotel she asked the doorman to get her a cab.

She was at the gallery in less than five minutes.

Thirty-Seven

It was as imposing an edifice as she'd ever seen. A massive grey building, its frontage decorated with stone pillars, its grounds were dotted with statues. The gallery itself looked as if it had been carved by some giant sculptor, minute details in the stonework wrought by caring as well as skilful hands.

Donna had only seconds to appreciate its beauty; she had other things on her mind. She paid the taxi-driver and walked briskly towards the main entrance of the building, slowing her pace as she reached the flight of broad stone steps that led up to the doors.

This was going to cause more problems than she'd thought, but it was the first place to try.

For one thing, there was no time in the diary for meeting Worsdale. Coupled with that, she had no idea what the man looked like.

As Donna climbed the stairs slowly she looked around at the dozens of people entering and leaving the building, wondering how the hell she was supposed to find someone she'd never seen before. Perhaps her husband and Worsdale had agreed a certain meeting place inside or even outside the gallery.

She entered the building, wondering how she was to find this elusive man, wondering again what she was going to tell him even if she *did* succeed in locating him.

She gazed around at the paintings which hung on the walls, looking but not really seeing.

It was quiet inside the gallery, an atmosphere akin to a library. That same hushed reverence pervaded the place. Donna glanced at the other visitors, noticing how diverse an audience were drawn to such a building.

There were people of all ages, wandering back and forth, some studying the paintings for long moments others just glancing, some checking their guides, some making notes.

As she looked up she saw what looked like a loud speaker in one corner of the room.

A public address system.

The idea hit her like a thunderbolt and she spun round, heading back towards the main entrance, remembering that there was an enquiries desk there. She could get them to broadcast an announcement for her, spread the word around the gallery that Mr James Worsdale was to come to the main entrance.

She smiled at her own ingenuity, the smile fading as she realized the ploy would only work if Worsdale was actually in the gallery. But, she thought again, her mind accelerating now, there was another way. She could leave a message at the desk. Get them to put a sign up telling Mr

Worsdale to contact the Shelbourne Hotel and ask for Mr Ward.

Pleased at her plan, she smiled as she approached the desk.

She'd find him yet.

There was a man seated behind the desk reading a book. He looked up as Donna approached and smiled at her.

She returned the gesture, struck by his good looks. He was in his late twenties, thick-set, dressed in jeans, with his long hair pulled back in a pony-tail.

'Can I help you?' the attendant said happily.

'Yes, I think you can,' Donna told him. 'I'm looking for someone. I'm supposed to meet them here but I've forgotten where,' she lied. 'I was wondering if you could put out a message over the public address system to tell him I'm here. If that's okay?'

'It's not supposed to be used for that, really,' he said apologetically. 'It's newly installed. We've had a couple of bomb threats lately and it's been installed to warn staff to clear the building. I'm sorry.'

'This is *very* important,' Donna insisted. 'Please.' She could feel her heart sink. If this failed she was lost.

'I shouldn't,' the attendant said, but then smiled broadly.

'But what the hell. What's the name of the person you're looking for?'

Donna smiled broadly.

'Thank you, I appreciate it,' she said, relieved. 'His name is James Worsdale.'

The attendant's smile faded rapidly and he looked at Donna with narrowed eyes.

'Are you sure?' he asked.

'Yes, I'm sure. Is there a problem?' Her own smile was replaced by a frown.

'I can put out the announcement but I don't think James Worsdale will show up.'

'Why not? How do you know?'

'Because he's been dead for over two hundred years.'

Thirty-Eight

The smile on the face of the attendant was a marked contrast to Donna's expression of shocked surprise.

As he saw her concern, again his smile faded.

'Well, let's say the James Worsdale *I* know has been dead that long,' he said apologetically. 'But if there's another . . .' He shrugged. 'It's an unusual name.'

Donna's mind was still reeling but she reached for her handbag, pulling out the diary.

'Look,' she said, thrusting the book at him and pointing at the entry. 'James Worsdale, Dublin National Gallery.'

'You're in the right place, then. His work is exhibited here. *He's* not.'

Donna shook her head, now totally puzzled by what she'd heard. She felt a little foolish, too.

'I'm sorry,' she said, and turned to leave.

'Wait,' the attendant said. 'Have you got five minutes to spare? You came here to see Worsdale's work; the least I can do is show it to you.'

She hesitated, then smiled thinly.

'Five minutes?' she repeated. 'I feel such an idiot,' she said.

'No need to. You wouldn't be the first one through these doors,' he nodded towards the main entrance and smiled broadly.

The gesture was infectious and Donna at last found herself grinning, too. The attendant clambered out from behind the counter, one of his colleagues taking his place. He walked around to where Donna stood and motioned for her to follow him. Again she was struck by his good looks and his relaxed, easy manner. He introduced himself.

'My name's Gordon Mahoney,' he told her.

'Donna Ward. How long have you worked here?'

'Six years. It pays to know whose paintings are exhibited here. People are always asking questions.'

'But not always looking for the artist,' she said.

Mahoney grinned.

'What makes Worsdale's work so interesting to

you?' he wanted to know as they walked through the gallery, passing among the tourists and the students and the other visitors.

'It was my husband who was interested in him,' she said a little sadly.

'Is he with you today?'

'He's dead.' She swallowed hard.

'I'm sorry,' Mahoney said quickly. 'Was he interested in obscure Irish painters, then?'

'Was Worsdale like that?'

'He wasn't one of our most famous painters. Maybe obscure is being a little unkind to him, though.'

They climbed a flight of stone steps and reached another floor. Mahoney moved briskly along, glancing at Donna every now and then. He finally came to a halt and made a sweeping gesture with his arm designed to encompass the array of canvases on the wall.

'This is some of James Worsdale's work,' Mahoney explained.

Donna stood looking at them, listening as the attendant pointed out each canvas in turn and told her a little about it. They were unremarkable works: landscapes, portraits and still-lifes. She could see nothing amongst them to explain why Chris should have been so interested in the artist's work. She knew very little about art and couldn't tell if the paintings were brilliant or not. To her, they looked accomplished but ordinary. What the hell made Worsdale so interesting to her late husband?

'What was your husband looking for?' Mahoney wanted to know.

Donna merely shook her head gently, looking from canvas to canvas.

'I honestly don't know,' she said quietly. 'Is this it? All of his paintings?'

'All *we* have. Well, nearly all. There's one in storage.' He smiled. 'In fact, it's permanantly in storage and it's probably the most interesting thing he ever painted, but the subject matter makes it a little, how shall I put it, undesirable for public display.'

'Why, is it obscene or something?' she asked.

Mahoney laughed.

'Anything but.'

'So why is it never put on show?'

'You could say it's something of an embarrassment.' He looked at her and held her gaze.

'Could I see it, please?' she asked.

Mahoney hesitated, his infectious smile fading.

'I don't know. Perhaps I shouldn't have mentioned it.' He looked around, as if afraid that someone might be listening to their conversation.

'It could be important,' she persisted.

He nodded finally.

'Okay. Come with me.'

Thirty-Nine

Nothing about the gallery had been how Donna had imagined it. It was not filled with crusty old men and women poring over the paintings; the whole building had a bright and open atmosphere, instead of the sullen brooding one she'd expected. Most of all, Mahoney didn't look like the sort of man who would work in an art gallery. He seemed too young and vibrant for work she had previously thought to be the province of uniformed men with starched collars and even stiffer demeanours. Every cliché she had held had been exploded by her visit.

The room where paintings were kept in storage was no exception. She had been expecting a small, dusty room filled with paintings draped in cloths that were thick with dust, where air would have a musty scent of old canvas and decay. Instead the room was light and airy, lit by fluorescent lights and smelling pleasantly of air freshener. There was a thermometer on the wall displaying the temperature, ensuring that it was constant so that the paintings were preserved correctly. There was an expel-air machine on a bank of filing cabinets which rattled in the stillness of the room.

The paintings were carefully stored in crates dependent on their size. Others were propped against the walls. These, she noticed, *were* covered by white dust sheets. Some appeared to be covered by what looked like cling film.

'How do you decide which paintings go on display and which are kept here?' she asked, following Mahoney through the room.

'We display them on a kind of rotation system,' he told her. 'Each artist is allocated a certain amount of space in the gallery. The paintings are usually left on display for three months, then one or two are replaced. Those not on show are kept in here.' He reached a canvas covered by a dust cover and paused. 'You wanted to see all of James Worsdale's work?'

She nodded.

'Like I said, this one is hardly ever displayed.' He pulled the sheet clear, exposing the canvas.

Donna took a step closer, her gaze travelling back and forth over the gilt-framed painting.

'Hardly what you'd call shocking, is it?' Mahoney said, smiling.

'Who are they?' Donna moved closer to the painting.

It showed five men in eighteenth-century garb, four seated, one standing, bewigged and splendid in their clothes and obviously, for their time, wealthy men.

'Five of the founder members of the Dublin Hell Fire Club,' Mahoney announced with a sweeping gesture. He pointed each one of the figures out individually, moving from left to right across the canvas. 'Henry Barry, fourth Lord

Santry. Colonel Clements. Colonel Ponsonby. Colonel St George and Simon Lutterell. Rakes and profligates, the lot of them.' He chuckled. 'And proud of it.'

'The Hell Fire Club,' said Donna quietly. 'I've heard of them.'

'Most people have, and know something about the legend attached to them. They were rich young men, out for thrills, out to shock the establishment. They used to pass the time being cruel to the poor, gambling, whoring and indulging in most other perversions you could care to name.' He smiled. 'A little like an eighteenth-century branch of the Young Conservatives.'

'Why isn't the painting displayed?' Donna wanted to know.

'The Hell Fire Club were something of a social embarrassment at the time. Lots of them were the sons of well-off men, politicians and the like. Not the sort of offspring you'd be proud of if you were in politics, or some other branch of the upper social orders. Their motto was "*Fay ce Que Voudras*", "Do as you will". And they *did*, most of the time.'

'Was Worsdale a member?' Donna asked, intrigued.

'No one knows for sure. That's the curious thing about this painting, though,' Mahoney said, tapping the frame. 'The two men responsible for actually starting the Dublin Hell Fire Club aren't in it.'

'Who were they?'

'Richard Parsons, the first Earl of Rosse, and Colonel Jack St Leger. You know the horse race, the St Leger? It was named after Colonel Jack's ancestor Sir Anthony. Jack lived near Athy in County Kildare, a great drinker and gambler.'

'What about the other one, Parsons?'

'He was the most vicious of the bunch, from what I've read. He had a fondness for setting fire to cats, apparently.'

Donna frowned.

'A lovely crowd they were. We've got a painting of Parsons here somewhere, a miniature done by another member of the club called Peter Lens. I'll see if I can find it.' Mahoney wandered off to another part of the room, leaving Donna to study the canvas more closely. She reached out to touch the surface, aware of a chill that seemed to have settled around her. As Mahoney returned she shook it free but her eyes remained on the painting.

What had Chris wanted here?

'Richard Parsons,' Mahoney announced, presenting the miniature.

Donna looked closely and frowned. She could feel her heart thumping that little bit faster against her ribs.

'I've seen this face,' she whispered.

Mahoney didn't answer.

Donna traced the features with one index finger but it was not the face that caused her hand to shake.

'Are you all right?' Mahoney asked, seeing the colour drain from her cheeks.

She nodded.

'I need to know about these men,' she said, suddenly looking straight into his eyes. 'About The Hell Fire Club. How much do you know?'

'I've read a fair bit about them. What's so important?'

'Will you meet me tonight, for dinner? I'm staying at the Shelbourne. Will you meet me there? Eight o'clock?'

It was Mahoney's turn to look puzzled.

He nodded gently.

'There's something I have to show you. Something I have to know. I think you might be able to tell me,' Donna said. Then she turned her attention back to the painting. Again she found that she was quivering slightly as she studied the picture of Richard Parsons.

On the index finger of his left hand he wore a gold signet ring.

It was identical to the one worn by the man in the photo she had back at the hotel.

Forty

Julie Craig rolled over on the large double bed.

She sat up, her breathing heavy in the stillness. She swung herself off the bed and padded, naked, across to the wardrobe, hesitating there for a second.

Apart from her own breathing, the ticking of the bedside clock was the only sound.

She opened the wardrobe and pulled the cord inside. The small bulb inside exploded into life, displaying his clothes.

His jackets. Shirts. A couple of suits.

Julie ran her hand across them, feeling the different materials, her fingers lingering over the silk of the shirts, stroking gently.

She pulled one from its hanger and rubbed it against her cheek, her eyes closed.

Enjoying the softness she allowed the material to brush against her breasts. The nipples stiffened and she squeezed her breasts through the silk, her breathing growing heavier as she kneaded the sensitive buds with her fingers, her excitement growing rapidly. As she stepped away from the wardrobe she felt the moisture between her legs. She drew one index finger through her dewy pubic hair, lifting the glistening digit, touching it very gently to her lips. She shuddered, then slipped the shirt around her bare shoulders before heading towards the landing.

She paused at the head of the stairs, as if expecting someone to ascend; the house remained silent save for the creaking of settling timbers.

Julie turned and headed back across the landing, down the short corridor towards the office.

Outside she hesitated again, feeling the silk shirt around her shoulders. She pulled it more tightly, rubbing her shoulders, allowing one hand to slide across her breasts and down her belly. Then she pushed open the door and stepped inside the office, flicking on the table lamp.

The dull light cast thick shadows in the small room where her brother-in-law had worked.

The atmosphere was slightly chilly but she scarcely seemed to notice it as she sat herself at Ward's desk. She ran one finger across the keys of his typewriter and looked across the room to the photo of him which hung on the wall, smiling.

She smiled back at it, licking her lips, her breathing now deep, almost laboured.

Julie stood up and faced the photograph, slipping the shirt from her shoulders so that once more she was completely naked.

She moved closer to the picture, her eyes never leaving Ward's face, her feet brushing against the soft silk as she walked over it.

She knelt before the picture as if in prayer, then slowly opened her legs, stroking the insides of her thighs with both hands. Julie had her eyes closed now and her head tilted back, so that her long hair dangled down and brushed against her arched back. Her mouth dropped open slightly, her breathing deep as she allowed her hands to slide up her body, cupping both breasts, rubbing both nipples with her thumbs. She opened her eyes, kept her gaze fixed on Ward's face and allowed her hands to glide over her smooth skin back down towards her pubic mound.

Her fingers stirred the tightly curled hair there,

one index finger probing more deeply, grazing the hardened nub of her clitoris, stroking gently before plunging further to stir the warm wetness of her vagina.

She began to make slow circular movements on her clitoris, gradually increasing the speed, sliding another finger into her slippery cleft. She felt a sensation of heat building up between her legs as she rubbed harder and faster and held her gaze on Ward's picture as the pleasure grew more intense.

'Oh, Chris,' she whispered as the beginnings of an orgasm made her shudder. 'Chris.'

Forty-One

'I owe you an apology,' Donna said, pushing her plate away and dabbing at the corners of her mouth with a napkin.

Mahoney looked puzzled but continued sipping at his soup.

'I never even asked if you had other plans for tonight,' she said.

'I can live with it,' Mahoney told her, smiling.

'I'm not in the habit of picking up men I've just met,' she told him.

Especially when my own husband has only been dead for just over a week.

'I'm not complaining.'

Donna smiled thinly and watched him as he finished his soup.

He was dressed in a black jacket and black shirt, immaculately pressed, as were his trousers. His shoes were shined to perfection. The long hair she'd admired was still drawn back in a pony-tail. They'd drawn the odd inquisitive glance as they'd entered the dining-room of the Shelbourne, but Mahoney had been convinced that was because of the way Donna looked. She would have turned heads anywhere in a navy blue backless dress which rose just above her knee. Moving elegantly on a pair of high heels, she looked stunning. Her long blonde hair, freshly washed, seemed to glow in the dull light from the chandeliers.

Donna looked at him again, wondering why she felt so guilty to be sitting at the table with this man. Perhaps it was because there had been such a short gap between this meeting and the burial of her husband.

Do you think Chris ever felt guilty when he was with Suzanne Regan?

She tried to push the thought from her mind but found that it persisted.

'I used to work here, you know,' Mahoney said, pushing his bowl away and glancing around him. 'I was a trainee chef for six months.' He raised his eyebrows.

'What happened?'

'I managed to tip half a pint of *crème brûlée* over the manager one evening when he came in to see how I was getting on. They sort of decided for me that it wasn't my perfect vocation. I was sacked.' He raised his wine glass in salute. 'Cheers.'

She echoed the toast and drank.

'From there to the National Gallery,' she said.

'Via half a dozen other jobs. I've been a barman three times. There's always plenty of vacancies for bar work here. We like our drink, the Irish. More drinkers call for more barmen. It's a simple equation.'

She found him looking at her a little too intently and lowered her gaze.

'What made you come here?' Mahoney wanted to know. 'You said your husband was working on a book but that doesn't explain why *you* came to Dublin.'

'I wanted to find out what he was working *on*,' she said as the waiter removed the plates and tidied the table for the main course. 'The entries in his diary were all I had to go on. I think he was researching something, but I'm not sure what. That's why I had to find out who James Worsdale was.'

'And now you do?'

'I'm none the wiser, unless his work was something to do with the Hell Fire Club. It seems the most likely explanation now. Tell me what you know about them, Mr Mahoney.'

'Call me Gordon, please. I've never felt very comfortable with formality.'

She nodded and smiled.

'Gordon,' she said.

He raised his hands.

'There's so much to tell, Mrs Ward,' he began.

'Donna,' she told him. 'I thought we'd dispensed with formality.'

Mahoney grinned.

'The subject is vast,' he began. 'It depends what you want to know. It also depends on whether or not I can *tell* you what you want to know. I don't profess to be an expert.'

'You said you'd read a lot about them.'

'I've seen a lot of horse races but that doesn't make me a jockey, does it?'

She smiled again and reached for her handbag, sliding the diary free, laying it beside her as if for reference. The photo was in there, too, but she left it for the time being.

'I know more about the Dublin Hell Fire Club, obviously,' he continued. 'They were just one of the off-shoots. There were a number of branches affiliated to the main club in England. They had individual leaders at each club but one overall head. The affiliates were known as cells. As far as I can tell there were cells in London, Edinburgh and Oxford as well as here in Dublin.'

Donna swallowed hard, one hand involuntarily touching the diary. She remembered the entries.

Edinburgh.

London.

Oxford.

Her husband had been to all those places shortly before his death.

'Where were the meetings?' she wanted to know.

'In Ireland, usually at a place called The Eagle Tavern on Cork Hill. That's where Worsdale's painting was done. They also met at Daly's Club, College Green. That's where Parsons picked up his charming habit of setting fire to cats. He'd pour scaltheen over them first.'

'What's that?'

'It was a mixture of rancid butter and raw Irish whiskey, I believe. It's no wonder members of the Hell Fire Club were crazy if they drank that.'

The main course arrived and Mahoney sat back in his seat, seeing how intently Donna was looking at him, hanging on his every word. She glanced irritably at the waiter, barely resisting the urge, it seemed, to hurry him up so that her companion could continue. He finally left and Mahoney continued.

'Their favourite meeting place, though, was Mountpelier Hunting lodge near Rathfarnham. The ruins are still there today. Kids drive up there at nights and try to spot ghosts.' He smiled.

Donna didn't.

'How was it destroyed? You said there were only ruins there now.'

'One of the Hell Fire Club members, Richard Whaley, accidentally set fire to it one night. Well, he supposedly had drink spilled on him by a coachman so, by way of revenge, he poured brandy over the man and ignited him. Whaley got out but quite a few of the others didn't.'

'How difficult is it to reach?' Donna enquired.

'It's easy. You can drive up there. It's only twelve miles or so. They reckon on a clear day you can see the ruins from O'Connell Street.' He smiled again.

'Have you ever been up there yourself?' she wanted to know.

'When I was a student. Half a dozen of us went up there one night.' He shrugged. 'The only spirits *I* saw were Jamesons and Glenfiddich.' He chewed a mouthful of food.

'So what did they do at these meetings?' Donna persisted.

'Orgies, mainly. They drank a lot, they gambled, supposedly they practised the Black Mass. Their object was to undermine society, the Church in particular. But most of all it was just an excuse for an orgy.'

'What about the other clubs?'

'They were the same, but all the other cells were presided over by the man who founded the order at a place in England called Medmenham Abbey. They were called "The Monks of Medmenham". One man was responsible for starting the Hell Fire Club. A man called Francis Dashwood.'

Dashwood.

D.

Beside every entry. *D.*

'Dashwood was the President of the club. He used to travel around all the other cells to make sure they were carrying out their objectives.'

Mahoney chuckled. 'They had a nickname for him. They called him The King of Hell.'

Forty-Two

Gordon Mahoney held the brandy glass in his hand and swirled the amber fluid around gently before sipping at it.

The dining-room was almost empty; just one other couple occupied a table on the far side of the room now. Mahoney felt exhausted, as if he hadn't stopped talking since he sat down earlier that evening. Donna's questions had been unceasing, her curiosity boundless. He regarded her over the rim of the brandy glass, captivated by her looks. She certainly was a beautiful woman. As she drank her coffee Mahoney looked at her, studying the smooth contours of her legs, noticing the way the dress clung to her slim hips and waist. He felt an embarrassed stirring in his groin and shifted position in his seat.

'Did Dashwood ever come to Dublin?' Donna asked.

Mahoney sucked in a deep breath, preparing himself for the next round of questions.

'I would think so. Like I said to you earlier, he visited the cells all round the country. Parsons spent some time in England, too. They were powerful men. Dashwood was Postmaster-General of England at one time. Most of the members were wealthy young men. They were bored, I suppose. Nowadays the rich snort coke; in those days they got drunk and had orgies.' He smiled.

'What about the witchcraft side of it?' Donna wanted to know.

'They were perverts. It just gave them an excuse to do what they wanted in the name of the Devil. A lot of what went on was based on gossip, most of it spread by members themselves.' He drained what was left in his glass.

'What happened to Dashwood and Parsons?' Donna wanted to know.

'No one knows for sure. Parsons just disappeared, not long after the fire at Mountpelier lodge. Dashwood died, supposedly, of syphilis. The clubs broke up when too much political pressure was put on them, when it came out that some of their leading members were important social figures. The scandal ruined them.'

Donna nodded slowly, drawing her finger around the lip of the cup.

Mahoney watched her intently.

'Could there be a Hell Fire Club today?' she asked finally. 'Now, in the twentieth century?'

Mahoney shrugged.

'Anything's possible, but if there was I think *The News of the World* would have found them by now.' He chuckled.

'I mean it,' Donna snapped.

The Irishman was surprised at the vehemence in her voice.

'A group of men meeting together to get drunk and cavort with women? I should think that happens quite a lot, but I doubt they'd call themselves The Hell Fire Club. You can see that on any guy's stag night.' He shrugged. 'Dashwood and Parsons had political objectives; they wanted to do genuine damage to society. The clubs helped them recruit supporters.'

'So you're saying that couldn't happen now?' she said challengingly.

'No, I'm not saying that. All I'm saying is, I doubt if there are men practising the Black Arts and meeting on a regular basis for drunken orgies the way Parsons' and Dashwood's men did. I said it was unlikely; I didn't say it was impossible. Supposedly there was a Hell Fire Club in London in 1934, but what they were getting up to no one knows.'

Donna reached for her handbag and took the photo out. She pushed it across the table towards Mahoney.

'That's my husband,' she said, jabbing a finger at the image of Chris. 'I don't know who the other five are.'

Mahoney inspected the faces carefully, pausing at the two blurred images.

'Look,' said Donna, pointing at the first of the fuzzy figures. 'The ring on the left index finger. It's the same as the one worn by Parsons in that painting you showed me. The other man is wearing one, too.'

Mahoney frowned.

'They certainly look alike,' he mused.

'They're the same,' she snapped angrily.

'What are you trying to say, Donna?' he asked.

'Identical rings, one worn by a man in a painting done two hundred years ago, another worn by a man photographed less than six months ago. It's a hell of a coincidence, isn't it? I think that someone found the rings that belonged to Parsons and Dashwood. Those men in that photo. I think my husband knew that. I think he knew who they were. I'm sure that's what he was working on. All the places you mentioned that they used to meet, my husband had been there recently. I think he'd found a new Hell Fire Club.'

Mahoney didn't speak, mainly because he wasn't sure what to say. He could see the sincerity in her expression and hear the belief in her voice.

'I'm going to drive out to Mountpelier Lodge tomorrow,' she told him. 'Will you come with me?'

'What are you hoping to find there?'

'I don't know. Some answers?'

Mahoney exhaled.

'I told you, it's just a ruin,' he said wearily.

'Will you help me? Yes or no?'

He nodded.

'Pick me up at eleven,' he said. 'At the Gallery.'

'Eleven.' She nodded. 'Gordon, there's something else.' She licked her lips before she spoke. 'Were women allowed to join The Hell Fire Club as members?'

Could Suzanne Regan have introduced Chris to the others?

'No. It was strictly a male preserve,' he said, smiling. 'A couple of the high-ranking members like Parsons or Dashwood had what they liked to call "Carriers" but that was it. The carriers were women chosen to be impregnated, made pregnant by members. The children they bore would be used in ceremonies.'

'Jesus,' murmured Donna, taking a sip from her cup and discovering that the coffee was cold. She winced and pushed it away from her. She glanced up at the clock on the wall opposite.

It was 11.46 p.m.

'Gordon, I don't know how to thank you for your help,' she said.

'I could think of a couple of ways,' he said, smiling.

Donna looked at him coldly.

He raised his hands as if in surrender, then got to his feet.

'Shall I get them to call you a cab?' she asked.

'I'll be okay. The walk will clear my head.'

She walked to the main doors with him and said a quick 'Goodnight', reminding him that she'd pick him up at eleven the following morning.

Mahoney thanked her for the meal and left, stepping out onto the pavement. The fresh air hit him and he sucked in lungfuls and drank them down. After a few moments he began walking, pausing once to look up at the grand façade of the Shelbourne. He wondered which room she was in. Mahoney smiled to himself and set off. He should be home in less than thirty minutes.

Not once did he notice that he was being followed.

Forty-Three

Donna left the hazard lights of the Volvo flashing as she hurried up the steps towards the main entrance of the Dublin National Gallery. As she reached them she glanced back at the hire car, knowing that she couldn't leave it there for long. She hoped Mahoney would be ready to go.

She'd called Julie that morning to make sure she was all right, and that there had been no more trouble. Julie had told her she was fine. Donna, satisfied that her sister was well, asked the hotel to get her a hire car for the next couple of days. The Volvo had arrived less than twenty minutes later.

Now she reached the main doors and walked in, eyes flicking over the sea of faces in search of Mahoney.

He had told her a lot the previous night, too much for her to take in, but the salient points stuck out clearly in her mind. She had sat up that night in her room, sitting on the bed scribbling notes on one of the Shelbourne's notepads. She'd finally drifted off to sleep at about two, woken an hour later feeling cold and slipped under the covers, resting fitfully until room service brought her breakfast at eight.

She moved through the gallery quickly, looking for Mahoney but unable to find him. Finally she returned to the information desk where she'd first encountered him the previous day, and found a pretty young woman sitting there stacking up guide books on Dublin.

'I'm supposed to be meeting Gordon Mahoney here at eleven,' Donna said.

'He'll be back in a minute,' the young woman told her, still stacking.

Donna glanced agitatedly at her watch and walked to the main doors, trying to see the Volvo parked in the street beyond.

When she turned again she saw Mahoney approaching the desk. Donna smiled and approached him.

'Are you ready?' she asked.

He looked at her blankly.

'Can I help you?' he said flatly, his gaze barely meeting hers.

'Gordon, it's eleven o'clock. I've got the car outside. Come on.'

The girl stacking the guide books looked at both of them but said nothing.

'I can't go,' he said sharply. 'I'm working.'

'What the hell is wrong with you?' Donna demanded, irritated by his coldness.

'I'm busy.' He reached for a sheet of paper, picked up a pen and began writing.

'Was it something I said, last night?' she wanted to know. 'Why are you acting like this?'

'I don't know what you're talking about.' She could hear a note of disinterest in his voice, but something else too.

Fear?

'I've got work to do if you don't mind. I'm sorry,' he told her and continued writing.

The girl finished stacking the guide books and slipped out from behind the desk.

'I'll be back in a minute,' she said.

'Gordon, tell me what's wrong? Why are you doing this?' Donna said through clenched teeth.

Mahoney looked directly at her, his eyes blazing.

'Get out of here now,' he snarled. 'Leave me alone.'

Donna held his gaze, her own anger boiling.

'Get the fuck away from me,' he said vehemently. Then he looked around quickly. 'Get away from *me*, get away from this *place*, get away from *Dublin*.'

Donna frowned, opened her mouth to say something but was cut short.

'Go. Go now,' he said, still not looking at her. 'What do I have to say?'

She turned and walked briskly away from the desk, out of the main entrance and down the steps back to the car. She slid behind the wheel and started the engine, pulling away so sharply she caused the car behind to sound his horn as he braked to avoid her. Her mind still racing, she glanced down at the map on the passenger scat and then headed towards the road that would take her to Mountpelier Lodge.

Forty-Four

Perhaps it was her imagination, she thought.

Maybe she didn't really feel a chill in the air. After all, the sun was out and high in the sky. It was just her imagination working overtime.

Donna tried to convince herself of that as she walked slowly around the ruins of Mountpelier Lodge. Perched high on a hill, the remains of the place overlooked Dublin like some skeletal sentinel. The whistling of the wind was low, disappearing as quickly as it came, ruffling her hair. She pulled the collar of her jacket up. Evil places were said to retain an aura of Evil and, from what she had learned of this place from Mahoney, if ever that aura was present then it would dwell easily here.

The stone walls, what remained of them, were weather-beaten but untouched by overgrown weeds. In fact there were no plants anywhere near the ruins. Nothing grew in or around the stonework and, as she wandered around, she was aware also of the silence. A stillness which seemed to bear down on her like a physical presence.

No birds nested here.

Nothing living, it seemed, would come anywhere close to this long abandoned dwelling.

Mahoney had told her that the lodge had been built on the site of a demolished *cromlech*, a tower erected for the worship of native Irish Gods. Parsons and his followers had found it ironic that their place of depravity should be built on what had previously been Holy Ground.

As she walked, inspecting the ruins, she thought of Mahoney. Of their evening together, of how forthcoming he'd been with his information. How easy to talk to he'd been, generous in his desire to tell her what she wanted to know.

So why the change of attitude? What had happened to make him treat her so badly? It was another in a growing catalogue of mysteries and unanswered questions. Donna feared they might remain unanswered forever. At least some of them. One thing she *was* sure of was the purpose of her husband's visit here. Donna was convinced that he was investigating The Hell Fire Club or some organisation like it. What she didn't know was why.

Christ, there were so many whys and wherefores.

Why had he been having an affair?

There was always *that* question.

She crouched and picked up part of the brickwork that had crumbled away from a supporting pillar. Holding the stone in her hand, feeling its texture, she looked around the hilltop. Still she felt that breeze ruffling her hair, biting at her nose. Donna shivered and decided to head back to the car, not even sure why she had come here in the first place. Perhaps Mahoney might have been able to point out something to her, tell her more about the site. But Mahoney wasn't here, was he? She tossed the stone aside and headed back to her car, looking round again, even more aware of the silence and lack of birdsong. The only bird she saw was a crow flying high above, its black outline alien and unwelcome against the clear blue of the sky.

Donna slid behind the wheel of the Volvo and sat there for a moment, looking back at the ruins. She wondered exactly what kind of depravities had occurred inside that place when it was standing. She tried to imagine what an imposing building it must have been in its time. Ironic that so noble an edifice should house so vile an organisation.

She started the engine and swung the car around, catching a last glimpse of the place in her rear-view mirror.

Inside the car it seemed to warm up. In fact

the further from the ruins she got, the warmer she grew.

Imagination?

Donna adjusted the fan inside the car and headed back towards Dublin. She glanced into the rear-view mirror, convinced that hers was the only car on this lonely road.

Exactly where the black Audi had come from she had no idea.

There were numerous dirt tracks leading off from this road, but she didn't recall seeing it parked in any of them as she passed. All she knew was that the vehicle was behind her now. And, as she peered more closely into the mirror, she could see that it was drawing closer.

Accelerating.

Donna frowned and put her foot down, coaxing more speed from the Volvo, her eyes flicking back and forth from windscreen to rear-view mirror.

The Audi was still gaining on her.

She tried to look over her shoulder, to see the face of the driver, to mouth some kind of warning to him but she could see nothing. A combination of the sun on the windscreen and the tinted glass made it impossible.

The Audi was only yards from her now and Donna decided to pull in and let it pass.

It was then that it slammed into the back of her.

Forty-Five

The impact flung Donna forwards in her seat, the safety belt preventing her from hitting the windscreen.

She looked round, seeing the Audi reverse slightly.

'What the hell are you doing?' she screamed to the unseen driver as the black vehicle came hurtling towards her once more, this time clipping her offside light. She heard the crash of shattering glass as the cars clashed.

The Audi reversed a few yards. This time Donna stepped on the accelerator and the Volvo shot forward, dirt and stones spraying up behind it as she guided it back onto the road. She glanced in the rear-view mirror to see that the Audi was in pursuit.

She pressed down harder on the gas pedal, coaxing more speed from the car, trying to put more distance between herself and the maniac in the Audi, but whoever was driving the pursuing car had no intention of letting her get away. The black car swerved out in an attempt to get alongside her.

The road was scarcely wide enough to accommodate two cars travelling abreast but the Audi ploughed up a grass verge. Earth was sent flying upwards in a dirty wall as the wheels spun on the damp ground; puddles of water at the roadside splattered up the sides of the vehicles.

The Audi slammed into the side of the Volvo and Donna had to use all her strength to keep control of the car. Again she glanced at the windscreen of the other car but she could see nothing through the darkened glass. She spun her own wheel, smashing into the Audi. It skidded slightly and slowed down.

Donna accelerated, seeing a crossroads ahead.

She prayed there was nothing coming the other way.

The Volvo shot across the junction doing sixty.

The Audi followed.

Donna could feel perspiration soaking into her blouse and droplets beading on her forehead. When she turned her head her hair was matted to the nape of her neck. She gripped the wheel, looking alternately into the rear-view mirror and ahead, searching for a turn-off where she might be able to lose the chasing Audi.

The road forked about two hundred yards in front of her and Donna leant forward in her seat, willing the car to greater speed.

The Audi slammed into her again, the jolt almost causing the Volvo to skid, but she regained control and drove on. Her mind was blank. She was functioning on instinct alone. Self-preservation kept her going.

There was the renewed sound of breaking glass as the cars clashed again.

The fork was coming up.

Which way to go? Right or left?

She pulled hard on the wheel and took the left fork.

The Audi followed, spinning slightly on the wet road, the back end swinging round as the driver revved too hard. The momentary lapse gave Donna time to edge away and she pressed so hard on the accelerator she feared she might shove her foot through the very floor of the car.

The road was beginning to rise slightly, an incline that led to a gentle crest. Donna didn't slow up as she roared up the slope. She was doing seventy when she reached the top.

The Volvo left the ground for precious seconds, flying through the air before finally crashing back down to earth with a sickening jolt that jarred every bone in her body. She winced in pain as she felt a shock across her back at the impact.

The Audi came hurtling over the rise, too, one hubcap spinning away from it as it landed.

Donna grabbed the gear stick, simultaneously pressing hard on the brake.

The Volvo skidded for about fifty yards, its speed gradually slowing.

Donna jammed it into reverse. 'Come on you bastard,' she shouted and pressed down hard on the gas. The Volvo hurtled backwards and Donna gripped the wheel tightly, knowing that this particular ploy was going to stop the Audi or kill them both. She didn't know which.

The impact was massive.

The speeding Audi and the Volvo slammed into each other with sufficient force to buckle the Audi's grille and shatter both headlights. The Volvo fared little better but Donna closed her eyes tightly as the impact hurled her forward again and sent her crashing against the steering column with enough force to knock the breath from her. But she forced the Volvo into first, the engine screaming as she drove fifteen or twenty yards down the road. There was a loud crunching of gears as she forced it into reverse again, then sent the car hurtling again into the now stationary Audi, shunting it several yards further back. More glass covered the road; she heard it crunching beneath the tyres. There was steam coming from beneath the bonnet of the stricken Audi, water gushing out like blood from a wound. When the black vehicle tried to move away she heard a horrible clanking sound and saw the bumper come free.

The driver reversed and the whole thing came away, dragged for a few feet by the car.

Donna sent the Volvo crashing into the Audi again, then shifted up through the gears and drove off.

The Audi tried to follow but it could not muster its previous speed. Donna saw it in the rear-view mirror, convinced and elated that she'd done it crippling damage. She shouted defiantly for a second, tears forming in her eyes, tears of terror and relief. Her body was drenched with sweat; it was glistening on her legs and she felt moisture beneath her on the seat. Donna wasn't sure whether it was perspiration or if she'd wet herself in the hectic chase. For now, all she could think about was getting away. Getting back to the hotel. Calling the police.

She looked again at the rear-view mirror and saw that the Audi was turning into a side road, allowing her to go.

Her breath coming in short gasps, she drove on.

Forty-Six

The bathwater lapped gently up around her neck as she slid deeper.

Donna pulled the flannel from the water, wrung it out and placed it over her face. Her breathing was slow and steady, the only accompaniment being the slow dripping of one of the taps. Steam from the water had clouded the mirrors in the bathroom; condensation had formed a dewy veil over the tiles. It had run down in rivulets here and there like tears.

Donna pulled the flannel from her face and put it on the side of the bath. She felt drained.

How she had ever managed to get back to

the Shelbourne, she didn't know. It was as if her legs had turned to ice. She could barely feel the pedals beneath her feet. She'd left the smashed car outside and staggered inside, drawing disapproving glances from the other guests. Once inside her room she'd called reception and told them to get the police. She ordered herself a brandy and downed it a little too fast.

She'd been sitting on the edge of the bed when they'd arrived, two large uniformed men. One of them looked at her as if she were mad as she recounted the story. Donna smiled at the recollection. Why shouldn't he think her mad? The story sounded crazy enough. The entire scenario *had* been insane. Who would want to run her off the road the way the Audi had done?

No, he wasn't trying to run her off the road; he was trying to kill her. Don't fuck about. Face it. Whoever was driving the car had been trying to kill her, it was as simple as that. But why?

First the business with Mahoney, then the Audi. What was going on?

The police had apologized for the incident as if they were personally to blame, their apologies becoming even more profuse as they told her that, without a number plate (which she had been unable to remember) to trace, there was little chance of them finding the car, let alone the driver. Donna had nodded understandingly, anxious only then that they should go.

Alone in the room she had stripped naked and

run herself a bath, trying to wash away the sweat and relax after her ordeal.

She considered what she had discovered, her mind racing like a Roladex.

She was convinced now that her husband had been working on a book about The Hell Fire Club and . . .

And what?

That was it. The only other things she had were guesses and suppositions.

He *might* have discovered a modern-day equivalent of the Club.

It's *possible* they killed him (even though the police in England were convinced his death was an accident).

Gordon Mahoney had gone, overnight, from being helpful to being downright rude. *Why?*

Someone had tried to kill her that very morning.

Why?

Someone had broken into her house, apparently searching for something. *Why?*

Questions. But no answers.

Donna closed her eyes again.

Her husband had been having an affair with Suzanne Regan.

That was about the only other thing she knew for sure. She wondered how the other woman was involved in this chain of events. Had she been to these places *with* Chris? Had he shared information with her he wouldn't share with his own wife?

Donna clenched her fists beneath the water.

The knowledge of his affair still ate away at her, and it was knowing that she could never speak to him about the affair that hurt most.

No, not hurt, *angered* her.

He had escaped her wrath when he died. Both of them had. They'd been wiped off the face of the earth before they could taste her fury. That was what truly enraged her.

She sat up, splashing her face with water, catching a glimpse of herself in the steam-clouded mirror. Her reflection looked distorted. She hauled herself out of the bath, pulled on a bathrobe and wandered through into the sitting-room. She picked up the phone and reached reception, asking them for the phone number of the Dublin National Gallery.

Perhaps if she could speak to Mahoney again, tell him what happened out by Mountpelier that morning, he would tell her more.

She got the number, thanked the receptionist then jabbed the digits, reading them carefully from her pad.

A voice told her she'd reached her chosen number.

'Can I speak to Gordon Mahoney, please?' she said.

She was asked to hang on for a moment.

Donna shifted the receiver to her other ear and began doodling on the pad.

The other voice returned.

Gordon Mahoney had gone home about an hour ago.

'Could you give me his home number, please?' she asked.

The voice at the other end of the line obliged and Donna pressed down on the cradle to sever the connection before ringing the new number.

She waited for the phone to ring at the other end.

Waited.

It was finally picked up.

'Gordon Mahoney, please,' she said.

Silence at the other end.

'Hello.'

Nothing.

'Gordon, it's Donna Ward.'

She heard the click as the phone was replaced.

'Shit,' she murmured and punched the same digits.

Dead line.

She heard nothing but the endless whine over the wire. After a moment or two she replaced the receiver.

It was dusk by the time she checked out of the Shelbourne; night was approaching rapidly. The sun left a red stain behind as it retreated below the horizon.

The taxi took her to the airport. By the time the plane rose into the air it was dark.

Donna closed her eyes as it climbed through turbulence.

The flight to Edinburgh should take less than an hour.

Forty-Seven

The pistol was pressed against his cheek so hard that it almost broke the skin.

The sudden cold chill against his warm flesh woke him but, as Martin Connelly tried to sit up, shocked into consciousness by the sensation, the muzzle of the .45 was jammed against his face with incredible force.

In the darkness, and still half-asleep, he was unable to focus immediately on the figures standing around his bed.

All he was aware of was the deathly cold of the gun barrel. For a fleeting second he wondered if he might be dreaming, but this time he had woken *into* a nightmare.

Connelly blinked myopically, trying to clear his gaze, trying to figure out what the hell was going on. He felt his bowels loosen, felt the hairs on his neck and forearms prickle as he saw the face of the first intruder, the one who held the gun.

'Get up,' hissed Peter Farrell, stepping back. He kept the gun pointed at Connelly's head the entire time, the barrel never more than inches from his face. The muzzle seemed to expand, to grow into a vast black tunnel before his eyes.

'Move,' Farrell continued, grabbing Connelly

by one arm and jerking him towards the door of the bedroom.

The other man picked up the dressing gown lying on the end of the bed and threw it at Connelly. He looked at Farrell as if asking permission to put it on, to cover his nakedness; although, at the moment, decency was the last of his worries. Nevertheless he pulled it on and padded out onto the landing. Farrell kept close by, the gun still held at his head.

'I told you before I don't know anything,' Connelly said quietly, his voice cracking. His mouth felt dry, as if someone had filled it with sand.

Farrell grabbed the back of his hair and yanked his head back, forcing the gun hard against his temple.

'I didn't believe you then and I don't believe you now. I want some fucking answers,' he hissed.

'For Christ's sake . . .'

He was cut short by a shove in the back that nearly made him overbalance and fall down the stairs.

He shot out a hand and caught the banister, steadying himself. On shaking legs he began to descend.

Farrell and the other man followed him.

'Have you been in contact with the woman?' Farrell wanted to know.

'Which woman?'

'Ward's widow, who do you think?'

'Why should I have been?'

Farrell drove a foot hard into the base of Connelly's spine, the impact knocking him off balance. He toppled forward, pitching off the steps. He crashed against the wall then fell, rolled the last few stairs to the hallway.

Farrell was on him in an instant, dragging him upright, the gun held beneath his chin.

'Have you been in contact with her?' he repeated.

'No,' Connelly said, hurt by the fall. 'Look, I swear to you, I don't know anything.'

Farrell pushed the agent's head back sharply, banging it against the wall with a sickening thud. For a second Connelly thought he was going to pass out, but a hard smack across the face kept him conscious. Farrell grabbed him by the shoulder and pushed him towards a closed door leading off the hallway.

'What are you doing?' said Connelly, realizing which room he was being shoved towards.

'Move,' snapped Farrell.

Connelly was about to push the door when it was opened from the inside and he found a third man there.

Farrell pushed the agent inside and was joined by the other intruder.

All four men stood in the room and Farrell raised the pistol once more so that it was aimed at the agent's head.

'What the fuck are you playing at?' Connelly babbled timorously.

'We're not playing, Connelly,' Farrell told

him and pulled him across the hot and clammy room.

The kitchen was large but the air was warm and dry.

Connelly didn't know how long the rings of the electric cooker had been on but one of them was almost white-hot.

Forty-Eight

'No,' Connelly shouted as he saw the glowing rings and felt their heat.

Farrell took a step towards him and swung the butt of the .45 hard, catching him across the forehead.

The agent went down heavily, a gash on his head weeping blood down the side of his face. He rolled on the floor, moaning, and Farrell nodded to one of his companions.

'Shut him up,' he said. The second man reached into his pocket and pulled out a long length of what looked like ribbon. He slipped it around Connelly's chin and tugged it tight across his mouth, gagging him, then he dragged the agent upright. The other man moved over to join them, gripping Connelly's right arm so that his hand was groping at empty air. Farrell held the gun steady and looked directly at Connelly.

'I'm only going to ask you these questions once,' he said, 'so listen. When I ask you to answer, the gag will be removed. If you attempt to shout for help, I'll kill you. Do you understand?'

Connelly nodded, the action making his head ache. Blood had begun to run into the corner of his eye and he blinked to try and clear his vision.

The heat from the cooker was intense and sweat already beaded his forehead and face.

'Where is the book?' Farrell said.

The gag was pulled free.

'I don't know,' Connelly said, his eyes filling with tears of terror. 'I don't . . .'

The gag was pulled tightly back into position.

Farrell nodded.

The man holding Connelly's arm pushed it forward, forcing it down onto the largest of the electric rings, holding it there.

Searing, excruciating agony ripped through his hand and up his arm until it seemed to engulf his entire body. His scream was muffled by the gag; the sound was like a child shrieking inside a locked room.

As the hand was held on the blazing ring, the stench of burning flesh was clearly noticable in the hot air.

As the hand was finally pulled away, flesh stuck to the ring as if welded there by the heat. Tiny pieces of skin shrivelled and cooked on the red-hot ring and wisps of smoke rose into the air.

Connelly felt himself losing consciousness but he was aware of being slapped hard across the face, even if the pain of the blow was negligible compared to the mind-numbing suffering he felt from his burned hand. Blisters rose immediately, some of them in the shape of the ring. He felt as if his entire arm and hand were ablaze; as if someone had turned a blowtorch on them.

'Where's the fucking book?' Farrell snarled, moving closer. 'What did Ward do with it?'

'I don't know,' Connelly sobbed, tears mingling with the blood and sweat on his face. There was a dark stain on his dressing gown and he could feel urine running freely down his leg.

'Tell me,' Farrell said, glaring at him.

'He never told me about his work. I swear on my fucking life I don't know where it is.' His eyes bulged madly in their sockets, like bloodshot ping-pong balls threatening to burst from his skull. 'I don't know anything about the book, I don't even think he'd started writing it.'

Farrell looked puzzled but merely nodded to his companion.

The gag was tugged back into place, cutting off Connelly's exhortations for mercy. The muffled scream rose in his throat again as he felt the heat growing more intense, the closer to the blazing rings his hand was pulled.

Three inches.

He would rather died on the spot than endure that pain again.

Two inches.

The man tugged harder, using his immense strength to force Connelly's hand down towards the large ring.

One inch.

'Where's the book?' Farrell said again.

As his hand was crushed down onto the red-hot ring again, Connelly's body jerked convulsively and so savagely that the man holding him up was almost knocked off balance, but he stood his ground while his companion pressed down on the limb.

Blisters which had formed the first time now burst, weeping clear fluid onto the burner which hissed like an angry snake. The whole hand turned a deep shade of scarlet, the flesh itself heating up. Connelly, barely conscious now, felt as if his blood was boiling, as if his bones were calcifying under the incredible heat. Pain hit him in one intolerable wave and he blacked out.

The mercy of unconsciousness was denied him; as one of the men slapped him while the other threw water from the tap over him, also tugging his hair in an effort to bring him round.

He awoke to screaming pain in his hand, which hung uselessly at his side. The palm and most of his wrist were scorched black, the flesh seared into thick red welts. And again there was that sickly sweet stench of cooked flesh which clogged his nostrils and made him want to vomit. When his head lolled back, his hair was seized and tugged hard.

'Last chance,' Farrell said flatly. 'Where's the book?'

Connelly was sobbing uncontrollably now.

'You can't do this, please stop, Jesus fucking Christ, I don't know. Oh God,' he whimpered, tears pouring down his cheeks.

The man holding him tugged his hair and yanked his head back.

'Ward hadn't even written the fucking book, I swear to God.'

Farrell pushed his companion aside and grabbed the agent by the throat, almost lifting him off his feet, staring right into his bulging eyes.

'What do you mean he hadn't *written* the book?' he said.

'He was still researching it.'

'He stole it.'

'Stole what?' Connelly babbled frantically.

'He stole the book. He took it from us.'

'I don't know what you're talking about.'

'Liar,' snapped Farrell. He pushed Connelly's head towards the cooker, determined to push his face against the blistering rings.

'I don't know,' he shrieked, the screams cut off by Farrell's free hand. The muffled bellows were the only sounds he could make as his face was pushed closer and closer to the glowing rings. He could smell his own burned flesh on them, could see blackened streamers of skin sticking to the metal.

'Ward stole the book from us,' Farrell said. 'Where did he hide it?'

The heat was unbearable. Connelly used every ounce of strength he had to push himself away from the cooker, but Farrell was a powerful man and forced the agent's face ever closer to the ring. Another two inches and the burning cooker ring would be against his flesh.

'Tell me where he hid it,' Farrell urged.

One inch.

'He doesn't know,' said one of the other men, smiling thinly as he watched the agent struggle.

Connelly was fighting as hard as he could but it was useless. The heat made him feel faint; as his face was moved closer, he could actually feel the blistering heat drying his eye.

It was over now.

Farrell suddenly yanked him upright, away from the cooker. As he did he drove a fist hard into Connelly's face, the impact propelling him across the kitchen. He slammed into a wall, his head snapping back to crack against the plaster, then he fell forward.

'Bring him,' Farrell said, nodding towards the door. 'We're taking him with us.'

Forty-Nine

At first he thought they'd blinded him.

Martin Connelly was sure that his eyes were open, yet he could see nothing. It took a few seconds after he regained consciousness to realize that he was blindfolded. The cloth had been knotted tightly round his head, cutting into his temples. But the discomfort was mild compared to the pain which engulfed the rest of his body, filling his veins like liquid fire. His head throbbed mightily from the blows he'd received, and the continuous agony of his burned hand made him feel as if the limb was swelling to gigantic proportions. Soon it would simply burst.

Connelly flexed his fingers and toes and felt renewed pain, a feeling of weightlessness. A terrible strain on his shoulders and neck. As if . . .

He was suspended in mid-air, dangling there like a useless, discarded puppet. He had no idea where he was and no idea how far off the ground he was. It could be two or three inches, it could be several hundred feet. Also, he was suddenly aware of the numbing cold. As a cool breeze swathed his sweat-drenched body he realized they had taken his clothes.

Martin Connelly dangled naked in the air, supported only by two thick pieces of hemp, wound so tightly around his wrists that they chafed the skin raw.

Help me.

He noticed the smell.

A rank, fetid odour clogged his nostrils and reminded him of bad meat. It seemed to be coming closer to him. Perhaps the mad fuckers had hung him in an abattoir. His mind began to race, all the possibilities hurtling through his consciousness. If he was hanging in a slaughterhouse, then might they not choose to use the implements of the slaughterer on him? The cleaver. The butcher's knife. The skewers.

Connelly felt sick and tried to twist himself free, his legs swinging helplessly beneath him. His ankles were unbound; it made him think he was higher off the ground than he would have liked. Perhaps they reasoned that even if he managed to slip clear of the ropes he would have so far to fall it wouldn't matter. The agent stopped struggling and hung there, aware of the pain in his wrists and the rasping against his skin, but even more conscious of the massive welts and blisters that covered his throbbing hand.

The silence was unbroken but for his own laboured breathing.

He let out an involuntary groan of pain and desperation.

'Where is the book, Mr Connelly?'

The voice lanced through the blackness, close to him and below him to the right.

He looked in that direction but the blindfold prevented him from seeing who had spoken.

'Where is it?'

Another voice. This time below to his left.

It was like the first. Slow, deliberate. Slightly mucoid. As if the speaker had a mouthful of phlegm.

'The book.'

Connelly felt a sudden stab of fear and also of

quite irrational embarrassment. The pain seemed to take a back seat momentarily, then he moved his right hand and it came thundering back into his mind.

'Christopher Ward took it from us, you know that,' the first voice said. Connelly was aware of that rancid stench growing stronger. It was closer to him now. So close, he could feel breath on his thigh.

On the thigh.

That meant that, unless the one standing to his right was abnormally tall, he couldn't be suspended more than about six feet off the ground. It was the only crumb of comfort he could salvage from the ordeal. He clung to it.

'We want to know what Ward did with the book. We want it back,' the second voice said.

'We *need* it back,' the first voice told him. 'Where is it?'

Connelly cleared his throat.

'I swear to you I don't know what book you're talking about,' he said. 'I know Ward was writing a book, but he hadn't even started it, he was still doing research.'

'We don't care about the book he was *going* to write,' the first voice snapped angrily. 'We want back what is rightfully ours.'

'He stole it and hid it somewhere. We need to know where so we can recover it,' the other voice added.

'Tell me about the book,' Connelly said, the last vestiges of reason working in his tortured mind. *Could he possibly talk his way out of this situation?* 'I may be able to help.'

'He doesn't know,' the first voice said.

'He's lying,' said the second.

'Ward was his client, he must have known,' intoned a third voice. A harsh voice that Connelly recognized as belonging to the tall man with the dark, close-cropped hair. 'He knows where it is,' Peter Farrell insisted.

'I don't know anything about a stolen book,' Connelly bleated.

'Then you are no use to us,' the first voice said.

'Wait,' Connelly said, panicking.

There was silence for a second, only his rapid breathing filling the air.

'His wife knows where the book is,' Connelly lied. 'Find her and she'll lead you to it.'

Would they believe it? Come on, convince them.

He realized that his last chance was to make his captors believe that Donna knew where the book they sought was hidden, whatever it was. If they thought that *she* knew, they might let *him* go. To hell with Donna. He had to save himself.

'Ward told her everything. He would have told her where your book is,' the agent continued, the lies falling easily from his lips. 'Find *her* and you'll find the book.'

'You're lying,' snapped Farrell. 'We didn't find it at Ward's house.'

'Well, he wouldn't keep it *there*, would he?'

Connelly hoped they couldn't hear the desperation in his voice. 'Besides, he owns another place, a cottage in Sussex. It could be there. Look, she's gone to look for it. His wife is searching for the book because Ward told her he had it. He told her he stole it. It's *her* you want, not *me*. She knows.'

'Where is this house in Sussex?' Farrell demanded.

Connelly searched his mind desperately, trying to remember. He almost smiled when he did, quickly imparting the information to them.

'It could be there but I doubt it. She was going to Ireland to find it. I asked her if she wanted me to go with her but she said no. She said she had to find the book, but that it was a secret between her and Ward. She's in Ireland now.'

'She *was*,' Farrell corrected him. 'She was seen near the lodge at Mountpelier yesterday.'

'I told you,' Connelly blurted.

'Shut up,' hissed Farrell, striking him hard across the stomach.

'Is this true?' the first voice asked. 'She was at the Lodge?'

'She left on a plane from Dublin last night. She's being followed,' Farrell explained.

Merciful fucking Christ, I think I've done it. They believe me, Connelly thought as he tried to suck in breath, tasting the rancid atmosphere as thickly as if it were smoke.

'I told you,' he said wearily. 'She knows where it is.'

'You would betray this woman to save yourself?' asked the first voice. A chuckle. It was a sound that made the hair at the back of Connelly's neck rise. 'You really have *no* honour, do you? I like that.' Another laugh. And another. The whole room seemed to be filled with it. Raucous, insane laughter that drummed in the agent's ears until he feared he would go deaf.

It gradually died away. His body swayed gently back and forth on the ropes.

'I've helped you,' he said. 'Let me go, please.'

'And if we do? We are to expect you to keep quiet? What do you think we are?' the second voice snorted. 'Your treachery is matched by your stupidity. If we release you, you will try to expose us the way Ward was going to.'

'How can I?' bleated Connelly. 'I haven't seen who you are. Please.'

He felt hands tugging at his blindfold.

'Look upon us,' the voice said and the agent opened his eyes.

'Oh God,' he whispered as he stared at his captors, his eyes bulging madly.

He gaped round the small room, realizing that he was suspended from a ceiling only fifteen feet high. There were a dozen or more people in the room, all seated, all staring at his dangling, vulnerable form.

'You have been a help to us and now we are

done with you,' said the first man, smiling up at him.

'No,' shouted Connelly.

He heard the sound of liquid slurping in a metal container as Farrell approached him from behind.

'What are you doing?' he shrieked, twisting about madly on the ropes that suspended him.

He felt cold, thick fluid being splashed on him.

He smelled the petrol as it covered his skin.

'No,' he bellowed. 'For God's sake, please don't. Please.' His voice cracked as it rose in pitch. More of the reeking petrol was doused over him. It matted the hair on his chest and ran down over his pubic hair and penis, dripping from his feet.

Tears of helplessness and terror welled up in his eyes.

'You can't do this, please,' he wailed.

The first figure struck a match and held it up in front of him, the tiny yellow flame glowing brightly.

'No,' Connelly screamed, his yell so loud it seemed his lungs would burst.

'Thank you for your help,' said the figure, and tossed the match at him.

The petrol ignited immediately, a loud whump filling the room as it consumed Connelly's body, which twisted insanely on the ropes as he screamed in uncontrollable agony.

From those watching there was movement.

They stood and, as one, began to applaud. There was some laughter.

Connelly's body continued to burn.

Fifty

It was raining outside, a thin veil of rain that was blown by the wind so that it appeared to undulate in the air like gossamer curtains. Droplets of fluid formed on the window and trickled down, puddling on the sills.

Donna Ward glanced distractedly out of the window for a second, her mind racing, her hand on her book.

The pages were stiffened with age and the tome smelt fusty, like a damp cloth left to dry on a radiator. Some of the words on the pages were faint, barely legible. Donna had squinted at them as she'd read. Some of the words did not even make sense to her but, through the confusion, she'd been able to salvage enough to piece together roughly the contents.

If not for the help of the librarian she might not even have found the book.

After checking into The Holiday Inn, Edinburgh, she had travelled to the library indicated in Ward's notes and diary, not really sure what she sought. The library was large and, rather than hunt through the endless rows of volumes dating as far back as 1530, she had sought the help of the librarian. The woman was in her mid-thirties, dressed in a black trouser suit and white sweater. She was a little overweight, her hands a touch too pudgy when she reached for various books and took them from the shelves. The badge she wore on one lapel proclaimed that her name was Molly. She seemed eager to help and selected half a dozen books for Donna to look at concerning The Hell Fire Club. She herself knew little or nothing about the organisation, and Donna wished she could have happened upon someone as knowledgeable on the subject as Mahoney had been.

This time she was on her own.

There were only a handful of other people in the library reference section; the normal air of peace and quiet one would expect in such a place seemed to have become an unnatural silence. Donna glanced round at the other occupants of the room but they were all hunched over their chosen books, seated at the wooden desks. Every so often the sound of a dropped pencil or pen would break the solitude, but apart from that the only sound was that of the wind outside, whipping around the building, hurling rain at the windows so hard it sounded as if thousands of tiny pebbles were being bounced off the glass.

Donna returned to the book, bending closer to make out the words:

Initiates into these clubs did undertake to join in deeds most foule to Christian Man. Some such as cannot bee described. The Acts demanded of them were as different as those Clubs themselves. Of the Clubs in existence there were the Mohocles The Blasters, The Bucks, The Bloods and, most vile of all The Sons of Midnight. These Heathen groups practised rites som would pray God not to here.

Donna flicked ahead a few pages but could see no way of hastening her search for the information she sought. She continued to read;

Those who joined were forced to fornicate in the presence of others. Some would beat the women afterwards. But these vile tasks were as welcome to them for they knew no love of God nor worship of Him. Only the pleasure of the flesh and pleasing their Masters was their joy. They killed too and found pleasure in it. After fornication with a woman then the one who would join would show his love of the Unholy by taking a child and killing it. The skull he would keep in his abode. A sign and an offering to those he wanted to join. Som would kill the unborn child or children of women and som ript open their bellys to take the child as offering. The skull of that child would always be theres. A sign of their villainy and proofe of their love of Evil.

Donna chewed her lip contemplatively as she read, forced to run her index finger beneath the words, so jumbled and irregularly formed were they on the faded page.

All these Evils are set down in great and Anciente Bookes called Grimoires. These books much prized by thes societys were filld with incantations and secrets known only to those who trod the dark pathes. Each club had a GRIMOIRE and where in every member would write his name as to show love of Evil and to show kinship with others of Evil.

Donna fumbled in her handbag, looking for a piece of paper and a pen. She found a notepad from the Shelbourne and scribbled the word Grimoire down.

She wondered where they kept the dictionaries.

The hand on her shoulder made her jump.

She turned to see Molly standing there.

'Sorry if I startled you,' she said, smiling. 'I just wondered how you were getting on.' She nodded towards the books in front of Donna.

'I'm okay,' she said, her heart slowing slightly. She administered herself a swift mental rebuke for nervousness. 'I need a dictionary, please.'

Molly nodded and hurried off to fetch one, returning a moment later. She handed it to Donna and stood by her as she flipped through it, running her finger down the columns of words until she found what she sought.

GRIMOIRE; *(Archaic) (Grim-wah) Old Norman French word*; (i) *A Book of Spells and invocations*.

(ii) *A book supposedly used for contacting Devils and Demons. Usually ascribed to Witches or Satanists*.

She re-read the definition, then closed the book and handed it back to Molly who smiled.

'Can I help you with anything else?' she wanted to know.

Donna ran a hand through her hair and sighed wearily. Her shoulders felt stiff and she could feel the beginnings of a headache gnawing at her skull.

'No thanks,' Donna said gratefully. 'I think I've finished.'

She glanced at the books in front of her, then at her watch.

It was approaching 4.15 p.m. She'd been in the library for close to four hours now.

All the reading and yet she wasn't even sure she'd made any progress. Because she wasn't sure what she was looking for. She knew more about The Hell Fire Club; she was certain that was what her husband had been working on. She knew that members had to fornicate and kill a child to gain entry. She knew that they relied on a book called a Grimoire for their contact with Evil.

Donna sat back.

In the cold light of day it all seemed so ridiculous.

Contact with Evil.

Hell Fire Club.

What had any of this to do with her husband's death or affair, she asked herself?

Perhaps she should be reading about infidelity instead of impiety. Widowhood instead of Wizardry.

And yet there were things wrong somewhere. Nagging doubts in her mind.

The police were convinced that her husband had *not* been murdered.

She *wasn't* convinced.

Why had masked men broken into her house? What had they been looking for?

Who were the men in the photo with Chris? Why did one of them look like a man who had supposedly been dead for over two hundred years?

Why had she been chased and nearly killed in Ireland?

Why had Mahoney withdrawn his offer to help so suddenly and unexpectedly?

Why? Why? Her life was turning into a series of unanswered questions.

Donna rubbed her eyes and got to her feet, picking up the piece of paper and putting it in her handbag.

On her way out of the library she thanked Molly for her help.

Donna hesitated on the steps of the library, looking out into the rain, seeing people caught in the downpour hurrying past. The cold wind closed around her like an icy fist, chilling her to the bone.

There had to be an answer to all this somewhere. She just wasn't sure where to find it.

Not yet.

Fifty-One

Julie Craig heard the car pull up in the driveway and hurried across to the landing window to look out.

She saw the Jaguar parked there but couldn't make out the identity of its occupant. The man was alone; he looked alternately towards the house and then down, as if searching for something on the dashboard.

She saw him rub one hand across his forehead, as if wiping away perspiration. Still he remained seated behind the steering wheel of the Jag.

Should she go downstairs, outside and ask him what he wanted? No. Let *him* make the first move. She was suddenly aware how ridiculous she was becoming. Why should there be anything sinister about him? She tried to think more rationally, to dismiss the darker possibilities from her mind, but after what had happened here in the past week or so she found the worrying thoughts came more easily. After all, hadn't men broken into the house? He might be one of them, come during the day to catch her off guard.

She watched as the man swung himself out of the car.

He was dressed in a suit that looked as if it needed pressing. Indeed, as he shut the car door, he brushed at one sleeve as if to remove wrinkles as well as fluff. She watched as he stood beside the car for a moment looking up towards the house.

She stepped back a pace and watched as he looked across at the Fiesta then at the house once more.

He began walking towards it and she saw that he had one hand inside his jacket, as if reaching for something.

She moved to the head of the stairs and looked down into the hallway, listening to his footsteps approaching the front door.

He rang the bell.

Julie froze, gripped the banister tightly and waited.

He rang again and waited.

She moved quickly but cautiously down the stairs and stood close to the front door, edging towards the spy-hole, squinting through it.

The man she saw on the other side was in his late thirties, his hair receding slightly, but what hair he did have was thick and lustrous and reached the collar of his shirt. He was thin-faced, a little pale.

He shifted from one foot to the other as he waited for the door to be answered.

As Julie saw him reach for the doorbell a third time she opened the door and eased it back to the extent of the chain.

The man peered through the gap and smiled politely at her.

'Good morning,' he said. 'I'm sorry to disturb you. I was wondering if I could speak to Mrs Ward. Mrs Donna Ward.'

Julie eyed him suspiciously for a moment.

'My name is Neville Dowd,' he continued. 'Sorry, I should have introduced myself first.' He smiled warmly.

There seemed to be no threat in his manner.

Julie nodded a greeting.

'I was Mr Ward's solicitor,' he explained.

'Can I help you?' Julie wanted to know.

'I needed to speak to *Mrs* Ward, actually. I should have called round sooner but I've been on holiday and only returned yesterday to hear the news. It must be a very difficult time for her. I was going to call her into my office but I thought that would be a little heartless.' He smiled thinly, as if expecting praise for his gesture of concern.

Julie nodded.

'That's very good of you,' she said, some of her initial apprehension disappearing.

'May I ask who you are?' he said.

'I'm Donna's sister, Julie Craig.'

He extended a hand, tried to shake hers through the gap in the door. Julie slipped the chain and opened the door to its full extent.

'Sorry for the greeting,' Julie said, 'but you can't be too careful.'

'I agree. A woman here in a house like this, I

don't blame you being wary. Is Mrs Ward here, please?'

'She's away for a couple of days. Can I give her a message? I could get her to ring you when she gets back.'

Dowd looked perplexed.

'No, it's all right. Thank you, anyway. I don't want to keep intruding; she must have other things on her mind. It's just that there were some things I needed to clear up with her about her husband's estate. Some items I'd been holding for him. She should have them.'

'What kind of items?'

'I really shouldn't discuss that with anyone else but Mrs Ward. I'm sorry, I don't mean to be rude.'

'I understand.'

He looked down at his shoes which, unlike his suit, looked well-cared for.

'However, if you're not sure when she's going to be back . . .' He allowed the sentence to trail off. 'As long as she gets the items, that's all that matters. If you'd be so kind, you could pass them on to her from me. If she needs to get in touch with me for anything, she has my number.'

Julie nodded.

Dowd reached inside his jacket and pulled out a thick brown envelope. He handed it to Julie.

'Mr Ward said that this was only to be given to his wife in the event of his death,' the solicitor said.

'I'll see she gets it.'

Dowd extended a hand which Julie shook.

'Thank you for your help. Please pass on my condolences and tell her to call me if she needs any help.' He smiled, told Julie how delightful it had been to meet her and headed back to his car. She watched him slide behind the wheel of the Jag and start up the powerful engine. He turned the vehicle round in the drive and drove off. Julie closed the door again and slid the chain into place.

She lifted the envelope, testing its weight, then she moved across to the phone.

Running her finger down the notepad beside it, she found the number she sought and pressed the digits.

At the other end it began to ring.

Fifty-Two

6.46 p.m.

Julie cradled the mug of tea in both hands and looked at the wall clock on the other side of the kitchen. She checked her own watch.

'Come on,' she murmured irritably.

The phone on the wall close to her rang and she picked it up at the second ring.

'Donna?' she said.

'Yes,' the voice at the other end said.

'What kept you? I called this morning.'

'I've only just got back to my room and picked up your message. What's wrong?'

'Nothing, as far as I know. I've had a visitor today. Chris's solicitor, a man called Neville Dowd. Do you know him?'

'I met him a couple of times. What did he want?'

Julie looked at the envelope lying on the worktop. She told Donna about it.

'What's in it?' Donna asked.

'It's private. You didn't expect me to open it, did you?' Julie said, surprised. 'You'll have to look when you get back. How's it going, by the way?'

Donna told her sister what had happened in Ireland, the information she'd accumulated about The Hell Fire Club and also what she'd found in the library in Edinburgh. She explained a little about The Hell Fire Club itself.

'So that's what Chris was working on?' Julie said finally. 'Who the hell were the men who attacked you in Ireland?'

'I don't know. I don't know if it's linked to Chris's work either.'

'Can't the police do anything?'

'They can't act on maybes, Julie. I haven't got any concrete proof to show them.'

'Someone tried to kill you; how much more concrete does proof have to be?'

'Listen, I've been thinking about Chris's work. You know how deeply involved he got with it; he had on other books. I think he might have discovered some kind of organisation *like* The Hell Fire Club. A modern day off-shoot of it. I'm not sure.'

'Then why didn't *he* go to the police if he had?'

'I don't know.' Donna sighed. 'I don't know what he was trying to do. I don't know if *she* was involved with it.'

'Who?'

'Suzanne Regan.'

'For Christ's sake, Donna, I thought you'd forgotten about that.'

'Forgotten about it? My husband dies in a car crash with his mistress and you think I can forget about it?'

'I meant about his love life. I thought you were supposed to be finding out what he was working on, not going on about what he might or might not have done with Suzanne Regan.'

'I think she was involved with it, too,' Donna said.

'How?'

'Some of the things I found out from books here today. I think Chris was using her to get himself accepted into the organisation, whatever it was.'

'You mean he was trying to join them?'

'It's possible. She could have been his way in.'

'What would he have gained by joining a group like that?'

'That's what I have to find out. I thought Martin Connelly might know, but I've phoned his office and his home a couple of times and there's never anyone there. Have you heard from him?'

'Why would he call *me*?' Julie said defensively.

'He might want to find out if *I* was back yet. If he *does* call, tell him I'll speak to him when I get back.' There was a pause, then the silence was finally broken by Donna. 'I think Chris was involved in something, Julie. Something dangerous. Perhaps that envelope Dowd brought round will answer some questions.'

Julie looked at the envelope lying on the worktop.

'There's nothing more for me here,' said Donna wearily. 'I'm coming home tonight. I'll get a shuttle flight.'

'Do you want me to pick you up from the airport?'

'No, I'll get a cab. I'll see you later. Take care.'

'You too.'

Donna hung up.

Julie gently replaced the receiver and walked across to the envelope. She picked it up, feeling the weight of it. It was packed tightly with papers and . . .

She ran her fingers gently over the manila surface and felt the outline of something small and cold inside. She pressed it with the tip of her index finger, trying to figure out what it could be. She frowned, gliding the pads of her fingers across the shape like a blind person reading braille, feeling every contour.

Fifty-Three

'She must die.'

The voice floated through the air like smoke, the words almost visible in the heavy atmosphere.

'Not yet,' another said. 'Not until we have the book.'

The room was large, the walls oak-panelled on two sides. The other two were dark brick. Paintings hung on them, large canvases in gilt frames. The room was lit by a number of small reading lamps, none powered by anything stronger than a sixty-watt bulb. It gave the room an artificially cosy feel, which was added to by the open fireplace and the array of expensive leather furniture that dotted the floor, spread out on thick carpet as dark as wet concrete.

The air was thick with cigarette and cigar smoke; a number of the twelve men seated there puffed away quite happily while they talked. They sat at different places in the room, most of them also with drinks cradled in their hands.

The house in Conduit Street was just two minutes walk from Berkeley Square in one direction and, in the other, the bustling thoroughfare that was Regent Street. The house and the room within were like a peaceful island in the sea of activity that constituted the centre of London.

The room was on the second floor of the three-storey building, its curtains drawn, its inhabitants hidden from those below. Windows like blind eyes reflected the lights of passing cars.

One of the men in the room got to his feet and crossed to a well-stocked drinks cabinet, refilling his glass, offering the same service to his colleagues.

They had been drinking for the best part of an hour but none were drunk. Even so, large quantities of brandy and gin were consumed as the men talked.

There was a large table in the centre of the room, made of dark polished wood. Two men sat at its head, their faces reflected in the gleaming surface. As the first of them drank, thc gold ring on his left index finger clinked against the crystal.

'What if Connelly was lying?' said the one seated next to him. 'What if the woman doesn't know where the book is?'

'She knows,' the other said with an air of certainty. 'She was at Rathfarnham, wasn't she? She went to the lodge at Mountpelier.'

'I want to know why she wasn't stopped there,' an angry voice from the other side of the room interrupted him.

'Those responsible for the mistake have been dealt with,' another said. 'Besides, we can't kill her until she's led us to the book or at least told us where we can find it.'

'If Ward *did* tell her about it then she might go to the police,' a third voice said.

'Let her,' chuckled another. Several others joined in the laughter.

One of the men at the head of the table brought his hand down hard on the table-top and the sound ceased.

'Enough of this. We need the book and we need it quickly. There isn't much time left.'

'We'll get it,' said another man, approaching the table. 'We'll get her *and* the book.'

The other occupants of the room gradually moved across to the table, each of them taking a seat around it.

'It must be in our hands within seven days,' one of the men wearing the gold rings insisted angrily.

'It will be.'

There was a note of certainty in Peter Farrell's voice.

'I hope for your sake that it is, Farrell. I hope for *all* our sakes it is.'

'What if *she* uses the book the way Ward was going to?' another voice added with concern. 'If she knew about the book, he may have told her about the contents, too.'

Farrell waved a hand dismissively.

'She's being followed now. There are two men on her. They'll find the book. They'll *make* her tell them where it is. And then they'll kill her. End of story.'

'What if they fail?' a worried voice interjected.

'They won't,' Farrell snapped irritably.

'You said that about the men who went to her house to search. *They* failed. Perhaps we underestimated her.'

'She's a woman,' Farrell chuckled. 'Just a woman.'

A chorus of laughter greeted his remark.

'So, we are agreed,' said one of the men at the head of the table. 'Once she tells us where the book is or she leads us to it, she dies.' He looked around at his companions. 'Yes?' He looked at each man in turn and waited for their compliance.

They nodded slowly, solemnly, like a jury passing sentence.

Farrell merely smiled.

'Perhaps we should have brought her here,' said one of the men. 'Let her enjoy our company for an evening.'

There was more laughter.

One of the men at the head of the table rose, his glass in his hand, the gold of his ring clinking against the crystal.

'A toast,' he said grandly.

'To the Death of God, the destruction of morality and to The Sons of Midnight.'

Francis Dashwood spoke the words with a grin on his wrinkled features.

Beside him, Richard Parsons echoed the toast, and so did the other men in the room.

'To The Sons of Midnight.'

Fifty-Four

The shuttle flights from Edinburgh to London were booked up right through until eleven that evening. Donna rang the station and discovered that there was a train to King's Cross leaving at 8.27 p.m. She booked a seat on it and took a taxi to the terminus.

Trains out of Waverley were running fifteen minutes late by the time she got there, but she didn't care. She wandered across the concourse to the Travellers' Fare buffet and sat warming her hands around a cup of coffee while she waited for her train to arrive.

She sat in the window, watching the streams of people coming to and from the trains. Taxis waited in a long queue to ferry them away, while others struggled up the stairs with cases or bags, determined to make their way by other means. She wondered how many of them were going home. Home to relatives, to loved ones. *To husbands?*

Donna felt a twinge of sadness and stared down into the depths of her cup, picking up the spoon and stirring unnecessarily, watching the dark liquid drip from the plastic utensil.

On the concourse people stood around gazing up at the departure and arrival boards, checking times of trains. She saw a young man squatting on a rucksack, eating a bar of chocolate and looking at the board. Close by a couple were kissing, holding each other close to ward off the cold wind that had sprung up. Donna watched them for a moment, then looked away.

One of the station employees was following a discarded wrapper across the concrete, trying to pick it up but thwarted every time by a fresh breeze that blew the litter out of his reach. Cursing, he continued his pursuit.

Donna finally got to her feet and wandered outside, glancing up at the board, noticing that her train was due in about five minutes.

She left the buffet and headed for the small John Menzies shop opposite.

She didn't notice the thick-set man dressed in jeans and a long dark coat get up and follow her out. He stood by the exit, watching, cupping one hand around the flame of his lighter as he lit up a Marlboro.

Donna glanced at the paperbacks on the bestseller stand as she entered the shop. Only six months earlier her husband's last book had occupied a prominent position on that stand and hundreds like it up and down the country. Again she felt that twinge of sadness. She selected three magazines, paid for them, then made her way back out onto the concourse.

The man outside the buffet sucked on his cigarette and watched her as she headed towards the gates and the platforms beyond. She paused to roll up the magazines and push them into her handbag, rummaging for her ticket.

The man in the long dark coat glanced at Donna, then back towards the Menzies shop.

Another man, dressed in a leather jacket and trousers that were too short, was walking briskly across the concourse, his eyes fixed on Donna. In fact so engrossed with her movements was he that he bumped into a young woman who was struggling with an impossibly heavy suitcase. He almost knocked her over but continued walking, ignoring her angry shouts. Other heads turned towards the commotion; indeed, even Donna looked round briefly. But she only saw the girl who had now returned her full attention to the case.

Other passengers for the train were forming a queue. Donna joined it, filing past the barriers, showing her ticket and heading down the platform towards the First Class carriages. As she passed the buffet car her stomach rumbled, as if to remind her she hadn't eaten since lunchtime.

She opened one of the doors and climbed up, selecting a double seat for herself, sliding her suitcase between two seats.

Further down the train the man in the long dark coat also climbed aboard.

The man in the leather jacket stood on the platform for a moment longer before stepping up into the carriage next to Donna's.

She spread her magazines out on the table and removed her shoes, massaging her toes as she waited for the train to pull away. There were perhaps half a dozen other passengers in the carriage, all spread out. Some read newspapers; one fiddled with a Walkman, adjusting the volume.

Donna shivered slightly, noticing how cold it was on the train.

The journey should take a little over six hours. She glanced at her watch as the train pulled away from the platform.

The man in the leather jacket walked to the door that linked the carriages and looked through, seeing where Donna was seated. Satisfied he knew her position, he returned to his seat.

There was plenty of time.

Fifty-Five

Apart from Donna there were only two other people eating in the train's dining car. They sat at the far end of the carriage, talking in hushed tones. Each man had a portable phone on the table beside him.

Donna enjoyed her meal, luxuriating in the warmth of the carriage. She felt tired and wondered if she might manage a couple of hours' sleep before the train reached London. It was about forty miles from York at present, so she had plenty of time.

She glanced up briefly as David Ryker passed

her, his leather jacket undone. As he passed by, Donna noticed that his trousers didn't touch the top of his shoes. She looked at his broad back, then at the short trousers, and smiled to herself, returning her attention to her coffee. When the steward returned with a steaming pot she had another cup.

Ryker passed her once more, glancing at her, cradling a plastic beaker of tea in his hand. As the train thundered over a set of points he steadied himself against her seat for a moment, then wandered off down the aisle.

Donna ordered brandy from the steward and sat gazing at the window of the train.

Apart from lights from distant towns, all she saw was her own reflection in the dark glass. The train sped along, countryside flying by in the gloom outside.

She moved across to the window, cupping one hand over her eyes so that she could see out, but there was little to see. They passed through a small station and she caught a glimpse of a couple of people standing on the windswept platform, but other than that there was nothing to see. She sat back and reached for her brandy. She closed her eyes and allowed her head to loll back against the pillow.

Was she any closer to a solution, to finding out why her husband had died?

He died because his car hit a wall.

But why? Was it *really* an accident?

The incidents in Ireland told her it wasn't, yet

she had no proof to support the fact that he had been killed. She was beginning to wonder if her trip had been worthwhile. She had also wondered if seeing the places he went might make her feel closer to him, but it hadn't. She was left with still more unanswered questions. Most of all, she was no wiser as to his involvement with Suzanne Regan.

Donna missed Chris badly. At nights, particularly, she had felt loneliness so great it was as if a hole had been torn in her soul, something irreplaceable had been ripped from her. Knowing of his involvement with another woman, however, had meant that that hole was in danger of being filled with hate, not sorrow. If only she'd had the chance to ask him why he'd had the affair.

She felt cheated, when she should have felt despair.

Just one chance to ask him.

One chance to say goodbye.

She sat forward and opened her eyes.

David Ryker's reflection filled the window beside her as he passed. For a second Donna thought he'd been standing there looking at her, this man in the leather jacket and trousers which were too short.

He retreated back down the aisle again.

Donna decided to take her brandy back to her seat with her. She paid the bill and walked back through the dining car, drawing glances from the two men at the other end with the portable phones. Both of them looked at her for a second, then continued their hushed conversation.

She made her way back to her seat, noticing that the man with the leather jacket was seated about five rows behind her.

Donna made herself comfortable and prepared to sleep, wondering, despite the fact that she was tired, whether or not the thoughts tumbling through her mind would be still long enough to allow her two or three precious hours' rest. She drained what was left in her glass and set it down.

'Mind if I join you?'

The voice startled her. She looked round to see Ryker standing there. His face was expressionless.

Without waiting to be invited he sat down beside her and crossed his legs, the trousers riding up almost to his calf.

'I saw you in the dining car,' he said. 'I thought you were travelling alone.'

'I prefer travelling alone,' Donna said, trying to be as tactful as possible. She smiled thinly at him.

'Can I get you a drink?' Ryker asked. 'I was going to have one.'

'No thanks, I *was* going to try and get some sleep,' she told him, an edge to her voice.

'I can't sleep on trains,' Ryker said.

And it doesn't look as if I'm going to be able to either, thought Donna irritably.

'I get bored,' he continued, looking up, noticing that another man was approaching.

A man in a long dark overcoat.

Donna saw him, too. Saw that he was looking at her.

She sat up, the puzzled look on her face turning to one of irritation.

The second man sat opposite her.

'I don't want to seem rude,' she said, 'but I was hoping to travel on my own. I . . .'

Ryker cut her short.

'Shut up,' he whispered. 'Just shut it.'

Donna turned to say something to him.

As he opened his jacket she saw his hand close over the hilt of a knife.

Opposite, the man in the long dark overcoat was smiling.

'We need to ask you some questions,' he said. 'We need your help.' He unbuttoned his coat and reached inside.

'And what if I call for the steward?' Donna said defiantly.

Stuart Benton pushed back his coat slightly so that she could see that he too carried a knife.

'If you do,' he said softly, leaning towards her, 'we'll slice you up like a joint of meat.'

Fifty-Six

'Who are you?'

Donna regarded the two men warily, her

gaze flicking from one to the other in quick succession.

'We need your help,' said Benton, staring at her. 'And you're going to give it. You're going to tell us what we want to know.'

Donna looked up and saw the steward coming up the aisle.

Could she alert him to her danger? *Should* she?

Ryker saw him too and nodded towards him.

Benton glanced over his shoulder and saw the man.

'Don't even think about it,' he said, his eyes blazing. 'I'll kill him, too.'

The steward smiled as he passed, glancing at the two men sitting close to Donna.

Benton watched him go.

'Well done, Mrs Ward,' he said, smiling.

'Don't patronize me, you bastard,' she snarled. 'And how do you know my name?'

'We've been following you since you left your hotel yesterday,' Ryker told her. 'The library, everywhere.'

'Was the book in the library?' Benton said.

'There's lots of books in libraries, you half-wit. You should try looking some time,' Donna said with gleeful malice.

'You fucking cunt . . .' Benton snapped, lunging forward.

Donna sat back in her seat, her heart thudding hard against her ribs. But it was Ryker who sat forward to restrain his companion.

'We can't hurt her,' he said quickly, hoping Donna hadn't heard. 'Farrell said not to hurt her yet.'

'Bitch,' hissed Benton. 'Fucking rich bitch.' He nodded slowly. 'Mouthy, just like your old man.'

'You knew my husband?' she asked.

'I saw him a couple of times. Flash cunt. Thought he owned the place. Too much mouth.'

'Did you kill him?' she wanted to know.

'No,' said Benton, 'but I wish I had. Perhaps I'll have to make do with killing his missus. Now, tell us where the book is. Are you going to pick it up now?'

'I don't know what book you're talking about,' she said.

The steward passed by again and Donna even managed to smile at him. She felt suddenly more secure despite the fact that she was flanked by men with knives. The train wasn't stopping until it got to London; there were other people in the carriage and surely these men wouldn't dare try anything here, now. If they harmed her there was no way they could get off the train other than jumping and, with it travelling at over ninety-five miles an hour, that didn't seem a very good idea. If she could call their bluff she might just be able to slip away.

Play for time.

She knew she had to keep her nerve.

Easier said than done.

'Do I take it that you work for the same

man as the two who broke into my house?' she asked.

Benton looked at his companion, who merely wrinkled his brow.

'I mean, they seemed to be incompetent morons like you. It's an understandable supposition. Don't you agree? Or would you prefer me to stick to words of one syllable?'

Benton leaned forward again, his face contorted with anger.

'I'm going to enjoy doing you,' he said angrily. 'I might even slip you one before I do.' He rubbed one hand across his groin. 'Right up your tight, rich twat.'

'And what do you think the other passengers are going to do? Just look the other way?'

'You think anyone's going to help you? Do you think anyone gives a fuck what happens to you? Nobody cares. They'll be too busy looking after themselves,' Benton hissed.

He and Donna locked stares for long moments.

'Where's the book?' Ryker said, jabbing her in the ribs with his elbow.

'Get off me,' Donna hissed.

'Where is it?' he asked, jabbing her again.

She tried to move away from him.

'Come on, bitch. Tell us.'

'Fuck you,' said Donna and kicked out hard under the table.

Her foot connected hard with Benton's right shin and he yelped in pain, reaching down to massage the throbbing limb.

Ryker jabbed her again with his elbow.

'Where is it?' he persisted.

'I'm going to fucking cut you,' Benton said, wincing in pain. 'I don't care what Farrell says.' He leaned closer. 'Get on your fucking feet, we're going for a walk.'

'I'm not moving from here,' Donna told him, meeting his steely gaze and holding it.

'Get up,' Benton repeated. 'I'll kill you, I swear I will.'

'You can't kill her,' Ryker reminded him. 'Farrell . . .'

'Fuck Farrell,' he grunted. 'We'll tell him she made a run for it, we had no choice.'

'He wanted her alive,' Ryker persisted.

Benton pulled the knife free of his belt, leant forward and touched the blade to Donna's left knee.

She felt the point against her stockinged leg.

'If you're not on your feet in five seconds I'll open your leg to the bone. You got that?'

Donna regarded him blankly for a moment, then nodded.

She stood up and squeezed past Ryker, picking up her handbag in the process. Throwing it over her shoulder, she set off down the aisle, the two men close behind her. As she passed the steward she nodded. He returned the gesture, looking at her two new companions.

Donna swallowed hard.

As long as she was on the train she was safe. Well, reasonably safe, anyway. There were other passengers around. What could they do to her?

The lights flickered briefly as the train entered a tunnel.

Donna kept on walking, aware that her two unwanted attendants were no more than a foot or so behind her.

The buffet car was up ahead; there was a young woman buying a drink and some sandwiches. Donna passed her, squeezing by. Ryker and Benton followed.

As they reached the area between two carriages Benton told her to stop. He pushed her towards the door, then reached into his coat pocket and took out a packet of cigarettes. He lit one, standing beside Donna, blowing smoke out of the window. Cold night air rushed in, ruffling her hair and making her eyes water.

What to do?

Ryker was standing by the door to the compartment, watching both ways for anyone approaching.

'Now, we'll start again,' Benton said, gripping Donna's wrist in one powerful hand. 'Where's the book?'

'I don't know,' she told him, trying to shake loose.

Benton leaned closer so that his face was only inches from hers.

'Have you ever seen anyone stabbed?' he said, spittle flying into her face. 'Do you know how much knife wounds can bleed?'

Donna pressed herself against the wall in a bid to move away both from his presence and his foul-smelling breath.

'I have to go to the toilet,' she said.

'What, so you can get in there and pull the emergency cord? Fuck off.'

'Then I'll have to piss all over your shoes, won't I?' Donna said defiantly.

Benton moved back slightly, then his lips curled into a crooked smile.

'You can go,' he told her. 'I'll stand in there with you. To make sure you don't come to any harm.' He chuckled and pushed open the lavatory door for her. 'Keep an eye open,' he told Ryker, pushing Donna into the small cubicle in front of him and pulling the door shut behind.

'Benton,' said his companion, grabbing the other man's arm. 'Don't kill her. I mean it.'

'I'll handle this.'

'Well then, *you'll* have to handle Farrell if you kill her. He said he didn't want her harmed until we find out what she knows about the book. Just go fucking steady, will you?'

Benton shook loose.

'And you just keep your eyes peeled. Right?'

There was scarcely room for one inside the cubicle, let alone two. Donna found the big man pressed close to her.

'What are you going to do? Stand there and watch me?' she demanded.

'I'm not going to turn my back on you, if that's what you were hoping. Go on, get on with it. Or do you want a hand?' He chuckled. 'I'll close my eyes, how's that?'

He did.

It was only a split second but it was all Donna needed.

She lashed out with her right foot, driving it into Benton's groin with all the power she could muster. She actually felt the bottom of his pelvic bone thump against her foot as she slammed his testicles up against the bone.

He howled in pain, the sound lost as the train hurtled into a tunnel.

Donna lunged at him, aware that his face was unprotected as he clutched at his genitals with both hands.

She raked his face with her nails, digging at his eyes, making him scream in renewed agony as she sheared a portion from his lower eyelid. Blood ran down his face. He tried to fight back, clutching at her throat and digging his thumbs into her Adam's apple, but she bit into his thumb until she drew blood, kicking again at the big man. She drove three kicks into his shins and smashed her handbag into the side of his head. Possessed of a strength born of fear and rage, she rained blows onto him, pushing him against the lavatory door, which flew open.

His face scratched and bleeding, contorted in a grimace of pain and anger, Benton toppled backwards, one hand reaching for the knife.

The train was still inside the tunnel, the wind howling like a mad banshee through the open windows. The lights flickered on and off.

Donna threw herself clear of Benton's groping hands.

She spun round and brought one heel down with tremendous force onto his outstretched hand.

The point of the heel crushed the tip of his index finger, splitting the nail as far as the cuticle. Blood burst from the shattered digit and Benton screamed again.

Donna turned as Ryker came at her, avoiding his clumsy attempts to grab her.

She was not so lucky with Benton, who sprang up and crashed into her, his arms locking around her waist, their combined momentum slamming them against the door.

The impact caused it to fly open. For what seemed like an eternity both of them were suspended in mid-air, filthy fumes pouring into the carriage from inside the tunnel.

Then the second passed.

Ryker tried to grab them but was too late.

They toppled out.

Fifty-Seven

She knew she was going to die.

In that split second, as she and Benton fell from the train, Donna *knew*.

The stench of the tunnel filled her nostrils; the roar of the train drummed in her ears. She felt weightless as they pitched into empty air.

Benton, in his terror, released his grip on her waist. His scream echoed madly inside the tunnel as he fell was slammed against the brickwork then bounced back against the speeding train, his body pulped by the impact.

Something inside Donna's mind, some shred of self-preservation, made her shoot out a hand.

She managed to grip the frame of the window on the door which was flying open now, banging against the side of the train.

Hold on, her mind screamed. *Hold on.*

She used all her strength to grip the frame, her body buffetted by the high-speed wind that swept against the train as it roared along. Her hair whipped around her face; she felt the icy chill filling her. Her fingers were beginning to go numb.

She was losing her grip.

The train burst free of the tunnel and Donna shouted in defiance, managing to get her other hand onto the frame, too. But all she could do was hang there from the side of the speeding train, unable to move, knowing her strength would eventually fade. It was only a matter of time before she fell.

'Grab my hand,' roared Ryker, extending a hand. 'I'll pull the door shut.'

He gripped the open door and pulled, one of his hands closing over Donna's.

She had visions of him slowly unpeeling her fingers, prising them from the door until she fell.

But instead he used all his strength to heave the door shut, battling against the onrushing wind as the train continued to hurtle along.

Donna felt faint; she thought her grip was failing.

HOLD ON.

Ryker pulled the door another few inches, pulled her closer.

If only she could hang on . . .

She felt her feet trailing through the weeds that grew at the side of the track, nettles and thistles tearing her skin as she was dragged through them at high speed.

'Take my hand,' Ryker shouted, bellowing to make himself heard. 'I'll pull you in.'

Donna didn't have time to think. She hadn't the luxury of considering her options.

She gripped his hand as tightly as she could, feeling a terrific wrench on her shoulders as he tried to haul her in, steadying himself against the door to ensure that he didn't end up suffering the same fate as his companion.

'Your other hand,' he shouted. 'Give me your other hand.'

She had one hand clamped in Ryker's, the other wrapped round the door frame. If she relinquished her grip on the door she was completely at his mercy.

'Come on,' Ryker screamed at her.

There was another tunnel approaching, looming large and dark, ready to swallow her and the train.

She heard a loud roar and realized that the 125 was sounding its air horn. A warning as it entered the tunnel.

She looked ahead, saw the yawning black mouth and the dark hillside around it.

Saw the lights.

Lights which got brighter as they came closer.

There was another train coming the other way on the track next to her.

It would leave the tunnel as her own train entered.

There would be less than five feet between the massive engines.

She would be crushed between them.

Donna let go of the door and allowed Ryker to grab her other hand.

He pulled as the two trains drew closer.

'Come on,' he screamed and heaved her upwards, clutching at her dress to pull her inside while she held his arms, squirming her legs through the window.

They both fell in an untidy heap on the floor.

The other train swept past with a roar and a deafening hiss of air. Then it was gone.

Donna rolled onto her back, her eyes half-closed, her limbs numb. She could feel nothing but the cold, that seemed to have filled every pore of her body. Her ankles and shins were scratched and bloodied, her stockings shredded by the trackside weeds and nettles.

Ryker knelt beside her, shook her, rubbed her arms as if trying to restore the circulation. She was still cold. Numbingly, almost painfully cold and some of it was shock.

'Why did you save me?' she said quietly, looking at Ryker.

'Because I need you alive,' he said, still rubbing her arms.

'I need information from you.' He looked worried.

'Who are you?' she slurred, close to fainting.

He struck her hard across the face to prevent that.

Then she felt his arms beneath her shoulders, lifting her, pushing her into the lavatory, locking it behind him. He sat her on thc seat and stood looking down at her.

She glanced up and saw the knife hidden inside his jacket.

A thought occurred to her and she almost smiled.

Out of the frying pan into the fire.

Don't all laugh at once.

Donna rubbed both hands across her face, her body quivering as she began to regain some warmth, some feeling in her extremities. Her shoulders ached; her hands and legs were throbbing.

'I saved your life,' said Ryker. 'Now tell me what I want to know.'

She closed her eyes.

The banging on the door made her open them again.

Fifty-Eight

'Conductor,' the voice outside called.

Ryker shot an angry glance at Donna and mouthed something she couldn't make out. She held his gaze then called, 'Just a minute.'

Ryker looked at her with sheer hatred. For one terrible second she thought he was reaching for the knife.

'Open it,' she whispered, nodding towards the door.

'I'll kill you and whoever's outside that door,' Ryker said.

'You wanted me alive, you said,' Donna told him defiantly. 'Kill me and you don't get your information. Now open the door.' They glared at each other for a second longer, then Ryker turned the lock and pushed the door open.

The conductor looked in on them, eyebrows raised.

'What the hell is this?' he said irritably, seeing the two dishevelled occupants of the lavatory. 'What's going on?' He saw the cuts and scratches on Donna's legs. 'I've heard about this sort of thing before,' he said, as if realizing what he'd stumbled on, or at least what he thought he'd stumbled on. 'Very funny. I know what you've been up to. Another couple tried it on one of my trains a month or so ago. I caught them, too.'

'It isn't what you think,' Donna said, running a hand through her hair.

'No, I'm sure it's not,' the conductor said disbelievingly.

'I can explain,' Donna assured him.

Ryker said nothing.

'I fell, I hurt myself,' she said. 'This gentleman,' she nodded towards Ryker, 'he helped me. I needed to sit down for a minute. I must have fainted, I think. This was the nearest seat.' She smiled and patted the toilet beneath her.

The conductor looked at Donna, then at Ryker.

'Is this true?' he asked the other man.

'Yes,' Ryker said sharply, trying to hide his anger.

'Then why was the door locked?' the uniformed man wanted to know.

'I didn't want anyone bursting in and getting the wrong idea, like you have,' Donna said, smiling again.

'Well,' said the conductor, 'it does look a bit suspicious, you'll admit. Two people in one lavatory, I mean . . .' He allowed the sentence to tail off.

'I agree,' Donna echoed. 'If I could just go back to my seat I'll be okay. Could you help me, please?' she asked the conductor.

Ryker regarded her furiously as the uniformed man extended a hand to help her up.

'Are you two people not together, then?' the conductor asked.

'No,' Donna told him, smiling. 'It was just lucky for me this gentleman was passing.' She looked at Ryker. 'I hurt my ankle when I fell. The floor was harder than I thought.' She looked down at her scratched and grazed legs.

'Would you like me to see if there's a doctor on the train?' the conductor asked as he walked back through First Class with her. 'I can get them to call it out over the loudspeaker.'

'No thanks, I'll be fine.'

Ryker trailed along behind, his expression one of growing agitation. His chance, it seemed, was gone. How the hell was he going to get the information he required from her with the conductor prattling about? He clenched his fists in frustration and annoyance. *And fear?*

What would Farrell do if he failed?

The conductor saw Donna to her seat and ensured she was comfortable.

Ryker sat down opposite her, his eyes still blazing.

'Would you like a brandy?' the conductor said. 'It'll calm your nerves. I can get you one from the buffet car.' He winked. 'On the house.'

'That's very kind of you,' Donna told him. 'Thank you.'

He scuttled off to fetch it, leaving them to face one another across the table.

'I'm going to kill you,' Ryker hissed.

'You're not going to do anything,' Donna told him, anger in her voice. 'You said you needed me alive, that *you* wanted some answers. Well, so do I. I want to know who you are and who you're working for, and don't fuck me around or I'll have this train stopped. Tell the truth or the law will be here before you can make a move. I'll tell them you pushed that other bastard out of the train and tried to kill *me*.' She looked at him with a challenging stare. 'Who's Farrell? You said Farrell didn't want me harmed. Who is he? The man who sent you?'

'Fuck you,' Ryker said.

She leaned closer.

'No, fuck *you*. You're scared of him, aren't you, whoever he is? That's why you didn't want that other moron to hurt me. It's why you pulled me back inside the train when you could have left me to die. You're not going to get another chance to threaten me. This train doesn't stop until it reaches London now, and I'm not moving from this seat. If you want to risk killing me, that's fine, but you're going to have to kill the conductor and the other passengers in this carriage, too. Have you got the stomach for that, or are you only brave when you're threatening a woman?' She sat back, smiling. 'You blew it. You should have let me fall, like your friend. But you daren't, dare you? You gutless piece of shit.'

Ryker leaned forward menacingly, anger colouring his face.

'One brandy,' the conductor announced, returning with the drink and handing it to Donna.

She thanked him.

'Will you stay with me for a minute? This other gentleman is going back to his seat now,' she said, smiling at Ryker.

'I can stay,' he said through clenched teeth.

'No,' said Donna, making a great show of concern for him. 'I'll be fine now. Besides, I just need to relax. I might even get a couple of hours sleep before we reach London. Thank you for your help.'

Ryker hesitated a moment, then got to his feet. He paused, looked at her then stalked off down the aisle.

Donna took a sip of the brandy, feeling it burn its way to her stomach.

Most of the chill had left her now and, with Ryker's departure, she felt more comfortable. Nevertheless, she realized that she was only safe until the train reached King's Cross. Once in the capital, she was fair game once more. She had to find a way to escape him.

'Are there phones on board this train?' she asked.

'I'm afraid not,' the conductor said.

Donna felt her heart sink.

'I've got one of these bloody things, though, if you want to borrow it,' the uniformed man said, pulling a portable phone from his pocket. 'We use them for getting track information and arrival times, that sort of thing. I can speak to the driver on it if I want to,' he said, smiling. 'Not that I want to, miserable bugger.'

Donna felt her spirits rising again.

'The reception's a bit haywire sometimes, especially in tunnels, but it should be okay,' he reassured her.

'Thank you,' she said, taking the phone from him. He checked that she was all right, then told her he'd be back in a while and wandered off down the aisle.

Donna called to him.

'What time do we get to King's Cross?'

He checked his watch, then pulled a timetable from his jacket pocket. He ran his finger down the list of times.

'We've made up some time,' he informed her. 'As long as there's no hold-ups, we should be in about 1.30 a.m.'

She thanked him, then turned her attention to the phone, punching in digits.

She glanced at her watch.

10.16 p.m.

At the other end, the phone was picked up.

'Julie, it's me.'

'Where the hell are you? I . . .'

The line crackled.

'Just listen to me, I haven't got time to explain. I'm on a train from Edinburgh, it arrives at King's Cross at 1.30. Julie, you *must* be there to pick me up. Do you understand? You *must* be.'

'Donna, what's going on . . .?'

'I told you, I can't explain now. I'll tell you

everything when I see you. Julie, we've got to go to the cottage in Sussex. I want you to drive me from King's Cross down to the cottage, right? Just listen to me. Go into the wardrobe in our room, get the guns and the ammunition and bring them with you. Bring the letter from Chris's solicitor, too. Please, just promise me you'll do it.'

'Why can't you tell me . . .'

Donna cut her short angrily.

'Just do it, Julie. King's Cross at 1.30. For Christ's sake, be there.'

'I'll be there,' Julie told her.

Donna pressed the 'End' button on the phone and laid it on the table.

While she was on the train she was safe. Once they reached King's Cross she had no idea what Ryker would do. She looked at her watch again.

In less than three hours she'd know.

Fifty-Nine

Donna cupped one hand over her eyes and saw the lights of King's Cross through the window as the train slowed to a crawl, preparatory to gliding to a halt.

She was already on her feet, glancing back in the direction of the next carriage where Ryker was. There were a couple of men standing there by the door, waiting for the train to pull in and stop.

Of Ryker there was no sign.

She picked up her suitcase and made her way along the aisle, pausing to inspect the damage to her legs. She'd removed her ripped stockings earlier and now, as she looked down at the patchwork of scratches and grazes, she was relieved that there hadn't been more damage. There was one cut just above the ankle; it had bled only slightly. She shuddered when she thought what her fate might have been.

The conductor appeared, smiling broadly.

'Would you like a hand with that case?' he said.

She accepted the offer gratefully, feeling the train slow down even more as it cruised into the vast amphitheatre of concrete and glass that was the terminus itself. Other trains, some also newly arrived, stood emptily by platforms, their passengers long since departed. At this early hour there weren't that many people on the concourse. It wouldn't be so easy to melt into the background.

She glanced behind her to see if she could catch a glimpse of Ryker.

Still he was nowhere to be seen.

She looked at her watch; they were on time. She prayed that Julie was waiting for her.

The conductor was babbling on good-naturedly about long train journeys but Donna scarcely heard what he said. She smiled and nodded as he wittered on, moving towards the door as the train drew into the platform. The conductor pushed the door open and peered up the train to see that others were doing the same.

It finally bumped to a halt. All the doors were thrown open and the uniformed man climbed down first, offering Donna his hand as she stepped onto the platform.

The first thing that struck her was the cold. It was freezing inside the huge building; it was as if someone had sucked every ounce of warm air from the interior and replaced it with icy breath. As she exhaled, her own breath clouded before her.

It was quiet, too, every sound echoing around the cavernous dome. Footsteps on the dark concrete platforms seemed to reverberate inside her head.

She walked quickly beside the conductor, who carried her case towards the barrier. There was no guard there to check tickets. Donna glanced around, looking for Ryker amongst the three or four dozen other people who had left the train along with her.

He was nowhere to be seen.

They were drawing closer to the barrier now and Donna began looking for Julie, praying that her sister was waiting, hardly daring to contemplate what she would do if she wasn't.

The conductor was still chatting happily. Donna didn't even bother to acknowledge his ramblings now, her mind was too occupied. Her eyes were too busy picking out faces amongst the other passengers.

Where was Ryker?

She glanced over her shoulder.

He was less than ten yards behind her, hands dug deep into his jacket pockets, walking fast, gaining on her. He pushed past an old woman in his haste to reach Donna, looking at the woman angrily as he nearly tripped over her suitcase.

Donna tried to quicken her pace, hoping the conductor would do likewise.

Ahead of her were half a dozen people, two of them pushing trolleys laden with luggage. Donna looked back at Ryker, then ahead once more.

She quickly slipped ahead of the trolley pushers as one of them blocked the exit, manoeuvring his way through. Those behind were prevented from going any further.

Including the conductor.

He walked to the barrier and handed Donna her case over the rail.

'I'll be okay from here,' she told him, seeing Ryker drawing nearer. 'Thank you for your help.' She took the case and spun round.

The first trolley was still stuck, its owner now flustered, aware that he was blocking everyone else's way.

Ryker pushed against the back of a man trying to get through and got an angry glare for his pains. He could see Donna on the other side of the barrier heading towards a dark-haired woman, whom she embraced.

They headed for the car park outside.

Ryker vaulted the barrier and ran after them,

slipping one hand into his jacket, touching the hilt of the knife.

He ran out through the main doors and looked to his right and left.

No sign of them.

He scurried over to the taxi rank. None of the vehicles had just picked up. There was no sign of Donna or the other woman. He stood on the pavement, hands on his hips.

'Fuck,' he rasped, knowing he'd lost them. He turned and walked slowly back into the station, heading for the payphones. He found one that took money rather than a card and dialled a number.

His hands were shaking.

It was picked up after a couple of rings.

'Farrell,' the voice at the other end said.

'It's Ryker,' he said, trying to control the anxiety in his voice.

'Well?'

'We lost her.'

At the other end the phone was slammed down.

Sixty

The headlights of the Fiesta cut through the darkness.

It was almost 2.45 a.m. The roads were all but

deserted south of London. The deeper into Kent Julie drove the more the two women began to feel as if they were the only people left on earth. Nothing was moving on the roads apart from them, it seemed.

Perhaps it was a good thing.

It was all Julie could do to concentrate on driving, as she listened incredulously to the chain of events her sister recounted.

Donna felt exhausted, drained both physically and emotionally. She lay slumped in the passenger seat, a jacket around her knees to keep her warm. The heating was on inside the car but it did little to drive out the chill that seemed to have settled in her bones. Recalling what had happened to her, especially on the train, served to intensify that cold.

She had come so close to death.

She shuddered.

Was that how Chris had felt seconds before he died?

She closed her eyes for a moment.

'We should call the police,' said Julie.

Donna ignored her.

She was thinking of what had happened on the train. About the two men, their threats. Their fear of the man who had sent them to find her. What had Ryker said his name was?

'Donna, I said we should call the police. This is too serious now,' Julie persisted.

Farrell. She opened her eyes, her tired mind gradually focusing on that name.

On that face.

'My God,' she whispered. 'It was the man at the house the day Chris was buried.'

'What are you talking about?'

'I told you that one of the men on the train kept saying that *Farrell* needed information from me, that *Farrell* had said I wasn't to be killed. That day at the house, the day of the funeral, I caught a man in Chris's office going through his papers. *His* name was Farrell. Peter Farrell.'

'It could be a coincidence.'

'It could, but I doubt it. He was looking for something that day; he said it was a book. Those men were looking for information about a book. Farrell sent them. It's the same man, I'm sure of it.'

'Even if it is, what does it prove?'

'It proves that Chris had something Farrell wanted. Something he thinks I've now got. Something which he was prepared to kill for.'

'Then call the police,' Julie insisted.

'They haven't been able to protect me so far,' Donna snapped.

'So what are you going to do with the guns? Shoot anyone who attacks you?'

'Did you bring them all?'

'Yes, and the ammunition. They're in the boot. You didn't answer my question.' She looked across at her sister. 'Donna, you can't take the law into your own hands. This isn't America. It's not some bloody film where the heroine straps on a gun and blows away the bad guys. This is reality.'

'And it was reality on that train when I was nearly killed,' Donna answered angrily.

'Who do you think you are? A female Charles Bronson? Call the police, for Christ's sake.'

'Julie, whoever those men are, whoever this Farrell is, they want something badly enough to kill for it. They might have killed Chris. They've *tried* to kill me. If they try again, they might not be too fussy about who they hurt in the process.' She looked at her sister. 'You're in danger, too. Perhaps it would be best if you left me at the cottage and went back to London. I've already involved you more than I should have. You should get out while you still can.'

'You really think I'd leave you now?' said Julie softly.

'I wouldn't blame you if you did.'

'I'm staying with you, Donna. No matter what. But I'll tell you something, I'm scared and I don't mind admitting it.'

'Join the club,' Donna said flatly.

They drove most of the remainder of the journey in silence, speeding through Kent into West Sussex, along roads flanked by hedges and trees, past isolated houses and farms.

It was approaching 3.15 when the headlamps picked out a sign that proclaimed:

WARDSBY 15 MILES

CHICHESTER 18 MILES

Donna instructed Julie to take the left-hand fork in the road.

Sixty-One

The ferocity of the assault lifted Peter Farrell off his feet.

He was slammed into the wall with crushing force and enough power to knock the wind from him. Reeling from the onslaught, he toppled forward but managed to keep his feet until a second attack pinned him to the wall and held him there.

'You said you would get the book,' snarled Francis Dashwood, gripping Farrell by the collar. 'We relied on you and you failed.'

Farrell recoiled, not from the verbal tirade but from the rank stench that wafted over him every time Dashwood spoke. It was a smell like rotting meat, a rancid, cloying odour that made him nauseous.

'I'm sorry,' he said breathlessly, trying to inhale as little of the fetid air as possible.

'Your apologies are no good to us,' roared Richard Parsons. 'We need the book, not your pathetic excuses.'

Dashwood let out a howl of frustration and hurled Farrell across the room. He crashed into a table, somersaulted over it and landed heavily on the carpet. He lay there for a moment before rolling over and getting to his knees.

The other two men advanced upon him.

'It has kept us alive for over two hundred years,' Dashwood told him. 'Get it.'

Farrell clambered to his feet, breathing heavily, forced to inhale the reeking smell. He looked at the other two men. There was a yellow tinge to their skin. Parsons' eyes looked sunken, with blue-black rings around them making him look badly bruised. The flesh of his hands appeared loose, as if it didn't fit his bones.

The skin beneath his chin hung in thick folds that swayed back and forth as he walked.

Dashwood looked even worse. A sticky, pus-like fluid dribbled from the corners of both his eyes. The orbs themselves were bulging in sunken sockets, criss-crossed by hundreds of tiny red veins, each one of which looked on the point of bursting. Like Parsons, his skin was sagging in places like an ill-fitting suit. In others it had begun to peel away in long coils. One of these coils hung from his left cheek like a spiral, frozen tear.

The stench inside the room was practically intolerable.

'Your men failed at the house and then on the train,' Dashwood reminded him.

'We will not tolerate another failure. *You* must get the book and bring it to us personally,' Parsons told him. 'Do you have any idea how important it is? Not just to us, but to everyone connected with this organisation?'

'If the contents were to be known, as Ward wanted them to be known, the results would be catastrophic,' Dashwood reminded him. 'Get the book.'

He shoved Farrell, who fell backwards, colliding with a chair and almost falling again.

'It isn't at the house,' he said, looking at each of the men in turn. 'We've already checked. She didn't have it with her . . .'

Dashwood cut him short.

'Are you sure of that?' he snapped.

'I'm not *sure*, but . . .'

Farrell was interrupted by a powerful blow across the face. As it landed he felt the repulsively soft feel of Dashwood's skin against his own.

'You know what will happen to us if the book is not found,' snarled Dashwood. 'You can *see* what is already happening.'

He grabbed Farrell again and pushed his face within inches. 'Look.' He touched the coil of rotting flesh with his free hand, pulling it slowly free. The skin tore slightly, leaving a red mark. Dashwood pushed it towards Farrell's lips, jamming the length of putrid flesh into the other man's mouth.

Farrell closed his eyes as he tasted the rotting matter on his tongue.

'Taste our pain,' hissed Dashwood, gripping Farrell's chin, forcing him to chew on the strand of flesh. As he spoke his foul breath swept over Farrell in a noxious cloud. 'Smell our suffering.'

Farrell knew he was going to be sick.

He felt Dashwood's index finger inside his

mouth, pushing the slippery piece of skin further into the moist orifice.

'Swallow it,' Dashwood demanded.

Farrell did as he was told and retched violently, falling away from Dashwood, feeling his stomach churn, eager to be rid of the disgusting matter inside it. He bent double and vomited, falling to his knees in the puddle of his own regurgitated stomach contents. The bitter stench mingled with the odour of putrescent flesh and he almost retched again but found that there was nothing left to bring up. His muscles contracted but could force nothing else out.

He sucked in deep, racking breaths and looked up at the two men.

Could the word be accurately applied to these two apparitions?

'Where is the woman now?' Parsons wanted to know.

'She hasn't been back to her house,' Farrell said. 'Someone picked her up at King's Cross. Another woman.' He wiped his mouth with the back of his hand. 'They could be anywhere.'

Dashwood took a menacing step towards him.

'My guess is they've gone to the other house,' he said quickly. 'The one Connelly mentioned before he died. If they have, we'll find them. *And* the book.'

'If you don't, it will mean *your* death as well as ours,' Dashwood told him. 'Now go.'

The stench of death hung in the air like an odorous, invisible cloud.

Sixty-Two

The cottage stood about two hundred yards back from the road, accessible only by a narrow drive flanked on both sides by stone walls. The walls extended round not only the front garden but the entire property, stark grey against the white walls of the cottage. The slate roof was mildewed in places and the guttering shaky, but otherwise the place was in a good state of repair.

Ward had bought it four years earlier with part of the advance on one of his books. He and Donna used it during the summer, making frequent weekend trips; Ward himself had written at least two books there. The cottage had no phone, something he had insisted on to prevent interruption when he was working. The nearest neighbour, a farmer well into his seventies, was more than five miles and a range of low hills away.

Donna guessed that it was more than two months since she had been to the cottage.

She wondered if he had ever brought Suzanne Regan here and found it more than usually difficult to wipe the thought from her mind. Even the stress of the past few hours had not removed the memories of his betrayal.

She stood in the small sitting-room and ran her finger along the top of a sideboard, drawing a line in the dust that had accumulated. The room was about twelve feet square, furnished with old, antique oak merchandise they'd bought from a shop in Chichester during their first visit to the place. It had few ornaments: a vase or two, an ashtray and a couple of ceramic figures. The windows were leaded.

The ground floor consisted of just the sitting-room and a large kitchen. The entrance hall seemed disproportionately large. There was a trap-door in the centre of the kitchen floor, which led down to a deep cellar. Ward kept old manuscripts down there. He also kept a substantial store of wine in the subterranean room. He had never been a great wine drinker, but on every visit to the Mayfair Hotel in London (which he used often) he was presented with a complimentary bottle of wine. He never drank them but always brought them home with him to add to the array in the cellar.

The floor of the lower ground room was of earth. Donna rarely ventured down the wooden ladder into it; it was not well lit and, despite Ward's attempts to convince her otherwise, she was certain that the entire cellar was seething with spiders, creatures she was frightened of.

A bare wood staircase led up to the first floor, which comprised a bathroom and two bedrooms. In the first bedroom a door opened onto a short flight of rickety steps that led to an attic. Ward had often threatened to have it converted into a work room but, as is the case with most attics, it remained nothing more than a storehouse for junk that wasn't wanted elsewhere in the cottage.

The obvious thing seemed to be to retire to bed; both women felt crushing exhaustion. But they seemed to have reached that point where they could not sleep despite their tiredness. Donna took a hurried bath, Julie made them some tea and, as the hands on the clock above the open fireplace crawled round to 3.56, they both sat down, one on either side of the table in the centre of the room.

In the centre of the table were two aluminium boxes resembling metal attaché cases.

Donna flipped the first one open and lifted the lid.

In the half-light cast by the lamps the metal of the Smith and Wesson .38 and the Beretta 92s gleamed.

Donna took each weapon from the case in turn, checked it and replaced it. She then opened the second case and performed a similar ritual with the .357 and the Charter Arms .22.

She flipped the cylinders from the revolvers and checked the firing actions, listening to the metallic click of the hammers on empty chambers. She worked the slide of the Beretta, then took fifteen rounds from the box of 9mm ammunition. She thumbed them into the magazine before placing it carefully back in the box with the weapon.

She loaded the revolvers, too, leaving the chamber beneath the hammer empty. Those two she replaced, then carried upstairs.

'I hope to God you know what you're doing,' said Julie when her sister returned.

'This is life and death, Julie,' she said solemnly.

'Then why don't you just call the police?' the younger woman said, agitated.

Donna didn't answer; she merely sipped her tea.

'I think you want it to come to this, don't you?' Julie snapped. 'You don't care if you kill them.'

'They tried to kill *me*.'

'And if you do kill anyone, *you'll* be the one who'll go to prison.'

'I'll take that chance.'

'Let's just hope it doesn't go that far.'

'It already has.'

They regarded each other for long moments, then Julie reached into her handbag for the envelope. She handed it to Donna, who turned it over in her hands, seeing Ward's handwriting on the front. She smiled thinly and ran her index finger over the Biro scribble.

I miss you.

'It can wait until morning,' she said quietly. 'We should get some sleep.'

Julie agreed.

Donna took the envelope upstairs with her and laid it on the bedside table. Before she got into bed she touched it once, running her fingertips over the smooth manilla package. Then, naked, she slipped between the sheets.

Her last waking thought was of her dead

husband. As she drifted off to sleep, a single tear rolled from her eye.

I miss you.

Sixty-Three

The book is called Domus Vitae, which is translated as 'The House of Life'. It was written by a man called Edward Chardell in 1753. Only one hundred copies were printed. The copy I discovered is, as far as I know, the only one in existence. It is vital to the members of The Sons of Midnight. Vital to their survival and also to their protection.

Every member of the club, from its formation back in 1721 right up until the present day, is forced to write his name in the book. I have those names. I know those names. That is why I stole the book and that is why they want me dead and why they need the book back. If its contents were released then they would be destroyed; but also the repercussions would be enormous.

The actual content of the book itself consists of a series of spells and invocations designed to be used at meetings of the club, just as similar books were used at meetings of The Hell Fire Club all over Britain and Ireland. Each club had one of these books which they called Grimoires, and the loss or destruction of these Grimoires has accounted for the disappearance of other branches of The Hell Fire Club over the years. The Sons of Midnight are the only remaining group I know of, still linked to the original Hell Fire Club. I have researched everything about them, their customs, their members and their motives. They trusted me enough to allow me into their ranks, but when I saw what they were planning I knew that the only answer was to destroy them, expose them.

They must be stopped. Their aims are sedition. They have infiltrated everywhere. Every branch of the Media, Politics and the Church. They are more powerful than anyone can imagine, more dangerous than anyone could realize. Perhaps I might be able to stop them by exposing them but I don't think they will allow that to happen. However, I have made contingency plans. Even if they kill me there are still ways to stop them.

Destroy the book. Destroy that and you destroy them. Especially Dashwood and Parsons. They need the book to live. Its very existence guarantees them life. Without it they are dead.

But don't look to anyone for help. They have members everywhere. No one can be trusted. Fight them alone. I tried and I would have succeeded. I hid the book from them, I covered my tracks as well as I could.

The location of the book I felt was too important to put down in this note. The key you will find enclosed fits a safety deposit box in the Chichester Branch of Lloyds Bank. Take the key and remove the contents of the box then find the book. Directions and instructions and also a description of the Grimoire itself are contained in there. The bank manager, Maurice Langton, is under orders not to allow anyone to open the door except you, Donna. Take this letter with you when you go there.

I pray that it is you reading this, my darling. If not then nothing I have written before matters. If it is you, then do this for me.

I love you. I will always love you, more than I thought it was possible to love anyone.

Christopher Ward.

Sixty-Four

Donna put down the note and ran her hands over the paper, as if trying to smooth out the creases. She was shaking slightly. Julie could see the tears in her eyes as she re-read the sheet of paper, touching her dead husband's name with her fingers as she read.

'Oh, Chris,' she murmured quietly, wiping one eye with the back of her hand.

He loved you. Then why did he have an affair?

Jesus, even now it plagued her. She lowered her head.

'Donna, are you all right?' Julie asked, slipping one arm around her sister's shoulders.

Donna nodded.

'We have to go,' she said, sucking in a deep breath, folding the note again. She looked at the small key on the table, then dropped that into the envelope with the note.

'No one can be trusted,' Julie said, echoing the words on the paper. 'You were right not to call the police.'

'Is my paranoia catching?' Donna laughed humourlessly. 'I've said it to you before, but I'll say it again. If you want to leave I'll understand, but you're the only one I can trust now.'

Julie touched a hand to her cheek.

'We'll do it together,' she said softly, holding Donna's gaze. The older woman stood up and the two of them embraced, holding each other tightly, neither wanting to let go, united in their grief and also in their determination.

'Come on,' said Donna finally. 'Let's get to that bank.'

In the daylight Julie could see the holes in the road which, the previous night, she'd only been able to feel. The surface was badly pockmarked and the car bumped and bounced over the uneven thoroughfare, its journey only becoming smoother as they reached the main road that would lead them into Chichester itself.

Along the way they passed through one or two collections of houses masquerading as villages. The sun managed to escape the shackles of dark cloud every now and then; when it did, glorious golden light fell across the countryside.

But for the most part the land remained in shadow.

As they drew close to the outskirts of Chichester itself rain clouds were gathering. As Julie finally found a parking space close to the bank the first droplets of rain were striking the windscreen of the car, like oversized tears.

The two women hurried across to the main doors of the bank. It was quiet inside. At the 'Enquiries' desk a young man with a strange, flattened haircut looked up from behind the counter. He smiled, ran swift appraising eyes over both women and coloured immediately.

'Can I help you?' he asked.

'I want to see the manager, please,' Donna told him.

'Can I ask what it concerns?'

'Could you just fetch him, please? It *is* important. Tell him my name is Donna Ward. My husband was Christopher Ward.'

The young man nodded and scuttled off, returning a moment later with a much older man in tow. The older man regarded the two women expressionlessly for a moment, then stepped forward. Donna made quick introductions. Thc man told her in a broad Scots accent that he was Maurice Langton, the manager. Then he invited them both through into his office.

'I was very sorry to hear about your husband, Mrs Ward,' Langton said, closing the door of his office and ushering them towards two chairs.

'My husband kept a safety deposit box here,

didn't he?' Donna said. She reached into her handbag and took out the key. 'I need to see the contents.'

'There are one or two forms to be signed first . . .' Langton began but Donna cut him short.

'That's all right,' she said briskly. 'It's important.'

Langton looked at her for a moment, then reached into his desk. He produced the necessary documents and handed them to her, pointing out where she should sign. She did so and handed them back to him, her irritation scarcely hidden.

Langton realized her impatience and ushered them out of the office towards another door, which he opened with a heavy key he took from his pocket. Beyond it fell a flight of stone steps which led down to the bank's vault. The walls on either side of the stairwell were dazzling in their brightness. Led by the bank manager, the two women descended to a corridor and more antiseptically white walls that seemed to crowd in on them like banks of snow. Langton led them through two more doors, finally coming to a small room with a desk and two chairs. To the right was another door; beside this one stood a uniformed man in what looked like a Securicor outfit. He looked impassively at the trio of visitors as they approached.

Julie waited outside while Donna and Langton passed through the last door into the vault itself. She saw hundreds of drawer facings, row upon row of safety deposit boxes. Langton led her to the one she sought.

'Your key, Mrs Ward,' he said.

Donna just stared at the box.

'I need your key,' he said, almost apologetically.

She nodded, handed it to him and watched as he put her key into one of the locks and the duplicate he carried into the other, turning both simultaneously. He pulled the drawer free and carried it outside for her, setting it on the desk.

'Just call me when you've finished,' he said and stepped back.

Donna sat looking at the box for long moments. Then, finally, hands quivering slightly, she reached for the contents.

All it contained were two envelopes.

Two flat, white envelopes.

'What the hell is this?' said Julie. '*This* is the big secret?'

Donna slipped the envelopes into her bag and called Langton back over.

'Did you know what was inside the box?' she asked him.

The manager looked aggrieved at the suggestion he might be privy to the contents of one of the high-security lockers.

'You knew there were just two envelopes in there?' she continued.

'I had no idea what was in there,' he said.

'Was my husband alone when he brought them

in?' Donna wanted to know. *Or did he have another woman with him?*

'Most certainly,' Langton told her. 'Is there something wrong, Mrs Ward?'

She shook her head, thanked him for his co-operation and then headed for the way out. Julie followed closely behind. They passed back the way they had come, past the gleaming white walls and up the stairs. Donna thanked Langton again and the two women left the bank.

Inside the car, Donna glanced at the two envelopes then slipped them into her handbag.

'Get us home,' she said, 'as quick as you can.'

Sixty-Five

By the time Julie parked the Fiesta outside the cottage the sky was a mass of dark cloud. Rain was falling fast now, drenching the countryside, turning the road that led to the cottage to mud, puddling in the ruts.

The two women jumped out and sprinted for the front door of the cottage, Donna struggling with the key. She finally pushed the door open and they both tumbled gratefully inside. Donna hurried through into the kitchen and sat down at the wooden table, pulling the envelopes from her handbag. For long moments she stared at them, as if reluctant to open them. She knew for sure that one contained the means to finding the Grimoire. The contents of the other was a mystery.

'Open them, Donna,' said Julie, her impatience getting the better of her.

Donna looked at her sister reproachfully.

'Give me time,' she said quietly.

A part of her didn't want to; in some strange way it meant severing her links with Chris. As long as there had been secrets, she had felt close to him but now, with the opening of these two slim packages, the last of those secrets would be gone. Just like *he* was gone. Her hands were shaking as she reached for the first of the envelopes.

It looked relatively new. The paper was untainted by age. She wondered how long they had lain in the safety deposit box.

There was a single sheet of paper in the first one.

It bore a name and an address.

'George Paxton,' she read aloud. 'Wax Museum.' And then an address in Portsmouth.

'That must be where he hid the book,' said Donna. 'He wrote a novel about a waxworks a few years ago. Chris said he'd become friendly with the owner; that must be who this Paxton character is.'

'Why hide it there?' Julie wondered.

Donna could only shrug.

'We don't even know what the bloody thing looks like,' Julie added. 'It could be anywhere there. Paxton might even have it himself. How the hell are we going to find it?'

There was more writing at the bottom of the sheet.

'The Crest on the Grimoire is a hawk, family crest of its author,' she read. She looked at Julie, her eyes alight. 'A hawk?' Donna reached into her handbag and pulled out the photo of Ward and the five other men. She looked carefully at the picture, studying the rings on the index fingers of the two shadowy figures.

They too bore engravings of some kind.

She squinted more closely.

'A hawk,' she said triumphantly, jabbing the picture with her index finger. 'The crest on those rings shows a hawk. You can see the wings.'

Julie squinted at them.

'Jesus,' she murmured.

Donna was already opening the second envelope.

It was another single sheet of paper, this time with typed letters on it:

RATHFARNHAM, DUBLIN.

BRASENOSE COLLEGE, OXFORD.

REGENCY PLACE, EDINBURGH.

CONDUIT STREET, LONDON.

Dublin, Oxford, Edinburgh and London. *And beside each entry D.*

'Chris was at all these places shortly before he died,' Donna said. 'They must have been meeting places for The Hell Fire Club he discovered.'

D for Dashwood?

'We have to get to Portsmouth,' Donna said, 'and find that book.'

'We can't go in this weather,' Julie said, looking out of the window. The rain was coming down in a solid curtain. It was as if God had kicked a bucket of water over. 'We'll be stranded, with the state of the roads around here.'

'As soon as it stops,' Donna said.

'If it stops,' Julie added quietly, gazing up into the heavens.

The rain continued to pour down.

7.08 p.m.

The sky still wept.

The ceaseless deluge had turned the small front yard of the cottage into a swamp. Water poured through the guttering and splashed noisily from the eaves. It was falling so fast that rivulets of rain streaming down the window-panes made it difficult to see out at all. Darkness had come prematurely with the deluge, the gloom summoned early by such an abundance of black cloud. The sky looked like one massive mottled rain cloud.

Donna sat in the sitting-room, glancing endlessly at the sheets of paper they'd picked up from the bank that day and also at the notes Ward had left. She knew the words off almost by heart.

'*Destroy the book and you destroy them.*' She exhaled deeply and massaged the back of her neck with one hand.

'*They must be stopped.*' A throbbing headache was beginning to gnaw at her.

'*They have infiltrated everywhere.*' Donna closed her eyes for a moment.

'*No one can be trusted.*'

'Donna.'

Julie's shout caused her eyes to snap open. She looked round and saw her sister standing at the window, gazing out.

'Come here,' the younger woman said, a note of urgency in her voice.

Donna did as she was asked and stood beside her sister, peering through the rain and darkness.

Two cars were moving towards the house, both with their lights turned off.

'Who are they?' Julie wanted to know.

Donna was reasonably sure she knew. When she spoke, her voice was low.

'Lock the doors and windows,' she said. 'Hurry.'

Sixty-Six

The cars stopped about twenty yards from the front of the cottage. One of them parked across the narrow track leading away from the building; it acted as a barrier.

Donna saw men scuttle from the vehicles, two of them running towards the house, slipping in the mud but keeping their balance.

She recognized one of them as Peter Farrell.

Julie was busily locking the doors and windows, sliding bolts and turning keys. Donna seemed transfixed by the approaching men. She saw two more of them move towards the sides of the cottage. She turned and ran upstairs.

'What's happening?' Julie asked breathlessly, hurrying to secure a window-lock on one of the kitchen windows.

The face loomed up out of the darkness and leered at her through the rain-soaked glass.

Julie screamed and took a step back.

The man held something in his hands.

Something he was swinging towards the window.

The iron bar struck the frame and the glass simultaneously, shattering the glass, sending shards spraying into the kitchen.

Julie screamed again and threw herself to one side, hissing in pain as a silver of broken glass sliced through the flesh on the back of her left hand.

The man outside struck at the window again, smashing more of the wooden frame, then he dropped the iron bar and snaked one hand inside, trying to slip the catch.

'No,' shouted Julie. She picked up a knife lying on the draining board by the sink, and drove it towards the man's hand. She heard him shriek in agony as the blade pierced it, cutting through the web of skin between his thumb and index finger. Embedded in the wood, it momentarily skewered him to the window-frame. Julie saw blood pumping thickly from the wound.

With a shout of pain he tore his hand free, the flesh ripping as he dragged himself away from the knife, leaving it embedded in the wood.

Julie snatched at the knife as the man disappeared back into the blackness outside. Rain now poured in through the broken window, the wind also whipping through, buffetting Julie as she moved across to the back door.

The impact against it was enormous.

It seemed to bow in the centre; for one terrible second she thought that it was going to split.

The second blow sent the door flying open. For fleeting seconds Julie found herself staring into the rain-soaked face of the intruder. He fixed her in a maddened stare and she saw the blood running from his gashed hand.

'Fucking bitch,' he hissed and lunged towards her.

On the cooker to her right stood a frying pan the two women had used for their meal less than an hour ago.

Julie snatched up the heavy skillet and swung it with all her strength.

It smacked savagely into the man's face, flattening his nose. The bones splintered under the force of the blow and blood spilled down his chin and the front of his jacket. He staggered.

She struck again, wielding the frying pan like a club, bringing it down hard on the top of his head with a blow hard enough to cut his scalp.

He dropped to his knees and tried to scramble away but Julie hit him again, kicking him hard in the ribs as he fell to the ground.

She dropped the frying pan and used both hands to push the back door shut, heaving with all her strength as the man tried to block it with his body.

She pulled the door back a foot or so then slammed it forward, catching him between the heavy wooden door and the frame. He grunted in pain.

She slammed it on him again.

And again.

He let go and ducked back into the driving rain.

Julie banged the door shut and slid the bolts into place.

Donna had been rummaging beneath the bed upstairs, where she'd pulled out both of the metal cases. She flipped one open and took out the Beretta and the .38, jamming one into the waistband of her jeans. Then she rushed back towards the stairs, almost falling in her haste to get back to the ground floor.

As she dashed into the sitting-room she heard movement outside the front door and immediately swung the automatic up into firing position.

It had been a while since she'd fired a pistol and the initial retort took even *her* by surprise. In the confines of the cottage the noise was thunderous.

The 9mm bullet left the barrel travelling at over

1,200 feet a second and cut a hole through the door. She fired again, and again.

Movement by the window.

Donna fired.

The glass exploded outwards and rain suddenly came pouring in through the hole. The curtains billowed madly as the wind caught them and Donna dashed across to the light switch and slapped it hard, plunging the room into darkness.

With her ears ringing from the massive blast of the weapon she threw herself down and crawled across to the wall by the front door, able to see back through the sitting-room to the kitchen.

She could see Julie also crouching down, one hand closed around the handle of the frying pan.

Outside she heard footsteps in the sucking mud.

The lights upstairs were still on; if she could only get to a window she might be able to see what the men outside were doing.

Rain continued to sweep into the cottage, driven by the strong wind that screamed around the building.

For interminable seconds the only sounds were the wind and rain and the heavy beating of her own heart.

Donna crouched where she was, the Beretta held close to her, the stink of cordite strong in her nostrils.

The attackers had obviously been surprised by the ferocity of their defence. Perhaps, she reasoned, they had left, not expecting to be greeted with guns.

There was no sound from outside, although it was difficult to pick out anything in the torrential rain that battered both cottage and landscape.

Donna got to her feet, still keeping low, and moved towards the small round window close to the front door in the hall.

If only she could get a look, see what they were up to . . .

It was pitch black; she could scarcely see a hand in front of her. Her breathing was deep and she tried to control it, tried to stop herself hyperventilating. She gripped the pistol more tightly as she reached the wall beneath the window and rose slowly.

Just one quick look.

Her heart thudded madly against her ribs and the blood sang in her ears.

She steadied herself, ready to look through the window.

Then the first burst of gunfire tore across the front of the cottage.

Sixty-Seven

The roar of the UZI sub-machine gun was deafening. In the howling wind and driving rain the burst of 9mm fire looked and sounded like man-made thunder and lightning. The muzzle flash illuminated Farrell and the yard around him for several feet as he raked the sub-gun back and forth, spent cartridge cases spewing from the weapon; smoke and steam rising into the damp air.

Windows were blasted inwards by the fusillade. Bullets drilled into wood or stone or sang off the walls with a loud whine. Lumps of plaster were torn free. Part of the guttering at the front of the cottage was blown away.

The hammer finally slammed down on an empty chamber. Farrell angrily ripped the empty magazine free and rammed a fresh one in.

A dark figure appeared at his side, limping.

'She locked the back,' said Frank Stark, wiping blood from his broken nose away with the back of his hand.

'I didn't expect her to have a gun,' said Brian Kellerman, peering at the cottage, shielding his eyes from the driving rain.

'I don't care if she's got a fucking cannon in there,' Farrell snapped, pulling back the slide on the UZI. 'Get inside.'

He fired another short burst from the sub-gun, blowing in an upstairs window.

Fragments of glass and shattered window-frame fell. He raised his eyebrows.

The porch was directly beneath the window. Anyone managing to get on top of the porch could easily clamber up through that bedroom window.

Farrell grabbed Kellerman and pointed at the window.

'You and Stark get in through there,' he said. 'Ryker, you go round the back again. Listen, all of you, we need Ward's wife alive, got it?'

'What about the other woman?' Stark wanted to know.

'Who gives a fuck?' said Farrell and opened fire.

More bullets spattered the front of the cottage, drilling lines back and forth in the stonework. Dust was washed away as the rain continued to pelt down.

Stark and Kellerman ran towards the house, keeping low, as anxious about Farrell's erratic covering fire as they were about Donna's possible retaliation.

Three bullets suddenly hit the ground only inches ahead of Stark.

The muzzle flash that accompanied their arrival came from inside the house.

He pitched forward, throwing himself down in the glutinous mud, covering his head with his hands as Farrell replied, bullets slicing through the air and singing above the prone man's body, missing him, it seemed, by mere inches. He kept his face pressed to the muck as bullets drilled holes in the wall and door. Lumps of wood were blasted free.

More shots from the Beretta came back, one of them striking the car. The 9mm slug exploded one of the Orion's headlights, smashing the housing and causing Farrell to jump back and seek cover behind the vehicle.

Kellerman reached the porch and hauled himself up onto it, hoping that the wooden canopy would take his weight. He looked down and saw his colleague still lying in the mud, not daring to move. Kellerman wondered if he'd been hit. He turned and saw that the window ledge was about three feet above him. He steadied himself, then shot out both hands and gripped it, hauling himself up the wall to the beckoning entrance.

Farrell saw him and smiled.

Donna scrambled through the hall to the sitting-room, the automatic smoking in her hands.

'How many of them are there?' Julie asked frantically.

'It's hard to tell,' Donna said breathlessly. 'I think I might have hit one of them.' She crept towards the shattered front window and peered out.

Stark was no longer lying in the mud.

'Shit,' snapped Donna, sinking back down to the floor.

Rain was still driving through the broken window.

'Oh God,' gasped Julie, pointing towards the kitchen.

Donna saw it too and her eyes widened in panic.

One of the men had set fire to the kitchen curtains.

Flames were licking hungrily at the material; it was blazing fiercely. She could smell petrol.

'Put it out,' she screamed at Julie as another burst of fire from the UZI spattered the cottage.

Donna sucked in a deep breath and headed for the stairs, intent on getting a clearer look at what was going on outside. From a vantage point up high she would be able to see their attackers.

Julie meanwhile was filling a saucepan with water, trying to stay clear of the flaring curtains. Thick black smoke spread through the room, thousands of tiny cinders filling the air like black snow. She coughed as she felt the heat searing the air in her lungs. It made her eyes water but she stayed where she was until the saucepan was full, then tried to douse the flames. One curtain went out, extinguished by the shower of water. Julie tugged hard at the remains of it and pulled it down. The other one continued to burn. She refilled the saucepan, sweat soaking her body despite the cold wind and driving rain blasting through the smashed window.

Ryker loomed at her through the flames and she hurled the water both at him and at the fire.

He grinned. She dropped the saucepan as she saw him raise the pistol and aim at her.

He fired twice and Julie threw herself down as bullets ploughed into the kitchen table. Another hit a vase on the sideboard. It promptly disintegrated in a cloud of dust, pieces spinning in all directions.

He fired again.

Julie rolled over, finally propping herself against the back door, touching the bolts there to reassure herself that it was locked.

She almost screamed when she felt the blows raining against it.

Donna emerged on the landing, momentarily frozen, unsure what to do. She had heard the shots from downstairs, heard Julie's shouts, but what to do? Go back downstairs or try and get a better shot at one of the bastards from up here?

She chose to move on.

The door to her left was open slightly; she could feel cold air blowing through.

Donna shoved the door open, steadying herself against the frame, the Beretta raised.

Stark was caught completely by surprise.

For one moment he looked as if he was raising his hands in surrender, then he leapt forward.

Donna got off two shots before he crashed into her.

The first missed and blasted a hole in the far wall.

The second caught Stark in the left shoulder. The bullet ripped through his deltoid muscle and pulverized part of the scapula as it exited, the impact enough to spin him almost three hundred and sixty degrees.

He yelled in pain, then crashed into Donna, both of them falling, hitting the floor with a thud that knocked the wind from her.

The Beretta flew from her hand, bounced against the wall and skidded down the stairs.

She reached for the .38 jammed into her waistband, trying to pull it free as Stark grabbed for her throat.

Donna didn't manage to get her finger around the trigger but she did pull the weapon clear, closing her hand around it and using it as a club.

She drove it into the side of his head as hard as she could, hearing a crack as she smashed his temporal bone.

Stark fell to one side and Donna scrambled out from beneath him. He tottered drunkenly to his feet and reached inside his jacket. She saw his fingers close around the butt of a .45.

Donna fired twice.

From point-blank range the first bullet hit him in the stomach, doubling him up as it punched a hole just to the left of his navel, ploughing through intestines before lodging close to his spine.

The second hit him in the right shoulder, the impact lifting him off his feet and sending him toppling towards the head of the stairs.

He threw out a hand, clutching at empty air, then fell backwards, tumbling head over heels down the steps, finally crashing to a stop at the bottom, where he lay in a spreading pool of blood.

Downstairs, Julie looked across and saw Stark hit the floor, her attention diverted only momentarily from the blows still raining against the door.

She felt sure that, any second, the wood must splinter and the attacker would be inside.

She looked around desperately for something to defend herself with.

The tool box was lying in one corner of the room, close to the cellar hatch.

Jesus, the cellar.

That was it.

She crawled across the floor in the darkness, her body drenched in sweat, her eyes stinging from all the smoke.

She grabbed a hammer from the tool box and crawled back towards the cellar hatch. Lifting it, she peered down into the blackness below, feeling the first rung of a rickety ladder as she dangled her foot into the yawning gap.

She eased herself down a few rungs, praying it wouldn't collapse under her.

The stench of damp that enveloped her was noxious; she tried to take short breaths. Gripping the hammer in one fist and propping the hatch up with her free hand, she crouched low so that she had about an inch gap through which she could see the back door.

The door was starting to split from its merciless battering.

One of the hinges was coming loose.

Julie gripped the hatch and waited. She almost screamed when she felt something soft touch her face.

A spider the size of her thumbnail dropped past her in the gloom, its legs brushing her cheek.

She gripped the hammer and waited.

The door was practically off its hinges now. One more blow and the attacker would be inside.

Julie swallowed hard, closing her eyes.

There was a final crash and the door, and Ryker, hurtled into the kitchen.

Upstairs, Donna heard the sound of forced entry, her eyes still fixed on the barely moving form of Stark.

Had she turned round quicker, she might have seen Kellerman advancing upon her.

Sixty-Eight

The attacks happened simultaneously.

Kellerman launched himself at Donna.

Ryker crashed into the kitchen, looking for Julie.

Donna heard a grunt as Kellerman grabbed her, pinning her arms by her sides, lifting her off her feet. She could not raise the pistol to use against him.

She found herself looking directly into his face as his arms tightened around her in a bear hug that threatened to crush her ribs.

With horror she realized he was carrying her to the top of the stairs.

Donna twisted in his grip but could not free herself.

She screamed loudly, but it was a bellow of rage not helplessness.

Kellerman grinned at her but the gesture faded instantly as Donna spat in his face, the mucus sliding down his cheek thickly like gelatinous tears. She snaked her head forward and bit hard into his nose, biting down with all her strength, ignoring his shrieks of pain, trying not to gag on the blood that filled her mouth.

He let go of her and staggered back, reaching for his gun.

She ran at him now, driving one foot up, kicking him with all her force between the legs.

He groaned and dropped to his knees, grabbing her other leg and pulling hard enough to send her flying. She hit the floor with a bone-jarring thud and lay there, momentarily dazed. Kellerman leapt on her, his weight pressing down. She jabbed two fingers into his eyes and he screamed and rolled off her, trying to rise to his feet, blinded by her attack. Her stabbing nails had torn his left upper eyelid and blood from the wound dribbled down the side of his face, some of it running across the orb itself, turning one half of his world crimson.

Donna tried to raise the .38, anxious to get a shot at him, but he knocked her hand down and the gun discharged into the floor. The thunderous retort deafened them both momentarily. He struck out again, this time with the back of his hand, catching her a blow across the face which split her top lip and sent her reeling. But she still held the gun and, as Kellerman turned on her, Donna shook her head clear and fired at him.

Luck playing a somewhat greater part in the matter than judgement, the bullet struck him in the calf, tore through the muscles there and exited, spattering the wall behind with blood and pink tissue.

He screamed and almost lost his footing as he made for the stairs.

Donna, her head spinning, tried to follow but he was halfway to the bottom before she managed to get off another shot. The heavy-grain slug powered into the wall inches above Kellerman's head. He looked up at her, teeth gritted, his face a mask of blood from his injuries.

She saw him stop and slide an arm around Stark's waist, carrying his companion towards the front door, both of them leaving a trail of blood behind.

Donna tasted her own blood as it ran into her mouth from the cut on her lip.

She tried to follow and almost fell down the stairs, gritting her teeth to prevent herself passing out.

She had to get to Julie.

As Ryker came careering into the kitchen, Julie threw back the cellar hatch and came hurtling forth like a maddened trap-door spider, brandishing the hammer.

So startled was he by this sudden onslaught, Ryker momentarily froze, rooted to the spot.

Julie swung the hammer with all her strength and caught him in the mouth with its gleaming head.

She heard teeth shatter under the impact, saw one of them driven through his top lip. Saw blood burst from the cut.

He reeled backwards, one smashed incisor falling from his bleeding, pulped gums.

Julie struck again, this time catching him just above the right eye, tearing the flesh. The hammer carved through his eyebrow and opened up a cut as deep as the frontal bone it cracked.

Julie spun the weapon, bringing the clawed part down on his hand as he raised his fists in defence.

The metal tore into his flesh, ripping it away, slicing effortlessly through skin and muscles, exposing a portion of the middle-finger knuckle.

Ryker ran for the shattered back door, out into the driving rain and the darkness, which suddenly seemed welcoming.

Julie stood by the back door, rain drenching her, mingling with the tears of rage and fear on her cheeks. She tasted blood and thought that it was Ryker's, but then realized that her own face was gashed just below the left eye, she guessed by flying glass.

Panting breathlessly, she turned from the door and moved through to the hall, where Donna was trying to make her way down the stairs.

From outside, they both heard the sound of car engines.

Julie, still gripping the bloodied hammer, looked cautiously through the window by the front door.

She saw two cars disappearing down the dirt track, away from the cottage, their tail-lights gradually swallowed by the gloom and the relentless downpour.

'Donna,' she gasped.

Donna said nothing; she just dropped to her knees, the .38 still gripped in her fist, face bruised, her lip bleeding.

Julie dropped the hammer and found she was sobbing uncontrollably. She was standing in a pool of blood.

Sixty-Nine

It wasn't a matter of *if* they would return; it was merely a question of *when*.

Donna sat at the sitting-room window, the Beretta on the sill in front of her. On the coffee table to her right lay the .38 and the .357. All had been reloaded.

On the sofa behind her Julie was sleeping fitfully, a blanket covering her, her face pale and drawn, dark rings beneath her eyes. The cuts on her hands and arms had been cleaned and bathed, then covered with plaster. She'd been fortunate to escape more serious injury from the flying glass.

Donna herself touched her lip tentatively with one finger, feeling how it had swollen. There was a dark bruise surrounding it; she hoped that the discoloration wouldn't last too long. Her sides ached when she inhaled, and when she moved too quickly she felt a sharp pain in her lumbar region. As the night wore on it began to diminish. There were more bruises on her arms and legs, and some on her shoulders.

The house had been cleaned as well as was possible. The broken windows had been boarded up with pieces of wood from the attic. Donna had re-attached the back door to its frame as well, while Julie mopped up the blood in the hallway – although she finally passed out during the task. Donna had helped her onto the sofa, woken her gently but then realized that she was becoming hysterical. She had been forced to slap her face to quieten her. Tears had followed, both women understandably shaken by their ordeal, by the knowledge of how close to death they had come.

And of how close they might come again.

Donna felt herself dozing and sat upright, shaking her head free of the crushing tiredness that threatened to envelope her. Another fifteen minutes and she would wake Julie. They had agreed to keep the vigil between them. One would watch for two hours while the other slept.

Donna reached out to touch the butt of the automatic, as if the feel of the cold steel would somehow shock her from her lethargy.

How easy it would be to surrender now, she thought, not only to sleep but also to the demands of these men. How easy to give them the book they sought, to be done with the entire affair.

And just walk away?

Donna knew that was impossible. Even if she did tell them the whereabouts of the Grimoire, there was no way they were going to spare her *or* Julie. Too much damage had been done; she knew too much about them now. They would have to kill her.

As they had done her husband?

She still didn't know for sure if Chris had been murdered. The police had been convinced it was a genuine accident that took his life

(*and that of his mistress*)

but after what she'd been through, after what she had discovered, Donna could not believe that men willing to kill for the possession of a book had not taken the life of the man she'd loved.

Once loved? Before his affair?

She administered a mental rebuke. She and her sister had almost been killed only hours earlier and all she could think about, it seemed, was her dead husband's infidelity.

No one can be trusted.

How prophetic had been those words he'd written. How apt. How irritatingly, fittingly, fucking appropriate. She gritted her teeth in anger and pain.

And frustration?

No. She would not give in to these men. She would not let them have the Grimoire.

She wanted it. Not because she needed it, but because she was determined no one else should have it. It was like a prize. This hunt for the book had become a contest and Donna intended winning.

Life and death.

Win or lose.

There was no turning back now, even if she wanted to.

Life or death.

She looked at the guns.

Seventy

'Farrell, he's dying.'

'What do you want me to do about it?'

'Help him.'

Brian Kellerman looked down at Frank Stark, then at Farrell.

Stark was lying on his back in the motel room, his shirt open to reveal the bullet wound close to his navel. Blood pumped slowly from the hole, which was tinged black and purple at the edges.

Kellerman himself looked bad. His nose was little more than a bloodied lump and the bruising around his left eye was so severe he could barely see out of it. He had two or three minor cuts and grazes on his cheeks; they looked as if someone had pulled a fork through the flesh.

On the other bed in the double room of the Travelodge David Ryker sat, head bowed, hands clapped to both sides of his skull. Every now and then he would spit blood onto the carpet. He had bandaged his cut hand so tightly his fingers were beginning to go numb. He touched his shattered front teeth with his other hand, feeling part of one smashed incisor come free. He spat out enamel and blood.

Farrell was sitting at the table in the room, thumbing 9mm bullets into two magazines for the UZI. Each held thirty-two rounds.

Fucking women, he thought, pushing the high calibre shells into the box magazine. Fucking bloody women. They were spoiling everything, those two troublesome cunts. He gritted his teeth, loading the bullets more quickly. Jesus, he'd make them pay. Especially Ward's wife. That fucking bitch would wish she'd never seen the book or *him* or anything to do with it. He'd put a bullet in her brain himself. No, he'd put several in. Hold the UZI against the base of her skull and let rip. Blow her fucking head right off. Turn her face and head into confetti. He slammed the full magazine into the weapon and gripped it for a moment, the veins in his temple throbbing angrily.

On the bed Stark groaned loudly and clapped hands to the wound.

'We've got to do something about him,' snapped Kellerman.

'Have you got any suggestions?' Farrell wanted to know 'Do you want to call the ambulance yourself? Why not call the police, while you're at it? Tell them how he was shot. What he was doing when that crazy mare put three fucking bullets in him. Go on, call them.' He banged his fist down on the table and glared at Kellerman.

'We'll have to leave him here,' said Ryker, probing another loose tooth.

'And when he's found?' Kellerman asked. 'What then?'

'We'll be long gone,' Farrell said. 'There's nothing to link him to us. We'll take his ID with us so they won't be able to identify him.'

Stark coughed, a sticky flux of phlegm and blood spilling over his lips. The movement made the pain worse and he groaned even more loudly.

Farrell regarded the man impassively.

'I didn't expect them to have guns,' said Kellerman, gazing down at his stricken companion.

Farrell didn't answer.

Ryker got to his feet and wandered into the bathroom. He inspected the damage to his mouth again, wincing as he saw just how much destruction Julie had wrought with the hammer. His lip was torn, a flap of skin hanging uselessly from it. The area between his gashed top lip and his nose was heavily bruised. Blood had congealed on his other front teeth; when he licked his tongue back and forth he could taste the coppery tang. He allowed a long streamer of mucus to hang from his mouth, watching as it struck the white enamel of the sink and trickled slowly into the plughole, leaving a crimson slick behind it.

'So we leave him here?' Kellerman protested. 'Just leave him to die . . .'

'Do you want to stay with him?' hissed Farrell, turning the UZI on Kellerman. 'Do you?'

Kellerman looked at the dying man, then stepped away from the bed.

'What about the women? Do we go back there? Try again?' Ryker asked, returning from the bathroom, wiping his mouth with the back of his hand.

Farrell shook his head.

'We follow them. Let them lead us to it. Then we'll take care of them.' He stroked the short barrel of the sub-machine gun. His eyes strayed to the telephone. The other two men saw him looking at it.

'What makes you think they'll try to get it?' Ryker asked. 'After what happened tonight they might have had enough.'

'This isn't over until we've got that book. Besides, Ward's wife will want to get her hands on it. She's stubborn, like her fucking old man was. She won't give up now.'

He looked at the phone again then lifted the receiver, aware that his hand was shaking.

He dialled the number and waited.

Seventy-One

Julie Craig sat at the wheel of the Fiesta, her head bowed. She sucked in a deep breath then looked up, squeezing her eyelids tightly together as if to clear the fuzziness which clouded her vision. But it wasn't her vision that was affected, she realized; it was her mind. She felt as if someone had wrapped her thoughts in a blanket. Reasoning seemed difficult; actions were a major effort.

'Do you want me to drive?' Donna asked, looking across at her sister.

'No, it's okay,' Julie replied, starting the engine.

The rain slowed to a fine drizzle which hung over the countryside like a dirty curtain. The yard in front of the house and the dirt track were little more than liquid mud. The rear wheels of the Fiesta spun, trying to gain purchase in the sucking ooze. Finally Julie stepped harder on the accelerator and the vehicle moved off. She flicked on the windscreen wipers. One of them squeaked but neither woman seemed to notice the irritating sound. Both kept their eyes fixed firmly ahead.

Donna dared not settle herself too comfortably into her seat in case she dozed off. She doubted she'd had more than three hours sleep the previous night, and Julie only a little more. It showed, too; despite their make-up, they both looked pale and wan. Donna had managed to disguise the worst of the bruising on her top lip beneath some foundation cream and a little rouge had given at least some artificial colour to her cheeks, but as she pulled down the sun-visor on the driver's side and peered into the mirror she realized she *looked* as tired as she *felt*.

She had no idea how long the drive into Portsmouth would take. Two hours, perhaps less? The road conditions and Julie's emotional state weren't going to help. Again Donna asked if *she* should drive but Julie merely shook her head.

'This man at the waxworks,' she said. 'What's his name? Paxton? Have you ever met him?'

'No, but Chris got on well with him. He helped him a lot with research about the history of the building, how the models are made, that sort of thing.' She sighed. 'Chris must have trusted him in order to hide the Grimoire there.'

No one is to be trusted.

'But he didn't say whereabouts he hid it?'

'No. I doubt if Paxton knows either,' Donna said, looking at the piece of paper she'd collected the day before. Beside thc address of the waxworks, it also had two phone numbers. One she guessed was the owner's home number; as it was Sunday, she might well need it. Off season, she doubted if the attraction would be open. It was hardly the weather to attract day-trippers, either.

'So what do we do when we find it?' Julie asked.

'I wish I knew,' Donna confessed. 'Read it?' She smiled thinly.

She glanced at the dashboard clock.

1.56 p.m.

By the time they reached the outskirts of Portsmouth the rain had practically stopped, but the sky was still slate grey and threatening. There wasn't much traffic on the roads until they approached the city centre, and then roads became a little more clogged. Julie had cold air blowing into the car in an effort to keep them both alert. The crushing weariness was a formidable enemy, though, and she felt her eyelids drooping as if they'd been weighted.

'I'm going to have to stop for a while, Donna,' she said finally. 'I'm practically driving asleep.'

'I know how you feel,' her sister said, pointing at something up ahead. 'There's a café there. Let's get a coffee.'

Julie checked the rear-view mirror and prepared to swing the car across the road into a parking space. At the last moment she stopped the manoeuvre and drove on instead.

Donna looked at her in bewilderment.

'I thought you were stopping,' she said.

Julie didn't answer, but drove on towards the traffic lights, glancing again in the rear-view mirror. They were amber as she swung the car round to the right and through them, heading down a side street, taking another right then another until they were back on the street where they'd started.

'I appreciate the tour of the block,' said Donna, smiling, 'but what's wrong?'

'We're being followed,' Julie said flatly.

Donna's smile faded immediately. She sat forward so that she could see into the Fiesta's wing mirror.

'How can you be sure?' she wanted to know.

'Because whoever's driving went through a red light to keep up with us.'

'Which car?'

'The Granada,' Julie said, and Donna saw the dark blue vehicle behind them.

'What shall I do?' Julie asked.

'Pull in,' Donna said unhesitatingly. 'See what he does.'

Julie nodded, indicated again and this time swung the car into a gap in front of the café.

The Granada drove past, disappearing around a corner.

'They spotted me,' Brian Kellerman said into the two-way radio.

'Where are they now?' Farrell wanted to know.

Kellerman told him.

'All right, we'll follow them from here. You keep out the way. I'll let you know where we're heading, but keep back. If they spot you again we might lose them.' Farrell switched the two-way off and jammed it into the seat pocket beside him. He gave Ryker directions, then sat back in his seat.

'Now we'll see,' he murmured.

Seventy-Two

They sat at a window table in the café looking out, watching every car that passed.

Donna warmed her hands round her tea and glanced at her watch again.

4.26 p.m.

They'd been in the café for over thirty minutes now, with only the sound of a fruit machine and the loud chattering of a group of youngsters in their late teens for company. A couple were playing the fruit machine; every so often, a cacophony of bells and buzzers would go off. The place smelt of damp clothes and cigarette smoke. There were a few curled-up sandwiches in a glass-fronted cabinet beneath the counter and a cheese roll that looked like it had been hewn from granite rather than baked with dough. Bottles of Coke, Tizer and Pepsi were lined up, along with a few token bottles of Perrier and Evian. The Formica-topped tables were scarred with cigarette burns and discoloured by spilled coffee. A woman in her forties was busily scrubbing tables at the far end. Donna thought she would need more than hot, soapy water to remove the accumulated grime.

Julie did not take her gaze from the window. Every vehicle that passed she scanned, every passer-by she scrutinised.

The Granada hadn't been past. But it could be lurking up ahead somewhere, Julie reasoned, waiting to continue its pursuit. Or worse.

'We can't sit here forever,' Donna said finally. 'Come on.'

'They could be waiting,' Julie said warily.

'We'll take that chance.' As she opened her handbag to retrieve her purse, Julie saw the Pathfinder .22 nestling inside.

Donna paid for the teas and the two women walked out to the Fiesta and got in.

Julie's hand was shaking as she pushed the key into the ignition but she sucked in a deep breath and started the car, checking her rear-view mirror both for approaching traffic and, more particularly, for that Granada.

'How much further?' she wanted to know.

Donna consulted the directions on the sheet of paper and realized that they must be pretty close to their destination. She checked street names carefully, peering at a sign indicating an approaching roundabout. She pointed to the turn-off they should take.

'We're close now,' Donna said.

They were still on the outskirts of thc city centre itself and Donna wondered what something as strange as a waxworks was doing so far from the city centre, even what it was doing in a place like Portsmouth. She could understand the existence of such an attraction at a seaside resort, but this traditionally nautical stronghold could hardly be classified as such. She wondered how Paxton made it pay.

'There,' Donna suddenly shouted, jabbing a finger against the glass.

Julie looked to her left and caught a glimpse of what looked like a large terraced house fronted by a blue and white canvas awning. There was a small paved area in front of it and a low wall. The paved area had several figures on it. A ticket booth was guarded by two of these figures dressed as policemen.

HOUSE OF WAX proclaimed the sign on the awning.

The shutters were firmly closed at the ticket booth, the waxwork policemen staring with sightless eyes at passers-by. The street was more or less deserted.

There were more shutters at the windows of the building, only one of which was open. Leaning out of it the figure of Charlie Chaplin waved to anyone who cared to look up, frozen forever in that pose.

'Now what?' Julie asked, seeing that the place was closed.

'Let's find a phone box,' Donna said. 'I'll call Paxton.'

They finally found one two streets away. Julie pulled in and her sister ran across to the two booths, pulling the piece of paper from her handbag, finding Paxton's number. She touched the .22 Pathfinder for reassurance as she removed the sheet.

The first phone was broken and the second took only phone cards. Donna rummaged in her purse and found hers. She pushed it into the slot and dialled, dismayed to see she only had six units left. She hoped he picked up the phone quickly. She hoped he was there. The phone continued to ring.

'Come on,' she muttered.

Another unit was swallowed up.

The phone was picked up.

'Hello,' the voice said.

'Mr Paxton? George Paxton?'

'Yes. Who's this, please?'

Another unit disappeared.

'I'm in a call box, I can't speak for long, just listen to me, please. My name is Donna Ward, Chris Ward's wife. You knew my husband very well; he wrote a book about waxworks and you helped him with his research. He left something inside your waxworks. He hid something. A book.'

Silence at the other end as another unit was consumed.

'Mr Paxton, I need your help, please. It's very important.'

'Where are you?' he wanted to know.

'In a call box, I told you.'

'Meet me outside my waxworks in an hour, Mrs Ward,' he said.

Donna hung up, left the phone card in the box and hurried back to the car.

Julie drove off.

* * *

'We've got them,' said Peter Farrell into the two-way. He gave Kellerman the location. 'Get here as quick as you can, but stay out of sight. We don't want to fuck it up now.' He looked at Ryker and nodded in the direction of the Fiesta. 'Don't lose them, but be careful.'

Ryker guided the Orion into traffic, keeping well back from the Fiesta.

Farrell watched as the smaller car parked across the street from the waxworks. He saw the two women sitting there as the Orion glided past and disappeared up a side street. Satisfied that they were staying put, he flicked on the two-way again.

'It's Farrell. We've got them under surveillance. They won't get away this time.'

'We'll be there in about thirty minutes,' the voice on the other end said, then there was a sharp hiss of static followed by silence.

Farrell reached inside his jacket, his fingers touching the butt of the .45 in his shoulder holster.

No escape, he thought, smiling. Not *this* time.

Seventy-Three

The office was small, less than fifteen feet square, dominated by a large antique desk piled high with correspondence. A glass paperweight in the shape of a tortoise held the letters down. Framed photos on the walls showed the front of the waxworks. Set out in chronological order, the first picture had been taken in 1934, then, every ten years until the most recent one. The building itself had changed little, apart from a lick of paint here and there; it still reminded Donna of a huge terraced house.

There were cabinets set against one wall, each filled with photos and biographical details from figures in history and the media, politics and sport – everyone from Clement Attlee to the Greek god Zeus.

'My grandfather started the museum,' said Paxton. 'He saw a number of them in America when he visited during the Thirties. When he died it was passed on to my father and then to me. It doesn't make much money now, just enough to keep it running, but we break even every year. I wouldn't want to close it down.' Paxton smiled affectionately and touched the picture of the Wax Museum taken in 1934.

He was a tall, attractive man in his mid-forties, the grey hair at his temples giving him a distinguished look. More so than the bald patch at the back of his head. He wore an open-neck shirt and trousers that needed pressing, but he'd apologized for his 'unkempt' condition when he'd first greeted them, explaining that he'd been decorating at home and had pulled on the first things to hand in his haste to get to the waxworks.

'We used to make all the figures here ourselves,' he said. 'There was a workshop in the basement.

My father employed three people to create them. I don't need them any more. I simply write to Madame Tussaud's and put in a list of requests for figures.' He smiled. 'They send me the ones I need. They sometimes suggest figures I should have here. You know, the 'Famous for fifteen minutes' type. The pop stars, the TV celebrities or sportsmen. I put them in my Warhol Gallery. That's what I call it.' He smiled again. 'Everyone will be famous for fifteen minutes,' he mused. 'I usually replace them after a month or so.'

'Mr Paxton, how well did you know my husband?' Donna asked.

'How well do *any* of us know someone else, Mrs Ward?' he said philosophically. 'I got on well with Chris while he was here doing his research. He spent about a week with me, learning about the running of the place, things like that.'

'How much did you know about the book he hid here?'

'Nothing at all. He rang me one day and asked if he could bring something down. He wouldn't even tell me what it was over the phone.'

'How long ago was that?'

Paxton shrugged.

'Six or seven weeks,' he said. 'All he told me was that the book was important to him and to some other people.'

'He didn't say which people?' Donna interjected.

'No. He just asked if he could hide it in the museum. I agreed. He said he'd pick it up in a month or so. Then, of course . . .' He allowed the sentence to trail off.

'Did you see the book? Do you know where he hid it?'

'I haven't got a clue. It could be anywhere in the museum.' He paused for a moment, looking almost apologetically at Donna. 'Would it be rude of me to ask who he was hiding it from?'

'I'm not completely sure,' Donna told him, 'but I need to find it.'

She felt it unneccessary to mention some of the incidents that had taken place over the last few days, least of all the confrontation at the cottage the previous night. She merely told him that the book bore a crest, an embossed crest of a hawk. It was very old, too, she said.

'I know that's vague,' she said, 'but it's all I know.'

'I'd like to help you look if I can,' Paxton volunteered.

Donna smiled.

'That's very kind of you. Thank you.'

Paxton slid open a drawer in his desk and took out what looked like a floor-by-floor plan of the three-storey building. He laid the diagram out on the desk-top, weighting each corner down with a pile of papers.

'The museum is divided into galleries,' he said, jabbing the plan. 'It makes it sound grand, doesn't it? Museum.' He chuckled. 'My grandfather thought that wax museums should be places of learning, too. Three-dimensional temples of knowledge, he used to call them.'

Donna and Julie were more interested in the layout of the building than in Paxton's nostalgic musings.

'Is this the ground floor?' Donna asked, prodding one part of the map.

'No, that's the basement. It's where we keep our Chamber of Horrors. No waxworks is complete without one. It's always the most popular area, too. It brings out the morbid streak in all of us, I'm afraid.'

'And you've no idea where Chris could have hidden the book?' Donna repeated.

'None at all.'

'We'll have more chance of finding it if we search separately,' Donna suggested. 'Julie and I will start on the top floor, then work our way down.'

'I'll meet you on the second floor. If we miss each other we'll meet back in this office in three hours.'

'Miss each other? Is that likely?' Julie wanted to know.

'There are two sets of stairs into and out of every gallery,' Paxton explained, 'So that if we get too many visitors it doesn't get too congested as people move around. It's quite possible we could pass each other and not even realize it. It's dark in the galleries, too, apart from the lights on the figures.'

Julie felt her heart beating faster.

'If one of us finds the Grimoire, we call out to let the others know, then bring it back here to this office,' Donna suggested.

Paxton nodded.

He left the office first, waiting for the two women to follow him out before closing the door again.

There was a flight of stairs directly to their right.

'Follow the stairs straight up to the third floor,' he said. 'I'll go that way.' He nodded in the direction of an archway. Through it, Donna could see the first of many wax tableaux showing famous film stars. The atmosphere was thick and gloomy. She hugged her handbag tightly to her sides, comforted by the thought of the Pathfinder inside.

Two or three feet away, standing by the entrance to the waxworks, were the figures of Laurel and Hardy. In the darkness they seemed not the amusing and loveable clowns they were meant to be but somehow menacing. Their glass eyes regarded the group blindly. Julie again felt a shiver run up her spine. She glanced up the stairs; the top of the flight almost disappeared into the dimness.

'Back here in three hours,' said Donna, her voice sounding loud in the unyielding silence. 'Unless one of us finds the book.'

Paxton nodded.

They set off.

The hunt began.

Seventy-Four

Marilyn Monroe gave him no clues. John Wayne offered no help. Neither did Marlon Brando or any other member of the Corleone family.

Paxton stood in the middle of the tableau entitled:

THE GODFATHER

and moved between the figures of James Caan, Al Pacino and Marlon Brando, all of them identified by name plates at their feet.

In the display the Godfather's desk had a number of books on it; the waxworks owner reached for them one by one. They were encyclopaedias or dictionaries with the dust jackets removed. Not wax but real books.

The figure of Robert Duvall was holding a briefcase; he glanced inside but found nothing but a sheet of blank paper. He moved on, past Indiana Jones and Rambo until he came to a display of THE EXORCIST.

It featured a bedroom and figures of Max Von Sydow, Jason Miller and Linda Blair in her possessed incarnation. The waxwork of Von Sydow held what was supposed to be a Bible but Paxton wondered if Ward might have substituted the Grimoire for the Holy Book. After all, he had no idea how big it was. He stepped in amongst the figures, moving around the bed until he reached the kneeling wax effigy.

The book it held was indeed a Bible.

Paxton moved on.

It wasn't just the silence Julie found overwhelming, it was the claustrophobic atmosphere of the place. The solitude and the almost palpable darkness combined to create the feeling that they'd been drapped in a blanket. The carpeting of the floors served to enhance the illusion; they could not even hear their own footsteps as they moved around.

Julie walked quickly, keeping within two or three feet of Donna. Even so, her sister was a barely glimpsed shadow most of the time.

They passed through an archway into a display of great sporting figures. The waxworks were arranged in groups beyond a rope, which was supposed to separate them from their admirers. In a mock-up of a boxing ring stood Henry Cooper, Mohammed Ali and Mike Tyson. At the edge of the ring Joe Louis and Rocky Marciano glared glassily at her. Julie found herself drawn almost hypnotically to the blank stares. She could see herself reflected in the glass orbs, a distorted image.

Ahead, Donna was standing beside Pelé and George Best. Kenny Dalglish and Eusebio looked on impassively. Johan Cruyff, one foot perched on a football, regarded her with the same emotionless expression as the rest.

Further along there was a model of Sir Francis Chichester; on what was supposed to be the deck of his yacht lay a number of books. Donna climbed into the exhibit and began inspecting them. She found to her annoyance that they were all books about sailing.

She pressed on.

Julie followed, her passage unnoticed by Lester Piggot and Willie Carson.

A flight of three steps led up into another gallery, this one depicting great artists.

They moved on.

Sean Connery, George Lazenby, Roger Moore and Timothy Dalton stood around Paxton as he searched through the drawers of M's desk, but the James Bond tableau was no help to him either.

So many places to look. So many places Ward could have hidden the book.

As he walked among the figures Paxton wondered what could be so important about this missing book. What could be so vital to send him and two women trekking around the place?

Opposite him a display showed Gene Kelly, Fred Astaire and Ginger Rogers all dancing together, watched by a group of admiring figures. One of the figures was of a child; at its feet were a set of school books. He strode across to it, climbing into the little set-up. The child was Shirley Temple and the books were spilling from her satchel. He began sorting through them.

Danny Kaye, Liza Minnelli and Judy Garland

looked on blankly as he sifted through the books. Again he found nothing.

The hand grabbed his hair.

So surprised by the movement he felt as if his vocal cords had frozen, Paxton hardly moved as his head was yanked hard backwards.

The knife flashed in the spotlight, glinting viciously before the razor-sharp blade was drawn across his throat.

Blood erupted from the wound that opened like a grinning mouth, spewing crimson over the lifeless figures.

Peter Farrell held tightly to Paxton's hair, careful to avoid the jetting blood. He heard the soft hiss as the waxwork owner's sphincter muscle collapsed. Then he allowed the body to drop to the floor, watching it twitch for a second before stepping back into the shadows from which he'd emerged. He pulled a two-way radio from his pocket and flicked it on.

'I'm on the ground floor,' he whispered into the machine. 'Paxton's dead. Split up and find the other two.' He paused a moment, still looking down at the body, the head in the centre of a spreading pool of blood. 'Keep them alive until I get there,' he added as an afterthought.

He put the two-way back in his pocket and slipped away, swallowed by the gloom.

Behind him, Paxton's body lay amongst the frozen dancers and entertainers smiling down blankly as if welcoming him.

Blood from the hideous wound washed over

the title plate of the tableau, which proclaimed happily:

GOTTA DANCE.

Seventy-Five

Second floor.

The top storey had yielded nothing. Outside, the rain which had been falling when they entered the building seemed to have eased. Night had invaded the heavens, closing around the waxworks like a black fist as impenetrable as the umbra that seemed to fill every inch of the museum. The exhibits were small islands of light within a sea of shadows.

Donna paused at the bottom of the flight of steps and looked to her right and left.

To her right was a gallery featuring GREAT EVENTS IN WORLD HISTORY; to her left, THE ENTERTAINMENT WORLD.

'Do you want to check one side and I'll check the other?' she asked Julie.

'No. I'm staying with you,' the younger woman said, horrified at the thought of being alone in one of these darkened rooms. Donna gripped her hand briefly to reassure her, but the gesture did little to ease Julie's fear. Donna, too, felt the hairs on the back of her neck rise as they moved into the right-hand gallery.

A mock-up of the front benches of the House of Commons displayed a dozen of the country's most important politicians. Behind them were older, more famous ones. Gladstone, Disraeli and Lloyd George all stood in judgement, silent and unmoving as the two women passed by.

The next exhibit showed Napoleon's final trip to St Helena. He was in a cabin on board the ship with several figures standing around him.

There were books on the desk at which the effigy of the Emperor sat.

Donna wasted no time checking them out.

Julie, meantime, took a couple of paces across the gallery towards a group of world leaders, past and present, gathered around a desk.

She shivered as she felt so many sightless eyes boring into her.

A board creaked beneath her feet and she sucked in a startled breath.

Adolf Hitler stood, arms folded, beside Benito Mussolini. Stalin and Trotsky stood to their left.

Julie could see bookshelves behind them.

The Grimoire could be there.

'Donna,' she whispered.

No reply.

She looked round to where her sister was searching through the other books.

'Donna,' Julie repeated.

There was no sign of the older woman.

Julie felt as if someone had suddenly pumped her full of ice water.

'Oh, Jesus,' she murmured, fearing she was alone. 'Donna.' She raised her voice slightly.

There was a chipboard wall between the exhibits and Julie turned and moved towards it.

She could hear sounds on the other side.

The breath was stuck in her throat and her mouth felt dry.

It was if someone had filled it with sand. In the deafening silence inside the gallery she could hear her heart thumping madly against her ribs.

'Donna,' she said again, the word sounding thunderous in the solitude.

Close by a floorboard creaked.

Julie swallowed hard.

'It's not here.'

Donna stuck her head out from behind the chipboard wall.

Julie just managed to stifle a scream. She raised a hand to her forehead and let out a breath which seemed to empty her lungs.

'For Christ's sake,' she murmured.

Donna saw the exhibit her sister had been looking at and crossed to it. She looked up at the books on the shelves and reached for the closest.

She flipped it open.

Blank paper.

So was the next.

And the next.

Every book on the shelf was a volume of blank sheets.

Donna sighed wearily and prepared to continue the search.

Julie suddenly grabbed her arm.

'Listen,' she whispered, her eyes bulging in their sockets.

'What . . .'

'Just listen.'

They stood as motionless as the wax figures surrounding them, ears alert for the slightest sound, eyes roving around the darkened gallery for any trace of movement.

Donna heard it too.

The unmistakable creaking of floorboards.

Someone was on the floor above them.

'It must be Paxton,' Donna said quietly.

'He was below us,' Julie protested.

'He said that we could pass each other without knowing. Perhaps he went up to double check, in case we missed something.'

The footsteps receded.

The two women remained motionless, gazing up at the ceiling as if to trace the source and direction of the footsteps.

There was one more protesting creak, then silence.

'I'm sorry,' said Julie none too convincingly. 'This place . . .' She allowed the sentence to trail off.

Donna squeezed her hand and nodded.

They paused a moment longer, then moved further down the gallery, inspecting each exhibit, checking any books which could be the hidden

Grimoire. Finally satisfied that these tableaux held no secrets, they turned round and headed back towards the gallery marked THE ENTERTAINMENT WORLD.

At the top of the stairs between the two galleries Donna paused and peered into the thick shadows, listening for movement from either above or below. She heard nothing. She wondered if she should call out to Paxton, just to find out where he was. She decided against it and walked through the archway to be confronted by the figure of Elvis Presley.

Julie followed, past the cast of *Dallas*, glancing at figures of Rod Stewart, Tina Turner and Madonna.

So many eyes watching them.

These exhibits were mostly just single figures, not set out in any kind of tableau, but isolated in their stage clothes with just a name plate for company.

Kate Bush stood defiantly before them, her hair frozen in an imaginary breeze, curling in the air like the deadly locks of a Gorgon.

Bob Hope was leaning on a golf club.

Frank Sinatra was holding a microphone.

Donna moved quickly through the gallery.

'There's nothing in here,' she said. 'Let's try the next floor. Perhaps Paxton's found something.'

'He would have called, wouldn't he?' Julie enquired.

'Perhaps we didn't hear him.'

At the top of the stairs just beyond the archway at the exit from the gallery stood figures of Michael Jackson and Stevie Wonder.

The former of the two was in a glass case.

Donna moved close to it, peering in at the finely sculpted features, momentarily distracted by the sheer artistry of the effigy.

She and Julie moved nearer to the glass.

Julie touched it.

The figure turned and looked at them.

Seventy-Six

Julie could not suppress a scream this time.

Her shriek of surprise echoed around the building, drumming in their ears, amplified by the stillness.

The figure turned stiffly and fixed them in a sightless gaze.

It took Donna a moment or two to realize that it had been activated by some kind of electric eye. When the glass was touched, the mechanism was set in motion. The figure swayed slightly on its base, then was still.

Julie ran a hand through her hair and closed her eyes, her heart racing.

'Oh God,' she murmured.

Donna too felt her heart thumping; the sudden shock made her tremble. She squeezed Julie's hand and motioned for her to follow down the stairs that led to the ground floor.

They were halfway down when the thought struck her.

Why had Paxton not come to find the source of the scream? Why, at least, had he not called out? There was no question of him hearing the noise in the stillness of the waxworks. Where the hell was he?

Perhaps they had been his footsteps they'd heard above them earlier. But even so, why had he not come running to find out what was happening?

Donna licked her tongue across her dry lips and stopped at the bottom of the stairs. Julie joined her.

'What now?' Julie wanted to know.

Donna glanced across into the gallery on the ground floor then at another doorway ahead of them marked PRIVATE.

She crossed to the door and found that it was unlocked. It opened out onto a narrow flight of stone steps. There was a cloying fusty smell rising from below, like drying clothes. It was cold in the narrow stairwell; the metal banister was freezing when she touched it.

'Come on,' she said. 'This must lead to the basement.' She began to descend, and Julie followed. They trod carefully on the bare stone until, finally, Donna pushed open the door at the bottom and stepped out.

The smell here was even stronger. The odour

of decay as well as damp was strong in her nostrils. She looked round.

The door from which they had emerged was also marked PRIVATE.

To the left was a light, well-illuminated area that contained various electronic games and fruit machines.

To the right, a set of steps led down into what looked like seething blackness. The darkness was so total that she wondered if they would even be able to proceed without the aid of a torch. There was a sign on the wall beside this entrance:

ALL THOSE WISHING TO LEAVE THE WAXWORKS HERE, KINDLY USE THE APPROPRIATE EXIT. IT IS RECOMMENDED THAT YOUNG CHILDREN OR THOSE OF A NERVOUS DISPOSITION LEAVE NOW.

Donna took a step closer to the top of the steps and peered down.

There were five stone stairs leading down to a wooden floor and a narrow stone corridor.

The smell of damp and rot seemed to waft from the doorway as if expelled from putrid lungs. There was a sign just inside the doorway, suspended from the ceiling by two rusty chains. Donna read it aloud.

'Abandon hope, all ye who enter here.' She smiled. 'It would have been just like Chris to hide the Grimoire down there,' Donna said, pointing towards the abyss beyond the steps. 'It would have appealed to his sense of humour.'

'What is it?' Julie wanted to know, wrinkling her nose at the smell.

Donna raised her eyebrows.

'The Chamber of Horrors.'

Seventy-Seven

It was like stepping into empty space.

Donna, who couldn't see her feet beneath her, moved cautiously for fear of slipping on the stone steps. Julie followed behind, steadying herself against the wall, recoiling slightly as she felt the moistness of the stone.

Paxton must have had the place treated with something, Donna thought. She was sure the basement that housed the waxworks' grisliest exhibits was not naturally damp and decaying. Part of the process of making the viewing experience all the more real and eerie was the smell which went with the darkness and unbearable silence. There were companies in the film business who made fake blood; why not someone to recreate the smell of damp and neglect? Perhaps that odour could indeed be bottled and sold. Paxton must have bought a crateful.

Fake cobwebs had been sprayed over the walls, too, although how much of the gossamer-like material was real and how much was fake she wasn't sure. There would be no need to clean this part of the waxworks. Grime and the odd spider could only serve to enhance its appearance.

The figures of the murderers themselves were arranged behind what looked like rusty prison bars. These too were covered by cobwebs both fake and genuine.

Dependent on their stature or the nature of their crimes, figures were enshrined within their own individual displays. Others were grouped together, usually with a newspaper of the day framed beside them proclaiming their arrest or, in the case of those before 1969, of their execution.

How perverse, Donna thought, that there should even be a hierachy amongst killers. Men like Denis Nilsen, Peter Sutcliffe and John George Haigh were presented in tableaux of their own, while those who had killed only once or twice, or who were there more for their notoriety than their savagery, merited a smaller setting where they were crowded together. Ruth Ellis, Lee Harvey Oswald and the Kray Twins stood together.

Christie was displayed surrounded by his nine victims, portions of them visible from gaps in the walls and floor of the mock-up of his front room at Ten Rillington Place. Behind him stood Timothy Evans, the man wrongly hanged for a murder Christie committed.

If the atmosphere in the rest of the waxworks had been unsettling, in this odorous basement it was close to oppressive. These glass eyes stared out with a venom and hatred that matched those of their inspirations. Julie felt her skin crawl.

Nilsen stood at the cooker where he'd boiled down the remains of his victims.

Sutcliffe gripped a claw hammer and a screwdriver, his face twisted into a half-smile.

Haigh, dressed in a leather apron, was in the process of dissolving one of his victims in an acid bath.

Julie tried to swallow but felt as if someone had blocked her throat.

Beneath the model of Eichmann were newspaper cuttings about Auschwitz; yellowed with age like some of the other clippings, they were still as abhorrent, even after all these years.

Dr Crippen was standing by a desk on which lay a pile of books.

Donna looked for a way in to the exhibit. The only door was in the side of the cage-like display, at the end near the exit. In order to reach the figure of Crippen she would have to pass the other figures, too. She turned and headed for the door immediately, relieved that it was open when she pushed. She stepped inside.

Julie gripped the bars, wincing as she felt how cold and wet they were, watching as her sister drew closer, pausing to look at the tableau of Christie. There were many cupboards in the display; Ward could have hidden the Grimoire in any one of them.

Donna opened them but found that they were

empty. She glanced at the figure of Christie and walked on. Past Haigh. Past Nilsen.

The figure of Peter Sutcliffe was standing over the body of a woman, old newspapers beneath his feet. Donna paused to lift the newspapers and look beneath them.

Julie sucked in an anxious breath, her eyes fixed on the model of Sutcliffe.

The head moved a fraction.

She opened her mouth to shout but no sound would come.

Donna was still at his feet.

Julie blinked hard and looked at the waxwork again.

This time she saw no movement. A trick of the light? A trick of her mind? A little of both, she fancied.

'Come on, Donna,' she said, her breath coming in gasps.

Her sister nodded, got to her feet and finally reached the Crippen figure. She looked at the books on the desk: a medical book and a book on anatomy.

The third had a picture of a bird on it. *A hawk?*

Was this the Grimoire?

Her hands were shaking as she lifted it.

A *picture* of a hawk, not an embossed crest.

Could it be . . .

She opened it.

Blank pages.

'Shit,' she muttered angrily and replaced the

book. She hurried out of the cage and rejoined Julie. Ahead of them was another wall with a small gap in it; barely five feet high and three across, it formed a doorway into the last part of the exhibit. The Torture Chamber.

Donna advanced towards it.

There was a red light over the narrow opening. As she waited for Julie to join her, the light bathed her in crimson so that it looked as if she'd been drenched in blood. She looked down into the Chamber and saw that the same inky blackness awaited them. Only the models were lit, but this time by even weaker beams from hidden spotlamps in the low ceiling. This was the only entrance in *and* out. Donna led the way, glancing at several severed heads arrayed before a guillotine. Nearby a wax body dangled from a hook embedded in its side. Behind them a display featured a man with rats trying to eat their way through his stomach while imprisoned in a red hot cage.

Burning out the eyes.

Driving needles beneath the fingernails.

Tearing off the nose with red-hot pincers.

The horrors came thick and fast, vying with each other.

A man being boiled alive in what looked like a massive metal bowl.

A man with a steel ring through his tongue, the ring attached to a metal ball by a chain.

The revulsion Donna felt was tempered by her recognition of the skill with which these monstrosities had been constructed. They were obscenely realistic.

The two women turned a corner and Julie groaned aloud.

THE MURDER OF SHARON TATE proclaimed the plate on the bars of the enclosure that housed one of the most horrendously realistic exhibits in the building.

In front of the tableau a newspaper of the day headlined the slaughter of the Hollywood star and four others by members of the Charles Manson family. The figure of Manson himself, eyes wild, hair flying behind him, watched over the scene. It showed the living-room of the Tate residence with the film star's killers, armed with knives and guns, and the other people who died with her. Whoever had modelled it had certainly been painstakingly accurate in the depiction, anxious to show that Sharon Tate had been eight months pregnant when she'd been hacked to death, her blood used to write the word PIG on the wall.

'Jesus Christ,' Julie whispered, her attention drawn to the vile display.

Donna had her eye on something else.

Further down the corridor another, larger exhibit showed the Spanish Inquisition. It featured several hooded figures and a victim being racked, while another was being hung from the ceiling on chains, his glass eyes fixed on a cowled figure carrying what looked like a set of rusty garden shears. The intention was castration.

Another hooded figure sat at a desk, a book open before it.

A book of Latin phrases. An old book.

Donna looked round frantically for the entrance to the exhibit and found it nearby in the form of a metal door. She opened it and stepped inside, making for the book. She pulled it towards her and flipped it over, looking at the cover.

The crest showed a Hawk.

The cover felt cold and clammy, as if the book had been in a damp hole for months, years even. The pages were stiff with age, some of them split at the edges. Some of the writing was in Latin, the rest in the same quaint script she'd seen in the book in the library in Scotland.

'Julie,' she called.

Her sister hurried over.

'I've found it,' Donna said triumphantly. 'This is the Grimoire.'

It was then that the hooded figure at the desk leapt to its feet.

The cowl slipped away to reveal the face of Peter Farrell.

Seventy-Eight

Farrell lunged at her, his face contorted in an expression of pure hatred.

His grunt of anger mingled with Donna's own shout of surprise and Julie's scream.

Donna jumped back, pulling the book with her, allowing it to fall to the floor with a crash.

Farrell leapt over the desk, not sure which to grab first, Donna or the Grimoire. He launched himself at Donna, who managed to avoid his rush, seeing him crash into the figure holding the castrating irons. An arm broke off and the metal implement went skidding across the dusty floor. Donna snatched it up as she saw Farrell reaching inside his jacket, pulling the .45 free.

She swung the castrating iron with all her force and caught him across the back of the hand, the clang of metal on bone reverberating through The Torture Chamber.

The gun flew from his grasp, but instead of trying to retrieve it Farrell came at her again.

Donna swung the iron again. This time she caught him in the face with it.

The blow split his cheek almost to the bone and blood burst from the wound and ran down the side of his face. Grabbing the book, Donna dashed past him towards the door where Julie was waiting.

'Get them,' roared Farrell. As if from nowhere, Ryker and Kellerman appeared from the shadows. Like two spectres rising from the umbra they rose up before the women.

Donna pulled the .22 Pathfinder from her handbag, thumbed back the hammer and fired twice. The first shot carved a path through the shoulder of Ryker's jacket without touching flesh; the second missed both men and blew the head off the model of Torquemada.

Ryker dived to one side but swung his foot at Donna and managed to trip her.

She pitched forward, the gun falling from her grasp and skittering across the floor. As she hit the ground, she fell on top of the Grimoire.

Ryker leapt on her, trying to wrestle the book from her grip.

Julie kicked out at him, catching him in the groin, but then she felt powerful hands fastening around her throat as Kellerman grabbed her.

'You cunt,' he hissed, squeezing until his fingers pressed deep into her windpipe.

White stars began to dance in front of Julie's eyes; no matter how she scratched at his hands she could not break his grip.

She was helpless, supported by the hands but dying because of them.

Donna pushed Ryker off her and scrambled to her feet, seeing that Farrell was now about to free himself and join the fight, blood pouring down his face. But it was Julie she was concerned with.

Kellerman was tightening his grip on her throat, squeezing until Julie's eyes bulged madly in their sockets as she fought for breath.

Donna looked around for the gun and saw it. She dived onto the floor, snatched up the Pathfinder and rolled over. She fired once, and more by luck than judgement the bullet hit Kellerman in the shin, just below the left knee. The sound of the pistol was deafening inside the chamber, but even above the roar she could hear the strident crack of splintering bone as the tibia was shattered by the bullet.

Kellerman shrieked and released his grip on Julie, clapping his hands to the wound. Blood ran through his fingers as he crashed to the ground, clutching the ragged hole.

Julie, too, had fallen to the ground, barely conscious. Donna tried to help her up but felt herself grabbed from behind by Ryker.

She pushed herself backwards and both of them went hurtling over the low chain that separated them from the exhibits. Donna landed on top of Ryker, winding him as he took her elbow in his chest. Again the gun slipped from her grasp.

Farrell was out of the cage by now, racing towards Julie, the .45 out and lowered at her.

He grabbed her around the waist and lifted her to her feet, the barrel of the pistol pressed to her temple.

'No,' Donna shouted, trying to struggle away from Ryker, 'leave her alone.'

Kellerman was groaning loudly, his lower leg smashed by the bullet.

Ryker made a grab for the book but missed and overbalanced, crashing into the guillotine display. He cracked his head on one of the sharp corners and went down in a heap, clutching his throbbing skull.

'Stop.'

The voice boomed out, filling the chamber.

Both Donna and Farrell turned towards the entrance.

Francis Dashwood moved slowly into the chamber, closely followed by Richard Parsons.

Dashwood was smiling.

Seventy-Nine

The stench was appalling.

Donna noticed it as soon as Dashwood and Parsons entered the chamber. The unmistakable rank odour of death.

'You have something which belongs to us,' Dashwood said, jabbing a finger towards the book she held.

'Your husband stole it from us,' Parsons added.

'Return it.'

Donna swallowed hard, her stomach somersaulting as she inhaled the rancid stench that emanated from the two men.

'Who are you?' she asked, seeing the pallid skin that hung in festering coils from their faces. Dashwood's forehead was dotted with boils, one of which had recently burst. Thick pus seeped down towards his eyebrow.

'Friends of your husbands,' Dashwood told her, smiling, lips sliding back to reveal blackened teeth. 'Now give me the book.' The smile faded to be replaced by a look of anger. He held out a hand.

Donna kept a tight grip on the Grimoire.

'I'll blow her fucking head all over the wall,' hissed Farrell, pushing the barrel of the .45 forcefully against Julie's temple. 'Now give him the book.'

'Fair exchange, Mrs Ward,' Dashwood said. 'You have something *we* want. We have something *you* want. Give me the Grimoire.'

'If I do you'll kill us both,' Donna said, trying to swallow.

'And if you don't, Farrell will shoot you. *Then* we'll take it,' Dashwood told her.

'Fair exchange. Her life for the Grimoire,' Parsons added, nodding towards Julie.

'Why does it mean so much to you?' Donna asked, taking a step backwards, the book in her arms.

Dashwood advanced a pace, his eyes fixed on the Grimoire.

'Give it to me,' he rasped. She heard the anger in his voice but there was something else there, too.

Fear?

'Give him the book or I swear I'll kill her,' Farrell said, looking first at Donna, then at Dashwood.

Donna moved back another step.

'Tell me why it's so important,' she demanded, opening it at the first page, smelling the musty odour that rose from the parchment-like paper. She closed her hand on the top sheet.

'Don't damage it,' shouted Dashwood. Now Donna was sure it was fear she heard in his voice. He moved closer to her but she merely held her ground, one hand poised to rip the page free. 'Don't damage the book,' Dashwood repeated. 'You can both go, just don't damage the book.'

'Let her go, or I'll rip this page out and all the others,' Donna said defiantly, looking at Farrell.

He kept his grip on Julie, the gun still pressed to her temple.

'Shoot her,' Parsons snapped.

Dashwood shot up a hand.

'No,' he hissed.

'I'll destroy the book,' Donna threatened. 'Let her go.'

'You couldn't rip up a dozen pages before I killed you both,' Farrell said, not impressed by her show of bravado.

'Let her go,' snarled Dashwood, glaring at Farrell.

He hesitated a moment then released his grip on Julie, pushing her away from him. She stumbled and fell to her knees, one hand massaging her bruised throat.

'Drop the gun,' Donna said.

Farrell did as he was told.

'Now back off, all of you,' she continued, moving across to her sister, the Grimoire still held in her hands.

Dashwood didn't move but his rheumy eyes followed the book.

Farrell, Ryker and Kellerman, still clutching his knee and the wound just below it, moved out of the chamber, leaving the two women to face Parsons and Dashwood. The stench seemed to grow in intensity.

'We made a bargain,' said Dashwood. 'Give me the book.'

Donna glanced quickly to one side and saw the .45 that Farrell had dropped. It was a couple of feet to her right.

'Give me the book and I'll tell you why it's so important to us. You said you wanted to know.'

She edged closer to the automatic.

Julie was leaning back against the wall, her head spinning, her eyes filled with tears of pain and fear.

'A bargain, Mrs Ward,' Dashwood continued.

Donna dropped to one knee, snatched up the .45 and then straightened up with the barrel pointed at Dashwood.

He chuckled.

The sound echoed around the chamber. Donna felt the hairs on the back of her neck rise.

'Take the fucking thing,' she hissed and hurled it at Dashwood.

He grabbed it and pulled it close to his chest, his eyes blazing.

Donna raised the .45 until it was level with his head and steadied herself to fire.

'Stay back,' she said, teeth gritted, her finger resting on the trigger.

'I have what I want now,' Dashwood told her, moving towards the exit.

'They'll kill us,' Julie croaked.

'No, not *us*,' Dashwood smiled. '*We* will not touch you.'

Donna frowned.

What the hell did he mean?

She had the sights directly over Dashwood's forehead; all she had to do was tighten her finger and she'd spread his brains all around the chamber.

Perhaps she should.

He was still hugging the book to him as if it were a nursing child.

'Your husband was inquisitive, too,' he said, smiling, showing his array of blackened teeth. 'Perhaps you're like him. You want to know about the Grimoire?'

She nodded slowly.

'Then I'll tell you.'

Eighty

Kill him.

Donna felt as if a tiny voice were whispering in her ear. She kept the automatic raised as Dashwood ran his hand over the cover of the Grimoire.

Blow the fucker's brains out.

'You killed my husband,' she said quietly, the words sounding more like a statement than a question.

Dashwood shook his head.

'It was none of our doing,' he said. 'He brought about his own death because of his betrayal.'

'You murdered him.'

'Is that what the police told you? That he was murdered?'

'They said they were reasonably sure he *wasn't*. That his death *was* an accident.'

'Then why don't you believe them?' Dashwood asked, smiling thinly.

'I don't know what to believe any more,' she said, keeping the gun trained on the other man. 'All I know is his death is linked to that book.' She nodded towards the thick volume.

'Possibly. As I said to you, it *is* very important to us.'

'And just who are you?' she wanted to know.

'Surely you must know by now. We are The Sons of Midnight.' He spoke the words with reverence. 'And always will be.' Again that smile. 'At least now we have our Grimoire back we can be safe again. Safe from men like your husband, who sought to expose us.' He eyed Donna impassively. 'Do you have any idea of the power this book contains? No, you couldn't. Your mind isn't capable of comprehending such power. The power of life. The power to *give* life.'

He looked down at the cover of the Grimoire and touched the crest lovingly. Even in the darkness Donna could see his eyes blazing with a ferocity that belied the appearance of the rest of his body.

'Edward Chardell, the author of this book, believed that life was immortal. Not so much in *time*, as in *essence*. This book,' again he held it up, 'was published as Chardell was dying. It contains his theories and his researches. The sum total of knowledge he'd spent years accumulating. He says that life exists outside and independent of Creation, and independent of birth too.'

Donna looked puzzled.

'He says that life can, and does, attach itself to inanimate as well as animate objects. Organic life can exist, can be *made* to exist, anywhere and within everything. Within the bricks and mortar of a house. Within a jewel.' He smiled. 'Within a car.' He paused a moment. 'Do you believe in ghosts, Mrs Ward?'

Donna shrugged.

'As far as Chardell was concerned, a ghost was merely living consciousness without a body to house it. The body can function without consciousness, in a state of coma or sleep. Why should consciousness not function without a body? It becomes a separate entity, able to enter objects at will, or if guided. Guided by men like myself. I'm not saying I can bring the dead back to life; there are limits even to *my* abilities.' He chuckled. 'But I have studied the words within this book and I can bring life to what were otherwise lifeless objects.'

He pointed at the gun.

Donna felt something pulsing in her hand, as if she held a beating heart. The sensation was vile. As she looked down she saw the .45 moving slightly, the butt throbbing in her grip.

She did see it, didn't she?

The barrel seemed to twist, snake-like, the muzzle opening up like a mouth, growing wider.

Donna dropped the weapon and stepped away from it.

The .45 lay at her feet.

She blinked hard and looked at it again.

'No, you didn't imagine it,' Dashwood said. 'The Church would call it a miracle.' Both he and Parsons laughed aloud. 'Fascinating, isn't it?' Dashwood said, smiling. 'Your husband thought so, too. That was why he sought us out, why he wanted our knowledge.'

'He was going to destroy you,' Donna said. 'He

knew you needed the book to survive; that was why he took it from you.'

Dashwood raised his eyebrows questioningly.

'He wanted knowledge. He wanted to learn and he would do *anything* in order to gain that knowledge. He threatened to expose us, yes, but in order to expose us he first had to join us. To learn about us. The best way to destroy is from within. Your husband knew that.'

Donna felt her heart beating more rapidly.

No, this couldn't be.

'He wanted what we had,' Dashwood said. 'He wanted to *be* one of us.'

'No,' Donna murmured, shaking her head.

'How well did you know your husband, Mrs Ward?'

Donna was quivering.

'How do you think he knew so much about us? Why should we consider him such a danger unless he could damage us?'

'He took the Grimoire. That was why you wanted him dead,' Donna said.

'But how do you think he got close enough to take it in the first place?'

Donna shook her head.

'What did he tell you?' Dashwood asked. 'Did he tell you he was one of us?'

Donna didn't answer.

'No. He didn't, did he?' Dashwood said, smiling.

'He couldn't have been,' she shouted. 'I know about you. I know about what you do. You kill.'

‘Some things are worth killing *for*,’ Dashwood told her. ‘Some knowledge has a high price.’

‘He wasn’t one of you,’ she said defiantly. ‘He wouldn’t have done the things he . . .’

‘What things, Mrs Ward?’

‘The initiation rites. I read about them.’

‘What *wouldn’t* he have done?’ Dashwood chided.

‘He wouldn’t have killed . . .’ The sentence trailed off.

‘Killed a child?’ Dashwood smiled broadly. ‘He wouldn’t have killed a child, is that what you were going to say? He wouldn’t have fornicated in front of us, he wouldn’t have taken the life of a child, he wouldn’t have urinated on the cross. You think he wouldn’t have pissed on Christ.’ Dashwood bellowed the final words, the noise echoing around the chamber. ‘How well did you know your husband, you bitch? How well did you know him? Could you see into his mind? You ignorant, stupid bitch.’

Donna leapt forward, grabbing the .45.

She rolled over, aiming it at Dashwood, squeezing the trigger.

Nothing happened.

He merely stepped back, away from her through the exit.

As he did she saw him raise his hand, the index finger pointing at something behind her.

Donna kept squeezing the trigger until, finally, she hurled the automatic away with a wail of despair.

The door of the chamber was slammed shut. She and Julie were trapped.

They ran to the door but it was firmly closed, unyielding despite their frantic efforts to open it. Julie turned, sliding exhausted down the damp wood, her back to the door. Donna continued thumping at the recalcitrant partition.

'Donna.'

Julie could scarcely force the word out. She grabbed her sister's leg, waiting until she'd turned before pointing at something inside the chamber.

'Oh, Jesus,' Donna whispered.

Was this imagination? Or madness?

The wax figures in the tableau of Sharon Tate's murder were moving frenziedly.

Rooted to the spot, their limbs jerked insanely, as if charged with some kind of kinetic energy. Arms and legs thrashed wildly.

Then the sounds began.

Screams of pain and terror rose from frozen throats and drummed in the ears of Donna and Julie.

Those who'd died that night in 1969 were dying again, their agony finding a new voice.

Donna watched, her eyes bulging in their sockets, her throat constricted.

Julie too found that she was paralysed by the sight.

Only when the figure of Charles Manson turned and looked at her did she finally allow her own scream to escape. It mingled with the others in a hideous cacophony of suffering.

The figure took a step towards them.

Eighty-One

In some obscene parody of a child's first steps, the Manson figure lurched from its position on the display, steadying itself against a wall.

From the tableau itself the large figure of the man who had been known as Charles 'Tex' Watson also struggled free and turned on the two women. Both the effigies held knives.

Donna, her mind still reeling, looked around for the discarded .22 Pathfinder.

It lay ten or twelve feet away, beneath the rack of the Inquisition victim.

To reach it she would have to pass the figures of Manson and Watson.

Donna ran towards the weapon, but Manson moved towards her. The waxwork moved with surprising speed; Donna felt cold hands grabbing at her.

The knife slashed down and carved through the air only inches from her face. She turned and lashed out, feeling her hand connect with the hard wax of the face. The eyes fixed her in their glassy, stare, the eyes of a dead fish on a skillet.

The screams continued, over and over again.

Manson grabbed her by the wrist and pulled her towards him.

Towards the knife.

Donna managed to twist in his grip and drove a foot into his midriff, knocking him backwards. He crashed into the effigy of a torturer burning the eyes from his victim.

Donna lunged towards the gun and scooped it into her hand, rolling over in time to see Watson bearing down on Julie.

The younger woman avoided the knife-thrust and hurled herself to one side, rolling beneath a table on which a man was being subjected to the Chinese Water Torture.

The dust and grime was thick beneath the table and Julie coughed as it clogged in her throat and nostrils.

Watson turned and came at her again, his movements thankfully slow.

Donna rose to one knee and swung the Pathfinder up into position.

She fired twice, the retort, even from a pistol as small as a .22, quite deafening within the confines of the chamber.

The first bullet struck him in the back of the head, the second in the side of the face, blasting most of the area from the temple to the chin away. Fragments of wax flew into the air.

Watson continued moving towards Julie.

Donna thumbed back the hammer and pumped two shots into Manson with similarly useless results. She saw the body quiver, saw the burns on the shirt of the mannequin. She even heard the sharp crack as the slugs thumped into the hard wax. The figure did not pause, merely raised the knife and lunged forward.

Donna rolled away beneath the table and came up on the other side.

The Manson figure made a sudden movement and the knife came hurtling down, burying itself in the wood, missing her hand by inches.

Donna made a grab for the knife but Manson's hand closed over hers. Again she felt the clammy chill of wax; it was like being touched by a dead man. She struggled to escape the grip. Using the pistol as a club she slammed it into the side of the figure's head with such force that one of the glass eyes popped out, the wax around it splintering.

The grip on her hand was released and she backed off.

The Manson figure kept coming.

Julie scrambled to her feet, pushing other figures over in an effort to halt the inexorable progress of Watson, who had the blade brandished high.

The screaming continued, great racking caterwauls of agony that deafened the women as surely as the retorts of the pistol. The backdrop of sound was intolerable.

Donna ran towards a scene showing the execution of Mary Queen of Scots. As the Manson figure advanced on her, she dragged the axe from the frozen grip of the headsman. It was heavy, the razor-sharp blade comfortingly lethal.

With all her strength she swung it, burying the blade in Manson's chest.

The figure wobbled.

Donna struck again, her own shouts of defiance and fear mingling with the screams all around her.

The next blow sheared off an arm.

Manson still advanced.

'Bastard,' roared Donna and struck his head from his shoulders.

The effigy flew into the air, the wax head spinning, the fake hair flowing out wildly.

The waxwork toppled over and lay still.

'Donna,' shrieked Julie, and she looked over to see her sister trapped in a corner, the Watson figure only a couple of feet away.

Watson swung the knife, the cut slicing through the material of Julie's shirt and gashing her forearm. She looked up into the sightless glass eyes, unable to move as the knife was raised again.

Donna ran at the figure, bringing the axe down with manic force. The blow was so powerful it cleft the wax head cleanly in two and bit into the torso as deep as the shoulders.

Watson swayed uncertainly for a second then fell backwards, the axe still embedded.

Donna sucked in the stale air, perspiration soaking her T-shirt, matting her hair at the nape of her neck.

Julie shook her head, the tears running down her cheeks. Donna dropped to her knees and the two women embraced, blood from the wound on

Julie's arm smearing Donna's clothes as they held each other tightly.

The screams continued to echo around them.

Eighty-Two

She woke with a start, looking around her frantically, disorientated, unsure of her surroundings. She felt her heart beating madly; the fear she had come to know only too well enveloped her like a cold glove.

Julie Craig sat forward on the sofa and rubbed her eyes, still trying to shrug off that twilight state between dreams and awareness.

'Shit,' she murmured, exhaling deeply.

Her faculties seemed to return slowly. She shook her head, as if that simple action would clear her mind. Immediately she became aware of a dull ache in her right forearm and looked down to see the bandage wound round it from just above the wrist to the elbow.

'You okay?' Donna asked her quietly.

'I dropped off. I'm sorry,' Julie apologized, rubbing both hands across her face, pulling her long dark hair back from her forehead. 'What time is it?'

'Just after one,' Donna told her. 'I flaked out, too, when we got back.'

They had returned to the cottage almost two

hours ago, exhausted, drained and frightened. Both of them had fought against the sleep they so desperately craved, but eventually it had overtaken them. Through that troubled sleep the events of the night returned to them. The drive to the Wax Museum, the slow exploration, the meeting with Dashwood and Parsons and the terrifying aftermath. All of it was re-run through their subconscious like a video recording. Their escape from the waxworks, through a small window which opened out into a side alley, and then the long drive back to the cottage.

Donna wondered if, indeed, she had just awoken and the entire bizarre chain of events had been the product of her fevered mind.

If only that were the case.

She need only look at the cuts and bruises on her own body and on Julie's to know that the events had been all too real.

'We have to leave here tonight,' Donna said.

'We need to rest,' Julie protested.

'We can rest when we get back to London. I don't think they will, but if they come looking for us and find us here . . .'

She allowed the sentence to trail off.

Julie closed her eyes for a moment.

'The police will come,' she said.

'That's another reason we have to get out of here,' Donna said.

'Why? When they come, you can tell them what happened. Tell them everything. Like you should have done in the first place.' There was a trace of anger in her voice. 'Let *them* take care of this business now, Donna.'

'No. It isn't *their* business. Besides, if they find out what happened there'll be problems. How the hell are we supposed to explain what happened at the waxworks? They'll lock us both up. They'll think we're insane, and I wouldn't blame them if they did.' She regarded her sister for long moments then spoke again. '*We* have the advantage now. Dashwood and his men think we're dead. They won't be expecting us to go after them. They think they've got rid of us. They'll be off guard.'

'What the hell are you talking about, "Go after them"?' Julie said incredulously.

'Like I said, they think we're dead. They won't be expecting us,' Donna said almost excitedly.

'You're mad,' Julie said quietly. 'Donna, for God's sake, they've already tried to kill you Christ knows how many times, and you're still not satisfied. Do you *want* to die?'

'I want *them* to die,' she rasped.

'Forget it, it's over. They've got the bloody book, that was what they wanted. Let them have it. Let them keep it. We're alive, that's all that matters.' The anger had turned to desperation.

'It's not about the book, Julie, it never was.'

'No, it's about revenge. Your need for revenge. It's become an obsession with you, Donna. It's eating you away and you don't even know it. First it was Chris's affair, and now it's that book, and even after everything we've been through that's not enough for you. You won't be happy until you've got us both killed.'

'You don't know what I'm feeling,' she said angrily. 'It was bad enough knowing about the affair, then being involved in something which could have caused our deaths, but now I find out my husband could have been a murderer, too. You heard what Dashwood said tonight. Chris was *one* of them.'

'And you believe that?'

'I'm going to find out and I'm going to wipe those bastards off the face of the earth.'

'You can't even *see* what it's doing to you, can you? You can't see what it's made you. All that matters to you is this ridiculous need for revenge. You couldn't have it against Chris or Suzanne Regan so you used the hunt for the book, instead. And now that's gone you've found another excuse to carry on.'

'Perhaps that's all I've got left, Julie.'

'Well, I won't help you. I'm sorry but I can't take any more. I'm not going to be there when you get yourself killed. I won't watch you die, Donna.'

'Part of me died when I found out about Chris and Suzanne Regan,' Donna said. 'And perhaps you're right, perhaps this whole thing has been about that, an extension of the anger I felt. Somebody had to pay for it. Somebody *will* pay for it. And if *you* won't help me, then I'll do it alone. I can't stop now. Not until this is over.'

'It *is* over,' Julie shouted, tears running down

her cheeks. 'Jesus Christ, how many more times? How much more pain can you stand? You were looking for the truth and you thought you'd found it. Well, you didn't.' She sniffed back more tears. 'He wasn't having an affair with Suzanne Regan. He was having an affair with *me*.'

Eighty-Three

Silence.

The words Julie had spoken brought only silence from her sister. For dreadful seconds Donna was reminded of her first sight of the policeman on her doorstep bringing her news of her husband's accident. How long ago was that? A month? It felt like years. Suffering had a way of distorting even time.

Now she looked blankly at her sister, momentarily unsure she'd heard right. The words gradually found their way into her consciousness. They began to take on their full meaning.

She swallowed hard.

'I don't believe you,' she said finally, her voice a hoarse whisper.

Julie sucked in a weary breath.

'It's true. Do you want dates, times, places? What do I have to say to convince you?' Julie answered wearily. She sank back on the sofa, one hand over her eyes.

She waited for the explosion of rage and recrimination.

It never came.

Donna sat at the other end of the sofa, hands clasped around one knee.

'How long had it been going on?' she wanted to know.

'Nine or ten months.'

Donna felt as if she'd been struck by an iron bar. Her head was spinning.

'Jesus,' she murmured, trying to recover her wits. 'Why?'

'I don't know. It just happened, I . . . We never intended it to happen.' She looked at her sister, her own shame intensified by the confession. 'I'm sorry.'

'So am I,' Donna said. Then, more vehemently, 'Did you love him?'

'I don't know.'

'I wouldn't have thought that was a multiple-choice question, Julie. You either did or you didn't.'

The younger woman shook her head.

'Did *he* love *you*?' Donna persisted.

'No.'

'You sound very sure. Ten months is a long time; are you telling me you never felt anything, either of you?'

Julie didn't speak.

'It was just sex then, was it?' Donna hissed. 'No love, just plenty of fucking. Was that it?'

'Donna, he loved *you*. I knew he'd never leave you, he always made that clear.'

'Did you want him to leave me? Were you trying to get Chris away from me?'

'No, I would never have done that. It was *his* decision. Like I said, he loved you.'

'But you hung around, just in case he changed his mind, right?'

'It wasn't like that.'

'Then tell me what it *was* like, Julie,' Donna hissed.

'We were more like friends.'

'Friends don't fuck each other.'

'Sex wasn't important.'

'But when you did it, was it good? Did you enjoy it? How did you rate him? Did he do things to you other men hadn't? Did he make you come? Was he considerate, caring? Tell me, Julie.'

The younger woman had no answers.

'What attracted you to him in the first place, or did *he* make the first move?'

'I had an exhibition of some of my photographs in a gallery in Knightsbridge. Chris came along, we chatted. He took me for a coffee.'

'And that was when you decided, was it? That was when you thought you'd start fucking your sister's husband. Well, was it? Come on, I'm curious. Did he suggest going back to your place or did you tell him to come round when he felt like it?'

Julie was about to answer when Donna's face darkened.

'Did you ever fuck him in *our* house?' she demanded, anxious that the betrayal should not have entered her most private domain.

Julie shook her head.

'It was usually my flat, sometimes my studio,' she said. 'Like I said, Donna, it wasn't that often.'

'It doesn't matter if it was once or a hundred times, you still did it.'

'He was an attractive man, for Christ's sake,' Julie said irritably, as if that were some excuse to explain what had happened. 'He was hard to resist. We'd always got on well, you know that. I admired his attitude to life, perhaps that was what attracted me to him. He didn't give a fuck about anyone or anything. If he wanted something, he got it. I'd never met a man so ambitious, so determined.'

'Yes, Chris always got what he wanted. Did that include *you*?'

'I know it was wrong and if there was anything I could do to change things I would, Donna.'

'Would you really? Are you trying to tell me you regret the affair? Or are you sorry Chris is dead because *you* lost him as well as I did? *Do* you regret it?'

'I regret hurting you.'

'Then why tell me? Was your conscience pricking you? I find that difficult to believe, after ten months. I would have thought you'd have come to terms with the guilt by now. Pushed it to the back of your mind. Did you ever think about me when you were with him? Did you ever once stop and think what you were doing?'

'No,' Julie said flatly.

'Ever since Chris died my life has been one continual round of suspicion, mistrust and deceit. And now I find out that it extends into my own family. With my own fucking sister.' Donna looked at the younger woman with an expression that combined rage and bewilderment. 'How long would it have gone on, Julie, if he hadn't died? A year? Three years? The rest of our lives? Or just until I found out?'

'It would have petered out. Like I said, we didn't love each other.'

'There must have been something between you to keep it going for ten months. Don't tell me it was just because Chris was good in bed.'

'*We didn't love each other*. How many times do I have to say it?'

'It's easy to say that now, because it's over. But if it had gone on you might have. Then you might have tried to get him away from me. But that's something we'll never know, isn't it?'

The two women faced each other for long moments.

'Did anyone else know what was going on?' Donna said finally, angered by the fact that the secret might have been shared.

'Martin Connelly knew,' Julie confessed. 'Chris took me out for dinner one night and Connelly was in the same restaurant. He didn't say much. I don't know what Chris told him.'

'I wish you could feel what I'm feeling now,' Donna said vehemently. 'Anger, sadness – and I feel like a fool, too. I feel as if you've been laughing at me. I feel as if everyonc's been laughing at me. Was it because your own marriage failed, Julie? You couldn't stand to see anyone else happy after what happened to you? Was that it?'

'I've told you the reasons and I know it's pointless to say it but I'm sorry, Donna.' She got to her feet. 'I'll go now. You won't see me again, I promise you.'

'No. You're not walking out on this, Julie,' Donna rasped. 'You say you're sorry.'

'I am. I know you don't believe me, though. You never will.'

'Make me believe.'

'How?'

'Stay and help me destroy The Sons of Midnight.'

'I can't.'

'You mean you *won't*?' Donna glared at her sister. 'It would be so easy for you to walk out, wouldn't it? Well, if you want to show me you're sorry then you'll help me.'

'That's emotional blackmail.'

'Too fucking right it is. Anyway, you're not giving yourself an opportunity to get over your guilt if you walk away. Stay and help me.'

'We could both be killed.'

'Look on it as paying back a debt,' Donna said, her eyes narrowed. 'You *owe* me that.'

Eighty-Four

The .357 bucked violently in her fist as the hammer slammed down.

The retort was massive. Even with her protectors on, Donna could still hear the dull ring as the heavy grain slug struck the back wall of the range travelling at over 1,450 feet a second. As another bullet left the barrel she felt a spattering of tiny metal fragments bounce off the wooden wall of the booth and pepper her hand. The smoke from the round cleared. She jabbed the red button on the control panel beside her to retrieve the target. It whirred back up the range towards her. As it drew close she laid the Magnum down and leant forward to inspect the grouping of her shots.

On the man-sized target she had put three shots through the centre, two in the outer ring and one low, in the groin.

Donna shook her head, reached for the roll of sticky white spots and covered each hole, jabbing the red button once more to send the target back up the range.

She pushed six more of the hollow-tipped shells into the cylinder and steadied herself, squinting down the sights.

These next six she fired off quickly and brought the target back, her hand still slightly numb around the base of the thumb where the recoil of the Magnum had slammed the butt repeatedly against her palm.

All six shots were in the central area.

Donna nodded and removed the target, selecting another and pinning it to the black rubber backboard.

She was the only one in the range. She usually was during the day; the clock outside, beyond the double-thickness bullet-proof glass panels, showed that it was just 11.15 a.m.

She had risen early that morning, despite not getting back to the house until almost four. Sleep had eluded her for all but a couple of hours. Despite that, she felt fresh and alert. She turned to look out at Julie and caught a glimpse of her own reflection in the plate glass. There were dark rings beneath her eyes and her skin was pale. She might not *feel* tired but she looked as if she'd been without sleep for days.

Julie.

Donna had given up even trying to suppress her anger towards her sister. They'd exchanged words only briefly that morning, most of them unpleasant.

Now Donna turned back to face the counter where the .357, the .38, the Beretta and the Pathfinder were laid out. She selected the .38 and began thumbing in bullets from the box to her left.

She still felt numb from the revelations of the previous night.

Her own sister involved in an affair with Chris.

Donna shook her head.

Perhaps it *would* have been easier just to let Julie walk away. Walk out of her life. If she did, there would be no one left for her. Better the company of one she hated than complete loneliness.

Donna snapped the cylinder shut.

Did she hate Julie? Hatred was a very strong emotion. Stronger, she was beginning to think, even than love. But did she truly *hate* the younger woman?

She raised the .38 and took aim, firing off the six rounds evenly.

No one is to be trusted.

Christ, how prophetic the words in Chris's letter had proved to be.

She brought the target back and looked at the damage. Two in the centre, two in the head. Two in the groin. She covered the holes with white spots, sent the target away again and began pushing 9mm shells into the magazine of the Beretta.

How many times had she done this when Chris had been with her?

She almost smiled.

They'd been coming to the shooting club in Druid Street for almost three years. As she thought of her husband she felt a familiar but fleeting twinge of sadness but it was rapidly replaced by anger.

She hated Julie for what she'd done. She hated

Chris for his part in the deception. She hated The Sons of Midnight for what they too had done.

Someone had to pay for her anger; someone must be forced to suffer for her pain. It would be that organisation. Those who had tried to tell her that not only was her husband a liar and adulterer, he was capable of murder too.

Adulterer.

The word seemed peculiarly archaic.

Murderer *didn't.*

That was one of the things which *really* troubled her. She didn't find it easy to dismiss the suggestion as effortlessly as she would have liked. Why would Dashwood lie? Some kind of psychological trick? But why taunt her about facts she could never prove or disprove? Why?

Why?

There were so many questions; she knew that she would never know answers to most of them.

She continued thumbing bullets into the magazine.

Why had Chris decided upon an affair with Julie?

There were ten in the magazine now.

What had been so wrong with their marriage to make him do such a thing?

Eleven. Twelve.

Had Dashwood been telling the truth? Had her husband not merely wanted to expose The Sons of Midnight? Had he joined their ranks?

Thirteen.

Had the man she'd loved been capable of murder?

Fourteen.

And there still remained the mystery of Suzanne Regan. If it had been Julie embroiled in the affair with Chris, then why had Suzanne Regan been with the writer when he died?

Was there no end to these mysteries? No end to the pain?

She pushed in the last bullet, slammed in the magazine and worked the slide, cocking the weapon. She raised it, drawing a bead on the centre of the target.

If there were answers she would find them.

And then?

What was there to live for after that?

Donna gritted her teeth and tried not to think about it. For now she had something to drive her on.

The desire for vengeance. And she would not stop until it was hers. Someone was going to suffer for her torment and she didn't care who it was.

She fired off all fifteen rounds with remarkable rapidity and accuracy, the shots shredding the centre of the target, the pistol bouncing in her grip, empty shell-cases flying from the weapon until finally the slide shot back, signalling the weapon was empty. Donna lowered it, her breathing heavy, the stench of cordite strong in her nostrils.

Dark smoke surrounded her like a dirty shroud.

Eighty-Five

'It has to be the place in Conduit Street.'

Donna prodded the sheet of paper with the locations on, her eyes moving swiftly back and forth over the names:

RATHFARNHAM, DUBLIN.
BRASENOSE COLLEGE, OXFORD.
REGENCY PLACE, EDINBURGH.
CONDUIT STREET, LONDON.

The meeting places of The Sons of Midnight.

'How can you be sure?' Julie asked. 'What about Oxford?'

'London would have been easier for them to reach after leaving Essex but,' she exhaled deeply, 'I can't be *sure*. All we can do is check it out. If they're not there, we'll keep looking.'

Julie regarded her impassively across the table. The tension between the two women was almost palpable.

'Didn't Chris ever mention them to you?' Donna asked, not looking at Julie. 'Did he ever talk about his work to *you*?'

'No. He wouldn't discuss something with me that he refused to discuss with you, would he?'

'I don't know. I thought I knew him up until the last few weeks. Now I'm not sure of *anything* he would or wouldn't do.' She looked at Julie irritably. 'I thought I knew *you* too, Julie. Looks like I was wrong about both of you.'

'Why do you want me around, Donna?' Julie demanded. 'You can't stand me near you any more because of what happened. It would be best for both of us if I left.'

'I told you why. You *owe* me your help, *because* of what happened between you and Chris.' Her eyes narrowed. 'Don't think I enjoy looking at you and imagining what you and he used to get up to, but I'm damned if I'm going to let you walk away from what you did. You'd like that, wouldn't you? To think it was over and you'd escaped the consequences.'

'I'm not proud of what I did, Donna. If you think I am then you're even more fucked up than I imagined.' She spat out the words angrily.

Donna allowed her fingers to touch the butt of the .357 that lay on the table but she kept her gaze fixed on Julie.

'Why don't you use the bloody gun on me,' Julie said challengingly. 'That'd solve your problems, wouldn't it?'

'Don't think I haven't thought about it,' Donna told her. 'Don't think I haven't imagined how much I'd enjoy killing you.'

'I can understand that. Revenge seems to be the most important thing in your life now, Donna,' said Julie sardonically.

'Perhaps it's because there's nothing else in my life any more,' Donna told her. 'Chris is gone, even my memories of him might as well be gone.

You destroyed them, Julie. When I think of him I think of him with you. I think of his deceit. *Your* deceit. I *shared* him for ten months with you.'

'I saw him once a week, if that,' Julie said. 'In all that time, if you add up the hours I spent with him it's probably no more than two weeks.'

'And that's supposed to make it more acceptable, is it?'

'Look, Donna, I thought you wanted to destroy this group of men. I thought you wanted revenge on them. That's your *mission* now, isn't it?' She made no attempt to hide the sarcasm in her voice. 'Then concentrate on *that*.'

'And forget everything else?' She smiled thinly.

They sat in silence for what seemed like an eternity.

'So what do we do?' Julie asked finally.

'We find them. All of them.'

'And then?'

Donna looked down at the .357.

'Kill them.'

'I think the police might have something to say about that,' Julie observed.

'To hell with the police,' Donna snapped.

'Wasn't there something in Chris's notes about destroying the book?' Julie asked.

' "Destroy the book and you destroy *them*",' Donna muttered, as if she'd learned the words by heart. 'And you think they're going to let us walk in and do that without a fight?'

The two women regarded each other across

the table. Julie's eyes roved over her sister's outfit. The two shoulder-holsters she wore looked strangely incongruous.

Beneath one arm she carried the Beretta. As Julie watched, she slid the .357 into the other holster.

'Mrs Rambo,' Julie said almost scornfully. 'Do you have any idea how ridiculous you look?'

Donna eyed her malevolently.

'People are going to die, Julie,' she said quietly. 'Maybe you and me, too.' There was angry resignation in her voice. 'But who cares?'

She got to her feet, glancing at her watch.

It was 7.46 p.m.

Eighty-Six

The drive into Central London took less than fifty minutes. Traffic was relatively light, even in the centre, and Julie parked the Fiesta on the corner of Conduit Street and Mill Street.

'It's not too late to stop this bloody insanity,' Julie said, looking at her sister.

'We'll leave the car here,' Donna said, ignoring her.

She reached beneath her jacket and gently touched the butts of each gun in turn.

'We don't even know which house it is,' Julie protested.

There weren't many to pick from. Most of the buildings that occupied the street were shops or offices, their stonework grimy with years of accumulated muck. Donna gazed at the frontages of the buildings, her eyes finally coming to rest on a dark brick edifice sandwiched between a jeweller and a travel agent.

'From Chris's notes, it has to be that one,' she said.

The house had three stone steps leading up to its black front door. There were two windows downstairs, three on the first floor. Shutters were pulled tight across all of them, preventing prying eyes from seeing in. A length of iron railings ran in front of the building, some of them rusted, the paint having peeled away. Stone steps led down to a basement.

'What do we do? Just ring the doorbell?' Julie asked cryptically.

'There has to be a back way in,' Donna mused, studying the other structures nearby. She saw what appeared to be a narrow passageway leading alongside a building about twenty yards down the street. 'Come on,' she said and swung herself out of the car, leaving Julie to follow.

They hurried across the street towards the passage, Donna pausing briefly before stepping into the dark walkway. It smelt of stale urine. Donna wrinkled her nose as she made her way along, with Julie close behind her.

The passageway opened out into a large, square

yard. Surrounded on all sides by buildings, it had a claustrophobic atmosphere. Donna shivered involuntarily as she moved over the damp concrete towards the rear of the house.

Another heavy wooden door confronted them, and two ground floor windows. The building appeared to be in darkness. No sounds came from inside, either.

'It's not this house,' Julie said flatly.

Donna moved closer to the window and slid her fingers carefully beneath the sash frame.

To her surprise it moved slightly.

She tried again and a gap about two feet wide opened.

Wide enough for them to slip through.

Donna hesitated.

This was a little too easy, *wasn't it?*

Perhaps they were expected.

And yet, as she'd said to Julie before, as far as Dashwood and the others were concerned both women had died in the waxworks.

And yet . . .

Could it be a trick?

'Do we go in?' Julie wanted to know, her heart thumping that little bit faster.

A trick?

They had to take that chance.

Donna eased the window up a fraction more, then swung herself over the sill and into the room beyond.

Julie followed.

* * *

The woman lay on a rug in the centre of the floor.

She was naked.

So was the man who lay beside her.

The room was silent apart from their low breathing.

The watchers made no sound.

The man finally looked up, as if seeking permission to begin.

Francis Dashwood, seated at a long oak table at one end of the room, nodded slowly, a crooked smile on his face.

As the man in the centre of the room moved onto the woman, his erection bobbing before him, a great cheer arose.

As he thrust hard into her a chorus of handclapping and cat-calls accompanied his actions.

The noise began to build to a crescendo. In the brightly lit room sweat glistened on the couple in the centre of the floor.

Donna stood in the darkened room, listening for any sounds of movement. Apart from Julie scrambling through the window, there were none.

Donna closed it behind her.

'No alarms?' Donna mused quietly.

Julie didn't answer. She was squinting around the room, trying to pick out details in the gloom.

The walls were oak-panelled, hung with large paintings in ornate frames. Shelf after shelf of books loomed from the blackness on two sides of them. There was a fusty smell inside the room; it reminded Donna of the odour from the Grimoire. Ancient paper, now yellowing, expelled its stench like decaying flesh. There were four or five high-backed leather chairs in the room, too; the arms were worn, the furniture very old.

On the other side of the room was another door.

Donna moved towards it. Julie followed, glancing up at the stuffed birds that lowered down from the corners of the room like silent sentinels. She recognized the birds as hawks.

There was a strip of light beneath the door and Donna paused, wondering what lay beyond the wooden partition. She could hear no sound from beyond. Even the noise of traffic passing down Conduit Street outside was barely audible, so thick were the walls of the dwelling.

She knelt, trying to see through the keyhole, desperate to know what lay beyond.

She could see nothing.

Just that strip of light beneath it.

Again, almost unconsciously, she allowed one hand to stray inside her jacket and brush against the butt of the .357.

If there was anyone beyond this door she would be ready for them.

She placed her hand on the doorknob and turned it.

Eighty-Seven

It looked like a hallway.

As Donna eased the door open and peered through she saw a large area of black-and-white tiled floor with three doors leading off it. To the right was a staircase. The hallway was twenty feet across, perhaps a little more. It was brightly lit by two enormous crystal chandeliers hanging from the ornate ceiling. Donna could see the clusters of lights reflected in the tiles.

There were no shadows in which to hide.

She eased the door open a fraction more and looked round at the staircase. It looked like bare mahogany. No carpet covered the highly polished wood. The walls were a dark colour completely devoid of decoration of any kind. Not one single painting hung either in the hallway or on the stairs.

Donna eased the .357 from her shoulder holster and steadied it in her hands.

'What are you doing?' Julie wanted to know.

'We've got to get across that hall,' Donna told her. 'If anyone comes out of any of those doors, I want to be ready.'

She took a step out into the brightly lit hall.

Her eyes darted back and forth over the three doors, then up the stairs. She inclined her head, a signal for Julie to follow her towards the stairs.

Donna's eyes never left the top of the flight as they climbed; Julie kept her attention riveted to the doors.

They climbed slowly, step by step, their progress agonizingly slow. Donna was aware how hopelessly exposed they would be, should anyone either enter the hall or approach from the head of the stairs. She could see a large landing at the top with more rooms leading off it.

A step creaked protestingly beneath Donna and she froze. The sound seemed to echo around the hall.

She gripped the revolver tightly, looking quickly around her.

'Come on,' whispered Julie, her own heart beating faster. 'Move it.'

Donna remained motionless. After what seemed like an eternity, she began to climb once more.

Julie followed gratefully.

'Listen,' said Donna.

Julie heard nothing at first then . . .

Breathing.

It sounded as if there was someone close to them, breathing. A low, almost inaudible but laboured breathing.

'Where the hell is that coming from?' Julie said frantically, trying to keep her voice low.

Donna had no answer. All she could do was look around, trying to find the source of it.

Was someone watching them?

The breathing sounded close, as if someone were standing right next to them. Yet they were the only ones on the staircase.

Donna felt cold fingers of fear plucking at the hairs on the back of her neck. She moved further up the stairs until she reached the landing.

The breathing continued, a little more faint now, though. The two women looked round at the doors on the landing. They were all tightly closed. The breathing didn't seem to be coming from any of them.

It still seemed as if it was from an invisible source right beside them.

Imagination?

Julie looked back and forth anxiously. Their assailant could be behind any one of the doors. Just waiting.

'Donna . . .'

Her words trailed off as she heard a sound below.

One of the doors leading into the hall had opened.

The two women ducked down against the landing rail and watched as a smartly dressed man emerged from a room beyond the hall, his shoes beating out a tattoo on the polished floor. He vanished beneath them, then returned a moment later carrying a bottle of brandy. He disappeared back into the door through which he'd emerged.

For what seemed like an eternity Donna and Julie crouched where they were, watching the closed door. Then Donna raised herself up slowly, moving to the head of the stairs.

'Come on,' she said quietly. 'We'll see where he's gone.'

They began to descend, Donna holding the pistol at the ready should the man or any like him appear again.

As they reached the bottom of the stairs Donna heard the low breathing again. She tried to ignore it but she couldn't. Her heart thumped hard in her chest as she looked around.

'I can still hear it,' Julie said, as if to affirm what her older sister already knew.

Donna nodded slowly, and moved across the hall towards the door through which the smartly dressed man had disappeared only moments earlier.

The chandeliers above them pinned them in bright light; Julie could see their reflections in the fine crystal.

There was still no sound except for that infernal low breathing. The entire house seemed to be deserted, but after the appearance of the smartly dressed man, they knew that to be untrue. Could Julie be right? Could this be the wrong house? What if The Sons of Midnight didn't frequent this building? What if they only gathered at certain times?

What if?

There was only one way to find out.

Donna grabbed the door handle, swallowed hard and pushed.

Eighty-Eight

The corridor beyond the door was less than six feet wide and it stretched about twenty feet ahead of them. The walls on either side were bare. Unlike the hallway, it was lit only by two wall lights, one at either end of the corridor. The far end boasted another closed door. The man they'd seen must have come and gone via the door ahead. There was nowhere else for him to go.

Donna wondered how big the place was. It didn't seem this big from the outside.

Where the hell was everybody?

Apart from the smartly dressed man, they'd not seen nor heard a living soul.

Heard nothing apart from that low breathing.

Julie looked into the dark corridor with trepidation.

How much longer was this going to go on? She feared that the end would be signalled by *their* deaths.

Donna moved into the darkened corridor, stepping cautiously, as if she were walking on squeaking floorboards, not carpet-covered concrete.

The wall lights didn't seem to be powered by anything more substantial than forty-watt bulbs. The glow they cast was a sickly yellow light that barely illuminated the narrow walkway from one door to the other.

The two women moved cautiously along, Donna keeping her eyes ahead, Julie occasionally glancing at the door behind.

Donna put out one hand as if to steady herself against the wall.

Something moved beneath her fingertips.

'Jesus,' she hissed, moving away from the wall and looking down.

'What is it?' Julie wanted to know, her eyes wide with fear.

Donna didn't answer. Instead she carefully replaced her hand on the wall where it had been seconds earlier.

She felt it again. Once more the sensation caused her to pull her hand away, as if she'd received an electric shock.

Was she going insane?

She touched the wall again, but left her hand there until she was sure beyond any doubt.

The stonework, the very plaster, was throbbing gently, as if the bricks and mortar contained some kind of pulse.

Donna could see no movement but she could feel the slow, even thudding against her hand.

Dashwood's words came flooding back to her:

'*Organic life can exist, can be made to exist, anywhere and within anything. Within the bricks and mortar of a house.*'

Donna raised the barrel of the .357. Using the

blade foresight as a tool, she drew the sharp fin across the wall.

'Oh God,' whispered Julie.

Blood oozed from the mark on the wall.

It welled thickly in the narrow mark Donna had made, then dribbled down the paintwork.

She repeated the action on the other wall.

The same thing happened.

She closed her eyes for long seconds, praying that when she opened them the blood would be gone.

It wasn't. The thick crimson fluid ran down the wall in rivulets.

Donna swallowed hard and moved forward, towards the door at the end of the dimly lit corridor.

One of the lights flickered.

They froze momentarily as the bulbs went into a kind of stroboscopic dance before flaring full on for a few more seconds.

Then they went out completely.

The two women were plunged into total darkness.

Julie backed up and touched the wall, feeling the pulse in it, scarcely able to stifle her scream of terror. She bit her fist to muffle the sound.

Donna gripped the .357 tightly and moved towards the door at the far end of the corridor.

'Let's get out now,' hissed Julie.

Donna's answer was to shoot out a hand and grab her sister by the arm, pulling her along with her.

The end of the corridor couldn't be more than about six or seven feet away, she reasoned.

The lights stayed off. Darkness wrapped itself round them like an impenetrable shroud.

They moved forward in the gloom, nearer and nearer to the door.

The light at the far end of the corridor flickered briefly and Donna saw they were a couple of feet away.

'Come on,' she whispered, trying to reassure herself as well as Julie. Her own breathing was heavy now.

She touched something cold and realized that it was the door handle. No light showed beneath. She could only guess at what lay beyond it. *More darkness?*

The lights flickered again and went out. Flashed on.

They enjoyed a few seconds of light, then blackness returned. But at the far end of the corridor there was illumination.

The two women were relieved to see light, until they realized that the door through which they'd entered was slightly open.

Had someone slipped into the corridor behind them while the lights were out?

Donna pushed Julie aside and raised the pistol, sighting it at the far end.

She could see nothing. No dark shape moving furtively in the shadows.

Nothing.

It appeared that they were alone in the corridor.

She turned back to face the next door.

Gripping the gun tightly, Donna took the handle and twisted it, pushing the door open. She stepped through.

Eighty-Nine

The flight of stone steps seemed to stretch away into the subterranean shadows. The bottom of the staircase was barely visible. Only the merest hint of sickly yellow light seeped upwards, barely penetrating the umbra.

Donna moved cautiously down the first few steps, glancing back to make sure Julie was following. She was, her face pale and drawn, ghost-like in the darkness.

She heard breathing, as she'd heard before.

This time it seemed louder, more pronounced, as if some invisible phantom were treading the steps with her. Donna swallowed hard, gripped the .357 more tightly and continued to descend.

The staircase was narrow. More than once she was forced to brush against the wall.

She shuddered with revulsion as she felt the cold stone pulsing. Like a gigantic brick heart it pumped against her. Even beneath her feet she felt a rhythmic movement.

She closed her eyes for a second, still not convinced it wasn't her mind playing tricks.

If only it had been.

Behind her Julie was looking down at her feet, being careful not to slip on the narrow steps. She too felt the thudding. Sweat beaded on her forehead despite the chill in the basement.

They were halfway down the stairs now, within sight of the bottom. Donna saw that it was a hallway similar to the one upstairs. Instead of being lit by chandeliers, however, this one was illuminated by the dull glow of three candles. Halos of subdued light flared from the small flames that flickered and threatened to blow out.

The breathing continued, but Donna was aware her own laboured exhalations were now adding to the sound that filled her ears.

In the silent blackness it seemed deafening.

They reached the bottom of the stairs. Julie looked round to check that no one had slipped through the door behind them, but it was so dark on the steps it was difficult to see anything at all. She stared at the sea of shadow, trying to spot any deviation in a wall of gloom, as if part of that false night might at any second detach itself.

She saw nothing.

Donna stood motionless, surveying the basement area.

The two women stood in an area roughly twelve feet square. Behind them was the staircase. To the right and left were solid walls; straight ahead, they faced three doors. Beside each stood a candle, helping to light the underground chamber.

Which door first?

She listened, trying to hear over the insistent breathing.

Christ, it was getting louder.

If Dashwood had been right about inanimate objects being given life, then they must be at the very centre of the house. It was, she imagined, like walking around inside a huge chest cavity. The infernal pulsing continued, too. Donna thought she could see undulations in the very umbra itself.

She felt perspiration on her palms, the metal and wood of the gun against her flesh. She shifted it to the other hand and wiped her palm on her jeans. She repeated the action with the other hand.

Which door?

She could hear no sound behind any of them. Could the basement also deserted, she wondered? But they had seen the smartly dressed man come down here. There was no other way out but through these three doors.

But which one?

She took a tentative step towards the one on the left, her eyes fixed on it.

The flame of the candle closest wavered, as if disturbed by a breeze. For a second it sputtered but then it flared again. A plume of black smoke rose into the darkness and was absorbed by it.

Donna took a step closer.

Behind her Julie watched, then advanced cautiously, her eyes darting back and forth between the three doors.

Donna was within two feet of the left-hand door.

It was then that the middle door opened.

Light and sound suddenly flooded into the darkened hallway. The figure silhouetted against the sudden explosion of brightness stood motionless, looking first at Julie, then at Donna.

His surprise lasted only seconds.

Peter Farrell reached for his gun.

Ninety

The movement was smooth and efficient.

Donna raised the .357, steadied herself and fired off two rounds.

The roar as the weapon spat out the high-calibre shells was intolerable in the confined space; both she and Julie were deafened by the thunderous retort. The muzzle-flashes seared white light onto their retinas and the stink of cordite filled the air.

The impact lifted Farrell off his feet. The first bullet struck him in the chest, the second hit him just below the chin.

He was slammed back against the wall, blood spouting from the wound in his throat. For long seconds he stood there, eyes gaping wide, his body twitching.

Donna fired again.

The third shot caught him in the face slightly to the left of his nose. The bullet drilled the eye socket empty, powered through the brain and exploded from the back of his skull, carrying a confetti of pulverized bone and sticky pinkish-red matter with it. Farrell pitched forward, what was left of his head smacking hard against the floor, blood pouring from the remnants of his blasted cranium.

Donna stepped over the body and into the room from which he'd emerged, her ears still ringing.

Julie followed, glancing down at the body as she passed.

The room beyond was large and well lit, particularly the area in the centre. It was there that Donna saw a naked man scramble to his feet, a look of horror on his face as he saw the gun. The woman beneath him, also naked, rolled over and tried to get up but she slipped, screaming in terror.

Donna saw perhaps a dozen men in the room, most dressed in suits. And instead of attacking her and Julie, they were fleeing.

A door at the far end of the room seemed to be their only means of escape. They rushed at it *en masse*, struggling with each other in their haste to get out.

Donna spun round, the gun levelled.

Dashwood and Parsons stood immobile at the head of a long table.

The Grimoire was on the table in front of them.

There was another thunderous roar of gunfire. Donna hurled herself to the ground as the bullet sang past her, slicing empty air before blasting a hole in the wall.

David Ryker got off two more rounds before Donna managed to return fire.

The room was filled with the massive sounds, thundercracks of noise that threatened to burst the eardrums.

The naked man ran towards Ryker.

He shot him.

Donna looked on in bewilderment as Ryker put two shots into the man's chest. She saw him hurled backwards by the impact, one shell erupting from his back close to the right scapula. Gobbets of lung tissue sprayed across the room as he fell.

The woman who had been with him went on screaming until Ryker shot her, too, one .45 slug in the head. It smashed in her temple as surely as if she'd been hit with a sledgehammer.

Donna fired and hit Ryker in the shoulder. He dropped his gun and clapped a hand to the wound, feeling jagged bone against his fingertip as his index finger slipped inside the hole.

'Get the book,' Donna shouted to Julie, who sprinted across the rapidly emptying room.

The other people who had been in the room had mostly scrambled through the door at the far end.

Julie picked up a chair and hurled it at Dashwood, who raised his arms to shield himself, falling back.

Parsons snatched at the Grimoire, catching Julie across the face with a swipe of his hand. She shouted in pain, feeling her bottom lip split under the impact.

Parsons gripped the book in his gnarled hands.

Donna stood up and fired at him.

The shot caught him in the left arm, tearing through the bicep.

Blood exploded from the wound, thick, dark blood that spattered the wall behind him.

He dropped the book and Julie made a grab for it, knocking it away, sending it skidding across the floor.

Parsons shouted something and leapt after it.

Donna drew a bead on him and fired.

The hammer slammed down on an empty chamber.

She threw the .357 away, pulling at the other shoulder holster, freeing the Beretta.

Parsons shouted in triumph as he reached the book but Donna swung the 92S into position and pumped the trigger.

One, two, three times she fired.

Parsons was hit in the chest and thigh. The third bullet missed and buried itself in the far wall.

Four, five, six.

The room had become like the inside of a cannon barrel, the noise incessant and deafening. Julie screamed but could not hear her own cry.

Parsons had fallen face down on the floor across the naked woman, his body torn and bleeding from the impact of the 9mm bullets. He reached out towards Donna, his fingers gradually twitching less and less.

He lay still.

Smoke hung like a gauze net across the room.

Julie, on her hands and knees, looked around for the Grimoire. Donna could see that the only living people left now were herself, her sister, Ryker, who was slumped against an overturned table holding his smashed shoulder, and Dashwood, who stood defiantly facing her.

Donna's breath came in gasps as she looked from one man to the other.

The floor was awash with blood from the dead man and woman and from Parsons.

The Grimoire lay in the centre of the floor.

A prize.

The trophy in a game of death.

No one moved.

The retorts of the guns still filled their ears, the muzzle-flashes still flamed in their eyes. But the room was all but silent.

Donna could see that Ryker's .45 was lying within two or three feet of him. She saw his eyes dart to one side.

He moved very slightly towards the weapon, still holding his shoulder. Blood was pumping through his fingers; every movement clearly brought him fresh agony, as the two pieces of his shattered clavicle grated together.

Nevertheless, if he could just reach the gun . . .

Donna shot him three times.

His body jerked as each bullet thudded into him, then he slid to one side and lay still, his chest and face covered in blood. It looked as if someone had upended him and dipped him in the crimson fluid.

Donna aimed the pistol at Dashwood.

Julie was crying softly now. Her hearing all but gone, her eyes stinging from the smoke, she could only watch helplessly as Donna and Dashwood faced each other.

He was smiling.

Ninety-One

'You should have been dead by now,' Dashwood told her. 'Both of you.'

Donna kept her eyes fixed on him and the automatic aimed at his head.

'What did you hope to gain by this little show?' The words were heavy with scorn. 'You think what's happened here tonight will make any difference? Do you think you can stop us? Your husband thought the same thing, and he ended up joining us.'

'No,' said Donna, shaking her head.

'Why do you find it so hard to believe?'

Dashwood asked. 'Did you know so little about him? Or were you too stupid?' He glared at her. 'He knew *this* place well enough. And our other meeting houses. He wanted our knowledge and he found it. He paid the price to be one of us. He abandoned *all* he believed in, all his morals, all his ethics. He had nothing left but us.'

'It's not true,' Donna said tearfully.

'He knew a woman called Suzanne Regan,' Dashwood said flatly, as if he were telling her something she didn't already know.

The surprise registered on her face and Dashwood saw it.

'True?' he continued.

She nodded.

'Do you know what she was? She was what this woman was to have been.' He nodded towards the corpse of the naked female at Donna's feet. 'She was a carrier. She had been for a number of our other members. And she was for your husband.' Dashwood held Donna's gaze. 'You said you had read the initiation rites. You knew of the fornication, the offering of a child, the need to keep that child's skull. Suzanne Regan carried a child for your husband. A child he then killed.'

Donna's body stiffened. She felt an icy coldness envelope her, as if she'd been wrapped in a freezing blanket.

'He knew he had to sacrifice a child as an offering to us,' Dashwood told her. 'He made Suzanne Regan pregnant. She knew what would happen to the baby, but it didn't bother her. She handed it over willingly, so your husband could kill it. He killed it in front of us, just as he had copulated with Suzanne Regan as we watched. He cut the child's head from its shoulders as we watched.' Dashwood shrugged. 'We welcomed him into our ranks and then he betrayed us. He stole the Grimoire and threatened to expose us, as I told you. He knew too much about us.'

'You're lying,' Donna said, wishing she could inject more conviction into her voice. She had lowered the gun slightly.

'You traced us, you learned about us. You know that every member of The Sons of Midnight entered his name in the Grimoire. Your husband's name is there. Look at it.'

He motioned towards the book.

Kill him.

'Go on, look,' he urged.

Kill him and destroy the book.

She had to know.

Donna moved towards the Grimoire and flipped it open. There were hundreds of names there, some faded from the passing of time.

'The last name,' Dashwood told her.

She turned a couple of pages and looked at the list.

'Oh God,' she whispered. She felt the freezing blanket being drawn tighter.

On the parchment-like paper she saw her husband's name, recognized his handwriting.

Donna took hold of the page and tore it out.

Dashwood shouted in pain, his teeth gritted, as he looked at the ripped-out page.

Donna folded it and pushed it into the back pocket of her jeans.

She tore out another page.

'No,' shouted Dashwood. A deep gash appeared above his left eyebrow, as if slashed by an invisible blade.

He lunged at Donna, trying to get hold of the book.

'Leave it, you bitch,' he roared.

She hurled the book away and fired at it, putting two bullets into the ancient tome.

To her surprise and horror, blood exploded from the book.

Dashwood screamed and clapped hands to his chest.

Blood was jetting from two wounds there.

Donna fired more shots into the book.

Pieces of it flew into the air, propelled by the dark blood pumping from it.

Dashwood dropped to his knees, holes appearing in his leg and stomach.

More of the crimson fluid spilled over his lips. He turned to face Donna.

'You know the truth now,' he grimaced, teeth clenched, bloodied. 'Search your house. The cellar.' His eyes blazed. 'He was one of us,' he roared.

Donna shot him in the face as he knelt in front of her.

He raised his hands towards her and she saw

the skin beginning to yellow, to peel away from his fingertips. A nail came free, pus and blood spewing from the digit. Huge pieces of flesh began to curl away from his cheeks, leaving the network of muscles beneath exposed. One eye burst in its socket. Dark fluid began to run from both his nostrils and suddenly the room was filled with an overpowering stench of decay, a nauseating odour that made the two women feel sick.

Dashwood clapped his hands to his face and pulled them away dripping. Flesh was liquefying on his bones, the bones themselves crumbling.

In a corner of the room the Grimoire was dissolving into a seething puddle of reeking muck, a gelatinous mess that looked like the contents of a huge, freshly milked boil.

Dashwood fell forward and his body seemed to fold in on itself, his chest collapsing, lungs transformed into reeking sacks which burst, spilling more black fluid into the cavity of the torso. His legs seemed to shrivel, shrinking up inside his trousers, already stained with blood.

Donna finally managed to stagger away from the sight. Julie followed.

They headed for the door through which they'd entered, hurdling the body of Farrell, aware now that the breathing that had been ever-present since they entered the house had stopped.

Blood oozed from the walls.

All the way up the flight of stone steps and along that corridor the dark fluid coursed down the plaster and stone.

They burst free into the hallway, then through into the room beyond, and struggled out of the window by which they'd first entered.

The cool night air washed over them but could not drive the stench of decay from their nostrils.

Julie was already running for the alleyway that ran alongside the house. Donna took one look back at the building, then ran after her.

The wailing of sirens already filled the air.

It would be a matter of minutes before the first police car arrived.

Ninety-Two

From where they sat they could see the uniformed men approaching the house in Conduit Street. Donna watched them scrambling out of their cars, running towards the front door. Others headed off up the alley at the side of the building.

She watched impassively, her mind blank, her eyes devoid of emotion. She felt as if every last ounce of feeling had been sucked from her. She was drained, incapable of movement let alone rational thought.

And yet still Dashwood's words echoed in her mind:

'*He was one of us*.'

She lowered her head momentarily and closed her eyes.

'The police will be looking.'

Julie's voice seemed a million miles away.

Donna raised her head and looked at her sister.

'The police will be looking for whoever killed those men,' the younger woman continued.

'They won't be looking for *us*,' Donna said.

Julie gazed at her for long moments.

'Are you satisfied now?' she said finally.

Donna didn't speak.

'They're dead. You've got what you wanted. How does it feel?'

'We have to go back to the cottage,' Donna said quietly. 'Dashwood said I'd find the truth in the cellar. Only the cottage has a cellar. We have to go back and look there.'

'Not *we*, Donna. *You*. I'm finished. I'm leaving now. If you want to stop me, you'll have to kill me.' There were tears in Julie's eyes.

Donna looked wearily at the younger woman.

'I wanted to hate you for this,' she said softly. 'For what you did. For taking Chris from me.'

'I didn't take him,' Julie protested.

'I know he didn't leave me, but like I said to you before, you shared part of his life. A life that should have been just mine and his. And I *do* hate you.' She felt her own tears beginning to run warmly down her cheeks. A bitter smile creased her face.

'You'll never see me again, Donna, I promise you,' Julie said, wiping her eyes. She opened the car door.

'You think I'd just let you walk away?'

'What else are you going to do? I'm sorry. Believe that, at least. I *am* sorry for what I did.'

Julie held her sister's gaze for a moment, then moved to pull herself out of the car.

'I can't let you walk away, Julie,' Donna said almost apologetically.

'You can't stop me,' the younger woman said, and swung herself out of the car.

Donna slid her hand inside her jacket and pulled out the Beretta, keeping the pistol low, aimed at Julie's stomach.

She shook her head, tears streaming down her face.

A look of fear flickered behind Julie's eyes.

'You're right,' Donna said, her voice cracking. 'It *is* all over.'

Donna turned the gun round quickly, bent her head forward and opened her mouth.

She pushed the barrel into her mouth and squeezed the trigger.

Ninety-Three

Julie wanted to scream but the sight of her sister with the pistol jammed in her mouth seemed to freeze her vocal cords.

Instead she made a frantic grab for the Beretta as Donna fired.

The hammer slammed down on an empty chamber.

The metallic click reverberated inside the car as Julie tore the pistol from her grip and stood panting beside her.

Donna merely looked at the younger woman, then leaned across and pulled the passenger door shut.

Julie looked down helplessly at the gun she now held in her hand.

'Donna, I . . .'

The sentence trailed off, lost in the sound of the Fiesta's engine as Donna started it up.

She guided the car away from the kerb, away from Julie. As she pulled away she glanced one final time in the rear-view mirror.

Julie was standing on the street corner, the empty gun clutched in her hand.

Donna drove on.

The journey became a blur of passing traffic and dark roads.

She didn't look at the clock when she left London; she had no idea how long it would take her to reach the cottage. Donna merely drove, her mind spinning. Two or three times she had to brake sharply to avoid hitting vehicles in front of her. She considered stopping at a service station for a coffee, but then decided against it. If she stopped she'd never start again. It was as if she was being forced on by instinct alone. All she felt was a crushing weariness, a similar feeling to the one she'd felt in the days after her husband's death. A feeling that she had become an empty shell, sucked dry of feeling, unable to think straight.

She stopped for petrol, standing on a deserted forecourt, the cold wind whistling around her. She shivered but the chill she felt came from within.

She had achieved her goal. Parsons and Dashwood were dead. Farrell was dead.

Why then did she not feel a sense of triumph?

Perhaps because she felt that she *too* should be dead.

All she felt was a growing feeling of desolation. Death and loss had become engrained in her life.

She had no one now.

She thought how easy it would have been to drive the car into a tree. She gripped the wheel more tightly and drove through the night.

Ninety-Four

It seemed like years, not days, since she'd been to the cottage.

The assault on the property, which could have cost her and Julie their lives, seemed to have faded into the mists of time. Supposedly the mind pushes unpleasant things to one side in an effort to forget them. Donna had tried to do that with the events at the cottage, but as soon as she saw the building the memories came flooding back in an unwelcome tide.

She sat in the Fiesta gazing at the structure. Even in the darkness she could see bullet holes in the stonework. The wood she'd used to board up the windows was still in place, although a couple of the sheets had come loose. One was slapping against the frame each time the wind blew.

Donna slid out from behind the wheel and approached the cottage, fumbling in her pocket for her key-ring. She selected the front door key, pausing for a moment before turning it, images of her last visit running through her mind like a video recorder on fast-forward. She could see Farrell and his men trying to break in. She could see the blood. She could see Julie.

Julie.

Donna closed her eyes tightly, then took a deep breath. The image faded slightly. She entered.

There was broken glass in the hallway, still. It crunched beneath her feet as she walked, moving through into the sitting-room, not bothering to turn on the lights. She moved quickly and assuredly in the gloom, heading for the kitchen.

There was a torch in one of the kitchen drawers. She retrieved it, flicking it on, allowing the powerful beam to cut through the blackness.

She trained it on the cellar trap door.

'*Search your house. The cellar.*'

Donna hooked a finger into the ring on the trap and pulled, opening it. She shone the torch down into the underground chamber, ignoring the smell of damp that wafted up from below. She tucked the torch into the waistband of her jeans as she eased herself onto the ladder, climbing down slowly, afraid, as she'd always been, that the wooden rungs would give way. A spider's web brushed against her face as she neared the bottom. Donna snatched at it, anxious to brush it away. The floor of the cellar was partly earth; it was the damp soil that she could smell so strongly.

Donna took the torch from her jeans and shone it around.

The cellar was less than fifteen feet square but it was crammed with tea chests and boxes, some of which were damp and mildewed. Spiders' webs seemed to link the boxes like membranous skin. She shuddered as she looked around. It was the first time she'd had a proper look inside the underground room; already she felt a sense of claustrophobia. Nevertheless she moved towards the first pile of packing cases, rummaging through them, not really sure what she was looking for but fearing what she might find.

The boxes were mostly full of old newspaper, which had been used as padding around items of value. There didn't seem to be much else lurking in there.

She heard a noise from above her and froze.

Instinctively she switched off the torch, standing completely still in the cloying darkness, her heart thudding against her ribs.

Whatever it was appeared to be coming from the sitting-room, above her to the left.

She heard it again.

Donna suddenly realized the source of the disturbance.

It was a piece of wood banging against a window-frame, blown by the wind.

Flicking the torch back on she continued her search, checking more boxes, feeling her feet sinking into the earthen floor. The dirt stuck to her trainers. She muttered to herself, scraping the sticky mud off against a wooden box.

Her efforts to remove the earth caused the box to topple over and Donna saw, beneath where it had stood, a piece of metal; a sheet of rusted iron about a foot square, only part of it showing through the dark earth. She aimed the torch at it, then dropped to her knees and began pulling at the clods. The odour of damp was thick and noxious but she continued with her task, finally exposing the metal sheet.

It was covering a small hole.

Donna laid the torch beside the hole, slipped her fingers under the sheet of iron and lifted, flipping it over.

She snatched the torch up again and shone it down into the hole.

The object inside was small, perhaps twice the size of a man's fist, and wrapped in plastic.

Her heart beat faster as she reached for it.

Leave it. Go now. Walk away forever.

She hesitated a moment.

Get out now and never return.

Donna had to know. She snatched up the

object, pulling the plastic from it like a child would unwrap a Christmas present.

The skull was unmistakably that of a baby.

Parts of it were not even completely formed. The fontanelles had not yet joined.

The child must have been very young indeed.

Days old when . . .

When it was killed?

She dropped the skull and closed her eyes, tears beginning to form behind her lids. When she looked down again the skull had fallen back into the hole, the eye sockets gazing sightlessly up at her.

'*He was one of us*.'

She sat down on the wet earth, the torch still gripped in one hand, tears coursing down her cheeks.

Donna felt something digging into her backside and realized that she still had the folded pages of the Grimoire stuffed in there.

Including the page which bore her husband's name.

She pulled it out slowly and unfolded it, shining the light over the other names on the list.

Other members of The Sons of Midnight.

'*They have infiltrated everywhere*.'

Donna read the first of the names.

'Oh, Christ,' she murmured.

She heard the creaking above her, spun round and looked up.

There was a torch beam shining in *her* face

now, held by the figure on the edge of the cellar opening.

It was Detective Constable David Mackenzie.

Ninety-Five

'Come up here, Mrs Ward, and bring the pages from the book with you.'

Mackenzie's words seemed to echo inside the small cellar.

As Donna looked more closely, she saw that he was holding a gun, too. The .38 glinted in the torchlight.

Without a second thought she began to climb the steps, the pages of the Grimoire held in her hand. There was no point in trying to run. Where the hell was she going to go?

She pulled herself out of the cellar and stood facing him, noticing that he'd taken a step back, that the pistol was levelled at her.

'You're part of it,' she said flatly.

'Drop the pages on the floor in front of you and step back,' Mackenzie told her.

She did as instructed, tossing the parchment away as if it was infected with some vile disease.

Mackenzie picked the discarded paper up without taking his eyes off her. He stuffed the pages into the pocket of his coat. He moved away from her again.

'You knew right from the beginning,' she said. 'You knew that first night at the hospital when I came to identify Chris. You were a part of it then. *You're* one of them, aren't you?'

The policeman smiled thinly.

'One of who, Mrs Ward?' he said.

'The Sons of Midnight, or whatever the hell they call themselves.'

'You saw some of the other names on the list,' he said. 'You can't even begin to imagine how far this goes. Who *is* involved. How high up it goes. You've only scratched the surface. I'm a *very* small part of it but there are others who must be protected until the time is right. Your husband knew that, too. He knew who was involved, how important some of the higher ranking members were.'

'That's why you killed him?'

'I told you, his death was an accident.' The policeman smiled. 'Perhaps he was lucky. He died before we got to him.'

'And now it's my turn?'

'Why should I kill you?'

'I've seen the names on the list. I know what's going on.'

'You've seen some of the names, but you have no idea of what's going on. You can't begin to imagine what is going on and who else is involved. Like I said, you couldn't begin to imagine how high this thing goes.'

'*No one can be trusted.*'

'Who would you go to with your revelations? The press? Television?' There was a mocking tone in his voice. 'Who'd believe you?'

He backed towards the kitchen door, the gun still levelled at her.

'Everything you've done has been for nothing,' he told her. 'You wasted your time.'

Donna watched as he opened the door, then stepped outside into the night. She heard his footsteps in the mud beyond, heard a car engine start up, the vehicle pull away.

She walked through to the sitting-room and peered through a crack in the boarded-up window, watching the car's rear lights disappearing into the gloom.

The package was standing on the table.

Donna saw it. Saw the small red lights winking on it.

She smelled something.

A sickly sweet smell that reminded her of marzipan.

Her husband had once told her that plastic explosive smelled like marzipan.

She guessed that the bomb was about fifty pounds.

There were two red lights on it, and one of them had begun to flicker madly.

Donna took a step towards it.

In the back of the Orion, Mackenzie pressed the red button on the small control panel.

The explosion was thunderous.

Even seventy yards from the cottage the car was showered with debris.

Mackenzie didn't bother to look back; he merely slid the control panel back inside his jacket and nodded to his driver.

The car moved off, swallowed by the night.

'Whom God wishes to destroy, he first
makes mad . . .'

Euripides.

Nemesis

For Belinda

with love

August 15, 1940

They were getting closer.

There was no doubt about it.

The rumbling which filled the subterranean corridor seemed to emanate from every brick, swelling around him like an approaching storm.

George Lawrenson knew that the tunnel which he now hurried along was at least seventy feet beneath the pavements of Whitehall, but still the reverberations rocked him as he walked. Flecks of dust floated from the ceiling every now and then, tiny pieces of plaster, dislodged by the incessant shaking detached themselves and fell like solid snow. Lawrenson wiped some of the dust from his jacket as he walked, looking up as the lights flickered once.

Below ground there was light. On the surface all was darkness.

The peculiar reversal of roles, the dislocation of normality which everyone had been living through for the last few weeks was illustrated perfectly by this particular example, Lawrenson thought. Where there should be blackness there was light. Where street lights should be burning there was gloom.

The only light on the surface was that which came from the fires.

From the incendiary bombs which the Luftwaffe dropped. From the blazing wreckage of houses and factories.

It had been like this every night for the past two weeks

and no one knew how much longer it would go on. The skies above London were full of German planes, pouring bombs onto the capital, transforming it into a gigantic torch which flared with the flames of a thousand fires.

Lawrenson walked on, the file gripped firmly in his right hand. He turned a corner and proceeded down another long corridor. Above him the lights dimmed briefly then flared into life once more.

The bombs were falling on the embankment now.

Coming closer.

How many would emerge from the relative safety of the underground stations the following morning to discover that their houses no longer existed? That the places they had called homes had been reduced to piles of blackened brick.

Every night they poured down the steps and onto the platforms of the stations, there to spend the night sleeping or lying awake listening to the pounding from above. Then, the following morning they would emerge from below ground like a human tidal wave.

Like souls let loose from hell.

Only they were climbing the stairs *into* hell.

Into streets cratered by bombs, littered with human remains and obliterated vehicles.

But, for now, they were below ground like so many rabbits and all they could do was wait and hope. And pray.

Lawrenson thought briefly about his own wife as he strode along the corridor. His home was in the country, about forty miles from the capital. Unlike others, he was reasonably sure she was safe. He spoke to her by phone every evening and she had told him that she had seen the crimson glow which came from the city. She had told him she was frightened. Afraid for his safety. But, every night he told her not to worry then he retreated below ground like some kind of be-suited troglodyte, there to sit out the fury which Hitler's air force unleashed with the coming of night.

The rumbling grew louder and the lights dimmed once again but this time Lawrenson walked on without slowing his pace. He held the file close to his chest, as if protecting it from the tiny pieces of debris that fell from the ceiling.

As he turned the corner the two figures seemed to loom from the walls themselves and, despite himself, Lawrenson faltered.

He nodded a cursory greeting towards the first of the uniformed men then reached inside his jacket for his security pass. He held it up for inspection, allowing the senior of the two men to scrutinise the small photo which adorned the pass. He glanced at the picture then at Lawrenson as if to reassure himself that the man who stood before him was indeed who his pass declared him to be. Satisfied with that fact, the soldier turned towards the door, knocked once then stepped back, ushering Lawrenson through.

On the other side he was greeted by a third uniformed man. An officer.

The military man nodded affably and then returned to the table to his left where he and two other men were gathered around a map which was spread out before them.

Maps covered the wall too. The room was about twenty feet square and it seemed that every single inch of wall space was covered by maps and diagrams. Lawrenson spotted one which showed the British army's withdrawal to Dunkirk.

The room smelt of coffee and cigarette smoke and he waved a hand before him as if to dispel the odour. The men inside the room glanced quizzically at him, those who hadn't seen him before, others who knew him nodded greetings. No one smiled.

Lawrenson brushed a stray hair from his forehead and approached the large table which was set in the centre of the room. Two men stood behind it, looking down at yet another map. As Lawrenson approached they both looked up and the elder of the two nodded deferentially. He glanced at the file which Lawrenson held, watching as it was laid before him.

Others now gathered around the table, as if the file were acting as some kind of magnet, drawing them from all corners of the room. But only the older man sat, rubbing his eyes briefly then re-adjusting his glasses.

Outside, the earth shook as another shower of bombs fell.

Inside the subterranean Headquarters Winston Churchill began to read the contents of the file marked 'Genesis'.

One

The car came within inches of his motorbike and Gary Sinclair swerved violently to avoid being struck by the speeding vehicle.

'You stupid bastard!' he bellowed at the retreating tail lights but, in seconds, the car had disappeared around a bend in the road, swallowed up by the night.

Gary sucked in a deep breath, both shocked and angered by the near miss. Hadn't the driver seen him? Maybe the stupid sod was pissed. Either way it had been a close thing. Another couple of inches and he'd have been off. The bike juddered beneath him as if sharing his apprehension and, instinctively, he glanced down at the fuel gauge. The needle was almost touching red, the tank close to being empty. Gary muttered to himself and eased off slightly on the throttle. Perhaps, he thought, if he took it steadily, he'd get home before the bike packed up on him. When he'd taken it for a couple of test runs he'd been sure that the fuel tank was leaking but his brother, who'd sold him the bike, had assured him there was nothing to worry about.

Nothing to worry about, Gary thought irritably, glancing down once more at the gauge. He had another five miles to go before he reached Hinkston, he doubted if he'd make it.

As if to reinforce his doubts the bike slowed noticeably and refused to speed up even when he twisted the throttle violently. The engine spluttered dismally then died. Gary instinctively allowed his left foot to drop to the ground to steady himself as the Kawasaki came to a halt.

He grunted in annoyance and swung himself off the saddle. Then, propping the bike up against the hedge which ran along the roadside, he pulled his helmet off and glared at the bike. He drew his fingers through his shoulder length brown hair and squatted down beside the 750. Inspections, mechanical or otherwise, seemed somewhat pointless at this stage, he thought after a moment. He was stuck five miles from home. There was nothing else to do but wheel the bloody bike back into town. He pulled a packet of cigarettes from one of the side pockets of his leather jacket and lit one, allowing the smoke to burn its way to his lungs, then he took hold of the handlebars and guided the bike away from the hedge, the helmet hanging from the throttle.

A strong breeze had blown up in the last hour or so and it caused Gary's hair to flap around his face like so many writhing snakes. He pulled some strands from his mouth, cursing his brother once more for selling him the bike. It would take him more than an hour to walk into Hinkston from his present location and the weight of the bike made that journey all the more uncomfortable. He stopped every few hundred yards and drew in a couple of deep breaths.

The wind was keen and he was glad he wore a sweatshirt beneath his jacket. However, pushing the bike kept him warm, it was just his face that felt cold.

On both sides of him trees bowed as the wind grew in strength. The moon had retreated behind a bank of thick cloud. The road was dark, flanked by tall hedges beyond which stood the trees that rattled their branches almost mockingly at him. Low hills rose to his right, masking the approaches to the town of Hinkston, hiding the glow of street lights and making it seem as if he were much further than five miles from the town. He glanced down at his watch and saw that it was almost 12.15 a.m. And he had to be up at six in the morning. He cursed his brother once more. He'd be lucky to reach home before 1.30 at this rate. Four hours sleep if he was lucky – Christ, he'd be wrecked by tomorrow. He thought about ringing in and saying he was ill but he decided against that. The job at the bakery was the first he'd had since leaving school two years earlier. Jobs weren't easy to come by and he couldn't afford to be choosy. An eighteen year old with two CSE's and negligible work experience wasn't exactly an employer's dream.

He guided the motorbike around a bend in the road, kicking several tree branches aside. The wind must have been stronger than he thought. It whistled through the tall hedges, a shrill banshee wail. Gary trudged on, now feeling quite warm from the effort of pushing the Kawasaki.

The car was parked about two hundred yards ahead of him.

There was a kind of makeshift lay-by, little more than a gap in the right hand hedge with a muddy verge before it but the vehicle was standing motionless there, lights on, smoke rising from its exhaust.

Gary smiled thinly to himself. Maybe the driver would give him a lift into Hinkston. He could wedge the 750 into the boot. Surely the bloke wouldn't mind. He increased his pace in an effort to reach the car before it pulled away.

There was something familiar about it.

Something . . .

He was about fifty yards away when he realised it was the same car that had almost forced him into the hedge further back on the road.

Gary felt the anger rise within him briefly but he fought it back. If the driver was willing to give him a lift then the previous aberration could be overlooked. He might mention it in passing, just as a joke. But, he reasoned, why make an issue out of it?

He drew closer to the car and heard the engine idling in the stillness of the night.

Maybe the driver wasn't alone. He might have his girlfriend in there with him. Maybe he'd pulled over for a quick one. Gary chuckled then shook his head. If they were romping about on the back seat the driver wasn't likely to have left his engine running and all his lights on.

The dull purring of the car engine continued to fill the otherwise noiseless night.

The wind had slackened slightly although the tree branches still swayed as if pulled by invisible strings.

Gary rolled his bike up to within twenty feet of the car and peered into the vehicle.

It was empty.

The bloke must have nipped behind the hedge for a slash, he thought, moving closer. He'd just wait until he came back then ask for a lift.

Gary leant the bike against the hedge and walked closer to the car, admiring the sleek bodywork, deciding that he would start saving up for driving lessons. He liked the bike but a car had more class. He walked around it, patting the bonnet as if he were inspecting the car with a view to purchase.

The engine continued to purr.

Gary glanced behind him towards the hedge, wondering where the driver could have got to. He sighed and continued with his tour of inspection of the vehicle, sliding his hand almost unconsciously to one of the handles.

The door opened as he pulled.

He frowned.

This was weird, he thought. It was bad enough leaving all the lights on and the engine running but to leave the car unlocked too? The driver was either very trusting or very stupid. Gary tried the rear door.

That too was unlocked.

He walked around to the driver's side and tried that door as well.

Not surprisingly he found it unlocked.

The car moved.

Only a matter of inches but the motion was enough to startle Gary who took a step back, realising that the handbrake must be off. The car came to a halt a couple of inches further on, engine still ticking over. Gary stepped forward again, reaching for the handle, deciding he'd at least reach inside and pull up the handbrake, stop the car rolling down the slight hill which sloped away ahead of it. He reached for the door.

Hands gripped the back of his head.

He felt uncontrollable force and strength at the base of his skull as two strong hands fixed themselves around his neck, fingers digging into his throat.

Taken by surprise he was helpless, unable to stop himself as the hands forced him forward with incredible speed, slamming his head into the driver's side window of the car.

The impact opened a hairline cut across his forehead and a thin trickle of blood oozed down his face.

As he shouted in pain and surprise, he felt himself being propelled forward a second time, with even more force.

His face was driven into the top of the car door and he felt searing agony fill his head as two of his front teeth were shattered, one of them forced backwards into his tongue. Blood filled his mouth and spilled down his chin as he tried to twist, to fight off his attacker.

But his hidden assailant was taking full advantage of Gary's helplessness and another sickening contact with the car roof splintered two more of the youth's teeth and chipped the bone of his lower jaw. He tried to scream but the pain had already driven him to the edge of consciousness. As the hands relaxed their grip on the back of his neck, Gary Sinclair fell across the bonnet of the car then slid to the ground, his vision clouded by agony. He rolled onto his back on the muddy verge, looking up at his attacker who stood over him for brief seconds then knelt beside him, grabbing a handful of his hair, lifting his bloodied face as if to inspect the damage.

It was then that Gary saw the knife.

The blade was about ten inches long. Slightly thicker than a knitting needle.

Gary opened his mouth, moaning as he felt fresh waves of pain from his smashed jaw. He tried to squirm away from the hand which held him so firmly but it was useless.

The point of the knife actually brushed his upper eyelid and he felt his bowels loosen as fear overcame him.

The wickedly sharp point of the knife punctured the bulging orb of his right eye effortlessly.

It was pushed with no haste. It wasn't driven into the writhing boy's eye, it was *inserted* with a kind of sadistic precision.

And now he did find the breath to scream but the frantic bellow was cut off abruptly as two more inches of the blade disappeared into his eye socket, pushed with an even pressure.

Two inches.

Three.

Four.

Vitreous liquid spurted onto his cheek, mingling with the blood which already covered his skin.

The eye seemed to burst like a water-filled balloon. The white turned red and the orb seemed to collapse in upon itself as the blade was pushed deeper. One final surge of pressure and it punctured the frontal lobe of the brain.

Gary Sinclair shuddered then lay still.

The knife was pulled free then the driver of the car calmly unlocked the boot and pushed it open.

It took only a moment to lift Gary's body and push it

unceremoniously into the rear compartment of the vehicle. The lid was slammed down and the driver walked unhurriedly around to the door, slid behind the wheel and guided the vehicle back out onto the road.

Once again, the tail lights were swallowed by the blackness.

Two

It looked as if someone had been shading beneath her eyes with charcoal.

Susan Hacket looked at the reflection which stared back at her from the mirror and sighed. She picked up the brush which lay on the dressing table and swept it through her hair, listening to the static electricity crackling. She fluffed up her shaggy locks with her fingertips then reached for her make-up. She plucked a brush from the hand-shaped container on her left and began applying foundation to the pale visage which confronted her. The brushes and the make-up had been a present for her twenty-fifth birthday, just seven months earlier. But, at the moment, she felt a hundred and twenty-five.

Susan sighed again, tiring of her own efforts to brighten her appearance. She got to her feet, crossed the landing to the bathroom and washed the foundation off, towelling her face dry, glancing at herself in the bathroom mirror this time.

She was grateful that she didn't feel as rough as she looked.

Even the ravages of so much worry, so many sleepless

nights, could not hide her natural attractiveness. She rarely wore heavy make-up. People were always telling her she didn't need it. But, in the last couple of months she had taken to wearing it on these nightly visits. Taken to making an effort. He had always liked her in make-up before, had always complimented her on her appearance. What reason was there to stop? Just because . . .

She splashed her face with more water, dried it a second time then returned to the bedroom where she hastily but expertly applied some mascara and eye-liner. The dark smudges beneath her eyes didn't look too bad she told herself. A few good nights' sleep and they would vanish. Exactly when those nights would come she had no idea.

She pulled on a sweatshirt and jeans, stepped into a pair of short suede boots and headed back out onto the landing once more. The door directly opposite her was slightly ajar. Sue crossed to it and moved silently into the room, careful not to collide with the half-a-dozen mobiles which hung from the ceiling. Snow White and the Seven Dwarfs. Dumbo. Postman Pat. All swayed gently in the slight breeze which wafted through the window. Sue rubbed her hands together, thinking how cold it was turning. She crossed to the window and closed it, pressing a hand to the radiator as she stepped away.

She moved close to the bed and crouched down beside it, pulling the sheet back from the tiny sleeping form cocooned within it.

Lisa Hacket lay still as her mother gently brushed some strands of fine, silver-blonde hair from her face. Then Sue leant across and kissed her four-year-old daughter on the cheek.

'I love you,' she whispered, then slowly straightened up and crept out of the room.

At the foot of the stairs she picked up her handbag and

jacket then popped her head round the door of the sitting room.

'I'm off now, Caroline,' she said, smiling. 'I'll be back in a couple of hours.'

From the sofa, Caroline Fearns turned and smiled. A bright, pretty, sixteen-year-old with uncomfortably large breasts, she nodded and smiled broadly at Sue.

'I really am sorry I had to call you at such short notice,' Sue said. 'But John's got a meeting at the school and I'm not sure what time he'll be back. If he gets back before me could you tell him I've left some food in the oven for him, please?'

Caroline nodded briskly, smiled again then turned her attention back to the TV screen. She enjoyed baby-sitting for the Hacket's. They paid her well and they had a colour TV as well as a video. Her own father refused to buy a colour TV despite the fact that, during snooker matches, he spent the entire time complaining about not being able to figure out which balls the players were trying to pot. But besides the money and the TV there was an added bonus. Mr Hacket always insisted on taking her home in his car after the baby-sitting was over. Caroline found him unbearably sexy (even though he *was* pushing thirty). She wished *her* English teacher looked like him.

She heard the front door close and glanced at her watch.

6.35 p.m.

She'd wait until the soap opera she was watching had finished then she'd make a cup of tea. She stretched out contentedly on the sofa.

As Sue stepped out into the night she shivered. The wind whistled around her and she pulled up the collar of her jacket as she headed for her car, fumbling in her handbag for the keys. She slid behind the wheel of the Metro and started the engine, checking her reflection briefly in the rear-view mirror. Cheerful enough? No cracks in the mask?

She pulled away, making a note to stop off at the garage and get some flowers.

Flowers were so important.

They saw her leave.

Hidden by the darkness, sitting in the car parked about fifty yards down the street, they watched her as she pulled away.

6.38 p.m.

One of them glanced at the house, at the light burning in the front room.

They would wait a little longer.

Three

He heard the thud from above and squinted at the ceiling, as if expecting it to cave in. But no cracks appeared, there was no rending of beams or crashing of concrete. The ceiling remained as unblemished now as it had been ten minutes ago when he'd first fixed his eyes on the spot above his head.

John Hacket draped one arm across his forehead, catching sight of his watch in the process. The ticking sounded thunderous in the relative silence of the bedroom. As even as his own low breathing.

'Penny for your thoughts.'

The voice came from beside him, a slight Irish lilt to it.

Hacket turned his head slowly to look at Nikki Reeves.

She was looking at him with those large brown eyes, fixing him in the kind of gaze which had first drawn him to her. There were a thousand clichés for those eyes, for that look. *Come to bed eyes. Hypnotic glances.*

Hacket almost laughed.

How about, *Screw me and to hell with your wife eyes?*

She asked him again, brushing hair from her face.

'What are you thinking about?'

Hacket shook his head dismissively, watching as she raised herself up onto one elbow to look down on him. Her right hand rested on his chest, her index finger tracing patterns across his skin. He could smell her perfume. He knew the smell well. He should do, he'd bought it for her. The delicate aroma mingled with the stronger musky scent of their own post-coital exertions.

'What makes you think I've got something on my mind?' Hacket asked her, raising one finger and gently running it along her bottom lip.

She flicked out her tongue and licked the tip of the probing digit.

'Because you're quiet,' she said, smiling.

He shrugged.

'Be thankful for small mercies.'

Hacket lay still while she continued stroking his chest, only now his eyes were on her, taking in the details of her face and upper body. The sheet had slipped down to reveal her breasts, the nipples still erect. He looked at her face and, again, found himself lost in those eyes. His finger strayed from her lips and he took to stroking her cheek, enjoying the smoothness of her skin. And, all the time he could smell her perfume. It was one of the things which had first attracted him to her. The fact that she was good-looking had seemed almost secondary. Romance begins in many different ways and Hacket could think of a thousand more clichés to describe that particular peculiarity which men and women put so much faith in. But he knew that this was not romance. It was an affair. Pure and simple.

He almost smiled again at the irony of that phrase. There was nothing pure about it and simplicity was rapidly eroded when a man took a lover.

She was twenty-two, eight years younger than Hacket. The affair had been going on for the past three months. Ever since . . .

He tried to push the thought from his mind but it persisted.

Ever since Sue's father had become ill.

Hacket wondered if he was trying to justify his actions to himself. Even trying to shift the blame for his indiscretions onto his wife.

Her father was dying. She was worried. She hadn't enough time for Hacket so he'd found a lover. There, he thought, bitterly, it *was* simple when you thought it through.

Nikki leant across him and pressed her lips to his. He felt her tongue flicking urgently against his teeth then it slipped inside his mouth, stirring the warm wetness. Hacket responded fiercely and when they finally separated both were breathing heavily. He could feel her nipples pressing into his chest, his own erection now nudging her belly as she lay closer to him.

After a moment or two she pulled herself across him and sat on the side of the bed.

'Was it something I said?' he asked, watching as she got to her feet and reached for a baggy T-shirt on the chair nearby.

She smiled and slipped it on, the voluminous folds hiding her shapely figure as she padded towards the door. She paused there, silhouetted by the soft light which was spilling from the sitting room.

'I'm hungry,' she told him. 'Do you want something?'

He shook his head.

'No thanks I'll . . .' He coughed. 'I'm fine.'

I'll have something to eat when I get home. I'll eat the food that my wife has prepared for me, Hacket thought. He exhaled deeply, almost angrily, and sat up, reaching for his cigarettes, pulling the packet from the pocket of his trousers. He lit a Dunhill and sucked hard on it. Sue would be at the hospital by now, he thought, glancing at his watch. The nightly vigil. Christ, why did she torture herself like that? Every single bloody night she was at the hospital. He blew out a stream of smoke watching it dissipate slowly in the air. And how much longer was it going to last? No one knew, no one could tell her. The same way no one could tell *him* how long his affair with Nikki was going to continue. Nagging doubts at the back of his mind told him he should end it now. But the doubts only came when he was at home, when he was away from her. When he was with her the desire to end the relationship wasn't so pressing. He didn't love her, that much he knew, but he felt for her more strongly than he should have done. She filled a gap in his life, a gap which should never have been there to begin with. Was he blaming Sue again? The role of neglected, misunderstood husband didn't suit him particularly well.

How about husband who's feeling sorry for himself?

Hacket took another drag on the cigarette.

How about unfeeling, selfish bastard? That seemed to suit him perfectly.

Hacket's philosophical musings were interrupted by Nikki's return. She was carrying a glass of milk and a plate with a couple of hastily-made sandwiches stacked on it.

She shivered, commented how cold it was in the kitchen then sat down on the bed beside him and took a bite from one of the sandwiches.

'Pig,' he said, watching her as she ate.

'Oink, oink,' she replied, giggling.

He snaked an arm around her waist and drew her closer to him, kissing her ear. She put down the sandwich, kissed him lightly on the tip of the nose then reached for the glass of milk. She took a mouthful but didn't swallow it. Instead she leant closer to him, the white liquid staining her lips. As she kissed him he opened his mouth and allowed her to pass some of the milk to him. When they parted she was smiling broadly. She allowed one hand to drop to his thigh, stroking the hair which grew so thickly there. Then her fingers were exploring higher, her nails gently raking his scrotum before gliding around his stiffening penis.

'I'll have to go soon,' he whispered as she gripped his shaft more tightly, working up a rhythm, coaxing him to full hardness.

'Soon,' she breathed in his ear.

They lay back across the bed, bodies entwined.

Four

The houses in this particular part of Clapham all looked similar. Terraced and semi-detached, inhabited by unremarkable people with unremarkable lives.

People like John and Susan Hacket.

It was their home which the men in the grey Ford Escort had been watching for the last twenty minutes.

As if some kind of silent signal had been given both of them swung themselves out of the car and walked unhurriedly up the path towards the passageway which led towards the back garden of the Hacket's house. The street lamp outside the house was off, and it afforded the two men the cover they needed. The curtains of the houses on either side were drawn. It was too late in the day for people to be peering out checking on callers. A couple of doors down a dog barked but the two men paid it no heed. The first of them, a tall man with what seemed like abnormally long arms, gently lifted the catch on the passage door and opened it.

His companion followed him into the enveloping gloom.

The passage was about fifteen feet long, the floor of chipped concrete. The two men moved cautiously along the narrow walkway, careful not to create any noise as they made their way to the back of the house.

The garden was in darkness.

A rusted tricycle stood close by and the first man pushed it with his foot, ignoring the protesting squeal from its wheels. He smiled broadly and looked at his companion but the other man was already trying the back door, finding, not surprisingly, that it was locked.

The knife he took from his belt was about eight inches long, double-edged and wickedly sharp.

He stuck it into the frame of the window, working the blade expertly up and down until the window lock finally came loose. He nudged it gently and the window opened a fraction.

Peter Walton smiled and nodded to his companion who squatted down, clasping his hands together to form a stirrup. Walton put his foot on the helping hands and allowed himself to be hoisted up onto the window-sill. He paused there for a moment then swung himself inside, the sound of the TV reaching his ears as he eased himself down onto the tiles. He stood in the darkened room, watching as the tall man followed him inside.

Ronald Mills moved with remarkable dexterity for a man of over six feet. He clambered through the window and joined Walton in the kitchen, taking a step towards the closed door. He too could hear the sounds coming from the lounge.

Walton chewed his bottom lip contemplatively. He hadn't expected anyone to be at home. His expression of bewilderment gradually melted into a grin of satisfaction. This was an added bonus.

He looked at Mills and nodded, reaching for the handle of the door.

It opened soundlessly.

Both men stepped into the hall, the staircase to their right.

The sound of the TV was louder now.

Caroline watched the end credits of the soap opera. She even watched the adverts after it had finished. It was like seeing them for the first time watching them in colour. But finally she decided to make herself a cup of tea then check on Lisa. She hadn't heard any noise from the girl's bedroom, she never had any trouble with her, but she thought it part of her duty as baby-sitter, to actually check her temporary charge. Caroline stretched then got to her feet, glancing back at the television, as if reluctant to leave it for too long. She pushed open the door and walked out into the hall, slowing her pace.

It was dark.

And yet, hadn't Mrs Hacket left the hall light on when she'd gone out?

Caroline was actually reaching for the switch when the hand grabbed her by the throat, stifling any attempt at a scream. She was yanked backwards, almost lifted off her feet by the hand which held her.

She felt something cold against her cheek and realised that it was a knife.

Ronald Mills pressed the razor sharp blade against her flesh and whispered in her ear, his voice low and rasping.

'You make one sound and I'll cut your fucking head off!'

August 26, 1940

She wouldn't stop screaming.

Lawrenson had tried to calm the woman, tried to reassure her, but his efforts had been useless.

They couldn't stop her screaming.

'Give her an epidural for God's sake,' snapped Maurice Fraser. 'She's in agony.' He bent close to the woman's face, seeing the pain in her bulging eyes, as if he needed further proof that she was indeed suffering.

'No pain killers,' Lawrenson said, quietly, his eyes never leaving the woman. She was in her mid-twenties but the pain etched on her face gave her the appearance of someone ten years older. Her feet were secured in the metal stirrups by thick straps, her arms also held firmly. Despite the restraining straps though, she jerked and shuddered incessantly as wave upon wave of pain tore through her.

The white gown which she wore had slipped away from her lower body, exposing her swollen belly and, as Lawrenson watched, he could see the sometimes violent undulations from inside her abdomen.

It looked as though the baby was trying to tear its way free.

A particularly violent contraction tore through her and she unleashed a scream which reverberated around the room. Lawrenson felt the hairs at the nape of his neck rise.

'She's losing a lot of blood, doctor,' Nurse Kiley told him, watching the steady flow from the woman's vagina. Several swabs had already been used, unsuccessfully, to stem the outpouring of crimson fluid, they now lay discarded in a metal receiver like thick placental fragments. Another pint of blood was attached to the drip which fed blood into the prone woman by way of a twisted tube to her left, the needle jammed securely into the crook of her arm.

'Remove the baby, for God's sake, Lawrenson,' Fraser said. 'Perform a Caesarian before it's too late. We'll lose them both.'

Lawrenson shook his head.

'It'll be all right,' he said.

Another piercing scream filled the room and drummed off the walls.

Nurse Kiley, who was standing between the woman's legs, peered towards the weeping vagina then glanced at Lawrenson.

'It's starting,' she said.

Lawrenson moved closer, anxious to see the birth.

Fraser gripped the woman's shoulder, trying to offer some comfort but she continued to scream in pain as the contractions became more violent. She felt something inside her tearing, as if part of her insides were detaching themselves then, incredibly, the pain seemed to intensify.

Lawrenson saw the top of the baby's head, the lips of the woman's vagina sliding back like fleshy curtains to expose the first couple of inches of the child. The bloodied lips reminded him of a mouth, trying to expel something bloated and foul tasting. The labia swelled until it seemed it must tear, until it appeared that the woman would begin to split in half. Blood pumped from the widening cleft which was now opening ever wider to release its precious load.

The woman began thrashing madly on the bed, so ravaged by pain that she actually managed to pull her left arm free of the restraining strap. As she waved it before her, the drip came free and blood spurted madly from her arm and also from the end of the tube. Nurse Kiley hurried to re-attach it.

'Come on,' shouted Lawrenson, watching as more of the baby's head came free. 'Push. It's nearly over.'

There was a soft, liquescent spurt as the woman defecated, the waste mingling on the reeking bedclothes with the blood which still streamed from her vagina.

The head was free now, the child itself twisting from side to side, as if anxious to escape its crimson prison. The woman's labial lips spread ever wider as the child slithered into view. Lawrenson reached for it, ignoring the blood which drenched his hands.

He lifted the child, the umbilical cord hanging from its belly like a bloated snake, still attached to the placenta which, seconds later, was expelled in a reeking lump.

The woman's head lolled back, sweat covering her face and body, her hair matted to her forehead.

Fraser turned to look at the child which Lawrenson held aloft, gripping it like some kind of trophy.

'Oh Jesus,' murmured the doctor, his eyes bulging wide.

Nurse Kiley saw the child and could say nothing. She turned away and vomited violently.

'Lawrenson, you can't . . .' Fraser gasped, one hand clapped to his mouth.

'The child is all right, as I said it would be,' Lawrenson beamed, holding it up, not allowing it to squirm out of his grip. The umbilical cord still pulsed like a thick worm. It looked as if a putrescent parasite was burrowing into the child's stomach.

He held it towards the mother who had recovered sufficiently to look up. Her eyes were blurred with pain but as she blinked the clarity quickly returned and she saw her child.

'Your son,' said Lawrenson, proudly.

And she screamed again.

Five

Walton guessed that the girl was seventeen, maybe older. He didn't care.

She stood before him, hands clasped, shuffling her fingers like fleshy playing cards. There were tears in her eyes as she looked back and forth at the two men who stared so raptly at her. One of them, the taller one, kept wiping the back of his hand across his mouth and Caroline was sure he was dribbling. His breath was a low rasping wheeze, like an asthmatic gasping for air.

'You're pretty,' said Walton, touching her cheek with the point of the knife.

Caroline tried to swallow but her throat was dry. She closed her eyes and, this time, the tears did flow, running down her cheeks.

Walton pressed the knife against her flesh, allowing one of the salty droplets to dribble onto the metal. He withdrew the blade and licked the moisture with his tongue. Then he smiled at Caroline.

'Take your blouse off,' he said, softly, still smiling.

'Please don't hurt me,' she said, wiping the tears away with the back of her hand.

'Take the blouse off,' Walton urged, his voice now almost inaudible. He took a step closer to her, his face close to hers. He breathed stale cigarettes and tooth decay over her.

Still she hesitated.

'Take the fucking thing off or I'll take it off for you,' he hissed through clenched teeth.

Caroline reached for the top button, her hands shaking uncontrollably but, slowly, she managed to undo the fastener then repeated the procedure until the blouse hung open. Even through her fear she blushed.

'I said take it off,' Walton reminded her. 'Do it.'

'Please . . .'

'Do it,' he snarled.

She eased first one shoulder then the other out of the flimsy material, allowing it to drop to the floor in front of her. She sniffed, trying to fight back the tears but not succeeding.

'Please don't hurt me,' she whimpered, looking at both men as if expecting to find some trace of compassion. There was none.

'Why are you crying?'

It was Mills who asked the question this time.

He moved closer to her, and rested one hand on her left shoulder, peering at her breasts, which she attempted to cover.

He slapped her hands away and pulled at the strap of her bra.

'You've got lovely hair,' he told her, winding it around his hand, pulling her head to one side, towards his face. 'Kiss me.' He smiled broadly then looked at Walton, who nodded as if to urge his companion on.

'Well, go on, kiss him,' Walton said.

'Please . . .'

She got no further.

Mills pulled her round to face him, pushing his mouth against hers. She gagged as she felt his thick tongue pushing against her lips, his spittle running down her chin.

'A virgin. Never been kissed before?' Mills asked, pressing the point of the knife under her chin, digging it into the flesh gently at first. He watched as tears mingled with his own sputum.

'Take your bra off,' Walton said. 'Show us your body.'

Caroline shook her head almost imperceptibly, sobbing now.

'You said you didn't want us to hurt you,' Mills reminded her, grabbing a handful of her hair once again. He pressed the razor sharp knife against her taut locks and sliced effortlessly through, pulling the handful of hair free. 'Hair today, gone tomorrow,' he chuckled, looking at Walton who merely nodded.

'Take off the bra,' he snapped. 'Now.'

She tried to plead, tried to beg but no words would come. Instead she reached behind her and unfastened the clasp of her bra, holding it for precious seconds before releasing it, pulling the garment free and exposing her breasts.

Walton rubbed his growing erection through his trousers.

'Now the jeans,' he said.

She was crying softly all the time now, tears pouring down her cheeks.

The two men stood a couple of feet back, watching the obscene strip-show with growing excitement.

'Don't kill me,' she sobbed, standing before them in just her knickers. 'I'll do what you say but don't kill me.'

'Take off your panties,' Mills told her. 'Slowly.'

She hooked her thumbs into the elastic and eased them down over her hips and thighs, shrugging them off to finally stand naked before her tormentors. She raised a hand to cover her sandy pubic hair but Mills gripped her wrist, lifting her hand instead to his own crotch, forcing her to touch the throbbing erection he now sported.

'Have you got a boyfriend?' Walton asked, pressing himself against her.

She didn't answer.

'Have you?' he snarled, jerking her head around so that she was looking directly into his staring eyes.

She shook her head, her eyes now clouded with tears, her whole body shaking.

'So you don't know what it's like to be touched by a man?' Walton said, softly. 'You don't know what you're missing.' He chuckled and gazed at her breasts for a second.

'Now if you're good we won't hurt you. Are you going to be good?'

She tried to nod but it was as if her body was paralysed. She thought she was going to faint.

'Dance for us,' said Mills, smiling.

'I can't,' she wailed, close to breaking point.

'Come on,' he said, chidingly, pressing the knife to her left cheek. 'Every young girl can dance.'

'You said you wouldn't hurt me. Please . . .'

Walton bent down and picked up her bra on the end of his knife. He dangled it before her like some kind of trophy.

'Dance,' he said.

'Mummy.'

All three of them heard the word.

Mills spun round, a faint smile on his thick lips.

'Who else is in the house?' snarled Walton, grabbing Caroline by the hair.

'It's a child,' said Mills, his eyes blazing.

'Where is she?' Walton rasped.

'Upstairs,' sobbed Caroline.

Again the plaintive call.

Mills moved towards the door.

'Don't hurt her,' Caroline shouted but the exhortation was cut short as Walton clamped his hand over her mouth and forced her down onto the sofa, the knife held against her throat.

'I'll see to her,' Mills said, softly, heading out of the room and towards the stairs.

'He's very good with little children,' Walton informed her, fumbling with the zip of his trousers. 'Now, you just stay quiet for me, all right?'

Mills reached the bottom of the stairs and paused, listening to the calls from upstairs then, slowly, he began to ascend.

He reached the landing and moved towards the door which was slightly ajar.

He saw the child sitting up in bed as he opened the door, his frame silhouetted against the light.

The child was silent as he walked into the bedroom.

'Hello,' he said, gaily.

Lisa looked puzzled by this newcomer. She'd never seen him before but she remained silent as he knelt beside her bed.

'You're a very pretty little girl,' Mills breathed. 'What's your name?'

She told him.

'What a pretty name.' He pushed her gently back into bed, looking down at her, smiling, wiping his mouth with the back of his hand.

Then he reached for the knife.

Six

The ward sister nodded politely as Susan Hacket passed her. She managed a smile in return and walked on up the corridor.

A tall nurse also smiled at Sue. Most of the staff recognised her by now. After all, she'd been coming to the hospital every night for the last six weeks. If was as if she belonged there. As she pushed the door to room 562, she wondered how much longer she would be repeating this ritual.

She paused in the doorway for a moment, closing the door slowly behind her.

The air carried the familiar smell of stale urine and disinfectant, but tonight it was tinged with a more pungent odour. Sue recognised it as the stench of stagnant water. The flowers which stood by the bedside were wilting, some of them weeping their shrivelled petals onto the cabinet. The water was cloudy. It was three or four days since she'd changed it.

She walked towards the bed, aware of the chill in the air. She shuddered involuntarily and noticed that the window was open slightly.

She murmured something to herself then shut it, keeping back the cold breeze which had been hissing under the frame. Then she turned towards the bed.

'Hello Dad,' she said, softly, smiling as best she could.

He didn't hear her.

Over the past two weeks he'd been slipping in and out of consciousness more frequently. Sometimes it was the extra doses of morphine they gave him, at other times his body just seemed to give up, to surrender to the pain and seek release in the oblivion of sleep. Sue reached across and touched his hand. It felt like ice. He had only one blanket to cover him and this she hastily pulled up around his neck, easing both arms beneath it too.

As she leant over him she smelled the stale urine more strongly. As his condition had deteriorated they had fitted him with a catheter and now she glanced down to see that the bag was half full of dark urine. Sue swallowed hard, thinking how undignified they were. It was as if the bag was one of the final concrete illustrations that he was helpless, unable even to reach the toilet. He never left his bed now. When the illness had first struck he had been able to walk up and down the corridor, even take the odd trip into the hospital gardens but, as the cancer had taken a firmer hold, all he had been able to do was to lie there and let it devour him from the inside.

She stood by the bedside for a moment longer gazing at his face. The skin was tinged yellow, stretched so tightly over the bones it seemed they would tear through.

Tom Nolan had never been a big man even when he was in the best of health but now he looked like an escapee from Belsen. His eyes were little more than sunken pits, the lids slightly parted as if he were watching her. Watching but not seeing. She could hear his low rasping breaths, and only the almost imperceptible rise and fall of his chest, accompanied by those grating inhalations, told her he was still alive. His thinning white hair had been swept over to one side of his head, a couple of strands having fallen untidily onto his forehead.

Sue reached into the drawer in the bedside cabinet, took out a comb and carefully ran it through the flimsy hair. As she withdrew she found that her hands were shaking. She stood gazing at him for a moment longer then picked up the vase with the dead flowers and threw them into the waste bin nearby. She then washed the vase in the sink and arranged the flowers she'd bought on her way to the hospital.

As she was replacing the vase she noticed that there was an envelope on the top of the cabinet. Sue opened it and pulled out a card which bore the words 'HOPE YOU'RE SOON FIGHTING FIT'.

Underneath was a picture of a boxer. She flipped it open, her teeth clamped together as if to fight back the pain. Sue didn't recognise the name inside, didn't know who'd written 'Get well soon'.

She tore the card and the envelope up with almost angry jerks of her arm then tossed the remains into the bin with the dead flowers.

'Get well soon,' she repeated under her breath, her eyes fixed on the shrivelled, shrunken shape which was her father. She almost smiled at the irony. You didn't 'Get well soon' when you had lung cancer, she thought. You didn't get well at all. You did what her father was doing. You lay in bed and let the disease eat you away from the inside. You let it transform you into a human skeleton. You let it tear you apart with pain.

The tears came without her even realising.

Every night she saw him, sat by him and, every night she swore she wouldn't cry but, again, the sight of him lying there waiting for death proved too much. She sat on the edge of the bed and pulled a handkerchief from her pocket, wiping her eyes.

Her own subdued whimperings momentarily eclipsed the low rasping sound coming from her father. She clenched her teeth hard together, until her jaws ached, then she blew her nose and sighed wearily. How much longer was this going to go on? How many more nights of waiting? There had been times, especially during the last couple of weeks, when she had felt like praying for his death. At least it would mean the end of his suffering. But when she had thoughts like that she swiftly rebuked herself. Life was so precious that it was something to be grasped, to be retained no matter what the indignities, no matter what the suffering. Life with pain was better than no life at all.

She wondered if her father thought the same.

Sue squeezed his hand through the thin material of the blanket and felt again how thin he was. It was like clutching the hand of a skeleton, hidden beneath the cover she could easily have imagined that no flesh covered the bones and that to exert too much pressure would crush the hand. She held him a second longer then wiped her eyes again, the initial outpouring of emotion now passed. All that was left was the feeling of helplessness, the feeling which always came after the tears. An awful weariness and, at the same time, bewilderment that, after so long watching him wither away before her, she still had tears to offer. Every night as she arrived at the hospital she told herself that she would not cry, that she had become used to his appearance, to the knowledge that she was marking time waiting for him to die. But, every night, when she saw those ravaged wasted features and realised again that he would soon be gone forever, the tears came.

She knew she was the only one who ever visited him. It had been the same when he'd been in his flat in Camden, prior to being struck down with the illness.

Sue had a sister a year older than herself who lived about forty miles outside London, less than an hour's drive but she had visited the hospital only twice, at the beginning. Before the cancer took a real hold. Sue didn't blame her for that. She knew that there were practical reasons which prevented more frequent visits. And, besides, over the last two or three weeks, she had come to feel that the nightly visits were almost a duty. She came out of love but also because she knew she had been the one her father had doted on when she'd been growing up. She was still his 'little girl'. She *had* to be there for him.

She sniffed back more tears and clutched his hand again. He felt so cold, even when she took to rubbing his hand with her own, he still seemed frozen. It was almost as if he were sucking in the chill air and storing it in his waxen skin.

There had been none of this interminable waiting when her mother died. A stroke had taken her nine years earlier. The swiftness of it had been devastating but now, as Sue sat with her father she was beginning to wonder which was preferable. Although she, like everyone else, knew that there was *no* preferable way. Death brought pain and suffering, whichever guise it chose to arrive in. After her mother's death, Sue had realised both the awful finality of it but also how empty it leaves the lives of those who remain. She had seen the devastating effect her mother's death had wrought on her own father. The flat where they had lived for thirty years, where they had raised a family, had become a prison for him. A cell full of memories, each one of which held not joy but pain because he had known that memories were all he had. There was no future to look forward to, only the past to dwell on.

Sue knew that feeling now. There had been good times with her father but, once he was dead, there would be just memories and memories sometimes faded. Even the good ones.

This thought brought a fresh trickle of tears which she hurriedly wiped away with the back of her hand.

She touched his cheek with the back of her hand, stroking gently, feeling the prominent cheekbones, tracing the hollows which had formed in his features. This time no tears came, and she remained like that for the next fifty minutes, stroking his face and hair, clutching his hand.

Sue finally glanced at her watch, saw that visiting hours were over, and heard others leaving, making their way down the corridor outside. Slowly she got to her feet then pulled up the blanket again, tucking it around him to keep out the cold. Then she leant forward and kissed his forehead.

'Goodnight, Dad,' she whispered. 'See you tomorrow.'

She turned and did not look back, pulling the door open and slipping out silently, as if not to disturb him.

Seven

He pulled on his shirt, tucking it into his jeans as he heard the sound of the shower from the bathroom. Through the open door he could make out the blurred silhouette of Nikki behind the frosted glass.

Hacket buttoned his shirt then pulled on his trainers and started tying them. He sat on the edge of the bed, glancing up as he heard the shower being turned off. A moment later, Nikki stepped from inside, her body glistening with water, and Hacket admired her figure for a few seconds before she wrapped herself in a towel. Her hair was hanging in long tendrils, dripping water onto her shoulders as she walked back into the bedroom. She crossed to Hacket and kissed him softly on the lips, some of the water from her wet hair dripping onto his shirt. She slid the bath towel from around herself and began drying her arms and legs. He watched her for a moment longer, still sitting on the edge of the bed.

His eyes were fixed on the gold chain which she wore around her neck and the small opal which dangled from it. Another of his gifts to her. *If you're going to have an affair then do it with style*, he reminded himself. Buy her things. Show her that you care. Hacket almost laughed aloud at his own thoughts. *Care*.

What the hell did he know about caring? If he cared for anyone he'd be at home now, not preparing to leave the flat where his lover lived.

The self-recrimination didn't strike home with quite the vehemence it was meant to. He exhaled deeply, reaching out to touch her leg as she raised it, placed her foot on the bed and started to pat away the water with the towel.

'Do you have to go now?' she asked him.

Hacket nodded.

'Sue will be back from the hospital soon,' he told Nikki. 'I'd better make a move.'

'Won't she wonder where you've been?'

'I told her I had a meeting.'

'Is she trusting or just naive?' There was a hint of sarcasm in Nikki's voice which Hacket didn't care for.

'Do you really want to know? I thought you didn't want to hear anything about my wife,' he said, irritably.

'I don't. You mentioned her first.' She finished drying herself and reached for her housecoat which she pulled on, then she began drying her hair. 'Do you think about her when you're with me?'

Hacket frowned.

'What is this? Twenty questions?' He rolled up the sleeves of his white shirt revealing thick forearms. They regarded each other silently for a moment then Nikki's tone softened slightly.

'Look, John, I didn't mean to sound so bitchy,' she said.

'Well you made a bloody good job of it,' he snapped.

'I want you. I don't want to know about your wife or your family and if that sounds callous then I'm sorry. You chose to have this affair, just like I did. If you've got second thoughts, if you feel guilty, then maybe you shouldn't be here.'

'Do you want me here?' he demanded.

She leant forward and kissed him.

'Of course I do. I want you whenever I can have you. But I'm no fool either. I know this affair won't last. It can't. And I'm not going to ask you to leave your wife for me. I just want to enjoy it while I can. There's nothing wrong with that is there?'

Hacket smiled and shook his head. He got to his feet, enfolded her in his arms and kissed her, his tongue pushing past her lips and teeth, seeking the moistness beyond. She responded fiercely, the towel falling to the floor, her breasts pressing against his chest. When they parted she was breathing heavily, her face flushed. She looked at him questioningly and Hacket was held by the intensity of her stare.

'What do you want, John?' she asked him. 'What do you get out of it? What am I? Just a quick fuck? A bit on the side?' Her Irish accent had become more pronounced, something he always noticed when she was upset or angry.

'You're more than a bit on the side,' he told her. 'Christ, I hate that expression.'

'What would you call me? A lover? Makes it sound more respectable doesn't it? What about a Mistress?'

'A mistress is an unpaid whore,' he said, flatly. 'What do names matter, Nikki? You ask too many questions.' He stroked her gently beneath the chin with his index finger.

She caught the finger, raised it to her mouth and kissed it, flicking the tip with her tongue.

'You spend your money on me,' she said, touching the opal necklace. 'Don't hurt me, John, that's all I ask.'

He frowned.

'I'd never hurt you. Why do you say that?'

'Because I'm scared. Scared of becoming involved, of starting to think too much of you. You might hurt me without even knowing it.'

'It cuts both ways. I can't turn my emotions on and off Nikki. I'm at as much risk as you. And I've got more to lose. If I fall in love with you I've got . . .' He allowed the sentence to trail off.

'Your wife and daughter,' she continued.

'Yeah, wife, daughter and mortgage to support,' he said, smiling humourlessly.

'So we carry on,' she said, pulling him closer. 'Like I said, I want you whenever I can have you. I just have to be careful.' She kissed him.

Hacket looked at his watch then headed for the door.

She wrapped the towel around her again and followed him out to the hall.

'When will I see you?' she asked.

He paused, one hand on the door knob.

'Tomorrow at the school. We can walk past each other and pretend we've never met just like we always do,' he said with a trace of bitterness in his voice.

'You know what I mean. Will you call me?'

He nodded, smiled at her, then he was gone.

Hacket took the lift to the ground floor then walked across to his car. He slid behind the wheel of the Renault and sat there for long moments in the darkness then, he glanced behind him, towards the window of Nikki's flat where the light still burned. He exhaled, banging the steering wheel angrily. He cursed under his breath then, with a vicious twist of his wrist, he started the car, stuck it in gear and drove off.

If the traffic was light he should be home in less than forty minutes.

Eight

The first police car was parked up on the pavement close to the street entrance.

Susan Hacket drove past it, noticing the uniformed men inside it as she drew closer to her house. However, she was almost blinded by the profusion of red and blue lights which seemed to fill the night. On top of ambulances and police cars they turned silently and, with the men around them moving about in relative calm it looked like a scene from a silent film. Sue frowned, suddenly disturbed by the sight of so many official vehicles.

It took her only a second to realise that they were parked outside her own house.

'Oh God,' she whispered under her breath and brought the car to a halt. She clambered out from behind the wheel and hurried across to the pavement where a number of uniformed policemen were standing around in well ordered groups, most, it appeared, guarding the gates of the other houses. Sue could see lights on in the front rooms of the other houses, could see faces or at least silhouettes peering out into the night, anxious to see what was happening.

Uncontrollable panic seized her as she saw two ambulancemen entering her house.

She broke into a run, pushing past a policeman who tried to bar her way.

Two more men moved to intercept her as she reached the front door.

'What's going on,' she blurted, her passage blocked by a burly sergeant. 'Please let me in. I live here. My daughter is inside.'

It was another man, a man in his mid-thirties, dressed in a brown jacket and grey trousers, who finally spoke. He appeared behind the sergeant, eyeing Sue up and down appraisingly as if trying to recognise her.

'Mrs Hacket?' he finally said.

'Yes. What's happening, please tell me?'

The sergeant stepped aside and Sue rushed into the hall.

The smell struck her immediately.

A pungent stench of excrement, mingling with a smell not unlike copper.

The man in the brown jacket now barred her way and, as she tried to push past him, he caught her arms and held her. His face was pale, his chin dark with stubble. Even in such a tense moment Sue noticed how piercing his eyes were. A flawless blue which seemed to bore into her very soul. They were sad eyes.

'Please tell me what's happening,' she pleaded, trying to shake loose of his grip.

'You are Mrs Susan Hacket?' he asked.

'Yes, please tell me what's going on.' She practically screamed it at him. 'Where's my daughter?'

It was then that the ambulancemen emerged from the sitting room and Sue became aware of the smell once more, stronger now.

On the stretcher they carried was a sheet which, she assumed had once been white. It was soaked crimson and Sue realised that the thick red stain was blood. Her eyes bulged madly and she moved towards the stretcher.

The man in the brown jacket tried to hold her back but she wrenched one arm free and tugged at the sheet, pulling it back a few inches.

'No!' she shrieked.

As the ambulancemen hurried to cover the bloodied body of Caroline Fearns, Sue felt the bile clawing its way up from her stomach. In that split second she had time to see that Caroline's face had been slashed in a dozen different places, her lips clumsily hacked off so that only a hole remained where her mouth was. Her hair was matted with blood which had pumped from the wounds which had caused her death.

The man in the brown jacket tried to guide Sue into the kitchen away from the sight of Caroline's body but she seemed to resist his efforts until he practically had to lift her bodily from the hall.

'Where's Lisa?' she gasped, unable to swallow.

'Mrs Hacket, I'm Detective Sergeant Spencer, I . . .'

Sue wasn't interested in the policeman's identity.

'Where's my daughter?' she shrieked, tears beginning to form at her eye corners.

'Your daughter's dead,' Spencer said, flatly, trying to inject some compassion into his words but knowing it was impossible.

He held on to Sue for a moment then she shook loose and stumbled back against the table. For a moment he thought she was going to faint but she clawed at one of the chairs and flopped down on it.

'No,' she murmured.

'I'm so sorry, Mrs Hacket,' he said, gripping her hand.

She felt so cold.

'Where is she?' Sue demanded, her face drained of colour, her eyes searching Spencer's face imploringly for an answer.

'She's upstairs,' he told her then, quickly added, 'we've been trying to reach your husband . . .'

'I must see her,' she blurted. 'You must let me see her. Please.'

She got to her feet and tried to push past Spencer who, once again acted as a human barrier.

'Let me pass,' she shouted. 'I have to go to her.'

Spencer pushed the kitchen door shut behind him, penning her inside the room with him.

'There's nothing you can do,' he said. 'Your daughter is dead.'

Sue suddenly froze then, with a final despairing moan, she *did* pass out.

Nine

By the time Hacket arrived home there was just one police car parked outside the house. He gave it only a cursory glance as he walked towards the front door, fumbling for his keys, remembering he'd left them in his other jacket. He rang the doorbell and waited, blowing on his hands in an effort to warm them.

The door was opened by Spencer.

Hacket looked aghast at the policeman, standing on the doorstep even when he was ushered inside.

Across the road a curtain moved as the family opposite tried to see what was happening.

'Mr John Hacket?' Spencer asked.

The teacher nodded, finally finding the will to step over the threshold. The front door was closed behind him.

'Who are you?' he said, falteringly.

Spencer introduced himself.

'I don't understand. Why are you here?'

Hacket found himself manoeuvred into the kitchen where another plain-clothes man waited. The second man introduced himself as Detective Inspector Madden. He was older than his subordinate by five years, his hair greying at the temples, a stark contrast to his jet black moustache and eyebrows which knitted over his nose giving him the appearance of a perpetual frown. However, there was a warmth in his voice that seemed almost incongruous to his appearance. He asked Hacket to sit down and the teacher obeyed, finding a mug of tea pushed towards him.

'Will someone tell me what the hell is going on?' he said, irritably. 'Has there been an accident? My wife, is it my wife?'

'Your wife is with your next-door neighbours,' Madden told him, softly. 'She's been sedated, she's sleeping now.'

'Sedated? What the fuck are you talking about? What's happening?' His breath was coming in gasps now, his eyes darting back and forth between the two policemen.

'Your house was broken into tonight,' said Madden, his voice low and even. 'We found two bodies when we arrived. One we believe was a girl named Caroline Fearns, the other we think was your daughter. They're dead, Mr Hacket, I'm sorry.'

'Dead.' The word, the very act of speaking it seemed to drain all the anger and irritation from Hacket. His head bowed slightly. He tried to swallow but it felt as if his throat had filled with sand. When he spoke the word again it came out as a hoarse whisper.

'I'm sorry,' Madden repeated.

Hacket clasped his hands together before him on the table, his gaze directed at the cup of steaming tea. He chewed on one knuckle for a moment, the silence enveloping him.

Both policemen looked at each other, then at the teacher, who finally managed to croak another word.

'When?'

We think between seven and eight this evening,' he was told.

Hacket gritted his teeth.

'Oh God,' he murmured, feeling sick, wondering if he was going to be able to control himself. He closed his eyes, squeezing the lids together until white stars danced before him. Between seven and eight. *While he was with Nikki.*

He rubbed his face with both hands, still fighting to control his nausea. His mouth opened soundlessly but no words would come. He wanted to say so much, wanted to know so much but he could not speak. Only one word finally escaped.

'Why?' he asked, pathetically. 'Why were they killed?'

The question had an almost child-like innocence to it.

Madden seemed embarrassed by the question.

'It looks as if someone broke in with the intention of robbing the house,' he said. 'When they found your daughter and the young girl they . . .' He allowed the words to fade away.

'How was it done?' said Hacket, an unnerving steeliness in his tone, despite the fact that he could not bring himself to look directly at either of the policemen.

'I don't think you need to know that yet, Mr Hacket,' Madden said.

'I asked how it was done,' he snarled, glaring at the DI. 'I have a right to know.'

Madden hesitated.

'With a knife,' he said, quietly.

Hacket nodded quickly, his gaze dropping once more.

In the resultant silence, the ticking of the wall clock sounded thunderous.

It was Spencer who finally coughed somewhat theatrically, looked at his superior then spoke.

'Mr Hacket, I'm afraid that your daughter will have to be formally identified.'

Hacket let out a painful breath.

'Oh Christ,' he murmured.

'It has to be done within twenty-four hours if possible,' Spencer continued almost apologetically.

'I'll do it,' Hacket said, his words almost inaudible. 'Please don't tell my wife. I don't want her to see Lisa like that.'

Spencer nodded.

'I'll pick you up tomorrow morning about eleven.'

'Would you like one of my men to stay outside the house tonight, Mr Hacket?' Madden asked. 'It'd be no trouble.'

Hacket shook his head and, once more, the three of them endured what felt like an interminable silence finally broken by Madden.

'We're going to have to ask you to leave the house too, Mr Hacket, until the forensic boys have finished. Is there somewhere you can stay? It'll only be for a day or two.'

Hacket nodded blankly.

'Just let me see it,' he murmured.

Madden looked puzzled.

'Where it happened,' the teacher said. 'I have to see.'.

'Why torture yourself?'

He turned on Madden.

'I *have* to see.'

The policeman nodded, watching as Hacket walked out of the kitchen and through into the sitting room.

The sitting room had been wrecked.

The furniture had been overturned, ornaments smashed, television and video broken, but it was not the wanton destruction which shocked Hacket – it was the spots of blood on the carpet, so delicately covered with pieces of plastic sheeting. He pulled one of the armchairs upright and flopped down lifelessly in it, gazing around the room, his eyes bulging wide, looking but seeing nothing. He sat there as the minutes ticked by, surrounded by silence. Alone with his thoughts. Then, slowly, he hauled himself to his feet and walked towards the hall, pulling the sitting-room door closed behind him.

He hesitated again at the bottom of the stairs, as if the climb were too much for him or he feared what he might find at the top but then, gripping the bannister, he began to ascend.

He faltered again when he reached the landing, looking at the four doors which confronted him.

The door to Lisa's room was now firmly shut, but it was towards that one which he advanced, his hand shaking as it rested on the handle.

Hacket turned it and walked in.

More plastic sheeting.

More blood.

Especially on the bed.

He felt a tear form in the corner of one eye and roll slowly down his cheek. As he turned to step back out of the room his foot brushed against something and he looked down to see that it was one of his daughter's toys. Hacket stopped and picked up the teddy bear, holding it before him for a second before setting it on top of a chest of drawers. Again his gaze was drawn to the bed.

So much blood.

He felt more tears dribbling down his cheeks as he stared at the place where she had been killed.

How much pain had she suffered?

Had she screamed?

He clenched his fists together, each question burning its way into his mind like a branding iron.

How long had it taken her to die?

Does it matter? he asked himself. All that matters is that she's dead.

Perhaps if you'd been here . . .

The thought stuck in his mind like a splinter in flesh. He turned and closed the door behind him, wiping the tears away with one hand, sucking in deep breaths.

* * *

He undressed swiftly and slid into bed beside her, feeling the warmth of her body against him. She murmured something in her sleep and he gently placed one arm around her neck, wanting to hold her more tightly. Wanting *her* to hold *him*.

She woke up suddenly, as if from a nightmare then, immediately, she saw him and Hacket could see that her face was unbearably pale and drawn. Even in the darkness he could see the moisture on her cheeks.

'John,' she whispered, her voice cracking and now he held her tightly, more tightly than he could ever remember. An embrace more intense than any born of love. She looked so vulnerable. And he felt her tears on his chest as he held her, his own grief swelling and rising once more.

'If only we'd been here,' she whimpered. 'If I hadn't been at the hospital and you hadn't been at that meeting she'd still be alive.'

Hacket nodded.

'We can't blame ourselves, Sue,' he said but the lie bit deep and he finally lost control. Hacket could, and did, blame himself. 'Oh Jesus,' he gasped and they both seemed to melt into one another, united in grief.

September 10, 1940

The voices outside the room grew louder.

One he recognised, the other he had not heard before.

Garbled, angry words then the door swung open as he rose.

'I tried to stop him, George,' said Lawrenson's wife, Margaret, looking helplessly at her husband who merely smiled and nodded at her.

'It's all right,' he said, eyeing the other newcomer with suspicion. 'You can leave us.'

She hesitated a moment then closed the door behind her. The veneer of civility which Lawrenson had managed to retain dropped sharply.

'Who are you?' he demanded. 'How dare you burst into my home like this?'

The man who faced him was tall but powerfully built, the thick material of his uniform unable to conceal the muscles beneath. He had a long face with pinched features and his cheeks looked hollow, giving him an undernourished look which was quite incongruous when set against the rest of his physique. He strode across to Lawrenson's desk, a steely look in his eye and, even as the doctor noticed the man's rank, he introduced himself, albeit perfunctorily.

'Major David Catlin,' he announced, stiffly. 'Intelligence.'

Lawrenson didn't offer him a seat but Catlin sat down anyway.

'And to what do I owe this intrusion?' Lawrenson wanted to know.

'I'm here on official business, from the Home Office. It's about project Genesis.'

Lawrenson shot him a wary glance.

'Your work on the project is to stop as of now,' said Catlin, his eyes never leaving the doctor.

'Why?' Lawrenson demanded. 'The work has been going well, I've made great strides. Is someone else being put in charge?'

Catlin shook his head.

'The whole project is being shut down,' he said.

'You can't do that. You mustn't do that, I'm close to finding an answer. There are certain things which need perfecting, I know . . .'

The Major cut him short.

'The project is to cease immediately, Doctor,' he snapped. 'And I can understand why.'

'The Army, the Home Office, everyone was behind me at the beginning,' Lawrenson protested.

'That was until we saw the results,' Catlin said, quietly. 'Lawrenson, listen to me, if the public found out what this work involved there would be massive outcry. No one would stand for it, especially if the press got hold of it. Can you imagine the repercussions if a newspaper managed to get some photos of your work?' He shook his head. 'Work. God, I don't even know if that's the right word for it.'

'The Government encouraged me to perfect Genesis,' Lawrenson insisted, leaning on his desk and glaring at the officer. 'They funded me while I was researching.'

'That funding is also to be withdrawn,' Catlin informed him.

'Then I'll carry on alone.'

'Lawrenson, I didn't come forty miles to *advise* you to stop work on Genesis, I'm ordering you.'

The doctor smiled thinly.

'I'm not in your army Major, you can't give me orders,' he said.

The officer got to his feet.

'You are to stop work immediately, do you understand?'

'I've only been working under laboratory conditions for a month, less than that. You can't judge the results as early as this. It's unfair.'

'And what you're doing is inhuman,' snapped Catlin.

The two men regarded one another angrily for a moment then Lawrenson seemed to relax. He moved away from his desk towards the window which overlooked his spacious back garden. In the splendour and peacefulness of the countryside it was difficult to believe there was a war on, that, forty miles away in London, people would soon be preparing themselves for the Luftwaffe's nightly onslaught.

'What is more inhuman, Major,' Lawrenson began. 'The work that I'm involved in, work that could help mankind, or the senseless slaughter of millions in this bloody war we're fighting?'

'Very philosophical, Doctor but I didn't come here to discuss the rights and wrongs of war.'

Lawrenson turned and looked at the soldier.

'I will not stop my work, Major,' he said, flatly.

'Is it that you *cannot* or *will* not see why Genesis must stop now?' the officer asked.

'When I first began work on the project everyone backed me. I was hailed as a saviour.' He laughed bitterly. 'And now, I'm to suffer the same fate as the first saviour, metaphorically speaking.'

'Even you must realise the risks,' Catlin said. 'If details of your work were discovered there's no telling what would happen. That is why you must stop.'

Lawrenson shook his head.

'Tell the Home Office, tell your superiors, tell the Prime Minister himself that I will continue my work.'

Catlin shrugged.

'Then I can't be responsible for what may happen.'

Lawrenson heard the iciness in the soldier's voice.

'Are you threatening me, Catlin?' he snapped.

The Major turned and headed for the door, pursued by Lawrenson.

The officer strode towards the front door, past Margaret Lawrenson, who had emerged from one of the rooms leading off from the large hallway.

Lawrenson caught up with him as he reached the front door.

'Tell them to go to hell,' he roared as the soldier walked briskly across the gravel towards his waiting car. The driver started the engine and the officer slid into the passenger seat.

'You keep away from here, Catlin,' Lawrenson shouted as the car pulled away.

As he watched it disappear down the short driveway towards the road he wondered who the man in the back seat was.

The man who stared at him so intently.

Ten

Christ he needed a cigarette.

Hacket fumbled in his pocket for the fifth time and then glanced across the small waiting room at the sign which proclaimed, in large, red letters, 'NO SMOKING'.

Had it not been for the circumstances he may have found the irony somewhat amusing. Cigarette smoke was hardly likely to damage the residents of this particular building.

He sat outside the morgue, eyes straying to the door through which, minutes earlier, DS Spencer had disappeared. It felt as if he'd been gone for hours. Hacket felt utterly alone despite, or because of, the smallness of the waiting room. It was painted a dull, passionless grey. Even the plastic chairs which lined the wall were grey. The lino was grey. The only thing that wasn't grey was the NO SMOKING sign which he glanced at again, shifting uncomfortably in his seat.

Outside he heard an ambulance siren and wondered, briefly, where it was going. To an accident? A road smash?

A murder?

Hacket tired of sitting and got to his feet, pacing steadily back and forth in the small room. There weren't any magazines to look at to pass the time, no three-year-old copies of *Readers Digest* or *Woman's Own*. For some absurd reason a joke sidled into his mind. A joke about a doctor's waiting room. *Two men talking, one said I was at the doctor's lately, I read one of the newspapers there. Terrible about the Titanic isn't it?*

Terrible.

Hacket fumbled for his cigarettes once more and, this time he ignored the sign and lit up, sucking deeply on the Dunhill. He blew out a stream of grey smoke which perfectly matched the colour of the walls.

He found, when he took the cigarette from his mouth, that his hand was shaking. Neither he nor Sue had slept much the previous night. She was at the house now, still sedated. A neighbour was sitting with her. Hacket wouldn't have wanted her here with him, he wasn't even sure how *he* was going to stand up to seeing his daughter laid out on a slab. For fleeting seconds he wondered if the Fearns family had identified Caroline yet. Had they felt like he felt now? Had they stood in this same waiting room wondering, fearing what they were going to see?

The thought faded, merging into thousands of others which seemed to be whirling around in his head. And yet despite all the apparent activity inside his mind there was a peculiar emptiness. A numbness. He sat down again and almost reached out to touch the chair beside him to reassure himself it was actually there. He was a million miles away, his mind sifting through details with a swiftness that created a vacuum. He took another drag on the cigarette then stubbed it out beneath his foot.

He felt sick and rubbed a hand across his forehead, feeling perspiration. He'd rung the school earlier that morning and said that he wouldn't be in for a few days. No details. A family bereavement he'd said, wanting to keep it simple. He didn't want too many questions asked. They'd find out soon enough when the story appeared in the papers. Then would come the questions, the enquiries, the consoling handshakes. He sighed and looked at the door again.

It opened and Simpson emerged, raising his eyebrows in a gesture designed to beckon Hacket forward.

He'd been waiting for this moment, wanting to get it

over with, but now he would have given anything to sit for a while longer in that grey room in one of those grey chairs. He walked purposefully towards the door and entered.

The morgue was smaller than he'd imagined. There were no rows of lockers, no filing cabinets for sightless eyes. No white-coated assistants wandering back and forth with hearts and lungs ready to weigh.

And there was only one slab.

On it was a small shape, covered by a white sheet.

As he drew nearer to it, Hacket visibly faltered, he felt the colour drain from his face and his throat seemed to constrict.

Simpson moved towards him but he shook his head gently and advanced to within a couple of feet of the slab and its shrouded occupant.'

The coroner, a short man with heavy jowls and a balding head attempted a smile of sympathy but it looked more like a sneer. He looked at Spencer who nodded.

He pulled back the sheet.

'Is that your daughter, Mr Hacket?' the DS asked, softly.

Hacket let out a breath which sounded as if his lungs had suddenly deflated. He raised one hand to his mouth, his eyes rivetted to the small form on the slab.

'Mr Hacket.'

She was as white as milk, at least the parts of her which he could see through the patchwork of cuts and bruises. Her face and neck were tinged yellow by bruises and, across her throat was a deep gash which curved upwards at either side like some kind of blood-choked rictus.

'Why are her eyes still open?' he croaked.

'Rigor mortis,' the coroner said, quietly. 'The involuntary muscles sometimes stiffen first.' His voice trailed away into a whisper.

'Is it your daughter, Mr Hacket?' Simpson persisted.

'Yes.'

The detective nodded and the coroner prepared to pull the sheet back over Lisa but Hacket stopped him.

'No,' he said. 'I want to see her.'

The coroner hesitated then, slowly, he pulled the sheet right back, allowing Hacket to see the full extent of his daughter's injuries.

Her chest and stomach were also covered in dark blotches and deep gashes. The area between her legs was purple and he noticed that the inside of her thighs were almost black with bruising. The contusions continued right down her legs to her feet. Hacket looked on with lifeless eyes, there was no emotion there. It was as if the shock of seeing her had sucked every last ounce of feeling from him. He looked repeatedly up and down her tiny corpse.

'How was it done?' he asked, his eyes still on his daughter. 'Have you done the post-mortem?'

The coroner seemed reluctant to answer and looked at Simpson who merely shrugged.

'I asked you a question,' Hacket said, flatly. 'How was she killed?'

'No post-mortem has been done yet but, from external examination you can see . . . well, I decided that death was caused by massive haemorrhage, most likely from the wound on her throat.'

'What about the bruising,' he pointed to the purplish area between her legs. 'There.'

The coroner didn't answer.

Hacket looked at him, then at Spencer.

'You have no right to keep information from me,' he said. 'She was my daughter.'

'We thought that it would save you any more suffering, Mr Hacket . . .' Spencer said but the teacher interrupted him.

'You think it can get any worse?' he snapped, bitterly. 'Tell me.'

'There was evidence of sexual abuse,' said Spencer.

'Was she raped?' Hacket wanted to know.

'Yes,' the detective told him. 'There was evidence of penetration.'

'Before *and* after her death,' added the coroner by way of thoroughness.

Hacket gritted his teeth.

'Would she have felt much pain?' he wanted to know.

Simpson sighed wearily.

'Mr Hacket, why torture yourself like this?'

'I have to know,' he hissed. 'Would she have felt much pain?'

'It's difficult to say,' the coroner told him. 'During the rape, yes, probably, she may have been unconscious by that time though, she'd already lost a lot of blood before it happened. The cut across the throat would have sent her into traumatic shock. The rest would have been over quickly.'

Hacket nodded and finally turned away from the tiny body.

The coroner replaced the sheet and watched as Hacket strode out of the room, followed by Simpson.

The body was hidden from view once more.

Eleven

The drive from the hospital back to the house seemed to take hours, though Hacket assumed that it was actually less than thirty minutes.

Spencer drove at a steady speed and Hacket gazed aimlessly out of the Granada's side window hearing only the odd phrase which the detective spoke.

'. . . Positive identification of the killers . . .'

Hacket noticed a woman and her two children trying to cross the road up ahead, waiting for a break in the traffic.

'. . . Criminal records as far as we know . . .'

One of the children was only about four. A little girl and she held her mother's hand as they waited for the cars to pass.

'. . . No doubt that two men were involved . . .'

Hacket seemed to see nothing but children during the drive back. It was as if the world had suddenly doubled its population of four-year-olds.

With one notable exception.

'. . . Let you know as soon as we have any information . . .'

'What kind of man rapes a four year old?'

The question took Spencer by surprise and Hacket repeated it.

'You'd be surprised,' he said. 'Men you'd never expect. Fathers like yourself . . .' The DS realised his mistake and let the sentence trail off. 'I'm sorry,' he added.

'What are the chances of catching him?'

'Well, we got good dabs from around the house, blood type we know, approximate height, weight and age. We'll get him.'

Hacket laughed humourlessly.

'And if you do? What then? A ten-year sentence? Out in five if he's a good boy' he said, bitterly.

Spencer shook his head.

'It's not like that, Mr Hacket. He'll go down and he'll stay down.'

'Until the next time,' Hacket said, still looking out of the side window.

Hacket said a brief goodbye to the detective when they reached the house in Clapham and Spencer promised to be in touch as soon as he had any information, then he thanked the teacher for his co-operation, offered his sympathies once more and drove off. Hacket stood on the pavement for a moment then turned and headed towards the front door, letting himself in rather than ring the bell and risk disturbing Sue.

He found her sitting in the kitchen with the next-door neighbour, Helen Bentine. The two women, Sue a little younger, were sitting over a cup of tea talking, and Hacket thought how much brighter his wife looked. Granted she still had dark rings beneath her eyes and she looked as if she hadn't slept for a fortnight, but she actually managed a smile as he entered, rising to make him a cup of tea from the recently-boiled kettle.

Helen beat her to it, handed the teacher his drink then said she'd better go. They both thanked her, listening as the front door closed behind her.

'The doctor said you should rest, Sue,' he said, sipping his tea, loosening his tie with his free hand.

'I'll rest later,' she told him. 'I don't want to keep taking those pills he gave me, I'll get addicted.'

He sat down beside her, touching her cheek with his fingertips.

'You look so tired,' he said, looking at her.

She smiled weakly at him then took a sip of her tea.

Hacket knew she was about to say something but, when it came, he was still unprepared.

'What did she look like?' Sue wanted to know.

He shrugged, unable to think of a suitable answer.

Well, she was cut up badly, she'd been raped and the bastard had knocked her about so much there was hardly an inch of skin left unmarked, but apart from that she looked fine.

'John, tell me.'

'She looked peaceful,' he lied, attempting a smile.

'We'll have to tell the family, your parents, my family. They'll have to know, John.'

'Not just yet,' he said, softly, clasping her hand.

'Why did they pick on us?' she asked, as if expecting him to furnish her with an answer. 'Why kill Lisa?'

'Sue, I don't know. Would knowing the answer make it any more bearable? She's still dead, knowing why she was killed isn't going to bring her back.'

'But it isn't fair.' There were tears in her eyes now. 'My Dad's dying – that's hard enough to take – and now this.' She laughed bitterly and the sound caused the hair to rise on the back of Hacket's neck. 'Perhaps God is testing our faith.' She sniffed, wiped a tear from her cheek.'Well if he is he's going to be unlucky.' Hacket gripped her hand more tightly, watching as the tears began to course more freely down her cheeks. 'God is a sadist.' She looked at Hacket, her eyes blazing. 'And I hate him for what he's done.'

Hacket nodded, got to his feet and put his arms around her. They stayed locked together for some time, Sue sobbing quietly.

'I just wish that I could have said goodbye to her,' she whispered. 'To have held her just one last time.' She looked up into his face and saw the tears in *his* eyes. 'Oh, John, what are we going to do?'

He had no answer.

At first he thought he was dreaming.

The ringing sounded as if it were inside his head, but, as he opened his eyes, Hacket realised that it wasn't make-believe.

The phone continued to ring.

He rubbed his eyes and eased himself from beneath Sue's head. She had taken two of her tablets and been asleep for the last hour or so. He had dozed off as well, the strain of the last twenty-four hours finally catching up with him.

Now he stumbled towards the hall and the phone, closing the sitting room door behind him. He picked up the receiver, blinking hard in an effort to clear his vision.

'Hello,' he croaked, clearing his throat.

'Hello, John, it's me, Nikki. Look, I'm sorry to ring your home.' Her voice was low and conspiratorial.

'What do you want?' he said, wearily.

'I needed to speak to you,' she said. 'Someone at school said you weren't going to be in for a few days.'

'That's right, why is there a problem? Are you keeping a check on my movements or something?' The acidity of his tone was unmistakeable.

'What's wrong?' she asked. 'Are you all right?'

'Look, is this important? Because if it's not will you get off the line now.'

'I said I was sorry for phoning you at home,' Nikki said, both surprised and irritated by his aggressiveness. 'Is your wife there, is that why you can't talk?'

'Yes she is but that's not the reason. You shouldn't have called me.'

'We were supposed to meet tonight, I was waiting . . .'

He cut her short.

'Don't call me here again, all right?'

'I cooked us a meal.'

'Eat it yourself,' he rasped and slammed the phone down. He stood in the hallway, his hand still on the receiver, the residue of that soft Irish accent of hers still lingering in his ears.

He couldn't tell her the truth. How could he?

From behind him in the sitting-room he heard Sue call his name and he turned to rejoin her.

As he did he cast one last glance at the telephone, as if expecting it to ring again.

Twelve

The banks of black cloud which brought the rain also seemed to hasten the onset of night.

Like ink spreading over blotting paper the tenebrous gloom slowly seeped across the heavens above Hinkston. Icy rain came down in sheets, driven by a wind which cut into exposed skin as surely as a razor blade.

Bob Tucker pulled the scarf tighter around his chin in an attempt to protect himself from the elements and looked down into the grave.

The coffin was already hidden beneath a thin layer of muddy earth but the rain was rapidly washing it away, exposing the polished wood beneath. Bob shoveled a few more clods into the hole, paused to light a cigarette, then continued in earnest. The rain quickly extinguished the cigarette and he stuffed the sodden remains into the pocket of his overcoat, cursing the weather, his luck and anything else which came to mind as he toiled over the open grave. He knew he had to work fast. The rain falling on the excavated earth would rapidly transform it to mud. The soil in Hinkston was like clay at the best of times, but when it rained some parts of the town resembled Flanders in 1918.

Bob paused for a moment, straightening up, groaning as he felt the bones in his knees click. His back was beginning to ache as well. Occupational hazard, he told himself. He'd been grave-digger at Hinkston cemetery for the last twelve years. He liked the job too. Bob had never been much of a mixer, he enjoyed his own company and the job certainly gave him plenty of time alone. He had never married. Never wanted to. Approaching his fortieth birthday he was happy alone. He had a couple of friends who lived in the town, men he could share a drink with if he felt the need for company, but most of his time was spent in the small bungalow which overlooked the cemetery. It came with the job. He'd converted one of the sheds in the back garden into a workshop and he did his most precious work there. Carving shapes from lumps of wood he picked up in the cemetery. The thick growths of trees which populated the graveyard offered him plenty of raw material.The walking sticks he made from fallen branches he'd often sold at Hinkston's twice-weekly market. Some had fetched upwards of fifty pounds each, but it wasn't the monetary rewards which interested Bob, it was the craft itself.

He stood at the graveside a moment longer, peering through the rain towards the lights of the town. The street lights looked like jewels twinkling on a sheet of black velvet.

The cemetery was about half a mile from the town centre, on a steep hill designed to help drainage, but some of the older graves had begun to break up and sink and Bob feared that there might be some subsidence. However, the damage to the graves was not all attributable to natural causes.

There had been a spate of vandalism during the last three weeks. Gravestones had been smashed, flowers scattered from new plots, paint sprayed on headstones and, in the worst case, a grave had been tampered with. About two feet of earth had been excavated but, fortunately, the vandals had not dug down as far as the coffin.

Bob wondered what kind of people found pleasure from disturbing the dead and where they rested. The consensus of opinion in Hinkston itself seemed to point to youngsters. Bob had caught a young couple about a fortnight ago, laid out naked on top of one of the older graves but vandalism had been the last thing on their minds. He smiled at the recollection. Of how the boy had tried to run with his trousers round his ankles while the girl screamed and scuttled along beside him waving her bra like some kind of white surrender flag. Bob hadn't reported that particular incident to the police but the vandalism itself worried him. Many nights he'd left his bungalow and walked the tree lined paths through the cemetery in an effort to catch the vandals but his vigils so far had proved fruitless.

He continued to shovel earth into the grave, anxious to finish his task and return to the warmth of his home, to get out of his wet clothes.

The flowers from the funeral lay in a heap to one side of the hole, he would replace those when he'd finished. The rain tapped out a steady rhythm on the cellophane which covered the blooms, running off the clear covering like tears.

Bob shovelled more earth, trying to ignore the growing ache in his back.

The noise came from behind him.

At first he wasn't sure whether or not it was merely the rain pattering through the thick branches which hung overhead but, when it came again he was sure that the sound was coming from beyond the cluster of bushes which gathered around the grave like camouflaged mourners.

Bob stopped immediately and looked round, shielding his eyes from the rain and attempting to see through the darkness to the source of the noise.

He stood and waited but heard nothing.

After a moment or two he continued with his task.

Another foot or so and he would be finished, he thought, thankfully.

The noise came from behind him again, this time slightly to the left.

Bob dropped the spade and spun round, almost slipping on the wet earth.

It could be an animal of some kind he reasoned, taking a step towards the bushes. He'd found squirrels, even a badger during some of his nocturnal strolls through the cemetery. But, it was too early to be a badger. Despite the darkness his watch told him that it was only just 7.30 p.m.

Vandals perhaps? No, surely they'd wait until late, until they were sure no one was around.

He parted the bushes and eased through the first clump, surprised at how high they grew.

No one hiding behind them.

The rain continued to pelt down.

He felt something touch his shoulder.

Bob almost shouted aloud, his hand falling instinctively to the Swiss Army knife in his coat pocket.

The branch which had slapped against him had been blown by the wind.

The lower, leafless, branches were flailing about like animated flagellums and Bob shielded his face from the stinging twigs which whacked into him as he turned back towards the grave.

The figure which stood before him was holding the spade he had dropped.

In the driving rain Bob could not make out the features, he merely strode towards the figure, calling that it was private property and, besides that, to put his spade down.

The figure swung the spade in a wide arc which caught Bob in the side of the face. The powerful impact splintered bone and his left cheekbone seemed to fold in upon itself. The strident crack of bone was clearly audible over his strangled cry of pain. The figure advanced and stood over him for a moment, watching as blood from his pulverised face poured down his coat. Then the figure brought the spade down a second time, this time on his legs.

Both shin bones were broken by the blow and Bob screamed in agony, feeling one of the shattered tibias tear through the flesh of his leg.

He fell back into the mud, the merciful oblivion of

unconsciousness enfolding him, but seconds before he slipped away he felt his head being lifted almost tenderly.

Then he saw the long, thin, double-edged knife which, seconds later, was pushed slowly into his right eye.

The figure pushed on the blade until it felt the point scrape bone, then, as easily as a man lifts a child, the figure lifted Bob Tucker's body.

All that remained to show that a struggle had even taken place was the blood on the ground and, as the rain continued to fall, even that was soon washed away.

Thirteen

She looked at her watch and lit up a cigarette, puffing slowly on it, gazing at the phone as if it were a venomous snake sure to bite her the moment she extended her hand.

Nikki Reeves sat for five minutes until she finally picked up the receiver and jabbed out the digits. She waited, taking a last drag of her cigarette and stubbing it out in the ashtray. The tones sounded in her ear. She waited.

'Come on,' she whispered, ready to replace the receiver if necessary.

There was a click and she heard a familiar voice.

'Hello.'

She smiled.

'Hello, John, it's me, can you speak?' she said.

'If you mean is my wife here the answer is no,' Hacket said, irritably. 'I told you not to call me at home again, Nikki.'

'I had to speak to you. I have to know what's going on. You haven't been in to the school, I was worried.'

'I'm touched,' he muttered, sarcastically.

'John, what's wrong?' she wanted to know. 'I'm sorry for calling your home, I can understand you being angry about that.'

'When I told you not to call again I meant it. Not just here but anywhere.'

Nikki sat up, her brow creasing into a frown. She gripped the receiver more tightly.

'What are you saying? You don't want to see me again?'

There was silence at the other end then finally Hacket spoke again, his tone softer this time.

'You said you realised the affair couldn't go on indefinitely. I think it's time we stopped seeing one another.'

'Why the sudden change of heart?' she wanted to know.

'Things have happened that I can't discuss, that I don't want to discuss. It's over between us, Nikki. There wasn't much there to begin with, but I've been thinking and it's best ended now.'

'A sudden attack of conscience?' she snapped. 'It isn't quite as easy as that, John. We both knew what we were getting into. Why can't you talk to me, tell me what's bothering you?'

'For Christ's sake, Nikki, you're not my wife, you're just . . .' The sentence faded as a hiss of static broke up the line.

'Just a quick fuck,' she snapped. 'You don't have the right to just drop me like that. I'm not a tart you picked up in a bar. You didn't pay me. Unless that's what the perfume and the jewellery were.' She touched the onyx almost unconsciously.

'What do you want me to do, stick a cheque in the post?' Hacket said, angrily.

'You bastard.'

'Look Nikki, I made a mistake, right? End of story. My wife needs me now.'

'And what if *I* need you?' she said, challengingly.

'It's over,' he told her again.

'And what if I hadn't rung you. What were you going to do, hope that I'd forget what had happened in the last three months? Avoid me at work? You could have had the courage to tell me to my face, John.'

'Look, I can't talk any longer, Sue will be back any minute. It's finished.'

She was about to say something else when he hung up.

She gripped the receiver for a moment longer then slammed it down on the cradle, her breath coming in short gasps. Finished was it? Nikki lit up another cigarette and got to her feet, walking through to the sitting room where she poured herself a brandy, her hands shaking with anger.

Finished.

She fought back her tears of rage.

Finished.

Not yet, she thought.

September 23, 1940

George Lawrenson looked at the file marked 'Genesis' and nodded. The notes, the thoughts and theories contained within that manilla file were the sum of his work over the last ten or fifteen years. Only in the last few months had his ideas actually seen fruition.

And then, once those ideas had become facts, those who sought to control him had ordered him to stop the work which had been a greater part of his life. They had no right to stop him.

They had no understanding.

'Do you think they've changed their minds about the project?' Margaret Lawrenson asked, watching as her husband slipped the file into his small suitcase.

'I won't know until I get there,' he said.

The call from London had come late the previous evening. He had been told to come to the capital for 're-evaluation' (he hated their jargon) of his work. 'First they order me to stop and now they ask for more results.' He shrugged.

Margaret smiled and crossed to him, kissing him lightly on the cheek.

'You take care of yourself while I'm away,' he said, softly. 'Remember, there are two of you now.' He smiled and patted her stomach.

'What if they order you to stop, George?' she asked.

'Do you want me to stop?' he countered.

'I know you believe in what you're doing. *I* believe in what you're doing. Be careful, that's all I ask.'

He locked the suitcase.

'Where are the copies of my notes?' he asked finally.

'Hidden,' she assured him. 'If the originals are destroyed I've got the copies, don't worry.'

'They won't destroy them, they're not that stupid. Genesis is far too important for that and they realise it.' He picked up his suitcase and headed for the stairs. She descended with him, walking to the front door and out onto the drive. He slid the case onto the passenger seat of the car then walked around to the driver's side.

'Call me when you get to London,' she said, watching as he clambered behind the wheel and started the engine. Then she retreated to the front door and watched as he pulled away.

Lawrenson guided the car slowly down the driveway, turning to wave as he reached the end.

It was then that the car exploded.

The entire vehicle disappeared beneath a searing ball of yellow and white flame, pieces of the riven chassis flying in all directions. The concussion wave was so powerful that Margaret Lawrenson, standing more than fifty yards away, was thrown to the ground, her ears filled by the deafening roar as the car blew up.

A thick, noxious mushroom of smoke rose from the wreckage, billowing up towards the sky like a man-made storm cloud. Flames engulfed what little remained of the car, burning petrol spreading in a blazing pool around the debris. Cinders floated through the air like filthy snow and, as Margaret finally pulled herself upright and ran towards the flaming shell of the car she could smell burning rubber and a sickly, sweeter stench.

The odour of burning flesh.

The heat of the flames kept her back, away from the

twisted remains of the car which were now glowing white from the incredible heat. But inside she could see what was left of her husband, burned so badly he resembled a spent match, still clutching what was left of the steering wheel with hands that had turned to charcoal.

She dropped to her knees in the driveway, sobbing.

Other eyes had seen the blast.

More professional eyes.

The two figures who sat in the jeep across the road, hidden by trees, watched appreciatively as the car first exploded then blazed.

The first of them smiled, the second reached for the field telephone.

'Give me the Prime Minister's personal aide,' he said, in clipped tones. There was a moment's silence then he continued. 'Tell Mr Churchill that, as of 10.46 a.m. today, Project Genesis ceased.'

Major David Catlin replaced the phone and gazed once more at the flames.

Fourteen

Hacket felt as if he'd been hit with an iron bar. His senses were dulled, his head aching. He moved as if in a trance, stopping to hold on to furniture every now and then as if afraid he was going to fall.

On the sofa, Sue sat quietly, her face pale, her eyes red and puffy from so many tears. She looked exhausted, as if the effort of so much sobbing had sucked every last ounce of strength from her.

She still wore the black skirt and jacket which she'd worn to Lisa's funeral.

Hacket had tried to coax her into changing after the last of the mourners had gone but she had merely shaken her head and remained on the sofa, her eyes vacant. He had wondered a couple of times if she had slipped into shock but, each time he'd touched her she'd managed a smile, even kissed his hand as he'd brushed her cheek.

Now he stood in the kitchen waiting for the kettle to boil, hands dug in the pockets of his trousers.

The day had passed so slowly. It seemed that each minute had somehow stretched into hours, each hour into an eternity. The pain of their loss had become almost physical. Hacket rubbed a hand across his forehead and watched the steam rise from the kettle, just as he had watched it first thing that morning when he'd risen, dreading what was to come.

The arrival of the flowers.

Then the guests. (They had limited those present to his own parents and Sue's sister and her husband.)

And finally the hearse.

Hacket swallowed hard, fighting back tears at the recollection.

The huge vehicle had completely dwarfed the tiny coffin. Hacket had thought how easily he could have carried the box himself, under one arm.

He made the coffee, reaching into the cupboard for an aspirin in an effort to relieve the pain which still gnawed at the base of his skull. He took a sip of coffee, scarcely noticing when the hot liquid burnt his tongue.

And at the cemetery they had watched as the box was lowered into the grave, again so pitifully small. He had feared that Sue would collapse. She had spent the entire service crushed against him, weeping uncontrollably, but he had tried to fight the tears, to be strong for both of them. It had been a fight he had no hope of winning. As the small box had come to rest on the floor of the grave he had surrendered to the pain inside him and broken down. And they had supported each other, oblivious to those around them, to the empty words the vicar spoke. Words like 'resurrection'.

Hacket now shook his head slowly and sighed.

The service had seemed to take an age and finally, when it was over, both he and Sue had been led like lost children back to the waiting car and driven back to the house. The mourners, feeling as though they were intruding, had stayed for less than an hour then left the Hackets alone with their grief.

Sue had slept for a couple of hours that afternoon but Hacket could find no such peace. He had paced the sitting room, smoking and drinking, wanting to get drunk, to drink himself into oblivion but knowing that he had to be there when Sue woke up. She needed him more now than ever before.

Even more than Nikki needed him.

He pushed the thought to one side angrily, picked up the mugs of coffee and headed back towards the sitting room.

Sue had her eyes closed and Hacket hesitated, thinking she was asleep but, as he sat down opposite her she opened her eyes and looked at him.

'I didn't mean to wake you,' he said, softly, smiling.

'I wasn't asleep. Just thinking.'

'About what?' he asked, handing her the coffee.

'About that stupid phrase people always use when someone's died. "Life must go on." Why must it?' Her face darkened.

'Sue, come on, don't talk like that. We have to go on, for Lisa's sake.'

'Why, John? She's dead. Our child is gone. We'll never see her again, never be able to hold her, kiss her.' Her eyes were moist but no tears came. Hacket wondered if tear ducts could drain dry as he watched Sue wipe her eyes. She shook her head, wearily.

So much pain.

'I should go and see my father tomorrow,' she said, quietly.

'No. Not yet. You're not ready.'

'And what if he dies too? What if he dies when I should have been with him?'

Hacket got up, crossed the room then sat down beside her, pulling her closer.

'Your sister could have stayed for a few days, she could have visited him.'

'She had to get back to Hinkston, her husband has to work and they have a child, John. It wouldn't be fair to leave him alone.'

'You do too much, Sue. If ever anything's needed to be done, you're the one who's done it. Never Julie. You take too much responsibility on yourself.'

'That's the way I am.'

'Well maybe it's time you started putting yourself first in order of priorities instead of coming second to everyone else's needs.' He gently held her chin, turned her head and kissed her on the lips. She gripped his hand and squeezed.

'I love you,' she whispered.

'Then prove it. Come to bed, get a good night's sleep.'

'In a while,' she said. 'You go up, I won't be long.' She glanced down at the coffee table and noticed a letter addressed to her lying beside a card offering 'Sincerest Sympathies'. 'What's this?' she asked him, reaching for the letter.

'It came this morning. I figured you'd read it when you felt like it.'

'I don't recognise the writing,' she said, turning the envelope over in her hands.

'Can't it wait until the morning?'

'Just give me a minute, John. Please,' she asked softly and kissed him.

Hacket rose and headed for the hall.

'One minute,' he reminded her then she heard his footfalls on the stairs as he climbed.

Sue put down her coffee, let loose a weary breath then opened the letter. It was just one piece of paper, no address at the top and, as she glanced at the bottom, she noticed it wasn't signed either. She checked the envelope again, ensuring that it hadn't been delivered to the wrong house. Her name was there, the address was correct.

'Dear Mrs Hacket,' she read aloud, her eyes skimming over the neat lettering. 'I know what you will think of me for writing to you but I had a feeling you would want to know what has been going on between myself and your husband, John . . .' The words faded into silence as she read the remainder of the note, her mouth open slightly.

She read it again, more slowly this time. Then, she folded it, gripped it in her hand and got to her feet.

She paused at the bottom of the stairs, looking up towards the landing, then at the crumpled letter.

Sue began to ascend.

Fifteen

'I should have stayed with her for a couple of days,' said Julie Clayton, gazing out of the side window of the Sierra. 'I should have gone to see Dad too.'

'They're best left on their own, there's nothing you could do,' Mike Clayton said, glancing agitatedly at the car ahead of him. He indicated to overtake, saw that the car ahead was speeding up and dropped back again. 'Come on you bastard,' he hissed. 'Either put your foot down or get out the bloody way.'

He looked down at the dashboard clock.

10.42 p.m.

'We're not going to make it back in time at this rate,' he said, irritably. 'I said you should have come alone.'

'Sue *is* my sister, Mike,' Julie snapped. 'She needed me there.'

'Well your own son needs you now,' he reminded her, attempting to overtake the car in front once again. He stepped on the accelerator hard, easing the Sierra out into the centre of the road, ignoring the lights which he saw coming towards him.

'Mike, for God's sake,' Julie gasped, seeing the oncoming vehicle but her husband seemed oblivious to the approaching car. He pressed down harder, the needle on the speedometer touching eighty as he sped past the van ahead of him.

The car coming the other way swerved to miss the Sierra, the driver slamming on his brakes, simultaneously hitting the hooter. The car skidded and looked like crashing but the driver wrestled it back onto the road and drove on.

Mike Clayton, now clear of the van which had been blocking him put his foot down.

They passed a sign which read 'HINKSTON 25 MILES'.

Clayton shook his head, trying to coax more speed from the car.

Julie also glanced at the clock and saw that it was fast approaching 10.47. She guessed it would take another twenty minutes before they reached home, provided there were no more delays.

She swallowed hard and looked across at her husband who was gripping the wheel so tightly his knuckles were white.

She too was beginning to wonder if they would reach Hinkston in time.

She prayed that they did.

Sixteen

'Who is she, John?'

Sue stood in the bedroom doorway, the letter held before her like an accusation.

Hacket looked across from the bed and frowned, not quite sure what was happening. Sue crossed to the bed, standing beside it, looking down at him, a combination of anger and hurt in her eyes.

More pain.

The realisation slowly began to creep over him.

'I had a feeling you would want to know what has been going on between myself and your husband,' she read aloud.

Hacket exhaled deeply, wanting to say something but knowing that whatever words he found they would be inadequate.

'I do not care what you think of me,' Sue continued, reading from the crumpled letter. 'But I felt you had a right to know what has been happening between us.'

'Sue . . .'

She interrupted him.

'I do not like being used,' she read, her eyes still rivetted to the paper. Then, finally, she looked at him. 'Who is she?'

He knew that it was pointless to lie.

At least clear one part of your conscience, eh?

'Her name's Nikki Reeves,' he said, quietly. 'She works at the school.'

It was said. There was no turning back now.

'You had an affair with her?' Sue said and it was a statement rather than a question. 'How long did it last?'

'Three months.'

He watched as she sat down on the edge of the bed, the

letter still held in her hand. She had her back to him as if to look at him caused her disgust. He wouldn't have blamed her if disgust was the emotion she was feeling but he guessed it was more painful than that.

'Is it over now?' she wanted to know.

'Would you believe me if I told you?'

'Is it over?'

'Yes. I finished it a couple of days ago.'

She looked at him finally, a bitter smile on her lips.

'All those meetings at school you went to, you were really with *her*.' Her eyes narrowed suddenly. 'You never brought her here did you?'

'No, never.'

'And where did your little *liaisons* take place, John?' she asked with something bordering on contempt. 'In the back of the car? In an empty classroom or office?'

'Sue, for Christ's sake it wasn't as sordid as that. She has a flat . . .'

'Oh, her own place, how convenient. Somewhere to wash away the dirt afterwards.' The last sentence was barbed and it cut deep. 'How old is she?'

'Twenty-two. Is that really important?'

'I thought teachers were meant to have flings with pubescent pupils, nymphomaniac sixth-formers. Still, you always liked to do things differently didn't you, John. Why someone so young? Re-affirming your attractiveness now you're reaching the dreaded thirtieth birthday?'

'Don't be ridiculous.'

'Me? You're the one who had a bloody affair with a secretary at your school, John. I would have thought *that* qualified as ridiculous, wouldn't you?' She glared at him, her eyes moist.

'Don't patronise me, Sue,' he said, irritably. 'I know it was wrong and I'm sorry. If it's any consolation I feel pretty bloody lousy about it as well.'

'It *isn't* any consolation,' she snapped.

They sat in uncomfortable silence until Sue spoke again.

'Why, John? At least tell me that,' she said, quietly.

He shrugged.

'I don't know. I really don't know. Whatever explanation I give you is going to sound inadequate, pointless.' He sucked in a deep breath. 'I can't explain it.'

'Can't or won't?' she demanded.

'I can't,' he replied with equal anger, trying not to raise his voice but frustrated in the knowledge that whatever she said she was right. What he had done was indefensible. 'Look, I'm not proud of what I did. It just happened.'

'Affairs don't just *happen*,' she chided. 'What was the attraction anyway? Is she pretty? Got a nice figure? Is she good in bed? Not that you'd have known that until you got her back to her flat though, would you? Well come on, tell me, I'm curious. Did this pretty young thing just fall into your arms?'

He shook his head but didn't answer.

'Tell me,' she snarled, vehemently. 'Is she pretty?'

'Yes,' he confessed.

'*And* good in bed?'

'Sue, for God's sake . . .'

'Is she good? Come on, I'm curious, I told you. Is she good in bed?'

He smiled humourlessly.

'What do you want me to do, rate her one to ten?'

'Just tell me if she was good,' Sue snarled.

'Yes,' he said, almost inaudibly. 'It was only ever a physical thing. I didn't feel anything for her. I never stopped loving *you*, Sue.'

'Am I supposed to be grateful, John? You'll be telling me next that I should understand why you did it. Well, perhaps I ought to try and understand. Tell me why, make me understand.'

'Since your father's been ill . . .'

'Don't blame it on my father, you bastard.'

'Let me finish,' he snapped, waiting until she was looking at him once again. 'Since he's been ill you've been obsessed with him, with what he's got. You've been distant. Perhaps I felt neglected, I know it sounds like a fucking lame excuse but it's all I can think of.'

'Oh I'm sorry, John,' she said, sarcastically. 'I should have realised you weren't getting enough attention, it's practically my fault you had this affair. It sounds as if I forced you into it.'

'That's not what I'm saying and you know it.'

'You're saying that you couldn't have what you wanted from me so you picked up some little tart and fucked her,' Sue spat the words.

'She's not a tart.'

'Why are you defending her, John? I thought you said it was only a physical thing. If you wanted sex that badly you might as well have found a whore, paid for it. I do apologise for having other things on my mind, if only you'd let me know how you were suffering perhaps I could have fitted you in a couple of nights a week.'

'Now you *are* being ridiculous.'

'What the hell do you expect?' she yelled at him. 'Rational conversation? On the day my daughter is buried I find out my husband's been having an affair.' He saw her expression darken, her eyes narrow. Hacket could almost see the thoughts forming inside her mind. That final piece of deduction which would damn him forever. 'You were with her the night Lisa was killed weren't you?'

He didn't answer.

'Weren't you?' she hissed.

He nodded.

'I can't get that out of my mind,' Hacket whispered. 'The thought that if I'd been here it probably wouldn't have happened. You don't have any idea what that's doing to me, Sue.'

'I don't care what it's doing to you,' she said, coldly. 'You killed our daughter.'

'Don't say that,' he snapped.

'You didn't hold the knife but you're as responsible for her death as the man who killed her. Our daughter died for the sake of your bloody affair.'

She lashed out at him, wildly, madly, the suddenness of the attack taking him by surprise. Her nails raked his cheek, drawing blood. Hacket tried to grab her wrists, seeing now that tears were coursing down her cheeks. She struck at him again but he caught her arm and held it, getting a good grip on the other wrist too. She struggled frantically to be free of his restraining hands, wanting also to be away from the touch of his skin against hers. It was as if he were something loathsome.

'Let go of me,' she shouted, glaring at him. 'Don't touch me.'

He released her and she pulled away, moving from the bed, almost falling as she reached the door. Hacket swung himself out of bed and moved towards her but she held up a hand to ward him off.

'Don't you come near me,' she hissed. 'Don't.'

He hesitated, knowing that whatever words or actions he chose were useless. The two of them remained frozen, like the still frame of a film, then, finally, Hacket took a step back. A gesture of defeat.

'Sue, please,' he said. 'Don't shut me out. Not *now*. We need each other.'

She almost laughed.

'Do we? Why do you need me? You can go back to your whore can't you?' She glanced at him a second longer then turned and left the bedroom.

He thought about following her as he heard her footfalls

on the stairs but he knew it was useless. Instead, he spun round and, with a roar of rage and frustration, he brought his fist down with stunning force on the dressing table. Bottles of perfume and items of make-up toppled over with the impact. Hacket gripped the top of the dressing table, gazing at his own pale reflection in the mirror.

The face that looked back at him was despair personified.

Seventeen

The barking of the dog woke him.

In the stillness of the night it seemed to echo inside the room, inside his head and he sat up in bed immediately, glancing to one side, squinting at the clock.

1.46 a.m.

Brian Devlin thought about snapping on the bedside light but hesitated. He rubbed his eyes, the barking of the dog still reverberating through the darkness. The animal could be anywhere on the farm, perhaps even in one of the fields, noise carried a long way in the stillness of such a late hour.

Devlin hauled himself out of bed and padded across to the window which overlooked the main farmyard.

The porchlight which burned offered little by way of penetrative glow and Devlin could see no further than the land rover which was parked just outside his back door. Again he thought about putting on a light, but again he hesitated, reaching instead for the torch which stood on the floor beside the bed.

Then he slid a hand beneath the bed and pulled out the Franchi over-under shotgun. He broke the weapon, thumbed in two cartridges from the box in the bedside cabinet then moved quickly towards the stairs, the torch gripped in one hand, the shotgun cradled over the crook of his other arm.

At the back door he paused to step into his boots, pulling his dressing gown more tightly around him. It was cold and he cursed as his bare feet were enveloped by the freezing wellingtons.

Outside, the dog continued to bark.

Devlin unlocked the back door and slipped out into the night.

He stood still for a moment, squinting into the gloom, letting his eyes become accustomed to the darkness, then he headed off in the direction of the barking Alsatian.

Devlin was sure the sound was coming from the rear of the barn. From the chicken coop. He'd lost nearly a dozen chickens to foxes over the last month or so. This time he'd catch the bastard, blow it to pieces. The woods which grew so thickly on the eastern side of his land were perfect breeding ground for foxes and he had already searched part of them in an effort to track down the vermin, but so far with no success.

Other farmers, on the western side of Hinkston, had reported no such losses of poultry and that, in itself, irritated Devlin. He'd been running the farm for the past twenty years, ever since his twentieth birthday, he didn't have the resources that the farmers on the other side of the town had. His was a small concern built up over the years first by his father and now by himself. The farm was a consuming passion. So much so that his ex-wife had found it impossible to accept that the farm and farm business would always take precedence. Perhaps, Devlin had thought when she'd left him, she didn't like taking second place to a sty full of saddle-backs. He smiled at the recollection. Of how she had tried to play the farmer's wife, milking the cows, even mucking out the pigs but, after a year or so the novelty value had worn off and she'd seen it for what it really was. Bloody hard work. Devlin worked a sixteen-hour day sometimes to keep the farm ticking over. There was no time for a social life. It had been almost inevitable that the marriage should break up. There had been no children though, and consequently no complications. She was only too happy to leave and he was quite content to carry on devoting *all* his time to the farm. If he had one regret it was that they had been childless. The thought that, after his death, there would be no one to run the farm bothered him. But, he mused, when he was six feet under he wouldn't be worrying about anything anyway, would he?

Right now, all that worried him was the barking Alsatian.

He steadied the shotgun in his other hand, ready to drop the torch and fire should he see a fox, but as he drew closer to the barn and the chicken coop beyond a thought occurred to him. Surely the dog's insistent barking would have frightened the would-be predator away by now? Why was the animal still so agitated?

The barking stopped suddenly and Devlin found himself enveloped in the silence. He paused for a moment, waiting for the Alsatian to begin again.

It didn't.

The silence persisted.

Maybe frightened the bloody fox off, Devlin thought, chased it away and now it's going back to get some sleep which is what he himself ought to be doing. He was supposed to be up again in less than five hours.

Nevertheless he advanced towards the barn noticing that one of the doors was slightly open. He muttered to himself and moved towards it.

He was almost there when he tripped over something.

Cursing to himself he flicked on the torch, shining it over the ground around him.

The beam picked out the dead Alsatian.

Devlin frowned as he looked at the animal, leaning closer.

From the angle of its head he guessed that its neck had been broken. Its tongue lolled from one side of its mouth and he saw that blood was spreading in a wide pool around its head, spilling from its bottom jaw. The dog's mouth looked as if it had been forced apart, its bottom jaw almost torn off. Devlin prodded it with the toe of his boot, spinning round when he heard a rustling sound from inside the barn.

He was seized by a deep anger. Whoever had done this to his dog was probably still inside.

'Right, you bastard,' he hissed under his breath and blundered into the barn, shining the torch all around. Up to the second storey where hay and straw were kept. The light bounced off the row of tools which were lined up against one wall. The rakes, the spades, the cultivators, the sythes and the pitchforks.

Nothing moved.

'You've got ten seconds to come out,' he shouted, hearing a slight creak from above him.

There was someone up on the second storey.

It was accessible only by a ladder which led up through a trap-door and it was towards this ladder which Devlin now moved, anger at the killing of his dog overriding all other emotions. Whoever was up there was going to pay, one way or another he thought as he reached the ladder.

He paused, one foot on the bottom rung. Then he jammed the torch into the waistband of his dressing gown and gripped the shotgun in his free hand.

He began to climb.

'You're on private property,' he called as he ascended. 'What I do to you is *my* business. You're on my land.'

He was half-way up by now.

'You didn't have to kill my dog, you bastard.'

Devlin slowed down as he reached the trapdoor, pushing against it hard. It flew back and crashed to the floor with a bang that reverberated throughout the barn.

'I'll give you one more chance to come out,' he called, pulling himself through the narrow entrance. 'You can't get past me, this is the only way out.'

Silence.

'I've got a shotgun,' he called.

Nothing.

Devlin took a couple of paces towards where he thought he'd first heard the sound, holding the shotgun in one hand, playing the torch beam ahead of him, over the bales of hay and straw which were stacked like over-sized house bricks.

There were plenty of places to hide, he thought.

The beams creaked beneath his feet as he walked, stopping every few paces to shine the torch behind him, checking that the intruder hadn't tried to slip out through the trapdoor.

Below, the barn door banged shut.

Devlin spun round, running back to the trap door, peering through.

The door swung open again then crashed shut once more and he realized that it was the wind which had caused the movement.

He straightened up and continued with his search of the loft area.

Had his ears been playing tricks on him, he wondered? The loft seemed to be empty. No one hiding behind the bales. No sign of any disturbance. The barn appeared to be empty. Devlin shone the torch back and forth over the upper level once more then shook his head and turned, heading back towards the ladder.

He laid the torch and the shotgun on the rim of the trap door as he lowered himself onto the ladder.

The barn door creaked open again and remained open.

Devlin jammed the torch back into one of the pockets of his dressing gown and, holding the shotgun in one hand climbed down carefully.

He stood at the bottom of the ladder, listening.

Only silence greeted him.

Puzzled and a little disappointed, Devlin made for the door, closing it behind him. He turned, his torch shining ahead of him.

The body of the dog was gone.

There was just a puddle of crimson to show where it had been laying. The dead animal had vanished as if in to thin air.

Devlin sucked in an angry breath.

This had gone too far. If someone was pissing about with him then he didn't find it very funny. He stormed off back across the farm yard towards the house.

Behind him, the barn door opened a fraction.

Devlin pushed open the back door and stormed in, snapping on lights now, putting down the shotgun and cursing to himself.

The figure was standing in the kitchen

Devlin opened his mouth to say something but no words would come. He reached back for the shotgun but it was too late.

The figure lunged forward, driving the pitchfork before it like a bayonet.

The twin steel prongs punctured Devlin's chest, one of them skewering his heart, the other ripping through a lung, bursting it like a fleshy balloon. Blood erupted from the wounds, spraying the kitchen, and the farmer was propelled backwards with incredible force, driven by the sheer strength of the thrust.

He crashed back against the wall, blood spattering the plaster and leaving a red smear as he slid down to the ground, still transfixed by the pitchfork. He tried to scream but his throat was full of blood and, as he tried to move he could hear the air hissing through his ruptured lung, could feel the cold breeze gushing through the hideous rent. While, all the time, blood from his punctured heart fountained into the air as if expelled from a high pressure hose.

As unconsciousness began to overtake him he saw the figure standing over him.

Saw the long, stiletto blade being held before him.

Devlin found some lost reserve of strength and, even with the pitchfork still embedded in his chest, he tried to drag himself towards the open back door.

But the figure merely knelt beside him, like a priest administering the last rites.

Devlin felt his head being cradled almost lovingly in the intruder's hands and then, as he found the breath for one final scream of agony, he felt the knife being pushed slowly into his right eye.

Eighteen

In the days following Lisa's funeral Hacket found himself enveloped by a feeling similar to isolation. Despite his return to work (perhaps *because* of it – the endless chorus of condolence rapidly became tiresome) and the necessity to mix with people once more, he found that Sue was becoming even more distant. He felt like a lodger. She spoke to him as if he was a stranger for whom she existed solely to put food on the table and to offer perfunctory conversation.

Instead of returning to her own job as a secretary at a computer firm she had considered giving up work completely. Hacket had suggested that, under the circumstances, that might not be a very good idea. Something which had only served, it seemed, to push her into resignation more rapidly. The firm had given her four weeks' compassionate leave but Sue felt that wasn't enough.

And she had begun returning to the hospital on a nightly basis to visit her father.

His condition had deteriorated during the past week and it now seemed only a matter of days until the inevitable happened.

As Hacket sat staring blankly at the television screen he heard the door open and realised that Sue had returned from another of her nightly vigils. She closed the front door behind her and walked straight into the kitchen where she made two coffees, returning to the sitting room to set one of them in front of Hacket. He smiled gratefully but received no reciprocal gesture.

She sat down in one of the armchairs and looked, with equal indifference at the screen.

'Is there any change in your father's condition?' Hacket asked, watching as she kicked her shoes off.

Sue shook her head.

'Have they said how long?' he said, quietly.

'They can't be specific. Days, weeks. They don't know,' she told him, still gazing at the TV. She took a couple of sips of coffee then picked up her shoes. 'I feel tired. I'm going to bed.'

'It's only nine o'clock,' he said.

'I said I was tired.'

'Sue, wait. We have to talk.'

'About what?'

'You know what. About us. About what's happened. We can't go on like this.'

'Then perhaps we shouldn't go on,' she told him, flatly.

Hacket frowned, surprised by the vehemence of her words and disturbed by their implication.

'You mean you want us to split up?' he said.

She shrugged.

'I don't know, I haven't thought about it properly. I've got other things on my mind.'

'Listen to me,' he said, trying to control the tone of his voice. 'We've been married for almost seven years. I love you, I don't want to lose you. I want you back, Sue.'

'I want Lisa back but wishing for it isn't going to make it happen is it?' she countered, acidly.

'Lisa's dead,' he said, through clenched teeth and then finally, he raised his voice in frustration. 'Jesus Christ, Sue do you think you're the only one feeling that pain. You haven't got a monopoly on grief you know. I miss her as much as you do. She was my daughter too, in case you hadn't noticed.' His breath was coming in gasps.

Sue regarded him impassively.

'We've got to rebuild our own lives,' he continued, more calmly. 'I'm not saying we should forget Lisa, we should never do that, she was the most precious thing in both our lives. But now all we've got is each other.' He sighed. 'I know you still feel angry about what happened between me and Nikki but it's over now, Sue. I said I was sorry and I'll keep on saying it as many times as you want me to. For as long as it takes for things to go back to normal between us.'

'They can't ever be normal again, John,' she told him with an air of finality. 'We're not talking about just an affair. We're talking about the death of our daughter. A death you *caused* because of your affair.' She eyed him angrily.

'I have to live with that knowledge,' he rasped. 'I don't need you to remind me all the fucking time. Do you have any idea what I'm feeling? What it's like to carry that guilt with me all the time? Do you care?'

'No John, I don't. All I care about, all I know is that our daughter is dead. That you've wrecked our marriage. Don't mention love to me again, you don't know the meaning of the word.'

'So what's the answer?' he wanted to know. 'Divorce? Is that going to make things better? It certainly isn't going to bring Lisa back is it? And if that sounds harsh it's because it hurts me to say it. Hurts me more than you'll ever know.'

There was an uneasy silence, finally broken by Sue.

'I've been thinking it might be best if I go away for a while,' she told him. 'To stay with Julie in Hinkston. We don't see much of each other now. And I need the break.'

'What about your father? Who's going go visit him?'

'I can drive in from Hinkston, it only takes an hour.'

'How long will you go for?'

'As long as it takes.' She got to her feet, shoes in hand, and walked to the door.

Hacket sank back on the sofa, drained. He heard her footfalls on the stairs as she climbed. He stared at the TV screen for a moment longer, listening to the endless catalogue of strikes, accidents, murders, kidnappings and rapes that the newsreader was relaying, then finally he got up and switched the set off.

He sat in silence for what seemed like an eternity then suddenly got to his feet, walked through into the hall and picked up the phone.

'I'd like to speak to Detective Inspector Madden please,' Hacket said when the phone was finally answered.

Madden wasn't available.

'What about Detective Sergeant Spencer?'

The man on the other end of the phone told him to wait a moment.

Hacket shifted the phone from one hand to the other agitatedly as he waited.

DS Spencer was in the office, he was told, but the man wanted to know what the call was about.

'Is it important? I want to speak to Spencer. Just tell him it's John Hacket,' the teacher told him.

There was a moment's silence at the other end, a hiss of static then the other man agreed, announced he was connecting Hacket, and the teacher heard a series of crackles and blips. Then Spencer's voice.

'Mr Hacket, what can I do for you?' the policeman asked.

'Is there any news on the men who murdered my daughter?' he wanted to know.

'We're following several leads. It's still early days . . .'

Hacket cut him short.

'Have you arrested anyone yet?' he snapped.

Spencer sounded somewhat perplexed.

'I told you, Mr Hacket, we have leads which we're following up but no arrests have been made yet. We'll inform you as soon as anything happens.'

Hacket nodded, thanked the DS then hung up. He stood staring down at the phone for a moment then looked up the stairs towards the landing, towards the room where his wife slept.

He clenched his fists until the nails dug into the palms of his hands.

No arrests yet.

And when they did catch the men, what then?

Hacket stalked back into the sitting room, reaching for his cigarettes. He lit one and sucked hard on it.

What then?

The thought had come to him only fleetingly to begin with, but now, as he stood alone in the deserted sitting room, that thought began to grow stronger. Building, spreading like some festering growth within his mind.

And he nurtured that thought.

Nurtured it and clung to it.

May 7, 1941

The contractions had begun almost an hour ago.

Margaret Lawrenson hauled herself out of the chair, her bloated belly almost causing her to topple over. She paced back and forth for a few moments, trying to relieve the awful cramping pains which came so rhythmically. Over the last sixty minutes the contractions had become more frequent and more intense. Each one almost took her breath away and, twice she reeled as if she were going to faint.

She was alone.

No doctor had been called to the house. No doctor *would* be called. Her husband had assured her that the birth would be a straightforward one and she had believed him.

The thought of George Lawrenson made her momentarily forget even the pains of labour.

Her husband had been dead almost nine months now, and since his murder (she had no doubt that he had been killed even though the autopsy and examination of the car had suggested a faulty petrol tank) she had lived in the large house on the outskirts of Hinkston alone. She had become reclusive, venturing into the town itself as little as possible. She had no friends there so no visitors ever came out to the house. But Margaret had preferred it that way. She had remained in the large building like some kind of guardian, her husband's papers, his notes on Project Genesis, safe in her care.

As she struggled towards the lab her legs buckled and she fell heavily, falling on her side. She felt a sudden gush of liquid from between her legs and looked down to see a flux of thin, blood-flecked discharge spreading across the carpet. Margaret grunted and tried to pull herself upright but it seemed the weight of the child she was carrying prevented that action and she was forced to drag herself along the floor, gasping for breath as she drew nearer the lab.

If only she could reach its sterile environment, its pain killers.

A contraction so savage it practically doubled her up caused her to cry out and, for a moment, she stopped crawling. It was difficult enough with the huge weight of the child in her belly, but now the pain was coursing through her as if it were liquid pumped into her veins by some insane transfusion.

Pain killers.

She moaned in agony and felt more warm liquid spilling onto the inside of her thighs. She looked down to see that it was blood.

She was less than ten feet from the door of the lab but it may as well have been ten miles. Every inch took a monumental effort both of will and endurance.

Margaret Lawrenson suddenly surrendered to the pain, rolling onto her back, knowing that she was not going to make it. Excruciating pain seemed to numb her lower body and she gripped the carpet in anguish as she felt the child move, beginning its slow emergence. She tried to breathe as her husband had taught her, tried to think about him standing beside her. Tried to think about anything other than the savage pain which followed her and caused her to cry out.

She screamed as she felt the child's head push clear of her vagina and now she was unsure whether it was being propelled by her own muscular contractions or using its own strength to escape the prison of the womb. Blood spattered onto the carpet and she felt the incredible pressure ease momentarily as the child's head showed. It nestled between her legs, stained with blood and pieces of placental waste. Margaret gripped the carpet in both fists, her jaws clamped together to prevent the escape of another scream. Perspiration beaded on her forehead and cheeks then ran in rivulets down her face.

She pushed harder, her muscles finally expelling the child which lay on the floor beneath her, still joined to her by the umbilical cord.

Margaret tried to sit up, to reach the child and, as she did she felt the remains of the placenta burst from her vagina in a swollen lump. She swivelled round, her body still enveloped by pain and reached for the child. It was coughing, its mouth filled with blood and saliva. She took it into her arms, using her index finger to scoop the thick mixture of crimson mucous from its tiny mouth. It began to cry immediately.

She raised herself up onto her knees, the baby held in her arms, the umbilicus dangling from its belly. It had to be severed.

She laid the child down again then took the slippery coil in both hands and raised it to her mouth.

Ignoring the taste of blood she bit through the cord, bright flecks of crimson filling her mouth and running down her chin. But she fought the need to vomit and swiftly tied the cord, wiping her mouth with the back of her hand.

The child continued to cry and she smiled as she heard the sound. It was a healthy yell to signal its arrival in the world. Margaret looked down at it. At her son. He was perfectly formed, and as she picked him up his sobs diminished slightly. She rocked him to and fro in that cold corridor, her hair matted with sweat, her clothes drenched with blood. The coppery odour of the crimson fluid was strong in her nostrils but she ignored it. All that mattered now was that her son was alive.

The second wave of contractions took her completely by surprise, both because of their intensity and the unexpectedness of their arrival.

She looked down at her belly to see that the flesh was undulating slowly, swelling then contracting.

As the pains grew more severe she realised what was happening.

She screamed in agony as the head of the second child nudged its way free.

Nineteen

The drive to Hinkston took her about an hour due to the heavy traffic leaving London, but as she guided the car down the main street of the town Sue Hacket noted that it was still barely noon.

The sunshine which had accompanied her on the first part of the drive had given way to a cold wind and the promise of rain. She glanced at the shoppers in the high street, noses red from the cold, some walking briskly, others standing and chatting.

Hinkston was a busy little town close enough to London to qualify as green-belt commuterland but also with enough distance to rightfully be called a country town. Its population, she guessed, was around eight thousand. At least that's what it had been three years ago when she and Hacket had last visited.

Sue drove through the town, past a library, and found herself surrounded by houses which were beginning to take on a solid uniformity. She knew she had entered the estate where her sister lived. She found the street then slowed up, looking for the number of the house. She counted them off as she drew nearer, smiling as she saw Julie standing on the front doorstep talking to the window-cleaner. As Sue parked the Metro outside the house, Julie waved and walked out to meet her. They embraced, watched by the window cleaner who nodded affably as Sue approached him, carrying a small suitcase. Julie introduced her and the window cleaner smiled, making some comment about how alike they were and both so sexy. Julie laughed and slapped him playfully on the shoulder. Sue could see his blue eyes lingering on her own breasts, his attention caught by the fact she wore no bra beneath her blouse. She slid past the window cleaner, leaving Julie to pay him.

Sue stood in the hallway of her sister's home and put down her suitcase, glancing around at the entryway.

There was a chain-store copy of 'The Haywain' hanging on one side of the hall, opposite a particularly large cuckoo-clock which looked as though it could have comfortably housed a vulture. Sue noticed that it was almost twelve o'clock and moved towards the sitting-room to avoid the appearance of the noisy bird. Sure enough, the mechanical occupant of the clock duly shot forth on the hour and proceeded to fill the hall with the most unholy din as the hour hand touched twelve.

Inside the sitting-room Sue again glanced around, noting the fixtures and fittings which filled her sister's house. The room was overflowing with ornaments. Perched on every available ledge. On top of the TV, the wall units, the bookcase. There was even a plastic model of the Eiffel Tower on top of the stereo.

'Mike brought that back from Paris for me,' Julie announced, entering the room. 'He was there on business the other week. He doesn't like ornaments himself but he collects them for me whenever he goes away.'

Sue smiled and held out her arms to embrace her sister. The two of them clung to each other for a moment then Julie kissed her lightly on the cheek.

'I'm pleased you came,' she said, softly.

They exchanged pleasantries, chatted about the weather and Julie told her sister about the window cleaner, what a randy sod he was. She chuckled as she poured tea for them both as they sat in the kitchen. Sue listened and smiled when she felt she should but her mind was elsewhere. Something Julie wasn't slow to notice.

'I'm not going to ask you what's on your mind,' she said, finally. 'You don't know how sorry we were to hear about Lisa. I thought what I'd have been like if anything had happened to Craig.'

Mention of her nephew seemed to coax a smile from Sue and she looked across the table at her sister.

'Where is he?' she asked.

'He's across the road playing with one of his friends. It keeps him from under my feet while the school half-term is on. He'll be pleased to see you. I'll fetch him in a little while.'

Sue nodded and sipped her tea.

'Mike's working late tonight, so . . .'

Sue chuckled at her sister's words and Julie looked puzzled.

'I'm sorry,' Sue explained, sighing. *Working late. Meetings.* She thought of John and his lover. The perennial excuse. *I've got to work late.* She finished her tea and began tracing a pattern around the edge of the cup with her index finger.

'What's going on, Sue?' Julie wanted to know. 'When you rang and asked to stop with us it was all *I* need to get away, and *I* can't stand to be in the house anymore. You never mentioned John. He could have come with you, you know.'

'John was one of the reasons I had to get away,' Sue said, raising her eyebrows.

'Why? What's wrong?'

Sue exhaled wearily wondering whether she ought to burden her sister with her worries but knowing that she had to tell someone. She couldn't carry on bottling up her feelings.

'He had an affair, Julie.' The words came out with ease.

She went on to explain what had happened. The letter. The discovery. The row.

How she blamed him for Lisa's death.

Julie listened intently, her face impassive.

'That's why I had to get away,' Sue continued. 'To give myself time to think, to decide where I go from here.'

Julie still didn't speak.

'I don't know if I can ever forgive him,' said Sue. 'I don't even know if I *want* to.'

The two women regarded each other silently, across the table. Sue feeling slightly drained after relaying the revelations of the last few weeks, Julie not sure what to say.

The silence was broken by the sound of the back door being flung open.

Craig Clayton bounded in, spreading dirt over the kitchen carpet as he bounced his football. He was smiling happily, the football strip which he wore covered in mud, just like his face. He saw Sue and bounded towards her.

She held out her arms to grab him, lifting him up onto her knee and kissing his muddy cheek.

Julie could see the tears forming in her sister's eyes.

'How's my favourite nephew?' Sue asked, hugging him.

'I'm all right,' he beamed and slipped from her grasp, heading for the sitting room.

'Boots off, football kit off, and into the bath,' Julie said. 'Look at the state of you. I've told you not to come into the house with your boots on.'

'But Mum, Mark's just as dirty as I am,' he told her as if that information would somehow pacify her.

'Well it's a good job you didn't bring him over here with you then, isn't it. No dinner until you've had a bath.'

He shrugged and looked at Sue as if expecting her to offer assistance but when she only smiled he turned and stalked back outside to remove his football boots.'

'Kids,' said Julie, smiling. 'Sometimes . . .' She allowed the sentence to trail off, feeling suddenly awkward.

'I'm going to change,' Sue told her, getting to her feet. 'I know where the spare room is. You take care of Craig.' She smiled and walked through into the sitting room then beyond to the hall, where she picked up her case and climbed the stairs.

Julie sat at the kitchen table a moment longer then went to see how her son was managing with his football boots.

Outside, the first spots of rain were beginning to fall.

Twenty

She woke with a start, propelled from the nightmare with a force that shook her and left her trembling.

Sue sat still in the darkness, trying to calm her laboured breathing, worried in case she'd woken anyone else in the house. The silence which greeted her seemed to indicate that she hadn't. She lay back down, her heart still beating fast, perspiration glistening on her forehead despite the chill in the room. She shivered then swung herself out of bed and closed the window.

The rain which had begun as a shower had turned into a full-scale downpour with the coming of night and Sue stared out into the gloom for a moment, noticing lights on in other bedrooms in other houses on the estate. Aware suddenly of her own nakedness she reached for her dressing gown and pulled it on, realizing that she would not be able to find the comfort of sleep so easily now. Instead she walked, barefoot, from the bedroom and out onto the landing, passing Julie and Mike's room. She paused to listen for any sounds of movement, any indication that she'd disturbed them.

Silence.

She repeated the procedure outside Craig's room, pushing his door open slightly to look in on him.

Clad in pyjamas with pictures of motorbikes on them, he lay cocooned underneath his quilt, his mouth slightly open, his breathing even. Sue stood looking at him for a moment longer. He was just two years older then Lisa. A healthy, strong boy. Sue carefully pulled his door closed and made her way downstairs.

Craig's eyes snapped open, his mind instantly alert. He heard footsteps on the stairs which he knew didn't belong to his mother or father. He lay beneath the quilt, only his eyes moving.

Sue snapped on the light in the kitchen and sat at the table while she waited for the kettle to boil. When it finally did she made herself a cup of tea and drank it slowly, gazing into empty air, listening to the steady ticking of the clock on the wall behind her. As she got to her feet to return to bed she noticed that it was 3.11 a.m.

She drifted off to sleep after about ten minutes, the pattering of the rain on the window an accompaniment to her steady breathing.

The door to the bedroom opened soundlessly and Craig stepped inside, his gaze never leaving Sue.

He moved to within two feet of the bed, looking at her, watching as she moved restlessly. But even her movements did not prevent his silent vigil. He remained beside the bed.

Julie had heard the movement and eased herself out of bed, careful not to disturb Mike.

Now she made her way down to her son's bedroom and peered round the door.

She saw that the bed was empty.

'Oh God,' she whispered, swallowing hard.

She turned and headed for the spare room.

Craig was still standing beside Sue looking down at her, watching the steady rise and fall of her chest.

Julie crossed to him and gripped his shoulder firmly.

He turned round and looked at her, smiling. Then he looked back at Sue.

'No,' Julie whispered, shaking her head, trying to coax him out of the room.

He hesitated then allowed himself to be led away.

Julie glanced at her sister, ensuring that she was still asleep. Then she closed the door and ushered Craig back to his own room.

He climbed back into bed and slid down beneath the quilt.

Julie knelt close by him and once again shook her head.

'No,' she said, quietly. 'Not her.'

Twenty-one

He would kill them.

That was the only answer.

He had lain awake thinking about it, even at work the idea was constantly with him.

Somehow Hacket was going to kill the men who had murdered his daughter. He didn't know how and he didn't know when. All he knew was he was going to kill them.

Of course there was the matter of practicality. If the police didn't know who they were then how was he to find out alone? And, even if he succeeded, what then? What if he found them and actually managed to end their lives? It would mean arrest, imprisonment. No jury in the land, no matter how sympathetic they might feel to his predicament, would be allowed to bring in a verdict of not-guilty once he was tried. But Hacket didn't seem to care about that. The thought that by ending the lives of his daughter's killers he would effectively be ending his own life made little impression on him.

What had begun as a vague wish had begun to turn slowly but surely into an obsession. Scarcely an hour passed that he did not think about finding and killing the men. He considered how he would make them suffer. Plotting and planning ways to rid the world of them. He revelled in his own inventiveness. He rejoiced in his capacity to imagine what he might do to them. Castration.

God, how he would love to draw the knife so slowly around the scrotum of the one who had penetrated his daughter. To slice through that soft flesh and expose the reeking purple egg-shaped objects inside. He would cut them free one at a time then, while the bastard bled to death, Hacket would push the knife into his anus. Split his bowel. And finally he would take the penis, that vile member which had violated his little girl and he would insert the point of the knife into the slit in the glans and he would push. Push until he sliced the organ in two, cutting slowly and carefully, finally severing it at the root.

Jesus, the thought was a good one and, as he lay in bed gazing at the ceiling he smiled to himself.

At first he had been horrified that such thoughts should have found a home within a supposedly educated and civilised mind like his own but then, as the thought of his dead daughter flashed back into his mind more vividly, the sight of her tiny body on that mortuary slab, he had actively pursued the thoughts. Each method of torture and death had been dredged from blacker regions of his mind until he felt as if he were pillaging the thoughts of some degenerate sadist.

He enjoyed the thoughts.

He would destroy their eyes.

The organs with which they had first looked upon his little girl.

Hacket thought how he would take the blade and cut across the glistening orbs, or else he would carve them from the sockets.

He would cut off each of their fingers in turn.

Cut off their ears.

Shatter their knees with an iron rod then methodically break every bone in their bodies.

Make them eat their own faeces.

The thoughts tumbled around inside his mind, each one to be savoured. Punishment for him would be meaningless. Nothing the law could do to him could make him suffer more than the death of his daughter.

And, perhaps, he thought, with vengeance would come forgiveness. When Susan saw what he had done to the killers of their child she would love him again. She would want him back.

He knew now, more than ever before, that his only hope of atonement lay in finding and killing the murderers of his child.

He swung himself out of bed, reaching for the bottle of whisky on the cabinet beside. He drank straight from the bottle, some of the fiery liquid spilling down his chest. The amber fluid burned its way to his stomach and he sucked in a deep breath, holding the bottle before him. He grinned, seeing his own distorted image in the glass.

If madness was a mirror then Hacket was indeed studying his own reflection.

Twenty-two

It all had an appalling familiarity about it.

The flowers in their cellophane wrappers, the empty words of the priest. The tears.

And the grave.

The inevitability of Tom Nolan's death made the event no less traumatic and Hacket found that, even though he hadn't known the man that well, he was fighting back tears as he stood at the graveside beside Sue, Julie and Mike.

Sue stood motionless, gazing down into the grave as if trying to read the brass nameplate. Hacket thought how serene she looked but he realised that what he had mistaken for serenity was something bordering on shock. He felt like waving a hand before her to see whether or not she would blink.

Julie was crying softly, comforted by her husband who kept her in his arms throughout the ceremony.

Grey clouds rolled by overhead, spilling a thin curtain of drizzle onto the tiny band of mourners. There were others standing nearby although they seemed reluctant to move closer to the grave for fear of intruding. Hacket guessed they were friends of Tom's. One or two of them were crying also but their anguished utterances were carried away on the wind which whipped across the cemetery.

When the time came, Sue moved forward and gently tossed a handful of earth on top of the coffin then stepped back to stand beside her husband.

Julie did not move.

The vicar finished speaking, offered his usual perfunctory words of condolence then waddled off back towards the church to greet the next cortège which was just passing through the cemetery gates.

More pain, thought Hacket.

Even death had become like a production line.

'I'm going to take Julie back to the car, Sue,' Mike said, leading his sobbing wife away. He nodded to Hacket who managed a smile.

Sue continued looking down into the grave.

'I know this isn't the right time,' Hacket said, self-consciously. 'But can we talk?'

'Just give me a minute,' she said, without looking at him.

Hacket nodded and turned, walking slowly towards a seat beneath a tree away to his right. He brushed some fallen leaves from the seat and sat down, watching Sue who stood gazing down into the grave. Hacket could see her lips moving and wondered what she was saying. Her father's death didn't seem to have hit her as badly as Lisa's. Perhaps the end of his suffering had been something of a relief to her, he thought although he decided not to mention it. Instead he waited as she walked towards him.

He brushed the seat with his gloved hand and she finally sat down.

'Thanks for taking care of the funeral arrangements, John. I appreciate it,' she said, quietly.

'I knew you wouldn't be in any state to do it. I owed you that at least.'

'It doesn't earn you any gold stars,' she said, a slight smile on her lips but also he saw the tears in her eyes.

He moved towards her, wanting to hold her, she held up a hand as if to keep him at a distance. Hacket clenched his teeth.

'I'll be OK,' she said, quietly. 'What did you want to talk about?'

'I wanted to know when you're coming home.'

'I'm not.'

Hacket swallowed hard. Was that it, he wondered? The final pronouncement on their current state of affairs?

'You mean it's over between us?' he asked, almost incredulously.

'What I mean is I can't come back to that house, John. There are too many memories there.'

'So what will you do? What will *we* do?' he wanted to know.

'I'll stay with Julie for the time being. I know I can't do that indefinitely, but . . .' She sighed. 'Like you said, this isn't the right time to talk about it.' She moved to get up and Hacket reached for her arm, holding it for a moment.

She pulled free from his grip, glancing at him for a second. He saw something akin to hatred in her eyes and lowered his hand.

'Julie needs me,' she said. 'I'll have to go.'

'*I* need you,' he said, trying to control the anger in his voice. 'We have to talk, Sue.'

'But not now,' she repeated, walking away from him. He watched as she strode down the narrow path towards the tarmac area which served as a car park. He saw her climb into the back seat with her sister, then he looked on as the car turned and sped away.

Hacket stood alone for a moment, the wind whipping around him, then he too turned and headed back towards his car. There was so much he had wanted to say to her. To tell her that he would sell the house and move to Hinkston, that they could start afresh if she'd have him back. So much to say. But, more than words he had wanted to hold her, just to feel her in his arms for a moment.

He'd been denied even that simple pleasure and, as he climbed into the car and started the engine, he began to wonder if it was one which was to be denied him forever.

He'd lost her.

Hacket was convinced of it.

First he'd lost his daughter, and now his wife. There

wasn't the appalling finality of loss with Sue that there had been with Lisa but he was still sure that their relationship was over. She might as well be dead.

He sat alone in the sitting room of their house, a glass of scotch in one hand, his head buzzing from the amount he already drunk. Half a bottle remained from the full one he'd opened just an hour earlier.

Hacket looked around the room suddenly realising how much he hated it. Sue was right, it held too many memories. But it held them for him too, couldn't she see that? But he couldn't run from them. He could never escape the memories no matter where he went because the thoughts which tortured him were *inside* him. Eating him away as surely as the cancer had eaten away at Sue's father. And yet still he clung to the hope that revenge would be his salvation.

He took a long swig from the glass, some of the fiery liquid running down his chin.

Hacket let out a roar of rage and frustration and, as he did, he squeezed with even greater force on the glass.

It shattered. Thick shards of crystal tearing into the palm of his hand. Others flew into the air along with a mixture of whisky and blood which spurted from the savage gashes. He dropped the remains of the glass and slowly turned his palm to look at it. Glass had lacerated the flesh in several places and thick crimson fluid pumped from the wounds. A piece of crystal the size of his thumb had punctured the palm and was still protruding from the flesh. Hacket reached slowly for it and pulled it free, holding it before him for a second before tossing it aside.

He studied his bloodied hand then slowly raised it to his face and, with measured movements, he drew the torn and bleeding appendage across each cheek until his face was smothered with the thick liquid.

He sat motionless, like some war-painted Indian brave, the throbbing pain in his hand growing worse but dulled by the amount of whisky he'd drunk. The smell of blood was strong in his nostrils. He could feel the life-fluid congealing on his cheeks, while, by his side, it dripped from his slashed palm.

Hacket smiled then laughed. Stupidly, drunkenly.

And slowly the tears of laughter became tears of despair.

Twenty-three

To say that the dining room of The Bull was small would have been an understatement. It consisted of five tables and, as he pulled his chair out and sat down, Stephen Jennings tried to visualise the place full of diners. He doubted if that ever happened.

The Bull was what people like to refer to euphemistically as 'homely'. In other words it was cramped. A small, family run hotel (even the description seemed rather grand for somewhere as modest as The Bull) in the centre of Hinkston, it was cheap, immaculately clean and friendly. He had stayed in dozens like it and many much worse. Jennings had worked for the past three years as a rep for a company of jeans manufacturers. It wasn't the greatest job in the world but it got him around the country and he had a company car and a reasonable salary. However, now approaching his twenty-seventh birthday, he was wondering if the time had come to move on. Better himself, as his mother always liked to say. She was also fond of saying that he should settle down and marry, something which he had definitely *not* given any consideration to. He'd been in an on-off relationship for the last eighteen months, although his time on the road seemed to ensure that it was more 'off' than anything else. Still, he was too young to settle down, he kept telling himself. Too old to rock and roll, too young to die, he thought, and smiled to himself.

Casting aside his philosophical musings, Jennings picked up the menu and glanced at it for a moment before taking another look at the dining room of the hotel. Each table had a vase of flowers at its centre, every napkin and tablecloth was spotlessly clean. The lighting was subdued to the point of gloom. Perhaps to hide the state of the food when it finally arrived, he thought, returning his attention to the menu.

The choice was small but fairly adventurous for a place of The Bull's modest means. Steak in red wine and mushroom sauce. He glanced at the price. Expensive, but what the hell, it was going on his expense account. He checked the wine list.

'Hello.'

The voice startled him from his considerations and he looked up to see a young woman standing there. Woman was somewhat overstating the fact, perhaps and a quick appraisal told Jennings this newcomer was in her late teens. She smiled at him and he noticed the pad in her hand and realised that she was the waitress.

She was slim, that fact accentuated by the tight fitting black skirt and top she wore. A thick mane of shaggy blonde hair cascaded over her shoulders, framing her thin face from which two eyes like chips of sapphire seemed to shine as if lit from within. She wore no make-up and the freshness of her complexion seemed almost unnatural for a girl in the throes of pubescence. She stood beside the table patiently and Jennings glanced down to see that she was wearing not the flat shoes of a waitress but a pair of high heels. The girl was little short of stunning.

She smiled at him again when she noticed his surprise.

'Did I startle you?' she said, happily. 'Sorry. My Dad's always telling me not to sneak up on customers.'

Jennings returned the smile.

'Your dad?'

'Yes, he owns the hotel. Him and Mum have been running it for about twenty years, since before I was born.'

She kept those sapphire eyes on him, also appraising.

'You're new here aren't you?' she said. 'Just arrive today?'

He nodded.

'So, you know all the guests?'

'That's not difficult,' she told him. 'We hardly have any at this time of the year.' She looked more deeply at him. 'At least none like you.' No blushing. No quick glance down at her pad. The remark hadn't slipped out by mistake.

Jennings could not resist a sly glance at her breasts, the nipples pressing gently against the cotton of her blouse.

'Thanks for the compliment,' he said. 'Is that included in the price of the room?' He smiled.

'I had a boyfriend who looked like you,' she said, her gaze unwavering.

He raised his eyebrows.

'*Had*?'

'We split up. I got tired of him.' She smiled. 'He couldn't keep up with me. Not many of them can.'

Jennings coughed, trying to disguise the laugh which threatened to escape him. She wasn't flirting with him, she was practically propositioning him. About as subtle as a sledgehammer. But then again, as he looked at her face once more, the laugh faded. No doubt about it. She was stunning.

'I'd better order something,' he said, looking at the menu.

'Am I making you nervous?' she asked, brushing a speck

of dust from her skirt with exaggerated slowness, pulling the material tight at the top of her thigh to ensure he saw the outline of her suspenders through the skirt.

'No,' he told her, rather enjoying the game. 'But I don't think your Dad would like it if he walked in and heard the way you were talking to me. He'd probably ask me to leave the hotel.' He winked at her. 'Then what would I do for the night?'

'Dad doesn't care what I do,' she said, still gazing at him. 'Nor does Mum. So why should it bother *you*?'

He shrugged, again drawn to those blazing eyes. Jennings ordered then handed her the menu, watching as she walked away, unable to keep his eyes from her legs. She disappeared through into the kitchen leaving him alone in the dimly lit dining room.

'Would you like a drink while you're waiting, Mr Jennings?' Tony Kirkham called from behind the bar. 'I see Paula's taken your order.'

Another five minutes and she'd have taken my bloody trousers, Jennings thought with a smile.

He ordered a pint of bitter, retrieved it from the bar and returned to his table. Paula returned a moment later with his starter which she duly set down before him.

'Thanks. By the way,' he said, spearing a couple of prawns with his fork, 'is there any nightlife around here. I was planning on going out after I'd eaten.'

'There's a cinema down the street, a couple of discos,' she shrugged. 'Not much. We have to make our own entertainment.'

He smiled.

'I thought that's what you'd say. Maybe I'll wander down to the pictures. Thanks.' Jennings wasn't sure whether or not to continue the little game. A glance at her persuaded him. 'It's a pity you're working. You could have showed me around.'

'I still can,' she whispered. 'Later.'
He nodded.
'I'll keep that in mind.'
She turned and left him alone.

He finished his meal, drank a couple of brandies, then decided to venture out and sample Hinkston's somewhat limited nightlife.

As he stepped out of the hotel the wind whistled around him and he pulled up the collar of his jacket. Then, hands dug deep in his pockets, he set off down the street.

Hidden by the darkness of the bedroom, Paula Kirkham watched him disappear out of sight.

Twenty-four

'No'.

'He has a right to be told.'

The two men faced each other across the small office, cigarette smoke floating lazily in the air like a grey shroud.

'I said no,' DI Madden snapped, stubbing out the Dunhill and pushing the overflowing ashtray towards the edge of his desk.

'Why can't we tell him?' Spencer wanted to know.

'Because we'd be breaking the rules.' There was a note of sarcasm in the senior officer's voice.

'To hell with the rules,' Spencer rasped. 'Hacket's daughter was butchered by this fucking maniac.' He held up the arrest sheet, brandishing it before him as if it were some kind of accusation.

'We can't prove that, yet,' Madden reminded him, getting to his feet. He lit up another cigarette.

'Then why did we even bother pulling him in? Was that *procedure*?' Spencer glared at his superior. 'We can hold him for twenty-four hours and then we have to charge him. Only we've got nothing to charge him *with*. So what happens?'

'He walks,' said Madden, flatly. He sucked hard on the cigarette then wearily blew out a stream of smoke.

'Call Hacket,' Spencer insisted.

'What good would it do?' Madden wanted to know.

Spencer continued to gaze at his companion, his expression challenging.

Madden shrugged then, slowly, pushed the phone towards Spencer.

Twenty-five

The man was tall, powerfully built, larger than Hacket. Subduing him had been difficult. The wounds on the side of his face and his scalp testified to the number of blows from the hammer it had taken to finally batter him into unconsciousness.

Now Hacket stood over the man who was beginning to come round, his eyes rolling in their sockets like the reels of a fruit machine. He blinked hard, trying to clear his blurred vision and, finally, he looked up at Hacket.

The man tried to straighten up but found that his arms were secured by rope, tied so tightly that the hemp bit into his flesh when he squirmed to escape the bonds. His ankles too were similarly secured. He was spread-eagled on the floor of what looked like an abandoned warehouse.

And he was naked.

Hacket held the claw hammer in his right hand and took a step closer to the prone figure, then he twisted the tool so that the steel prongs of the claw were facing his captive. With a blow combining incredible power with uncontrollable rage, Hacket brought the hammer down onto the right knee-cap of the bound figure.

The claws shattered the patella, tearing through the cruciate ligaments at the back of the knee and almost ripping the knee cap itself off. Blood from the hideous injury ran freely from the site of the damage and the man on the ground screamed in agony as he felt Hacket trying to pull the hammer free. The claws had wedged behind the knee cap and, with each tug on the shaft, the flat piece of bone rose a few more millimetres until Hacket realised he was levering it free. The sound of tearing ligaments was almost audible above the man's insane screams. Hacket put more weight behind the hammer, determined to lift the patella free.

It came away with a vile, sucking sound, the shattered bone skittering across the floor, pieces of it dangling on the end of tendrils formed from ripped muscles and ligaments.

The man on the floor writhed in uncontrollable pain and Hacket looked at his face, wanting to see the agony register.

But the man *had* no face.

Where the features should have been there was just smooth skin.

No eyes. No mouth.

The screams seemed to be coming from inside Hacket's head as he stood over the man, the hammer dripping blood.

No face.

Hacket began to laugh, the sound joined by the faceless man's terrible screams. And by a new noise.

By the strident ringing of the telephone.

Hacket sat up in his chair, his face bathed in perspiration, his cut hand still throbbing madly.

Momentarily disorientated, he looked around him, looking for the claw hammer. For the faceless man.

Neither was present and, as the phone continued its monotone screech, he realised that he'd been dreaming. All that *was* real was the pain in his hand. He winced as he dragged himself out of the chair, wrapping a handkerchief around the swollen appendage.

The phone continued to ring.

Hacket staggered across the room, towards the hall wondering why his face felt so stiff but then remembering the congealed blood which caked it. He scratched at one cheek with his index finger and saw some of the dried, mud coloured mess come away beneath his nail.

He blundered through the doorway to the hall and snatched up the phone.

'Yeah,' he panted. 'Who is it?'

'Mr Hacket?' the voice asked.

'Yeah.'

'It's Detective Sergeant Spencer. I'm sorry to disturb you but you did say you wanted to know if there were any developments in your daughter's case.'

Hacket gripped the phone more tightly.

'And?'

'We've got a suspect in custody. We think he might have been involved in your daughter's murder.'

Twenty-six

It was almost 10.30 when Jennings returned to The Bull. He'd decided to by-pass the cinema in Hinkston. The idea of sitting through the umpteenth cinematic episode of 'Star Trek' hadn't appealed to him. He'd eventually ended up in a pub a couple of streets away called 'The Badger's Set.' There he'd spent a couple of reasonably diverting hours with a couple of the locals discussing topics ranging from the possibility that Margaret Thatcher was a man to Liverpool FC's latest trophy-winning exploits.

Now he pushed open the door which led into the reception area of The Bull and withdrew his hands from his pockets, feeling the welcoming warmth.

Irene Kirkham was behind the desk. A rotund woman in her early forties who still had a pretty face. Perhaps Paula inherited her looks from her mother, thought Jennings with a grin. He wondered who she'd inherited the sexual precocity from but decided it had been nurtured rather than inherited. He crossed to the desk and asked for his key and an alarm call for the morning.

'Is there any chance of something to eat?' he asked. 'Just a sandwich would be fine, thanks.'

'You go to your room and I'll take care of it,' Mrs Kirkham told him, handing over the key.

He thanked her and bounded up the stairs to the first floor, the boards creaking beneath his feet as he entered his room. He closed the door behind him and pulled off his coat, throwing it onto the bed, then he flicked on the TV and wandered into the bathroom to relieve himself.

He was half-way through draining his over-filled bladder when there was a knock on his door. He finished then hastily zipped up his jeans, cursing as he caught a pubic hair in the metal teeth. Re-adjusting himself he crossed to the door and opened it.

Paula stood there holding a tray which bore a plate of sandwiches and a glass of milk.

She had changed from earlier. Now she wore a pair of faded jeans which bit into her crotch so deeply he could practically see the outline of her labia. It was obvious she wore no panties. Just as she still wore no bra, a fact attested to by the prominence of her nipples which strained against her white T-shirt. She was barefoot.

'Room service I presume,' he said, smiling, stepping back to allow her entrance, his eyes flicking admiringly over her bottom as she wiggled past.

'Where do you want it?' she asked, raising her eyebrows.

Ha, bloody, ha, thought Jennings. More games.

He decided to play.

'On the bed?' he chuckled then shook his head and motioned to the dressing table. She set down the tray and looked at the various toiletries on show. There was some anti perspirant, some after shave. Paula unscrewed the lid of the bottle and sniffed it.

'Well,' she said. 'How did you enjoy Hinkston's nightlife?'

She sat down on the stool which faced the dressing table, one leg drawn up beneath her.

Jennings hesitated a moment then closed the door of the room. She smiled as he crossed to the dressing table and picked up a sandwich. As he stood before her she reached up and ran one hand gently across his thigh, allowing it slide higher towards his penis.

Game on. Your move, Jennings told himself.

He swallowed the remains of the sandwich and looked down at her. She didn't attempt to stop her firm stroking and, despite himself, Jennings felt a tightening in his groin.

Paula smiled up at him, those chips of sapphire pinning him again in that electrifying gaze.

'What about your parents?' he said, quietly, his erection now painfully constricted by his jeans.

'I told them I was going to bed after I'd given you your food. They won't check on me.' She began to rub more firmly over the bulge in his jeans, outlining his stiffness with her thumb and index finger then she loosened the popper on his waistband and, slowly eased his zip down.

Jennings sighed as the pressure was relieved, that sigh of relief turning to one of pleasure as she eased his pants over his hips exposing his throbbing erection. She bent forward and closed her lips around the bulbous head. He moved closer as she flicked her tongue around the glans, allowing her fingers to trace a pattern across his tightened scrotum. He began to thrust gently in and out of her mouth as she covered his throbbing member with her saliva, still sucking greedily at it.

He slid his hands through her hair, amazed at the fineness of it. Then his hands slipped to her shoulders then down to seek her breasts which he kneaded through the material of her T-shirt, coaxing the nipples to even greater stiffness.

She pulled away suddenly, allowing his penis to slip from her mouth. Then, with a grin on her face she pulled the T-shirt off and moved swiftly across to the bed. Jennings stepped out of his jeans, tugged his socks off then removed his shirt, watching mesmerised as she shrugged off her own jeans, undulating and writhing on the bed, peeling them off like a snake sloughing its skin.

Naked, they were joined on the bed.

He cupped her left breast in his hand and squeezed, his tongue flicking over the stiff nipple, teasing it between his teeth before repeating the procedure on the other. Her hand found his shaft and she enveloped it in her fingers, beginning a rhythmic motion which brought him immense pleasure. He twisted round so that his face was between her legs, nuzzling his way through her tightly curled pubic hair until he found her swollen vaginal lips. He flicked his tongue along each in turn before seeking her clitoris, drawing back the fleshy hood with his teeth, feeling the firmness against his tongue.

Her cleft wept moisture into his mouth as he brought one hand around and began softly stroking the inside of her thighs. Her breathing became deeper.

Then she rolled over, pulling him onto his back, lowering herself onto his face, pressing her wet pubis against his mouth for a moment longer before sliding down his chest, leaving a moist trail. She straddled him taking his penis in one hand, guiding it towards her wetness, rubbing his swollen glans against her clitoris. Using him to stimulate her further. If this was still a game then he was playing by *her* rules now.

'Fuck me,' she gasped, insistently and lowered herself onto him, enveloping his penis with her cleft so that it felt as if he was being seized by a slippery glove which tightened more as he thrust up to meet her downward movement. She gasped and ground against him harder, moaning as he rubbed her swaying breasts, knowing that he was close to orgasm himself.

Paula leant forward and kissed him, her tongue pushing into his mouth, flicking across his lips as she rode him faster. She sucked his tongue into her mouth and he felt it against the hard edges of her teeth. Felt her own tongue retreat to allow *his* to probe deeper.

Felt her front teeth closing on his tongue.

Felt the uncontrollable agony as she bit through it.

Blood burst from the tumescent appendage, filling his mouth and hers, spilling over his chin to stain the sheets beneath.

She sat back, swallowing the tongue with one huge gulp

then she bent towards him again, still riding his now shrinking penis, still feeling the uncontrollable pleasure building within her as he bucked beneath her.

Her orgasm came as she tore off his top lip.

She took it between her bloodied front teeth and bit deep, pulling. Shaking her head from side to side until it came away. She chewed once and swallowed that too.

Her pleasure was limitless now.

The shattering power of her climax sent what felt like an electric charge through her body and, as blood from his severed tongue spilled down her naked torso, she rocked back and forth on top of his writhing body, her arms holding him down with surprising strength.

He tried to scream but the blood flooded back into his throat.

She slid off him, reaching for the vase on the bedside table, bringing it down with terrifying force on his head.

The vase shattered, the blow opening another savage gash on his forehead.

His eyes rolled upwards in the socket as she clambered back onto him, like some unsatisfied lover in search of gratification.

She used the jagged, broken edges of the vase to open his stomach, the muscles and flesh splitting like an overripe peach.

She thrust one hand inside the reeking cavity, her fingers closing around a length of intestine. It felt like a throbbing worm, bloated and slimy but, undeterred, she pulled hard, ripping the bulging length free. Paula raised it to her mouth and bit into it ignoring the blood which poured down her arms and torso. It trickled through her pubic hair like crimson ejaculate and she slid back and forth in the reeking mess, her eyes closed in ecstasy. Her mouth bulging as she filled it with the dripping entrails, chewing happily.

Jennings had stopped moving. Even the muscular spasms which had racked his body having ceased.

He was dead by the time she began peeling pieces of skin from his face, pushing them into her mouth with a gourmet's fervour.

It was as she reached for his eye that the door opened.

Twenty-seven

'Who is he?'

Hacket's voice sounded like gravel as he sipped at the coffee, gazing through the two-way mirror into the interrogation room.

The room was bare but for a table, two chairs and three men.

A uniformed sergeant. Detective Inspector Madden and a third man.

'His name's Peter Walton,' said DS Spencer, looking down at a sheet of paper fastened to the clip-board which he held. 'Age thirty-two, no fixed abode. Eleven previous convictions. All small-time stuff though. Handling stolen goods, mugging, that kind of thing.'

'You call mugging small-time?' said Hacket, his eyes never leaving Walton. He studied every inch of the man's face as he sat toying with an empty packet of cigarettes. The lank hair, streaked with grey here and there. The sallow complexion, sunken eyes. Unshaven. His lips were thick and puffy, as if he'd been chewing the bottom one repeatedly until it swelled. He had a dark birthmark on the left side of his neck, just below his jaw. Hacket noticed with disgust that there was some hardened mucous around one nostril. When he tired of playing with the cigarette packet, Walton began picking at that particular nostril, examining the hardened snot before wiping it on his trousers.

Spencer had not expected the school teacher to drive to the police station after the phone call. He was even more surprised by his appearance. Hacket's hand was crudely bandaged, the blood still seeping through. His hair was uncombed and the dark rings beneath his eyes made him look as though he hadn't slept for a week. Spencer noticed the smell of whisky on his breath but made no comment. Instead he had shown the dishevelled man straight through into the office which looked onto the interrogation room, watching as Hacket sat down, his eyes never leaving Walton. As if he were trying to remember every single detail about the man.

Hacket himself had washed his face when he'd finished speaking on the phone to Spencer, scrubbing the dried blood away. The he'd bandaged his hand, pulled on a jacket and driven to the police station. The cold night air combined with the news he had just heard had served to shock him out of his stupor even though he was still aware of the smell of drink on his breath.

Now the two men sat in the small room gazing through the two-way mirror as if they were watching fish inside an aquarium.

'We picked him up in Soho,' said Spencer. 'He was trying to sell some videos. Cassettes which had been stolen from your house.

'You said that there were lots of fingerprints in the house when Lisa was killed.'

'There were. Unfortunately, none of them match with Walton's.'

Hacket exhaled deeply.

'You must be able to hold him on something,' the teacher rasped.

'Apart from receiving stolen goods, there's nothing.'

'You mean you're going to let him go?' Hacket snarled, turning towards Spencer for the first time. The DS saw the fury on the teacher's face. 'He killed my daughter. You can't let him go.'

'We can't prove that, Mr Hacket. Not yet. And, until we can, we can only hold him for forty-eight hours. After that he's free.' Spencer shrugged. 'I don't like it any more than you do but it's the law. *He* has his rights, regardless of what you or I think.'

'And what about my daughter?' Hacket muttered through clenched teeth. 'What about *her* fucking rights?'

'Look, I told you that we thought two men were involved well, perhaps Walton can lead us to the other man. To the one who really murdered your daughter.'

'How do you know it wasn't him?'

'Because his blood group is different to that of the man who raped your daughter.'

Hacket swallowed hard and turned away, his attention returning to Walton. He could see the man nodding or shaking his head as Madden asked him questions. He didn't seem very concerned. At one point he even smiled. Hacket gripped the arms of the chair until his knuckles turned white. What he wouldn't give for ten minutes alone with the bastard.

Forty-eight hours and he would be free again.

Hacket closed his eyes tightly, as if hoping the rage would vanish but, when he opened them again Walton was still there. The rage was still there.

The pain.

And the guilt.

He got slowly to his feet, wiping one hand across his face.

'What did you do to your hand?' asked Spencer, nodding towards the bandaged appendage.

'Just an accident.' Hacket turned towards the door.

'One of my men could drive you home, Mr Hacket.'

The teacher shook his head, pausing with his hand on the door knob.

'You let me know what happens. Please,' he said, without looking at Spencer. 'If you manage to hold him. If he spills the beans on his . . . partner. You'll let me know?'

'Yes,' said Spencer, watching as Hacket left.

The schoolteacher paused a moment on the steps of the police station, sucking in deep lungfuls of night air. As he stood there a police car pulled up and two uniformed men got out, running past him into the building.

Another emergency?

Hacket walked to his car and climbed in, sitting there for a moment before starting the engine. As he twisted the key it purred into life.

'Peter Walton,' he said under his breath.

He had a name and he knew what the bastard looked like.

It wasn't much but at least it was a start.

He pulled away, guiding the car out into traffic.

Twenty-eight

Her fingernails were deep inside his eye socket.

Like hooks, ready to pull the orb free of his skull but, as she heard the door open, Paula Kirkham turned, her blood spattered hand falling to her side. She chewed slowly on a portion of Jennings small intestine, pieces of it sticking to her chin. Her torso was smothered in his blood. The room smelled like a slaughterhouse. Crimson had soaked the bed itself, elsewhere it had sprayed up the walls as if directed by a hose. Some of it had even spattered the sandwiches which Jennings had asked for.

Paula swallowed what was left of the intestine and looked blankly at her parents.

Tony Kirkham slipped inside the room, pulling the door shut behind him. Irene crossed towards the bed, towards Paula and the mutilated remains of Stephen Jennings. She smiled benignly at her daughter and held out a hand, watching as the young girl slid from Jennings' torn body. Irene wrapped a blanket around her then gathered up the clothes which lay in an untidy bundle on the floor, some flecked with blood.

Paula smiled lovingly at her parents and, as she passed him, she paused and kissed her father softly on the cheek.

He smiled and touched her hair. Hair that was matted with blood.

Irene led her from the room and Tony was left alone with the remains of Jennings.

He wasted little time.

First he wrapped the body in the sheets and covers from the bed, cocooning it. Then he reached into his jacket pocket and pulled out the string he carried, wrapping long lengths around the bloodied corpse to keep the covers in place. The stench was appalling but he continued with his task, fetching Jennings' small suitcase from the wardrobe. Into it he pushed the dead man's clothes, his shoes, and anything else he could find which gave the appearance that someone had stopped in the room. He moved through into the bathroom, scooping up the rep's toothbrush and razor. Those too he tossed into the suitcase.

The mattress was sodden with blood, Tony made a

mental note to burn it later. The large wood-burning stove in the basement of the hotel would be more than adequate for that task.

He would dispose of Jennings' body in there too. And his clothes.

As for his car, that could wait. He would drive it out into the countryside in the small hours and dump it. Even when it was found there would be nothing to connect it to the hotel, to the Kirkham family.

To his beautiful daughter.

Tony smiled as he looked down at the blood-drenched parcel of bedclothes which formed a shroud for Stephen Jennings. Some blood was beginning to seep onto the carpet. He would have to move fast before it left too indelible a stain.

The crimson which had spattered the walls would also need to be washed off.

He left the room for a moment, hurrying along the corridor to a utility room from which he took a mop, bucket, several cloths and dusters. By the time he returned to the room, a puddle of thick red fluid was beginning to spread out around the corpse. Tony muttered to himself, knelt down and lifted the body. He was a strong man and the weight bothered him little. He carried Jennings into the bathroom and dumped the corpse unceremoniously in the bath, looking down at it for a moment before returning to the bedroom.

As he picked up one of the cloths to wipe down the dressing table, the door of the room opened and Irene walked in.

'How is she?' he asked.

'She's sleeping now. I cleaned her up first then put her to bed.' She surveyed the blood spattered room indifferently. 'How long will you be?' she wanted to know.

'Give me an hour,' he said.

Irene nodded and glanced at her watch.

11.57 p.m.

She turned and left Tony to his task, hurrying down to reception. She ran her finger down the guest register and found Jennings' name. Then, with infinite care she changed the date of which he was due to leave. If anyone came looking for him, which was doubtful, they would say that he didn't stop the night, that he had to leave suddenly. That he hadn't left an address where he could be contacted.

That task done she scuttled back upstairs to her husband who was washing down the walls.

'What about the body?' she asked.

'I'll take care of it in a minute,' he said, calmly. 'There's no rush.'

No rush. No fuss.

They were used to the ritual by now.

12.57 a.m.

He'd said an hour and he'd been right.

The body was gone, all of Jennings' belongings were gone.

Irene Kirkham looked at her husband, who nodded.

She reached for the phone and dialled.

Twenty-nine

The house was large. An imposing edifice with a mock-Georgian front, its stonework covered by a creeping blanket of ivy. The windows peered from beneath this canopy like questing eyes, gazing out into the darkness. During the hours of daylight it was possible to see over most of Hinkston from the main bedroom of the house. The building set, as it was, on one of the many hills which swelled around the town.

A gravel drive curved up towards the house from the main road which led down into the town. Hedges which had once been subject to the complex art of topiary had been allowed to merge into one and now formed a boundary along the bottom of the spacious lawn and also on either side of the curving drive.

There was a pond in the centre of the lawn but it was empty of fish. A couple of weatherbeaten gnomes stood sentinel.

The house boasted eight bedrooms but, at present, only one was used. Downstairs there was a sizeable library, a sitting-room which again looked out over Hinkston itself, and a kitchen.

The surgery had been installed over twenty-three years ago. It had been constructed from two other rooms, one turned into an office, the other a waiting room.

It was in the surgery that Doctor Edward Curtis sat, his jacket off, his sleeves rolled up.

He was cradling a glass of gin in one strong hand, massaging the skin above his eyebrows with the other.

Curtis was a tall, lean man in his late forties. His brown hair was cut short, his skin smooth apart from the moustache which covered his top lip. He turned the glass slowly in his hand, looking down into the clear liquid and telling himself that he would go to bed when he'd finished his drink.

He'd said that after the first two. Now, gazing at his fourth, he determined to keep to his word. He took a sip of the gin.

The house was particularly quiet at this time. Not even the creak of settling timbers disturbed the solitude. Curtis enjoyed silence. He was grateful that the house was set outside the town itself, more than half a mile. Of course a frequent bus service brought his patients to him during surgery, those who didn't drive. But, apart from his work, Curtis was rarely disturbed. He was on call, naturally, twenty-four hours a day, preferring not to employ a locum as the surgeries in town did. Many of his patients called him by his first name and he had found that his rapport, carefully cultivated over the years, helped them to relax. Perhaps, he reasoned, private practice offered more time than that available to his overworked colleagues working for the NHS but it was something which Curtis found both rewarding and necessary.

He had been practising in Hinkston for the last twenty-one years, ever since his return from medical school and he was now a well established member of the community, his skills sought by both old and young, not just in Hinkston but also further afield. There was one woman on his books who came from London to see him, such was her faith in him.

Curtis employed just two people, both on a part-time basis. A receptionist and a housekeeper, although it would be more appropriate to call her a cleaner. But he disliked the term, finding it demeaning to the woman who performed such a necessary task. She cleaned both the surgery and the house itself.

But not the cellar.

The subterranean part of the house was the private domain of the doctor. He had installed a simple but sophisticated store of machinery and equipment which allowed him to perform some fairly complex tests. His ability to test for diseases such as diabetes and various renal problems, to name but two, removed the need for patients to travel to hospital and so cut down the time they had to wait for results. He even had a small X-ray unit down there. Blood tests and urine tests could be analysed on the spot, the patient able to know the results before they left the surgery.

Most of the money to set up the surgery, and certainly to install the equipment, had come from his parents. Now both dead, they had left him not only the house but a sizeable amount of money which Curtis had invested wisely. His fees were more than reasonable and, living alone, he had minimal overheads. Just the wages of his two staff and his everyday living requirements.

He took another sip of the gin and glanced at his watch.

1.36 a.m.

He rubbed his eyes and yawned.

The door to the surgery opened and Curtis looked up as the newcomer walked across to the desk and sat down opposite him.

'Join me?' Curtis asked, pushing the bottle and a glass towards the other occupant of the room.

He filled the glass, watching as his companion drank.

'Sorry if I woke you,' he said.

The other merely shrugged.

'I had to go into Hinkston. An emergency,' he explained, finishing his drink.

The figure also drained the glass and pushed it towards Curtis, who promptly re-filled it.

'I'm going to bed,' Curtis announced, yawning again. He got to his feet, picked up his jacket and headed for the door that led through the waiting room and beyond to the stairs.

The remaining occupant of the surgery sat drinking, only the sound of low, rhythmic breathing breaking the deathly silence.

Thirty

She guessed she'd slept less than three hours all night.

Sue Hacket splashed her face with cold water, dried it then wandered back into the bedroom to apply some make-up. She inspected the dark rings beneath her eyes before adding eye-liner and a touch of lipstick. She rubbed her cheeks, noting the paleness of her skin and finally gave in to the temptation of touching on some rouge.

Downstairs she could hear the sound of the radio, the vacuous ramblings of the DJ periodically replaced by the even more vacuous music he played. She slipped out of her housecoat and pulled on jeans and a sweater, stepping into her shoes before she made her way downstairs.

'Well, come on then,' she said to Craig who was sitting at the kitchen table trying to fasten the laces on his shoes. 'You've got to show me the way and we don't want you being late do we?'

'I won't be late,' he assured her, jumping down from the chair and rushing into the sitting room to retrieve his satchel.

'Thanks for taking him to school, Sue,' said Julie who stood at the kitchen sink, her face looking distinctly haggard. 'Mike would have stayed off work but he says they've got a big contract to finish . . .'

Sue held up a hand to silence her.

'Leave the washing up, I'll do it when I come back,' she said.

'No. I'd rather keep myself occupied. It stops me thinking about Dad,' Julie told her.

'I know what you mean.'

'I'm ready, Auntie Sue,' announced Craig, appearing in the doorway like a soldier ready for inspection. Sue smiled and heard the front door open as he rushed out to the

Metro to wait for her. She turned and looked at Julie then followed him out.

Craig sat in the passenger seat beside her, well strapped in, happily telling her directions to his school, pointing at friends he knew as they passed them on the journey.

Sue saw mothers with younger children and her expression hardened.

The emotion she was feeling was something close to resentment. That others should be enjoying the simple pleasure of walking their children to school while she would never know that joy. Was it resentment she asked herself? Envy or jealousy? It all amounted to the same thing.

'That's Trevor Ward,' Craig announced pointing to a tall, thin child with glasses who was crossing the road ahead of them. 'He picks his nose and eats it.'

'Does he really?' Sue answered, deciding that kind of personal detail didn't interest her too much.

'His Mum and Dad can't afford a car,' said Craig with glee.

'Not everyone is as lucky as *your* mum and dad, Craig,' she told him, the merest hint of rebuke in her voice. Some people aren't even lucky enough to have children she felt like adding, administering a swift mental slap for the feelings of self-pity she felt surfacing. But, surrounded by children as she was, it was difficult not to feel the resentment which Lisa's death had brought. Sue suddenly felt very weary.

She brought the car to a halt outside the main gates of the school and leant across to unlock the door for Craig.

He told her he'd get a lift home with a friend of his. His mum always picked him up. Sue told him to get a teacher to ring if there was any change of plan. He nodded happily, unfastening his seat belt and pushing open the door.

'See you later,' she said, smiling. 'Don't I get a kiss goodbye?'

He looked at her and chuckled, as if it were something he'd meant to do but it had just slipped his mind. She turned her face slightly to allow him to kiss her cheek.

Craig took hold of her chin, turning her face back towards him then, kneeling on the seat, he kissed her full on the lips, pressing his against her own for what seemed like an eternity.

Then he pulled away and jumped out of the car.

Sue watched him run off into the playground, still shocked at his response, still able to feel the pressure of his lips against her own.

She raised two fingers to her mouth and gently ran them across her lips.

As she did she saw that her hand was shaking.

Thirty-one

Hacket stared down at the black marble stone and glanced at the inscription, feeling the tears begin to prick his eyes. He sniffed them back, holding the small bouquet of violets in his hands. The right one was still heavily bandaged and, even with the benefit of pain killers, he could feel a dull throbbing pain coming from it.

The sun was out but it was cold, the light breeze occasionally intensifying into a chill wind which caused him to shiver. The flowers which already stood in the small pot on Lisa's grave had wilted, some shedding their withered petals, and it was these petals that the wind scattered like discarded confetti.

Hacket stood for a moment longer looking down at his

daughter's grave then he knelt and began removing the old flowers from the pot, laying them on the wet grass.

The sunshine and the Sabbath day had coaxed a number of people to the cemetery and he glanced around to see others performing tasks similar to his own. Replacing flowers, pulling unwanted weeds from plots. He saw an elderly woman cleaning a white headstone with a cloth. Not far from her a man in his early forties stood, hands clasped before him, gazing down at a grave. Hacket wondered who the man had lost. A wife? A mother or father? Perhaps even a son or daughter like himself. Death held no discrimination for age, sex or creed.

Hacket began placing the new flowers in the pot his mind full of thoughts. Of Lisa. Of Sue.

Of the phone call he'd received earlier that morning.

DS Spencer had phoned about ten a.m. with the news that, due to lack of evidence, Peter Walton had been released.

Hacket had barely given him time to finish speaking before angrily slamming the phone down.

Released.

The bastard had gone free, just as Spencer had warned.

So, now what?

Hacket continued pushing flowers into the pot, the question eating away at him.

Did he go looking for Walton? Try to trace him? Spencer had said that his address had been unknown so where did Hacket begin? He had no doubt of his own ability to kill Walton should he find him but his first, main problem, was actually hunting the bastard down. And Hacket was no detective. Where did he start? He exhaled wearily. In films it was so simple. The avenging angel always knew where to find his intended prey. Everything always went according to plan. Only this *wasn't* a film, this was real life with all its attendant complexities.

Hacket had no doubt he could kill Walton.

No doubt?

He had fantasised about it, dreamt of the most elaborate ways of inflicting pain on the killer of his child and yet, if the time came would he have time to make Walton suffer as he wished him to? Would Walton kill *him*?

And Spencer had also said that another man could be involved.

What then?

What? If? How? When?

Hacket turned and hurled the dead flowers into the nearby waste bin. He turned back and looked at the grave, massaging his forehead gently with one hand. He could feel the beginnings of a headache, the pressure building slowly but surely. Just as it was building within him until all he wanted to do was scream and shout. Anything to release the pent up emotion which swelled like a malignant tumour. Only *this* cancer was eating away his soul.

He looked down at the grave and thought of Lisa.

Of Sue.

Hacket had never felt so lonely in his life.

He turned and walked slowly back towards the car.

Thirty-two

The crying awoke her.

Michelle Lewis sat up quickly, rubbing her eyes as she heard the howls from the bottom of the bed.

Beside her, Stuart Lewis grunted and swung himself out of bed.

'The joys of parenthood,' he said, smiling thinly.

Michelle also clambered out of bed and moved towards the cot which held their child.

Daniel Lewis was crying loudly, his face creased and red.

'He looks like a bloody dishcloth,' said Stuart, yawning, looking down at the screaming bundle which his wife carefully lifted into her arms.

'You probably looked like that at six weeks,' she told him, rocking the baby gently back and forth.

'Thanks,' he muttered, watching as she unfastened her nightdress and eased one swollen breast free, raising the child to the nipple it sought.

He had been a large baby, over nine pounds at birth, but Michelle had been fortunate. The delivery had been an easy one. She had always had what Stuart referred to as 'child bearing hips' which was his way of saying she needed to lose a little weight. But she had already begun her exercise classes to lose the pounds she'd gained while carrying Daniel and she was confident she'd soon have her figure back. After all, she was only just past her twentieth birthday, her body was still very flexible.

'I'm going to make a cup of tea,' said Stuart, running a hand through his hair. 'Do you want anything?'

She didn't answer, merely hissed in pain as Daniel chewed rather over-enthusiastically on her nipple, coaxing the milk from the large bud and gurgling contentedly. However, after a moment or two, Michelle removed him from her left nipple, noticing as she did how red it was. The baby yelled for a second but soon quietened down as she lifted him to the right nipple, allowing him to close his mouth over that. He began sucking vigorously, his eyes darting back and forth as he accepted her milk.

'It's a pity *you* can't do this,' said Michelle, smiling.

Stuart rubbed his chest and shrugged.

'Sorry, love,' he said. 'Empty.'

They both chuckled.

Daniel continued to suck with ever increasing vigour.

'I'm sure he's getting some teeth,' Michelle observed, feeling the soreness beginning around her nipple.

'He's too young for that isn't he?' David asked, deciding not to bother with the tea. Instead he sat down on the edge of the bed beside his wife, watching as she nursed the baby. He remained there for a moment longer then got up and wandered along to the bathroom where he urinated gushingly.

Michelle held the baby to her breast, aware of a growing pain around her nipple.

The child had gripped the mammary in both tiny hands and was clinging on like a leech, his mouth still sucking hard. She was sure that he had some teeth, he must have. His jaws continued to move up and down, swallowing the milk greedily. Another minute or so and she'd move him back to the other nipple again, the right one was becoming painfully sore. Besides, he should have had enough by now.

She held him gently, frowning as she felt the pressure on her breast increase. His tiny fingers raked across the flesh leaving four red lines and she winced.

'I think you've had enough, young man,' she said, and prepared to transfer him back to the other nipple, if not to terminate the feed there and then. She lifted him gently.

He did not release her nipple.

'Daniel,' she said, softly, easing him away.

The child continued to suck.

Michelle took hold of one of his tiny hands and tried to pull him away but he wouldn't budge.

She felt a growing pain in her breast as he continued to suck.

'Daniel, that's enough,' she said, more urgently.

He seemed to be nuzzling against her with renewed vigour, pushing his head against the mammary, closing his jaws even more tightly over the protruding nub of flesh and muscle.

She let out a yelp of pain as she felt a sharp stab around her nipple. As if he were biting her. Using his teeth. Teeth which, by rights, he shouldn't have.

Michelle for some inexplicable reason felt suddenly worried. The child would not let go of her nipple and as she tried to pull him free she felt the skin stretching, most of it still held in his mouth.

The pain was growing.

'God,' she hissed as Stuart re-entered the room and looked at her.

He saw the baby pushing hard against her breast, saw the skin of that breast being pulled taut, saw the pain on Michelle's face.

Then he saw the blood.

It trickled from the baby's mouth, mingling with the overflowing milk to create a pink dribble which dripped onto the bed.

'What's wrong?' he said, worriedly, taking a step towards the bed.

Michelle didn't answer, she merely continued to tug at the baby who was now hanging on grimly, using both hands to anchor himself.

The pain spread across her chest until it felt as if her entire torso was ablaze and, finally, unable to bear it any longer, she pulled the child hard.

As she did, Daniel bit through her nipple, severing it.

Blood jetted from the swollen tissue, spraying the child and the bed, soaking into the sheets.

The baby swallowed the nipple with one gulp, blood and milk dribbling over its chin.

Michelle screamed and looked down at her torn breast, a flap of skin hanging over the lacerated mammary. Blood was pumping furiously from the wound and she hastily laid the baby down and tugged the sheet to her chest, pressing it against the wound which bled profusely.

Daniel lay contentedly on the bed, his eyes still as bright and alert.

'Oh Jesus,' gasped Stuart, moving towards her. 'I'll get an ambulance.'

He looked once more at his child, its face soaked in blood, still chewing on a piece of skin which had come free with the nipple. Then he dashed for the phone.

'No,' Michelle called. 'Not the ambulance. Not yet.' She was pressing the sheet to her mutilated breast, trying to stem the flow of blood as best she could. 'You know who you've got to call.'

He hesitated a second longer then stabbed out the digits.

Behind him on the bed, the baby gurgled contentedly.

Thirty-three

Stuart Lewis looked at his watch and then continued gazing out of the front window. Every few moments he would step back to take a drag of his cigarette but then anxiety would force him back to his vigil.

He checked his watch again.

5.46 a.m.

He had made the phone call more than twenty minutes ago.

'Come on, come on,' he whispered, agitatedly, his face pressed to the glass of the window again.

Finally the car swung round the corner and came to a halt outside the house. Stuart moved towards the front door and unlocked it, opening it as the occupant of the car clambered out.

Doctor Edward Curtis strode up the path and through the front door.

'Upstairs,' Stuart said, and the doctor followed the younger man as he bounded up the narrow flight, hurrying towards the bedroom where his wife waited.

As Curtis entered the bedroom he was struck by the strong smell of blood.

The sheet which Michelle Lewis held against her breast was soaked in the crimson fluid, some of it beginning to congeal on the material. There were spots of it on the wall and carpet. It looked as though she was wearing red gloves.

The child lay beside her, its shawl similarly dotted with crimson, its face and hands stained dark with its mother's blood.

It was the baby that Curtis approached first.

'How long ago did this happen?' he asked, unfastening the black bag which he carried.

Stuart told him.

'And you haven't called an ambulance?' Curtis wanted to know, smiling relievedly when Stuart shook his head.

Curtis reached into his bag and took out a syringe. He quickly took it from its plastic wrapping then pulled out a bottle full of almost colourless liquid. He upended it, jabbed the needle through the top and drew off 50ml then he gently took hold of the baby's arm, found a vein and ran the needle into it.

The child didn't murmur as Curtis pushed the plunger, expelling the liquid into its veins.

He waited a moment then withdrew the syringe, dropping it back into his bag. Only then did he turn to Michelle who was still holding the sheet to her chest in what looked like an exaggerated attempt at modesty.

'Let me look,' said Curtis and she lowered the blood spattered sheet.

Not only had the nipple been torn off but a piece of flesh as large as the palm of Curtis's hand had also been pulled from the breast. He could see muscles and vein networks exposed. Blood was still oozing from the wound, dribbling down Michelle's stomach.

Curtis reached into his bag once again, this time pulling out some gauze and bandages.

'I'll dress the wound as best I can,' he said. 'You'll need to go to the hospital, you've lost a lot of blood.'

Michelle nodded obediently as Curtis pressed a gauze pad to the place where her nipple used to be then hastily wrapped bandages around to keep it in place.

'Tell them whatever you have to,' he said. 'Whatever you can think of. The child will be fine now. But he's not to be left alone for a while.' The doctor looked at Stuart who nodded. 'He'll sleep now.'

Curtis got to his feet and headed for the door.

'Wait five minutes then call the ambulance,' he said. They heard his footfalls on the stairs, the sound of his car engine as he drove off.

Both of them looked into the cot where the baby lay, already beginning to drift off to sleep.

They smiled down at him then Michelle wet the tip of her finger and wiped some blood away from his mouth.

He was really such a beautiful child.

Thirty-four

She had hesitated for a long time before finally deciding to call him.

It had been over a week since her father's funeral and she hadn't spoken to him since then, but now Sue Hacket sat beside the phone looking down at it as if expecting the digits to reach him without her having to touch them. She hadn't even been sure at first if she *wanted* to speak to him but she had found that loneliness is a truly contagious disease and Sue was finding it creeping into her life despite being surrounded by Julie and the family. She had tried rehearsing what she should say to her husband, even got as far as lifting the receiver once but then replaced it and resorted to pacing the floor of Julie's sitting room surrounded by the dozens of ornaments.

Julie was out shopping. Craig was at school and Mike at work. She was alone with only her thoughts for company.

Finally, almost reluctantly, she lifted the receiver and slowly pressed the numbers which would connect her with Hacket's school.

The connection was made, she heard the dial tone.

'Can I speak to John Hacket, please?' she asked when the phone was finally picked up.

The woman at the other end apologised but Mr Hacket had taken a week's holiday. She could leave a message if she wanted to, the secretary had his home number.

'No thanks,' said Sue and replaced the receiver, looking down at it for a moment before lifting it to her ear and jabbing out the digits of her home number.

Home. The word seemed curiously redundant.

The phone was answered almost immediately.

'Hello.'

She recognised his voice and, for a second, thought about putting the phone back down.

'Hello, John, it's me.'

'Sue? How are you?'

'I'm OK I rang the school, they said you were off for a week.'

'Yeah, I can't seem to concentrate. It's not fair on the kids if I'm not giving it a hundred per cent, besides I've got things to do around the house. I put it on the market, there's been three or four prospective buyers round already.'

'Any interest?'

'One couple seemed fairly keen until they found out what had happened here.' He was quiet for a moment. 'Some bloke came just *because* of what happened here, morbid bastard. I haven't heard anything from the others yet.' There was another awkward silence. 'You say you're all right, you sound tired.'

'I am. I haven't been sleeping too well.'

More silence.

Christ, it was excruciating, as if each was trying to think of something to say. They were like strangers.

'How's Julie and Mike?' he asked.

'They're not so bad.'

'And the boy?'

'He's all right too.' She didn't mention the incident in the car, having since tried to dismiss it from her mind.

'Good,' he said, wearily. 'So everyone's OK'

'Listen John, I had to speak to you. It's about you and me. I told you I couldn't come back to that house and I can't.'

'I understand that but things might not be that cut and dried. I mean, it's not just the house you're avoiding is it? It's me.'

She swallowed hard.

'I might *just* have managed to forgive you for the affair, John,' she said. 'But I'll *never* forgive you for what happened to Lisa. And, yes, I still blame you. I always will.'

'You phoned to tell me something I already knew?' he said, trying to control the irritation in his voice. 'How do you think *I* feel? I can't forgive *myself*, I don't need you to remind me all the time. It's me who's living in the house now. I'm closer to the memories. You're the one who ran away from them, Sue.'

'I didn't run away. If I hadn't got out I'd have gone crazy.'

'I know the feeling.'

There was another silence.

'John, the real reason I rang was to tell you that one of the schools down here in Hinkston has a vacancy for an assistant headmaster. Apparently there's a house included with the job.'

'Why Hinkston?'

'Because I don't want to live in London anymore, I told you that,' she snapped.

'And the two of us? If I got this job would you be willing to start again? A new environment, a new life perhaps?' He sounded hopeful.

'Maybe. We couldn't start from the beginning, John. Things would never be the same between us again.'

'We can try for Christ's sake,' he insisted. 'I still love you, Sue. I need you and I think you need me, whether you admit it or not.'

She sat in silence for a moment, knowing there was some truth to his words.

'It'll take time, John.'

'I don't care how long it takes.'

She gave him the address and number of the school.

'Let me know how it goes,' she told him.

'Maybe you could meet me when I come down for the interview.'

There was a long silence. For a moment he thought she'd gone.

'Yes, I will,' she said, finally.

'Sue, if you're not sleeping, love, it might be an idea to take something. Go and see a doctor. You've got to take care of yourself.'

'I was thinking of seeing Julie's doctor actually.'

Another long silence.

'I'd better go, John,' she said. 'Call me when you're coming down for the interview.'

'Sue, thanks for calling.'

'I'll see you soon.'

'Sue.'

'Yes?'

'I love you.'

She gripped the receiver tight for a second.

'See you soon,' she said, softly then put the phone down.

It was as if the conversation had drained her of strength. She sat back, looking down at the phone, feeling as if she'd just run a marathon. It was fully five minutes before she got to her feet and wandered into the kitchen. He was right, perhaps she should see a doctor. A few sleeping pills wouldn't hurt her. there was a small booklet lying on the kitchen table with a picture of a smiling cat and the legend 'Important People' embossed on it. Another of Julie's organisational aids. The address book contained numbers for everyone from the Gas board to the local vet. All in alphabetical order. Sue flicked through until she came to the 'D's'.

She found the name she sought almost immediately.

DOCTOR'S SURGERY.

And beneath it:

Doctor Edward Curtis.

Thirty-five

It was a feeling Hacket thought he'd forgotten and he smiled as he drove, glancing out at the scenery which sped past him. The sun was high in the sky as if its emergence were purely to mirror his state of mind.

He hadn't felt this way for many months, years even. It was something like anticipation only it was more heightened, more acute. There was anxiety there too, naturally but, he actually felt reasonably happy and that particular emotion was one which had been intolerably absent from his life of late.

As he drew nearer to the outskirts of Hinkston and houses began to appear in greater abundance, he thought what his prospects were. If he could secure the job at the school and the house which Sue had told him went with it then he had a chance of rebuilding his marriage too. Hacket felt the surge of adrenalin once again and realised that it wasn't anticipation it was, in all senses of the cliché, a ray of hope.

He'd rung the school immediately after he'd finished speaking to Sue and had been surprised to find that they were prepared to interview him the following day. He'd expected a wait of a week at least but apparently they were anxious to fill the post, and consequently wanted to begin seeing applicants as soon as possible.

Hacket was also glad to be out of the house for a day. He hadn't felt like being surrounded by people, that was why he'd taken the week off work, but being imprisoned in the house, alone with just his thoughts, had proved almost as intolerable. The trip to Hinkston and the possibility of a new job had lifted his spirits a little. He'd even found it possible to face some music and had jammed a cassette into the machine as he drove. However, as he drove further into the town he switched the cassette off and contented himself with glancing around at the buildings which were beginning to form more regular patterns on either side of him.

As he paused at traffic lights, Hacket checked the location of the school on the piece of paper he'd written it down on. He wasn't far away now, he realised.

He felt nervous, though not about the interview. He knew his own capabilities, knew he was as able, if not more so, than most to fill the post but his anxiety grew from knowing that if he didn't get the job then his chance of rebuilding his marriage was also in jeopardy. He could stand to lose the job but not to lose Sue.

The lights changed and Hacket drove on. He guided the car through the town centre, looking around at what appeared to be a bustling community. There was an open market in the paved square, the awnings fluttering brightly in the light breeze. He could hear the shouts of traders as they vied for custom.

The school was on the other side of town, about five minutes' drive from the centre, and he finally spotted the iron railings which rose from the concrete like rusted javelins. The playground was empty but past a large red brick building he could see beyond to a playing field where a number of children were kicking a ball about. Hacket swung the Renault into the car park and switched off the engine. He glanced at his reflection in the mirror, running a hand through his hair, then he climbed out and strode through the main doors of the school in search of the headmaster's office.

A young woman in her mid-twenties passed him and smiled and, for fleeting seconds, Hacket caught himself gazing at her shapely legs as she passed him.

A little like Nikki?

He sucked in an angry breath, mad with himself for even

thinking about her, but her image would not fade from his mind as quickly as he would have liked. He walked on and finally came to a door marked: D. BROOKS. HEADMASTER

He knocked and walked in, finding himself in an outer office.

A tall woman smiled at him, trying to shovel the final piece of a Kit-Kat into her mouth, chewing quickly enough to ask him what he wanted. Hacket smiled and spared her the trouble.

'My name's John Hacket. I've got an appointment at ten about the deputy Head's job.'

She continued chewing furiously, nodding vigorously as she swallowed the pieces of biscuit.

'Excuse me,' she said, wiping chocolate from her lips. 'I'll tell Mr Brooks you're here.' She smiled again and knocked on the door behind her, walking in when called. Hacket was left alone in the outer office.

He glanced around at the diagram of the school which covered one wall, the paintings which adorned another. Each one had a small plaque beneath it which Hacket read. The paintings had been done by pupils, each one a prizewinner in a different age group.

One of the paintings showed an owl perched in a tree holding something small and bloodied in its claws. Hacket leaned closer, unable to make out the shape.

'If you'd like to come through, Mr Hacket,' the tall woman called, interrupting his inspection of the painting.

'Thank you,' said Hacket, taking a final look at the painting.

As he moved away from it he finally realised what the small bloodied shape was in the painting. He frowned.

In its talons, the beautifully painted owl held a torn and bleeding human eye.

Thirty-six

The heat inside the office was stifling.

Hacket felt his skin prickling as he walked in, and he was aware of his cheeks colouring from the warmth.

The man who faced him across the wide desk, by contrast, was pale and, as he shook Hacket's hand, the younger man noticed how cold the others' touch was.

Donald Brooks was in his early fifties, his immaculate appearance spoilt only by a few flakes of dandruff on the collar of his grey suit. He was an imposing-looking individual despite his pallid appearance, and the eyes which looked out at Hacket from behind spectacles were an intense green. His handshake was firm, his smile friendly. He invited Hacket to sit down, noticing the scarlet tinges on the younger man's cheeks.

'Sorry about the heat in here,' Brooks said. 'I'm a little anaemic and I tend to feel the cold more than most.'

'I'd noticed,' Hacket said, smiling.

'My wife's always complaining about it at home,' Brooks went on. 'Even in the summer we have the central heating turned on.' He shrugged almost apologetically. He asked Hacket if he wanted a coffee and the tall woman in the outer office entered with one a moment or two later. He thanked her and she left the two men alone once more, allowing Brooks to flick through the two-page CV which Hacket had passed to him. The younger man sipped his coffee while Brooks nodded approvingly, reading the qualifications and commendations that Hacket had acquired over the last ten years.

'Very impressive, Mr Hacket,' he said, finally. 'Your qualifications are excellent and you have some very useful experience behind you. I see the school you teach at presently has over 900 pupils – that can't give you much opportunity for personal contact.'

'I'm afraid it doesn't. It's an occupational hazard I suppose, working in London schools. What's your pupil to teacher ratio here?'

'We average about twenty to a class, usually less. Most of the sixth-form classes have only three or four pupils.'

Hacket nodded approvingly and the two men talked for some time about the school, about Hacket's background in teaching and his desire for the present position.

'Are you married, Mr Hacket?' Brooks asked.

'Yes.'

'Any children?'

He hesitated a second, as if the word itself brought pain.

'No,' he said, sharply, reaching for his coffee and taking a sip, wincing when he found it was cold.

Stone cold. As cold as the grave.

As cold as Lisa.

'Have you had many applicants for the position?' Hacket asked, anxious to steer the conversation onto other things.

'You're the fourth,' Brooks told him. 'And, I must admit I'm impressed. When could you start if you were given the job?'

Hacket shrugged.

'Next week,' he said. 'There's details to finalise about selling our house in London, but a week should be plenty of time.'

'Excellent,' said Brooks. 'Then I think it's time I showed you around the school. You ought to see where you're going to be working.'

Hacket smiled broadly, got to his feet and shook the older man's hand, again feeling the coldness of his skin but this time he ignored that small detail. He followed the Headmaster out of the office, pausing again to look at the painting of the owl which hung in the annexe beyond.

'Quite a talented artist,' Hacket said, nodding towards the painting, glancing at the name on the plaque beneath.

Phillip Craven.

Brooks glanced at the painting then walked out of the annexe without speaking.

Hacket followed.

The tour of the school took longer than Hacket had anticipated. The facilities were extensive and impressive and he thought that the school must be one of the few State-funded seats of learning not to have been decimated by Government cut-backs in the past few years.

He and Brooks walked past the red brick building Hacket had seen when first arriving at the school and the teacher was informed that it was a gymnasium. A class of girls were playing hockey on the nearby pitch, a shrieking horde supervised by a mistress who had thighs like a Russian shot-putter and shoulders slightly broader than Hacket's. He grinned as he watched her hurtling up and down the pitch, whistle clamped in her mouth.

'You may be asked to take on some of the duties of the Games masters,' Brooks said. 'I noticed in your CV that you'd done that at your last school. Are you a sporty man, Mr Hacket?'

'I played rugby and football for my school when I was a kid. I wish I was as fit now as I was then. But I can manage. No heart attacks, I promise.' He smiled.

Brooks looked at him as if he didn't understand the joke, then he shivered and turned away from the hockey match and strode across the playground with Hacket beside him. The sun was still out but Brooks looked frozen. His skin had turned even more pale and he kept rubbing his hands together as if to restore the circulation.

'As you're aware, there is a house with the position,' he said. 'I'll show you around that too.'

It was a white-walled building hidden from the school grounds by a high privet hedge which was somewhat sparsely covered for the time of year. But it was enough to offer protection from any inquisitive eyes within the school. There were a couple of willow trees in the front garden which had been allowed to get a little out of hand. The grass was about six inches long and there were weeds poking through cracks in the path which led to the front door but it was nothing which couldn't be put right in a weekend, thought Hacket.

As for the house itself, it looked in good repair, all the slates were on the roof. At least the ones he could see. The paintwork was good for another six months at least. The only thing which did stand out was the newness of the front door. It hadn't yet been painted the same dull fawn as the window frames and looked as if it had been affixed only days earlier.

Brooks fumbled in his pocket for the key and opened the door, ushering Hacket in.

The hall was narrow, leading to a flight of stairs carpeted with a rusty coloured shag-pile.

'How long has the house been empty?' Hacket wanted to know.

'About two weeks.' Brooks told him, pushing open the door to the sitting room.

There was no carpet on the floor in there and Hacket's feet echoed on the bare boards. There were, however, still some framed prints on the wall and a couple of armchairs.

They were covered by dust sheets.

'The teacher who lived here before,' Hacket began, glancing around the room. 'Why did he leave?'

Brooks rubbed his hands together again and shrugged, partly in answer to the question, mainly as a gesture to indicate how cold he was. He patted one of the radiators as he passed it as if hoping it would begin pouring forth some heat.

'It was very sudden,' he said, sharply and moved through into the dining room.

This room was also carpeted and Hacket wondered why just the sitting room should have been left bare.

There was more furniture, too, also covered by dust sheets.

'What was he like?' Hacket wanted to know.

'He did his job,' Brooks answered, as if that was enough.

'He left a lot of furniture behind. He *must* have left in a rush.'

They wandered through into the kitchen then back through the dining room to the hall and up the stairs to look into the three bedrooms.

'Did he have kids?' Hacket asked.

'He liked to keep his affairs private, Mr Hacket. I don't pry into the private lives of my staff,' said Brooks, stiffly.

'I only asked if he had kids,' Hacket said, somewhat bemused.

Brooks turned and headed for the stairs.

'Have you seen enough? I have to get back to work.'

'I understand,' Hacket said, shaking his head.

As they reached the front door once more Brooks locked it, pressing on the wood to ensure it was properly fastened.

'The teacher before you did what I believe is called a moonlight flit. I don't know *why*, Mr Hacket. I just hope you're more reliable.' He stalked off up the path, leaving Hacket standing on the front step.

'A moonlight flit, eh?' Hacket muttered to himself.

His thoughts were interrupted by the sound of a bell. The signal for lunch.

Within minutes, the playground was filled with children, the sound of their voices swelling the air.

Back in his office, Brooks pressed himself against the radiator, the colour gradually coming back to his cheeks. He stood there while Hacket thanked him for the tour of the school and the house then they said their goodbyes and Hacket left, weaving his way through the throng of children in the playground in order to get to his car. Only then did Brooks leave the radiator and move across to the window, watching as the teacher eased the car through the gates and onto the main road.

'I gave him the job,' said Brooks as the tall woman entered the office.

'Did he ask many questions?' she enquired.

Brooks nodded.

'He wanted to know about the teacher who was here before him, wanted to know why he left so suddenly.'

'What did you tell him,' the secretary asked.

'I didn't tell him the truth, if that's what you mean,' Brooks said, rubbing his hands together. 'I'm not *that* stupid.'

Thirty-seven

Hacket parked his own car behind Sue's Metro and then slid from behind the steering wheel. He glanced at the house, hesitating a moment before walking up the path to the front door. He rang the bell, feeling peculiarly nervous. Like a boy on his first date, afraid that no one will answer. He waited a moment then rang again.

The door swung open.

'Hello, John,' beamed Julie and kissed him gently on the cheek. 'How did it go?'

'Fine,' he said, stepping in past his sister-in-law. 'Is Sue here?'

'Go through into the kitchen,' Julie told him.

Sue was drying some dishes. She turned as Hacket entered the room, her smile rather thin.

He thought how beautiful she looked. It seemed like years since he'd seen her, not days. Even longer since he'd held her.

'I got the job,' he told her.

'That's great,' she said, her smile broadening a little.

Julie joined them, aware of the atmosphere. She filled the kettle and prepared three cups while Hacket sat down at the kitchen table. He told Sue about the school, about the job, the salary. The house.

She seemed pleased and even managed to laugh as he mentioned Brooks' obsession with the cold. They gazed at each other long and hard, Hacket searching for even a hint of emotion in her blue eyes. Some sign of love? Was that what he sought?

'Are you going back to London tonight?' Sue asked.

He nodded.

'I've got no choice. I'll have to arrange the move and there are people coming to view the house tomorrow. Why?'

She shook her head.

'Just curious.'

'If you two want to talk . . .' Julie said.

'No, don't be silly. You stay here,' Sue told her sister.

Hacket was a little disappointed but hid his feelings adequately.

'I'd like you to see the house next time I come down Sue,' he said.

'What did the headmaster say about the teacher who lived there before?' Julie asked.

Hacket grunted.

'Very little.'

Julie nodded almost imperceptibly and gazed down into her mug.

'Why?' Hacket asked, noting her expression.

'Perhaps I shouldn't say anything but I think he should have told you. Anyone from around here would have told you. It was all over the local papers at the time. Big news. The police never did find out why he did it?'

'Did what?' Sue wanted to know.

'One night, he must have gone crazy or something. He got a shotgun, killed his wife and his son and then stuck the barrel in his mouth and shot himself.'

Thirty-eight

Elaine Craven sat alone in the waiting room of the surgery.

Shafts of sunlight flowed through the wide windows illuminating the room, making it seem as if the white walls were glowing. Elaine glanced around her, smiling each time she caught the eye of the receptionist.

She was in her late thirties, dressed in a black skirt and a navy blouse, the left sleeve of which was rolled up to reveal a bandage which stretched from her wrist to her elbow. The limb was held stiffly across her chest and, each time she moved she felt a twinge of pain from the arm. Elaine glanced up at the wall clock above the receptionist's desk and noticed that she still had another five minutes before she was due in to see Curtis. She tried to move her left arm slowly in an effort to minimise the pain but it didn't work and she winced once again.

'What did you do to your arm?' asked the receptionist, noticing Elaine's obvious distress.

'A stupid accident,' she said, dismissively, and shrugged, but even that movement caused her pain.

The two women exchanged perfunctory conversation about the weather while they waited for Curtis to call Elaine in. Then, tiring of that particular topic the receptionist tried a different subject.

'How are your family? It's just the one boy you've got isn't it?'

Elaine nodded.

'Yes, Phillip. He's fine. My husband is fine. It's only me who goes around having stupid accidents.' She motioned towards the bandaged arm as if to remind the receptionist why she was here.

There was a loud beep from the console in front of the receptionist and she flicked a switch.

'Send Mrs Craven in, please,' said Curtis, his voice sounding robotic as it filtered through the intercom.

Elaine got to her feet and smiled at the receptionist once more as she passed through the door ahead of her marked 'Private'. It opened onto a short corridor which led down to another door. She knocked and entered.

Edward Curtis smiled as she entered his room. He invited her to sit down, his eyes drawn immediately to the heavy bandage on her arm.

'I hope your family are in better shape than you, Elaine,' he said, getting to his feet and walking around the desk to her. 'What have you been doing?'

'It was an accident,' she told him. 'It should never have happened.' She looked up at him and Curtis saw a flicker of something behind her eyes.

It looked like fear.

'Let me have a look,' he said, and she extended her arm until it was resting on his desk. With infinite care, Curtis began to unfasten the bandages, unravelling them as cautiously as he could, apologising when Elaine hissed with the pain. Finally he pulled the last piece free and exposed two large gauze pads which covered her forearm. He reached behind him, into a small tray on his desk, and retrieved a pair of tweezers. Then he took one corner of the first pad between the ends of the metal prongs and pulled gently.

'Good God,' he murmured, exposing the forearm more fully. 'How the hell did this happen?'

The skin which covered the forearm had been removed in several places. Not sliced or scraped but torn off.

The area around the first deep laceration was red and swollen and Curtis could see the first watery deposits of pus nestling beneath the torn flesh.

The second wound was even worse.

He pulled the gauze pad free and could not resist wincing himself at the damage which had been inflicted on the arm. Part of the flexor muscle closest to the ulna had been severed and the bone was showing clearly through the mass of twisted flesh and muscle. There was more pus forming on the extremities of the wound, this time thicker and more noxious. Some of it was already leaking into the savage gash.

He looked sternly at Elaine.

'When did it happen?' he said, harshly.

'Two nights ago,' she told him.

'Why didn't you call me?' he snarled. 'Was anyone else hurt?'

She shook her head, glancing down at the wounds which looked like dog bites, only made by some ravening animal unlike any ordinary pet. She gritted her teeth as he used sterile pads to clean the gashes.

'It was my fault, I know,' she said. 'I knew it was close to the time, I know I should have contacted you but he seemed all right.'

Curtis wiped away the pus, dropping the swab into his waste bin.

'The treatment must be kept up at regular intervals, you know that,' the doctor told her, repeating the procedure on the smaller gash. 'How *is* the boy?'

'Restless.' It was the only word she could think of.

'Bring him to me tomorrow, before this happens again.' He jabbed an accusatory finger at the two wounds.

Elaine nodded, watching as he re-dressed the torn forearm. When he was finished she got to her feet, pulled her coat carefully over her injured arm and turned towards the door.

'Tomorrow,' Curtis reminded her and she nodded, thanking him.

Thirty-nine

The sun was already bleeding to death as he left Hinkston. By the time he reached the outer suburbs of London the vivid crimson of the sky had given way to darkness.

Hacket was feeling a strange mixture of feelings. Anticipation, excitement and anxiety had all fused together inside his mind. Those three emotions were to do with the job and with the possibility of starting afresh with Sue but he also felt something else.

Suspicion? That wasn't the right word.

Unease seemed to better suit his mood.

Why had Brooks been so secretive about the previous occupant of the house? Granted, it wasn't the sort of thing which you told a man who was about to work for you, at least not in so many words. Hacket could understand how the headmaster had feared telling him about the double murder and suicide which had taken place inside the house. But why lie about it?

But, it wasn't Brooks' lies that bothered Hacket. It was the reason *why* the previous occupant had murdered his family then killed himself.

He pulled up at traffic lights, the thought tumbling around inside his head.

Pressure of work? That seemed a bit extreme.

Perhaps he didn't like her cooking, Hacket smiled grimly.

Maybe he'd had an affair and couldn't face her any longer.

A bit of a kindred spirit, eh?

Hacket tried to push the last consideration from his mind as the lights changed to green and he drove on.

As he drew deeper into the heart of the capital a curious but not altogether unexpected weariness began to close around him. Like some kind of cloying, unwelcome blanket, he had felt its folds slip from him as he'd left the city that morning, but now, as he drew closer to home he felt their invisible weight enfolding him again.

Perhaps it was the thought of returning to so many bad memories.

' . . . *But the night goes by so very slow* . . . ' came from the car radio.

' . . . *and I hope that it won't end though. Alone..*' Hacket switched it off.

He was less than five miles from home now and he glanced down at the dashboard clock.

8.38 p.m.

He yawned and drove on, slowing down as he came to a

Zebra crossing. A woman pushing a pram piled high with boxes crossed first then a young couple holding hands. Then, finally a tall, thin man who glanced at the car as he sauntered across.

In the light of the headlamps Hacket could pick out certain details of the individual.

The lank hair, the pale complexion, the sunken eyes.

There was something familiar about this man and Hacket felt his chest tighten, the hairs at the back of his neck rise.

It was then that he saw the dark birthmark on the side of the man's neck and, finally, he was in no doubt who the individual was.

Hacket gripped the steering wheel until his knuckles turned white, his eyes rivetted to the man.

To the man who had murdered his daughter.

Peter Walton sauntered past him.

Forty

Hacket was out of the car in seconds.

He hurled open the driver's door and scrambled out, pointing at Walton.

'You, stop,' he bellowed.

Taken aback by the shout, Walton didn't wait to find out who this madman was, he simply turned and ran up the street, bumping into people as he fled. He ran not even knowing why he ran, but he had seen the expression of pure hatred on Hacket's face and it had been enough to convince him that this man, whoever he was, was best avoided.

Hacket slammed his door and, ignoring the blaring horns of the cars behind him, ran after Walton.

Hacket didn't see the figure that followed *him*.

'Walton,' he roared as he pounded after the fugitive.

People on the pavement who saw him coming stepped aside, those who didn't were buffeted aside as the chase continued up the road to a junction.

Walton looked behind him and saw Hacket still hurtling after him. Without checking the traffic he ran into the road, a speeding Volvo narrowly avoiding him. A taxi coming the other way banged on his hooter as he also came close to hitting the running man. But Walton made the other side of the road safely and ran on, glancing over his shoulder to see that Hacket was still in pursuit.

The teacher also ran into the road without regard for the traffic.

A Capri slammed on its brakes and skidded to a halt just in front of him. Hacket leapt up onto the bonnet and slid off the other side while the driver yelled at him.

He hit the tarmac in time to avoid an oncoming mini which swerved, striking the pavement as it narrowly missed Hacket. He sucked in a deep breath and hurtled on, worried he might lose his quarry on the crowded street.

Up ahead, Walton dived to his left, into a cafe, pushing past the customers, bumping into a table and spilling the drinks that were there. One of the customers jumped up to challenge him but Walton merely pushed him aside and burst through the door which led to the kitchen.

Seconds later, Hacket entered the cafe, following his prey, also ducking through into the kitchen where he heard the cook yelling obscenities as he and Walton raced through and out the back door.

The cool air was a welcome change from the stifling heat of the kitchen but Hacket was already sweating profusely, the salty fluid running down the side of his face. However, he didn't slacken his pace.

Walton found himself in the alley which backed on to the café and he bolted down it as fast as he could, overturning dustbins in his wake. Anything to delay his pursuer, but Hacket merely hurdled the obstacles and ran on, desperate to catch his foe.

And when he did catch him? What then?

The thought faded as he stumbled over a box, almost falling. He shot out a hand to steady himself, tearing some skin from his palm on the brick wall of the alley.

Then suddenly, he and Walton were free of its confines, back on another street, amongst people again.

Walton slammed into a young lad, knocking him to the ground but he didn't stop, merely glanced round to see that Hacket was still after him. Walton saw a bus coming down the street and he ran into the road, running alongside it for a few yards before launching himself up onto the running platform.

He laughed as he saw Hacket running after the bus.

Up ahead, the traffic lights were about to change to red.

Stay on red, Hacket thought as he hurtled after the bus.

They did.

To Walton's horror the bus began to slow down and he looked ahead to see the glaring red light then back to see that Hacket was almost upon him.

Walton jumped from the bus, shaking loose of the conductor who tried to grab him. Then he jumped into the road and scurried back onto the pavement, the breath now searing in his lungs. His legs felt like lead weights and he didn't know how much longer he could run for.

Hacket was feeling the same. He could hardly get his breath but he ran on, his head spinning from lack of oxygen. Gulping in huge lungfuls of air in an effort to keep himself going. His heart was thudding against his ribs, threatening to burst but still he found more energy to continue the chase.

Walton looked up and saw what might be his sanctuary.

The neon sign for the Underground station glowed like a beacon in the darkness and he bolted across the road towards the entrance.

Hacket followed.

'Get out the fucking way,' shouted Walton, elbowing a passage through the gang of people emerging from the stairway. He battered his way through, slipping as he was five steps from the bottom. He toppled over, landing heavily on the dirty tiled floor.

Hacket ran on, taking the steps two at a time, ignoring the stench of stale urine and sweat which rose to greet him from the subterranean cavern.

Walton hauled himself upright and looked around, seeing the automatic barriers which led to the trains. He ran towards them, scrambling over, ignoring the protests of the man collecting tickets.

Hacket too vaulted the partition and hurtled after his quarry who was now heading for the escalator that led even deeper into the bowels of the earth.

Walton, scarcely able to walk now, staggered along on legs that felt like lumps of lead, struggling down the metal steps of the escalator, pushing past those who stood in his way.

Hacket followed, still unaware of the figure that pursued him.

He was panting madly, his throat dry and parched from sucking in breath, his muscles crying out for rest but he knew that if he could catch Walton on the platform he had him. There was nowhere for him to hide. No further he could run.

Hacket stumbled half-way down the escalator but steadied himself, seeing Walton reach the bottom and bolt to his right.

Over his own laboured breathing, Hacket could hear the rumble of an approaching train and a further realisation struck him.

Should Walton board a train before him then there was no way he'd catch the man.

The teacher forced what little reserves of strength he possessed into his screaming muscles and ran on.

There were about two dozen people on the platform, most of them moving forward as they heard the train drawing closer.

Hacket looked to his right and left, sweat now pouring from him.

There was no sign of Walton.

The train was emerging from the tunnel, its lights like the glowing eyes of some massive, fast-moving worm as it slid from the tunnel.

Hacket raced down the platform, looking frantically for Walton, glancing back over his shoulder as the train came to a halt and its doors slid open. Those already on the train watched with detachment as he ran back and forth up and down the platform, his face coated in sweat, his eyes bulging as he tried to get his breath.

Where the hell was Walton?

He heard the familiar whirring noise which came just prior to the doors shutting and, in that split second he saw the man he sought dive for the carriage at the far end of the train.

He got in just as the doors were sliding shut.

'No,' roared Hacket and leapt for the nearest door, jamming his hand into it, ignoring the pain, knowing it would force the doors to open fully once again. As they did he slipped inside.

Seconds later the train pulled away again, picking up speed as it entered the tunnel at the far end of the platform.

Hacket began making his way along the train towards the carriage where he knew Walton to be.

As he came to the door marked 'ONLY TO BE USED IN AN EMERGENCY' worried travellers watched him force the handle up and down until the door opened. He squeezed through, feeling the warm air inside the tunnel buffet him as the train sped along, threatening to shake him from his precarious perch. He struggled with the next door, anxious to get into the safety of the carriage, balanced on just the coupling which held the compartments together.

He almost had the door open when his foot slipped.

Hacket yelled in terror as he felt himself falling.

He shot out a hand and managed to grab the door handle which promptly twisted in his grasp.

The door flew open and he fell into the carriage, sprawling on the floor, watched by the other travellers but Hacket wasn't bothered by their stares. He dragged himself upright and struggled on, realising that they were only moments away from the next station. Once the train pulled in he could run along the platform to the carriage where Walton hid then he had him.

The train escaped the blackness and Hacket pressed himself to the sliding doors, ready to bolt out the minute they opened.

The train slowed down, came to a halt.

He was out in a flash, hurtling towards the front of the train.

Towards Walton.

His quarry, as if realising Hacket's plan, came flying from the foremost carriage, knocking a woman to the ground in his haste. He ran across the platform, through a narrow walkway and towards some stairs which led to a bridge across another track. Hacket followed, taking the stairs two at a time, his lungs now feeling as if someone had filled them with hot sand, his legs throbbing.

Walton looked round to see his pursuer was still there, still on his heels.

He jumped the last three steps, landing heavily on the concrete as Hacket ran on, now only yards from his quarry.

Walton turned to his right, onto another platform.

It may have been rancid ice cream, it may even have been a puddle of vomit left by one of the many drunks who frequented the underground complex. But, whatever it was, Walton didn't see it.

His foot slid in the slimy mess and he skidded, stumbled. Then, with a despairing scream, he pitched forward, arms flailing in the air for interminable seconds.

He toppled off the edge of the platform, onto the rails.

Hacket dashed to the edge as he heard the loud crack and the hiss of thousands of volts as Walton's body was scorched by the incredible electrical charge. His flesh was turned black in seconds, the blood boiling in his veins, and his body jerked uncontrollably as the current continued to course through it.

Hacket reached the platform edge and looked down.

Walton's body resembled a spent match.

With a gasp, Hacket sank to his knees, eyes rivetted to the blackened corpse which lay across the lines.

The stench of seared flesh and ozone was overpowering, and for a moment he thought he was going to be sick, but the feeling passed and he knew only the terrible ache in his muscles and the pain in his chest.

Somewhere down the platform a woman was screaming but Hacket didn't seem to hear it.

He looked down once more at the body of Walton and smiled.

He was still unaware of the figure who watched *him*.

Forty-one

Edward Curtis pushed another log onto the open fire then sat back in the high-backed leather chair, watching the flames dancing in the grate.

His face was set in hard lines and he reached for the brandy glass on the table beside him, sipping it, not taking his eyes from the leaping flames. His mother used to tell him that you could see shapes in fire, but the only shape that Curtis could see was the outline of Elaine Craven's mutilated arm.

'I think it's getting out of control,' said Curtis, quietly.

'You're the only one who can do anything about it,' said the other occupant of the room, seated on the other side of the hearth. But the other figure's eyes were fixed not on the fire but on Curtis.

'There have been too many incidents lately,' Curtis said. 'The Kirkham girl at the hotel. The Lewis baby and now this business with Phillip Craven.'

'They knew the risks, Edward, you can't blame yourself.'

'Blame isn't the right word. I don't feel any guilt for what has happened, for what is going to happen. As you say, they knew the risks. But that doesn't stop me feeling a little helpless. There's still too much I don't know.'

'Are you saying you want to stop?' the other said, challengingly.

Curtis looked at the figure and shook his head.

'There's too much at stake to stop now. Besides, I've gone too far to stop.' He sipped his brandy. 'We both have.' He re-filled his own glass and then the glass of his companion.

'It's what they would have wanted,' the other said. 'We owe it to them to carry on.'

Curtis watched as the figure got up and crossed to the

large bay window which opened out from the sitting room. Drink in hand the other pulled back one curtain and looked out over the lights of Hinkston which lay below.

'You make it sound like duty,' Curtis said. 'Saying we owe it to them.'

'Not duty, Edward. Love.' The figure swallowed a sizeable measure of the brandy. 'And something stronger.'

'Like what?' Curtis wanted to know.

The other figure did not look at him, merely kept on staring out at the lights of the town. The words were spoken softly.

'Like revenge.'

Forty-two

'What the bloody hell did you think you were doing?'

Detective Inspector Madden bellowed the words at Hacket who sat at the desk, his hands clasped around a paper cup full of black coffee.

'You're not a vigilante. This isn't New York,' Madden continued.

'Look, he fell . . .' Hacket began, but was cut short by the DI.

'Lucky for you he did. Also you should be thankful that there were plenty of witnesses on the platform to testify to that fact. We could have been forgiven for thinking you threw Walton on the line.'

The office inside Clapham police station was small, its confines filled with a thick haze of cigarette smoke. All three men were smoking. Hacket was sitting on a plastic chair in front of Madden's desk. The DI himself was pacing the floor agitatedly, and DS Spencer was leaning against the desk looking down at the teacher, a Marlboro jammed in one side of his mouth.

Hacket took a sip of the lukewarm coffee and winced.

'How long are you going to keep me here?' he asked.

'For as long as it takes,' Madden rasped.

'Takes for what?'

'As long as it takes for you to see sense. To keep your nose out of police business and stop acting like fucking Charles Bronson. Like I said to you you're not a vigilante and this isn't *Death Wish*.'

'I told you, Walton slipped. You know that. Why can't you just let me go?' Hacket asked.

'You're lucky we're not charging you,' Madden informed him.

Hacket spun round in his seat to look at the DI.

'Charging *me*?' he snapped, incredulously. 'With what?'

'Disturbing the peace. Causing an affray. Would you like me to carry on?'

'That bastard killed my daughter,' snarled Hacket getting to his feet. 'You couldn't do anything about it so I did.'

'You don't even know if Walton was the one who killed her,' Spencer interjected. 'There were two men involved in the murder.'

'Great. One down, one to go then.'

'I'm warning you, Hacket,' the DI said, sternly. 'You keep away from this case.' His tone softened slightly. 'I'm sorry, we're all sorry about what happened to your daughter but let the law take care of it.'

Hacket nodded.

'Let the law take care of it,' he echoed. 'And if you catch him, what then? He's not going to be punished is he? A few years in prison isn't enough for what he did to my little girl.'

'That's as maybe but he'll serve a *proper* sentence for his crime, proposed by a judge in a *proper* court of law. The Fearns family lost a daughter too didn't they? If you stop to remember that Hacket, two people died in your house that night. I haven't had any trouble from Mr Fearns wanting to be judge, jury and executioner.'

'If he can live knowing that his daughter's killer isn't going to suffer the way he should then that's up to him. I can't.'

'You've got no choice. I'm not *asking* you to keep your nose out of this case, Hacket, I'm *telling* you,' Madden snapped. 'The last thing I need is some self-styled avenger running around London. *We'll* take care of it.'

Hacket shook his head and took a final drag on his cigarette, grinding it out in an ashtray already overflowing with dead butts.

And what would you have done if it had been *your* child?' he said. 'Would you have accepted the judgement of a court?' His voice was heavy with sarcasm. 'Don't tell me you wouldn't have wanted to see the bastard suffer because I won't believe you.'

'And what if you'd caught up with Walton tonight?' asked Spencer. 'What would you have done? Killed him? That would have made you no better than him and you'd be in the cells now, under arrest.'

'Five minutes' satisfaction isn't worth ruining your life for,' Madden echoed. He took another drag on his cigarette then hooked a thumb in the direction of the door. 'Go on, go home before I change my mind and charge you with breach of the peace.'

Hacket paused at the door, turning to look at the two policemen.

'You know,' he said, smiling. 'I'm still pleased he's dead. I just wish he'd suffered more.' Hacket slammed the door behind him.

Madden dropped the cigarette on the floor and ground it out with his foot.

'Do you know the worst thing about all this, Spencer?' said the DI nodding in the direction that Hacket had gone. 'I agree with him.'

Spencer nodded slowly.

'Join the club.'

Forty-three

He stood outside the door for what seemed like an eternity. His eyes riveted to the doorbell, his hand wavering as he reached for it. Hacket wasn't sure if he was trying to summon up the courage to press it. Courage wasn't the word. Right now he didn't know what the word *was* and, what was more, he didn't give a fuck.

He pressed it and waited.

And waited.

He finally heard movement from the other side of the door.

'Who is it?'

He managed a thin smile as he heard the soft Irish lilt to the voice.

'It's Hacket.'

Silence.

'What do you want?' she finally said.

'I've got to talk to you,' he said.

Another silence then he heard the sound of a chain being slid free, of bolts being drawn back. The door opened.

Nikki Reeves stood before him in a long T-shirt which

was so baggy it managed to hide the smooth contours of her body. Her eyes were bleary with sleep and she rubbed them as she looked at Hacket, blinking myopically.

'Do you know what time it is?' she asked. 'Nearly midnight.' She remained at the door, leaning against the frame.

'Can I come in?' he asked, and as he spoke she smelled the whisky on his breath.

'What's wrong, all the pubs shut and your supply of booze run out at home?'

He looked at her but didn't speak. She sighed and stepped aside, motioning him into the flat. He wandered through into the sitting room where he sat down on the sofa.

'Make yourself at home,' she said, sarcastically. Nikki sat down in the chair opposite him, the T-shirt riding up over her knees, exposing a greater expanse of her shapely legs.

Hacket gazed at them for a moment then looked at her face.

'You've got a bloody nerve coming here, John, after what's happened,' she said, sternly.

'I wanted to talk to you,' he said.

'I thought you'd said all you wanted to say over the phone.'

'I just thought you might like to know that your *little note* had the desired effect. My marriage came close to breaking up, I'm still not sure it'll last.

She merely shrugged.

'I told you not to use me like a doormat. I was hurt. I wanted to hit back at you and it was the only way I could think of.'

'You heard what happened to my daughter?'

'Yes. I'm very sorry about that.'

'Well your *little note* arrived the day of her funeral,' he rasped. 'It didn't take Sue long to figure out that I was with you when Lisa was murdered.'

'Have they caught the killer yet?' she asked, conversationally.

He merely smiled humourlessly.

'One of them is out of action, to coin a phrase,' he chuckled, glaring at her once again. 'What you did was unnecessary, Nikki. If you wanted to hurt someone then you could have had a go at me, not Sue. She didn't ask to be involved in this.'

'It's not my fault your daughter's dead, John. I told you I didn't mean to be vindictive. I'm sorry for what happened.'

'Sorry,' he grunted. 'Really? Well, you're right about one thing, it isn't your fault Lisa's dead, it's my fault. My fault for being here with you when I should have been at home with *her*.'

'And you came over here tonight to tell me that? What is this, confession time?'

He sat on the sofa looking at her, smelling the booze on his own breath as he exhaled.

'Do you want a coffee?' she asked, almost reluctantly. 'You look as if you need one.' She got to her feet and padded into the kitchen. Hacket waited a moment then got up and followed her.

'Sorry I called so late,' he said. 'I mean, you might have had someone here. I wouldn't have wanted to interrupt.'

'By "someone" I gather you mean another man?'

He shrugged.

'Why not? You're a good looking girl. I'm surprised there *isn't* anyone here.' There was a vaguely contemptuous tone to his voice which she wasn't slow to spot.

'Is that how you see me?' she asked. 'In and out of bed with any man I find?'

'It didn't take you long to sleep with me. Three dates it

took, didn't it? Pretty fast going, Nikki.' He smiled, again without a trace of humour.

She made his coffee and shoved the mug into his hand.

'Drink that and go will you?' she snapped, walking back into the sitting room. He followed her once more.

'What did you hope to achieve by writing that letter to Sue? Just tell me that. Did you want to break up my marriage?'

'Just remember who started the affair, John,' she snarled. '*You* chased *me*, not the other way round. You knew the risks. We both did.'

'But you had to have your little bit of revenge, didn't you?' he said, bitterly.

'I don't like being treated like some kind of whore,' she rasped. 'You can't just pick me up, use me then throw me away when you feel like it.' She glared at him. 'Now drink your coffee and get out of here.'

Hacket put the mug down and got to his feet.

'Sue called you a tart and I defended you,' he said, shaking his head. 'I think she was right.'

'Get out, now.' She pushed him towards the door. 'Is that why you came here, tonight, John? For the same reason you wanted me in the first place? Because you still can't get what you want from your wife?'

Hacket spun round and lashed out, catching her with the back of his hand.

The blow was powerful enough to knock her off her feet and, as she fell to the floor, Hacket saw the ribbon of blood running from her bottom lip. She glared up at him then touched the bleeding cleft which was already beginning to swell up. She looked at the blood on her fingers and her eyes narrowed.

'Get out you fucker,' she hissed. 'Go on,' the last two words were shouted.

Hacket moved towards the door, pulled it open and

looked back at her. She still sat on the floor, legs curled up beneath her as she dabbed at her bottom lip with the end of her long T-shirt. Blood blossomed on the material. He hesitated a moment longer then walked out, slamming the door behind him.

He rode the lift to the ground floor and walked out into the chill night air, standing beside his car for a moment, looking up at the window of Nikki's flat. Then he slid behind the wheel, twisted the key in the ignition and drove off, glimpsing the block of flats in his rear view mirror. Then he turned a corner and it was gone.

Out of sight, out of mind, he thought, wondering why that particular cliché had come into his head.

He wondered if it would be as easy to forget Nikki.

Forty-four

She knew she was going to be sick.

She knew it and, what was worse, she knew there was nothing she could do to stop herself. Amanda Riley gripped the edge of the sink, ducked low over the porcelain and vomited. As she stepped back, moaning, she almost over-balanced. It felt as if the floor was moving beneath her although she couldn't be sure if that apparent undulation was due to her own inebriation or the pounding of the music from downstairs.

She ran the taps, washing the mess from the sink, glancing at her own haggard reflection in the mirror. She groaned again as she caught sight of the apparition which stared back at her. Pale skinned, eyes black from too much smudged mascara. Her hair, so carefully prepared before the party, now hung limply around her face. There were stains on her red blouse and also on her tight white skirt. She shook her head but even that minor act of disapproval caused her to reel once more. She had no idea how much she'd drunk, or even what she'd drunk. The party had begun four or five hours ago, she thought, but now she wasn't even sure of the time. Amanda glanced at her watch but it seemed to dissolve before her eyes. Her drink-clouded vision refused to clear and she sat down heavily on the toilet seat, feeling the vomit beginning its upward journey for the second time that night. She clenched her teeth together and the feeling passed momentarily. It felt as if her head was spinning around on her neck like some bizarre kind of top. She gripped the edge of the toilet seat for fear of falling off.

Amanda was beginning to wish she had never agreed to come to the party. She didn't like loud music, she didn't know many of the other guests and, ordinarily, she didn't drink much. Perhaps someone had spiked her drink, she pondered, rubbing her stomach with one shaking hand. Whatever the answer was she knew she couldn't stand another night of this purgatory. She felt her stomach contract suddenly, struggling to her feet just in time to reach the sink. She hung over it, waiting for the inevitable but the spasms passed and she began to straighten up. Again she caught sight of her reflection. God, she thought. She looked about fifty instead of nineteen.

There was a bang on the bathroom door.

'Amanda.'

She barely recognised the voice.

'Amanda. Are you all right?'

She blinked hard, trying to clear not only her vision but her head too.

Outside the door, Tracy Grant exhaled wearily and banged once more. She was beginning to wish she hadn't invited Amanda. If she threw up on any of the carpets there would be hell to pay. If her parents discovered she'd had the party in the first place while they were away for the weekend she'd be in big enough trouble but, if they came back to find puddles of puke everywhere then she may as well pack her bags and leave home. It would save them the bother of throwing her out. She banged again and repeated Amanda's name.

'Are you all right, I said?' she shouted, forced to raise her voice over the sound of the music thundering away downstairs.

There were a series of raucous cheers from below her and, despite her anger, she managed a smile as she heard the chugging rhythm of AC/DC's 'You shook me all Night long' and realised that her brother was more than likely engaged in his duckwalk dance.

Tracy heard the sound of a bolt being slid back and the door opened.

'You look awful,' she said as she saw Amanda swaying uncertainly before her.

'I *feel* awful,' the other girl told her. 'I'm going home.' She took a step forward, almost overbalancing.

Tracy grabbed her.

'Not in that state you're not,' she snapped. 'What have you been drinking anyway?'

Amanda could only shrug.

'I'll get Carl to drive you home,' Tracy told her. 'He's about the only one who's still sober.' She snaked an arm around Amanda's waist and the two of them struggled down the stairs. As they got to the hallway Amanda clenched her teeth together once more and put a hand to her mouth.

Tracy muttered something under her breath and dashed to the front door, pulling it open in time to allow Amanda to get her head out and retch violently into a rhododendron bush which Tracy's father had so carefully nurtured.

'You stay there,' said Tracy irritably and stalked off into the sitting room where the music was reaching ever more deafening proportions. Amanda gripped the door-frame as best she could, supporting herself while her stomach somersaulted, finding yet more fluid to expel should she lose control. A moment or two later Tracy returned with a tall youth in his early twenties, his face pitted around the chin from the ravages of acne. But, apart from that he had strong features and piercing green eyes which immediately focused on Amanda's backside and legs. He smiled appreciatively.

'Carl's going to drive you home,' Tracy announced.

'I don't want her throwing up in my car,' Carl Dennison said, suddenly realising the state of his intended passenger.

'Drive with the window open,' Tracy snapped, supporting Amanda with both arms as Carl scuttled along the path to his waiting Capri. He'd bought it off a friend about a week ago and the last thing he wanted was some boozed up bitch spewing up all over his mock-tigerskin seats. Still, he thought as he looked more closely at his drunken passenger, she should be all right until he got her home. It was after midnight, the roads in Hinkston would be quiet. He could make it in less than twenty minutes if he put his foot down. Carl slid behind the wheel and started the engine, glancing across at Amanda who had already wound down the window and was leaning out, trying to suck in lungfuls of air. As the car vibrated the girl felt her stomach turning more forcefully and, only by a monumental effort did she manage to retain its contents.

Carl drove off, seeing Tracy in the rear-view mirror. She stood there for a moment then disappeared back inside the house.

Carl looked across at Amanda who was groaning quietly as he drove. The wind was whistling through the open window, blowing her hair away from her face. She had her eyes closed. He took his eye off the road momentarily to glance down at her legs. She'd kicked off her high heels and one leg was drawn up beneath her on the seat. Carl turned a corner, saw that the road was deserted and slowed down slightly.

As the needle on the speedometer dropped to below thirty he reached across with his left hand and touched her knee, feeling the soft material of her stocking beneath his fingers. He grinned.

Amanda moaned and slapped feebly at his hand but there was no strength in the rebuff, she was more concerned with holding down her drink.

Carl's hand slid higher, towards her thigh.

She mumbled something and drew her head back inside the car for a second, glancing wearily at him.

He withdrew his hand, aware of the erection which was beginning to uncoil inside his jeans, pushing painfully against the denim as it became harder.

As Amanda put her head back out of the window he let his hand slip back onto her thigh, but, this time, he pushed it higher, allowing his fingers to brush against the sleek material of her panties.

Again she tried to slap his hand away but this time he hooked two fingers into the top of her knickers, feeling her tightly curled pubic hairs. Amanda shook her head.

Carl smiled triumphantly and pulled his hand away just long enough to unzip his own jeans and pull out his erection. He grabbed her right hand and wrapped the limp fingers around his stiff shaft. What the hell, she was so pissed she wouldn't even remember what she'd done in the morning.

She pulled her hand away but he closed his own over it, forcing her back to his penis, guiding her, using her to masturbate him.

Amanda grunted in disapproval, not sure whether she was more disturbed by the vomit rising in her throat or the fact that she was an unwilling partner to Carl's approaching gratification. She turned in her seat, her hand still clasped around his shaft, his own fist wrapped around hers moving it rhythmically.

'Go on, do it,' he urged, his breathing now becoming more heavy. He was staring ahead at the empty road, aware of the sensations building in his groin.

Amanda finally lost her battle.

She leaned towards Carl and vomited into his lap.

He yelled in rage and disgust as his jeans, the car seat and his throbbing penis were all covered in the copious regurgitation.

He slammed on the brake and leant across, pushing open the car door, digging his elbow into Amanda's side, shoving her from the seat.

She fell heavily onto the grass verge at the roadside and Carl himself felt his stomach spinning as the stench of her vomit filled his nostrils. It covered him like a sticky yellow blanket.

He shouted something at her then drove off, leaving her lying on the damp grass.

Amanda tried to rise, tried to call him back but her protests dissolved into a flood of tears. She thought she was going to be sick again but the feeling passed. Finally she managed to rise, aware that her shoes were still in the car, now disappeared into the night. She felt the dampness soaking through her stockings as she walked.

She had no idea where she was, not even which part of Hinkston. There was a garage about a hundred yards down the road, the forecourt in darkness. But, beyond it there were houses. If she could reach one of those she could use a phone, call her parents. They'd be mad at her. Furious. But she didn't care. She just wanted to get home to bed, to drift off to sleep and shut out this terrible feeling once and for all. Amanda began to walk, her gait shambling, as if her legs would not obey her brain. Twice she stumbled, almost falling. The second time she fell against a hedge, the leafless twigs snagging her stockings and scratching her skin. She moaned, her head still spinning, her plight, it seemed, intensified by the chill night air. She felt as if her head had been stuffed with cotton wool.

She glanced towards the petrol station again and something caught her eye.

A figure moved on the forecourt.

Perhaps it was someone walking their dog. Someone who could help her. She tried to quicken her pace.

The figure stepped back into the shadows at the side of the main building and disappeared.

A second later she saw car headlights lancing through the blackness. The vehicle swung out of the forecourt turned and moved unhurriedly towards her.

It slowed down as it drew level with her then it stopped, the engine idling.

Amanda couldn't see the driver, he was hidden by the gloom inside the vehicle.

She staggered towards it, both surprised and relieved when the passenger side door was pushed open as if to welcome her.

'Help me please,' she slurred, fighting back the nausea as she stuck her head inside the car.

The stench in there almost cleared her head.

She jerked upright still unable to see the driver, appalled by the smell, aware that it was going to make her vomit.

She tried to step back but a hand shot forward and clamped across her mouth, forcing back both the seething hot bile and her scream.

The long, double-edged stiletto blade darted forward and buried itself in her right eye.

Amanda was dragged into the car, the door slammed behind her.

The car moved away, the driver indicating thoughtfully as he turned a corner. Only then did he speed up.

Forty-five

She heard the thunderous blows on the front door as he tried to batter his way in.

Sue Hacket stood in the hallway for long seconds, mesmerised by the incessant pounding, her eyes fixed on the door which seemed to bow inward an inch or two with each successive impact.

Another second and he would be through.

She thought about screaming but realised that it would do no good. The house stood at least thirty yards from its closest neighbour, even if they should hear her cry for help it was doubtful if they would reach her in time.

He was nearly through the door.

Perhaps they had heard the banging, perhaps the police were already on the way.

Perhaps . . .

Sue spun round and caught sight of the phone on the stand behind her.

The thunderous blows on the front door seemed to increase and her eyes widened in horror as she saw the first split appear in the wood. It zig-zagged across the paintwork like a crack in a sheet of ice.

If she could reach the phone. Call the police.

Would they arrive before he got in?

Before he reached her?

She had one hand on the phone when one panel of the door was smashed inwards.

Sue screamed, dropped the phone and hurtled up the stairs as fast as she could, stumbling on the fifth step. She whimpered under her breath, glancing around to see his hand reaching through the pulverised wood, feeling for the lock and chain which secured the door.

He freed it and kicked the door open.

Sue screamed again and hauled herself upright, running for the landing, towards the bedroom as she heard him career into the sitting room. Then out into the hall once more, his footfalls pounding on the stairs.

She slammed the bedroom door and stood with her back against it, her breath coming in gasps.

He would find her.

He didn't even need to hurry. There were only four rooms on the first floor of the house. He would be able to move at will from one to the other until he found her and then she knew what would happen.

Just like the woman who had lived in this house before her she would die.

Slaughtered like an animal by the man who supposedly loved her.

The last occupant of the house had been a schoolteacher just as the new occupant was. Only this new occupant was her own husband.

It was John Hacket who prowled the landing stealthily, the double-barrelled shotgun gripped in his bloodied hands.

She heard him kick open the door of the bathroom, then the other two bedrooms.

She heard the creak of the floorboards as he stood outside the room where she hid. There was only three inches of wood between her and her husband.

Her and the shotgun.

Sue crossed to the window and tried to open it but the

old sash frame had been painted over and the emulsion secured it as if it had been nailed shut. Through the glass she could see the school beyond, its tall buildings rising into the night sky as if supporting the low clouds.

Hacket drove his foot against the door and the hinges groaned protestingly.

Sue spun round, knowing there was nowhere else to run. Knowing that this was the end.

She had just one comforting thought.

She would soon be with Lisa again.

Strange how, when death is near, the human mind clutches at even the most ridiculous notions to ease its fear.

Hacket roared with rage and drove his shoulder against the door.

It swung back, slamming into the wall and he stepped across the threshold, raising the shotgun to his shoulder, aiming at her head.

He was smiling.

Sue screamed.

Hacket fired and the scream was lost in a deafening crescendo of blazing lead as both barrels flamed.

The scream catapulted her from the nightmare.

She sat bolt upright in bed, perspiration covering her like a translucent shroud.

In the darkness of the bedroom she blinked, trying to readjust to the gloom, to push the nightmare from her mind, not sure for fleeting seconds what was real and what was a residue of the dream.

Like the figure which stood at the foot of her bed.

She blinked, expecting it to vanish.

It didn't.

Standing at the bottom of her bed, his eyes pinning her in an unblinking stare, stood six-year-old Craig Clayton. His body was quivering from head to foot.

Forty-six

Sue looked at the child through the darkness, barely able to make out his features, illuminated as they were by the thin shaft of light from the landing.

He seemed to be swaying gently back and forth at the bottom of the bed but, throughout the strange motions, his eyes never left her.

She pulled the sheet around her, aware of her nakedness and strangely uncomfortable beneath the unflinching stare of the boy.

'Craig?' she said, softly, as if trying to break his fixed concentration. To distract him from that piercing stare. He seemed almost trance-like.

She pulled her house-coat on hurriedly and swung herself out of bed, blinking hard to clear her vision.

As she approached him the door of her bedroom opened and Julie walked in.

Sue saw the look of shock on her sister's face as she looked at the boy and she motioned for Sue to stay back.

'I thought I heard him get up,' Julie said.

'When I woke up he was just standing there,' Sue explained.

'Come on, Craig,' Julie said, sternly, taking the boy by the shoulders as if to drag him forcibly from the room. 'You've disturbed your auntie now.'

'He didn't disturb me . . .' Sue began but then hurriedly closed her mouth as Julie shot her a withering glance.

'Craig, come on. Back to bed,' Julie snapped, pulling him with even greater urgency.

The boy wouldn't move. He shook loose from Julie's grip, his eyes never leaving Sue.

'Is he all right, Julie?' she asked, seeing the boy's expression darken.

Julie didn't answer, she merely gripped the boy by the shoulders and pulled.

He tore himself free of her hold, spun round and punched her in the side, his eyes blazing.

Sue looked on in shocked dismay.

'You'll have to help me,' Julie gasped, making another grab for the boy who was now facing his mother, his hands twisted into claws, as if ready to strike at her should she try to touch him again. Julie moved forward and Craig backed off, his back touching the wall. He glanced at the two women and Sue almost recoiled from what looked like pure hatred in those eyes.

'Mike, come here,' Julie shouted, rousing her husband.

She lunged forward and grabbed Craig, holding one of his wrists, but he gripped her hand, tugging at the skin on the back of it until his nails drew blood. Julie yelped in pain and withdrew her hand, the bloody furrows weeping red fluid onto the carpet. He looked at Sue as if daring her to approach him. She could see the first clear dribblings of sputum beginning to seep through his clenched teeth.

Mike Clayton entered the room, pushing past the two women, making straight for the boy, a look of determination on his face.

'Come on,' he snarled, grabbing Craig around the waist, lifting him into the air.

The boy writhed madly in his father's grip, trying to shake himself free, scratching at Mike's face.

'Get the doctor, now,' Mike hissed, struggling back through the door with the boy. 'Do it,' he snapped as Julie hesitated.

Sue, still bewildered by the tableau, followed Mike and his maddened son out onto the landing. Julie scuttled downstairs to the phone and frantically jabbed out the number, glancing behind her to see Mike carry the boy into his bedroom.

Watched by Sue, he threw the boy onto the bed then leapt on beside him, pinning the boy's arms to the mattress, using all his superior strength to prevent his son from moving.

The boy hawked loudly and spat into Mike's face.

Sue put a hand to her mouth, watching as the mucus dripped from Mike's cheek like a thick tear. But he didn't attempt to wipe it away, he seemed too concerned with restraining his son. The boy continued to twist and turn like an eel on a hot skillet.

'The doctor's coming,' shouted Julie, making her way back up the stairs, pushing past Sue, who could only look on in bewilderment.

'I hope to God he's quick,' Mike rasped. 'I can't hold him for much longer.'

Craig seemed to have found an energy and strength quite disproportionate to his age and size. A strength which took every ounce of his father's muscle to hold him down. Sue saw the veins standing out on Mike's forehead as he struggled to keep the boy pinned down.

Julie ushered her out of the room.

'There's nothing we can do until the doctor gets here,' she said, her face ashen.

'Whatever's wrong with him, Julie?' Sue asked, a note of fear in her voice. 'Is it some kind of epileptic fit?'

'Yes, that's right,' Julie said. 'A fit. He doesn't get them very often. I've never mentioned them to you. We thought he'd grow out of them.'

'But he's so strong.'

'He'll be all right when the doctor gets here,' Julie said, dismissing the observation.

Sue was about to speak again when she heard a deafening shout from the bedroom.

From Craig.

She felt the hairs on the back of her neck rise.

She felt suddenly afraid.

Forty-seven

The needle came free and Curtis quickly wiped the puncture in the crook of Craig's arm with a swab, pressing the pad of cotton wool to the tiny hole for a second.

The boy winced and moaned slightly but Curtis merely pressed the palm of his right hand to the child's forehead. He could feel beads of perspiration there but at least the spasms had stopped. Craig let out an exhausted sigh and his whole body seemed to go limp. Curtis covered him with a sheet, watching the steady rise and fall of his chest.

Mike Clayton looked down at his son then glanced at the doctor who had slipped the hypodermic back into his bag.

'Will he be all right now, doctor?' Mike asked.

Curtis nodded slowly and headed for the door.

'We've heard things,' Mike continued, falteringly. 'Rumours. About the others.'

Curtis turned and looked at him, expressionless.

Mike swallowed hard, as if intimidated by the doctor's unfaltering stare.

'What's been happening to them?' Mike asked.

'I don't discuss other patients, Mr Clayton,' Curtis said, dismissively. 'Your sister-in-law, does she know about the boy?' He nodded in Craig's direction.

'No,' Mike said, hastily. 'She saw what happened tonight. We found him in her room.'

Curtis shot the other man a worried glance.

'Nothing had happened,' he reassured the doctor. 'Julie

told her he suffered from epileptic fits. I think she believed it.'

'Good.'

He made for the landing, followed by Mike. They both descended the stairs, the doctor heading for the sitting room where Julie and Sue sat sipping cups of tea.

Julie stood up as Curtis entered but he motioned for her to sit once more.

'Is Craig all right?' she asked.

'He's fine. He's sleeping now.'

Julie looked relieved.

Curtis glanced at Sue and smiled and she returned the gesture, struck by the firmness of his features, the intensity of his eyes. Despite the late hour he looked perfectly groomed, as if he'd come from a dinner-dance instead of having been dragged from his bed by the emergency call. Julie performed a quick introduction and Curtis shook hands with Sue, gripping her hand in his own. She felt a pleasing mixture of strength and warmth there. She looked at him as he sat down, grateful for the cup of tea which Julie offered him. He seemed relaxed, almost at home in the sitting room. As if he'd visited it many times before.

'Do you live in Hinkston, Mrs Hacket?' Curtis asked.

Sue shook her head, unable to take her eyes from Curtis, her mind relaying facts back and forth as she tried to estimate his age.

'Not yet,' she said. 'We . . . I have a house in London but I'll probably be living in Hinkston soon.'

'Any family of your own? I see you're married,' he smiled and nodded towards her wedding ring.

'No,' she said, quickly. For fleeting seconds it occurred to her to mention Lisa but the memory was painful enough locked away inside her mind without exposing it to conversation. She contented herself with a sip of her tea.

'If you don't mind me saying, Mrs Hacket, you look a

little pale.' Curtis chuckled. 'An occupational hazard of being a doctor I'm afraid, I see everyone as a potential patient.'

Sue smiled too.

'I haven't been sleeping very well lately,' she told him.

'Well, if you do move to Hinkston then please feel free to come and see me. Your sister has the address of my surgery. Whereabouts in the town are you moving to?'

'My husband's a teacher. He's due to start work next week at the Junior school about half a mile from the town centre. You know the one? There's a house next to the school, it comes with the job.'

Curtis nodded slowly, his expression darkening slightly.

'I know the one,' he said, quietly. 'Well, the best of luck with your move.' He finished his tea quickly, as if the hospitality of the Clayton's was suddenly something he wished to be away from. He got to his feet and headed for the sitting room door.

'Don't forget, Mrs Hacket,' he said. 'Come and see me.'

'I will,' she assured him.

Julie and Mike followed him out into the hall.

'Thank you,' Julie said as he stepped out onto the front porch.

'Be careful,' Curtis said, looking at each of them in turn. 'Watch the boy closely for the next two or three days. Get in touch with me immediately if he suffers anything *like* a relapse. We were lucky this time.' He turned and strode off down the path towards his car, watched by the Claytons, who waited until he'd driven off before stepping back into their house and shutting the door.

Sue finished her tea then announced that she was going to bed. She left Julie and Mike sitting downstairs.

As she reached the landing she paused by the door to Craig's room. Hearing nothing she pushed the door slightly and peered in.

The boy was sleeping, his face peaceful. A marked contrast to the twisted mask which it had become only thirty minutes earlier. Sue closed the door and wandered across to her bedroom where she slipped off her house coat and climbed into bed.

As she lay there in the gloom she gazed up at the ceiling, waiting for sleep to come but knowing that it would not. She heard Curtis's voice inside her head.

'Come and see me'

She closed her eyes, seeing his face more clearly, remembering that mixture of warmth and strength in his grip. The penetrative stare.

Sue allowed one hand to slip beneath the quilt, to glide across her breast, the nipple already stiff and swollen. It was joined by her other hand which she pushed with exquisite slowness over her flat belly and into the tightly curled triangle of hair between her legs, her index finger probing more deeply until she found the bud of her clitoris. She began to stroke it gently, the moisture between her thighs increasing.

'Come and see me.'

She pushed one finger into her slippery cleft, her eyes closed now, the vision of Curtis' face filling her mind.

'Come and see me.'

Forty-eight

He had killed Hacket's daughter and now he would kill Hacket.

Ronald Mills had decided on his course of action with

ease. Ever since he'd seen Hacket pursue Peter Walton through the streets of London, ever since he'd seen his friend fall onto the tracks of the tube train. Mills had watched it all.

An eye for an eye, they called it. His mother had told him that came from the Bible. His mother had always quoted him lines from the Bible, and most of them he'd remembered. Like the one about suffer little children.

Mills chuckled.

God wanted little children to suffer did he? Well, if that was the case then God would love Ronald Mills. God would have looked down on him and Lisa Hacket that night and he would have smiled. He would have seen Mills clamp one hand across the little girl's mouth as he cut away her nightdress with the point of his knife. He would have watched it all. Watched as Mills climbed onto the bed beside her and unzipped his trousers.

Suffer little children.

Afterwards God would have watched as Mills cut the child repeatedly. He used the knife with almost surgical skill, pushing it easily through her flesh until the bed was soaked in blood, until she stopped writhing beneath him, until his penis was hard with lust again and he penetrated her warm but lifeless form for the second time that night.

Mills giggled again and inspected his hands. They were rough, calloused. The left one still bore the remnants of a tattoo but it hadn't taken properly and the skin had turned septic. In place of a snake coiled around a knife blade Mills sported a scab curled around a septic boil. He picked at the scab, pulling some pieces of hardened flesh off.

Mills and Walton had lived in the flat in Brixton for the last ten months. Neither of them had a job but they had made a living dealing in various illegal practices. Mills in particular had found a lucrative market in child pornography. He had become friendly with a couple of dealers and this little sideline had the added bonus of pandering to his own tastes too.

Walton had worked as a pusher around King's Cross, even done a little pimping.

It was on those proceeds that they'd bought the gun.

It was a .38 Smith and Wesson revolver and Mills gently stroked the four-inch barrel as he sat at the table occasionally glancing at the brown mess on his plate which, according to the box, was liver and onion. It certainly didn't look like the picture on the box. In fact, it looked as if someone had defecated on his plate. He prodded the cold food with the barrel of the pistol then wiped it on the makeshift tablecloth. Piled up on the other side of the table were some of the magazines he'd been intending to sell the following day. Every one featured photos of children, some as young as two years, engaged in various acts with both men *and* women. He had heard that one of his dealers could get hold of stuff which actually showed men and babies. Real, new born babies.

Mills smiled again, the stirring in his groin becoming more pronounced.

Suffer little children.

He picked up one of the magazines and leafed through it, his thick lips sliding back as he surveyed the pictures. Many were bad quality, grainy black and white shots taken by amateurs. Probably by those who participated, thought Mills, his erection now pressing uncomfortably against his trousers. But they served their purpose. He finished looking through the magazine and dropped it back onto the pile, picking up the gun again, turning the empty cylinder, thumbing the hammer back then squeezing the trigger.

The metallic click echoed around the small flat.

It had been lonely since Walton's death. Mills didn't enjoy being alone. Apart from Walton he had no friends and he felt as if Hacket had taken from him the one person he really cared about.

He would make him suffer for that.

As he'd made his daughter suffer.

Suffer little children.

God would be watching him again. God was on his side.

He would kill Hacket and God would be pleased with him for upholding his word.

Mills raised the gun and sighted it, thumbing back the hammer again.

'An eye for an eye,' he said, smiling.

Forty-nine

Birth, marriage and moving house.

Hacket was sure that was how the cliché went. They were the three most traumatic things in life. As he sat in the sitting room of the house, perched on one of the many packing cases that filled the place like an oversized child's building bricks he'd come to the conclusion that the former two paled into insignificance alongside the third. It had taken him more than three days to pack the cases, working for anything up to fifteen hours a day. Well, he had nothing else to do. It was better than sitting around in the old house with just memories for company. At least he didn't have to worry about selling the house in London before he could move into the one next to the school. No chain, no mortgage worries. The rent for the house was deducted from his salary every month. Once the house in London was sold the money would be straight profit. It was an enticing prospect.

The thought of the money together with the possibility of starting afresh should have left Hacket feeling elated but, as it was, he sat wearily on the packing case, holding a mug of tea and staring around the room his thoughts jumbled and confused.

He thought about Lisa.

About the deaths that had occurred in *this* house.

From one place of pain to another.

There was always pain.

And he thought about Sue.

He'd called her the previous night to let her know roughly what time he and the accumulated trophies of their life would be arriving but so far she had not turned up. He was beginning to wonder if she would. There was a phone box just across the street. Hacket glanced at his watch, decided to give it another fifteen minutes, then call her.

There was a knock on the door and the teacher jumped down from the box and hurried to the front door, a smile already beginning to form on his lips.

At last, now he wouldn't need to call her.

He felt his spirits lift as he fumbled with the catch.

Donald Brooks stood on the doorstep, immaculate as ever apart from the flakes of dandruff on his collar. The headmaster smiled at Hacket who just about managed to return the gesture, fighting to keep the disappointment from his face.

'Glad to see you arrived safely, Mr Hacket,' said Brooks. 'I won't come in. I just thought I'd say welcome and that I hope you'll be happy in your new home. You and your wife.'

'Thanks,' murmured Hacket, almost grudgingly.

'What does your wife think of the house?'

'She likes it.

'I won't disturb her, I'm sure she's busy unpacking. I'll go now. I look forward to seeing you on Monday morning.'

Hacket nodded and closed the door as the headmaster walked back up the path. The teacher sighed and wandered back into the sitting room. Perhaps he should phone Sue now. He glanced at his watch again. Give it another five minutes? He drummed agitatedly on the top of the nearest crate then the front door bell sounded again. This time he moved with less speed, pulling the door open wearily.

Sue smiled thinly as she saw his face.

'I was going to call you,' he beamed, stepping aside to allow her in.

She stepped over the threshold almost hesitantly, moving through into the sitting room, glancing around at the crates and packing cases.

'We'd better get started,' she said, rolling up the sleeves of her sweatshirt.

They worked in separate rooms, pulling the lids from the boxes and crates, unwrapping the contents as if they were Christmas presents. Sue worked in the kitchen while Hacket attended to the sitting room. He had ensured that the stereo was not left to the tender attentions of the removal men. He had transported that particular item himself on the back seat of the car. It had been the first thing he'd rigged up before unpacking and music filled the house as they worked.

Hacket had no idea of the time, surrounded by empty and half-empty packing cases, his ears filled with the music, his thoughts wandering aimlessly. He wiped his hands on his jeans and wandered across to the stereo, flipping the record before continuing his task.

Sue appeared in the doorway, her sweatshirt and jeans also covered by a thin film of dust. She had some dirt on one cheek and Hacket crossed to her to wipe it away.

She smiled thinly but pulled away and completed the task herself.

'There's a cup of tea in the kitchen,' she told him and walked across the hall.

'. . . But it was only fantasy. The wall was too high as you can see..'

sang Roger Waters from behind him.

Hacket wiped his hands again and wandered into the kitchen. He sat down opposite Sue and picked up his mug of tea.

'I've just about finished in here,' she told him. 'I'll do upstairs next.'

'There's no rush,' he told her. 'We've got plenty of time.'

'I want to get it finished, John. I don't want the house looking like a bomb site for too long.'

He nodded.

'Do you remember the first place we ever moved in to?' Hacket asked, a thin smile on his face.

She raised her eyebrows.

'The flat. Trying to lug furniture up three flights of stairs past the snooker hall, wondering if the blokes inside were going to rob us as soon as we got settled in.' She almost laughed. Almost.

'Listening to them playing bloody snooker all night. It kept us awake at the beginning didn't it.'

'As I remember we didn't mind being kept awake.'

Hacket smiled.

'It was a nice place,' he said.

'Apart from the noise,' she added.

'And the damp.'

'And the cold.'

'Yeah, a great place.' He chuckled. 'It doesn't seem like six years since we left there.' He put down his tea. 'Unpacking today it made me think about the flat, about our first place. It could be like that again, Sue. This house is new. Things don't have to change.'

'They already have changed, John. *We've* changed. Circumstances have changed. It can never be the same between us.' There was an appalling finality in her voice. 'I still love you but a part of that love died with Lisa. Because her death could have been avoided.'

'I don't need reminding, Sue. Do you think there's a day goes by that I don't think about her? About what might have been? I made a mistake and I'm sorry. God knows I'm sorry. Sorry for the affair, sorry for Lisa's death, sorry for the way I hurt you and damaged our relationship. I know I can't put those things right and I don't expect you to forget. But if you could find a little bit of forgiveness, Sue . . .' He allowed the sentence to trail off.

She took a sip of her own tea and shivered slightly.

'I feel cold,' she said. 'Is the heating on?'

Hacket sighed wearily.

'I'll check it when I've finished my tea.'

She got to her feet and headed out of the kitchen. He heard her footfalls on the stairs.

'Shit,' he murmured, also getting to his feet. He wandered back into the sitting room to be greeted by the music once more.

He began opening another case, noticing that there were several photos laid on the top of the other items. Framed pictures. He unwrapped the first of them and found that it was a photo of Lisa. Hacket smiled and set it down beside him, reaching for the next one. It was Sue, dressed in a low-cut black dress, taken about a year ago at a party. She looked stunning.

The music behind him was building to a crescendo.

He took out the last photo.

A young couple on it happy and smiling.

Their wedding photo.

'. . . *When I was a child I caught a fleeting glimpse, out of the corner of my eye. I turned to look but it was gone, I cannot put my finger on it now..*' Hacket frowned down at the picture. '. . . *The child has grown, the dream is gone . . .*'

The glass had shattered, two long thin shards had cut deep into the picture.

Fifty

She didn't know how long she'd been lying there listening to the slow, steady breathing of Hacket and the monotonously regular ticking of the clock. All Sue did know was that she was no closer to sleep now than when she'd first slid between the covers. It had been a tiring day, she had expected to be enveloped by sleep almost immediately, but it was not to be.

She lay still, hearing the house creak and groan as the timbers settled. After a moment or two of this she finally swung herself out of bed and crossed to the window, peering out into the darkness and the school beyond. She could just make out the shapes of the buildings in the gloom and she pressed her hands to the radiator, aware of a chill which had settled upon her. She had pulled on her house coat as she slipped out of bed, but the chill was present nonetheless.

Behind her, Hacket stirred, his hand reaching across for her. He opened his eyes slowly when he could not feel her next to him. The teacher sat up and saw his wife gazing out into the night.

'Sue,' he said, softly. 'What's wrong?'

'I can't sleep, as usual,' she told him, still continuing with her vigil.

'Come back to bed,' he urged.

She finally relented, sliding in beside him.

'John, it's cold in this house,' she said. 'I know the heating is on. It isn't that kind of cold. It's . . . well . . . as if there was some kind of atmosphere because of what happened here.'

Hacket sighed.

'I know what you think about things like that,' she went on, 'the eternal sceptic – but I can't help it. I felt like that in our house after Lisa . . . They say houses carry a residue of sorrow don't they?'

'Do they?' Hacket said, a note of irritation in his voice. 'It sounds like a line from a bad romantic novel. I can't feel anything, Sue, honestly.'

She shivered again.

'Relax,' Hacket said, sliding closer to her.

She flinched almost imperceptibly as she felt his arm glide across her stomach, around her waist. He pulled her to him. As their bodies pressed together she felt the beginnings of an erection beginning to press into her thigh. Hacket kissed her gently on the lips, his shaft growing stiffer.

Sue tried to move away but he held her more tightly, his hand now straying to her breast which he squeezed, thumbing the nipple.

'Not now, John,' she said, gripping his wrist.

But Hacket would not release her. He tightened his hold on her breast, kneading the flesh so hard that she almost cried out from the sudden pain.

'John, please,' she snapped, again trying to squirm away from him.

'I want you, Sue,' he said, raising himself up on one

elbow. He straddled her, his erection pointing towards her face, his hands gripping her wrists, pinning her to the mattress. She struggled but could not move him.

'Get off me,' she shouted, angrily.

In one swift movement his hands had left her wrists and fastened around her throat.

Her eyes bulged as he began to squeeze, his thumbs digging into her flesh.

'I want you,' he breathed, squeezing more tightly.

She tried to swallow but couldn't. Her head felt as if it were swelling and, all the time, the pressure on her throat seemed to intensify. She looked up into his face, her eyes blurred with pain and fear. She felt her body beginning to spasm, the muscles contracting violently.

Sue tried to scream but his vice-like grip prevented that action.

She bucked beneath him, trying to dislodge him, already growing weak but, finally, with one last reserve of strength she brought her knee up into the small of his back.

The grip was released and, in that split second, she found the breath to scream.

Hacket twisted round in bed as he heard the scream.

He saw Sue sitting upright, massaging her throat, perspiration beaded on her forehead and upper lip.

'What's wrong?' he asked, shocked by her appearance. He put out a hand to touch her but she drew back, as if frightened of his touch.

Her breathing was harsh and rapid, her eyes bulging, glazed.

Only gradually did she regain her senses as the last vestiges of the dream faded.

It was then that she began to cry.

Fifty-one

He felt the gun in his pocket.

As Ronald Mills stood looking at the 'FOR SALE' sign outside the house he gently traced his fingers over the .38.

There were no lights on in the house. Perhaps Hacket was in bed, he reasoned. After all, it was past midnight.

Mills walked past the house on the far side of the road, reached the bottom of the street crossed then walked back again.

Should he just knock on the front door? Wait until Hacket opened it and shoot him down on the doorstep? It would be simple but hazardous. Although he doubted that he would be caught. God had views about revenge too, Mills remembered.

Vengeance is mine saith the Lord.

He smiled as he remembered the quote from the Bible.

God would not allow him to be caught, after all, he practically had God's blessing for what he was about to do.

He glanced behind him, noting that the street was empty. Mills paused a moment then walked up to the front door of the house.

He didn't knock. Instead he pushed the letter-box open and peered through into the gloom beyond. He could see and hear nothing.

He moved along the front of the house to the bay window. Cupping a hand against the glass he looked through.

The sitting room was empty.

Something finally clicked inside Mills' rather dull mind and he glanced again at the 'FOR SALE' sign. He hurried around the side of the house, down the passageway which he remembered so well. He smiled as he thought of his last journey along this cramped stone corridor.

Smiled at the recollection of finding the child inside the house.

This time, however, it was not to be.

He peered through the rear windows only to have what he'd already surmised confirmed. The place was empty. Quiet as a grave. He smiled thinly, amused at his joke but angry that Hacket was not there. Mills scuttled back up the passageway, his hand touching the revolver in his pocket once again. He had intended to press the barrel to Hacket's neck or to his stomach, make him die slowly. Even shoot his eyes out. But now he had been cheated.

And so had God.

God wanted him to take revenge for the death of Walton. He knew that. He was only upholding God's law by killing Hacket. *His Will be done.*

Mills headed for the street, stopping beneath the sign again. This time, however, he pulled a piece of paper and a pencil from his coat pocket. Resting the paper in the palm of his broad hand he wrote: JEFFERSON ESTATE AGENTS, then the phone number.

Hacket may have left the house but he could be traced, thought Mills.

This wasn't over yet.

Fifty-two

The sun was doing its best to force a path through the clouds and, every so often, a shaft of golden light would lance into the kitchen, bouncing off Hacket's knife as he ate.

Sue sat opposite him as he ate, chewing indifferently on a piece of toast. She dropped the bread and ran a hand through her hair.

Hacket saw how dark she was beneath the eyes.

'How are you feeling?' he asked.

'Tired,' she told him. 'I'm going to the doctor this morning, see if he can give me something to help me sleep.'

'Be careful,' he said, guardedly.

'Careful of what?' she asked.

'Doctors like to give out prescriptions for sleeping pills and drugs like that. It's easier than talking to the patient about their problems.'

'I'm not going to him to talk about my problems,' she said acidly.

'If you're not careful you'll need a shopping trolley to carry the tranquillisers and anti-depressants.'

'Have you got a better idea, John?' she snapped. 'It's all right for you. You start a new job today. I'm the one who's going to be stuck in a new house with nothing to think about but my problems.' She took a sip of her tea. 'I'm seeing the doctor and that's all there is to it.'

'All right, I'm sorry. I'm just suspicious of doctors, you know that.'

'Well this one is good. He's Julie's doctor. I met him the other evening.' She explained briefly about Curtis' visit to the Clayton's home, deciding not to expand on Craig's condition.

Hacket listened dutifully, nodding occasionally. When she'd finished he looked at his watch.

8.30 a.m.

'I'd better go,' he said, standing up.

'I'll finish tidying up the house when I get back,' Sue told him.

'There's no need. We can carry on tonight.'

'I need something to occupy me, John. Now, go on or

you'll be late.' She brushed a hair from his collar, looking into his eyes briefly.

'Wish me luck,' he said, hopefully.

She smiled.

'You don't need it.'

He kissed her lightly on the lips and headed for the front door. She heard it close behind him then sat down at the kitchen table again, finishing her tea. She washed up, listening to the increasingly loud noise coming from the playground just beyond the tall hedge at the bottom of their garden. Then when nine o'clock came she heard the bell sound and the noise receded into silence again. Sue dried her hands and moved into the hall. There she found the number she wanted, lifted the receiver and pressed the digits.

It was answered almost immediately.

'Hello. Yes, I'd like to make an appointment for this morning please,' she said. 'I'd like to see Doctor Curtis.'

Fifty-three

The match made a dull hissing sound as it was struck, the yellow flame billowing from its head.

Phillip Craven held it before him for a second, then slowly lowered it towards the boy spread-eagled across two desks.

The boy shook his head, staring up at Craven with pleading in his eyes, but the other lad was interested only in the match, which he now held close to the chest of his helpless companion.

Four children held Trevor Harvey down, making sure that he couldn't squirm away from the approaching flame as Craven waved it over his pale, white chest. He suddenly lowered it onto Trevor's left nipple and the boy shrieked loudly.

Craven and the others watched mesmerised as the delicate skin turned first pink then bright red under the fury of the heat. He held the match against Trevor's chest until it went out. Then he lit another.

And another.

He pressed both of them to Trevor's stomach this time, below his navel, watching as the skin rose in a red welt, already blistering.

Trevor didn't shout so loudly this time. He merely grunted and tried to pull away from the others who held him down.

'Oh come on, Harvey, scream for us,' said Craven, grinning.

The rest of the class, girls and boys, all the same age as Craven, looked on with the fascination most children of thirteen display toward the suffering of others. Most were glad they were not the one being burned but many looked on the whole tableau as a diverting exhibition and Craven as a master showman.

He lit three matches and pushed them towards Trevor's right eye.

The boy's eyelashes had actually begun to smoulder when a shout from outside the room caused him to withdraw the matches.

Another boy came dashing into the classroom, almost falling over in his haste to get behind his desk.

'He's coming,' he said, and the four holding Trevor also bolted for their own places leaving Trevor to ease himself off the desks. He swayed uncertainly for a minute then a rough push from Craven sent him crashing into a nearby chair. He sprawled on the floor amid the cheers and laughter of the other class members.

Hacket heard the rumpus as he strode up the corridor, finally finding the room he sought. He swept in, smiling, closing the door behind him.

'You are form 3A, yes?' he asked.

'Yes, sir,' they answered in unison.

Trevor sat hunched over his desk, his shirt still unbuttoned, his eye streaming from the effects of the match. Still, he thought, wistfully, it could have been much worse.

It could have been like it was last week.

Hacket introduced himself to the class, still smiling broadly, told them where he was from, what they could expect from *him* and what he expected of *them*. Finally he walked to the centre of the room and, standing in front of the blackboard, looked around at the expectant faces.

'I want to get to know all of you so could you each stand up in turn and tell me your names, please? We'll see how many I can remember.' He rubbed his hands together theatrically. The gesture was greeted by good-natured laughter.

One by one the class obeyed and Hacket eyed each member. There were less than twenty of them, mostly sat in groups, apart from Trevor who sat alone at the front of the class, his head still bowed.

The list of names grew until there were just a couple left.

'Phillip Craven, sir.'

The boy sat down.

Hacket snapped his fingers, the name ringing bells of recognition in the back of his mind.

'The artist,' he said, smiling.

Craven looked bemused.

'I saw your painting in the annexe outside the headmaster's office. The one of the owl. It is you isn't it? There aren't *two* Phillip Cravens in the school?'

The rest of the class laughed, Craven turned scarlet and smiled.

'I was very impressed with the painting. A bit gory though, as I remember.'

'Life isn't always pretty, sir,' said Craven, his smile fading slightly.

'A philosopher too?' Hacket mused.

He looked at the last boy in the class. Trevor remained seated, his head still bowed.

'Your turn,' Hacket said.

The boy looked up at him but didn't move.

This one is either the comedian or the trouble-maker, Hacket thought. There was one in every class.

'Just stand up and tell me your name, please. It's quite simple.' He smiled.

'So is he, sir,' said Craven and the rest of the class laughed.

Hacket looked around at them and the noise died away.

Trevor rose slowly to his feet, his shirt undone, his hair untidy. There were stains around his crotch and, even from a couple of feet away Hacket could smell the odour of stale urine. The boy was a mess.

'What's your name, son?' the teacher asked.

'Trevor Harvey, sir,' he mumbled.

Hacket didn't hear and Trevor repeated himself.

'He's the village idiot, sir,' Craven called and the class broke out into a chorus of laughs and jeers once more.

'That's enough, Craven.' Then, to Trevor: 'All right, sit down.'

As the boy did so his shirt billowed open and Hacket winced as he caught sight of the red and pink welts on his skin. Some were purple, where scabs had formed over wounds only to be scratched off once more. He saw bruises too, and some cuts.

'What happened to you?' Hacket asked, shocked by the boys appearance.

'Nothing, sir,' said Trevor, trying to button his shirt. But Hacket stopped him, inspecting a burn on his chest more closely.

'Who did this?'

Silence had descended like an invisible blanket, all eyes on the teacher and the boy.

'Trevor, tell me who did this to you,' Hacket said, quietly.

The teacher caught a slight movement out of his eye corner, just enough to see Craven hurl a large eraser. It struck Trevor in the face but he didn't react, merely sat down.

Hacket spun round and glared at Craven.

'What do you think you're doing, Craven?' he snarled, angered by the look of defiance on the boy's face. 'Do you know anything about Trevor's injuries?'

'Why should I, sir?' the boy said. 'He probably did them himself and he's too stupid to remember.'

Trevor was busily buttoning his shirt.

Hacket looked at both boys in turn, aware still of the slight smirk on Craven's face. He held the boys's stare, a little unsettled when the youth didn't look away.

'This isn't a very auspicious start to things is it, Craven?' he said.

'I'll try to do better next time, sir,' the boy said.

Hacket nodded slowly then glanced at Trevor once more.

'Are you OK? Do you want to visit the nurse, get those wounds looked at?'

Trevor shook his head, pushing some strands of hair from his face.

Hacket glanced around the class once more then picked up the chalk and began writing on the blackboard.

The bell was the signal for a mass exodus from the classroom. Hacket dismissed the children, watching as they trooped past him. Craven avoided eye-contact this time as he passed.

Trevor was the last to leave, wiping his nose with the back of his hand.

'Trevor, wait a minute,' Hacket called.

The boy hesitated but didn't turn.

'Listen to me,' the teacher said, quietly. 'Those marks on your body. If you want to tell me who did it, if you want to talk to me then you know where to find me. Do you understand?'

Trevor nodded and sniffed back some more mucus. Then he turned and headed for the door, closing it behind him.

Carter exhaled deeply and wiped chalk dust from his hands.

As he looked up he saw Craven's face peering at him through the classroom window.

The boy was smiling.

Fifty-four

Gravel crunched beneath the wheels of the Metro as Sue Hacket brought the car to a halt. She switched off the engine and looked up at the house which towered over her like some kind of ivy-covered giant. It certainly looked more imposing than the usual doctor's surgery, she thought, as she climbed out of the car. The leaded windows and the hanging baskets which adorned the oak front door made the place look more like a country hotel than a place of healing. She wondered how much it must be worth, set, as it was, in about half an acre of its own grounds. Separated by wide lawns and immaculate hedges from the main road which led into Hinkston. Private medicine obviously *did* have its advantages for those who practised it, she mused.

The large oak door opened easily when she pushed it and Sue stepped into what looked like a hallway. To her left was a dark wood door, to her left a white one marked 'SURGERY'. She walked in.

The waiting room was empty apart from the receptionist who smiled with genuine warmth, and not the practised response which Sue had seen so many times before in women of the same profession.

They exchanged pleasantries and Sue gave her name then was told that doctor Curtis would be able to see her in a minute or two. He, she was informed, would complete a form with her help in order to register her as a patient.

The door behind the receptionist opened and Curtis appeared.

He smiled at Sue and beckoned her through.

Once inside the surgery Curtis sat down behind his desk and invited Sue to take a seat opposite. She slipped off her jacket and draped it over the back of the chair.

Curtis smiled at her once more and, again, Sue was aware of the combination of strength and warmth which flowed from his gaze. She looked at him, not wanting to make it too obvious that she was taking in details of his appearance. As with their first meeting she was struck by the youthfulness of his features. His smile was reassuring. Inviting even. As he folded his hands across his lap she noted how powerful his hands were, his fingers long and slender, the backs of his hands covered by thick dark hair. There was more than the power of a healer in them she thought.

Sue felt strangely light-headed, as if being with Curtis

were somehow intoxicating, his very presence a kind of drug.

An aphrodisiac?

She was aware that her nipples were beginning to stiffen. A welcome warmth began to spread between her legs as she continued to look at Curtis.

She tried to control the feelings, both puzzled and . . .

And what? Ashamed?

'Would you like a coffee while we talk?' asked Curtis.

'What about your other patients?' she asked.

'I don't have another appointment for an hour. That's one of the advantages I have over the National Health Service. I don't have twenty appointments an hour.' He smiled and buzzed through to the receptionist on the intercom.

'I'll just have to take some personal details if you don't mind,' Curtis informed her. 'Date of birth, medical history. That kind of thing.' He smiled that hypnotic smile once again and Sue answered his questions. The coffee arrived and the receptionist retreated back to the waiting room. Sue sipped from the bone china cup, watching as Curtis wrote on a pink sheet.

'If I recall, you were having trouble sleeping,' he said finally. 'Is that still the case?'

She nodded.

'Even when I do manage to get a few hours I seem to get woken up by nightmares,' she continued.

'What kind of nightmares?'

'The usual stupid things that make no sense in daylight,' she said, sipping her coffee as if anxious to avoid the subject.

'Have you any idea what's caused the disruption of sleep, Mrs Hacket?'

She put down her cup, avoiding his gaze for a moment.

'Trouble at home perhaps?' Curtis continued.

She took a deep breath, as if trying to summon up the courage to tell him.

'When we first met you asked if I had a family, any children and I said no. Well, I did have, *we* did have. A daughter. Lisa.' The words were coming with difficulty, as if she were learning some kind of new language. 'We used to live in London. A nice house. Respectable.' She smiled bitterly. 'Our daughter was murdered.'

It was said. Simple really.

'A few weeks later my father died of cancer, he'd been ill for months. The two things together were too much for me, especially with what happened to Lisa . . .' She found she could go no further.

'I'm very sorry,' Curtis murmured.

'Around the time of my daughter's murder, my husband was having an affair.' Again she chuckled but there was no humour in the sound. 'This sounds like a hard luck story doesn't it? Perhaps I should be telling an agony aunt instead of you.'

'A doctor should care for his patients' psychological welfare as well as their physical condition.'

'Everything seemed to happen at once. That was why I left London. If I'd stayed I'd have gone crazy.'

'That's understandable.'

Sue smiled at him, aware of how easily she was speaking. Secret thoughts which she had kept locked away were spilling out almost wantonly. And, as she spoke she felt a numbing weariness envelope her, as if talking about what she felt were draining her. It was like a criminal unburdening himself of guilt, glad to be given the chance to confess.

Was this what John had felt like when he'd confessed to the affair?

But it wasn't guilt she was purging herself of, it was an accumulation of misery.

She felt the tears forming in her eyes and pulled a tissue

from the pocket of her jeans. A couple more deep breaths and she had regained her composure.

Curtis looked on silently, his eyes never leaving her then finally, sitting forward in his chair he leant towards Sue.

'Have you thought of having another child?' he asked.

'I can't,' she told him. 'I mean, I want one but, after Lisa was born there were complications. My fallopian tubes were infected. I can't have children.'

This time when she looked at him she made no attempt to wipe away the tears.

'You don't know how much I want another child,' Sue continued. 'Lisa could never be replaced, you understand that. But I think her death hit me harder because I knew I couldn't have another baby. It made things even more final.'

'And does your husband feel the same way? Would he have wanted more children?'

She smiled wearily.

'John always wanted another daughter. We used to laugh about it. You know, how men are supposed to want a son to carry on the family name. Not John. He wanted another girl.' She sniffed.

Curtis was already writing out a prescription.

'Sleeping pills,' he announced, handing it to her. 'Only a week's supply. They can become addictive. I could have given you tranquillisers but they only help you live with a problem they don't remove its cause.'

'Then how can I ever go back to normal?' she wanted to know. 'I know what my problem is. I want another child but I can't have one. It's an insoluble problem.'

'How badly do you want it?'

'I'd give anything,' she said, flatly. 'Anything.'

Curtis smiled benevolently.

'Promise me you'll come back in a few days, even if you feel better. Just to talk.'

She nodded.

'You've been a great help, Doctor. Talking about it helps.'

'So you'll come back?'

'Yes.'

She got to her feet and slipped on her jacket. Curtis showed her to the door and opened it for her. He shook her hand and she felt the warmth in his grasp. He smiled once more and then she was gone.

As Curtis closed the door and turned back into the surgery his smile vanished abruptly. He crossed to the door to the left of his desk which was already opening.

'You heard that?' he asked as the other occupant of the house entered the office. 'She said she'd give anytning for another child. Anything.'

'Did you tell her?' the other wanted to know.

Curtis shook his head.

'She's got to be handled carefully but I think she's at the right stage emotionally. She seems particularly receptive.'

'When will you speak to her again?' the figure wanted to know.

Curtis heard the sound of Sue's car pulling away.

'Soon,' he murmured. 'Very soon.'

Fifty-five

Hacket felt the air rasping in his lungs as he inhaled. He hadn't realised until now quite how unfit he really was. As he ran back and forth across the rugby field, following the play he could feel his heart thumping protestingly against his ribs. As a younger man he'd played both football and rugby for his school but that had been more than ten years ago. He might only be twenty-nine, but he felt as if he had the lungs of an eighty-year-old.

The mud-spattered boys who swarmed over the field with him did so with more urgency, as befitted their age. There were those, as there always were, who struggled to keep up, who were constant targets of abuse from their fitter, more athletic colleagues. They too plodded through the mud puffing and panting.

Hacket watched as a boy he knew as Lee Vernon received the ball and began to run with it.

He'd got less than twenty yards when Phillip Craven came hurtling at him.

Vernon tried to avoid the tackle but Craven caught him just above the waist, slamming his shoulder into the other boys solar plexus with something akin to relish. They both went down in a muddy heap and Craven rose quickly, smiling as he looked down at Vernon who had had the wind knocked from him. He lay in the mud wheezing, trying to suck back the air which had been blasted from him by Craven's crunching tackle.

Hacket ran across to the boy and helped him up, bending him over and patting his back in an attempt to re-fill his lungs. The boy gasped, coughed then began to breathe more easily but pain still showed on his face. Hacket asked him if he was all right and he nodded and trudged back into position.

The match re-started and this time it was Craven's turn to catch the ball. He gripped it tightly and ran, barging past a couple of half-hearted tackles, ignoring the boy who had run alongside him to support.

Two opponents came at him and Craven struck out a hand, catching one in the throat. The other was less fortunate.

Craven's hand connected with his nose with such force that the appendage seemed to burst. Blood spilled from both nostrils, pouring down the front of the boys shirt, staining it crimson. He moaned and fell forward into the mud while Craven ran on to score.

Hacket blew his whistle to halt the game, running across to the boy with the bleeding nose. It looked bad and the teacher could see that the boy was struggling to keep back tears. It might even be broken. There was certainly enough blood.

'Put your head forward,' Hacket instructed while a number of the other boys gathered around.

Streams of blood ran from the boy's nose and dripped into the mud between his legs. The sight of his own life-fluid draining away made him feel sick and he went a sickly white colour. Hacket thought he was going to faint, but the boy retained his grip on consciousness.

Craven trotted over, grinning.

'A hand-off is supposed to be with the *flat* of the hand, Craven,' he snapped. 'Not a fist. You do that again and you're in trouble.'

'It's not my fault if he can't take it, sir,' said the youth, defiantly.

'Are you all right, Parker?' Hacket asked the injured boy. He pulled a handkerchief from the pocket of his track-suit and held it to the boy's nose. 'Go back to the school, see the nurse. You go with him,' the teacher said, pointing to another boy who seemed only too delighted to escort his companion off the field. At least it meant *he* was out of the action too.

Hacket watched them leave the field then re-started the game again.

The ball was lofted high into the air and it was Craven who caught it, running at speed towards the opposition. Hacket saw him pass two of them but a third, a powerfully built lad called Baker ducked low, beneath Craven's straight arm rebuff and gripped the other boy's legs. Hacket couldn't resist a slight smile as Craven went crashing to the ground, the ball flying from his grip.

'Good tackle, Baker,' shouted the teacher.

Craven tried to wrestle free of his captor, digging his boot into Baker's chest in the process. The other youth reacted angrily and, before Hacket could reach them, Baker had thrown a punch.

Craven jerked free and, instead of rolling away, he threw himself back at Baker, fastening his hands round his throat, bringing his face close to Baker's.

'Stop it,' bellowed Hacket, racing towards them, pushing past the children who had stopped to watch the fight.

Craven closed his teeth around the top of Baker's left ear and, as Hacket watched in horror, he bit through the fleshy appendage.

Baker screamed as the top of his ear was sheared off.

Blood spurted from it and ran down Craven's chin.

'Craven,' Hacket yelled, trying to reach the boy.

Baker continued to scream, looking up to see the portion of his ear still gripped in Craven's teeth.

He held it for a second then swallowed it.

'Jesus Christ,' murmured Hacket, finally reaching the struggling pair.

He hauled Craven to his feet, seeing the blood on the boy's face, the pieces of flesh between his teeth.

The grin on his face.

Baker had curled up into a ball, both hands clasped to his ear, or at least what remained of it. Blood was pouring down the side of his face, oozing through his fingers.

And he shrieked in pain.

'Go and get help,' Hacket roared at a boy close to him, still gripping on to Craven.

The boy ran off.

Another youth took one look at the bleeding mess which had once been Baker's ear and vomited.

Not only had the top half been severed, most of the remaining ear had been torn. The entire appendage was hanging, held to his head only by thin pieces of skin and muscle.

Hacket dragged Craven away.

Behind him, Baker continued to scream.

Fifty-six

'Don't you think you're over-reacting a little, Mr Hacket?' said Donald Brooks, apparently more concerned that mud from the teacher's boots was dropping onto his office carpet.

'Over-reacting?' Hacket gaped. 'The boy is a lunatic,' he hissed, trying to control his temper. 'I saw what happened. If you don't believe me then go and look at Baker, he's in the medical room now waiting for the ambulance to arrive.'

Brooks raised a hand as if to silence the younger man.

'I didn't say I doubted you,' he said. 'But it was an accident.'

'Craven bit Baker's ear off. He swallowed it for God's sake. Are you trying to tell me that's normal?' Hacket snarled. 'What does he do for an encore, pull the heads of babies?'

'Now you *are* over-reacting,' Brooks told him, irritably. 'What do expect me to do with the boy? Call the police? Have him locked up? I've already called his mother, she's coming to pick him up. I've decided to suspend him for a couple of days until all this blows over.'

Hacket shook his head wearily and brushed a hand through his hair.

Brooks huddled closer to the radiator as if fearing that Hacket's presence in the room was somehow sucking the precious warmth from the air.

'Have there been incidents like this before involving Craven?' Hacket wanted to know.

'Nothing,' Brooks told him. 'The boy is a good worker, a highly intelligent child.'

Hacket was unimpressed. He walked to the door of the Headmasters office and peered out. Craven was sitting in the annexe, looking at his own painting. He was smiling unconcernedly.

The teacher glanced at the boy then closed the office door again.

'He seems to be the dominant one in his class,' Hacket said.

'Intelligent children usually are. I don't have to tell you that, Mr Hacket.'

'What about a boy called Trevor Harvey? Craven was picking on him this morning. Is there some kind of antagonism between them that I should know about?'

'Harvey is a little *slow*, for want of a better word. Again, you know that children like that are usually the butt of jokes. You can't accuse Craven of persecuting Harvey as well. You seem to have taken a dislike to this boy, Mr Hacket and it appears to be clouding your judgement.'

'It's got nothing to do with judgement. I'm not talking about character references, for Christ's sake, I'm telling you what I saw today. And I don't like it.'

The two men gazed at each other for a moment, their concentration broken by a knock on the office door. Brooks' secretary popped her head around the door and coughed rather theatrically.

'Mrs Craven is here,' she announced.

Brooks smiled and instructed the secretary to show the woman through.

She was dressed in a loose fitting tracksuit and trainers. Hacket saw that part of a bandage showed beneath the left sleeve of the track-suit top. Her hair was long, jet black and tied in a pig-tail. She bustled into the room, smiling at Brooks then at Hacket. The headmaster greeted her then introduced her briefly to the younger man. Brooks offered her a seat but she declined.

'There's nothing wrong with Phillip is there?' she asked.

'There's been an accident, Mrs Craven,' said Brooks. 'Involving your son. A fight.'

'Is he hurt?' she asked, anxiously. 'I saw him sitting outside the room.'

'*He's* not hurt,' Hacket interrupted. 'But another boy is. Phillip injured him badly and I'm sure it was intentional.'

Brooks shot the younger man an angry glance.

'There was a slight fracas, Mr Hacket is right,' the headmaster said. 'We thought it best if Phillip stayed at home for a couple of days.'

'What happened?' Elaine Craven wanted to know.

Hacket told her.

She looked at him for a moment then turned to Brooks and smiled politely.

'I'll keep Phillip at home, if that's what you think is best. I hope the other lad is better soon.' Then she turned back to Hacket. 'I think you're a little too eager to blame my son for what happened.'

'I saw him do it, Mrs Craven.'

'He could have been provoked,' she said, defensively.

'Provoked into biting a boy's ear off?' Hacket shook his head.

She pulled up her sleeves and shrugged her shoulders, a gesture which signified defiance. Hacket caught sight of the heavy bandage which encased her left arm from wrist to elbow.

'I think it'd be best if I left now,' said Elaine. 'I'll take Phillip with me.' She turned and headed for the door, followed by the headmaster who waved Hacket back into the office. He waited there, listening to the mutterings coming from outside then he heard the door of the outer office close and, a second later, Brooks re-entered the room, making straight for the radiator. He pressed himself to it.

'Satisfied, Mr Hacket?' Brooks said. 'I believe you have a class to take.' He glanced at his watch. 'I trust there's nothing else you wish to discuss.'

'As a matter of fact there *is* something on my mind,' the teacher said. 'I'd like to know why you didn't tell me the truth about the previous occupant of my house.'

Brooks looked vague.

'The teacher who shot his wife and child then committed suicide,' Hacket continued.

'It's not something I like to talk about,' said Brooks rubbing his hands together.

'I had a right to know before myself and my wife moved in. Why did he do it?'

Brooks shrugged.

'You're asking me to give you answers I can't give now, Mr Hacket,' the headmaster said. 'Who am I to see into a man's mind? I had no idea he would do something like that. He may have been unbalanced. There were no outward signs. I'm a teacher not a psychiatrist.'

Hacket was silent for a moment, his gaze never leaving the headmaster.

'You should have told me,' he said finally.

'Would it have changed your mind about the job? Would you have decided not to live there if you'd known all the facts?'

Hacket shrugged.

‘I don’t know. It’s a bit late for that now though isn’t it? The main thing is, you should have told me.’

Brooks looked at his watch again.

‘Your class, Mr Hacket,’ he said, sliding his hands along the radiator.

Hacket hesitated a moment longer then turned and headed for the door.

Brooks turned his back and gazed out of the window. He could see Elaine Craven driving along the short drive-way that led past his office.

Phillip sat in the back, a slight smile on his lips.

As Hacket passed through the annexe he paused for a second and looked at the painting of the owl on the wall.

The owl holding the eyeball.

Phillip Craven’s painting.

Perhaps it would have been more appropriate if the owl had been holding an ear, he thought bitterly.

All around him bells sounded, signalling the beginning of another lesson.

Hacket looked at his watch.

1.30 p.m.

It was already turning into a long day.

Fifty-seven

As he pushed open the front door the smell of stew greeted him.

Hacket inhaled deeply, the mouth-watering aroma a most welcome one. He dropped his briefcase and sports-bag in the hall and wandered through into the kitchen.

Sue was standing by the cooker stirring the contents of a large saucepan.

'How did it go?' she asked, cheerily and Hacket was pleasantly surprised by the lightness of her tone. She was wearing a pink T-shirt and pair of faded, tight-fitting jeans. Both items of clothing served to highlight both the shapely curves of her figure and the fact that she wore nothing beneath the outer garments. She turned to Hacket and smiled.

He wondered if he'd walked into the wrong house.

It was as if time had somehow been reversed.

Her hair had been washed and, beneath the lights in the kitchen it seemed to glow. She wore just a hint of make-up on her eyes and her face looked as if it had been purged of any lines or shadows. She looked closer to twenty than twenty-five. And when she smiled at him he felt the breath catch in his throat.

It was like finding a long-lost possession again.

He moved towards her and kissed her, surprised when she stopped stirring the stew and, instead, snaked both arms around his neck, drawing him closer to her. Their lips brushed together and he felt her tongue flicking urgently against his teeth, pushing deeper to stir the moistness of his mouth. He responded fiercely, allowing one hand to fall to her bottom, squeezing its firmness. She ground herself against his groin, pulling away for breath, smiling as she felt his penis beginning to stiffen against her.

'The stew will burn,' she said, touching his lips with her index finger. Hacket backed off and sat down, a little bewildered.

Why the sudden change?

He looked at her and smiled.

'I asked how the day went?' she repeated.

He told her, deciding to skip details about Craven's antics on the rugby field. She listened intently, dishing up the dinner, sitting down opposite him as he spoke. Occasionally he would look up at her and, sometimes would find her gaze on him. Hacket's bewilderment at her change in attitude was rapidly overtaken by his joy and relief.

Was this the turning point?

'What about you?' he asked. 'What sort of day have you had?'

'I finished tidying up,' she told him. 'Things actually look respectable in the bedrooms now. I put your clothes away. There's just some stuff that needs to go up in the loft and that's about it.'

'And the doctor? How did *that* go?'

'Fine,' she told him, getting to her feet and scraping the remains of the stew into the waste-bin.

'Did he give you any pills?'

'Sleeping tablets. And don't worry, I won't get addicted.' She smiled.

Hacket looked at her for a moment then he reached out, pulling her to him. She didn't resist but instead allowed him to lift her onto his knee. She put her arms around his neck, feeling the strength in his grip as he held her. He wanted to speak, wanted to say something to her, to tell her how she'd changed. Tell her how much he loved the change. But the words wouldn't come. Hacket was worried that if he spoke to her about her change of mood then she would revert to the way she'd been before. He was both elated and frightened by this new face she was showing.

Face or mask?

She kissed him and he felt sure that it was with genuine warmth.

Had he been forgiven?

He doubted it but he didn't question, he merely enjoyed the moment, savoured the sensations he was feeling.

He wanted her badly.

When he felt her hand gliding across his groin he knew the feeling was reciprocated.

She stroked the inside of his thigh then trailed her fingers across his penis, squeezing it through the material of his trousers, coaxing its stiffness. She took one of his hands and raised it to her breast, anxious to let him feel her own excitement. He kneaded her breast gently, feeling her nipple stiffen and swell. She moaned softly and they kissed, deeply, wantonly. She slid from his lap onto the floor beside him, unzipping his trousers, easing his penis from the confines of the material. Then she leant forward and took the bulbous head in her mouth, slowly lowering her head until more of his stiff shaft disappeared into the warm orifice.

Hacket gasped as he felt her tongue lapping around his glans while, with her free hand, she gently rubbed his testicles. He unfastened his trousers and eased them down, not wanting to disturb her then, as she continued sucking he reached down and pulled at her T-shirt, easing it over her head.

She kneeled beside him, moving back slightly, allowing him to reach her breasts, to squeeze them in his eager hands, to tease the hard nipples between his thumb and forefinger.

She stood up and unzipped her jeans, wriggling out of them until she stood naked in front of him.

Hacket stood too, slipping out of his trousers and pants, allowing Sue to unbutton his shirt and tug it free.

Naked, they embraced and he felt her hand close around his shaft, urging him towards her slippery cleft, demanding that he penetrate her.

She moved back, her shoulder blades against the wall, raising herself up onto her toes as he took his place between her spread thighs.

His penis nudged the entrance of her vagina for a moment

and she gasped as it rubbed her hardened clitoris then, with a grunt, he slid into her.

It was a pleasure he'd almost forgotten.

She raised one leg, snaking it around the back of his calves, allowing him deeper penetration, gripping his buttocks, unable to stand the torment any longer. He began to drive into her, long slow strokes which caused them both to gasp. Hacket bent his head to her breasts taking each nipple between his lips in turn, flicking his tongue over the hardened buds. Licking the mounds until they glistened with his saliva.

Sue looked into his eyes, her own eyes glazed as if she were in a trance, aware only of the thrusting of his penis and the sensations which were building between her legs.

She pressed her head against his shoulder as he increased the speed of his movements. Looking beyond him her eyes opened for a second.

'*Come and see me*'.

She knew that this was her husband who held her but she felt another.

'*Come and see me*'.

Curtis.

She mouthed his name as her ecstasy grew. Mouthed it but did not speak it.

And as the orgasm grew in intensity she closed her eyes, saw Curtis driving into her. Felt him bringing her to the brink.

She heard her name whispered but it seemed vague, muffled.

She cried out as she climaxed, reaching down to squeeze those swollen testicles.

Hacket felt her body trembling with the exploding pleasure, heard her moan her joy. Then, as her hand grasped him gently he too felt the beginnings of his orgasm. He thrust harder into her until he poured his thick fluid into her.

She groaned once more as she felt him come.

The image of Curtis filled her mind. It was *his* penis which throbbed inside her. *His* semen which filled her.

'*Come and see me*'.

Hacket slowly withdrew, his breath coming in gasps. Both of them were covered in perspiration but, even as he tried to pull away she gripped him hard, pulling his face close to hers, kissing him deeply.

Then she leant forward, licking his chest, lowering herself slowly, her tongue flicking over his belly until it reached his flaccid organ, now wet with secretions. She took it into her mouth, tasting herself on him. She licked, sucked, coaxed.

She demanded him again.

And Hacket responded, surprised at his own recuperative powers. He felt the stiffness beginning to return.

She led him, almost dragged him, towards the sitting-room and there they loved again. More slowly this time but with as much intensity.

Hacket felt as if the night had blurred into one long bout of glorious copulation.

Nothing else seemed to matter. He found reserves of strength he didn't know he had, spurred on by Sue's insatiability. She was tireless.

'I love you,' Hacket whispered as she lay with her head on his chest, licking the beads of perspiration from his flesh.

Her eyes were open, her breathing low. She didn't answer him.

All she could think of was Curtis.

And it began again.

Fifty-eight

It had all been so easy.

Much easier than he'd anticipated.

Ronald Mills sat at the table in the flat, smiling, looking down at the objects which lay before him.

At the .38 and its ammunition. The knife. The pad which bore the one word: HINKSTON.

Walton had always done most of the thinking when he'd been alive. Any deals to be worked out, they had been Walton's province. Any financial connivings, Walton had sorted them out, but now Walton was dead and Mills had to think for himself.

He spun the cylinder of the .38 then snapped it back into position, raising the gun so that he was squinting down the sight. He aimed at a dirty vase which stood on top of the sideboard and squeezed the trigger.

The metallic click sounded loud as the hammer slammed down on an empty chamber.

He put down the gun and picked up the knife, holding it almost lovingly in his hand. The hand which still festered from the tattoo. He grunted and picked a piece of the scab off, rolling it between his fingers for a moment before dropping it onto the floor. Then he reached for the sharpening stone, and began carefully drawing the blade back and forth across it, pausing every now and then to press his thumb to the edge.

After nearly five minutes of this task he pressed his thumb to the blade once more.

The knife split the skin effortlessly, opening the pad of Mills' thumb from the nail to the first joint.

He held it before him for a second, watching as the blood welled from the split and ran down his hand. Then he pushed the digit into his mouth, tasting the salty crimson fluid as it flooded onto his tongue. He sucked it as a child would suck on a nipple, coaxing more fluid from it.

Finally he lowered his hand, lowered the knife, his gaze drawn once more to the pad.

He had rung the estate agents and asked about Hacket's house. Said that he wanted to put in a bid for it. And they had believed him. Those fucking idiots who only cared about their commission, who only cared if they sold the house or not. They didn't care who bought it, who enquired, as long as there was the possibility of some money at the end of it all.

'Easier for a camel to pass through the eye of a needle than for a rich man to enter the kingdom of God,' chuckled Mills.

He didn't want money. He didn't care about money.

He wanted revenge.

He wanted Hacket.

The estate agent had tried to arrange a meeting with him, to show him round the house but Mills had hesitated. He had asked to speak to Hacket personally, he wondered if he would be willing to take a smaller offer.

The estate agent thought it might work.

Mills had smiled.

He had asked for a way of getting in touch with Hacket.

The estate agent had given him a phone number and an address in a place called Hinkston.

Ask and ye shall receive.

Mills looked at the word written on his pad then at the gun and the knife.

And at his bleeding thumb.

He knew where Hacket was, all he had to do was find him.

Slowly, Mills wiped his thumb across the pad, leaving a thick red stain.

It was just a matter of time.

Seek and ye shall find.
He began to laugh.

Fifty-nine

The frost crunched beneath his feet as he walked from the back door of the house.

Curtis made his way across the large lawn at the rear of the building, moving slowly, inhaling deeply. The early morning air smelt clean and unpolluted. When he exhaled his breath clouded before him. A watery sun was dragging its way up into the sky but, with dawn having broken scarcely fifteen minutes earlier it seemed to be finding the climb difficult. It wasn't yet strong enough to melt the frost.

The silence in the back garden, indeed all around the house, was almost total.

It was too early for any traffic to be either leaving or entering Hinkston, and the house was set sufficiently far back from the road to mask the sound even if some early morning traveller *was* passing.

The only sounds which Curtis heard as he made his way across the back garden were those of birds singing in the trees around him. Just two or three of them. A sparrow paused in its early morning song to peer quizzically at him as he passed beneath the branch where it sat.

Curtis drew closer to the bottom of the garden, towards the high, perfectly cropped privet hedge which towered a good nine feet.

There was a wrought iron gate set into it, supported on

a wooden frame, the paint of which was blistered and peeling in places. Curtis opened the gate which squealed protestingly on its hinges as he walked through.

The area beyond the hedge was roughly twelve feet square. Surrounded by more hedges, these not quite as well cared for. They were neat but not immaculate. The grass which grew within the shaded square was that little bit longer than that of the lawns, not as neatly cropped. Weeds were poking through it in places. Curtis administered a swift mental rebuke as he surveyed the square because this was caused by *his* neglect. *He* was responsible for the care of this part of the garden.

The gardener wasn't allowed through the gate.

Curtis stood by the gate for a moment, looking around at the tall hedge, also covered by a thin coating of frost. The privet grew three feet taller than him here too. It sheltered the square perfectly.

He walked slowly towards the middle of it, towards the piece of stone which lay there.

The stone was cracked in places due to the ravages of the years and the weather. Moss had begun to grow on it here and there, infesting the cracks in the stone like gangrene infects a wound.

Curtis looked down at the name on the stone.

Below the name was a rose bowl, flecked with rust and, from this he took half a dozen dead stalks of flowers, gathering them up in one hand.

He replaced them with the fresh flowers which he held in his other hand, arranging them so that the red roses seemed to glow against the dull background of the stone.

They looked like a splash of blood on the grave.

Curtis straightened up, walked to one corner of the sheltered green square and dropped the dead flowers into the metal incinerator that stood there, then he brushed his hands together and returned to the graveside, gazing down once again at the name on the stone.

He stood there for what seemed like an eternity, his mind at peace, all thoughts banished. Again, the only sounds he heard were those of birds, his meditative state uninterrupted by nature's extraneous sounds.

Then he heard the footsteps beyond the gate.

Beyond the hedge.

Heavy footfalls which broke the blanket of frost.

Curtis turned his head towards the gate as the footsteps drew closer.

He heard the latch of the gate rattle, then the dull clank as it opened.

The figure walked through to join him.

Curtis turned back to the grave, hands clasped before him once more.

'I heard you leave the house,' said the figure, standing at his side.

'Sorry, I didn't want to disturb you.' the doctor said, softly, almost reverently, as if to raise his voice would have been to defile the sanctity of this very private area.

The two of them stood silently for long moments, both gazing down at the stone.

And the name it bore.

'I've never thought this was right,' said Curtis nodding towards the grave. 'To lie here, even though it *is* our home.'

'Better here than with the others,' said the figure, defiantly.

Curtis nodded in agreement.

'Have you made up your mind what to do about the woman?' the other wanted to know.

'Mrs Hacket?'

'Yes.'

Curtis smiled thinly.

'Yes I have,' he said, his eyes still on the gravestone.

'She's due to visit me again today.' His smile broadened. 'I think the time has come.'

Sixty

The woman was struggling with the books as she climbed the stairs, and Hacket could see what was going to happen.

As she reached the top step he saw the first of the heavy textbooks begin to topple from her hands. Five or six more followed it, landing with a thud on the floor. She muttered something under her breath and began retrieving them. Hacket scuttled up the stairs beside her and began picking up books too.

He glanced across at her as she shrugged and smiled.

She was very attractive. In her early twenties he guessed. Shoulder length brown hair and wide grey eyes. A nice figure too.

A little like Nikki?

He pushed the thought to the back of his mind, angry that it had even surfaced.

'You look as if you could do with some help carrying these,' he said, picking up half a dozen of the books himself.

'If you've got a fork-lift truck handy, it'd be most appreciated,' she told him, smiling. 'You're new here aren't you?'

He nodded.

'The new boy. Yes.' He extended his free hand, balancing the pile of books on the crook of his left arm. 'John Hacket.'

She took the offered hand and shook it.

'Josephine Milton,' she told him. 'But please call me Jo.'
She scooped up the rest of the books and they began climbing the stairs towards the second landing.

'What do you teach?' he asked.

'Biology. I dissect things,' she chuckled. 'What about you? English isn't it?'

'English *and* games,' he told her. 'I've got the strained muscles to prove it.'

She laughed.

'Of course, you took over from Ray Weller didn't you? I suppose you know the story?'

'About him killing his family then committing suicide. Yes.'

'Isn't it creepy living in a house where someone has died?'

'You get used to it,' said Hacket sharply. *Especially when you've lived in the house where your own daughter was butchered. It's a piece of cake*. 'How much did you know about Weller?'

She shrugged.

'Not much. Not enough to know why he should want to murder his family if that's what you mean. He was a nice guy. About your age, easy to talk to. He never struck me as a lunatic.' She raised her eyebrows. 'I haven't really been much help have I?'

Hacket smiled.

'It's probably not important,' he told her, pushing open a set of double doors to allow her through. Four classrooms led off from the landing they stood on.

'My little darlings are in there,' said Jo, nodding towards the door ahead of her. 'If you wouldn't mind just helping me in with these books.'

Hacket watched as she walked to the door and opened it, trying to keep his eyes away from her shapely legs and tight buttocks but he lost the battle, content instead to admire them. She pushed open the door, expecting to be greeted by the usual cacophony of sound but there was only silence. The twelve girls in the class looked up as she entered.

All except one.

Emma Stokes remained at the bench, looking down at the white mouse which lay before her.

Its paws had been swiftly and effectively nailed to the bench, spreadeagling it.

Its stomach had been slit, the raw edges peeled back to reveal the network of intestines within.

It was these small tendrils of entrail which the girl was teasing from the ruptured belly of the mouse much as she might pull threads from a torn piece of material.

Hacket, close behind Jo, noticed with revulsion that the animal was still alive. Its head jerking back and forth, its small body quivering as the girl pulled ever longer lengths of intestine from it.

'What are you doing?' Jo snapped, dropping the books on the desk. She moved towards Emma who finally looked up from the eviscerated mouse and pinned the teacher in an unblinking stare. 'Give me that scalpel,' hissed Jo, holding out her hand to take the lethal blade from the girl who Hacket guessed was about twelve.

Emma hesitated.

'Give me that scalpel now,' Jo said, angrily, her attention flicking momentarily to the mouse.

Emma jabbed it towards Jo's outstretched hand.

The razor sharp blade cut effortlessly through the ball of her thumb and she hissed in pain as blood spurted from the cut.

She pulled the scalpel from the girl, dropping it onto her own desk. Hacket dragged a handkerchief from his pocket and passed it to Jo who pressed it against the wound, watching as blood soaked through the material.

'I'm all right, John,' Jo said. 'I can handle it now.'

He hesitated, looking first at the teacher's bleeding hand then at the girl who merely looked back indifferently at him.

He thought for a second he caught a hint of a smile at the corners of the girl's mouth. Not unlike that he'd seen on Craven's face.

The rest of the class remained silent.

Time seemed to have frozen.

Emma Stokes sat over the dying mouse, her face impassive.

Jo stood before her, blood soaking through the handkerchief.

Hacket hesitated a second longer then touched Jo's arm.

'Are you sure you're OK?' he murmured.

She nodded.

'You go. I'll take care of it.'

Hacket glanced around the class once again then walked out, closing the door behind him. He paused, peering through the small piece of meshed glass in the door, watching the tableau he'd left behind.

'Now Emma,' he heard Jo say. 'You tell me what you're playing at.'

He didn't wait to hear the answer.

He had a class of his own waiting for him.

Sixty-one

'John, I want another child.'

At first Hacket thought he had misheard, or perhaps that his hearing was playing tricks with him. Lying on his back, pleasantly drained by their lovemaking, he heard Sue speak the words but it was as if they wouldn't register. She had her head resting on his chest, running one index finger up and down his belly, twisting the hairs around his navel.

The ticking of the clock beside the bed was the only noise in the room apart from their low breathing. No, he was sure now, he hadn't misheard.

'Sue,' he raised his head and began to speak but she looked up at him and pressed a finger to his lips to silence him.

'I know what you're going to say. I know what you're thinking,' she told him. 'But that's what I want. I *need* another child, John.'

Hacket exhaled deeply as she slid up the bed so that they lay face to face. He took her in his arms.

'Sue, it's impossible, you know that. After you had Lisa, after the infection, they told you there couldn't be any more children.'

'I know what they told me,' she said, a little more forcefully.

'Then why torture yourself like this?' he asked, softly. 'Why even think about it?' He stroked her hair softly then brushed her cheek with the back of his hand.

'I went to see doctor Curtis again today,' she informed him, rolling onto her back.

Hacket propped himself up on one elbow, looking down at her.

'I told him how badly I wanted another child,' Sue continued.

'Did you tell him what the other doctors had said?' Hacket wanted to know.

'Yes I did. But it doesn't matter, John,' she said, smiling. 'He said that I *could* have another child. That there *was* a way.'

Hacket frowned.

'How?' he demanded. 'He has no right to tell you things like that, to raise your hopes.'

'I believe what he said and he says I can have another child.'

'It's not possible,' Hacket said, defiantly. 'I don't understand how he can tell you it is, not when half-a-dozen other doctors have said you can't. *You* know you can't. What makes you believe him?'

'Because I'm not the first. He's treated other women who were thought to be infertile, barren, not able to have children. Call it what you like. He's treated women in Hinkston and outside and those women have had babies.'

'Treated them how? He's a GP, Sue, not a surgeon. Your problem particularly is a surgical one. An *irreversible* surgical problem. How can he hope to treat a condition like yours?' There was a trace of anger in Hacket's voice.

'One of the women he treated was Julie,' she said, flatly.

'Your sister?' Hacket muttered, incredulously.

'She and Mike were told that they couldn't have children. But after doctor Curtis had treated her she had Craig. You know how healthy *he* is.'

Hacket shook his head.

'He's offering us hope, John. Can't you see that?' she demanded.

'I don't know what I can see.' He stroked his chin thoughtfully.

'I want to try, John. I have to. I know another child could never replace Lisa, could never wipe out the memory of what happened but we have to at least try. Don't deny me that.'

Hacket saw the tears forming in her eye corners.

'What about you? Don't you want another child?' she wanted to know. 'What have we got to lose?'

He struggled for the words but none would come. The idea seemed simultaneously ridiculous and inviting.

Another child, if it were possible might well bring them together again. It might go some way to helping them rebuild what they'd lost together.

But if it failed.

The pain would be unbearable.

So much pain.

'What have we got to lose?' she repeated.

The words hung in the air like stale smoke.

Sixty-two

The petrol tank was full.

He'd have plenty of fuel to reach Hinkston *and* complete the return journey to London.

Ronald Mills glanced down at the fuel gauge and smiled. He'd anticipated having to fill up during the drive but he'd been lucky. The car he'd stolen had a full tank. He'd probably dump it in Hinkston.

Once he'd found Hacket.

Dump it then steal another to return to the capital.

The .38 was in the pocket of his jacket.

The knife jammed into his belt.

He drove with his lights on full beam, ignoring those drivers who flashed their headlamps at him when he dazzled them.

Fuck them.

There wasn't that much traffic leaving London, but streams of it moved through the night towards the capital.

A car overtook him but Mills hardly gave it a second glance. He was in no hurry. He had plenty of time.

He smiled to himself, glancing briefly down at the map on the passenger seat. He had ringed Hinkston with a large biro circle. The drive would take him about an hour he guessed.

There was no need to rush.

Ahead of him he saw the lights of a service station. The neon figure of a chef beckoned him from the road and he swung the car into the slip-road without checking the rear view mirror. The driver behind banged on his hooter as Mills cut across but he ignored the irate motorist and guided the car into the carpark of the service station.

A dog in the back of the vehicle he parked next to began to bark at him as he clambered from behind the steering wheel.

Mills stood looking at the animal for a moment, smiling as it barked and snarled, unable to reach him. Then he raised his hand as if to strike at the dog, driving it into an even greater paroxysm of anger. It threw itself against the glass in its efforts to reach him but Mills merely grinned and walked off, the dog's barks dying away behind him.

The service station restaurant was relatively quiet.

Half-a-dozen lorry drivers, a couple of families, one or two suited men. They were the only customers. None paid him any attention as he sat down and flicked through the menu, wiping the tomato sauce from one corner with his finger.

The waitress ambled over, stifled a yawn and asked him what he wanted.

He ordered then sat back in his seat, glancing around him.

One of the families sitting about twenty feet from him had two children. A boy and a girl. The girl was no more than eight, he assumed. Pretty. Long plaited hair.

Mills clasped his hands together, leant his elbows on the table top and fixed his stare on her.

She was sucking milkshake through a straw, swinging her legs beneath her seat.

Pretty.

He smiled thinly as he watched her, feeling the beginnings of an erection pressing against the material of his trousers. His gaze travelled from her face to her torso, then down to her legs, which were encased by woollen tights.

So easy to cut those tights away.

To feel her skin.

His erection grew more prominent and he slid one hand into his pocket, rubbing it.

'Here we are, sir.'

The voice startled him and he looked up to see that the waitress had returned with his order which she set down before him.

He took it without thanks, eating as if he was ravenous. She turned and walked away, glancing back at him as he shovelled food into his mouth, his eyes still straying back to the little girl every now and then.

When he'd finished he crossed to the pay desk, put down the exact amount and walked out.

Back inside the car he sat, watching the restaurant exit, watching for the little girl.

She and her family emerged ten or fifteen minutes after him and Mills watched them climb into a Volvo and drive off.

He looked down at the map, tracing his route with one index finger.

About thirty miles and he would be in Hinkston.

He started the engine.

The dog in the car next to him continued to bark.

Sixty-three

Hacket smiled as he watched Sue cross to the front window and pull back the curtains, peering out into the night.

'Sue, he'll be here,' said the teacher. 'Don't worry.'

She looked back at him, shrugged and moved away from the window.

'You're like a kid on Christmas Eve, waiting for Santa to appear.'

They both laughed.

Hacket beckoned her to him and she sat beside him on the sofa, moving closer as he snaked one arm around her shoulder.

'I know how much this means to you,' he said, quietly. 'I feel the same way. If there is the possibility of us having another child then I'd be as happy as you.' He sighed. 'I just don't want you to raise your hopes.'

'Doctor Curtis wouldn't have told me about the treatment if he'd thought there'd be any doubt about its success, John,' she said, confidentially.

'What exactly *did* he tell you about the treatment?'

She shrugged.

'He didn't give any details, I suppose that's why he's coming to see us here, to explain it to both of us.'

Hacket was unimpressed.

Sue heard a car pull up and got to her feet again, crossing to the window. This time she saw Curtis walking up the front path. She felt that familiar shiver run through her as she watched him. He was dressed in a pair of dark trousers and a dark jacket.

She hurried to open the door, releasing the latch before he'd even knocked. Hacket heard them exchange greetings, then Curtis entered the living room.

Sue made the introductions and Hacket shook the doctor's hand, impressed by the firmness of the other man's grip.

Curtis declined Hacket's offer of a drink, settling instead for a cup of tea. The three of them finally sat down, Curtis aware that the eyes of the other two were on him.

'Well, I won't waste your time,' he said, smiling. 'Mr Hacket, I don't know if your wife has mentioned anything about our conversation the other day.'

'She said that you told her she might be able to have children again,' Hacket explained.

Curtis nodded and sipped his tea.

'That's right. She told me about your daughter. I'm very sorry.'

'Thanks,' snapped Hacket.'Can you get to the point? Please satisfy my curiosity.'

Sue glared at her husband for a second, annoyed by his abruptness. Then she returned to looking at the doctor, enraptured both by his words and his appearance.

Christ, it was like some schoolgirl crush, she thought, barely suppressing a smile.

'My wife, as I'm sure you're aware, was told that she couldn't have any more children. Several doctors told her that,' Hacket continued.

'But you want another child?' Curtis said.

Hacket opened his mouth to speak but the doctor continued.

'*Both* of you?'

'Yes,' Hacket said, quietly, meeting the doctors gaze.

'I've treated a number of women successfully over the past seventeen or eighteen years, Mr Hacket. They too had been told they couldn't have children, also by other experts.' There was a hint of sarcasm in the last word.

'Whatever it takes, we want another child,' Sue interjected.

Curtis smiled benignly at her, as a parent might smile at a child.

Hacket held up a hand, his eyes still on Curtis.

'Just a minute. Excuse my scepticism, doctor. It's not that I doubt your methods or your expertise but I'm concerned for my wife. If the treatment doesn't work then it could do her untold damage psychologically.'

'Don't talk about me as if I'm not here,' snapped Sue. 'I know the risks. I'm prepared to take them.'

'Please,' Curtis said. 'I didn't come here to start any arguments. I can see both points of view. If you'll just listen to what I've got to say.'

'I apologise for my husband, Doctor,' Sue said and, this time, it was Hacket's turn to feel the anger.

'You want to know about the treatment,' Curtis said.

Hacket nodded.

'I can't see how you can achieve anything without the use of surgery,' the teacher said.

'That is the advantage, Mr Hacket. The treatment can be completed at my own surgery. There is no need to involve a hospital or any other outsiders.'

'Why are you so anxious to exclude outside help? What's so special about this treatment?'

Curtis wasn't slow to pick up the note of challenge in Hacket's voice.

'Because it's *my* treatment, Mr Hacket. This is *my* project. I've done most of the work on it, I don't intend to let others start sticking their noses in where they're not wanted.'

'*Your* treatment. You've worked on this alone then?'

'Yes, for as long as I can remember. Ever since I qualified. It's been mine. My theories, my work. I've seen the results. I know it's successful. You can see the results for yourself, here in Hinkston. Some of them at your school.'

Hacket frowned.

'What do you mean?' he wanted to know.

'I said I'd treated a number of other women over the years. Some of the children they gave birth to are at the school where you teach.'

Hacket sat forward in his seat, his hands clasped together.

'Like who?'

'Phillip Craven. Emma Stokes.'

'Jesus,' murmured Hacket under his breath.

Craven. And he knew that other name too. *Emma*. What the hell had been her surname? *The girl who had been pulling the entrails from the mouse. The one who had slashed open Jo Milton's hand with a scalpel.*

'How old is the girl?' he asked.

'About twelve. A pretty girl. Long black hair,' said Curtis smiling.

Hacket nodded. It *was* her.

'Who else have you treated?' he wanted to know.

'A young couple, recently. Stuart and Michelle Lewis, they have a baby now. The Kirkhams, the couple who own The Bull in town, the hotel. They have a daughter, Paula, thanks to my work. And, as well as the Cravens' and the Stokes' families, there are a number of other children at your school whose mothers I treated. And of course there was Ray Weller.'

Hacket felt the colour draining from his cheeks.

'The man who lived here before us? The one who killed his wife and child then shot himself?'

Curtis nodded.

'A tragedy,' he said, wistfully, a faint smile on his lips. 'She really was such a beautiful child.'

Hacket felt the hairs at the back of his neck slowly rise.

Sixty-four

'Why did he do it?' Hacket wanted to know. 'Why did Weller kill his family then himself?'

'I'm not a psychiatrist, Mr Hacket,' Curtis said, finishing his tea and setting the cup down. 'I thought you wanted to know about the possibility of your wife having another child, not about the misfortunes of this building's previous occupant.

Hacket looked coldly at the doctor for a moment then nodded.

'Yes, I do,' he said, wearily. 'We both do.'

'When could the treatment start?' Sue wanted to know.

'As soon as you agree to it.'

'You still haven't explained exactly what this treatment is,' Hacket reminded him.

Well, without going into too much technical and biological detail, it involves an injection into the wall of the uterus,' said Curtis. 'It's as simple as that. There isn't necessarily any need for a local anaesthetic. The whole process is over in less than fifteen minutes.'

'But Sue's fallopian tubes were blocked, how can the egg travel from the ovaries?'

'It doesn't have to.'

Hacket frowned, his look of incredulity turning to one of near mocking.

Curtis continued.

'A hormone is injected into the wall of the uterus, it stimulates growth. The foetus gestates in the womb as normal but the fallopian tubes become unnecessary.'

'So it's a kind of artificial insemination?' Hacket said, quietly.

'No. In the case of insemination, sperm is introduced directly into the ovaries. The egg grows there then travels along the fallopian tube to the womb where it grows naturally. As I said earlier, this process eliminates the need for that part of the cycle.'

Hacket shook his head.

'So how is the egg fertilised?'

'By your sperm, within the vagina, as in normal intercourse. The egg is already removed, again by drawing it off using a needle, then replaced in the uterus where it is *then* fertilised. Gestation is accelerated by the second injection which initiates growth.'

'What do you mean "accelerated"?' Hacket said, warily.

'The gestation period is shortened. The time varies according to the individual subject and how well they respond to the drug.'

'It's not possible,' Hacket murmured.

'On the contrary, Mr Hacket, it's not only possible but it works. You can see the examples for yourself. The Craven boy, Emma Stokes and the others I've mentioned to you.'

Silence descended as Hacket struggled to come to terms with what he'd heard and Curtis sat back almost smugly, glancing first at the teacher then at Sue who returned his smile warmly.

Hacket stroked his chin.

'I don't know what to say,' he muttered. 'If this process works then why haven't you done more with it? Brought it to the attention of the medical authorities? It could benefit women all over the country if it works.'

'You still continue to say '*if*', Mr Hacket,' the doctor observed. 'What will it take to convince you? Won't you believe it until you're holding your own child in your arms?'

Hacket swallowed hard.

'I suppose I'm frightened to believe it,' he said, quietly. 'It sounds too easy. *Too* simple. What are the risks to the child?'

'No more than in normal pregnancy.'

'I said I'm willing to take those risks, John,' Sue said, defiantly.

'Well I'm not sure *I* am,' Hacket said, flatly.

Curtis glared at the teacher for a moment.

'You still haven't told me enough.'

'It isn't only your decision,' Sue said, angrily. 'It's me who's got to carry the baby. I'm the one who's got to give birth. I told you, I *need* that child.'

Curtis got to his feet.

'I think it would be best if I left now,' he said, making for the door.

Sue hurried after him. Hacket sauntered to the door where he shook hands with Curtis once more.

A chill breeze blew in through the open front door and Hacket felt his skin rise into goose-pimples.

'Take your time and think about what I've said,' Curtis told them, but his eyes were on Hacket when he spoke. 'It's a chance to start again, Mr Hacket. Not many people get that.'

He said goodnight to Sue then turned and headed down the path to his waiting car.

Hacket stepped back inside the house, Sue stood on the step watching as the car disappeared into the night.

When she entered the sitting room, Hacket was sitting in front of the electric fire warming his hands.

'You were rude to him, John,' she said, irritably. 'Like he said, he's offering us another chance. We have to take it.'

Hacket inhaled, held the breath for a moment then let it out in a long sigh.

'Sue, it might be coincidence, maybe I'm overreacting but the kids he's treated . . .' He struggled to find the words. 'There's something strange about them.'

'And what about Julie's son, Craig? Is he strange too?' she snapped, choosing to ignore the night Curtis had been called to the boy. 'It's not you that's overreacting, John, it's your imagination. Perhaps you've been a teacher too long, reading books too long. The name of this town is Hinkston not Midwich. These children aren't the children of the damned, they're not artificially created by some mad doctor.' She was angry, the anger mixed with scorn. 'They're the last hope for their parents. Just like Curtis is *our* last hope. She got to her feet and made for the door. 'I'm going to bed, John. If you want to sit up and think then fine, but just think about one thing. I'm having this child whether you want me to or not. And I won't let you stop me.'

Sixty-five

Curtis drove slowly through the streets of Hinkston, only speeding up slightly when he reached the road that led towards his house.

The massive building was almost invisible in the gloom but for a couple of lights burning in one of the rooms on the first floor. However, as he drew nearer the outline of the house became visible against the black velvet backdrop of night.

The doctor swung his car into the driveway, brought it to a halt before the front door and switched off the engine. He sat for a moment, head bowed, then he swung himself out of the car, locked it and headed for the house.

His footsteps echoed on the polished wood of the hall floor as he entered and, as he made his way towards the sitting room he slowed his pace, glancing towards the stairs.

Listening for any sign of movement from above.

There was none.

The house was silent.

Curtis entered the sitting room, feeling the warmth from the dying embers of the open fire. They still glowed red in the grate and he moved across towards them, warming his hands close to the coals. In the red light which they cast it looked as though his face had been splashed with blood.

'What did she say?'

The voice came from behind him, from the high-backed leather chair which stood close to the fire. Curtis hadn't seen the figure sitting in it when he'd entered the room and the words startled him momentarily. He exhaled deeply, looking at his companion for a moment before once again turning his back and warming his hands.

'The woman is enthusiastic,' he said. 'She *has* been from the beginning. It's her husband who's resisting.'

Curtis got to his feet, crossed to the ornate drinks cabinet and poured himself a whiskey. He raised a glass, inviting the other occupant of the room to join him.

The figure nodded and Curtis handed him a drink.

'How much does he know?' the figure asked.

'He knows about Weller,' Curtis announced, then he swallowed a large measure of the whiskey.

'You expected him to, didn't you? A murder and a suicide in a small town like this are bound to be common knowledge.'

Curtis raised his eyebrows quizzically.

'Murders but not disappearances?' he mused.

'Hacket knows that Weller killed his family,' the figure said. 'What he mustn't find out is *why*.'

Sixty-six

He stood beside the bed for what seemed like an eternity, watching the steady rise and fall of her chest as she slept.

Finally Hacket undressed and slipped into bed beside Sue. He lay back, one arm across his forehead, gazing at the ceiling, listening to Sue's shallow breathing.

Could what Curtis said really be true?

Was it even feasible?

Hacket exhaled deeply and rubbed his face.

He knew that the child was important to Sue. No, important was the wrong word. It had become an obsession. He wondered if he could stop her from undergoing Curtis' treatment now even if he wanted to.

But did he want to?

He knew the child meant everything to her and he also knew that it did offer their only chance of returning to anything like a normal existence. To be given the chance to start again. It was a chance which *he* dare not forego either.

But the risks.

Small compared to the joy which would come with the birth of the child.

What exactly was the treatment?

Curtis had described it. A form of artificial insemination. Only this was less clinical, less mechanical.

The foetus grows at an accelerated rate. Why?

Hacket sat up in bed and looked down at Sue. He reached across and gently pulled a strand of hair away from her mouth.

The thought of the child meant everything to her. He had no right to deprive her of that joy.

The children born because of Curtis' treatment were violent.

Only the ones you know about, he told himself. *Just two out of possibly dozens. It could be coincidence.*

It *had* to be coincidence.

'Oh God,' he murmured, irritably. The questions and queries could torment him forever if he thought about them. The only thing that mattered was that they had a glimmer of hope.

The chance of another child.

The risks . . .

'To hell with it,' he whispered to himself and swung out of bed.

It was then that the phone rang.

Hacket glanced down at the clock.

11.56 p.m.

He looked at Sue but the persistent drone of the phone didn't seem to have disturbed her.

It kept ringing.

Hacket got to his feet and padded down the stairs, shivering slightly from the cold as he reached for the receiver.

'Hello,' he said, quietly.

Nothing.

'Hello,' he repeated, wearily.

Silence.

Hacket put down the phone and shook his head.

Wrong number no doubt he thought as he turned and ascended the stairs once more.

He was half way up when the phone rang again.

'For Christ's sake,' he muttered and retraced his steps, snatching up the receiver once again.

'Yes,' he hissed.

No answer.

'Look, if this is a joke.'

His angry protestations were cut short.

'John Hacket?' said the voice at the other end of the line.

It was the teacher's turn to stand there in silence.

He didn't recognise the voice, hardly surprising, really, from the utterance of just two words.

'Is that John Hacket?' the voice repeated.

'Yes, who is this?'

Click.

The line went dead.

Hacket held the receiver away from his ear as if it were some kind of venomous reptile then, slowly, he replaced it. He stood looking at the phone for a moment, as if expecting it to ring again. When it didn't he made his way slowly back up to bed.

Sixty-seven

The smell reminded Sue of a hospital. The strong odour of disinfectant. A scent that was both reassuring and repulsive.

Sue thought of her father, lying alone in that hospital room, waiting to die. It was this smell which must have filled his nostrils for so long.

The memory came unexpectedly, all the more painful for that and she tried to push it from her mind. She sat in the waiting room of Curtis' surgery, nervously clasping and unclasping her hands, glancing alternately up at the wall-clock above the receptionist's desk and at the door which led through to the surgery.

She seemed to have been waiting hours, although she knew that barely five minutes had slipped by since she'd arrived and the receptionist had retreated into the surgery proper to tell Curtis of her arrival. Sue wasn't sure what was making her more nervous, the thought of the treatment or the nagging doubt that it would fail.

She brushed the hair from her face, noticing as she did that her hand was shaking.

Hacket had wanted to come with her but she had assured him she would be fine alone. She trusted doctor Curtis. Felt safe in his hands.

'Come and see me'.

The door to the surgery opened and the receptionist ushered her through, finally leaving her alone in the office. Although it looked different from the other times she had visited. For one thing there was no sign of Curtis. Sue saw a door leading out of surgery and she heard footsteps approaching that door. A second later the doctor entered. He was wearing a white lab coat over his clothes but that was the only item of protective clothing in evidence. He greeted Sue warmly and invited her to follow him through the door which she did.

It opened onto the cellar.

The white-washed walls almost glowed so dazzling bright were they painted. In the centre of the room was a couch, covered by a white sheet and, beside it, a trolley which sported a dizzying array of surgical implements.

Sue swallowed hard as she saw them, and glanced anxiously at Curtis, who merely smiled and led her to the lower level.

It was unexpectedly warm down there and she could hear an almost monotonous drone of something which she guessed might be a generator. Access to it though was hidden by a series of screens which surrounded the couch.

'How are you feeling?' Curtis asked, smiling warmly, and Sue, once again, was captivated by his eyes. She felt as if she were drowning in them. Floating.

'A little nervous,' she confessed.

'Then the sooner we get started the better,' the doctor

said. 'Are you warm enough? I want you to be comfortable. The procedure doesn't take more than about five minutes.' He touched her arm softly. 'And I'm sure you'll find it worthwhile.'

She smiled, relaxing visibly at his touch.

'If you could undress for me,' he said, quietly.

Sue nodded almost imperceptibly. The words were spoken slowly, almost tenderly. The words of a lover, not a physician. He handed her a white gown from another of the trolleys which she laid on the couch. Then she began unbuttoning her blouse, glancing at Curtis as she did, surprised that she didn't feel the slightest twinge of embarrassment.

Curtis turned his back as she pulled the blouse free of her jeans. He bent over the trolley, inspecting a number of syringes which were laid out, it appeared, in descending order of size. The largest was over eight inches long, the smallest no bigger than his index finger.

'Is your husband still opposed to this treatment?' Curtis wanted to know, his back still to her.

'He wasn't really opposed to it,' Sue informed him, unhooking her bra. 'He was worried because he didn't know all the details.'

'I told him as much as I could.'

'I know that.'

'Does it worry you?' Curtis asked, turning round.

Sue stood before him, naked from the waist up but she made no attempt to hide herself. Instead she stood facing the doctor, almost willing him to inspect her breasts, aware of the tightening and swelling of her nipples.

'I want a child,' she whispered, removing her shoes. 'I don't care what it takes.' As she spoke she began to unfasten the zip of her jeans, easing them down over her slender hips until she stood before him in just her panties.

The droning of the generator continued, a low hum which matched Sue's increasingly deep breathing.

As Curtis turned away from her for a second she was aware of the tingles running up and down her spine, of the growing excitement which was spreading through her body. As she prepared to remove her panties she felt the wetness between her legs.

Completely naked she swung herself up onto the couch.

Her breathing was coming in shallow gasps, her chest heaving almost expectantly.

'Slide your bottom forward to the edge of the couch and open your legs,' Curtis said, softly, laying one hand on her thigh to aid her in that simple manoeuvre. As he moved between her legs he could smell the musky odour of her sex. She shuffled around, gyrating her hips slightly, trying to slow the pace of her breathing.

'I'm going to give you a local anaesthetic,' he told her, quietly. 'Just relax.'

She eased her legs further apart, inviting him to move closer. Sue was gazing at the ceiling, she didn't see Curtis reach for one of the smaller syringes.

With infinite care he parted her outer labial lips, already swollen and red, slick with the moisture of her excitement. They had parted like the petals of a flower and he saw her stomach muscles contract as he gently moved the needle closer to her vagina.

The steel point slid easily into the tumescent flesh and Sue sucked in a deep breath as it penetrated her, holding that breath as Curtis pushed on the plunger, emptying the contents of the shaft into her. Then he withdrew the glistening needle carefully and laid it on the trolley.

'You might feel a little groggy,' he told her. 'If you do just let yourself fall asleep. There's nothing to worry about.'

She smiled.

'I know,' she whispered, closing her eyes, waiting for the next, deeper penetration.

'This time,' Curtis breathed and brought the largest of the syringes closer to her slippery cleft, pushing the needle inside until he felt it press against the spongy tissue of her endometrium. Sue arched her back slightly as the syringe was pushed deeper into her uterus and she felt fluid filling her. Felt a warmth spreading up from her thighs and across her belly. Her nipples ached, such was their stiffness, and she brushed one breast with her hand, suppressing a gasp as her fingers raked against the hard bud.

Curtis remained between her thighs, squeezing the last drops of fluid from the thick container, finally withdrawing it carefully.

Sue let out a long breath, her eyes flickering shut.

Curtis looked down at her and smiled.

'It's done,' he told her, watching as a smile spread across her face.

He reached for the gown and gently laid it over her.

'Rest for a little while,' the doctor said, standing over her until he saw that she was slipping off to sleep. Then he pulled off the rubber gloves he'd been wearing and tossed them into a nearby waste bin, washing his hands in the sink at one corner of the cellar.

He had his back to the door when it opened.

Curtis only heard the footsteps behind him, moving towards the couch.

Towards Sue.

He turned slowly to see the other figure standing over her.

They exchanged glances and Curtis merely nodded, a silent affirmation of what the other wondered. Like the mute answer to an unasked question.

The figure reached for the gown and pulled it up, inspecting Sue's body, gazing at her full rounded breasts, flat stomach and the small triangle of light hair between her legs. Legs which were still slightly parted.

Curtis, still drying his hands, joined the newcomer, who was still looking appreciatively at Sue's naked body.

'It won't be long now,' Curtis said, quietly.

The other nodded.

Sixty-eight

'That's about the tenth time you've checked your watch and we've only been out here for ten minutes,' Jo Milton said, smiling.

Hacket shrugged and dug his hands in his pockets as they walked.

'I promise not to look again,' he said, smiling.

All around them the sound of children playing, shouting, arguing, laughing and sometimes fighting merged into one endless cacophony of noise. Break-time, twenty minutes in which to unleash the furies built up during class, thought Hacket looking round at the children.

A group of boys were kicking a ball against a wall to his right. To his left three or four girls were standing around peering at a magazine. One of them looked at Hacket as he passed and smiled. The others dissolved into a chorus of giggles.

'Seems you've got an admirer,' said Jo, chuckling.

Hacket shrugged.

'Catch them young, that's my motto,' he told her. 'What about you, Jo? Any entanglements?'

'A boyfriend you mean?' She shook her head and sipped the tea she was carrying. 'Nothing serious.'

Hacket glanced at her, struck, as he had been at their first meeting, by her good looks. Her face was full but not fat, her pointed chin making her look much more thin-featured than she actually was. Her high cheek bones accentuated the look.

Was this how it had started with Nikki? A casual conversation?

Hacket tried to push the thoughts aside, but they persisted. Jo was very attractive indeed, and as she looked at him he found himself gazing deep into her eyes, stumbling through the clichés to find one that described them.

Inviting eyes?

He'd played this game before.

Come to bed eyes?

He forced himself to look away from her, glancing around the playground once again at the noisy throng of children.

'How long have you been married, John?' she asked.

'Five years,' he told her, again avoiding her eyes

'Happy?'

'What makes you ask that?'

'It's an innocent enough question isn't it?' she said, defensively.

Well go on then, tell her, his mind prompted. *Tell her you're happily married. It's just that you wouldn't refuse if she was available would you?*

Or *would* you?

'Jo, can I ask you something,' he said. 'In your official capacity.'

She smiled.

'That does sound grand, John. What is it?'

'Is it possible for a foetus to gestate inside the womb without having travelled along the fallopian tubes?'

'Is that a trick question?' she chuckled. 'What's the next one? Who won the FA cup last year?'

'I'm serious. You're a biologist.'

'I *teach* biology, there's a difference.'

'But is it possible?'

'Through certain forms of artificial insemination yes.'

'You mean that the egg is planted directly into the womb?'

She nodded.

'Is it fertilised first?' he wanted to know. 'I mean, the egg couldn't be placed in the womb then fertilised by normal means?'

'No,' she said, flatly. 'There are certain nutrients and proteins found in the ovaries and the fallopian tube which are essential to the development of the foetus.' She looked hard at him. 'If you don't mind me saying, John, this is a little *deep* for this time of the day isn't it? We're doing playground duty not "Mastermind".'

'Just humour me will you? What about the growth rate of the foetus, is there any way it could be speeded up? To cut the gestation period for instance?'

'Well, theoretically, yes.'

Hacket looked at her, stopped walking and gripped her arm.

'How?' he wanted to know.

Some of the children nearby saw him grab Jo's arm and turned to look but the two teachers moved on after a moment or two.

'How could it be done?' he repeated.

'Growth is regulated by the pituitary gland. Too little causes dwarfism, too much causes the opposite and disfiguring disease called acromegaly. The gland secretes the hormones that regulate growth.' She looked puzzled. 'I don't know what you're getting at, John.'

'Could the gestation period be altered by these pituitary hormones?' he wanted to know.

'Yes, but no one has ever done that.'

Hacket sucked in an almost painful breath.

'Why do you ask?' Jo persisted.

Hacket didn't answer.

All he was aware of were Curtis' words ringing in his ears.

'This is *my* project, Mr Hacket. *My* treatment.'

Sixty-nine

He pulled a piece of the scab from his hand, picking away at the crusted flesh until it came free.

His eyes, however, did not leave the playground.

So many children, thought Ronald Mills, smiling.

They ranged in age from eight up to about fifteen, he thought, watching as they cavorted noisily around in the school yard.

A tall privet hedge formed a boundary between the school field and the road on one side but Mills could see easily over this barrier as he walked along, glancing at the children as he did.

Groups of boys were playing football, girls were skipping or chasing each other or merely standing around talking.

Mills stopped as he caught sight of two young girls no more than nine years old. The first of them had gleaming blonde hair, so pure it looked almost silver. It reached to the middle of her back and, as she stood talking to her friend, she would occasionally toss the mane of hair with one hand. Her companion was slightly darker and a little taller.

Mills smiled as he gazed at them, feeling the first stirrings in his groin. He slipped one hand into his pocket, rubbing his stiffening penis.

Across the road from the school there was a row of houses, each one painted white with tedious uniformity. It was from the bedroom window of one of these houses that a woman watched Mills.

He stood staring at the children for a moment or two then moved on, looking behind him as he did so.

He saw the woman standing at the window.

She froze as she realised he'd seen her, attempting to duck back behind her curtain, but Mills merely stood gazing up at the window, as if challenging her to re-appear.

She didn't.

After a moment or two he moved on, glancing one last time at the two children in the field beyond.

It took him less than fifteen minutes to wander around the entire perimeter of the school and he came to the gates where he had begun his vigil earlier. There he lit up a cigarette and continued gazing into the playground.

He recognised Hacket immediately.

The teacher was with a woman, walking slowly, talking to her.

Mills sucked hard on his cigarette and watched Hacket with the same determined intent as a predator watching its prey.

He didn't know how long he stood there, but finally the sound of a bell disturbed his observations.

The children flooded towards the school buildings, Hacket and the woman were caught up in the flow and, in moments, they too were gone.

The playground was empty again.

Mills finished his cigarette then turned and headed back to his car.

He was smiling as he slid behind the wheel.

Seventy

The house was in silence when he entered.

Hacket paused by the front door, listening for any noise from within but, upon hearing nothing, he gently closed the door and walked into the sitting room.

Sue was lying on the sofa, her eyes closed.

Hacket looked at her worriedly and immediately crossed to her, kneeling beside her, shaking her gently to rouse her. She opened her eyes, looked up at him and smiled.

'Are you OK?' he asked, softly.

She nodded and sat up, rubbing her temple.

'Just a bit of a headache,' she told him.

'How did it go this morning?' he wanted to know. 'With Curtis? I thought you might have phoned when you got back.'

'I didn't want to disturb you. Besides, there was nothing out of the ordinary. Everything was fine. I *feel* fine.'

'How long did it take?'

'I was back home within two hours. Doctor Curtis told me to take it easy so I did. I must have dropped off.' She began to rise. 'I'll get the dinner.'

'No, Sue, leave it. Just sit,' Hacket told her, crossing to the drinks cabinet. He poured himself a large whisky and Sue a Martini. Then he sat beside her on the sofa, easing one arm round her shoulders.

'What happened?' he wanted to know.

'It was simple, just like Curtis said it would be.' She told him what had happened. The injection. The period of sleep which followed. Hacket listened intently, sipping his drink occasionally.

'Did Curtis say anything more about the nature of the treatment? What it involved?'

'He told us about it the other evening, John,' she said, wearily.

'He didn't tell us everything,' Hacket protested.

'You're never satisfied are you?' she snapped. 'Why do you need to know so much? Surely the most important thing is that we can have another child.'

'I don't like the idea of you being used as a guinea pig.'

'Don't be ridiculous. You speak as if I'm the first he's treated. We know the treatment works.'

'Yes, we just don't know what the treatment *is*.'

She shook her head.

'I've been thinking about it,' Hacket continued. 'I was talking to one of the other teachers today.'

'About *this?*' Sue blurted, angrily. 'It's *our* business, John.'

'Calm down, Sue, I just needed to know a few things. I think I might know what Curtis is doing. What some parts of the treatment are. One of the biology teachers, Jo, she said . . .'

'*She?*' Sue interrupted. 'It's always a woman isn't it? You always seem to get on better with women, John. Is it easier to talk about your problems to a woman than another man?'

He knew where this was leading.

'She was better qualified to answer my questions,' he said, irritably.

'Well, a teacher is a step up from a secretary isn't it?' said Sue, acidly.

'For Christ's sake.'

'A little talk. Is that how it started before? With the other one?'

Hacket glared at her, his anger mixed with the guilt which still plagued him. He resented Sue for making him feel that guilt again. He got up and poured himself another drink, his back to her.

'Are we going to talk about this or not?' he asked.

'What? You mean about what your lady friend told you today? Or about our baby? Except you seem to be more interested in your little chat.'

Hacket turned slowly.

'I don't want to argue, Sue. Especially when we've nothing to argue about. I just want you to hear what I've got to say.'

She exhaled deeply.

'Go on.'

'The treatment which Curtis perfected, from what he told us, it sounds like some kind of growth drug. He said the foetus would develop at an increased rate. I think I know what he's doing. What he's using.'

Sue looked on impassively.

'The drug must contain some traces of pituitary secretion in order to cause that acceleration.'

'So what if it does?' she said, flatly.

'The baby could be affected by it. If the dose was wrong it could be too small, perhaps even deformed.'

'And your *friend* told you this, did she?' said Sue, her voice heavy with sarcasm.

'I mentioned it to her, she gave me her opinion,' he said.

'I don't care, John. I knew the risks, we both did. Do you honestly think that a man of Curtis' expertise is going to give me the wrong dose? He said himself he'd treated other women. He's not some mad scientist from a bloody horror film, he's a trained doctor and I don't care what your friend says. I'd trust Curtis with my life. Mine and our baby's.'

'Just try to see my point of view,' he asked. 'I love you. You're all I have since Lisa died. I don't want to lose you too.'

Sue got to her feet and headed for the hallway.

'If you don't want to lose me, then don't stand in my way,' she said. 'Let me have this baby.'

He heard her footsteps as she climbed the stairs.

Hacket waited another moment then poured himself some more whisky, downing the contents of the tumbler in one gulp.

He suddenly felt very alone.

Seventy-one

Ronald Mills pulled the .38 from beneath the pillow and flipped out the cylinder, turning it slowly. Then he snapped it back into position and pushed the gun back out of sight.

Whenever he left the hotel he would take the gun with him, stuffed into the pocket of his jacket. The knife he would slide into his belt but now, he didn't intend leaving The Bull for the rest of the evening so he left the weapons beneath the pillow.

He crossed to the window which looked out onto the main street of Hinkston and peered down at the dozen or so people passing by. It was late, almost 10.30 p.m., the cinema down the street had emptied out about fifteen minutes earlier and the disco didn't open during the week, so the street was quiet.

Mills glanced across at the phone beside his bed.

There was a knock on the bedroom door and he opened it.

Paula Kirkham stood before him holding a tray.

She smiled broadly, shaking her head gently, allowing her long hair to cascade over her shoulders. She wore no bra beneath her T-shirt and Mills noticed that her nipples were straining against the material.

He stepped back to let her into the room, watching as she set the tray of food down on the bedside table.

'Will there be anything else?' she asked, smiling.

'No,' said Mills, holding the door open, as if to emphasise the fact that he wanted her out.

She looked most put out and wiggled past him, glancing briefly at him. He closed the door and she heard him lock it.

Paula hesitated outside the door, ear pressed close to it.

The man didn't seem attracted to her.

He'd been a guest at the hotel for the last five days, keeping himself to himself, ignoring the other guests and her own advances. She didn't think too much of him. Ugly bastard really.

But, he was single.

Alone.

He was a perfect choice.

Just like the man before him.

She struggled to remember his name.

Jennings, that was it. She smiled as she remembered.

The ones before Jennings she could *not* recall.

There had been too many.

She stood for a moment longer outside the door then slowly made her way along the corridor to her own room.

Mills heard her footsteps as she wandered away, only then did he turn his attention to the plate of food which she'd brought him. He nibbled at one of the sandwiches, his eyes flicking back and forth towards the phone every now and then. Finally he pushed the remains of the sandwich into his mouth and reached for the receiver.

Pulling the number from the pocket of his jacket he dialled.

And waited.

'Come on you fucker,' he murmured, listening to the purring at the other end.

The phone was finally picked up.

It was a woman's voice on the other end.

Mills sat listening to her, his breathing subdued, the smile spreading across his face.

'Who is this?' she asked.

He put the phone down.

Another five minutes and he called again.

This time he recognised Hacket's voice.

'Who's there?' the teacher snapped.

Mills sat on the edge of the bed, the phone held slightly away from his ear.

'Can you hear me?' Hacket rasped.

Mills put down the phone.

He chuckled, the grin slowly fading.

The game was nearly over.

Hacket's time had come.

Mills held the knife up before him.

And then there was the woman.

Paula Kirkham stood naked outside the door, her breathing low and rapid, like an animal in the heat.

She glared at the door as if trying to see through it to the man beyond.

To Ronald Mills.

She pressed herself close to the cold wood, feeling her nipples stiffen as she rubbed herself gently against the smooth paintwork, feeling the moistness between her legs.

Her mouth hung open, streamers of sputum dripping from it as she salivated madly.

She wiped her mouth with the back of her hand and smiled.

Seventy-two

She heard movement on the landing.

Julie Clayton sat up, her ears alert for the slightest sound.

Footsteps on the carpet.

She swung herself out of bed, jabbing her husband as she did so.

Mike rolled onto his back and groaned, rubbing his eyes.

'What is it?' he croaked, seeing Julie pull on her dressing gown. He glanced at the clock and saw that it was almost 3.36 a.m. 'Shit.'

'Mike, hurry,' she said, moving towards the bedroom door.

The expression on her face told him how frightened she was. He hauled himself out of bed, following her out onto the landing.

She was approaching Craig's room, aware of the sounds coming from within.

'Oh God,' murmured Mike. 'Not again.'

Stuart Lewis stood over the baby, looking down, his eyes fixed to the blazing stare which seemed to pin him as surely as light draws a moth. He could not look away from his son.

The baby was gurgling loudly, rocking itself back and

forth in its cot frenziedly, grasping at the sides with its tiny fingers.

Michelle joined him, reaching for the baby but Stuart put out an arm to hold her back.

'He needs me, Stuart,' she protested but her husband merely remained where he was, looking down at his child, watching as the boy suddenly stopped thrashing about and lay still, gazing up at his parents. His eyes flicking back and forth from one to the other.

Lewis shook his head slowly.

'It's not *us* he needs,' he said, quietly.

And she understood.

Elaine Craven picked up the phone immediately it rang. Despite the fact that it was so early in the morning she knew who it would be, and she was not wrong.

The voice at the other end belonged to Patricia Stokes.

It was her daughter, Emma, she said.

Elaine said she understood.

Patricia wasn't sure what to do.

Elaine tried to reassure her, touching her own bandaged arm as she spoke.

Upstairs she could hear the shouts and snarls.

She spoke calmly and slowly to Patricia who seemed to relax a little, the longer the conversation went on. Finally she said goodbye and returned to her own problem.

To her Emma.

Elaine waited by the phone a moment longer then she took a deep breath and made her way back up the stairs.

It had happened so quickly this time.

The shouting continued.

As she reached the landing she had to steady herself against the bannister, noticing that her hands were shaking.

She thought she had become used to it by now, but, somehow, the fear still remained.

Seventy-three

She hadn't mentioned the pain to Hacket.

Hadn't thought it worth talking about the silent twinges which she felt around her vagina, especially during their lovemaking.

But now, as Sue Hacket reached for the can on the shelf before her, she sucked in a deep breath, reacting as if she had been punched. The pain was sudden and severe. She gripped the shopping trolley for a second, waiting for the discomfort to subside, which, thankfully, it did. A woman passed and glanced at her, noticing the look on Sue's face and, for a moment, Sue thought the woman was going to stop, but she merely smiled and carried on with her own shopping.

Sue dropped the can into her trolley and walked on, parading up and down each aisle, filling the trolley, trying to ignore the stabs of pain telling herself that they were lessening.

Curtis had said nothing about side-effects. Nothing about pain. If she still felt as bad when she reached home she would call him. Visit him if necessary.

However, as she reached the check-out the pains did indeed seem to be diminishing in severity. Sue ran a hand across her belly almost unconsciously as the woman ahead of her packed her groceries into a succession of carrier bags. Sue shuffled uncomfortably as she waited her turn, brushing a speck of dirt from the leg of her jeans.

She waited for the pain to return.

It didn't.

She began unloading her shopping onto the conveyor belt.

If she'd mentioned the pains to Hacket he would have panicked, she thought to herself. He would have started complaining about the treatment again. Why couldn't he just be happy in the knowledge that they were to have another child? Why all the questions and doubts?

She packed the groceries away then paid the cashier, using the trolley to transport the goods out to the car.

As she unlocked the back of the car the pain struck her once more.

A deep burning sensation between her legs and she gripped the trolley for a second until it subsided.

Sue put the groceries in the back of the car then turned to return the trolley.

The man seemed to loom from thin air.

He was carrying an armful of shopping which promptly fell from his grip as he collided with Sue.

'I'm sorry,' she said, dropping to her knees to help him gather up the spilled groceries.

Her own handbag had also fallen in the collision and she scrabbled to retrieve its spilled contents.

'It was my fault,' said the man, shoving tins back into the shopping bag. 'I wasn't looking where I was going.'

The combination of food and the contents of her handbag had rolled for several feet around the car, some beneath it, and it took about five minutes to pick up everything. Everything except a couple of squashed peaches which had fallen from the man's bag. He looked down at them and shrugged.

'I was eating too much fruit anyway,' he said, wistfully.

Sue smiled, the expression twisting slightly as she felt more pain.

'Are you OK?' the man asked, seeing her wince.

She nodded.

'Thank you, yes. I'll be fine.' She managed another smile. 'Sorry again about . . .' she motioned to his squashed fruit.

'No problem,' he told her, smiling as she climbed into the Metro and started the engine.

He was still smiling as she drove off.

He watched her turn a corner and disappear and, as she did he slid a hand into his pocket and pulled out the prize he'd taken from her handbag in all the confusion.

The purse looked small in his large fist.

Ronald Mills wondered how long it would be before she realised it was gone.

Seventy-four

It was happening too fast.

It was as if someone had pressed the fast-forward button on life, and now events were moving at break-neck speed, faster than he could comprehend.

The ambulance, its siren blaring loudly, took the corner so fast it almost overturned.

Hacket gripped one edge of the stretcher to steady himself, with the other hand he held onto Sue's outstretched fingers. Her face was milk white, a thin sheen of perspiration covering her. She had her eyes closed tightly, her forehead wrinkling as each fresh spasm of pain racked her body.

'Isn't there anything you can give her?' Hacket asked the ambulanceman who rode in the back of the vehicle with them. But the uniformed man merely shook his head and looked on impassively.

'We're almost at the hospital,' he said, flatly, glancing at his watch.

Sue gripped Hacket's hand more tightly and he felt helpless to comfort her. All he could do was to wipe the sweat from her face with his handkerchief.

'It won't be long now,' he murmured. 'Hold on.'

Jesus, he felt so fucking useless. There was nothing he could do to ease her suffering. Nothing to stop the pain.

So much pain.

Her body stiffened then relaxed, as if someone were jabbing her with a cattle prod. The spasms became more frequent, more severe until finally she shouted aloud from the pain which raged inside her swollen belly.

Hacket pulled the sheet down and looked at her stomach. It was bloated and, as he watched, he could see the skin gently undulating.

'How much further?' he rasped, glaring at the ambulanceman.

'Not far,' the man said, also glancing at Sue.

'John.' Her voice rose in volume, dissolving into a scream of pain.

Hacket saw the first droplets of blood dribble from between her legs and she stiffened, her body jerking every few seconds.

She began to breathe rapidly and loudly, holding Hacket's hand so tightly it seemed she would break his fingers.

'It's starting,' she gasped, raising her legs and opening them.

'Help her,' Hacket snarled at the uniformed man, his face pale as he saw a steady flow of crimson beginning to pump from Sue's distended vagina. The outer lips seemed to swell and open like a blossoming flower and the sheet beneath her was stained by her life fluid as the contractions became more savage.

The ambulanceman struggled towards the far end of the vehicle, almost overbalancing as it took another corner doing over fifty. He retrieved some oxygen and stuck the plastic mask over Sue's face, but she merely pushed it away, beyond help now, knowing that there was no turning back.

A searing pain filled her lower body and she felt an incredible pressure building between her legs.

Hacket held her hand, his eyes rivetted to her swollen vagina.

A moment later he saw something white appear between the folds of flesh. Something white and bulbous.

The baby's head.

Pieces of placenta were draped over the skull like bleeding streamers, some of which dangled from Sue's vagina as the child fought to free itself.

The head burst free.

Hacket sucked in a deep breath, watching as the torso began to emerge.

'Nearly finished,' he said. gripping Sue's hand even more tightly. 'Nearly . . .'

The words trailed away and he felt the bile rising in his throat, felt his eyes throbbing in their sockets.

The child had a large hump on its back, just below the nape of its neck.

A hump large enough . . .

Hacket shook his head in horrified disbelief as he saw the child emerge.

Sue was still contracting her muscles, as if anxious to expel the child from her body.

The ambulanceman looked on, his face also pale, his eyes wide.

The hump on the child's back wasn't skin and muscle.

It was bone.

Thick bone.

A second head.

The eyes had formed but where the mouth should have been was a gash. No lips, just a rent across the lower face. But the eyes were open, blinking away the blood and fragments of placenta which coated it.

And, in that brief instant before he finally surrendered

to his revulsion and vomited, Hacket noticed that the obscene hole which passed for a mouth was curling up at either side.

The eyes fixed him in a blazing stare.

The second head was smiling at him.

He sat bolt upright in bed, his breath coming in gasps, his heart thudding madly against his ribs.

He turned to look at Sue, surprised to find her sitting up looking at him.

She was smiling.

Seventy-five

Hacket wiped a hand across his face and sighed, the last vestiges of the nightmare gradually slipping away.

'Jesus,' he murmured. 'I had a bad dream. About you and the baby.'

She held his gaze for a moment then slowly leant across and kissed him, her tongue flicking against the hard edges of his tongue before sliding into the warm moistness beyond. Hacket responded, feeling her arms glide around his shoulders. He lay down beside her, raising one knee so that his thigh was rubbing against her vagina. She was already wet and he felt her moisture dampen his leg as he ground it against her, his own movements matched by her slow rhythmic thrusting. She moaned in his arms as he allowed one hand to find her right breast, teasing the nipple between his thumb and forefinger, then kissing the swollen bud for a moment before transferring his attention to her left breast.

Sue reached down and cupped his testicles, rubbing gently, grazing the base of his shaft with the nail of her index finger.

Hacket felt a familiar warmth beginning to spread around his groin.

Sue arched her back as he slid down the bed, his tongue flicking across her nipples while his probing fingers gently outlined the edges of her vaginal lips, parting them, spreading the tumescent flesh like the petals of a musky flower.

'Love me,' she murmured, her eyes closed.

Hacket felt her hands on his back. Felt her nails raking his skin.

'Jesus,' he hissed as she pulled her nails hard across his shoulder.

She raised the hand before her and saw the tiny pieces of his flesh hanging from her nails. She smiled down at him and Hacket looked into her eyes.

He could feel the grazes on his shoulder.

The tiny dribble of blood from the four places she had scraped him.

He slid back up the bed, kissing her breasts again, this time returning to her mouth. They kissed feverishly, his tongue plunging deep into her mouth.

She took his bottom lip between her teeth, sucking gently, then chewing.

She bit hard.

'Sue, for Christ's sake,' he hissed, drawing back. He put a finger to his lip and found that there was blood dribbling from it.

'Please, John, just love me,' she gasped, a note of pleading in her voice, 'Like you were doing before.'

Hacket hesitated a moment then slid down her body once more, blood from his cut lip staining her breasts and belly as his tongue flicked over the warm flesh. He probed inside her navel with his tongue, slowing his pace as he drew nearer to the spot he sought. The tightly curled hair between her legs through which his fingers were already gliding. He withdrew one from her vagina, drawing a glistening trail across her belly with her own moisture. She gasped and pushed him further down towards her burning desire.

Hacket licked her belly again, tasting her wetness which he had smeared there.

The skin of her stomach rose a fraction beneath his tongue.

At first he thought it was a muscular contraction but, when it happened a second time he sat up, looking down at her belly.

'What's wrong?' she said, quietly. 'Don't stop now.'

Hacket rubbed the palm of his hand gently over her stomach.

He felt the movement beneath his palm.

Like..

Like what?

Like the first movements of a growing child?

'It's impossible,' said Hacket, as if in answer to his own thoughts.

'John, what's wrong?' she wanted to know, watching as he moved away slightly, his eyes still on her stomach.

Was this another dream?

'I felt something,' he said. 'Like..' He was struggling for the words, aware of how ridiculous it sounded. 'Like a baby moving.'

'Isn't it wonderful?' she beamed.

'Sue, it's not possible,' he snapped. 'Curtis treated you two days ago.'

'*Accelerated growth.*'

Hacket shook his head. No, this wasn't real. The foetus

couldn't possibly have developed at such incredible speed. He had imagined it. Yes, that was the answer. He had imagined it.

Her stomach moved slightly again.

Sue pressed her fingers to the spot and smiled.

'Aren't you happy, John?' she said, smiling broadly. 'I am.'

'This isn't normal, Sue. I don't know what Curtis has done to you but it's not right . . .'

She cut him short.

'I'll tell you what he's done,' she snapped. 'He's given me what you never could give me. He's given me hope.'

'At least let another doctor examine you,' Hacket pleaded. 'There could be complications. Something could have gone wrong.'

'That's what you want isn't it?' she snarled. 'You want something to go wrong. You want me to lose this child don't you?'

'Don't be ridiculous, Sue. I'm worried about your health.'

'No you're not. You just don't want me to have another child. Well I'll make sure I don't lose this one. It was your fault Lisa died,' she hissed, hatred in her eyes. '*You* killed her.'

'Sue,' he said, his own anger building.

'If it hadn't been for you she'd still be here now.'

'Drop it,' he told her.

'If not for you and your whore.'

'I mean it,' he said, angrily. 'Shut up.'

'You killed our first child, I won't let you kill this one.'

'SHUT UP.'

He acted instinctively, not even realising what he was doing.

Hacket struck his wife a stinging back-hand blow across the face.

She fell back on the bed, glaring up at him.

Despite his anger he felt the remorse immediately.

'Oh God, I'm sorry,' he whispered, moving towards her.

'Get away,' she roared. 'Leave me alone. Leave me and my baby alone.'

Hacket looked at her. The blazing eyes, her hair coiled around her face and shoulders like damp reptilian tails. She looked like some modern-day Gorgon.

'What's happening to you, Sue?' he asked, quietly, his voice cracking. 'I'm losing you again and I don't want that.'

'Then stay out of my fucking way,' she snarled, getting to her feet. She tugged a sheet from the bed and wrapped it around her.

Hacket could only watch as she padded towards the door.

He heard her cross the landing then heard the door of the spare room slam shut.

Alone, he knelt on the bed, head bowed.

As if in prayer.

Seventy-six

It was almost noon when she heard the knock on the front door.

Sue frowned and got to her feet, lowering the volume on the stereo as she passed.

It was too early for Hacket to be back for lunch. For one thing he hardly ever left the school during the lunch hour and, also, he had his key. He'd have no need to knock. She wasn't expecting Julie until later that afternoon.

She reached the front door and opened it.

The man who stood there looked vaguely familiar to her.

'Mrs Hacket?' he asked.

She nodded, somewhat tentatively.

'Yours I believe,' said the man and held out his hand.

Sue smiled as she saw her purse cradled in the palm of the visitor.

'You dropped it the other day when we bumped into each other,' said Ronald Mills, smiling. 'I'm afraid I looked through it in the hope of finding your address. I wanted to return it to you.'

'You're very kind,' said Sue, beaming. 'I thought I'd lost it.'

Mills shrugged, smiled even more broadly and handed her the purse.

As he did, Sue noticed the tattoo on his hand. The rough design, the discoloured flesh and the raw skin beneath where the scab had been picked away. He turned to leave but she stopped him.

'Look, I really am grateful. I don't know how to thank you,' she said. 'Would a cup of tea be enough? It doesn't seem like much of a reward, but . . .'

'That would be ample reward, Mrs Hacket,' said Mills, holding up a hand. 'Thank you.'

He followed her inside, his smile fading briefly as she turned her back on him.

The knife felt heavy jammed into his belt.

They exchanged pleasantries about the weather. He told her his name was Neville, that he was visiting relatives in Hinkston.

As he sipped his tea he glanced around the sitting room.

A photo of a little girl on the sideboard.

A little girl he recognised.

He felt the beginnings of an erection at the recollection of how close he had been to that girl. How close. How he'd held her.

He remembered using the knife on her.

The same knife which was now stuck in his belt.

'Your husband is out at work then?' he said, gazing at Sue.

'He's a teacher,' she said. 'He works in the school here,' she hooked a thumb in the direction of the building which backed onto their garden. 'That's why we moved here.'

'Your children must like it here,' he said, smiling, picking at the scab on his hand with his nail.

Sue smiled thinly.

'Your little girl, what's her name?' he asked.

'Lisa,' Sue said, quickly, then, trying to change the subject. 'Where abouts in Hinkston do your relatives live?'

'Lisa,' said Mills, ignoring her attempts to steer the conversation along different lines. 'How pretty. She's pretty too.' He got to his feet, crossed to the picture and picked it up. 'You don't mind do you?' he said, almost apologetically, regarding the photo carefully. 'Such a lovely child.'

With his back to Sue his smile faded once again.

So lovely.

'I can't thank you enough for bringing my purse back, Mr Neville,' Sue said, clearing her throat. 'I thought it had been stolen.'

'There are so many dishonest people in the world today, Mrs Hacket. You're lucky that it was me who found it. It could have been a criminal who picked it up.' He chuckled.

Sue found that his eyes were upon her once more, his stare unblinking.

'More tea?' she asked, anxious for the chance of a respite from those piercing eyes.

'Very kind,' he said, handing her the cup.

She took it and headed for the kitchen, aware of Mills behind her.

'You have a lovely house,' he said, stepping into the kitchen, watching as she poured him another cup of tea.

She thanked him.

'Lovely house. Lovely child.' He ran appraising eyes over her slim body. The tight jeans, the blouse which she always wore for housework, paint stained and threadbare in places. Her hair had been washed that morning and hung past her shoulders in soft waves. 'And you're lovely too if you don't mind me saying.'

She handed him his tea, beginning to feel a little uncomfortable. She sat down at the kitchen table.

Mills sat down opposite her, his eyes fixed upon her.

As he reached into his jacket pocket for his cigarettes his hand brushed the handle of the knife.

'You don't mind if I smoke do you?' he asked, lighting up. He offered her one and she declined, explaining about the baby. 'You are lucky. I love little children myself,' he said, grinning.

Sue shuffled uncomfortably in her seat, watching him as he sucked slowly on the cigarette. It seemed to take him an eternity to smoke it. Then, finally, he got to his feet and said he would have to go. Sue breathed an almost audible sigh of relief.

He followed her to the front door, standing behind her as she opened it.

She thanked him again and watched as he walked up the path, stopping half-way to smile courteously.

'Perhaps we'll see each other again,' he said. 'When we're shopping.' He chuckled.

Sue nodded, waved and shut the door.

She let out a deep breath, standing with her back to the door for a moment, listening for footsteps, almost as if she expected him to return.

He didn't.

She rebuked herself for feeling so uncomfortable in the man's presence, for being so jumpy.

Never mind, she told herself, he was gone now, *and* she had her purse back.

'Perhaps we'll see each other again,' she said, remembering his words. 'No chance,' she thought aloud.

It was then that the phone rang.

Seventy-seven

Doctor Edward Curtis glanced at the list of names written on the pad before him. He sighed as he ran his finger down the neatly written names. Finally he sat back in his chair, hands pressed together before him as if in some meditative gesture.

He was still sitting like that when the door opened and his receptionist popped her head round.

'Your next patient is here, Doctor,' she said.

Curtis nodded and sat forward, some kind of acknowledgement of the receptionist's presence. She retreated back to her own outer office and Curtis pushed the notepad bearing the names out of sight under a pile of papers.

He ran a hand through his hair and waited for the knock on his door.

It came a moment later and Sue Hacket walked in.

They exchanged greetings and she felt a peculiar pleasure from the fact that Curtis seemed genuinely pleased to see her.

He asked how she was feeling.

She mentioned the pains.

Always pain.

'I'd better check you over,' said the doctor, smiling. 'We can't be too cautious at this stage.' He motioned her towards the couch in the corner of his room and Sue paused beside it.

'Do you want me to undress?' she asked, her eyes never leaving his.

'Yes please,' he said, quietly.

She began unbuttoning her blouse.

Curtis, for his own part, turned to a tray of instruments covered by a sterile gauze sheet. As he lifted it up Sue saw two or three hypodermic needles lying there.

She pulled the blouse off and began unfastening her jeans, simultaneously kicking off her shoes.

'Did you tell your husband about the pains you were getting?' Curtis asked.

'No.'

'Why not?'

'He seems worried enough already, I didn't see the point in making things worse.' She pulled her jeans off and stood before him in just her bra and panties.

Curtis smiled at her and asked her to climb up onto the couch, which she duly did.

'Just relax,' he told her, his hands settling on her stomach. He began to knead the flesh gently, pressing occasionally, his fingers moving lower until he was brushing against the top of her knickers, stirring the silky strands of pubic hair which were in view.

'Show me where the pain was,' he said.

Sue took his hand and guided it between her legs, allowing him to rest against the warmth of her crotch. He pressed and stroked gently along her inner thighs and across her mound. She breathed deeply, her eyes closing. Keeping one hand on her warm vagina he took his stethoscope and pressed it to her belly.

Then moved it across. And down.

'Are you still getting pain,' he wanted to know.
'Only occasionally,' she breathed.
'The baby is fine, as far as I can tell. There's nothing to worry about,' he said, softly.
'When is it due?' she said. 'I know it's probably ages yet.'
'It needn't be,' Curtis said. 'If you want to accelerate the growth there is a way. If you're willing. It involves another injection though.'
'Do it,' she said, flatly. 'Now.'
Curtis smiled.
Sue hooked her thumbs into the sides of her panties and began to ease them over her hips, exposing her silky hairs and her vagina.
Curtis reached for the hypodermic, drew some fluid off from a bottle on the tray then eased the steel point past her outer lips.
She felt the steel penetrate her and it made her gasp. But there was little pain and, as he withdrew, she was smiling.
She dressed again slowly, almost reluctantly, then sat down opposite him at the desk.
'If you have any more trouble let me know,' Curtis said. 'Come and see me anytime.'
She thanked him and got to her feet, ready to leave.
'You don't know how much this means to me, doctor,' she said, pausing at the door. 'I don't know how I can ever thank you.'
Curtis smiled benignly.
Sue closed the door behind her and he heard her footsteps echoing away up the corridor.
His smile faded rapidly and he reached for the pad once more, his eyes skimming over the names he'd looked at a dozen times already that morning. The calls had all come in during a ninety-minute spell earlier that morning.
Calls from Elaine Craven. From Julie Clayton.

Stuart Lewis had rung. So too had Patricia Stokes.

All had been frightened.

Even the call from The Bull had sounded more urgent than usual. Could he come and see Paula, Mrs Kirkham had asked. It was very important.

Curtis knew it was important.

And he knew why.

He sighed as he re-read the list once more.

Had the time come again so soon?

Seventy-eight

Hacket prodded his dinner with his knife then looked across the table at Sue.

She was eating heartily, unaware of his stare.

'What else did Curtis say?'

Hacket finally broke the silence, dropping his cutlery on to the plate.

'He said the baby was fine,' Sue informed him. 'He said there was nothing to worry about.'

'And you believe him?'

She sighed.

'I have no reason to *disbelieve* him. John, I feel fine. I'm fine and the baby's fine. The only one who seems to have any problems is you.' She regarded him coldly for a second. 'He *did* say that the baby would be born earlier than we'd first thought.'

'How can that be possible?' he demanded.

Sue finished chewing the mouthful of food she had then put down her knife and fork.

'He gave me another injection,' she said, quietly.

'Jesus Christ. What of? More of his miracle fucking treatment? We don't know what's happening, Sue. Haven't you stopped to think about this? To think about what's happening to *you* as well as the baby?'

She didn't answer.

'You're changing, Sue,' he told her. 'Your attitude. Your temperament. Even your character, and it's all down to this fucking treatment.' He hissed the last few words through clenched teeth. 'You're blind to what it's doing to you. The only thing you can think about is that damned baby – you don't seem to care that Curtis could be doing you harm.'

'And all you seem to care about is yourself,' she countered. 'I thought you'd be pleased to think that we could have another child. You were the one who said you wanted to start afresh, a new beginning. And when that chance comes along all you do is criticise and complain.'

'I'm worried about you, can't you see that?'

'I can see your jealousy, John.'

'What the hell are you talking about.'

'You're jealous of Curtis.'

'Don't be so bloody ridiculous,' he snorted.

'It's *him* who gave me that hope. Is that what really hurts you? Is *that* why you're so opposed to this child?'

Hacket didn't answer. The muscles at the side of his jaw throbbed angrily and he pushed himself away from the table, getting to his feet.

'You don't understand do you?' he snapped, heading towards the sitting room.

Sue followed, watching him pour himself a large measure of whiskey. He downed most of it in one gulp and re-filled the glass.

'Are you going to get drunk now?' she asked.

'No. I'm going to have one more then I'm going to see Curtis,' he said, flatly.

The look on her face changed from anger to surprise.

'What for?' she wanted to know.

'I want to talk to him about a few things. Like what this treatment really is. What exactly he's been injecting into you and the other women he's treated. What is it that can make a child grow at five times its usual rate?'

'You can't just go barging into his house, John,' she said.

'Can't I?' he said, defiantly.

'This is because of that girl isn't it?' said Sue, acidly. 'That other teacher you spoke to. Until then you were as happy as I was about the possibility of having another child. But since you spoke to her you've changed your mind.'

'That's bloody stupid. It's got nothing to do with what she said.'

'Hasn't it?'

'You don't have to be a genius to figure out that things aren't quite right here. I don't like all the mystery surrounding what Curtis is doing.'

'There is no mystery.'

'He didn't tell us everything. He told us what he wanted us to know. Nothing more.'

Hacket finished his drink and slammed the glass down.

'Well, now I'm going to see what he's got to say.'

'No,' she hissed, blocking his path, her eyes narrowed in anger.

'Sue, get out of my way.'

She spread her arms so that he couldn't pass her.

'Come on,' Hacket said, quietly, a little unsettled by the look in her eye. 'You see what this is doing to *us* too. I told you, you're changing.'

'It's always me isn't it? Put the blame on me. As long as you don't have to face up to your own guilt. It's a wonder you didn't blame my father for Lisa's death. I mean, if I hadn't been out visiting him that night then you could have been with your bit on the side without having to worry. I'd have been in the house. You'd have kept a clear conscience.'

'Get out the way, Sue,' he snapped, gripping one of her arms.

She spun round, her left hand clawing at his face, her nails raking his cheek.

Hacket hissed in pain as he felt his flesh tear.

She struck at him again but he managed to deflect the second blow, gripping her wrists, holding her at bay.

He was surprised by her strength.

'Get off me,' she yelled at him, trying to shake loose of his grip.

She kicked out, catching him a stinging blow on the shin and he winced in pain, pushing her backwards, bolting for the door. She was at him immediately, gripping a handful of his hair, tugging so hard that several strands came away from his scalp.

Again he swung round, this time managing to pin her arms behind her back. He lifted her bodily and carried her back into the sitting room.

As he was about to drop her onto the sofa she spat in his face.

Hacket looked at her, both surprised and horrified by the savagery of her reactions.

He pushed her away from him as if she had some kind of contagion.

Then, as she struggled to get up he sprinted for the front door, opened it and hurried up the path towards the waiting car.

'You stay away from him,' Sue shrieked from the door, watching as the car pulled away, its tail lights swallowed up in the darkness.

She was weeping madly, tears of rage pouring down her cheeks. She stepped away from the door and slammed it, walking through into the sitting room, her fury unabated.

She crossed to the window and looked out into the night then she turned and glanced at the clock on the mantelpiece.

9.46 p.m.

She looked to the phone.

Should she warn Curtis?

She was moving towards the receiver when the first stab of pain tore through her.

Seventy-nine

Ronald Mills looked at his watch.

9.54 p.m.

He picked a piece of meat from between his front teeth and spat it onto the carpet of the room then he crossed to the bed and pulled the .38 from beneath the pillow.

He sat on the edge of the bed, dug his hand in his jacket pocket and took out six bullets. He flipped the cylinder out then carefully loaded the pistol. That done, he snapped the cylinder back into place and spun it, holding the gun at arms length, peering down the sight.

Not that he would need to aim.

He intended getting close.

And then there was always the knife.

He wanted to be near to Hacket, and to the woman as well.

Wanted to see their pain, feel their agony.

Just like he had done with their child.

The thought of the act he had already committed and that he was about to commit caused the beginning of an erection which he savoured, smiling as he felt the stiffness growing.

Perhaps he would gag them in case their screams were heard, but that, he reasoned, would deprive him of one of the most pleasurable parts of the exercise. Hearing them beg for their lives.

He would take off the woman's breasts.

He had already decided that.

Cut deeply and sever them both.

He would make Hacket watch while he performed the act, slicing each mammary in turn. Then he would cut her. Five, six, seven. A dozen times. He wanted her to die slowly. He wanted Hacket to see it.

Then he would kill Hacket.

He would carve the man's eyes from their sockets.

'If thine eye offend thee, pluck it out,' he chuckled.

He looked again at his watch then he headed for the door, locking it behind him, feeling the gun in his pocket, the knife wedged into his belt.

The drive to the Hackets' house would take him about fifteen minutes.

It was 10.01.

Eighty

The Renault skidded slightly on the road as Hacket spun the wheel and guided the vehicle into the driveway which led towards Curtis' house. The smoothness of tarmac was replaced by the loud crunching of gravel as Hacket drove on.

A powerful wind was gusting across the large open front garden bending a number of topiary animals to such extreme angles it seemed they would be uprooted.

Hacket heard the strong gusts hissing around the car but his attention was on the house itself.

The place seemed to be growing from the night itself. Only the dark outline showed that there was a building there at all, its frontage finally illuminated by the lights of Hacket's car.

There wasn't a light to be seen inside the house itself.

The teacher brought the car to a halt outside the front door, noticing immediately that Curtis' car was not in evidence. No lights. No car. *Nobody home?* He swung himself out of the Renault and crossed to the front door, the powerful wind buffeting him, blowing through his hair. He almost overbalanced, such was the force of the gusts. But, eventually he reached the large oak door and knocked hard, the sound dying away rapidly beneath the persistent howl of the wind.

There was no answer.

Hacket knocked again, harder this time.

Still no response.

He stepped back from the door and looked up at the windows. What little natural light there was reflected back off them and it reminded Hacket of staring into blind eyes. He looked around, wondering if there was access to the rear of the house.

To his right was a path which curved around one corner of the ivy-covered building. The teacher headed towards it. As he turned the corner the wind seemed to hit him with increased ferocity and he steadied himself against the wall of the house for a second before walking on. The path, sure enough, led to the back of the building but, as with the front, Hacket found it devoid of light.

Perhaps Curtis was out on a call, he reasoned. Well, if

that was so he'd wait for him. He'd wait as long as he had to in order to speak to the other man, to find out what the hell he was up to, to find out what he'd been pumping into Sue.

Hacket found the back door and pummelled on it angrily as if expecting his outburst to elicit some kind of reaction.

He stepped back, passing along the path, peering into a couple of the windows close by. He could see nothing through the gloom. His frustration and anger growing he turned away from the house, glancing out over the similarly well-kept back garden. The rockery close by, the lawn which sloped down towards the high privet hedge.

Hacket frowned, narrowing his eyes in an effort to see through the gloom.

Down by the high privet hedge something moved.

He was sure of it.

Maybe the wind had disturbed one of the well-kept bushes down there, he thought at first. Maybe.

He took a couple of steps onto the lawn, his eyes fixed on the spot ahead of him where he was sure he'd seen the movement.

Whatever he'd seen before stirred again.

Hacket froze for a moment, not sure whether to advance or remain where he was. He swallowed hard, his initial anger now tempered slightly by the realisation that he was trespassing. If Curtis chose to, he could prosecute.

The doubts vanished from Hacket's mind as quickly as they'd come. What the hell did he care about trespassing? He had more important things to worry about than that. Besides, if Curtis had nothing to hide then he would not object to this visit.

Fuck him, thought Hacket, heading for the bottom of the garden and the area where he'd seen the movement.

As he drew closer to the high privet hedge he heard a

high pitched squealing sound, carried to him on the blustery wind.

He squinted through the darkness once more and saw, a couple of feet ahead, a rusty metal gate set into the hedge.

It was a kind of entrance, he reasoned, the gate swinging wildly back and forth, flung helplessly by the wind.

Hacket paused as he reached the gate, gripping it in one hand to stop the maddening squeak of the hinges. He looked beyond into the area shielded by the high hedge.

Just a simple square of slightly overlong grass, a few flowers.

The flowers were scattered over the ground, tossed wantonly by the breeze.

He saw the piece of flat stone at the centre of the square.

Hacket let go of the gate, pulling it shut behind him as he moved towards the flat stone, finally glancing down at it. Even from so close it was difficult to read the words upon the marble. He knelt and fumbled in his pocket for his lighter. However, no sooner had he coaxed a flame from it than the wind blew it out. Cursing, Hacket leaned closer in an effort to read the words on the stone, realising, as he did, that it was a gravestone.

He ran his fingers across the stone, almost like a blind man, picking out each word carefully.

MARGARET LAWRENSON
BELOVED WIFE AND MOTHER
DIED JUNE 5th 1965

Hacket frowned.

'Lawrenson,' he murmured. He didn't see the connection.

He was still pondering this anomaly when he heard the sound of a car approaching from the front of the house.

Hacket got to his feet and sprinted across the rear lawn towards the house.

The sound of the engine grew louder, tyres were crunching on the gravel drive.

The teacher pressed himself against the wall and peered round into the drive.

Doctor Edward Curtis brought his car to a halt outside the house, switched off the engine then swung himself out from behind the wheel.

Hacket watched. Waited.

Curtis glanced across at Hacket's car but seemed to pay it little heed, something which puzzled the teacher. Instead, the doctor crossed to the front door and unlocked it, then he returned to the car and fumbled with the bunch of keys, selecting one and pushing it into the lock of the boot.

Hacket watched, unaware that he himself was the target of other eyes.

The figure watched.

And waited.

Eighty-one

'Bastard.'

She muttered the word under her breath, clutching her stomach with one hand, wincing with each fresh stab of pain. But it was not the pain to which she directed her anger. She glanced at the phone, wondering once again, if she should warn Curtis. Tell him that her husband was on his way. She looked at the clock. No, he'd have arrived at the house by now, surely.

Sue exhaled deeply, her mind turning over all the possible scenarios. A row. A fight even. She tried to push the thoughts from her mind.

Why was her husband so obsessed with the treatment she'd received? Why wasn't the gift of a child enough for him?

She felt another stab of pain. One which reached from her vagina to her naval and she sucked in a laboured breath, getting to her feet as if the movement would relieve the pressure on her belly.

The swelling there was only slight, as if she'd just eaten a heavy meal but it felt heavy. Sue felt bloated. Replete. As if the child she was carrying was growing not by the day but by the minute. Its progress to maturity accelerated beyond comprehension.

She walked across to the phone once more, her hand hovering over it for a moment.

Should she call Curtis?

She was still trying to decide when she heard the knock on the front door.

Sue froze for a moment, glancing down at the phone then at the door.

Could it be her husband? Had he finally seen the stupidity of his reactions? Perhaps their night would end in reconciliation instead of anger. She sucked in a deep breath and moved towards the door.

As she opened it she realised that if it had been her husband out there he would have used his key.

Ronald Mills stood on the doorstep, smiling.

Sue saw that he had a hand dug into his jacket pocket but, before she could speak he had pulled it free.

The .38 looked huge as it was pushed into her face.

'Don't scream,' snarled Mills. 'Just step back inside the house.'

She obeyed and he pushed her before him, stepping over the threshold.

The door swung shut behind them.

Eighty-two

The boot of the car opened like a large metallic mouth and, as Hacket watched, Curtis leant forward and scooped something up from within.

Something large.

Something which he struggled to carry.

The object was about five feet long, perhaps larger, thought Hacket. Wrapped in a blanket.

Curtis stood still for a moment, the wind swirling around him, as he braced himself to carry his heavy load.

His large load.

Hacket squinted through the gloom once more.

It was big enough . . .

'Jesus Christ,' he murmured.

Big enough to be a man.

Curtis crossed to the front door of the house and entered, bumping one end of the object he carried against the frame as he entered. Hacket stepped back around the side of the house, pressing his back against the cold stone of the wall, sucking in deep breaths. He stayed there for long seconds then peered around into the drive once more. There was no sign of Curtis, he had not returned to shut the car boot, obviously more intent on depositing his cargo inside the house first.

Hacket realised what he must do.

He scurried towards the open front door and paused by the threshold, enveloped by darkness. Curtis had not bothered to turn on any lights when he'd entered.

From inside the house Hacket heard movement.

He entered, pulling the door closed but not shutting it, momentarily silencing the wild howling of the wind. He stood in the hallway, looking around in the gloom.

To his right there was a wide staircase which looked as

if it had been plucked from some baronial mansion. It rose into even more impenetrable darkness.

To his left was a door.

It was slightly ajar.

Hacket advanced slowly towards it, hearing sounds from beyond. Another door being opened. The occasional bump.

He found himself in what he took to be Curtis' reception.

The door marked 'SURGERY' was open.

He moved through it, slowing his pace slightly as he came to the corridor which linked the doctor's office to the waiting-room. He moved slowly, trying to minimise the sound of his footfalls on the polished floor.

It was like being blind in the narrow passageway. No light to guide him.

It was then that he noticed the smell.

Hacket froze, his throat dry, aware of the pounding of his heart.

He recognised the smell.

Strong and coppery.

As he moved another step forward his foot slid in something wet and he almost overbalanced.

He stepped back, looking down at the spot which had caused him to slide.

He pulled the lighter from his pocket and flicked it on.

Illuminated by the sickly yellow flame was a puddle of blood about three inches across.

There were drops of it all along the corridor – they led to the door of Curtis's office.

Hacket flicked off the lighter and moved on, his initial anger now gradually turning to anxiety and something a little stronger.

Fear, perhaps

Why question it? he told himself. It *was* fear.

As he stood with his hand on the doorknob of the doctor's

office he felt the hair at the back of his neck rise. He pushed the door gently.

It swung open to reveal yet more darkness.

And more blood.

It had dripped onto the carpet. Hacket could see it glistening in the natural light which flooded through the study window.

Outside the wind battered against the windows as if trying to gain entry, its banshee wail rising as Hacket glanced around the room, his gaze eventually coming to rest on yet another door.

It was like a maze inside the house.

He moved towards the last door and peered through it.

This time there was light beyond.

Beyond and below.

He realised that he was looking down into a cellar, lit from overhead by banks of powerful fluorescents.

Of Curtis there was no sign.

Only the drops of blood which spattered the stairs leading down into the cellar.

Hacket waited and watched, backing off slightly when he saw the doctor struggle into view, still carrying the blanket covered form. He finally laid it on a trolley and stepped back, wiping his hands on a paper towel which he then screwed up and tossed into a bin.

Hacket was mesmerised by the tableau before him, his eyes fixed on the blanket-swathed shape.

The wind continued to scream, its cries masking Hacket's low breathing.

If not for the wind he might have heard the heavy footfalls on the wide staircase, descending slowly from above him.

Eighty-three

She knew she was going to die.

It was just a matter of when.

But the inevitability of it made it no more acceptable and her fear grew by the second.

Sue Hacket sat on the chair in the classroom looking at her captor.

Ronald Mills glared back at her, the knife held in one hand, the .38 laying on a nearby desk-top.

She had been surprised at how easily he had gained access to the school, pushing her before him, expecting alarm bells to sound when the main door was eased open. But only silence had greeted her wish. There had been no bells. No panic.

No rescuers.

Mills had dragged her through the deserted school, up and down corridors, up a flight of stairs, finally pushing her into a classroom, hurling her towards a chair.

Then he had pulled some rope from his pocket and tied her to it, pulling so hard on the hemp that it had cut into her wrists and ankles. She could see blood running onto her feet when she glanced down. It looked black in the gloom of the classroom.

'I suppose you wonder who I am,' he said, speaking the first words since he'd brought her to this place.

She tried to swallow but her throat felt constricted.

'Well, don't you?' he hissed.

She nodded.

He moved towards her, the knife pointing at her face. He touched the point to her cheek, drawing it gently, almost lovingly, towards her eye.

She closed her eyes, gritting her teeth against the agony she knew must come next.

He pressed the point of the knife against the corner of her eye.

'Open,' he whispered.

She couldn't. Her eyes remained tightly shut, as if the thin flesh of her eyelids would protect her from the razor-sharp point of the blade.

'Open your eyes,' Mills snarled.

Sue opened them slowly, tears beginning to form, to trickle down her cheeks.

'That's better,' he said, smiling. 'I mean, don't you want to see the face of the man who killed your daughter?'

She felt her stomach contract and her body felt as if it had been wrapped in a freezing shroud.

She stared at him through tear-filled eyes, the knife still pressed against her cheek.

'Now we're going to sit and wait,' he told her, trailing the knife down towards her mouth where he ran the tip across her bottom lip. 'Sit and wait for your husband.'

Eighty-four

Hacket took a step forward as he saw Curtis reach for the corner of the blanket. From his position at the top of the cellar steps, Hacket was hidden from the view of the doctor but still able to see what was happening. He looked on, his heart thudding against his ribs.

Curtis took hold of the blanket and pulled it free.

Hacket had to stifle a gasp.

Lying on the trolley was a man, he guessed in his mid-forties, dressed in a pair of trousers and a shirt, both of which were spattered with blood.

The long doubled edged stiletto blade still protruded from the dead man's right eye.

As Hacket watched, Curtis took hold of the blade and pulled, removing it from the eye with infinite care. He laid the knife on a table beside him, wiping some blood from it with a towel, then pulled off his own jacket and hung it on the back of a chair.

That simple task done he returned to the body and, using all his strength, turned the body over so that it was lying on its stomach.

Blood from the ruptured eye dribbled onto the trolley.

Curtis then pulled another, smaller, trolley towards him and Hacket could see the dozens of medical instruments laid out upon it. As he watched, the doctor reached for a scalpel; then he carefully pushed the hair away from the neck of the corpse and pressed the point of the scalpel to the nape of the neck, close to the base of the skull.

The razor-sharp blade cut effortlessly through flesh and muscle. More dark blood spilled from the incision.

Hacket gritted his teeth as he saw Curtis reach for a larger blade.

Hacket couldn't see but, from the vile sawing sounds which came from below he realised the blade had a serrated edge.

Curtis worked expertly with the tool, finally removing a piece of the occipital bone about two inches wide and three inches long. He discarded it into a metal tray close by.

Even from his high vantage point Hacket could see that the base of the victim's brain was exposed, and it took all the willpower he could muster to prevent himself vomiting. He gripped the door more tightly, hiding behind it, part of him wanting to run, to be away from this scene of butchery, the other telling, forcing him, to remain. Mesmerised by what he saw.

Using a pair of what reminded Hacket of pliers, Curtis cut through the spinal cord.

The snap of breaking bone echoed around the cellar like a gun-shot and the head of the man on the table seemed to collapse forward now, unsupported by the brain stem.

Hacket watched as blood oozed from the open skull, some of it covering Curtis' hands as he worked, but he seemed oblivious to the crimson weepings.

He reached for a small pair of tweezers and another scalpel, pushing the twin prongs deep into the thick grey-pink tissue of the brain, seizing something within its bloodied folds.

Curtis smiled as he gently gripped the pituitary gland between the prongs of the tweezers. One swift nick and the gland came free. He held it before him like some kind of trophy, admiring the swollen, dripping gland for a second before dropping it into a jar filled with clear fluid.

Hacket could stand no more.

He spun round and bolted back through the doctor's office, his only thought now to be away from this place, to tell the police.

To tell his wife.

Sue. Sue. What had Curtis done to *her*?

Hacket slipped on the carpet, fell but dragged himself upright again, not caring if Curtis heard him. He crashed through the door and out into the corridor, heading for the reception then the hall beyond.

If he could reach his car.

He heard footsteps behind him, heard Curtis hurtling up the cellar steps.

Hacket wrenched open the door which led out into the hall, glancing back, convinced that he could outrun the doctor. He was half-smiling when he blundered into the hall.

He collided with the figure.

It stood before him, blocking his path, barring his way to the front door.

Hacket had but one reaction as he looked at the figure.

His eyes bulged madly in their sockets, he fell back and, as he did, he screamed until he thought his lungs would burst.

Eighty-five

'I don't understand,' Sue Hacket said, quietly, tears spilling down her cheeks. 'Why are you doing this?'

Ronald Mills picked a piece of the scab from his left hand and rolled the hardened flesh between his thumb and forefinger.

'Why did you kill Lisa?' Sue persisted.

'Does it matter?' he asked, smiling, thinly. 'It's done now.' He moved closer to Sue, touching her shoulder, gripping it firmly for a second as if he were about to begin massaging it. Instead he pushed the knuckle of his index finger into the hollow beside her collar bone, digging hard until she winced in pain.

'She was pretty, your little girl,' Mills said. 'And so quiet too.'

Sue could not fight back the tears as he began to rub her neck, stroking his hand somewhat clumsily through her hair.

'When I went into her bedroom she didn't make a sound,'

he continued. 'Not even when I climbed onto the bed beside her.

'Please,' Sue said, softly, not wanting to hear.

'I asked her what her name was and she told me. Lisa. Such a pretty name.' He began to tug on Sue's hair then allowed his free hand to slide down the front of her blouse towards her breasts.

'Stop it,' Sue sobbed.

'She started to make a noise when I got out the knife,' Mills said. 'I thought she was going to cry then. That was why I had to put my hand over her mouth.'

The tears were pouring down Sue's face, dripping from her chin, some falling onto the back of Mills probing hand. He gripped one of her breasts hard and squeezed until she groaned in pain.

'She tried to scream when I used the knife on her,' he said, softly, his erection now throbbing against the inside of his trousers. 'But I kept her quiet.' He smiled. 'I pushed the knife into her throat. You should have seen the way her eyes opened up. It was like there was some kind of spring inside her head. I pushed the knife in and she opened her eyes wider. The further I pushed the wider they got. I thought they were going to fall out of her head.

Sue was sobbing uncontrollably now, Mills' hand still roughly kneading her breasts.

'And when I fucked her,' he sighed, wistfully. 'She was so tight. So beautifully tight.'

'You're fucking mad,' Sue wailed, her exhortations dissolving into racking sobs.

'Am I?' he asked, stepping back slightly. 'Could a madman have done what I've done? Tracked you and your husband to this place, planned revenge the way I have done?'

Sue merely shook her head, her cheeks burning, her eyes blurred.

'I'm going to kill your fucking husband,' he told her. 'Do you know why?'

She continued to cry.

'Do you?' he roared at her.

'No,' she yelled back, her body shaking violently.

Mills took a step forward, the knife held before him. He pushed it beneath Sue's chin, pressing just hard enough to puncture the skin. A tiny dribble of blood ran down her neck.

'Because he killed my friend. The only friend I ever had. Your husband killed him. Made him fall under a train. And I saw it all. I saw what he did and now he's going to pay.'

'Haven't you done enough to us?' she sobbed.

Mills smiled crookedly.

He began unbuttoning Sue's blouse.

'Done enough?' he hissed, a slight smile on his face. 'I've only just started.'

Eighty-six

Hacket was sure that his sanity had gone.

He was mad, that was the only answer.

A sane man would not have seen what he saw now.

He pushed himself back along the floor as the figure took a step towards him.

The teacher tried to pull himself upright but it seemed as if all the strength had drained from his body. He felt his bowels loosen, and the hair at the back of his neck stood up sharply. He shook his head slowly, wondering now if he was truly encountering madness.

The figure which faced him was not like those of a nightmare. No mind, however diseased, could conjure up an image like that which now confronted the teacher. No nightmare could be that bad.

It was fully six feet tall, about fifteen stone, perhaps more. A large man. *Man*? Hacket's tortured mind corrected itself. The monstrosity which stood before him was no man.

Supported on two legs the torso seemed much too broad, too heavy to be carried on even limbs as thick as those Hacket saw.

Its skin was pale, darkened only on the forearms by black hair. And there was power in those arms. Hacket could see each muscle clearly defined. Hands like ham-hocks swung from arms which looked a little too long, not quite simian but only a few steps removed. The torso seemed to widen as it reached the chest, and here, beneath the gauze-like shirt which the figure wore, Hacket could see several bulging growths. One on the right breast, another on the left shoulder.

It was the head which caused him to moan aloud as he stared at it.

Head?

Not one but two. Joined at the temple.

Four perfectly formed eyes fixed him in a freezing stare.

The mouths opened simultaneously and, had Hacket been in a position to reason, he may well have realised that the body was controlled by just one brain. The scalps were bald, graced only with fine whisps of gossamer like the hair of old men.

A growth the size of a fist swelled from the right cheek of the left head. Another from the other cranium. The flesh around the eyes was puffy, almost liquescent, as if it were filled with fluid waiting to burst. The growths looked like massive boils, replete with pus and ready to erupt.

The figure took another step towards Hacket who had

managed to drag himself up onto his knees into what looked like an attitude of prayer.

He watched as the figure advanced, its piercing gaze never leaving him. His mind was still reeling, but somewhere inside the madness a note of reason told him that he was looking at a Siamese twin. Two bodies supported by just one pair of legs. Two entities in a single body.

The twin reached for him, one powerful hand lifting him to his feet.

'What do you want?'

The two mouths moved in perfect unison, the words not slurred and laboured but crisply spoken, eminently understandable. Coming from such a monstrous source it made them sound all the more incongruous.

Hacket could not reply. His entire body was shaking.

A door behind him opened but he was scarcely aware of it.

Curtis dashed into the hall, slowing his pace when he saw that the teacher had been stopped.

The doctor nodded and the twin hurled Hacket to one side.

He crashed heavily against the wall and lay there as Curtis stood over him.

'You're trespassing, Mr Hacket,' said Curtis, calmly. 'You realise that?'

'What the fuck is going on here, Curtis?' Hacket gasped, his gaze drawn once more to the other figure. 'What is *that*?'

The twin moved forward angrily but Curtis stepped in front of it.

'*That*, Mr Hacket,' the doctor said, angrily. 'Is my brother.'

Hacket laughed uncontrollably. Was this the beginning of madness, he wondered, his eyes beginning to fill with tears. This was the laughter of the insane.

Curtis looked on impassively.

Hacket wiped his eyes and glared up at the doctor.

'One of your fucking experiments don't you mean?' he snarled. 'The product of your treatment. The same treatment you gave to my wife. Is that what she'll give birth to?' He pointed at the twin.

'I ought to kill you now,' the figure said, quietly.

Hacket swallowed hard, stunned once more by the figure's voice.

'Kill me like you killed that poor bastard in your cellar?' he hissed, looking now at Curtis. 'Who is he? Why did you kill him?'

'Call him a donor,' said Curtis, smiling.

Hacket looked vague.

'I couldn't expect a man of your limited perceptions to understand, Mr Hacket. Perhaps I at least owe you the privilege of some kind of explanation. Although I doubt it will mean much to you.'

Curtis glanced at the twin. 'Bring him.'

Hacket rose, but as soon as he was on his feet the other figure grabbed him, one powerful arm snaking around his throat the other hand clamping onto the back of his head.

'If you try to struggle,' the figure said, softly. 'I'll break your neck.' As it pulled him backwards, Hacket felt the heavy growths on its chest rubbing against his back.

Curtis set off for the cellar, followed by Hacket and the twin.

'Time for you to learn, Mr Hacket,' said Curtis, smiling. 'You should feel honoured.'

'And when I *have* learned?' Hacket said, struggling to speak because of the pressure on his windpipe.

Curtis didn't answer.

They began to descend into the cellar.

Eighty-seven

The stench from the body made Hacket feel sick, but held as he was by the twin he could not pull away. Instead all he could do was gaze helplessly at the corpse, his eyes drawn to the gaping hole in the back of its skull, and also to the small gland which still floated in the jar of clear liquid.

'From death comes life,' said Curtis, smiling, gesturing first to the body then to the gland. 'To coin a cliché.'

'What are you talking about, Curtis?' asked Hacket, wearily.

'I'm talking about hope, Mr Hacket. Something which you and your wife didn't have until *I* came along.'

'What have you done to her?' Hacket rasped, trying to pull away but finding himself restrained by the powerful hands which held him.

'I've done what she wanted me to do. I've given her hope. Her and dozens of women like her over the years. Women who couldn't have children. Women who now, because of me, are mothers.' He lifted the jar. 'And all because of this.'

'What is it?'

'The pituitary gland. Source of the body's growth hormones. I'll try to keep this simple Mr Hacket, otherwise I'll end up sounding like some kind of mad doctor.' He smiled. 'They belong in bad horror films.'

'And you belong in prison you murdering bastard,'

Hacket snarled. 'What about that poor fucker lying there? What about him? Where's *his* hope?'

'I said I'll keep this simple. I'll also keep it brief. My father began this work over forty years ago, on the directive of the British government. The project was called "Genesis". That name, I know, will mean nothing to you.' Curtis smiled. 'Except perhaps in its Biblical sense. The name was apt. Genesis describes the creation of life, and that was what Project Genesis was designed to do. My father perfected a fertility drug, refined from human pituitary glands. Given in the right doses it would cut the gestation period from nine months to three. In larger measures perhaps even to four weeks. And it worked.' The doctor's tone hardened. 'He did what *they* told him to do. The government, Churchill in particular, knew that the Germans would invade after Dunkirk. They also knew that there weren't enough men to combat an invasion. They needed my father and his work. Once the women had given birth the children would be regularly injected with the drug, their growth outside the womb would be as rapid as it had been while they were gestating. A child could grow into a man in less than two months.'

'You're mad and by the sound of it, so was your fucking father,' Hacket said.

The twin twisted his head sharply and Hacket felt excruciating pain in his neck and skull. He opened his mouth to scream but no sound would come.

'Another inch and I'll break your neck,' said the twin, leaning close to his ear, both mouths moving slowly.

Curtis held up a hand for the other to release the pressure and Hacket felt the force diminish somewhat. White stars danced before his eyes, and for a second he thought he was going to black out, but he kept a grip on consciousness, listening as Curtis continued.

'There was no madness, Hacket. Only supreme intelligence. But *they* couldn't see that. The men who had wanted his expertise were frightened by the success of his experiments. Some of the children were born deformed. Like my brother. Mentally they were perfect but their physical appearance was unacceptable.' He spoke the last word with sarcasm. 'They told my father to stop his work. He refused, so they had him murdered.' The knot of muscles at the side of the doctor's jaw throbbed angrily. 'My mother was left alone. She was pregnant at the time, carrying myself and my brother. She brought us up alone. Protected my brother, paid for me to go through Medical school. When the time was right she passed on our father's notes. I continued with his work. And, if people have had to die during the course of that work, then too bad. A few human lives are drops in the ocean. Besides, for every one that's died there's been another to take their place. A child where there would never have been one. Hope where there was only misery.'

'The grave in the back garden,' Hacket said, quietly. 'Who is it?'

'Our mother. Margaret Lawrenson. After we were born she gave us her maiden name. Curtis. Better for her to lie there than with others like those who had my father killed. The hypocrites and the doubters.'

'And she supported you? She knew what you were doing? Knew you were killing people?' Curtis asked.

'She knew that sacrifices had to be made if my father's work was to see true fruition. She believed, Hacket. Believed in *him*, believed in *me*.'

'And the children that were born by using your '*treatment*'? What happened to them?'

'All well. All thriving. There is one minor side-effect however. The introduction of so much growth hormone into their systems seems to stimulate other parts of their brains. Without regular treatment they revert to cannabilism.'

'And their parents *know* this?' Hacket gasped.

'Know it and accept it, Mr Hacket. How does the cliché go, love conquers all? Even the knowledge that your child may kill.' He smiled again.

'How come the police haven't found you by now?'

'If I told you that the wife of the local Inspector was one of my patients would that explain why?' Curtis smiled. 'They really do have the most beautiful young daughter. She's almost fifteen now.'

Hacket shook his head, his eyes screwed up tight.

'You *are* mad,' he murmured. 'This whole thing is insane. Weller thought so too, didn't he? The man who lived at the house before me. He knew didn't he?'

'Very astute, Mr Hacket. Unfortunately Weller wasn't prepared to live the kind of life necessary to protect his son. He was ungrateful. And he was a fool. He's better off dead. I gave him what he wanted and he destroyed it.'

'I won't let that happen to my wife. I'll stop her having that child.'

Curtis shook his head and sighed.

'I'm afraid you have no choice, Mr Hacket,' he said, his tone darkening. 'Besides, it's far too late to stop it now.'

Eighty-eight

The pains were growing worse.

Each fresh contraction caused Sue Hacket to wince. It felt as if someone were pulling her intestines out through her navel with red hot tongs. The burning sensation had spread to her vagina too and she shifted as best she could on the chair in order to try and alleviate the growing pain.

Ronald Mills walked up and down the darkened classroom agitatedly, glancing alternately out of the window then at his watch. He swore under his breath then strode across the room towards Sue.

'Where is he?' he hissed. 'Where's your fucking husband?'

She gritted her teeth as a fresh wave of pain swept through her.

'I don't know,' she grunted.

'Lying cunt,' he snarled and lashed out at her.

The blow with the back of his hand caught her across the left cheek. A blow so powerful it almost knocked her over.

'Where is he?' Mills repeated.

'I don't know,' Sue wailed, helplessly, the pain from her lower abdomen eclipsing that from her cheek. She tasted blood in her mouth as she licked her tongue across her bottom lip.

Mills gripped the knife before him, pressing it to her chest, prodding her bare breasts with the tip. He brushed it against her left nipple which stiffened with the cold touch of the steel. Mills grinned, feeling the first stirrings of an erection. How easy it would be to cut that fleshy bud off, he thought. The idea excited him even more. No. He wanted Hacket to see it. Wanted him to see his own wife in agony, bleeding. He wanted to hear her pray for death.

And then it would be Hacket's turn.

Mills had waited a long time for the moment and he intended savouring it.

He watched as Sue doubled over, a fresh jolt of pain filling her. Mills grabbed a handful of her hair and wrenched her upright, so that he was staring into her face. Tears were flooding down her cheeks once more.

'I want to know where your husband is,' hissed Mills.

'And I told you I don't know,' Sue sobbed. 'Why don't you believe me?'

Mills took the knife and carefully slashed the waistband of her skirt, tugging aside the material, leaving her in just her panties. Then he slid the blade under the elastic at the side and pulled them from her.

She continued to cry, now exposed to his leering stare.

'I don't think I can wait any longer,' said Mills, smiling, running approving eyes over her naked body. He could feel the erection pressing almost painfully against the inside of his trousers.

'I think I'll have to start without him.'

Eighty-nine

Hacket knew he had to break free but the task seemed impossible.

The pressure on his neck and throat reminded him of that.

Curtis regarded the teacher silently for a moment.

'What did you hope to gain by coming here tonight?' he said, finally. 'If it was the truth you wanted, then at least now you know it.'

Hacket's arms dropped to his sides, he didn't struggle against the pressure on his neck, merely stood there, half leaning, half-supported by the immense strength of the twin.

'And now I know?' he asked. 'Are you going to kill me?'

'What choice do I have?' Curtis snapped. 'I offered you

something more precious than you could have imagined, you *and* your wife, but you couldn't be content with that.'

'How many more people will you have to kill, Curtis, to carry on this fucking insanity?'

'As many as it takes. It's people like *you* who are mad, not me,' Curtis said, jabbing an accusatory finger at the teacher. 'What I do I do for the good of others. As I said to you, sacrifices have to be made.'

'Very noble,' Hacket chided, his hand brushing against the twin's leg. 'What about the families of the people you kill, do you ever think about what they must feel? You cause pain, Curtis. It's all you're any good for.'

So much pain.

Curtis glanced at the twin and nodded.

Hacket felt the pressure tighten on his neck.

It was then that he reached back and fastened his hands on the twin's testicles, squeezing as tightly as he could, gripping them in a vice-like hold which made the twin shriek in pain.

Hacket gritted his teeth and squeezed harder, pushing backwards.

The twin screamed again and the two of them fell to the ground.

Hacket felt the pressure on his neck released.

He struggled to his feet, turning swiftly to drive a powerful kick into the groin of his fallen captor. He turned back to face Curtis who had lurched towards him, his hand clasping the stiletto blade.

The doctor lunged at Hacket and the teacher shouted in pain as the blade sliced through his shirt, cutting into his forearm. Blood burst from the wound and Hacket jumped back, avoiding the twin's large hand as it grabbed for him. The monstrosity was raising itself up, trying to block his path.

Hacket lashed out again, kicking it in the chest this time but the impact had little effect.

Curtis struck at him once more, the blade carving through his shirt at the back this time.

Hacket screamed in pain as he felt the blade scrape his shoulder blade. The wound opened like a mouth, spilling more blood onto the already damp material of his shirt. He fell forward, crashing into a tray of instruments. Scalpels, forceps and syringes were sent skittering across the floor of the cellar and Hacket gripped one of the scalpels, turning to face the twin as it bore down on him.

He struck out wildly but the blow was effective.

The twin shrieked as the razor sharp blade cut through its calf. It staggered for a second, blood pouring from the wound, some of it spattering Hacket, who was now trying to reach the cellar steps.

He dragged himself to his feet and slashed at the twin once more.

Both mouths opened simultaneously to shout their pain as the blade sliced effortlessly through an outstretched hand. The palm was laid open to the bone, the thumb nearly severed.

Hacket edged backwards, Curtis and the twin advancing on him, blood from his own wounds dripping on to the floor. His left arm was beginning to go numb where Curtis had cut him, but he gripped the scalpel in his right hand, glancing from one attacker to the other, waiting for the inevitable rush.

Before it could come he took his chance and turned, running as fast as he could for the stairs.

He had reached the fifth one when the twin caught him.

Hacket felt a huge hand grab his arm, jerking him back but, as he fell he brought the scalpel around, driving it deep into the side of his attacker.

More blood spurted from the wound and onto Hacket,

who again struggled free, looking up to see Curtis preparing to strike.

The stiletto blade hurtled down, nicking Hacket's cheek. He felt warm fluid running down his face and knew that the cut was deep. As he sucked in a breath he could feel the cold air hissing through the wound.

Curtis pressed his advantage but Hacket ducked beneath the next swipe, striking upwards, catching the doctor in the thigh, burying the scalpel so deep he felt it scratch against Curtis' femur.

The blade remained embedded, quivering there as Curtis dropped his own knife and tried to pull the scalpel free.

From the amount of blood jetting from the wound he thought for one fearful second that his femoral artery had been severed. For fleeting moments he forgot all about Hacket, intent only on ripping the blade from his leg. It finally came free and Curtis screamed in pain.

Hacket, his throat now filling with blood from his slashed cheek, scrambled up the steps and managed to reach the cellar door. He tore it open and crashed through, feeling sick, his head spinning.

The twin, bleeding from the wound in its side, followed.

Curtis remained at the foot of the steps, using his handkerchief to stem the flow of blood from his thigh.

Hacket staggered on through the house, knowing his only hope was to reach his car, to get out of this house, away from this madness.

He blundered through the waiting room and out into the hall.

The twin followed.

Hacket ran for the front door and tugged on it.

It was locked.

He beat frantically against it, as if trying to smash his way free.

The twin reached the hall a second later.

Hacket turned to face it, watching as those two mouths turned upwards simultaneously in a grin of triumph.

'You should have stayed away,' the twin told him, clutching its injured side.

Hacket stood close to the door, the scalpel held before him, his breath coming in gasps, hissing through the savage gash in his right cheek.

As the twin advanced slowly, Hacket glanced to his left and saw another door.

He suddenly turned and bolted for it, crashing through into what, he guessed, was the sitting room.

The twin followed, shouting something after him.

There was a large bay window in the room and Hacket knew what he must do. There was no time for thought, no choice.

He ran towards the window and launched himself at it.

He screamed as he leapt at it, covering his face with his arms, hitting the glass like some kind of human projectile.

The window exploded outwards, huge shards of glass bursting into the cold night air.

Hacket hit the driveway outside with a sickening thump, dazed both by the impact and by the collision against the glass. He was close to unconsciousness, but the cold wind rapidly revived him and restored his senses. He rolled over in time to see the twin clambering through the remains of the window.

Hacket felt for the scalpel but he'd dropped it.

The twin was practically free of the window, ignoring the jagged pieces of glass which scratched it.

Hacket got to his feet and ran for his car, dragging open the door, jamming the key into the ignition.

The twin was pulling its bulk clear now, about to drop down onto the driveway.

Hacket twisted the key.

Nothing.

He gripped it harder and turned again.

The engine roared once then faded as his foot slipped off the accelerator.

The twin was lumbering towards him now, blood spilling not only from its hand and side but also from both of the mouths.

Hacket turned the ignition key again, the twin now less than twenty yards from him.

The engine roared into life.

Fifteen yards.

Hacket jammed the car into gear.

Ten yards.

The twin roared in defiance and ran at the car.

The Renault shot forward as if fired from a cannon.

It slammed into the twin, the impact so great that the figure was catapulted into the air, slamming down on the roof of the car before flying off. It crashed to the ground behind the Renault.

Hacket saw it in the rear-view mirror and reversed at top speed.

The second impact knocked the twin flat, the rear wheels running over the huge head.

It seemed to burst under the weight and pressure.

A vile flux of blood and brains exploded from the riven skull, some of the seething mixture flying up around the car as the back wheels spun impotently on the gravel drive for a second, then Hacket jammed the car into first and swung it around, heading for the main road.

Had he looked in the rear-view mirror he would have seen Curtis emerge from the house to see his dead brother then to bellow something after the fleeing car.

As it was, Hacket gripped the wheel as tightly as he could and pressed his foot down on the accelerator.

The car skidded violently as it reached the main road but the teacher kept control of it, guiding it towards Hinkston.

He seemed to forget his pain, even the horror of what he'd just experienced. It was all pushed to the back of his mind.

For now, all he could think of was his wife.

And the monstrosity she might be carrying inside her.

He drove on.

Ninety

12.08 a.m.

Hacket brought the car to a halt outside his house and glanced at the clock on the dashboard.

He swallowed, fighting back the nausea as he tasted blood. As he swung himself out of the car the wound in his back began to throb mightily, an accompaniment to the pain he was feeling from his gashed forearm. But fighting the pain as best he could he hurried to the front door and selected the appropriate key.

The house was silent as he walked in.

No TV.

Not even any lights.

Maybe Sue was in bed, he reasoned.

Hacket made his way up the stairs, his breath coming in gasps.

Half way up he called her name.

No answer.

As he reached the landing he stood against one wall, feeling a wave of pain wash over him, and for a second he thought he was going to faint; but the feeling passed and he moved into the bedroom, calling her name again.

The room was empty.

Hacket didn't even bother checking the other rooms, he hurried back downstairs, slapping on lights as he went, calling her name once again.

It was in the hallway he saw the blood.

There was more on the kitchen door.

He pushed it open.

The back door was open, banging gently against the frame as each fresh gust of wind blew it. The table and two of the chairs had been overturned. The room was a wreck.

He whispered her name under his breath, his eyes finally alighting on the piece of paper propped up on the draining board beside the sink.

He strode across and snatched it up, examining the large, almost child-like, letters. As he read the words he felt his body beginning to quiver.

COME TO THE SCOOL

COME AND GET YOUR

FUCKING WIFE

Ninety-one

Why hadn't the alarm gone off?

It was a curious thought, but one which nevertheless occurred to Hacket as he paused by the main door of the school, peering through the glass into the gloom beyond.

He could see smashed glass inside where his wife's kidnapper had broken in, but the alarm obviously hadn't gone off. He must have disabled it first, the teacher reasoned, pushing the door tentatively, wincing as it creaked slightly on its hinges. He slipped inside and stood in the entryway, ears alert for the slightest movement. The silence was chokingly oppressive. Like the darkness through which he moved, the solitude seemed almost palpable, holding him back from his quest.

Sue was in the building somewhere, along with the man who had abducted her. At least Hacket assumed it was a man. Just who it could be he didn't know. All he wanted to know was that she was alive. The questions could come later.

He gripped the carving knife he'd taken from the kitchen and made his way down the corridor to his left, peering into each darkened classroom in turn.

There was no sign of her.

He paused for a moment, aware of the burning pain coming from his wounds. But then he pressed on, checking the next corridor.

It was also empty.

Sandwiched between the two was the library.

Hacket pushed open one door and stepped inside, glancing around, squinting through the blackness.

He passed through the library quietly, as if preserving the usual reverence for a room normally silent. There was no sign of Sue in there either.

He wandered back up the corridor towards the dining room.

As he wandered around it the questions began to fill his mind.

Why had she been taken?

When?

By whom?

For what purpose?

Hacket leant against a door frame and sucked in a weary breath. There were so many questions. His head was spinning.

Was she still alive?

Was the child still alive? . . .

The child . . .

He shuddered as he thought about it, about what had happened at Curtis' house.

A noise from above him interrupted the whirlwind of questions spinning around in his head.

He pushed open the double doors which led through into the assembly hall. Hacket hurried across the varnished floor towards another set of double doors.

Beyond these were the stairs that led up to the first floor of the school.

He heard the sound again and slowed his pace, gripping the carving knife more tightly.

Hacket ascended slowly, eyes fixed ahead of him. He stumbled as he reached the half-way point, cursing when pain from the wound in his forearm shot through him. He turned a corner, trying to control his harsh breathing and the thudding of his heart.

He reached the top of the stairs and pushed the next set of double doors.

Four rooms faced him.

He checked them one by one.

Through the window in the door of the third room he saw Sue.

She was naked, tied to a chair, a gag stuffed unceremoniously into her mouth.

Hacket tried the door and, to his delight found it was unlocked.

He blundered in, tears filling his eyes.

She looked up and saw him but the look was not one of relief but one of horror.

Her eyes bulged and she shook her head.

'It's all right,' he whispered as he crossed to her.

She continued to shake her head, nodding towards him.

Towards him?

Her eyes were not on him but on something behind him.

As he reached for the gag he heard a metallic click.

The sound of a hammer being thumbed back.

'I've been waiting.'

Hacket spun round as he heard the voice.

'Drop the fucking knife.'

Hacket obeyed, watching as Ronald Mills stepped from the shadows, the .38 aimed at the teacher's head.

Ninety-two

'Get over there,' Mills snapped, motioning to the desk opposite Sue.

Hacket did as he was told, his eyes on the large man who held the pistol on him.

Sue moaned beneath the gag as another particularly powerful stab of pain lanced through her.

'Who are you?' Hacket wanted to know, watching as Mills moved towards Sue.

The big man removed her gag, pulling it free roughly.

'Tell him who I am,' he snapped, the gun still aimed at Hacket.

Sue hesitated, her words choked away by sobs.

'Tell him,' rasped Mills, pulling her hair.

'You bastard,' snapped Hacket and took a step forward but Mills levelled the pistol at arms length, drawing a bead on a point between the teacher's eyes.

'Tell him who I am,' Mills repeated. 'Tell him what I did.'

'He killed Lisa,' Sue sobbed, tears running down her cheeks.

'Oh Christ,' murmured Hacket, his voice low.

'Does the name Peter Walton ring a bell?' Mills said. Hacket didn't, couldn't answer.

'I'm talking to you, cunt,' Mills snarled. 'Peter Walton. Do you remember him? What happened to him?'

Hacket exhaled deeply, the feelings of frustration, helplessness and fear filling him in equal proportions.

'He was killed. Fell under a train,' Hacket whispered.

'No. You murdered him. I saw you. I saw you chasing him. Saw you push him.'

'He slipped. I didn't touch him.'

'You wanted to.'

'Fucking right,' snarled Hacket. 'And if I could I'd have put you under that fucking train with him, you animal.'

Mills tugged hard on Sue's hair, the gun still aimed at Hacket.

'You better shut your fucking mouth, Hacket,' he rasped.

'What are you trying to do to us? It's me you want. Let my wife go.'

'Fuck you. If she suffers, *you* suffer. You'll get your

turn, don't worry but I want you to see *her* die first. Just like I had to watch you kill Walton. He was the only friend I ever had. The only person I ever trusted or cared about. Who cared about *me*.' He shouted the last sentence. 'And you murdered him.'

'The police will come,' Hacket said, desperate for any idea which might save them. 'You'll be caught, perhaps even killed.'

'What do *I* care? At least you'll have died before me.'

'Just tell me one thing,' Hacket said. 'Why did you kill Lisa?'

'She was there. If it hadn't been her it would have been another girl. We broke in to rob you. Finding her was just a bonus.' He grinned broadly and, with his free hand, began unfastening his trousers. 'Now you watch me, Hacket.'

Sue looked imploringly at her husband, realising that he was as helpless as she to stop this madman. If he rushed Mills then he would either shoot Sue or the teacher himself. There was a chance he might just wound Hacket but, from such close range, Sue was as good as dead. Hacket could do nothing but watch as the big man tugged the rope from Sue's legs. He saw the red welts where the hemp had cut into her flesh.

'Open your legs,' Mills told her, unfastening his trousers to reveal a large erection.

Hacket understood.

'She's pregnant for God's sake,' he yelled.

'Shut up, fucker,' roared Mills, moving towards Sue. He grabbed her ankles and pulled her forward. He had to bend at the knees to manoeuvre his penis towards her vagina, all the time keeping the gun pointed at Hacket, who sucked in a painful breath.

Sue screamed as Mills drove into her, his shaft penetrating her deeply.

He began to thrust back and forth.

Sue felt him inside her and she sobbed helplessly, looking at the moon face before her but then she felt more contractions, a movement deep within her belly. Movement which seemed to transfer itself to her vagina.

Hacket looked on helplessly, clenching his fists until the muscles ached.

Dear God, just for one second . . .

Just one clear run at Mills.

Sue moaned aloud.

'I think she's enjoying it,' said Mills, still thrusting hard into her. He grinned again but the smile suddenly dissolved into a look of surprise.

Hacket looked more closely at him.

No, not surprise.

It was pain.

Mills thrust deeply once or twice more then tried to pull away.

But he couldn't.

Pain began to grow around his penis, spreading across his groin.

Sue had stopped crying.

She was smiling now as she watched the pain on the rapist's face.

He tried again to pull away and this time he screamed in agony.

His penis felt as if it were being squeezed inside her vagina. As if her inner muscles were contracting, closing like a fleshy vice. But the pain was sharper than that.

Mills pushed against Sue as the pain grew more intense.

Hacket looked on, mesmerised.

Sue merely continued to smile.

Mills shrieked uncontrollably as he felt the grip inside her vagina increase. As if he was being held by small hands.

The hands of a baby.

He felt pain unlike anything he'd ever experienced. An excruciating agony which almost caused him to faint.

Blood began to pump from Sue's vagina but it was not *her* blood. Mills was frantic now, desperate to be away from her, from that grip which was mutilating him. His knees buckled and he began to fall.

He fell backwards.

The scream which he uttered was like nothing Hacket had ever heard before. A bellow of absolute suffering torn from the depths of his soul.

As Mills fell onto his back Hacket could see that where the big man's penis had once been there was now only a spurting stump of shredded flesh. The big man put his hands into the wound as if trying to stem the flow of blood and recover his mutilated manhood.

He screamed and screamed, the sound echoing around the classroom, drumming inside Hacket's head as blood spurted from the savage wound. The teacher felt his own vomit clawing its way up from his stomach as he staggered towards his wife, stepping past the writhing shape of Mills but, as he drew closer, Hacket saw the final act of horror and, this time, he could not control himself.

The lips of Sue's vagina slid open and the torn off shaft of Mills' penis was pushed out to drop onto the floor amidst the puddle of blood which had formed there. Like a child spitting out a distasteful piece of food, the vaginal opening yawned wide to expel the remnants of Mills' manhood.

Hacket swayed then turned to one side and vomited until there was nothing left in his stomach.

Sue continued to smile, gazing down at Mills who was still screaming, his yells becoming fainter as the loss of blood gradually sapped his strength and his life gushed away through his fingers.

Hacket freed her, wrapping her in his shirt which he hurriedly pulled off.

Bloodied and dazed they stumbled past Mills.

'We have to get the police,' Hacket gasped, wiping his mouth with the back of his hand.

Mills' screams had degenerated into low burblings as they staggered out of the room.

Hacket didn't know how long it took a man to bleed to death.

They supported each other down the stairs and out of the school, heading back towards their house, sucking in the cold night air, as if wishing it could wash away the stench of blood and death from their nostrils.

Hacket shivered but he realised that it was not all a product of the cold wind.

Sue, bloodied and barely conscious, looked at him and smiled.

Hacket felt the hairs at the back of his neck rise.

They reached the house and blundered through the back door, Hacket slamming it behind them. Then they struggled through into the sitting room, the teacher slapping on lights as they went.

He froze.

Sitting in one of the armchairs, the stiletto blade held in his hand, was Doctor Edward Curtis.

Ninety-three

For long seconds Hacket couldn't speak, his eyes remained fixed on Curtis.

'My brother is dead, as you may have guessed,' the doctor finally said, his face emotionless.

‘It has to end, Curtis,’ Hacket said, leaning against the door frame to support himself.

‘I agree with you,’ the doctor echoed, rising to his feet, the knife held before him.

Sue looked first at her husband then at Curtis.

Then she felt the pain. So powerful she yelled in response to it.

‘You’ve done this to her,’ Hacket screamed. ‘God knows what she’s carrying. Something like your . . . brother? Help her. Abort the baby. Now.’

‘No,’ Sue moaned, her face twisted into a mask of pain. ‘Don’t let it die.’ She looked imploringly at Curtis. ‘Please.’

‘Kill it, Curtis,’ Hacket snarled. ‘It’s unnatural.’

Curtis took a step towards Sue, dropping the knife on the sofa.

‘I need it,’ she said. ‘Help it live.’ She gripped Curtis’ hand and pulled him closer to her.

Hacket stepped forward, pushing the doctor away, slamming him up against the wall, hands clasped around his throat. There was a look of hatred in his eyes. Hatred and something else.

Madness perhaps?

Curtis struggled against Hacket’s grip, supported by his hands but dying because of them. His head felt as if it were beginning to swell, and he was fighting for his breath as Hacket dug his thumbs deeper into the doctor’s windpipe, lifting him off his feet with the ferocity of his attack.

‘You’ve done this to her,’ snarled Hacket, exerting yet more strength on Curtis’ throat. ‘I’ll kill you.’ He bellowed the words into the other man’s face.

Hacket felt the pain in his lower back first.

Like a punch in the kidneys.

Then it came again. Harder this time and he felt the coldness now.

The third time he realised.

Sue drove the stiletto blade into his back, severing his spinal cord.

He lost his grip on Curtis then dropped to his knees.

As he did she brought the knife down again.

This time it powered into his neck, severing the carotid artery. A huge fountain of blood erupted from the wound, spattering Sue and spraying the wall of the sitting room crimson as surely as if it had been splashed with red paint. Hacket turned and looked at her, tears in his eyes, then he fell forward, his body jerking slightly.

Blood filled his mouth and he blinked hard as his vision began to cloud both with pain and tears.

How long would it take a man to bleed to death?

He would have the answer soon.

Curtis looked down at him, massaging his throat, scarcely able to speak.

Sue continued to sob, the knife still in her hands, crimson dripping from its point like thick teardrops.

'Why did you want to kill it, John?' she sobbed. 'Why?'

Hacket tried to speak but the only sound he could make was a liquid gurgle. Blood spilled over his lips, he felt it run from his nostrils. He reached out towards her, wanting to touch her hand, knowing he was dying. Along with the pain there was fear too.

'The child will live, Hacket,' Curtis said, rubbing his bruised throat.

'My child,' Hacket gurgled, but the effort of speaking only brought fresh pain and a massive heaving within his body. He began to shiver.

Curtis smiled down at him.

'No,' he said softly. 'Not *your* child. *My brother's*.'

Even through her tears Sue was smiling too.

John Hacket closed his eyes.

Some wounds never heal. Some pain
is never soothed.

Anon

Hatred shouldn't be forgotten. It
should be nurtured. And self-hatred
is the bloom which responds best.

Anon

I have looked into the mirror of madness
and seen my own reflection . . .

May 16, 1988